I0572100

A Company of Moors

A Company of Moors Copyright © 2010 by Justin Thomas. All rights reserved. No part of this book may be reproduced or utilized in any form or by any means, electronic or mechanical, including photocopying, recording, or by any information and retrieval system, without the written permission from the author.

978-0-9725548-9-3

Published by Twin Griffin Books

Cover art by The Writing Moor

www.TwinGriffinBooks.com

For the Griffin Company,

The Twin Moors,

&

Alexandre Dumas

Remember the adventures...

A Company of Moors

By

Justin Thomas

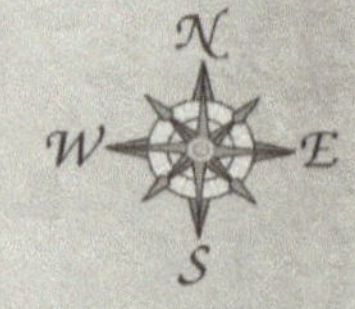

"The power of the piratical coast population of northern Africa arose in the 16ᵗʰ century, attained its greatest height in the 17ᵗʰ century, declined gradually throughout the 18ᵗʰ, and was extinguished only in the 19ᵗʰ century. From 1659 onwards the coast cities ... though nominally part of the Turkish empire, were in fact anarchical military republics that chose their own rulers and lived by plunder. The maritime side of this long-live brigandage was conducted by captains, or *reises*, who formed a class or even a corporation."
— *Encyclopedia Britannica* (1953 edition)

"In truth, the [North African city-states] seem to have been neither anarchical nor anarchist—but rather, in a strange and unexpected way, *democratic* ... in practice, the city-state was run by various 'chambers' of ... soldiers and corsair notables, who made their own policy—and sometimes sent the Sultan's representatives scurrying back to Istanbul with a blunt refusal to carry out the will of the Sublime Porte."
— *Pirate Utopias: Moorish Corsairs and European Renegadoes* (Wilson p.30)

Griffin
Twin
Books
PRESENTS

Chapter The First

North Africa, 1620

Sunset

This is al-Mari Ifriq, Moorish Africa, a small city dreaming for its borders to reach the coast. It is a city incomplete, but with still a beating heart. Its dusty, unpaved roads and small districts set the unofficial borders, and provided a reminder, of the minor squabbles initiated by the surrounding maritime companies that vie for control of each other, the city, and the entire region. The skirmishes were light, but heavy enough to impede the city's growth. The struggles halted the city's desire to stretch out and connect with the docks established at the coast, which lay not too far off in the distance. Al-Mari Ifriq, though wounded, incomplete in its structure, had its dream in reach.

Life bubbled in the small urban center, even now as the sun exhaled its final three hours of breath. The sun's light twirled in its final moments, beaming down and illuminating the deep red and brown roofs of Moorish houses and apartments. Their whitewashed walls glistened like fine crystal, gently touched by the illuminated tips of the sun's tendrils.

The sea's breeze modified the hot and desiccated climate, sparing al-Mari Ifriq's population of the dry, hot season they had been engaged in for several months. The crisp air was also a sign that the cool, wet season was approaching.

There was activity winding through the city. Children ducked in and out of alleyways, laughing aloud and out of breath as they played chase. The children were assorted in all ages, both genders, and the varying dark shades and brown hues that Africa had to offer.

The younger children played chase; the more mischievous children played snatch with the vendors' store goods. The teenage boys sparred with sticks, fencing with the mock grace of cultural heroes from stories heard in childhood. Some of them were teaching the younger boys the grace of the sword. The more jaunty boys spent time leaning against walls, armed with sly smiles and spry words, reciting to the young, teenage Moorish women gathered as an audience.

Older men, the color of midnight, who possessed wild, graying hair that resembled bursts of fire, squared off in chess matches outside a barber's shop. Young men, in their early twenties, with thick, long locks for hair, or woolen crowns shaped like billowing, black clouds, gathered outside the barbershop as spectators. Another group of young men huddled close to an alley. Elders accompanied them. The group debated the rules of chess and philosophically applied the game's rules to life. They also spoke in a scholarly manner on mathematics and the stars in between expressing exaggerated tales of women conquered and jokes told with coarse language, narratives that, of course, accompanied such conversations in the gatherings of men.

Several blocks away, women spoke about the influence of the stars on scandalous or amorous behavior. The women applied this astrology to particular subjects residing in their district. They tended to the braiding of young girls' hair, or ceremoniously locked a single area of coils on young boys' otherwise shaved heads. This was a young male tradition that extended all the way back to the ancient lands of Kemet and Nubia. Then, mothers started calling for their children as the sun dipped lower. The youthful activity through the streets came to a close.

There still was business on the outskirts of the city. Vendors from all over Africa gathered for the past seven days to display their goods at the al-Mari Ifriq Open Market. This was an annual event, and the imported goods at the market were not the only things vendors were showcasing. They hoped to be selected to permanently open a shop within the city walls. Each vendor stood tall, prideful, beside his or her goods. There was no indication on the vendors' visages that their hearts pounded nervously on the inside.

The city's most prominent company, the *Sa'ood Alliance*, led by Sa'ad al-Din Sa'ood, had the final say on selection. The *Sa'ood Alliance* was changing al-Mari Ifriq for the better. The company was hoping to achieve the city's dream—to grow to the coast. The vendors wanted to take part in that. There was great financial potential to have a steady shop in a growing city.

The market became a legitimate business eight years ago when Sa'ad, then a twenty-four year old businessman, steered his company toward the better interests of al-Mari Ifriq and its population. Contraband at the markets was in attendance less and less, but never a dismissed guest.

The *Sa'ood Alliance* was not another front company for Moorish corsairs and Mediterranean pirates, as most companies in North Africa had been for the last century. Sa'ad al-Din Sa'ood had plans to unite and legitimize the companies, ultimately creating an African state. Sa'ad was a different type of company boss. He was ambitious. He refused even the title *bey*, or chief. There was no hierarchy with him. He was well accepted by the companies. Business without warfare was appreciated. This, however, did not mean Sa'ad was never forced to prove he could command soldiers to kill.

The first six months of business almost degenerated Sa'ad to the level of the pirates and gangsters surrounding him. He did not succumb to their mentality, however, and all of the companies had Sa'ad's wife to thank for that. When he wanted to lead his soldiers into company war, his wife would soothe him. There were still too many times his hand was forced to act against the pride of an older company boss, a disguised corsair feigning legitimacy. But he calmed the tensions of the companies and took lead, bringing into his fold longtime friends to help him run his *Alliance*.

Sa'ad was not too conservative. He was even less religious, much to the chagrin of his advisor and lawyer Wakil al-Hakam, a devout follower of Mohammedan Law. Sa'ad was not completely turned off by piracy. His company had a minor claim of being built upon it. But that excursion was just he and his best childhood friend (now his second-in-command) being mischievous, or rather, adventurous. Sa'ad believed that piracy was not in the companies' best interest, at least not in acts against one another. He had no problem with taking a ship from any of the European nations. It was less expensive than buying from them. Willing pirates did not ask for much, and everybody could enjoy the spoils.

No company argued with the revenue Sa'ad generated for them. The prideful bosses that disappeared after failed negotiations with Sa'ad were neither missed nor mourned. But Sa'ad's *Alliance* was still having trouble persuading the remaining companies and new leaders to invest in al-Mari Ifriq, which would help increase the size of the city and its people's well being. There was still a lot of work to be done. In the last eight years, peace had been defined as best it could, and the city was thankful for that.

At the moment, Sa'ad's police stood guard as the vendors packed their goods, tents, mules, and camels. Some of the men had large caravans of goods. Servants did most of the packing. The final day was a complete reversal of the vendors' arrival seven days ago. Customers flowed away from the festivities of sale. The vendors packed up instead of pitching tent or setting up their vending stand. They would now be escorted and secluded to a section of the city, awaiting word by letter if they would be a permanent resident in al-Mari Ifriq.

The week was perfect for the vendors. No one was without sales. Money was made, and the travel was worth its headache. There was no loss even if the vendors were not selected. There was always next year.

The success of the vendors was because of a lack of participation at this year's market. There were only thirty-five vendors, most of them small outfits. This was down from over fifty, closer to one hundred every year prior. There were only rumors as to why this was. Some vendors had been re-routed. Rumors echoed that other vendors were scared away or even killed. In the last year and a half, Sa'ad's fortune, little as it was, started to turn. Ships too had been re-routed. Others were marked and plundered.

Pirate activity increased along company trade routes. Sa'ad sent spies to find the culprits. He could feel the heat of the other company bosses, knowing they were twiddling their fingers while they waited and judged his every move against the attacks. Now, matters were worse. Al-Mari Ifriq's current year did not enjoy a financial gain. The situation came to the attention of the Ottoman Turks, who not only had a company setup in the city, but claimed control of the entire region of Odongo-Mauharim, a small patch of land that was neither Tunisia nor Algeria but somewhere in between. It was this land where al-Mari-Ifriq was positioned. It was this land that Sa'ad sought to be strictly African, Moorish. He did not trust the Turks, and did not want the Empire to become a revenue-draining protectorate.

Some of the Turks that Sa'ad negotiated with were black Turks, with knowledge of their African selves, though Mohammedan in religion. But most of the head chiefs that made claim to the region were swarmahu Turks, closer in relation to what the Arab had become. They were swarthy, dusky in color, but tawny after years of mixing with whites or *tamahu*, an ancient word for 'white man' or 'stranger'.

Sa'ad was not going through this situation alone. His longtime friends and business partners were here with him. They surrounded him now in a small, well-decorated room situated on the second floor of the city's palace. He watched his associates while they shuffled through parchments, giving suggestions about the market and vendors.

Each gentleman sat on a wide, cushioned chair carved from fine wood. The room was circular. There were two doorways in the room, both in the shape of an upside-down 'U'. The door across from Sa'ad led to the hallways of the unfinished palace. The door directly behind Sa'ad led to the balcony, and, at the present time, was currently opened, inviting in the last rays of the sun's light. The companymen could hear their children playing in the courtyard below. The children's banter was soothing, actually relieving the men's headaches caused by business.

A small, round wooden table sat in the center of their council, parchments scattered on top. More parchments were being tossed, dealt like playing cards from the hands of the man sitting to Sa'ad's left. His name was Taran Zaher, a dark brown-skinned man wrapped in beige and light brown traditional cloths and garments. His head was oval like an almond, and he had wide eyes. His hair was cut very low, almost bald. Taran's mustache was the same, as was the low patch of hair on his chin. His ancestry, beyond the refugees from Spain, hailed from the east. He had Cushitic and Nubian blood flowing through him.

Sa'ad turned to Taran when he needed to negotiate with the Turks. Taran was the Commissioner for Foreign Affairs. He owned a tremendous amount of land in and outside of the city. Some districts of al-Mari Ifriq were built directly on his family's property. He would continuously use this knowledge of ownership against the Turks' pride and claim to the entire region. Regardless of his quick and sharp tongue in negotiations, the Turks favored Taran.

Wakil al-Hakam sat directly across from Sa'ad. He was the oldest of the gathered men. Wakil was thirty-six years old, and he was something no man or woman ever dreamed existed. He was a very humble and religious lawyer. But because his knees bent only to God, and his indulgence was only for the welfare of his family, he stood firm in the eyes of the law of man, and beyond that, Mohammed. Wakil was wrapped in black robes. He had a large head and a plump body. His hair, tightly curled, was already showing signs of ash, contrasting poetically with his black skin. At the time, his hair was up in a turban. His voice was just as heavy as his features. To see him smile and hear him laugh was like receiving a hug from thunder. He waited for the gentlemen around him to finish with their business so he could start conducting the legal side of the transactions.

The chair next to Wakil was empty. It was designated for Roberto Hamaat, a man who was in charge of the police. He was, at the moment, seeing that the traveling vendors were cared for.

Finishing the circle, sitting to Sa'ad's right, was his best friend Rashaad al-Hammon. His attire was no different than the rest of the men in the room. The color of Rashaad's clothes was tan, matching Sa'ad's. Rashaad had dark skin, a round face, and small eyes. He had a sportsman's physique, but his true power was in his smile, an instrument used to tame the most vicious pirates the Alliance negotiated with now and in their early days. The same smile allowed Rashaad to gain ownership of a small shipyard.

Rashaad was not always the best in negotiations, however. Sa'ad recognized that Rashaad's voice was smoother than his, more musical and less authoritative. Sa'ad's voice was better suited to engage the other company bosses. With the pirates, however, his voice was confrontational. They took to Rashaad's demeanor a lot easier. But, early on, Sa'ad carefully coached his friend before he went in for counsel with pirates. Rashaad followed a close script, and he learned cues from Sa'ad's inconspicuous hand gestures and eye movements. Rashaad was always amazed at the results. His understanding of negotiations increased in the last eight years, which gave him more confidence in his voice.

The men's conversation sounded like a giant sigh. There was nothing but bad news. Revenue could only afford them four stores to build. In past years the company had the money to build eight, even ten to give to the city. More products were being manufactured around the world— including in the colonies of the Americas. Al-Mari Ifriq was falling behind.

What made matters worse was the gentlemen knew where the problem lay. Their trade routes, by sea and land, were under attack. Worse than that, was the only solution they had. By the unanimous decision of the other companies, the Alliance was forced to take part in the presented solution. An invitation was extended to the Ottoman Turks to step into the matter. All power was about to be in the hands of the Turks. Another company was being created to oversee the annual operations of al-Mari Ifriq.

Taran and Rashaad were already speaking with the Empire's ambassadors.

Sa'ad wanted to seek comfort with the market's report. There was none. He leaned forward and sighed. He looked at the parchments piled atop the table in front of him and groaned, "Is this all we have to show?" Sa'ad leaned back in his chair and looked from Taran to Rashaad. He started to think. "There are a little more than thirty vendors. We can safely house three. If we force what little revenue we have, we can take in four." He rubbed his bearded chin and continued to ponder. He had an answer. "We'll take the best three of the regular eight we choose. With the other five, we will establish trade and expand stores already built."

Taran and Rashaad nodded. Rashaad turned to Wakil and asked, "Are there legal ramifications forcing partnerships to expand trade?"

Wakil answered quickly, "Not at all. I'm sure the stores chosen will welcome the extra product. They may have a hard time sharing the earnings with someone they are forced to be partners with."

"We just have to combine the right stores with the right trade," said Sa'ad. "We can increase the stores' tributes once a good trade market is established, when profits show that the goods are being sold."

"Do we have the money for extra storage houses or trade route employment?" Taran asked Sa'ad.

"Barely," said Sa'ad as he cleared his throat. "Once revenue picks up, that should get us over." He took a deep breath.

The room was silent again. No one wanted to bring up the next topic. The Turks. It was there, on everyone's mind. Each man knew the subject had to be discussed. Rashaad decided to address his fellow companymen with a tone representing the emotions stirred by the topic. "We do all this to help the Turks, not our city." He spoke his words through a heavy sigh.

Rashaad's expression of the matter was well appreciated. It was removed of all business and filled with sincerity. Sa'ad gave his friend a hard look and gritted his teeth behind closed lips. He shook his head; he was angry at the circumstances in which they now found themselves. The intensity of Sa'ad's gaze toward Rashaad started to grow as he pondered their predicament.

Sa'ad continued to shake his head. Water formed in the eyes of this hard-boiled Moor. He believed Rashaad was right. All their hard work came to this. It was this scenario Sa'ad was looking to avert eight years ago when he assembled the men in this room with the heads of the other companies. Now, Sa'ad sat silent, contemplating moves he could make before the Turks' arrival in two weeks. His conspiracy theorist mind considered recent piratic activity as part of a plot for the Turks to take over, rescuing al-Mari Ifriq from financial collapse, and buying the Ottomans another colony. He considered that the Turks were the ones behind the attacks on the company trade routes, re-routing or plundering ships and caravans. Sa'ad had his gut feeling investigated by Roberto Hamaat's second, and more covert, police force.

Behind Sa'ad, outside, through the door and beyond the balcony, he could hear the children playing in the courtyard. He stood up and walked away from the meeting. The other men gave Sa'ad the respect to leave for a breath of air.

The sun still held onto the day. The last toss of its rays touched Sa'ad's blue-black skin, creating a golden glow. Sa'ad could see the coast beyond the city limits. His eyes then narrowed down on the children. He spotted his son Nasir playing cheerfully with Rashaad's two boys, Maurice and Fusan. There too was Taran's daughter, Mehit al-Tarqiyya. The six-year old girl just became a big sister. Taran's wife had another girl. Wakil's children, two daughters and one son, frolicked about as well. His wife was expecting a fourth child. Wakil was the only man in the company dedicated to procreation. The other men, coming from the rougher side of business, considered having few children a safer road to travel. One child was enough; having two children was pushing it. But not even Wakil was brave enough to have more than one wife. Corsair politics did not allow a company boss to engage in such responsibility. Taran, for the sake of business, wanted to bring a professional attitude to the realm of taking on a second wife, but not even he could find the time.

Sa'ad reflected back to the frolicsome children. He remembered being the same age. He could remember being five and six years of age, wrestling with Rashaad. Their parents had moved into the same district on the same day, just two houses down from one another. The two families became friends. At that time, Sa'ad and Rashaad were only months old. They always tackled situations together from that time on. This was no different.

Sa'ad smiled at the memory of he and Rashaad, just twenty years old, commandeering a ship when the two were in Tunis. It was their first business venture. Their trade started by using that small vessel. Their business grew into a trade route that helped the two of them connect with a company in Algeria. Tunis had to be avoided for a while, as the original captain screamed for the heads of those who took his ship.

It was in Algeria where they caught up with Wakil. He was studying law there, almost finished. His services, however, were promised to a company captain in Algiers. Wakil reminded his two friends of Taran, a young man of their childhood that was now looking to jump into business. Taran was suggested as a substitute for Wakil, but Sa'ad wanted Wakil's pious sincerity on his team. It was then that Sa'ad reminded Wakil that he still knew the riffraff Roberto Hamaat.

Wakil was free from the captain's services the week before he graduated as a lawyer.

The captain's next of kin took over the company the same day.

The next of kin was not vengeful, but grateful for Sa'ad's actions. A partnership was formed. Sa'ad, Rashaad, and Wakil returned to al-Mari Ifriq with plans to become companymen. They made a promise that their home city would prosper for it. They invited Taran into the fold not too long after. Roberto and his gang were hired as police and guards.

Sa'ad sought the employment of another man, Ameer Las El-Behar. But that man's heart was too filled with delusions of revolution against Spain. Sa'ad made a second attempt to employ the Moorish rebel two years ago. Behar was in al-Mari Ifriq looking to recruit soldiers for his continuing war against Spain. He was helping small, Moorish taifas solidify their powers against the Spanish Crown. Behar would not settle down; he was in the middle of a personal war based on the Moors re-capturing the glory days of al-Andalusia. But he and Sa'ad were good friends and shared each other's company.

Sa'ad wondered how things might have been different with a mind like Behar in his service. Behar was a soldier. He was a wartime chief. That would not have been good for the times that Sa'ad's fiery temperament wanted to get the better of him. Rashaad was a better stand in, with no offense to the skills Behar might have brought to the table.

Rashaad's cool and friendly voice was always there to calm Sa'ad in times like this. It was either his friend or his wife. Sa'ad could not imagine a world without either of them. He sat on the balcony's banister and looked at Rashaad and started to feel guilty about putting himself in the situation he was in, and the decision that was made about it. Sa'ad's teeth tightened again. His anger rose. His eyes watered. His head shook. The situation was too much. He watched the others continue counsel but kept his eyes on his best friend and second-in-command.

It had been eight days since Sa'ad had come to terms with the fact that Rashaad al-Hammon, his closest friend, was the proven culprit that was aiding the Turks in re-routing and plundering the company trade ships. It had been two weeks since Roberto Hamaat delivered the devastating evidence that Rashaad was guilty. He was working close, perhaps too close, with the Ghanem Company, the already established company of the Turks.

Ghanem was partially owned by the interior kingdom of Odongo-Mauharim. The Djenhai Kingdom had investments with the company. The Djenhai's first ruler, wanting to connect with his Moorish brethren, took a Moorish woman as his second wife. The king devoted himself to Mohammed and created a bloodline of kings known as *The Kings of Two Worlds*. With his second bride, he was able to establish one of the first trading companies with Moors that were returning from al-Andalusia to populate the small land of Odongo-Mauharim. Al-Mari Ifriq was built. Marauders destroyed the trading company not too long after. Turks rebuilt the company when Moorish refugees of fallen Spain seeped back into Africa. Only recently did the Djenhai Kingdom's current ruler start to invest in the company, though the company was under new leadership and name.

Ghanem had gone through five leaders, now on their sixth. All of them were hardheaded. Their status as Turks, with an Empire behind them, was enough for Sa'ad to stay his hand. The company was just the eyes for the Turkish chiefs living off Odongo-Mauharim from far away. The Djenhai's investment meant little. The kingdom was going through restructure, only gaining from the company through very small revenue and even smaller trade. They were silent partners, completely unaware of the Turks' true intentions.

It was a loss. Sa'ad wanted to connect with the southern kingdom. Djenhai was crucial in making Odongo-Mauharim an independent state. The Turks blocked his advance. Now they too were making advances. They had control over someone close to him. The Turks were a power many of the company bosses told Sa'ad that he could not fight.

Sa'ad was not going to lose just yet.

He stood from the balcony's rail and stared into the distance again, watching the sun drop lower. "Two weeks," he said in a low voice. That's when he found out about his longtime friend. He made his move on a hunch, and unfortunately found out more than he bargained for. He just wanted to know if the Turks were indeed behind the marks on the company's trade vessels and caravans. They were. But they were working from the inside. Rashaad was supplying them with the most sacred routes for trade by sea and land. They were routes Sa'ad and his companymen swore an oath never to reveal. "Two weeks," he said again, teeth grinding against one another.

The vessel runners were trusted company captains. They were good friends with Roberto Hamaat. These captains, some dead, others recovering from wounds from the attacks, were the most cunning runners on the sea. They were both unlawful pirate and authorized merchant in one.

Sa'ad found out the company oath was broken two weeks ago. He had come to terms with the information, to some degree, not too long after. Sa'ad sighed and looked back at his friends, making sure not to concentrate his severe gaze too much on the guilty Rashaad. But he could not. His expression was not recognizable to the three men waiting for him, Wakil now up and lighting the lamps inside the room. Sa'ad managed to smile and nod his head when Rashaad did make eye contact, however. It was in that moment when Sa'ad came to complete terms about the knowledge of Rashaad's betrayal, at the very least, Sa'ad came to terms with the fact that he was going to kill him for it. The move was already in play. Roberto had his best man on it. Rashaad was going to die tonight.

There was a knock on the door, almost as if on cue of Sa'ad's thoughts. Wakil, having taken his seat again, looked over his shoulder at the door and then to Sa'ad. The company leader nodded his head and Wakil shouted over his shoulder, "Enter."

Roberto Hamaat came through the door. He was dressed like a scoundrel. He had on dark brown pants with brown boots that were only a shade lighter. A white silk shirt draped past Roberto's waist. Over the shirt, Roberto wore a vest the color of his pants. Roberto wore occult amulets around his neck, dangling from silver and gold chains. His fingers were adorned with rings decorated with symbols of theurgy. Attached to Roberto's belt was a short sword, sheathed in a decorated scabbard. A seaman's one-shot pistol was strapped to his right side.

Though Roberto was from a family of Moriscos—Moors that converted to Christianity—he was an occultist, and the leader of a dangerous sect of men and women. The rumors were true, if only spoken in low whispers. Roberto Hamaat was the leader of a group of assassins he called The Seventy-Two Points of the Universe. He held command of the local guards and police, but it was this clan that was his true outfit.

Roberto's clan was split into two teams of thirty-six. He called the two teams the Thirty-Six Seen, and the Thirty-Six Unseen. Each team consisted of twelve men called Suns, twelve women called Moons, and twelve initiates called Stars. Roberto led his clan with his mistress, Ilindia Kali. She was of Dravidian-Ethiopic extraction.

Sa'ad walked back into the room. Behind him, in the courtyard below, the wives of the men gathered the children to bring them inside. Sa'ad motioned to Roberto, waving his hand with the grace of a gentleman toward the occultist's empty seat. Roberto bowed at the neck, in respect to Sa'ad. He removed the leather satchel draped around him and placed it next to the empty chair. He then sat down at the unoccupied spot next to Wakil.

Sa'ad took his seat again and watched as Roberto amiably greeted Wakil with the Arabic phrase of *As-Sal mu `Alaykum*. Wakil replied back with a gentle smile, *"wa `Alaykum As-Salaam."* Wakil admired Roberto for being well learned. The lawyer did not let his devotion to Mohammed conflict with Roberto's devotion to the occult. The two found common ground in the simple nature of spirituality, the mythology surrounding the origins of the universe, and the wealth of history in Africa.

Roberto gave a nod and gesture to the other two gentlemen in the room. This was not a slight. Taran and Rashaad understood the friendship shared between the lawyer and the occultist. Roberto turned to Sa'ad and spoke factually, "The vendors are in their place, guarded well."

Sa'ad smiled. "Town reports?" he asked.

"There was a scuffle today," Roberto reported. "A group of boys, close to twenty in age," he continued. "A boy in one group had special tattoos; a boy in the other group had a brand. No symbols I recognize, nothing occult. I'm investigating gang relations—even more, if these two groups of boys are tied to any companies. I have some initiating of my own to do. Two Stars—young men that I have in training—will slip among their ranks."

Eyes went to Sa'ad. He took a deep breath and rubbed a flat hand against his chest while adjusting himself in his seat. "I can see the companies trying to use young men in gangs to claim territory. This year has been financially rough. Times are desperate. We have Turks coming in to handle the matter," Sa'ad rolled his eyes, "unfortunately. The smaller companies may want to strong-arm vendors and innkeepers under the nose of the Turks. The tributes that will be demanded by the Turks through their new company will break our treasuries more so. The smaller companies don't want to lose what little they have."

"The Turks understand that our company is the most prominent," Taran said. "We will be looked upon for all matters of the city, blamed rather."

Sa'ad lifted his hand and addressed Wakil. "I mean no offense to your faith, my friend. But I do fear the Mohammedan rules and laws that the Turks will try and implement."

"I agree," Wakil replied. "I believe religion should be for the search of spirituality not to rule the common man or woman. Though, I do believe there are some places for it that government can learn from."

"Government is one thing," Sa'ad exhaled. "These are pirates and gangsters. The citizens will respect any law given to them, but not these ruffians. We're lucky we got this far implementing law. Giving them God will be a miracle I'd like to see. Fortunately, our city was founded on law." The sun slipped away, substituted by the flickering lamps in the circular room. The room faded into shadows, carrying enough light for the men to see one another. "My greatest worry is Civan-el Bey." Sa'ad was naming the leader of the Ghanem Company. "He's a hard-boiled lot. He's even more hardheaded. I know he's excited about the opportunities that await him when the Turks arrive. There will be a full-blooded Turkish company."

"The Ahangar are on our side," Rashaad reminded Sa'ad of the Persian company allies. "Armed with them, we can keep the incoming Turks in line without averting to war. We can make sure that the Turks look to better al-Mari Ifriq and help re-establish our trade routes."

"We both know that's impossible," Sa'ad countered. "Our best trade routes are compromised; they will be under Turkish control. They will take the revenue for themselves." Sa'ad looked at Roberto and said matter-of-factly, "We will take care of Civan-el Bey before the Turks arrive."

Roberto acknowledged with a nod.

Rashaad's eyes went wide. "You plan to mark the head of a Turkish company?"

"I don't *plan* to do anything," Sa'ad said with a sly smile. "It's been done. He's marked. I only plan to carry it out."

Taran's mouth dropped as well. He was completely surprised by Sa'ad's openness with this plan. Sa'ad knew that Rashaad was a traitor; they all knew. His first course of action was to go straight to Civan-el Bey and inform the Turk of company plans. Taran wanted to ask him aloud what sense this made. His reaction, however, made him look just as surprised as Rashaad.

"Civan's successor is a man named Feroz Aunun," Sa'ad explained to Rashaad. "He is a trinity unto himself." Sa'ad played up his excitement, describing further, "His mother was a Moor. She was black and as beautiful as Africa. His father was a black Turk who was so dark he made the gods of midnight jealous. And by way of his wife, he is related to the nobles of the Djenhai court."

"Most importantly," interjected Roberto, "he's willing to help."

Sa'ad kept a sly smile. He watched Rashaad with an unassuming, judging eye. There was no movement from Sa'ad's friend that gave away any form of betrayal. Rashaad sat back and said, "We should be very careful about this."

"It will be a move to keep our control on the city," said Sa'ad. "We will be aligned with the Ahangar Company, the Ghanem, and be connected to the Djenhai court." Sa'ad could see hurt on Rashaad's face. He suspected it was because he played a move that countered the cunning betrayer. "I'm sorry I kept this information from you. You are a great negotiator. But I needed you like stone when you were speaking to them." Rashaad's eyes went to Taran. Sa'ad pointed to Wakil and Roberto. "Only Wakil, I, and Roberto were in counsel about this," Sa'ad lied. Taran knew, but Sa'ad insisted to Rashaad, "Taran didn't know." He looked to Taran and said, "I apologize to you as well."

Taran raised his lower jaw, still hanging in astonishment at the scene before him. He closed his mouth, swallowed and said, "I understand." He bowed at the neck politely.

Rashaad looked at Wakil and laughed, "And here I thought you were an honest lawyer." The group laughed with him. He put his eyes on Sa'ad. "We still need to talk further about this. I need to know everything."

"Most certainly," Sa'ad agreed.

Rashaad exhaled and managed to smile. He threw up his arms and said, "I hate to leave on this note, but it's getting late. My children are due for bed."

Rashaad rose from his seat. The other men followed, giving Rashaad salutation and safe travel for his family. Sa'ad commanded Roberto to escort Rashaad to the palace's front entrance. Roberto complied, relating that his best men would guard the family's caravan home. Rashaad and Roberto disappeared beyond the door.

Sa'ad, Taran, and Wakil took their seats again. Taran exclaimed, "You told him our plans!" He watched the tone in his voice so as not to sound too accusing against his company boss. Taran was also mindful that his voice would not carry beyond the door. "He may speak," Taran warned.

"He will only speak to angels or devils, depending on how he's judged," Sa'ad huffed. "I needed to get him out of here so that *we* can speak."

"But he may sell out our plans," Taran said again. "Forgive my voice."

"Forgiven," granted Sa'ad. "And he won't speak. He said he needed to know everything. He needs a plan to report. Besides, Civan is on his way back from Turkey. He's due to arrive several days ahead of the Turks. Rashaad will be dead by tonight."

Wakil said a silent prayer.

There was knocking heard.

"Enter," Sa'ad allowed.

Roberto stepped through and slipped back into his seat. He reached down and scooped up his satchel. He opened the leather bag and removed two sheets of parchment. He handed the parchments over to Sa'ad and stated, "Those were on Rashaad's contact. The contact has been disposed of." Roberto positioned his satchel next to the chair again.

"These are property statements," Sa'ad said aloud as he scanned the writing on the parchments. "Rashaad is being granted property that's in Turkey." He lifted an eyebrow. "And through French negotiations, the Americas." Sa'ad shook his head and sighed. "I don't believe the Turks will actually honor this. We're probably killing him sooner than they are."

"There's a second contact for Rashaad," Roberto reported further. Taran became curious. "I didn't get the information," the assassin concluded. "I'll continue investigations."

Taran's heart jumped and then relaxed. He was still clear and completely unsuspected for being tied with Rashaad and the incoming Turks. Taran considered himself smarter than Rashaad. He tried to warn him. Rashaad was set in his ways on how to handle things, however. They each agreed to play their own angles, allying with the Turks, only working together loosely. It was Taran's luck that he reacted the way he did when

Sa'ad spoke the company plans that marked Civan-el Bey. Sa'ad had to play with the surprised look and lie that Taran did not know. Taran did know. His best trait in business was to know when to remain silent. If Rashaad was going to die, so be it. Taran would bide his time and bite his tongue even with the Turks. He would allow Civan-el Bey, his close contact inside their Empire, to be extinguished. Taran played from both sides of business' coin.

Sa'ad's revelation to Rashaad, on company plans that marked Civan-el Bey, was not the most devastating news. The greater news came next. Sa'ad spoke slowly, "I will meet Rashaad tonight."

"Make it before midnight," Roberto reminded.

"I will meet him *at* midnight," Sa'ad said with great insistence. He could see the men around him wanting to protest his actions. Their eyes went wide simultaneously as they each correctly deduced Sa'ad's intentions for meeting Rashaad. Sa'ad explained to Roberto, "He may be familiar with his contact. Your man may frighten him off. He'll see what's coming."

Roberto's pride was offended. "With all respect, Company Boss, he *won't* see what's coming," he corrected elegantly. He shook his head and said, "Forgive my offense. But you…?" questioned Roberto.

Sa'ad took no offense. He understood the questioning. "It will put him at ease when he sees me. He will trust that I'm his new contact. He will be relieved. I will present to him these papers as proof." He extended an open palm to Roberto. "An instrument," he ordered softly.

Maybe Sa'ad needed answers, the others thought. But the sentiment was not pondered on too long. Roberto pulled out a small pistol from his satchel. He placed the weapon inside Sa'ad's palm. "It's a weak shot. Fire here," he pointed to the side of his head, at the temple. "You may have to do the rest with a knife."

Sa'ad assured he had a dagger. He stared at the gun contemplatively. This would be life number eight taken by his hands. Sa'ad contemplated no more. He put the weapon in his lap and stated the procedures. "Roberto, continue your duties with the guards and police. You will discover the body at dawn and alert Taran and Wakil." The occultist nodded at the command. "Taran and Wakil, you will bring the news to me. Come to the gates and call for my wife. I'll be in my study. I will give orders on Rashaad's family."

The two men acknowledged their company boss.

Sa'ad asked one more favor of Wakil. He wanted the pious lawyer to say a brief prayer for him, in private. Roberto and Taran were dismissed. A prayer was needed. There was killing to be done and forgiveness for it.

Night

Sa'ad leapt between shadows through dimly lit alleyways and dark streets. His robes fluttered elegantly behind him. He ducked through the alleys feeling nimble, as if ten years younger. The burden of the deed ahead of him did not weigh him down. He had been taking the back roads carefully. Rashaad was ahead of him, walking quickly. Sa'ad had been following him for the last ten minutes, starting from Rashaad's house. He allowed his friend a good lead before pursuing him on his way to his destination. Sa'ad at times took side streets, keeping a parallel track on Rashaad's progress, and then doubling around to be behind his friend again.

The only problems Sa'ad encountered were the bright lamps burning from stone pillars that were planted on the streets. He laughed silently at the irony. Sa'ad's company installed the street pillars holding lamps several years ago to keep the streets lit and prevent crime. He was now forced to outwit his own legislation. Rashaad exited an alley and walked casually onto a dusty road in a corner district. He looked both ways as he entered the street. Rashaad never looked behind him. It would have made no difference. Sa'ad was blanketed by shadow. He could see Rashaad. Rashaad would never be able to see him. They were still playing chase like little boys.

Rashaad then stepped forward and disappeared into the alley across the street. Sa'ad moved closer, removing a spyglass from his satchel. The purse also contained the property deeds, Roberto's small pistol, and a simple dagger. His eyes were well enough that he could see no movement in the alley beyond. There was a small area of the alley dimly lit by the flickering fire coming from posted lamps and torches. Sa'ad could see Rashaad. He looked as if he was sitting. He was still and waiting. Sa'ad looked through his spyglass and adjusted the lens. The image was dark, but close. This was Rashaad's destination. He was waiting for his contact.

Sa'ad had confirmation. He put the spyglass away and stepped backwards. His eyes remained on the alley across from the one he occupied. No shadows moved or silhouette stirred. Rashaad was stationary. Sa'ad had to act quickly. He turned around and made a journey that wound around the district he found himself in, and then crossed to the other side. He was quick in his travel, eventually finding a passage connecting to the alley where Rashaad sat still on a wooden crate.

Sa'ad continued to observe his friend from the dark. He stepped forward, his shoes slipping on the dust beneath him. A scratching noise was made and alerted Rashaad. He jumped to his feet and stepped back to keep balance. His eyes were wide as they stared into the darkness where eventually emerged Sa'ad. The company boss's face mirrored the expression Rashaad had, but he was only playing a part.

Rashaad didn't know what to do, confronted by his friend. But he saw the same look of surprise masking Sa'ad's face. He started forward and reached out to his friend. Sa'ad continued to play his part. He gave a soft smile and expressed in a very low whisper, "R-R-Rashaad?" Sa'ad stuttered with believable disbelief. "You're my contact? My goodness! They said I'd be surprised, but…"

Rashaad smiled and choked on excitement. He jumped to Sa'ad and threw his arms around him. "I can't believe it," he whispered back. "You have no idea how this comforts me." His embrace became tighter and then quickly loosened. Rashaad backed up. A worried look was on his face. "And also breaks my heart."

Sa'ad continued his performance. He sighed. "It's been hard. There are walls closing in. I have to get out, for the sake of my family."

Rashaad was relieved. He took his seat again on the wooden crate. It was large enough for Sa'ad to join him. Rashaad wiped his face with a hand, again exhaling relief. "I have felt the same way, my friend," he chuckled. "The Turks are advancing. They found our greater trade routes," he said not revealing how. Sa'ad just watched as Rashaad talked. His gaze was intense, waiting for his friend to burst into brimstone and turn into the devil himself. But there was no such luck. This was his friend. This was Rashaad. Sa'ad had to kill him as he was.

Rashaad's voice was smooth even in the act of betrayal. "Our treasury has been ransacked by businessmen," Rashaad articulated. "Our men are squabbling among each other. The companies are on the brink of war. And we are inviting swarmahu Turks to regulate us valiant Moors." Rashaad gritted his teeth in frustration. Sa'ad didn't know if this was an act or not. Rashaad, however, was leaving out his betrayal in all this.

Rashaad was now a master at the lie.

Sa'ad had no idea that Rashaad engineered a plan to kill him. The Turks were going to wipe Sa'ad away. Rashaad would be company boss. He would put Taran in charge, taking revenue and tribute while he lived far away. Rashaad would extinguish Wakil and round up Roberto's occult outfit, making sure the occultist met that great dark beyond that he always rambled on about.

Rashaad was not completely cold, though. He was going to take care of Sa'ad's family. He would take Afya—Sa'ad's wife—as a second wife; and he would raise Nasir as a third son. He wondered if Afya even remembered the night they already shared. Probably not. She was drugged. Afya did have spurts of memories. Rashaad convinced her that she started to breathe heavy, panic, and then fainted. It was not too farfetched. Afya had just given birth to Nasir; it was a complicated birth where she lost a good amount of blood. She was still recovering from the four-month-old trauma. In truth, she realized what Rashaad had done in drugging her. She tried to fight him, but the Asian-grown herb circulating through her bloodstream was too powerful. She passed out. Afya was Rashaad's for an entire night.

It should have been understood as to why. Sa'ad had taken Rashaad's wife to bed. It was innocent though. It happened when he and Sa'ad were playing scoundrel and pirates before settling down. She chose Rashaad after the affair. He was always second. He didn't care about that now. The sight of Sa'ad liberated him from guilt. This was his contact. The righteous Sa'ad was no better than him. He too was fighting to get out, no less through treachery and deceit than he. Rashaad thought to himself that Sa'ad would never make it. Sa'ad was marked.

"Yes," Rashaad heard Sa'ad agree. "All of Africa is in trouble."

Rashaad nodded his head. "They say the horrors of the African slave trade are true, and European eyes have spied Africa for the taking. They say that this time, with us in disarray, they'll do it. I can't have my family succumb to that."

"Well, at least we'll know for sure." Sa'ad removed the parchments from his satchel and handed them to Rashaad. "I have been given deeds as well. A man named Mahir gave them to us."

Rashaad took the parchments. "I was under the impression I was meeting him tonight." He looked through the deeds. Rashaad smiled and said, "Ah, America. Amexem." He then thought again about the fate of Africa. "It's as if the pride of al-Kahina scorched all of Africa." He looked at Sa'ad and asked, "So who will lead in your absence? I know you must have chosen a successor." Rashaad was unable to directly address Sa'ad with his next question. He turned away and asked with a haughty smile, "And when do you plan on abandoning al-Mari Ifriq?"

There was something in the line that angered Sa'ad. There was anger in him that he thought he would never aim toward Rashaad. It was even more intense than the anger that boiled in him earlier in the day. It was several times the mass of the sun, and far worse than the stage of anger he had journeyed through when he was informed of Rashaad's betrayal.

Rashaad's voice was no longer soothing; it was mocking. There was an arrogance detected. The same mocking tone that Sa'ad would hear in the voice of hardheaded men from other companies was now echoed in Rashaad's voice. Sa'ad would deal with his friend's mocking tone all the same.

Sa'ad took out Roberto's pistol from the satchel. He aimed it at Rashaad's temple, as instructed. His friend was looking away. Rashaad never saw the action. He only responded briefly, when before the weapon was fired, Sa'ad stated, "I hope our children can remain friends."

Rashaad's head turned into the blast. It snapped back with the impact of the small, compact projectile crashing into the left side of his head. The discharge's sound echoed through the alley and scattered out into the street like a crying ghost. Bursting sparks rained onto Sa'ad's sleeve and seared the edges of his garment; the burst of flames did the same to patches of Rashaad's hair. Blood and small, broken chunks of flesh covered the burns on Sa'ad's sleeve and parts of his hand.

There was not a lot of damage done to Rashaad. A tiny hole was tunneled into his head where the gun was fired, but blood poured from the wound like a waterfall. Rashaad's eyelids vibrated, fighting against closing and staying open. He was still conscious. Reality appeared fragmented— cracked and hazy—seen through his right eye. Rashaad's left eye was completely blind.

Sa'ad put the weapon back into his satchel, substituting it for his knife. He stood up and positioned himself in front of Rashaad's gyrating body. The company boss cupped Rashaad's mouth. Sa'ad forced his friend's convulsing, soon-to-be carcass against the wall of the building forming the alley. He put the tip of the knife against Rashaad's neck and eased it in. The sharpened blade slipped through the flesh with no difficulty. The body's convulsions increased. Rashaad's eyes went wide, but he was now completely blind. Sa'ad could feel Rashaad's mouth under his hand trying to open. The body continued to shake. Pain, shock, and fear at war with the body.

Sa'ad locked his teary, determined gaze with Rashaad's blank stare. Blood was coughed up onto the palm of his hand. Rashaad's eyes rolled back into his head and Sa'ad let go, allowing his friend's body to slump to the ground, carrying the dagger with it. Dust aired upwards with Rashaad's lifeless impact. Sa'ad knelt down and wiped the blood from his hands with Rashaad's garments. He searched the body for coin. There was none. He could not make the scene resemble a robbery.

Sa'ad exhaled a heavy sigh and sat back on the crate. He wished he had brought a flask with drink. Sa'ad leaned forward, elbows on his knees and hands locked together. "You were my brother, Rashaad," he spoke to the lifeless body. "I loved you."

He needed to leave. He needed to get back to his wife that lay in bed believing he was locked away in his study finishing up business. He wanted to be near his wife, sleeping next to her warm body. She was al-Mari Ifriq to him. She was Odongo-Mauharim to him. She was Africa to him, and Sa'ad would kill to protect her.

Sunrise

Sa'ad slept easy, exhausted from the previous day and night's events. He also found it easy to wash the blood from his hands. But he had his own ritual for mourning the death of his friend. He awoke next to his wife. He kissed her on the shoulder and then stood up from the bed. He slipped on his shoes and walked to the bedroom window. He opened the wooden flaps and let in the sun's light. A religious man howled in the distance to signal the city to come to activity. Sa'ad closed the flaps of the window when he heard his wife groan. He announced that he was going back to his study. Still dressed in his nightclothes, he left the room and wandered down the halls of the unfinished palace.

Sa'ad considered that the Turks who moved into the palace would probably finish it once he was removed from its residence. He knew they would set him up in a fine district. His company's influence would be reduced to a simple area of al-Mari Ifriq. He pondered this as he came to his study and walked inside. The room was larger than the council room. It too was circular, with parts of the walls carved out as shelves. They were lined with hundreds of books. In the center of the room was a circular bed draped with a canopy. Decorative pillows, in an assortment of sunrise colors, populated the bed. Thrown over them were his garments from last night. Near the window there was a low, wooden carved table and a wooden chair. Atop the table were two bottles of wine, smuggled into his room by command of servants.

Sa'ad took a seat after opening the window. He could see the gates and the courtyard. He took a deep breath. He needed to pass the time waiting for Wakil and Taran. So he decided to drink. It was planned anyhow. This was his mourning ritual. He took the first bottle and removed the cork. The wine's trapped aroma swiveled free from the bottle. Sa'ad tipped the opening of the slender bottle toward him. He looked deep inside the bottle of wine. He wondered if a djinn with comforting arms lay at the bottom. He knew the thought was ridiculous; but he wanted to drink. He wanted another excuse to drink. An excuse far different than the one he had. He wanted an excuse that would make him smile and forget. So he looked deep inside the bottle to find the spirit, the djinn. But the dark, purple liquid looked like the abyss of space. The bottle had no bottom in the view of the spying eye peering down from above. The bottle looked like it had a trapped, aqueous form of midnight. Sa'ad would reinvent the physics of this liquid cosmos, however. He would find the bottom of the abyss.

Sa'ad sipped the liquid and felt the burn of the dark, rich wine filter through his throat and then swirl inside his stomach. He imagined that the wine was the djinn spirit he was searching for, hot and fiery, and burning him for his sins. He looked to his right and saw the second bottle. One would not do. Two would be perfect. He turned his head to the left and looked out the window, watching the new day. Taran and Wakil were at the gates. The guards answered their presence, stepping forth. The two men summoned for Sa'ad's wife, as ordered. He watched Taran and Wakil speaking to his wife at the gate. Afya reacted in horror to the news she was given. Rashaad was dead, murdered in an alley last night. Sa'ad took another sip from his bottle, his eye watching his wife cup her mouth as she gasped. It would've been worse if his wife knew the truth, he thought.

Afya escorted Taran and Wakil inside. Sa'ad could see a blurry vision of the path they would take to his private chamber, the winding hallways, and the specific path to the front of his door. He saw each step; his vision becoming more and more blurry as he took more and more sips of wine. He timed his foggy breadth of view perfectly. At the very moment that Sa'ad imagined his wife, Taran, and Wakil approaching the outside of his chambers, there came knocking at the door.

"Enter," Sa'ad slurred. He straightened himself out, stood and smiled. His wife claimed the only genuine expression. Afya was fighting diligently to hide the hurt inside her. Terrible news was about to befall her husband, or so she thought.

Sa'ad stepped forward, carefully, his head light from the wine. He played sober well. He greeted his wife and friends. Afya bowed respectfully and then left the men to their business. Sa'ad's act dropped. He went back to his seat.

Taran and Wakil had an uncomfortable time sitting on the bed next to one another. It was comical. Sa'ad would have laughed if tragedy had not choked his humor. The two men awaited word from their company boss. "I will take Rashaad's family under my guard."

Wakil looked at Taran. The other could feel the lawyer's gaze. Taran confronted the stare and Wakil nodded his head, issuing Taran to speak. Sa'ad was not too bogged in wine to miss this movement. Taran turned to face Sa'ad. "Company Boss," he said humbly. "I will take Rashaad's children in." Before Sa'ad could protest Taran explained, "The burden is too great. Relieve yourself of some of it. I will take his wife as a second."

Sa'ad nodded his head, agreeing without protest. Maybe it was the wine. But he did have a stern warning. He took another sip from the bottle and pointed a finger. "When you take his wife, be there no scandal. Not even thought. Or I will repeat my act of friendship toward another dear friend."

Taran bowed at the neck with great respect. "Yes, Company Boss."

Sa'ad eyed Wakil. "You will shoulder Rashaad's duties. I will take control of his shipyard." Wakil agreed. "Send Roberto to me when he is through with processing the murder's location." He held the bottle of wine close to his chest and looked at the second bottle on the table. "Tell him to come for dinner. I will host everyone tonight. Our families. Rashaad's family. We will make way for a glorious funeral. Rashaad will be honored." Sa'ad cleared his throat and stared outside. "Tell my wife I want the cooks and servant-girls to prepare the finest meal. Tell her I wish not to be disturbed. You are dismissed."

Wakil and Taran stood from the bed, bowed with respect, and left the room. Sa'ad continued to drink. His thoughts strayed wildly but continued to sway back to a strange premonition telling him he needed to watch Rashaad's children. He should care for his friend's family. He tried to stay on the thought, drinking more and more, and believing that increasing the wine would open up his mind to understanding, like a religious sacrament taken for clarity. It was not guilt of his deed that made him believe that Rashaad's children should be taken under his wing. There was something wrong in Taran having possession of them. He heard something in Taran's voice. There again was that same arrogant tone of the hardheaded company bosses. He believed that he made the wrong move. He drank more, searching for a clear thought. The wine worked in retrograde to Sa'ad's intentions.

But there was a feeling. There was the sense that he let Rashaad's two boys, Maurice and Fusan, go into the hands of another betrayer—a betrayer with information that Sa'ad had killed the two boys' father, and information that could be twisted and used against Sa'ad, or even his young boy. The wine was now smothering. Sa'ad opened his mouth to let his accusing words escape and record his inclination into the ethers.

"Taran is too a traitor."

The words were free.

Unfortunately the revelation came when Sa'ad's brain was mired in alcohol. His ears did not hear the sentiment spoken by his lips, and he passed out. Dream and wine would wash away the accusation, a very brief moment of clarity swimming in an alcoholic haze. What would never be washed away, however, would be the guilt of the deed he accomplished the previous night. Sa'ad murdered his dear friend. The betrayal of Rashaad would never ease the pain. Regardless of the reason for his deed, Sa'ad would always shoulder the guilt. Worse yet, he knew there was another traitor in his close circle. By the afternoon, however, Sa'ad al-Din Sa'ood would no longer remember what he most certainly should not have forgotten.

Taran Zaher could not be trusted.

Chapter Two

Spain, 1640

"What did we Moors do for Spain?" asked the black Moor from his platform that was stationed in the small square at the heart of this Spanish city. The Moor played with the idea that he was in a time period not his own. To him, it was four hundred years ago. The city was dressed in the legends he had heard as a child growing up in the Moorish taifa, a remaining Moorish city-state in Spain. The era of the Moors was long passed, but its ghosts remained in the city's architecture, inspiring the Moor's imagination further.

The audience below him, a great gathering, like the gray clouds above, lifted fists toward him and hollered loud. The Moor took in the shouts beneath him, standing firm, hands behind his back. He equaled the crowd's rumblings with his voice. The Moor answered his own question. "All we did for Spain—*for Europe*—was provide light to its Dark Ages and halt its degeneration back into barbarism. They who deliberately turned away from the lessons of their highest cultures, the Greeks and the Romans, would be taught again by those who represented the descendants of those cultures' teachers. Ziryab, that man like a bird with black plumage—his color no different—single-handedly educated this world to music, botany, chemistry, table edict, and the aspect of fashion and seasonal dress. That was within the *first* hundred years of our seven-hundred-year reign.

"When the greatest of the white, European nobles were illiterate and living in a barn, we birthed palaces and libraries carrying hundreds-of-thousands of books, and sought knowledge rather than gold or land. We built the finest public baths when Europe looked upon cleanliness as a sin. We established drains when Europe was throwing its waste into the street. There were suburbs to our cities; there were districts; there were towering structures that surrounded great universities built for study of the finest arts and the greatest of sciences. We preserved the precise mathematics of the ancients, expounded upon their sciences, and the philosophical tenants of spirituality.

"We even extended the gifts of freedom. Women walked as doctors, lawyers, and soldiers. The Jew and the Christian were free to worship. And crime on the street could barely find shadows for comfort.

Ironically, we presented civilization like a tribute, as if Europe was the god and we its humble subjects. Perhaps then Europe was the embodiment of that black, Phoenician princess of mythology, of which whose name she so proudly continues to bare: Europa. All praises to the Mother Goddess. *I-sis! Emme Ya! Oya-Yasna! Kali-ah! Al-uzzah! Qre! Allah-t!* Praise even to your names unspoken, and to your three-fold Manat. Continue to anoint us with your oil—your petra—as you raise your true African descendants—*we Moors*—like a disgraced, single mother. Your Husband has been tricked into service by the pale religions and nations that have left a hulking scar on humanity's soul. You are invisible to Him now. A holy ghost beheaded like Medusa by the Greeks, they who so jealousy committed that heinous act to that beautiful, Negress-Goddess. We have been robbed of our medicine. I curse her cancer, her now blanched population. Let they remain as barren and recessive as the moon."

The crowd roared. The Moor pushed out his bare chest and again stood firm and tall. His height was not extended because of the stool beneath his feet, or the mounted public stage he and the stool were planted on. Nor was his height extended because of his wife's presence on the stage, kneeling and holding their two children. No, the Moor's height was extended by his words.

The Moor was not ashamed, and he let that be known. He stood upon the stool atop the wooden platform screaming his pride through the loop of a noose that he pretended was acting like a megaphone. It dangled in front of him, blaring his voice out to the hollering Spanish citizens that surrounded the gallows and called for his death. His hands were bound behind him, but his words were free to fly away.

Spanish soldiers were on either side of him. There was a soldier behind the Moor. Next to this soldier was a man ready to place the loop of the noose around the Moor's neck and kick the stool away. Five Spanish soldiers, armed with muskets, waited at the foot of the gallows. The Moor was found guilty of aiding and abetting five revolutionaries that had been robbing trade caravans of goods and weapons. The revolutionaries, at the command of their taifa's king, also conspired in a plot to target Spanish nobles.

The five Moorish revolutionaries were in attendance, peering up at the Moor and his family on the gallows' platform. For all their acts of rebellion, there was nothing more valiant than what played out on the stage in front of them. Even the elected king of their taifa, the man whom they served, did not die with such honor. None of the five Moors moved. Their faces were like stone. They might as well have been part of mythology, victims of the Greek's version of Medusa. Inside the revolutionaries, however, there was a different story. Their emotions were a whirlwind, at least with four of the Moorish rebels. These four men were young, just several years shy of thirty.

Ameer Las El-Behar was the leader and elder of the Moorish revolutionaries. He was fifty-eight years of age. His dark visage was chiseled by the drama of his small revolutionary deeds. His body, shaped with a warrior's physique, refused to ache from age. Behar was like iron. Though they followed an elect king—truthfully, a governor of a Moorish district outside the Spanish city—this was Behar's war. He was the true strategist in disrupting the Spanish Crown, which was why he and his closest lieutenants were receiving the harshest penalty. For the last ten days these five rebels were submitted to the viewing of multiple hangings of Moors from all extractions.

Moriscos were hanged. Moors with Arabian blood were hanged. Mohammedans of all creeds were hanged. Their governor, a Moor of Soudanese extraction, was shot and beheaded. Wives were brutalized publicly before burning. Even gracious European men and women of French, Dutch, and Spanish persuasion were executed for aiding the Moorish rebellion. Behar, over the past week, became numb to the sight of these executions, but this fellow Moor standing atop the gallows stirred Behar's blood.

Philip III, in his reign as King of Spain, and King of Portugal under the moniker of Philip II, expelled much of the Moorish remnants in 1609. The decision caused serious economic difficulties in the kingdoms of Valencia and Aragon, where the Moorish population held influence over the ruling nobles, and were used for cheap labor. These communities, made up of remaining Moors that did not flee into the mountains, another country, or back to Africa, were built outside Spanish cities. Some of these self-governing Moorish populations plotted rebellion. Piracy was committed on trade caravans. Thieves were blamed. Organized crime was whispered about throughout all of Spain. The taifas were never suspected, until recently.

Behar and his elected king stretched their arms too far in their activities. Their small population thrived too well as Moors. They should have been otherwise struggling. They were investigated, sold out by a few of their own, and rounded up. The last two weeks brought Spain back to the days of the Reconquest and the dreadful Cardinal Xemenos. One hundred years of slaughter were summed up in two weeks time. *Let not a black body be spared. Let the devils of Africa return to its fire."*—If, of course, they were not sentenced to slavery in the American colonies.

Slavery was the fate resigned for Behar and his lieutenants, the remaining soldiers of the unit that he called *The Griffins*. It was the thought of slavery that collapsed Behar's spirit. The crown could do to him as they wished, but not to these young men that he still viewed as boys. These scholars could not suffer such a fate. Behar referred to them as scholars because they were beyond warriors. He prompted each of them to study their family history as much as he made them study the blade and the gun. Behar wanted each young man to know what he was fighting for.

Standing to Behar's right was his second-in-command, al-Jeheuty Anhur Has. He was rich with brown skin, a triangular face, and facial hair so subtle a feature populating his chin that it could not even be described as a stubble. Al-Jeheuty was adorned with long flowing locks. Behar was surprised that the Spanish did not cut the young man's hair, taking away his might as though he were Samson himself. But there was no act against him, this proud negotiator, whose words saved his rivals in business from understanding he was an equally elegant swordsman. Al-Jeheuty was an executioner with words and actions. His word was his bond. He negotiated, not just to find a means to solve everyone's problems, or come to a common ground and understanding, but to keep alive the people with whom he negotiated. Crossing him was dangerous. He would annihilate any man should they prove unworthy, and so was he branded the name 'The Spear'.

Al-Jeheuty joined Behar's small army when he journeyed into Spain posing as a traveling student. He was twenty-two, struggling, and looking for sanctuary. Al-Jeheuty had been on the run for committing petty thefts and burglaries. These were activities he indulged in just to keep money in his pocket, and a little childhood mischief that he had yet to shake off. He held two professional jobs, but did not agree with the practice of his European employers. His employers were the targets of his mischief.

Al-Jeheuty was an actual student, a graduate from the University of Sankore. He became wrapped in mischief a year after schooling was finished. His family hailed from a small town on the eastern border of Morocco, close to Algeria. Al-Jeheuty already knew of his family heritage. They were of an African bloodline that stretched back to Abyssinia. Somewhere between the years 711 and 1241 the bloodline was swept up in the westward expansion of Mohammedanism and settled in Moorish Spain. His family tree migrated back to Africa before the fall of al-Andalusia.

Al-Jeheuty's wide, brown eyes stared up in amazement at his fellow Moor that performed for the gathered crowd. He was in awe at the Moor's last exertion. He asked himself if he could be so brave. He worried that his negotiations were not good enough. Someone had sold them out, their entire district. He wondered if his failed words would lead all the way to the death of his family.

Bo Yusuf ibn Tachfin al-Dume, Behar's captain-of-arms, stood to Behar's left. He was a year older than al-Jeheuty. His skin glistened like the African desert being struck by the high noon sun. A triangular beard decorated his rough, yet handsome visage. The top of Bo Yusuf's head was covered in tight coils of hair, sprouting from his head like Medusa's snakes. His eyes were like that of a hawk pursuing his prey. He looked so much like his father, one of Behar's best friends, now long gone in this Moorish rebellion. Bo Yusuf and his father kept the tradition of their family. They were descendants of honorable, Moorish warriors. And they did not take that knowledge lightly.

Bo Yusuf's political ideals and revolutionary fire longed to re-shape Spain into the old days of al-Andalusia. He was greatly in love with the romanticized tales his father told him as a youth. He wondered if he would die a soldier as brave as the Moor in front of him. Bo Yusuf understood the penalty given to him, Behar, and the rest of the lieutenants. He and his dearest friends would be made to suffer in servitude.

Bo Yusuf also understood that slavery would be a great offense to the lieutenant stationed behind him. His name was Rahmis Husani, a Moor that reveled in the information he discovered about his bloodline. Rahmis was connected to multiple nobilities that stretched from the Almohades Dynasty, the Sahelian-Ghanan Empire, and all the way to the kingdoms of ancient Africa. The fall of al-Andalusia disrupted this noble line, but the knowledge of Rahmis' nobility gave him a foundation. He lost his mother and father. His father was killed shortly after his birth. He was a proud man who, like many Moors, did not move from Spain when threatened. Rahmis' mother was too ill to care for him after his birth. She died alone. Somewhere. Rahmis was left in the care of a Moorish family that was close to Behar.

Rahmis was extracted from midnight. He was a shadow that defied the presence of light. He had a perfect oval-shaped head that was void of hair, save the thick patch that grew on his chin. His wide smile, bearing polished white teeth, was the only hint of white. But his mood now was somber, reflecting on how noble his fellow Moor was before death. There was nothing more beautiful, except perhaps the women Rahmis had conquered. Not even all their images could make him smile now. Not at this sight.

Behar's last lieutenant towered above everyone. There were definitely no intentions to shave Ojodo Yerodin's locks from his head. Behar understood why. Ojodo was a dangerous behemoth even when dressed in the heavy chains that weighed the black giant down. He knew much of his family history, architects and seafarers from Mali with a maritime business in Tunis. Ojodo did not go into the family business as an architect. The sea was more promising financially, and it also satisfied his adventurous heart. He joined his uncle's crew at the age of twenty. On the third day of his excursion, Ojodo learned that his uncle was more than a sea merchant. He was a smuggler. Ojodo learned the art of gunnery and smuggling. He was working with Behar two years after joining his uncle. That was eight years ago.

Behar's discipline for study wielded a love and appreciation for knowledge. Ojodo could not satiate his appetite for erudition. The giant devoured books like he devoured his plates of food. There was more that he wanted to do, though. There was more to discover. Eyes on the Moor, he wondered if he would die accomplished and complete.

The five rebels watched on. The executioner tightened the noose around the Moor's neck. He received no sack to cover his face. The citizens wished to see the black Moor become a gruesome sight. The crowd went silent. The Moor's wife turned her children away from their father's fate. She huddled with them, holding tight. Her tears dripped onto the gallows' platform, mixing in with the light rain. The stool was kicked out from under the Moor, and his wife closed her eyes in that instant. The body dropped, jerking back, the rope stretching the Moor's neck. There was a tearing sound, muted by the sudden ringing of a bell tower. Urine and feces slid down the Moor's pant leg, dripping and clumping onto the platform. His body gyrated and his eyes enlarged behind closed lids. The Moor's face rushed with blood and started to further darken to violet and purple.

The five rebels clenched their teeth in anger.

The Moorish wife opened her eyes. She kept her children turned into her embrace. The five-year old boy and ten-year old girl had their back to their father's swaying body. It jerked wildly, life keeping fight and breath in the Moor's body. He was a revolutionary to the last. The armed Spanish soldiers ascended the platform and assembled behind the Moorish wife and children. The boy looked up in horror. The Spanish soldiers aimed their muskets and fired a salvo of bullets into the hanged Moor. The rebellion was over.

The gunfire caused the Moorish wife to scream, her spirit finally broken. Her holler was deafened by the crowd's excited roar. The soldiers' captain quickly came up the steps and waved to the crowd with a smile. He motioned for the crowd to silence, waving his hands downward.

"Silence!" he yelled. "Silence," he continued. "There is more to do." He looked at the two soldiers standing beside the hanging Moor. "Remove these children. This is no place for them. We'll auction them off at the courts tomorrow."

The soldiers jumped to instruction. The armed soldiers stepped aside. The two soldiers wrapped their arms around either child and pulled them away from their mother. They screamed and locked their embrace tighter around the Moorish woman. She was too fatigued to hold them. She was crying, out of breath, and emotionally exhausted. But her children were strong enough to hold her body tightly, putting great restraint against the Spanish soldiers' tugs.

A soldier removed a pistol and fired into the back of the Moorish woman's head. It looked as if she leapt forward to attack the soldiers, but it was the force of the impact that pushed her body forward. Her body crumpled to the wooden platform. The soldiers carried the children away in separate directions. The children stopped struggling, accepting their fate. Their eyes were wide, swallowing the images of their dead parents.

The soldiers disappeared into the crowd with the children.

The five soldiers armed with muskets reloaded and aimed their weapons at the five rebels below. The captain motioned for the Moors to take the stage. "Come, come," he said with a sly smirk. Three more Spanish soldiers appeared in the crowd. Two had pistols, one a sword. The five rebels were prodded to the stage. The captain made his way down to the front of the gallows. Room was made for the rebels by removing the bodies of the hanged Moor and his wife. Their bodies were tossed into a cart and wheeled away.

The crowd gave the captain room. Citizens, gathered in the front of the crowd, removed small buckets of urine and held acrid clumps of feces in their hands. Others in the crowd did the same.

"Ready," the captain said to them. "Aim," he commanded next. The citizens prepared their excrement. "Fire!" shouted the captain, jumping out of the way of the tossed waste.

This ritual accompanied the executions every day for the last two weeks. A full hour passed before the citizens grew tired of yelling curses and tossing their waste. The five rebels were carried away. They were to be cleaned and prepared for departure to Portugal.

The water was refreshing as it slapped against al-Jeheuty's face.

Having his head forced down into the barrel of water, was not. But the water covering al-Jeheuty's face instantly removed the excrement tossed on him by the Spanish citizens. When his head was pulled back from the water he was shouted at by Spanish soldiers and spit on. He took in as many breaths as he could before being dunked back in again. Behar and the other lieutenants suffered the same cleaning routine just minutes before. Ojodo was a different story. Barrels were poured onto him while soldiers beat him with the butts of their muskets.

The Spanish soldiers punched al-Jeheuty in the ribs while his head was dunked below the water. He restricted his reflexes from inhaling after being struck by the blows. The soldiers were trying to make him draw in water and choke. But al-Jeheuty breathed out, forcing the water away from drowning him. A commanding officer finally ordered the soldiers to cease. Al-Jeheuty and the others were fated for service in the Americas. The soldiers could not go too far with their torture. The twenty-six year old Moor was dragged back to a small holding area, deep beneath a prison. The passageways looked like the city's sewer, and smelled the same.

The Moorish captives deduced that the underground holding area was part of the city's old sewage system. A true dungeon would have been squared out, instead of flowing with water mixed with other mysterious liquids. There were tunnels, not hallways, leading to cells. Al-Jeheuty, Behar, Bo Yusuf, Ojodo, and Rahmis shared a cell, wading in two-inch liquid. Al-Jeheuty was the last to be tossed inside. The cell door was locked and the soldiers walked away, their boots splashing in the reeking liquid.

Behar whispered, "They're taking us to Portugal."

Al-Jeheuty sat up against the wall. "Good. I hear it's nice this time of year."

"We can still escape," continued Behar, ignoring al-Jeheuty's cynicism.

"You have a lot of faith for someone who doesn't believe in the tenants of Moses, Christ, or Mohammed," al-Jeheuty voiced.

Behar's eyes focused on al-Jeheuty. "Do you feel I failed you," he asked with the greatest sincerity.

Al-Jeheuty shook his head. "No, my Captain. I'm just exhausted."

"As long as you're not defeated," Bo Yusuf spoke. He then exhaled, "We're heading to the colonies. Amexem: The Land of Dreams. I hear they're now investing in nightmares."

Al-Jeheuty's eyes looked across the small room. He spotted Bo Yusuf's silhouette. Al-Jeheuty smiled, even chuckled. "Ojodo," he then addressed the large Moor. "Is this adventurous enough for you?"

Ojodo muffled his laugh.

Al-Jeheuty then addressed, "Rahmis. Could your noble blood not ask for a finer place of rest?"

"I've become the Prince of Poop," Rahmis growled sarcastically. His fellow rebels exhibited low laughs. "I am the Sultan of Sludge."

They each rubbed their wrists, once clamped by heavy shackles. "Why can we still laugh?" al-Jeheuty asked.

Behar answered, "Because they can break every bone in our physical bodies, but they will never touch our spirits."

"They sure do give it the good academic try, don't they, Captain?" joked al-Jeheuty as he rubbed various aching areas on his body.

Behar grunted. His mind was contemplating. He looked up in thought. "From Portugal they will swing down to Africa where there is a slave port setup. We can escape there. We can fight."

"You don't believe they will go straight to the New World?" asked al-Jeheuty.

Behar shook his head. "No. They have other cargo, other Africans to market as slaves. They have money to make."

Al-Jeheuty re-considered his thought. He shook his head in agreement. "They need the winds coming off Africa to best reach Amexem anyway."

"And once we escape, what is our life then?" asked Bo Yusuf. "Where is the dream of al-Andalusia? Where is *our* dream? With no offense to my brothers, al-Jeheuty and Ojodo have a home to escape to. Rahmis and I have been orphaned."

Behar cleared his throat. He knew his eyes were probably not visible to Bo Yusuf. Light was scarce. No torches lined the tunnels. A small ray of light came from deep beyond the tunnel, spreading itself thin throughout the dungeon-made maze. Regardless, Behar put his eyes on Bo Yusuf. He was wholehearted in his voice. "Bo Yusuf, let Spain go. Africa is your home; Africa is your blood."

Bo Yusuf wrapped his arms around his knees, huddled. "Then that Moor died in vain today. They all did."

Al-Jeheuty snapped, "And you would wish more? You would risk more Moorish blood just to capture a moment in time that ended almost two hundred years ago? In a state of disarray, might I add?"

Bo Yusuf emerged from his huddle to raise a finger and sharply address, "That is not what we studied. We embraced the ideals of al-Andalusia's Golden Age."

"Well now we've hit the three-hundred year mark," al-Jeheuty countered. "Should we go back to where Tariq's glorious expedition captured Spain?"

"You have a home to go to," Bo Yusuf barked, keeping his voice low.

"And you are well invited," al-Jeheuty said with great intensity.

"The two of you," Behar chided. The brothers-in-arms relaxed and let their captain speak. "We plan escape first. There are kingdoms all throughout Africa for us to settle in. The ideals we fought for can still be applied. It does not always have to be a fight, a struggle." Behar sat up. He put his hands together and concluded: "We must find that point in the revolution where struggle becomes success and excel from there."

The four Moorish rebels pondered their captain's words. There was silence. Other scattered mutterings and conversations could be heard throughout the dungeon. Al-Jeheuty and Bo Yusuf relaxed. But there still was an unfinished matter. Al-Jeheuty could feel the heat of Bo Yusuf smirking at him.

"I'll slap it off your face," he told his fellow Moor.

The sound of chuckling came from the dark.

"There *are* advantages for being on your side," snickered Bo Yusuf.

Al-Jeheuty smiled. "You're the only one that doesn't see the tip of my sword when negotiations fail. You're lucky I'm unarmed. To an extent, anyway." Al-Jeheuty splashed a salvo of dirty water in Bo Yusuf's direction.

Bo Yusuf became drenched. He spit the foul water free before it could slip down his throat. He wiped the rest from his face and laughed a little harder. Behar silenced them again with a stern command. The water was filthy, and disease was something they could not afford to catch. Behar wanted them to have their strength. He encouraged his lieutenants to rest, especially their mouths. The latter part of their command caused a little laughter. The soldiers were quick to their orders.

The Moorish rebels rested for three hours before Spanish soldiers dragged them from their damp cell. Fifteen armed soldiers shackled and escorted Behar and his lieutenants up into the prison facility that once stood as a warehouse in times long passed. The rebels, along with seventy-six men, women, and children, were lined up in the streets. The day was still hazy. The rebels inconspicuously observed their surroundings. All of the women and children were African. The foreman called out their final destination as England. Twenty men were European, the rest were African men. The European men were criminals. The Africans were just in the wrong place at the wrong time. All the men were bound for the New World. The European criminals were separated from the rest. The groups were crammed into their respective prison caravans, setting out on a tiring eight-hour journey.

The prisoners were fed on the fifth hour of the journey. The meal was a bowl of cold, moist, unseasoned grains, and a cup of water. The meal interrupted the journey for two hours. The imprisoned took turns, being escorted out of their caravans in teams of three. None of the Moorish rebels were teamed together. Behar didn't know if that was purposeful. Luckily, the rebels shared the same caravan, but they decided to remain silent. Bo Yusuf wondered when they would find time to communicate. The rebels never had to escape before. Their strikes were quick, and then they rested. Being caught was not an option. The situation they were now in attested to that fact. Being caught only once resulted in the mass murder of hundreds of people.

One thing they always did was follow Behar's lead.

That's what the young men would do in this situation.

Al-Jeheuty could read Behar. There were situations when al-Jeheuty knew Behar's command simply based on the venerable Moor's body language. There was success every time.

But time was shortening. After the long eight-hour ride, and the dealings at the Portugal border, they headed to a port to be hauled away by cargo ship to an African slave-port. Bo Yusuf paid close attention to the exchange between the Portuguese and the Spanish soldiers. It was cordial, all directed toward the business of shipping slaves and servants.

Bo Yusuf remembered overhearing two Spanish soldiers' conversation while traveling. One commented that the *"Portuguese are good for something,"* in terms of hauling slaves. Some of the servants were being hauled to England. The Spanish soldiers also addressed the English with an air of disdain. There was no doubt that the English and Portuguese were speaking in the same manner about the Spanish before the Spaniards' arrival. Here now, in the business of lives, they were cordial. Wars were started over goods, land, philosophy, religion, and other trade. These warring European states, however, lowered their weapons and raised smiles when dealing with the lives of cultures unlike their own.

The caravan doors swung open. Spanish and Portuguese soldiers surrounded the captives with guns. It was night. The ocean provided a cool breeze. A Portuguese Captain commented on leaving before sunrise. The captives were split up again. England was in demand for Negresses and Negro children. The specific cargo was taken to a small ship. The criminals were stacked inside the same large merchant vessel that was making stops throughout the British Isles, extracting more criminals for indentured servitude. On the ship's way through, they would drop off the Negresses and Negro children.

The African men were separated from the rest of the captives. They were stripped of their clothes. Their mouths and anus were searched and fingered. A Portuguese man, who was neither soldier nor captain strummed al-Jeheuty and Ojodo's long locks. He told them in Portuguese that they would be cut before shipping to the New World. Bo Yusuf's coils would also be removed. The African men were fitted with more shackles and placed inside the cargo hold of a moderate-sized trading vessel. Boxes of other cargo were on board.

The African men were clothed with a thin loincloth and shirt. The cool air was now colder, biting. The shackles were like ice. A group of soldiers, armed with muskets, guarded them. The heavy ship moved away from the dock. The captives felt as if they lay in the belly of a drunken giant. The wood creaked as if it would fall apart at any moment. The ship's swaying motion seemed to push around the thick stench of previous captives and bodily waste present before these new captives arrived.

"We'll kill them all when we dock in Africa, our home," sang Behar in a language only the African men around him understood. He presented the words as a melodic song to escape detection that he was communicating with his fellow Africans. His voice resonated with such authority that no plan needed to be discussed. Each African man, beyond the Moorish rebels, was inspired by his musical words. *"Every man in here will bury their ego and follow me. Whosoever cannot bury their ego, will be buried in its stead."* Again, Behar's words were presented as a song, a sad lament.

The other men started to sing. *"We'll kill them all when we dock in Africa, our home."* It was inspiring. The armed soldiers guarding the captives gave one another a nervous look. The doors to the hull below were opened and the captain yelled, "What is that infernal racket?"

The captives' voices were released into the night air and crossed the sea to meet the horizon. Then appeared a ship's silhouette. The ship's pregnant sails looked like a black pyramid cropping up from the horizon. The ship started to draw closer to the Portuguese trading vessel. It was a small sloop. The captain was alerted and dismissed the singing men below. He commanded his crew to signal the sloop and quickly establish its intentions. The approaching ship was signaled. The Portuguese trade vessel, in return, was signaled with cannon fire.

"Pirates!" yelled the captain over another salvo of cannon blasts. He called for the gunmen to prepare return-fire. He shouted orders at his navigators to angle the ship to a degree in which minimal damage would be

sustained and major damage could be delivered. All the captain's orders were executed quickly, but his ship was not built for war, nor did it have much of a defense. It was a trade vessel built for cargo. It did not make well with speed either.

The captives continued to sing below, explosions beating into the ship's hull.

The attacking vessel moved closer, firing.

The trade vessel returned fire with little results.

The cannons mimicked the flash of lightning and echoed the sounds of thunder. The fire flashes existed in an instant of smoke and blazing theatrics, issuing cylindrical projectiles like magicians pulling objects from the air. The sound carried in the night, monstrous. Its reverberation hurdled through the air just as heavy as the cannonballs themselves. But the sound, though enormous, could only fly so long, eventually making an invisible splash into the sea. Air, mixed with sound, fell into the water's waves, an extra push to help the moon. By morning, these faded sounds of battle floated onto the shore of al-Mari Ifriq's *Guyotta Regency*, far, far away from where they originated.

Chapter Three

Here again is al-Mari Ifriq, Moorish Africa, with her borders now closer to the shore. Tall and mighty barriers constructed from stone were erected as guards against offshore attacks. At the docks stood large warehouses owned by the prominent companies of al-Mari Ifriq. The sun peeked over the horizon, rising from slumber as if awoken by the singing voice coming from a tower at the center of the city. The sun's rays sprinkled into the city, swimming through the streets, greeting citizens brightly.

Al-Mari Ifriq came to life. Its citizens circulated through its streets like blood through the body. The city was alive. Stores were opened for business. Fields and animals were tended and farmed. Select houses in different districts were opened for school and childcare. Workers boarded large, docked, merchant ships. Spanish Galleons commandeered and now under the command of Moorish corsairs, lifted anchor and set sail for plunder. Small galleys departed into the Mediterranean. Company bosses stepped into their warehouses to oversee business. This was an audit week. All the Moorish and Persian companymen were nervous, except one.

Sa'ad al-Din Sa'ood stood at the coastline. The sea's chilly waves rushed in and surrounded his shoes. He wore a merchant's suit made from foreign felt. He was clothed in beige, baggy pants, a tight waistcoat, and a short jacket with tight sleeves. Cloth was wrapped around his waist as a belt. Sa'ad was in his early fifties and graying. His physique was still strong, if not stronger. His blue-black skin, satiated with a healthy diet of the sun's rays, kept his appearance youthful. The venerable lines of wisdom did show, however, etched finely into his visage.

Sa'ad's oldest of two sons stood next to him. Nasir was now twenty-six years old. He was Sa'ad's partner in what little company he had left. Nasir's black skin vibrated with a green hue. Nasir's face squared at the chin, much like his father's. His brown eyes looked like permanent squints; he looked as if he was in perpetual contemplation, even more so with his sharp eyebrows. A thick patch of hair grew from his chin. There was no relevant shape. It was a messy tangle that he took pride in. The hair atop his head was a burst of coils resembling a burning bush. He was dressed identical to his father.

Staring out into the sea was now their morning ritual. It could not even be interrupted on this day when company audits were conducted by the ruling Turkish company, *The Four Winds*. The company had enough respect to allow some leniency for Sa'ad. Sa'ad trusted his companymen, especially his lawyer Wakil who was arranging the paperwork for The Four Winds Company.

Nasir appreciated his father's ritual. He reveled at the precise timing of the day's start. There first came the sun, a slow rise that seemed to increase with a sudden passing of minutes. Then came the angling of shadows, responding to the sun's position in the sky. Next was the call for morning. The harmonious voice resonated just as the shadows locked their position, the sun's movement slowing. Then the light sounds of activity came from the city, thumping and growing heavy.

The timing was perfect.

Al-Mari Ifriq was a functioning machine.

The well-orchestrated start of the day was all because of the man who stood next to Nasir, his father. Al-Mari Ifriq functioned because of Sa'ad's sacrifices. Nasir remembered everything changing when the Turk's Four Winds Company took control. He was six. The first thing that changed was his home. The Sa'ood family was relocated closer to the coast. Their new house was of moderate size. The company revenue kept the house stable. There were no more servants. Nasir's mother tried to keep two, but the servants were retained in service to the Turks. The house was again filled with various servants five years after the Turks took control. These servants were young Moorish men and women.

Nasir's father did not take all the revenue their family company earned. Sa'ad, also sharing the revenue with a close business consultant, Taran Zaher, put a lot of the money back into the city. The roads were not dusty pathways, but smooth and paved with large, rounded rock. The Turks were only interested in revenue. Nasir watched as his father tricked them into giving what little they would allow, back to the city.

The family company was reduced to control of a single shipyard. Nasir witnessed his father manipulate that too against The Four Winds Company. The Sa'ood Shipyard employed ship masons. The company loaned the ships they built. Nothing was sold. They even extended services to repair ships. Sa'ad and his friend Wakil would always laugh and recount the ways they outsmarted the ruling company. Nasir listened closely. The stories were greater than any adventure of the sea or swordplay that he had ever heard. Nasir asked to join the company business when he was eighteen. Sa'ad refused. *"There is more to this business, my son. There are things I do not want you involved in. There are dangerous men who do not always settle for verbal negotiations. I have made commands to kill such men."* He expressed these words with a sharp whisper that sounded like a cat's hiss.

Nasir remembered saying to his father in return, *"I am one of those men now to you. No word will dissuade me. How will you react?"* Sa'ad reacted with a smile. He took Nasir into his arms and into the company business. But Nasir never saw anything dangerous. He understood that the longtime servants and escorts helping around the house were tied to the former police captain, Roberto Hamaat. They were more than servants or escorts. They were well-trained, dangerous men and women. They were guards. Nasir realized they were everywhere, shielding Sa'ad.

Nasir took control of the daily operations of the company. He organized the warehouse labor and hired his younger brother, Zakiy. Nasir wished to take in his friends Maurice and Fusan, but they were busy planning their own company. Two years ago they accomplished their dream. It was more a tavern for weary travelers. It featured imported women for dancing and prostitution. It hosted card and chess games for gamble. Mostly riffraff of the sea gathered there. Maurice and Fusan seemed to like it. Fusan was able to form a crew and take to the sea in his ship. There were rumors about Fusan that Nasir wished to ignore. The rumors, accusations mostly, were of Fusan's maniacal behaviors at sea.

But Nasir kept his attention on doing business the way his father dealt with business. Some said that Sa'ad still ran the city. Sa'ad would tell the heads of The Four Winds, *"More for the city means more revenue. More revenue means more tribute."*

That saying always whet the financially avarice appetites of the company heads. They squeezed revenue dry, however. All the sly manipulation of their greed did not always have positive results. Al-Mari Ifriq could have been better, richer. But the revenue that was pooled into the city's infrastructure battled with increased tax and tribute. Trade routes by land and sea were taxed. Few traders journeyed to al-Mari Ifriq. Instead, pirates docked with enough plundered goods to pay for protection and service. The citizens' well-being was also taxed. Vendors were taxed. Schooling was taxed. It felt as if all movement was taxed.

Had these astronomical tributes gone to better al-Mari Ifriq, one could consider the sacrifice. But The Four Winds kept the tributes. Al-Mari Ifriq saw nothing. Sa'ad's intelligence, along with the few companies that were still allied with him, kept the city from crumbling. They even managed to make the city grow.

"We conquered and ruled lands across this sea," Sa'ad recounted to his son. "The African Moor ruled for seven-hundred years. The last great black kingdom, I say. Now, as refugees in our homeland, it is the sea we are set to conquer. Unless they take our hearts, they cannot have the sea." Sa'ad chuckled lightly. "You will enjoy this with *your* child, someday," Sa'ad expressed.

Nasir chuckled back, "Are you trying to find out when I will take a bride?" He raised an eyebrow and moved his eyes to spy his father.

"You need a woman to anchor you," said Sa'ad smiling at his son's ability to catch the undercurrent of his words. "You can't keep swinging around like some riffraff. People talk."

"Gossip," Nasir retorted. "Mostly among the religious," he continued as he rolled his eyes. "This city is half pirate, half pious. Both suckle gossip."

Sa'ad laughed at his son. "And where do you fall?"

"Somewhere in between," Nasir answered. "That's how life's suppose to be. After all, I'm young."

"You're twenty-six. Your mother was my bride when I was twenty-three."

"I'm learning the business first," Nasir defended. He was not offended by his father's chiding. This had become part of the morning ritual too. It always led to Nasir sharing with his father the latest woman he fancied. Nasir figured his father wanted to engage in bawdy talk to feel young. Wakil was too pious, Nasir believed. Taran Zaher was always busy with business. Nasir could see the sadness that sometimes haunted his father's eyes; he missed the company of his great friend Rashaad al-Hammon. A man long ago murdered.

"You also have to learn to balance a family with it," Sa'ad imparted.

Nasir considered his father's words and said, "I'll settle soon enough."

"Make certain that this company business does not settle you." Sa'ad's tone was sharp now. Nasir turned to his father as Sa'ad spoke, "Your mother saved me. Find someone who will do the same for you."

Sa'ad looked tired.

Nasir was about to address his father when a voice called, "Master Sa'ood!" The two of them looked up. Coming from the company house was Sa'ad's close escort and servant named Rasil. He was the same age as Nasir. Rasil was dressed in a long coat with a piece of cloth tied around his waist. His left pinky finger was decorated with a silver ring that had a black star carved into it. "I bring you a message," he said stopping in front of Sa'ad. He bowed.

Sa'ad and Nasir turned to Rasil. Sa'ad smiled gently. "Relax," he said as he smiled. Sa'ad's voice was deep, rich with age and experience. He rested a hand on Rasil's shoulder. The young man caught his breath.

"The Honorable Wakil al-Hakam needs to speak with you. He said the business is urgent." Rasil whispered, "It's about today's audit. The heads of The Four Winds want to meet with you."

There was nothing completely unusual about the request, but The Four Winds usually saved Sa'ad's audit and tributes for last. He was dependable. Sa'ad's papers about revenue were always well organized. There was no trouble in The Four Wind's inspection of Sa'ad's company. Sa'ad considered that today The Four Winds just wanted to get his business out of the way first. He ordered both Nasir and Rasil to follow him back to the company house. The two followed in tow. Sa'ad walked passed the docks and through the doors of his company house. He told Nasir to see to the daily activities, managing the labor. Rasil stayed close as Nasir bowed to his father's orders and disappeared.

Sa'ad stepped into his conference room. Wakil was waiting, standing near a large table. He was dressed in his traditional judicial outfit. He held two books under his arms; a book of religious scriptures was strapped to the belt around his waist. Sa'ad motioned for a stool and pleaded, "Take a seat."

Wakil bowed and sat down. A smile remained on his face the entire time. Sa'ad turned to Rasil and aimed a hand next to the door. The servant was not dismissed. Sa'ad was ordering him to take post next to the door. Rasil stood tall and did not move. Sa'ad turned his attention back to Wakil.

"My practice may jump-start again," the lawyer spoke, unable to contain his excitement. He pointed to Sa'ad. "You're making them look a fool."

"Who?" Sa'ad asked as he took a seat at another stool.

"The Four Winds," Wakil smiled and reverberated with a chuckle.

Sa'ad was confused.

Wakil explained to his friend, "They want you as a partner." The lawyer saw his friend's eyebrows rise in surprise. "A Portuguese ship was marked several days ago. The ship was transporting goods to the New World. It was bound for Africa-west to pick up slaves. They want you to bring in the shipment it was carrying. The word is it was hit last night. We're waiting word from a company in Algeria tied to the plunder."

Sa'ad lifted his shoulders. "How does that make me a partner?"

Wakil cleared his throat. "The heads want you to engineer a safe trade route for the plundered cargo—by land. This route will remain under your control, and then your control will branch to a maritime route. The trade will probably be contraband. I don't like that. But, the heads of The Four Winds have watched close. They see you make money. They want a part of it. They want to meet with you."

"How do you know," Sa'ad asked.

"Taran paid me a visit," Wakil answered. "He said he suggested your name to The Four Winds, but they already had you in mind."

Sa'ad pondered the information. He smiled. "He knows it's time to strike. There must be a weakness in the Turkish Alliance."

"We could bury our enemies," Wakil said with joy greater than a pious man should have possessed. But he understood that al-Mari Ifriq was about to collapse financially. The Turks' tributes were straining the city's economy. A righteous kill was needed. Even at the thought, Wakil said a silent prayer. He then said to Sa'ad, "We could take back this city before God takes us."

"In time," he said while standing up. "We would have to get them to trust us while we learn their movements. We'd need two months." He turned to Rasil and called for his escort's attention. Rasil took a step forward and waited to be addressed. "Rasil, tell your teacher, Roberto Hamaat, that I will need the service of the Seventy-Two Points of the Universe."

Rasil nodded and then stepped back to his position.

"I do have concerns, Sa'ad," Wakil voiced. "You've forced them to expand trade—"

"Their greed did that," Sa'ad corrected with a deep tone.

Wakil nodded, acknowledging Sa'ad's sentiment. The lawyer stated, "However, they may be trying to play you close."

Sa'ad waved his hands. "Of course they're trying to keep enemies close. We're doing the same. Two months. We may need an extra month to figure out how we frame their murders. We don't need more Turks coming in. Al-Mari Ifriq would become a military state. It would be against itself." He then contemplated. "We could blame pirates. But why would all four heads be sea bound? Perhaps an attack by French ships? But that would spark greater politics, and bring in the European." He became frustrated, though still excited about the turn of events.

"Guyotta Sahin-el Bey wants to meet with you tonight. The meeting will take place at his lodge outside the city," Wakil notified, routing Sa'ad's concentration back to current events. "He wants to begin discussing the route. He doesn't even care about the audit. He will collect his tribute from you after the route is successfully planned. The meeting is scheduled three hours after sundown."

Sa'ad bowed at the neck. He had a wide smile on his face. "Rasil will be with me, no one else. Not even you." Sa'ad swept a hand. "I want them to trust me and believe I am as naïve as can be. Rasil will watch close their movements. This is the beginning." He turned to Rasil and authorized, "Prepare mounts and tell my son I want to speak with him."

Rasil left the room.

Sa'ad then ordered Wakil, "Return my word that I accept Guyotta's offer."

Wakil stood up from his seat. "We still need a team to run a resurrected *Alliance*."

Sa'ad shook his head in agreement. "My son will help. But, yes, we need more heads, leaders." Sa'ad trembled with his next set of words. "Taran has become too close to Guyotta's regime. We have seen him less and less over the years. I can only make a decision about his well-being after we…re-name this regency."

"And if his loyalty is compromised," Wakil asked carefully.

Sa'ad managed to smile. The gesture conflicted with the sad look in his eyes. Sa'ad recalled old times. He put his hand on Wakil's shoulder and told him, "I've become an expert at dealing with those situations, even against dear friends that put me in them." He patted his friend's shoulder. "Now, go."

Wakil exited after a graceful salutation. Nasir appeared in his place, walking through the door and taking a seat on a stool. Sa'ad sat next to him. He was silent for a time. Then the words came to him. "You have watched me close, yes?" Nasir did not speak. He just nodded affirmatively. "Good." Sa'ad took a deep breath and asked his son, "Do you love this city?" Nasir nodded again. "I want you to pay close attention to my next moves. They are crucial." Sa'ad sighed. He put a hand on his son's knee and expressed in a fatherly voice, "I'm about to teach you the hardest lesson in our business. It's not just about death. It's about making sure the city does not collapse because of war."

"Is everything alright?" Nasir asked with great concern in his voice. His eyes were wide.

Sa'ad lifted his hand from his son's knee and waved his excitement down. "Not at all," he told Nasir in a voice that sounded more comforting than warning. "I just want to speak to you about consequence." He chuckled and then told his son, "It may seem cryptic. Over time, you'll understand." Sa'ad inhaled and pondered before talking. "Decisions can be more dangerous than dangerous men. What you decide will have its repercussions. You may feel that repercussion in your spirit; it may affect your emotions. Decisions can deteriorate you." Nasir watched in amazement as his father's bright glow became dull. Behind Sa'ad's watering eyes was a memory that no amount of negotiations would pull from him. Sa'ad sniffed back his teary eyes and shook his head. "Pray that is the worst your decisions bring if negative repercussions are inevitable. As a man, you will learn to carry burden. However, pray your decisions do not bring retribution to your front door; may they not touch your wife or children. More important, pray your decisions do not cripple this city and its people."

Nasir nodded again. He waited, silent, as his father looked away, centered on a far away thought. Only seconds passed before Sa'ad looked at Nasir and commanded for his son to stand. Both of them stood up. Sa'ad walked to the door, Nasir followed. "I have business tonight. In the morning, I want you to organize the labor so that they may carry on with work by themselves. I will need to talk to you about these great decisions." He said to his son in a whisper, "We are about to have a very silent revolution. The time has come for the Moors to take back their city."

Nasir knew all the actions and decisions his father had planned. Sa'ad interrupted Nasir from speaking. He said to his son, "Meet me here, tonight, hour eleven." Nasir bowed at the neck and his father commanded him to go back to his duties. Sa'ad was left alone in his office. He took a seat at one of the stools and started to strategize. He needed Roberto's Unseen to shadow the heads of The Four Winds Company. Their movements needed to be tracked. He needed the heads of The Four Winds to be routine in their daily behavior. One month would be to figure out if they had a daily pattern. A second month would be to see if the routine held strong. Sa'ad would strike on the third month. Until that day, Sa'ad had to figure out how he could make The Four Winds' heads disappear. What could be the plausible excuse for their death? What could he say to avoid the city being wiped out by the Turks far off, or sending in a military brigade to govern the city?

These questions haunted Sa'ad. He tried pacing his quarters for an answer. There came none. Rasil knocked on the door and was permitted entrance. The young inconspicuous guard mentioned to Sa'ad that the mounts were ready for the night's travel. Sa'ad ordered Rasil to then prepare whatever weapons necessary. Rasil left the quarters to equip arms. Sa'ad put the thought of revolution aside and pondered business. Tonight, he would discuss with his son the meeting he had with The Four Winds Company. In the morning, he, Nasir, Wakil, and Roberto Hamaat would begin forming the plan to rescue al-Mari Ifriq.

The headache of business, shipping, re-building, loaning, and taking in, did not permit more time to think about the night's meeting or its planned consequences. Sa'ad journeyed home with his two boys after the day's labor was finished. He informed his wife that he was meeting with the Regent Master. Sa'ad had three hours to rest, wash quickly, change robes, and perfume before being greeted by Rasil and two mounts.

Rasil appeared on time, waiting outside Sa'ad's house. The night was cool and without a cloud in the sky to taint the waxing, Gibbous moon and the stars that accompanied it. Zakiy was sent to meet Rasil and inform him that Sa'ad was on his way out. Sa'ad told his wife that Nasir would be meeting him at the company house down near the docks. He turned to Nasir and reiterated the time to meet at the company house. Nasir bowed his head and walked with his father out into the street.

Sa'ad greeted Rasil and saluted his son Zakiy. He jumped to his mount, a powerful Barbary steed, and nodded his head to his eldest son. Nasir saluted his father with a nod of the head. Afya joined them at the front and waved her husband goodbye. Nasir and his younger brother watched their father ride away through the city streets.

Sa'ad and Rasil were joined by The Four Winds' company guards just outside the city, beyond the eastern border of al-Mari Ifriq. There were fifteen mounted men armed with spears, short swords, and pistols. Their clothes were forest green. Atop their heads were turbans the same color, and they each wore a black wrap around their face. These soldiers were called The Green Army. Their Captain, Tous Zeki, a Four Winds' Head and Army Official, accompanied them.

Tous was the youngest of the four heads, in his mid-forties. He was dressed in the garments of a noble, rather an official lead officer. He possessed short, black hair that was curly. He had dusky skin and aquiline features. A thick beard covered his chin. His steed led the fifteen soldiers. He smiled politely and greeted Sa'ad and Rasil just the same. Sa'ad greeted the company head in return. Tous galloped next to him and said, "Tonight makes history." He sounded sincere. The tone in his voice made Sa'ad's heart skip. "Tonight, al-Mari Ifriq gets back on its feet."

The Army Official led the way to The Four Winds' lodge. Sa'ad rode next to him, Rasil and the soldiers in drag. "Was gold plundered?" Sa'ad asked.

"I believe so," answered Tous. "I do know that the marked vessel was hauling goods—and possibly live cargo—bound for the New World." Tous cleared his throat. "But the plunder has inspired Sahin-el Bey. He wants a new trade route established." He looked at Sa'ad. "He respects your understanding for trade. He needs your expertise." His eyes went back to the path in front of him. "And it's not just for this new route. He needs advice on stimulating trade along the other routes, land and sea." Tous sighed. He put his head down for an instant and then looked back to the gravely way that was now slowly turning into desert sands. "Sahin-el Bey is defeated."

Sa'ad cleared his throat. "Pardon my offense, Master Zeki, but has he ever considered that the taxes pressed on the trade caravans and sea merchants—"

Tous nodded his head. "He has. He has," Tous assured. "He understands the blame starts there. He is just an instrument of the harsh tributes, not their cause." There was another sigh. "We must look to his chiefs. The Ottomans are continuously reaping all reward from al-Mari Ifriq."

"They seem to allow the other territories leniency," said Sa'ad.

Tous shook his head. "Oh, Sale, Tunis, and Algiers get taxed too. Those pirates like to play as if they aren't under the constraints of the Sultan, his cabinet, and the chiefs." Tous rolled his eyes. "I thought our presence would alleviate the trouble. Most of the councils in the other regencies and republics are ruled not by the African Moor, but by the Turk."

Sa'ad wondered. *Could The Four Winds have just been the instruments, not the cause of al-Mari Ifriq's troubles?* He pondered further about if his hand was ready to slay the head of a dragon only to have another come in its place? *Was true war inevitable?* More questions. Sa'ad had three months to investigate.

"Sahin-el Bey aspires to be a statesman back in the Empire," Tous said with a half-hearted smile. His voice was sad. "He thinks he can change things. May God pardon me, but I don't believe he can do it." Tous then smiled warmly. "The only thing I do believe he will change is the company name. He wants to re-name the company *The Four Corners*. Sahin-el Bey wants to stretch his ambition to Asia and the New World." He sighed. "I will follow him to wherever his ambitions lead. I do hope that he—*we*, rather—have the resources to achieve such a dream."

The stone lodge appeared in the distance. A Green soldier darted forward, speeding toward the small house. The desert sand sprayed upward as the rider increased his speed. He slowed down, stopped outside the lodge, and dismounted from his steed. He knocked on the door. Tous maintained the troupe's current speed as they approached the lodge.

Sa'ad saw a man come from the lodge. He was tall, thin. This was

Guyotta Sahin-el Bey. This was the man whose name branded the region. Guyotta stepped up to meet Tous and his troupe as they stopped in front of the lodge. Guyotta's elegant clothes gave the illusion that he was gliding across the desert. The Army Official bowed at the neck, as did his soldiers. Sa'ad dismounted, a soldier holding his steed. He walked to the Regent Master and Company Boss and kissed his hands, concluding his greeting by extending to Guyotta an embrace and a warm smile.

The moonlight revealed Guyotta's dry, light brown skin that was ashy with age. He wore a turban not for religious reasons, but to keep him protected from the cool, night air of the desert. Under the turban was a fading mesh of white curly hair. Age lines marked his narrow face.

Hyle Tecer, the portly accountant, waddled from the lodge to greet Sa'ad. His fat face held a bright smile and he smelled of wine. Hyle commented that he couldn't wait for Sa'ad to give him something to count again. He made Sa'ad feel as if he was being used. Guyotta expressed that money was no longer an interest. The Bey declared that al-Mari Ifriq had to become an independent republic. "We must no longer send tributes to fat chiefs in another land," he continued. "Tonight, we start the beginning of plans for independence."

The lawyer named Aguyan Ozan appeared next. His skin was darker than the other company heads. He was mixed with black blood, his father being a black Turkish soldier. He bowed at the neck toward Sa'ad.

The Green Army dismounted and took a formation around the house. Two soldiers stayed close to Tous. The horses did not move. Rasil dismounted and took Sa'ad's side. A strong light glowed from inside the lodge.

Guyotta swung his arm wide and spoke, "Enter, Sa'ad."

The Moor stepped forward. He moved aside the door that was already partially opened and walked through the threshold. In front of him, in the one-room lodge, was a rectangular table with two lamps flickering brightly on top of it. Seated at either ends of the table was Maurice and Fusan al-Hammon. Taran Zaher sat on the far side of the table.

A thought stirred inside Sa'ad. He had considered that Taran may be at this meeting, but he did not expect to see Maurice and Fusan. Their presence made him pause in entering the lodge completely. Fusan, the large pirate with the burly beard covering a thick, black face, drank intensely. There was something about his sips that made Sa'ad recall the ritual he indulged in just after slaying the young man's father. On the other end was Rashaad's younger son, Maurice. He still had a boy's face, but he was a man as old as Sa'ad's son. Maurice was dressed in black, as if still mourning his father. His eyes resonated with intensity against his dark skin. He twirled a knife that had a piece of meat attached at the end. He took small bites. There was a plate with a loaf of bread in front of him.

Sa'ad was so struck by the young men's presence that he did not hear the scuffle behind him. A Green Army soldier grabbed Rasil from behind and covered his mouth to smother any screams. Rasil, though trained, could not move fast enough. The soldier's kris was stabbed into Rasil's back a total of five times. The kris' blade was then slammed into the escort's stomach. Rasil's bleeding body was pulled back and tossed to the sandy floor.

Then Sa'ad remembered. A faint voice yelled to him. It sounded incoherent, slurred. The voice was drunk. He listened, eyes locked onto Taran and Rashaad's two boys. The voice became louder, more coherent. Sa'ad then realized that the voice was his. The voice was from the past, sounding like a younger Sa'ad. It was warning him, *"Taran too is a traitor."*

And then the idea of a trap came to him.

A pistol went off.

The bullet tore through Sa'ad's throat. Blood was coughed up from his mouth, mixed with the projected blood that spilled from his throat, and crashed against the lodge's floor. Sa'ad dropped to his knees. He put out his hands to catch himself and stop his body from slamming onto the floor face first. But his strength was gone. Sa'ad crashed against the floor, his nose smashing inward, and the cartilage crumbling. There was a hole in his throat. He coughed instead of breathed. Blood streamed from his neck, mouth, and his nose.

Maurice and Fusan stood up from the table. They each held one-shot pistols. They thumbed back the hammers and both fired a bullet into Sa'ad's head. The force of the blasts broke Sa'ad's skull, and the top of his head erupted into an amalgam of liquid contents and chunks. The two young men sat back down. Fusan started to drink again.

The heads of The Four Winds stepped over Sa'ad. Tous commanded his soldiers to get rid of the bodies. The soldiers lifted Sa'ad from the house and dragged Rasil away. Four soldiers were told to take the bodies to the desert and dump them. As far as anyone would know, bandits attacked the company boss and his escort while they trekked alone to The Four Winds' lodge.

Each head then walked to a corner of the room and took a seat at stools planted there. The lodge's door was closed. The Regent Master and companymen were left to discuss the fate of al-Mari Ifriq. "What's next?" asked Aguyan to Guyotta.

"We'll wait three hours and then send a search party to find Sa'ad. We'll inform his family tomorrow when we find him. Then, we will nurture Sa'ad's son as he takes the reins from his father," Guyotta made clear. "And then like the priesthood to the boy-king called Tut-Anhk-Amen, we will bury the heir." Guyotta shook his head. He looked to the area of the floor where Sa'ad's body once lay. "Sa'ad, you poor, wretched goddamned boiling bloke."

Chapter Four

The four mounted soldiers dropped Rasil and Sa'ad's bodies and watched them smack against the gravely, sandy floor. The body's tumbled lifelessly. One soldier dismounted and removed a knife. He stabbed Rasil in the side. The blade jammed between two ribs. Sa'ad and Rasil's bodies were searched, mildly stripped, and then left alone. The sight was enough to allow the virgin viewer to believe there had been a robbery. The soldiers galloped back to The Four Winds' lodge.

The moon shined down on the two bodies.

The sea could be heard from far off, its waves ebbing and flowing to shore.

Rasil's arm moved slightly. His eyes moved. The world started to come into focus. He scanned the area to make sure that the soldiers were gone. He took small breaths. There was an excruciating pain violently grabbing his body. He felt like his deep and fatal wounds were bleeding fire. He felt like he was inhaling a mix of sand and jagged rocks. But, there was enough life in him to stir.

Rasil twitched. He rolled over onto his side and saw Sa'ad sprawled out beside him. The corpse was grotesque. Rasil pushed himself to his knees. He coughed. More blood streamed from his wounds. He rested in the sands for a minute, on his knees. He positioned one leg and felt the fire from his wounds heat up. He rested a hand on his knee and tried to lift. The fiery pain burned him again. The pain gripped him and held him in place. Rasil struggled against the intense heat of his wounds. Blood drenched his torn garments. It dripped onto the desert and formed an oasis.

Rasil gritted his teeth. He was not physically prepared for the techniques he was using to sustain his breath, life, and energy. Roberto Hamaat warned him and other training Stars about how painful this was, but it was something that could only be experienced. The ghost of a man he had assassinated two months ago appeared and started to laugh at him. Rasil had forgotten the man's name. He just remembered he was on orders to kill him. The captain was marked by his crewmembers. The seamen paid Roberto and the clan a good sum of money to take down their captain. Rasil shot and stabbed the man. He remembered the captain crawling in the small ship's cargo hold, wounded and begging. Rasil took an oil lamp and smashed it against the ship's wall. He took another small lamp and broke it against the burning fire. Rasil walked away from the captain, leaving him screaming, as the fire grew bigger, inevitably engulfing him.

That same fire now engulfed Rasil. The captain laughed, taunting Rasil as he struggled to stand. Rasil shook his head. He coughed. His wounds bled harder as a reaction. Then Rasil spotted Sa'ad's corpse. The sight of the dead company boss allowed Rasil to breathe in the fiery pain. He consumed the agony his body produced and used it as fuel. The ghost disappeared, its laughter gone. A cool, desert breeze surrounded Rasil. He controlled his breath and lifted himself to his feet.

Rasil was energized, but not overconfident.

He was dying.

There was just one last mission he had to complete.

Nasir was tired, but anxious to meet his father. He hoped the meeting would not take too long. He dressed quickly and set off from his house, through winding streets and out toward the city gates. The guards recognized Nasir. He did not have to reveal to the guards his purpose to take leave from the city, heading to his father's company house. The double turn of the gates was opened for Nasir and he walked free from the city. Nasir ventured toward the company house with neither torch nor lamp. He traveled to the shore, his hand resting on the hilt of his short-sword, at the ready. Nasir made his way to the company house and stood in front of the door, the keys to which were strapped to his sash. He lifted the key loop and stressfully thumbed through eight keys before finding the key he needed for the door.

Nasir heard something near the corner of the building. Someone was breathing heavy, panting. The young, black Moor stepped away from the door and substituted the loop of keys for his short-sword. He unsheathed his weapon and made his way around to the corner of the company house. Nasir took wide steps, his sword pointed in the direction of a potential attack. He saw the person's shoulder at the corner. Nasir looked closer. He recognized the person in front of him by just the light of the moon.

"Mehit," he called the woman's name.

Mehit al-Tarqiyya Zaher looked up. She was crying. Her face glistened with tears, illuminated by the moon's light. She was draped in a long, white dress with a tan waistcoat tied around her. Her head was wrapped in an elaborate, Moorish headdress draping with gossamer fabrics that fluttered in the night breeze. Nasir sheathed his sword and stepped forward. He waved her close. She stepped into Nasir's embrace as he asked, "What's wrong, *mora?*"

Mehit cleared her throat. "I had a fight with my father this evening." She sniffed. "He insists that I open my bathhouse for the Turk's use. He wants my girls to service the company heads and their soldiers. That fat, lecherous company head, Hyle Tecer, wants to rub up against one of my girls. You know Aludra? The linguist. He continuously hounds her. I keep her safe. She is allowed to stay in the guestroom of the bathhouse." Mehit sniffed again. "My father never liked the idea of me running my bathhouse." She stepped from Nasir's embrace.

No, Taran did not approve of his daughter's business, legitimate as it was. He wished his daughter pursued study at a university. Mehit tried, but Taran gave her little money. Her business venture, owning a bathhouse and salon that catered only to women, was supposed to help her with funds. The business generated so much revenue that Mehit did not pursue school. Her father still had her under a tight grip, living at home. He always shouted that there would be a scandal if she were to live unmarried and alone. Nasir always considered that Taran was sabotaging his daughter. He probably would've protested her schooling, depending on the subject she studied. With all of her father's insistence that Mehit attend a university, he allowed her little money to travel away and do so. He was trying to marry her off to a Turk, like her younger sister who now resided in Turkey as the fourth wife of a nobleman, a Four Winds Head associate who was many times her age. Mehit had not seen her sister in four years, since her wedding at the age of sixteen.

"Why did you come all the way out here?" Nasir asked.

"I've been here for hours, thinking," Mehit answered. "I was here after the close of your father's business."

Nasir became frustrated with Mehit. He stated in a stern voice, "It's dangerous for a woman to be alone beyond the city gates."

"Only to these superstitious people," Mehit wiped her tears clean. "They think this place is haunted." Her words stopped. Though she was not superstitious, she did not want to damn the dead by speaking ill against them. "Of course, even I won't go near the port, down by the docks." Her voice was sad as she remembered Maurice and Fusan's mother drowning herself five years ago. Men claimed they would see her apparition crying at night. Mehit would always escape here because no one dared to come near the docks after sundown. She started to believe that maybe they just saw her and perceived her the ghost of a sad woman.

Nasir reached for her. "Let me see you home. I have business here with my father—"

"Oh," said Mehit. "He's at a meeting with my father."

"I didn't know your father was going to be there," Nasir said surprised.

"Yes," spoke Mehit. "It's with The Four Winds Company."

Nasir nodded. "Well, let's get you home before your father arrives."

Mehit sighed.

Nasir waved for her. "Come. If my father is on his way, your father will probably be near home as well. Come. We don't need to escalate this any further. Your father will be worried if you're not home." Mehit grumbled and rolled her eyes. "You may not see eye-to-eye, but he is your father, and he still loves you. Now, come."

Mehit allowed Nasir to take lead, two steps ahead of her. She kept in pace behind him. His eyes watched the area closely. His hand rested on the hilt of his sword. Nasir now cursed at himself for not carrying a torch or lamp. The moon's light was a relief. They approached the city gate and were allowed in. Nasir delivered Mehit to her house. He kissed her forehead with the tenderness that an older brother would do to a sister, and then walked away, reversing his journey and returning to the company house.

Nasir waited inside his father's quarters. His eyes became heavy and he yawned. Nasir placed his back against the wall while seated at the stool. He tried to shake the weariness away. He started to drift into slumber when there was a sudden thud against the front door. Nasir stood up, alerted. The thud turned into a series of pounds. Someone was knocking frantically. Nasir again drew his sword. He rushed from his father's quarters and down a flight of stairs. He crossed the large holding area and stepped to the door. He opened a small panel carved into the door, and he peeked outside. There was Rasil. He was breathing heavy. He looked weak.

Nasir unlocked the door and opened it for the young man. Rasil collapsed inside the company house. Nasir's eyes went wide. Rasil was drenched in blood that seeped from open wounds around his torso and back. Nasir sheathed his sword. He dragged Rasil inside and knelt down next to the dying assassin. Nasir grabbed Rasil's hand and balanced his head in the cup of his arm.

Rasil's eyes were wild. He breathed in quick gasps. "Four Winds…killed…Sa'ad. Don't trust Taran…killed Sa'ad. Warn you…killed Sa'ad…Four Winds…Taran with them…Meeting…trap…killed Sa'ad… Four Winds…"

Nasir's breath was stolen from him. He could not believe what he heard. His father was dead. The Four Winds Company was responsible. Taran was an accomplice. The revelations dropped like the interior of a cave collapsing in on him. Rasil's words were an attack just as vicious as the young, dying man's wounds. Nasir gazed forward. He did not see Rasil anymore, though the guard's message echoed. Nasir's world went blank. He missed the gradual decrease in volume from Rasil's voice. He missed Rasil's inhale become heavier, breaths farther apart. Nasir was drawn back to reality when Rasil was silent and still. His eyes, wide, were staring up into nowhere.

Nasir dragged Rasil's body into the center of the large room. He shut the door and locked it. He looked around the wide storage area and came across several blankets. He wrapped Rasil's body inside them. Nasir contemplated his next moves while staring down at the mummified body. He wondered whom he could trust. Nasir could only think of two names: Roberto Hamaat and Wakil al-Hakam. He had to inform Roberto Hamaat about Rasil. He had to inform Wakil about his father. Wakil would then go through the legal procedures to make the company his. Nasir would continue his father's business and honor his father's plans by executing the heads of The Four Winds Company.

Nasir took a deep breath. He closed his eyes. He thought about how he loved Mehit like a sister. She was such a lovely woman, free and intelligent. Mehit's smile always warmed Nasir. Unfortunately, he had to mark her father too. Nasir pondered the morbid thought that Mehit might have gained sadistic pleasure at such a thing, considering her troubles with her father. He wiped the blasphemous notion away. He then thought about his father and started to cry. His legs trembled. Nasir felt like he could not get enough breath, no matter how deep he inhaled.

His father was gone.

Nasir coughed and choked tears. He then became angry. He looked at Rasil's body and imagined it was his father wrapped underneath the blankets. His tears dried. His thoughts became centered. He had to find Roberto and Wakil now. Nasir shook his head and stood. He started to pace.

"I can't get your master now, Rasil," he counseled with the cocooned body. "He's at the *al-Hammon Palace.*" As was called Maurice and Fusan's tavern. "It would arouse suspicion if I showed up there and asked for his presence. No. I'll contact Wakil. Your master will know of your fate, and the fate of my father, later tonight, when the time is right."

Nasir inspected his clothes. They were stained with Rasil's blood. He could not walk through the city gates covered in such a manner. He cursed and went upstairs, finding one of his father's robes stored in a closet. He wrapped himself in the robe, and tied the garment so as not to show the blood staining his clothes. He discovered a small amount of water filling the basin in his father's business quarters and washed his hands. Nasir then returned to the main floor and exited the company house. He locked up and returned to the city gates. There was a gathering of guards. Nasir walked up to them and was addressed upon arrival. The guards informed him about the disappearance of his father and that a search party was being formed. They asked to search the company house, and Nasir quickly informed them that his father was not there. The guards relayed word of The Four Winds' heads report that Sa'ad never made it to the meeting. It was all a lie, but the guards were ignorant of this. Nasir considered them just puppets. The guards were just instruments, not the cause. The cause lay with their masters. Nasir asked if his family was informed. The guards answered, 'yes'. They asked if Nasir required an escort to his house. Nasir accepted. Four guards encircled Nasir as he walked home. They left him at his house and went back to their duties.

Nasir stepped through the front door and made his way to the chief room. His mother and brother sat waiting, looking nervous. Candles and oil lamps lit the spacious room. They looked up at him. Nasir nodded and simply spoke, "I'm going to get answers." He saw his mother about to speak. He lifted an authoritative hand, surprising himself. "I will seek Wakil al-Hakam."

"At this late hour," Afya questioned her son. She noticed him wearing Sa'ad's old robe.

"Yes," Nasir replied with a look of desperation.

Afya studied her son's face. "What do you know, Nasir? I've seen that look on your father."

Nasir walked over to his mother and brother. He knelt down in front of his mother and held her hands. "I know," he said looking from his mother to his brother. "I know that I should prepare to inherit the company."

Afya gasped. She wanted to strike her son for concluding such an outcome about her husband's disappearance. But there was something in Nasir's expression; there was a sadness that was equipped with an unfortunate conviction of knowledge.

"You need me to come?" Zakiy asked with a firm, determined expression on his face.

Nasir shook his head. "No," he answered. He stood up, letting go of his mother's hands. "I need you to stay innocent in these matters," he commanded, not trying to imply an offense on his brother. "Guard our mother. I'll call on you tomorrow to help me run the company house. We'll probably have it closed. The ships that are due will be directed to other company ports."

Zakiy saluted with the nod of his head.

Nasir stepped away from his family. Afya jumped up and threw her arms around her son. "Are you sure," she said, tears streaming down her face. Her hold was tight. Zakiy walked over to his mother. He gently pulled her away from Nasir before his brother had a moment to break and confirm their father's death. Afya let go. Nasir walked to his room. He wrapped a long piece of cloth around his head. The lower half of Nasir's face was covered in cloth. He didn't want to be seen. He walked to the outside and made his way to the home of Wakil al-Hakam. He felt uncomfortable when he used the large knocker on the door. The clangs were too loud for the night, and Nasir felt as if he was disturbing the entire district. He lowered the cloth covering his face. Wakil's youngest son, Jabari, peeked out of a slide panel. The door was unlocked and Wakil's son greeted him with a smile and handshake.

"I seek your father's counsel," Nasir said to Jabari as his eyes fought against displaying the sadness he felt and the burden of his agenda.

Jabari sensed the conflict in Nasir. "Is everything okay? Enter."

Nasir stepped through the door. "I don't mean to disturb you."

"My mother sleeps," said Jabari. "My father is in his study." He turned and led the way to Wakil's chamber. There was no door blocking the wide upside-down, U-shaped passage to the study. A light curtain draped the passage, coupled with strings of beads. Jabari knocked on the wall and called, "Father. Nasir is here to see you."

"Oh," Wakil's voice came through the curtain. "Enter." Jabari swept the curtain and beads aside. Nasir walked inside the candlelit room. Jabari followed inside. Wakil had a curious look on his face. "Did your father send you?"

Nasir simply answered, "They killed my father." His voice trembled with each word. Wakil stood up and walked over to Nasir. His mouth hung low, his eyes wide with horror. Jabari's expression was no different from his father's; he was shocked by the news. "He's been reported missing but I know—" Nasir fought back tears. He recovered his voice. "They killed him. The Four Winds."

Wakil still drenched with shock, asked, "How do you know this?"

"I waited for my father at the company house," Nasir explained. "He wanted to talk after the meeting. He wanted to discuss revolution. It was time to strike, he said." Nasir's eyes went to the floor. Wakil waited patiently as the young man tried to straighten his words. "Rasil escaped. He was stabbed multiple times, but he persevered. His body is at the warehouse. He's dead. He warned me with his last breaths. Rasil told me everything. The meeting was an ambush. Taran was there." He opened his robe and displayed his bloodstained clothes. "This is Rasil's blood."

Wakil clenched his teeth. The reverent lawyer boiled with outrage. His anger ceased Nasir's emotions. The young man calmed immediately. He lifted a hand and bowed his head in respect, "Please, al-Hakam." The lawyer stumbled back. Jabari moved from behind Nasir and caught his father. He guided his father back to the multi-pillowed cushion in the room. Nasir followed. He knelt down in front of Wakil and said, "We need Roberto Hamaat. One of his soldiers is dead."

Wakil turned to Jabari. "Alert Sanura."

"Our servant girl?" Jabari questioned.

Wakil shook his head. "She's one of Roberto's students," he informed. "Tell her to find Roberto. He is most likely at *The al-Hammon Palace*." He looked at Nasir. "We'll meet at the company house." Wakil caught his breath and centered his emotions. He was still regretful that he allowed Sa'ad to go alone. He thought, because Sa'ad attended the meeting alone, that The Four Winds would only strong-arm him verbally. Wakil never suspected a fatal ambush. He stood up, shaking his head with an expression of sorrow. He patted Nasir on the shoulder and took lead from his quarters. "Come, the both of you." He paused and signaled his son. "Jabari, to your duties, and find clothes for Nasir. The two of you share the same size." He looked at Nasir. "We'll get rid of your attire. Leave your garments in Jabari's room for now."

Nasir agreed. He followed Jabari to his room. Wakil's son handed Nasir clothes and then dashed out of the room to find Sanura. Nasir changed clothes, leaving his garments piled next to Jabari's bed. He returned to Wakil, and the lawyer excused him from the house as he informed his wife that he was leaving. Wakil told his wife of the terrible news but ordered her to remain in bed and do her best to go back to sleep. Jabari stepped inside his parents' quarters, having returned from his errand. He said he would look after his mother. Sanura the servant-girl was off to find Roberto Hamaat. Wakil, knowing his family was safe, met Nasir outside. The two journeyed back to the city gates. There was a crowd of guards gathered. The guard-captain remarked the search for Sa'ad turned up nothing. Nasir stated his business to the guard-captain. He was supposed to meet his father at the company house. He would wait with Wakil there and report, should they find anything. The guards allowed the young man and the venerable lawyer through. Nasir and Wakil continued to the company house.

Roberto Hamaat waited patiently at the door, a bottle of liquor in his grip. He was informed by Sanura of Rasil and Sa'ad's fate. Now in his fifties, Roberto was heavier, a little wider. A small mustache patched his upper lip. Many believed his weight was an organic disguise. Roberto was still one of the most deadly assassins. Despite his heavier appearance, he remained a master of stealth.

The three men met one another with determined looks. They exchanged sorrowful hugs, handshakes, and pats. This was to honor both men slain. Roberto asked if Nasir was sure about the news of his father. Nasir answered affirmatively, telling Roberto about Rasil's escape and the young assassin's message. "He's inside," noted Nasir. "I wrapped his body in a blanket."

Nasir thumbed through his keys, unlocked, and opened the door. The three men stepped inside. Rasil's blanketed body was quickly visible. Roberto stepped over to the slain youth and shook his head in remorse. "Too soon a Star extinguished." He took a sip of the liquor and then performed a ritual by spitting in four directions. He swallowed a second sip. "Young Star, fade back into the Black Mother's embrace. Go back to the Black Parents above. From black, to starlight, back to the Great Black again." He performed another spitting ritual.

Nasir and Wakil bowed their heads respectfully as Roberto spoke his grace. Afterwards, Nasir lit several candles and oil lamps placed around the large storage house. Wakil closed the door, no longer needing the moon's light to see. Roberto approached Nasir slowly. He placed his hands on the boy's shoulders and said, "I will have soldiers guarding you. My best. Seen and Unseen alike."

Nasir shook his head. "I know. I suspected that."

"Wakil," the stocky assassin called over his shoulder. "Did you know about this meeting?"

"Yes," Wakil answered with shame in his voice.

"Don't feel guilty," Roberto said comfortingly. "We didn't see this coming."

Roberto straightened himself out. He spied Rasil's wrapped body. "We need to get him out of here. We need to toss Rasil's body far away. Somewhere it can be discovered." He turned around completely and walked to the body. "See now, if they suspect that he got away, because they know what they did with the bodies, then it's possible that he informed Nasir of what happened." Roberto looked at the young Moor. "These bastards can't think that, they'll kill you sooner."

Nasir nodded.

Roberto turned to Wakil. "Rasil told me that Sa'ad was going to need my service. I was informed of the purpose of his meeting with The Four Winds."

Wakil sighed. "I knew they were playing him close. I had a feeling. I just didn't expect them to strike so quickly."

"What was this meeting about?" Nasir asked. "My father was going to discuss plans with me here, tonight, after his meeting with The Four Winds. I do know he wanted to use this opportunity to eventually strike The Four Winds, and take back al-Mari Ifriq."

Wakil took seat on a crate. "The Turks wanted to open a new trade route. A Portuguese ship, bound for Africa-west, was marked. They wanted to establish a new delivery route. That would be the beginning of re-organizing their failing trade ventures." The lawyer's eyes swept the floor, but eventually his sad gaze looked up at Nasir. "They wanted to make your father a partner. He believed that he could get to know their movements once inside their circle. He was going to plot a silent rebellion. He marked the heads of The Four Winds. He planned for them to be dead within several months."

"Sa'ad was the last person to take shit from The Four Winds," Roberto remarked. "He was always pointing out that our city's failing economy was based on their taxes and tributes."

Nasir said with conviction, "And our company makes money. The Four Winds view that as a slap in the face."

"They had Taran deliver the message to me," Wakil said with a guilty tone. "Taran was there at the ambush."

"He'll die too," Roberto said as if making a casual checklist. He turned back to Nasir and asked, "Are you ready and willing to uphold your father's plans?"

Newfound pride fluxed through Nasir when Roberto asked him this simple question. Nasir did not smile, given the circumstances. He stood taller, though. He looked at Wakil and Roberto, two great professionals and loyal friends of his father. These venerable men, armed with great experience and wisdom, were his to command and learn from. "I will honor my father's wishes," said Nasir, "and I will execute his plan." He took a deep breath and added, "And I'm going to need your guidance more than ever."

"You should get home," stated Roberto. "You need to be with

your family. I'll clean up here. We'll find a good place for Rasil."

"I have papers to attend to," Wakil said. "I will work on making the company officially yours. Will you take the title of Bey?"

Nasir shook his head, no. "I will be company boss. No different than my father."

Wakil bowed at the neck. "Yes, Company Boss."

Nasir looked at Roberto. The assassin bowed his neck and saluted, "Company Boss."

"Everyone to there duties," commanded Nasir, feeling a little uncomfortable. He handed Roberto the keys to the company house and all three men left the storage area. The three men walked back to the town gates. There was still no word from the guards. Nasir said that his father never made it to the company house. Once inside the gates, the three men separated. Roberto headed to another district to find members of his clan. Wakil returned home, where he found Taran waiting. He delivered the news about Sa'ad missing.

Wakil wanted to choke him.

Taran was very good with his lie, though. His concern almost looked genuine, and may have persuaded the lawyer, if had he no knowledge of Taran's complicity in the murder of his friend. The lawyer informed Taran that he was waiting with Nasir at the company house. There was no sign of Sa'ad. Taran relayed that the heads of The Four Winds were upset.

"Their anger is for selfish reasons, though," Taran continued. "It comes at a time when they need Sa'ad for business."

"How treacherous of them," Wakil remarked sharply.

Nasir returned home. No word of his father came that night. In the morning, Nasir journeyed to the coast to watch the day begin. It was a new day, he was a company boss, and in the middle of a secret war he was not even supposed to be privy to.

Nasir's thoughts swayed back and forth between his father and war.

Sa'ad's body was discovered two hours after noon. Rasil's body was discovered facedown at the coast, just outside the borders of al-Mari Ifriq. A swift, deadly first move had been made. Nasir needed to act quickly before he was the next body discovered.

Chapter Five

Sa'ad was not buried in common ground. His body was entombed in a burial vault built within a chamber located near the company house. The Sa'ood Company closed its business for three days, not entirely for the purpose of mourning. The burial vault was opened on the first day after Sa'ad's body was discovered, and while the body was being prepared for service. Sa'ad's body, after discovery, was washed with warm water and rose water. His jaw was bound and cotton was placed at specific points of the body to keep its odor fresh. There was cotton in Sa'ad's ears, nose, armpits, and between his legs. Sa'ad was clothed anew, his merchant wear exchanged for the garments of a Moorish nobleman. A white cotton shroud covered Sa'ad's body. His head was wrapped to cover his terrible wounds, though they had been stiched as best they could.

Sa'ad's body was taken to the burial vault after preparation. Family and close friends observed Sa'ad's body on the morning of the second day. The burial vault was covered with candles and perfumed with incense. Roberto performed a ritual of sprinkling Sa'ad's body with water of orange-flower. Afya removed her shroud and placed it gently over her husband. She was sad, but she did not weep. Afya did not want her tears to interrupt the journey of her husband's departed soul. A lament had the power to call a person's soul back from the spirit realm, but unable to return to its body, and cursed to haunt the lamenter. Such was Moorish superstition.

Nasir and Zakiy splashed saffron water onto their father's chest. Wakil chanted Mohammedan prayers while Jabari, Taran, Maurice, and Fusan placed around Sa'ad's open funeral chest gifts from company bosses. The gifts were just small trinkets, gold rings or coins. Nasir, Wakil, and Roberto masked their offense at Taran's presence. They were, however, unaware of Maurice and Fusan's role in Sa'ad's assassination, the two of them having returned to their tavern thirty minutes after performing Sa'ad's mark. Wakil's other children, married and scattered about Africa, did not attend the service. Roberto had people from his clan seek them out to deliver the news.

Taran's wife and daughter waited at the entrance of the burial vault, standing next to Wakil's wife. The women were veiled. The attending men presented loaves of bread, dates, and figs. Mehit and her mother, along with

Wakil's wife, stepped forward. Afya accompanied them. The women placed down branches of myrtle and palm, and flowers.

Nasir and Zakiy escorted their mother from the burial vault. Jabari followed behind them, escorting his mother as well. Wakil and Roberto took turns exchanging prayers, Mohammedan and Occult. Taran met his wife and exited the burial vault. Maurice and Fusan flanked Mehit and walked from the vault. Wakil and Roberto, continuing their chants, extinguished the candles. Sunlight poured in. The two men closed and sealed Sa'ad's body within the burial chest and then exited in silence. They bowed their heads for the last time toward their dear friend and former company boss. They left the burial vault and locked the sanctuary behind them.

Wakil and Roberto emerged from the stone mortuary built into and underneath the sands. They regrouped with the others, and new groups were formed among them. Roberto took leave alone. Ilindia Kali claimed Rasil's body, posing as the young man's mother. The Seventy-Two Points of the Universe had a ritual to perform. Roberto's mistress was preparing the body in a secret location far from al-Mari Ifriq.

Nasir parted from his mother, taking Wakil's side. Zakiy escorted Afya to their home. Maurice and Fusan returned to the city with their foster mother and sister. Taran stayed behind, but was quickly dismissed by Wakil. "I am preparing the papers for Nasir," he told Taran in his husky voice that trembled with sorrow. "The city does not pause for our grievance. Inform the heads of The Four Winds that Nasir is company boss."

Taran bowed. "They want to meet with him tomorrow. I understand you will represent him."

"Yes," Wakil clarified.

"I will return with their orders. They will want to continue business." He gave what was almost a sincere apologetic look to Nasir. "I understand you're grieving. But these Turkish fiends were in the middle of business at the time of your father's murder. Their only act of generosity is to wave tribute in respect for your mourning. But the business they wanted to conduct with your father—"

Nasir nodded his head. "I know. I will continue business to honor my father's spirit."

Taran saluted the young company boss and then trekked over the sands, heading back to al-Mari Ifriq's gates. Nasir and Wakil waited for Taran to disappear over the sandy horizon, his figure shrinking as he journeyed back to the city. The two then turned and entered the company house and walked upstairs to what was now Nasir's private quarter. Wakil took a seat on one of the two large cushions. Nasir sat on the cushion opposite Wakil. A low, wooden table, piled with legal parchments, was situated between them.

Nasir looked toward the window. There was a beam of light shining through. He shook his head and exhaled deeply. "I can't believe he was there," he said speaking of Taran.

"It's all a part of his act," Wakil replied. He gave a low chuckle. "It's a good act."

Nasir didn't ponder the thought. He didn't want to give Taran any credit for his malicious ways. He stood from his rested position and walked over to the window, getting a view of the sea. His morning ritual was not interrupted even by his father's funeral. Nasir believed his father would not have allowed it. He could hear his father scolding him to simply, *"Bury the man and continue the plan."* Nasir managed a smile. There was only one problem to his father's plans. Sa'ad was going to negotiate a new trade route, one by land. He seemed confident that he could engineer a route that was not too long and did not venture into the territory of bandits and raiders. Wakil said he was unaware of any route, and there were no secrets between Sa'ad and Wakil.

Nasir turned to Wakil and asked, "Where do we begin? Should I campaign to the other company bosses that I'm now Sa'ood Company Boss?"

Wakil shook his head. "No need. They know." The lawyer reached for the pile of parchments on the low table in front of him. "I've been working on these the past few days. I will finish them tonight. The Four Winds will meet with us tomorrow. Will you keep the business closed for another day?"

Nasir nodded his head, yes. "Zakiy has been directing ships to the Ahangar Company. The Persian company has been generous in taking in our imports, or holding ships in need of repair. Company Boss Iraj is a good friend, and he's declared himself an ally. Ghanem has taken some of the burden too. We've given just a few to the al-Hammon Company. One more day and we will recover what time we've lost. I've already figured how to organize our workers to get us back on track. I will discuss this further with Zakiy."

Wakil cleared his throat. He was impressed with Nasir's drive to run the company under the stressful conditions, and with foreboding circumstances looming over the horizon. But there was still the question as to how much Nasir's younger brother was to be involved.

Wakil asked, "What about Zakiy and his involvement?"

"Company duty. No more," Nasir insisted. "He's not naïve," Nasir said, shaking his head. "Under no circumstances. But he is to have no involvement with the death of The Four Winds." Nasir's last sentence was barely an audible whisper. "I will increase his status once we have control of the city. I will bring Fusan and Maurice closer to me. I'll clean up *The al-Hammon Palace*. They will have a respectable business. Zakiy will have more control of the company while you and I unify the other companies' bosses. The original dream that you, my father, and Maurice and Fusan's father had for al-Mari Ifriq will be real."

Wakil just smiled. Nasir was still naïve to some things, despite his growing demeanor that was part desperation and part willing to prove that he was Sa'ad's son. Nasir, though, had no idea how Maurice and Fusan's father was killed. Sa'ad never imparted to Nasir that he was the assassin. Nasir had no idea about the betrayal of Rashaad al-Hammon. Pondering the past made Wakil wonder if Taran, a traitor as well, informed the two children that he had adopted as to how their father was truly killed.

"We should keep a careful eye on the al-Hammon brothers," suggested Wakil.

"Why?" Nasir asked, his voice sounding very young to Wakil's ears.

Wakil formed the words in his head, a complete confession. Something stopped his lips from making his thoughts audible. He realized quickly how hard confessing the truth could be if extreme, emotional consequences followed. Wakil understood all too well the consequences of words, having engaged in furious words with his eldest son, Laith, a little more than ten years ago.

Laith was fiery. He was hurt that Wakil and his associates, men carved from sterner stuff, did not take greater action against the Turks. Laith, when the he was nineteen years of age, approached his father about his feelings. Wakil let the wound in his ego get the best of him. He confronted his son's accusations as a lawyer, not as a father, trying to reason with him about the possible consequences of a full-scale war with the Turks. Wakil screamed at his son. Laith left shortly after, never to return to al-Mari Ifriq. There were letters sent from Mali. Wakil believed his son would join an army, rise in the ranks, and engage the Turks with great force. Instead, Laith studied finance and became part of an accountant and treasury system. He married, had a family, and settled in Mali. Jabari visited his older brother often. Wakil had few visits. Even with smiles and laughter, the visits were strained. Laith expressed no desire to return home.

These were the consequences of the wrong words, the wrong tone, and the wrong time. And this was certainly not the day for Nasir to learn that his father assassinated the father of two close friends. Even though Sa'ad had just cause, the day of his burial was not the time for this revelation. Nasir was already suffering enough, trying to exhale his mourning into determination and leadership.

"Their proximity to Taran makes them suspect, for now." This was all that the lawyer said on the matter. Nasir agreed, but argued that once all was said and done, the two brothers and their businesses would be let into the fold. Wakil hoped that his courage to reveal the truth would come beforehand. Nasir was then pensive. Wakil continued, "Your father figured it would take a month to track the heads of The Four Winds' movements. A second month would be used to time their marks perfectly. He also considered a possible third month." He then put his hand up and said, "We know what your father was planning. Roberto will have his men on it. We still need to generate a trade route. The Four Winds are obviously looking for one."

Nasir looked down, contemplating. "They enticed my father by making him believe they wanted him to build a new trade route. They were planning to kill him. Their plan was always for me to create the route." Nasir's gaze toward Wakil was stern. "A test or not, I will not submit. I will present them a route tomorrow. I will say it was part of a plan my father had spoken to me about."

"And where will this magical route travel through?" Wakil teased.

"Roberto must know a secret route," Nasir expressed. Wakil became interested. "There must be a travel route that he and his clan no longer use."

"It's possible," Wakil agreed. "There is some danger to worry about, though. Wandering tribes may now inhabit the route. They may consider Roberto and his clan friendly, but no one else. It might be overrun with bandits, or worse, tawny nomads." He shook a finger toward Nasir. "But I like how you're thinking."

Nasir bowed at the neck. "Thank you," he said. "But Roberto must know a route no longer in use. How long will the funeral for Rasil last?"

"It's not until midnight, truthfully," Wakil said. "He was just going to check if all had been prepared."

"Can he be called back?" Nasir asked.

Wakil nodded, yes. "I'll have Jabari track him down."

Nasir felt uneasy. "I don't mean to disturb Rasil's funeral. I gave Roberto a silver pot and an arrow as an offering to Rasil. No one but Roberto's clan is allowed to attend the service. I respect that."

"You have no idea the respect and loyalty Roberto had toward your father," Wakil said. "When other city-ports, regencies, and Republics were at war with Moriscos or condemning those who openly did not support Mohammedan law, your father washed all that away. He was more than just a company boss. He was this city's governor, unspoken as it was." Wakil then scoffed. "Your father hated that other regencies throughout Africa-north allowed the European to come and worship freely with any religion or ideal, but went to war with any man or woman with the hint of night in their flesh if they did not submit to Mohammed. Even I find that ridiculous." Wakil waved the thought away. "But, as for Roberto, his loyalty and respect are now transferred to you. Nasir ibn Sa'ad al-Din Sa'ood, if you so command it, Roberto will appear."

Nasir smiled warmly at the sentiment. "We have a long time until midnight."

Wakil lifted himself up from his cushion. "I will have Jabari find Roberto. I will send word to your house when Roberto has arrived. Until then, young Company Boss, be with your family."

Nasir stood up.

The two Moors bowed toward one another and then left the room and company house, traveling back to the city gates to enter, and depart in different directions. Wakil went to his home to command Jabari to find Roberto. Nasir returned to his house to mourn with his family.

Afya had prepared a large bowl of fruit salad and juice from a jug. Nasir and his family sat around a wooden table in the chief room and picked from the bowl of fruit. There was not much said. Afya tried a few words, remarking about the crime in al-Mari Ifriq. She spoke about how much Sa'ad, her husband, wanted to change that. She cursed the Turks' presence.

Nasir did not comment. He listened closely to his mother's tone. She was very intelligent. She was in no way ignorant of how Sa'ad handled business. Afya was the very reason that Sa'ad never slipped completely into the mentality of a maniacal pirate. Sa'ad confided in her about the decisions he had to make. She understood very well the possible repercussions of a hard-boiled company boss's disappearance, and the intended effect. Afya's intelligence, though, got ahead of her. Her intelligence rang far too loud in her remarks, and Nasir listened close. Afya wanted to see if Nasir knew more about her husband's death. After all, he knew her husband's fate before the city guards and police.

Nasir did not comment.

The raven-colored woman knew that she was just a mother to the new company boss. She was no longer someone's silent partner in company affairs. Sa'ad confided with Afya because he understood a woman to be his equal. He understood that his wife was his foundation, an ancient African understanding. Sa'ad was raised a Moorish Mohammedan, but he studied ancient African ideals. He was greatly influenced by Roberto Hamaat's ancient and occult understanding. Sa'ad's spirituality came from these ancient, occult lessons. These lessons influenced Afya's children. Afya understood that within those lessons was Nasir's knowledge that she and her son were not equals. She was his mother, something far greater than an equal. Nasir would protect her at all cost, even from the knowledge she desperately wanted.

Jabari, calling for Nasir from outside the front door, interrupted what little conversation the family had. Nasir asked his mother if she was well enough to be alone, Zakiy was needed to direct traffic to the other companies. Afya assured her son she would be fine. Zakiy stood up and took his brother's side. Afya looked up at them admiringly. The two sons bowed to their mother and left the chief room. They walked to the outside and found Jabari.

"I didn't mean to holler," said Wakil's son, an expression of embarrassment plaguing his visage. He shook his head as it hung low. "Where are my manners? And on this day," he continued.

Nasir laughed and excused his friend's behavior. "The day needs lightheartedness. My father would've appreciated it." He patted Jabari on the shoulder. "What is the situation?"

"Roberto is at the house," Jabari answered.

"Good," Nasir stated. He turned to his brother and said, "Four workers are to join you an hour after noon." Zakiy nodded. "The ships are not due until several hours after noon." Zakiy nodded again. "Take escort with a city guard on your way."

"I will," Zakiy said with a whine in his voice.

Nasir heard Zakiy's tone but gave it no attention. Zakiy walked away, heading to the company house for duty. Jabari escorted Nasir to his house. When they arrived and entered, Jabari's mother bestowed a gentle greeting. She gave Nasir a soft kiss and said a small blessing. Nasir thanked her, nodded, and then continued to Wakil's study. There inside he found the lawyer and the assassin. Wakil was seated. Roberto stood. Both men jumped to attention and bowed at the neck when Nasir entered.

"I informed Roberto of everything," Wakil explained.

Roberto stepped forward. "I got good news. There is a route no longer in use by my clan or bandits."

Nasir exhaled. He smiled and clapped his hands. "My man," he said excitedly.

"The trail is known as the African Black Bird. Legend says that warrior-priestesses blessed the trail. They were a faction of African women from the four corners of the continent." Roberto grinned. "Their spirits would love to be called upon to battle Turks. The African Black Bird is your trail. It extends all the way to Morocco."

Nasir approached Roberto. With each step his lip trembled and his eyes watered. He burst into tears as his arms wrapped around the husky assassin. Nasir held the assassin tight. All he could think about was his father.

Wakil walked over to Nasir. He patted the grieving young man on the back. Roberto embraced the young Moor harder. "Your father is still here, little Moor," spoke the clan leader. "Embrace his spirit and stab his enemies. We will help you."

Nasir let go. He stepped back. He looked at Roberto, his face, though dark as night, flushed red with rage. With tears still in his eyes he demanded, "You draw up that route." Roberto nodded at the command. Nasir turned to Wakil. "Tomorrow we will present it to these four devils and their slave, Taran. In two month's time, they will die."

The two men bowed again to the young company boss.

The rest of the day was busy for Nasir. He joined his brother Zakiy and a few company workers at the company house as they directed ships to other ports. Nasir mostly introduced himself as the new company boss to the few Moorish, corsair captains that floated in. He explained his father's fate, and the Moorish corsairs and their crews were saddened by the loss. The chief for the Council of Captains, a Moorish Captain named Hieremias Sunwil, who was a tall, imposing black man, submitted complete allegiance to Nasir when he heard the news. Nasir didn't divulge the true killers behind his father's murder to Captain Sunwil. But the corsair captain was now a full-fledged ally to the company. Nasir accepted Hieremias' pledge and took note of it.

Eight ships needed to be redirected. The activity lasted until sundown. Nasir met with the particular bosses whose companies hosted the ships. He explained to them that his company would re-open completely in the next two days. He instructed the other companies to help the re-directed ships distribute their goods to specific city stores. The ships in need of repair, and those ships handed in on loan, would be collected in two days.

Nasir had no problem speaking with the heads of the Ahangar, Ghanem, and al-Hammon companies. Fusan and Maurice were his friends.

They showcased remorse alongside Nasir and Zakiy. The head of the Ahangar Company, a young, Persian gentlemen named Isaiah Iraj, respected Nasir. Iraj now had the amity of another young, company boss. He was not exactly delighted about the circumstances that brought about this new turn of events, however. Iraj believed that Nasir's youth could challenge the hardheaded company bosses stuck in their ways, slaves to the ruling Turks. The Ghanem company head, the elder Feroz Aunun, was a black Turk, and he was open to Nasir's appeals. He was completely sympathetic.

However, Nasir's biggest challenge would come in the morning. The Four Winds called for a counsel with him. He had to present them with a route to bring in goods plundered from a Portuguese ship. Roberto drew up a map before Rasil's funeral. The parchment would not be presented to Nasir until the morning, before his meeting with The Four Winds.

Taran brought word to Wakil that the plunder from the Portuguese ship was waiting at a city-state in Algeria. The Four Winds were growing impatient. Not only did they want to meet with Nasir, they also wanted him to leave immediately and attempt any route planned. Wakil expressed to Nasir that The Four Winds were trying to test his efficiency. They would be very surprised. Nasir's resources, tapping the intellect of Wakil and Roberto, were almost without limit. Nasir was ready to prove that he would be a formidable foe. He still had his father's plan to honor. Killing the heads of The Four Winds Company was only the beginning. He had plans to make Wakil the *Beylerbey* of the entire region once The Four Winds were eradicated. The lawyer always aspired to become a politician. Nasir would grant him the chance.

Chapter Six

Nasir and Zakiy watched and listened to al-Mari Ifriq's day open and come to life. The next two days would test them both, and Nasir understood that. He brought his younger brother to the coast to calm him. Their company would partially re-open today. Zakiy would be in charge, manning the company servants and workers. Only half would be in attendance. Zakiy would have complete control over the company while Nasir dealt with The Four Winds' leaders.

Nasir made sure his brother was centered and ready to handle the day. He wiped Zakiy's shoulders and straightened out his merchant clothes. Zakiy protested, saying he was not a baby. Nasir teased his brother more, telling him he would always be just a baby to him. Zakiy laughed, retorting, "If you had not a meeting with gangsters, I'd wrinkle your fine suit and stain it with sand and water."

"Gangsters?" Nasir questioned.

Zakiy lifted his shoulders. "That's all those bastards are," he said noding his heads toward the palace in the distance. He gave Nasir a stern look. "Did they kill our father? Ma-ma believes so."

Nasir took a deep breath. "I suspect she had you ask me." Nasir guessed right, but Zakiy did not confirm. Nasir glanced over Zakiy's shoulder toward the company house. He then looked back to his brother. "I want you to handle company business. Let me worry about the company's, uh, *aggressive negotiations*."

"That's a wonderful euphemism," Zakiy retorted. "I hope you put on a better game-face then the one you wear now." Zakiy turned around and looked in the direction of their father's burial vault. "No time to mourn."

"I'll make time, Zakiy," Nasir assured.

Zakiy breathed back his tears. "Yes, well, to work." He cleared his throat. "Good day, brother."

"Good day," Nasir said back. The two brothers headed in different directions, Zakiy to the company house and Nasir back to the city. Once inside the gates, Nasir walked to Wakil's house. Roberto, three men, and one woman greeted him at the lawyer's front door. Roberto stepped forward, removing a parchment from his satchel. He extended the parchment to Nasir as he approached. "Company Boss," he said. "The route has been drawn."

Nasir took the parchment and nodded. He felt the need to tell Roberto, "No need with all the *company boss* talk. Nasir will do. You are my elder."

Roberto leaned closer and whispered, "Wakil and I will address you as Company Boss until we see the other company bosses and your companymen addressing you just the same, and with all sincerity."

"Yes, then," Nasir acknowledged humbly.

Roberto stepped back and then pointed Nasir's attention to the three men and one woman standing at the front door. "These are servants for you, Company Boss." Nasir nodded respectfully at the mention of his title. "Two are for you, one is for your brother, and the last is for your mother." Roberto again spoke in a hush voice. "They are from my clan." He winked. "Three Suns and one Moon." Roberto pointed to the first man and introduced him as Awa Abdule. He had blue-black skin, sharp features, and wild gray hair. He was short and thin, but muscular. He looked fit for a man nearing sixty. Awa was dressed in a long, dark, grey-blue cloth that draped around his body, over one shoulder, around his waist, and even down both legs. He wore over his clothes a brown burnoose. Dark sandals covered his feet. "Awa is your escort and servant," Roberto pointed out as Awa bowed graciously. He turned to another and said, "As well as this young gentleman here. His name is Tegu."

Tegu stepped forward and bowed. He was dressed in white, baggy pants, a shirt the same color, and beige shoes. A wrap covered the twists in his hair. He had dark brown skin, and a wide, toothy smile. He was tall, over six feet, and had a muscular build. The female was introduced as Biliqis Badra. She was slender and beautiful with her age. Her skin was very dark and she too, like Awa, had sharp features. Her head was triangular, and draping far past her shoulders were thin, coiled locks of hair. There was something sensual about her movements, her slender eyes and hissing voice. She reminded Nasir of a snake. Roberto assigned Biliqis to Nasir's mother.

The last was named Han Za. He was short with brown skin, a round head and bulging eyes. What he lacked in height he made up for with muscle and skill. He was assigned to Zakiy.

Nasir greeted everyone and thanked Roberto. He informed the assassin that his brother was down by the docks. Roberto bowed and continued to Nasir's house to introduce Biliqis to Afya, Han Za with him. Jabari came to the front of the house and allowed Nasir entrance. Awa and

Tegu waited patiently outside, on guard but inconspicuous.

Nasir greeted Wakil and the two of them went into the lawyer's study to inspect the route scribbled onto the parchment. The lawyer knew that the young company boss was nervous. He let Nasir have time to settle his thoughts, and so he said very little. Wakil had his servants prepared a ride to The Four Winds' palace. Nasir stayed silent, only commanding Awa and Tegu to take a mount and follow. Awa and Tegu insisted on walking, to blend more as servants than guards. Nasir didn't argue. He took to his mount and followed Wakil to the palace his family once occupied.

The palace's architecture had changed in the last twenty years, expanded with more columns and colonnades. The front was still a wonderful landscape, gated off from the outside and swarming with Guyotta's guards that were waiting for Nasir and Wakil's small entourage. Awa and Tegu, acting as servants, assisted Nasir from his mount. Wakil's servants did the same. The guards opened the gates and allowed Nasir and Wakil's entourage to pass through. Guyotta walked in a quick manner through the palace entrance. He held out his arms and rushed quickly to embrace Nasir. The young company boss accepted Guyotta's fabricated sympathy. Guyotta stepped back and bowed graciously. Nasir bowed his head in return. Guyotta and Wakil quickly greeted one another with Mohammedan salutations.

Guyotta's sympathetic conduct was flawless. Had Wakil or Nasir been ignorant of the Regent Master's involvement with Sa'ad's murder, they would have been completely fooled. Guyotta spoke with a hand to his chest and saddened eyes, "I mean no offense to your title, al-Nasir," he began. "But it pains me to call you company boss. Your father was a great man, though we did not always agree on politics. However, I am very humbled to understand that he was right all along. We must begin to reconstruct the infrastructure of al-Mari Ifriq. The city deserves tribute, not the Ottoman chiefs."

Nasir returned a smile. "I agree, Regent Master Sahin-el Bey."

Guyotta smiled warmly and put an arm around Nasir. "Enough with titles, al-Nasir. I am just Guyotta. Come." He led Nasir and Wakil inside the palace. Guyotta left orders with his guards to see that Wakil and Nasir's servants and mounts were taken care of. "You inherit your father's partnership. The Four Winds, an ambitious company, will now become *The Four Corners*. That, however, is not until we can establish ourselves in the four corners of the world, including the Americas."

The palace was finished on the inside. It was no longer barren, as Nasir's faint memories could recall. Its walls were bright with intricate designs and tapestries. The morning sun came through the windows and lit the elaborate hallways, a stunning blend of Turkish, Moorish, and Arabic décor. The sun's light, running through the many pathways the palace possessed, was the one thing Nasir remembered clearly. There was now ornamentation and color schemes to brighten and let shine. There also were far more servants running through the palace, more veiled women. None of the servants were Turkish. All were Moors.

Nasir couldn't help but feel robbed. Guyotta's voice sounded like he was gloating when he declared the palace as Sa'ad's greatest tribute to The Four Winds. Nasir did not react the way he wished. Guyotta continued his flattering ways as they walked into a counsel room. "Nasir," said the Regent Master. "Welcome home."

The room shined gold. The sun's tendrils ricocheted off the walls and brightened brass and copper vases sitting on marble pedestals. The light reflected off of gold shields that adorned the wall and kissed the tips of leaves in potted plants placed around the room. The rectangular, wooden table glowed with an earth-colored aura as the sun illuminated the furniture piece. Seated at the table were the other heads of The Four Winds and Taran. Nasir heard Hyle finishing a complement to Taran on allowing his daughter to open up her bathhouse to him and the Green Army soldiers. Nasir bit his tongue behind his closed lips. His anger rose just as Taran stood up and walked over to him. The ambassador beamed a smile at Nasir and embraced the young Moor. Taran stepped back and greeted Wakil and the Regent Master.

Guyotta acknowledged Taran's gesture and then graciously ordered him to sit. He waved his hand to guide Nasir and Wakil to a seat. They walked over to two seats on the right side of the table. Guyotta took the head. The company heads lifted from their seats and each greeted Wakil and Nasir. Hyle, Aguyan, and Tous expressed their sympathies concerning the death of Nasir's father. Nasir accepted their two-faced solace with a smile just as genuine and then took seat.

Guyotta continued to stand. He pointed to the bottle of wine and cups on the table and the fruit, cheese, and small treats occupying several plates. He looked to Wakil and said, "I understand we serve Mohammed's Law, but a small drink of wine never hurt anyone. I know you Moors are partial to wine."

Wakil lifted a hand and a smile. "Possibly after negotiations," he managed to say.

Guyotta did not take offense. He smiled and sat down and retorted, "There will only be a small need for negotiations. We are equals.

With that as our understanding and foundation, we are here to find an agreeable solution to al-Mari Ifriq's crumbling infrastructure. We are in need of a market that has been non-existent for the past five or six years. Trade import is low. Our shops struggle to maintain goods. Few ships dock in our ports, and few corsair captains seek protection in our hood. Gang activity, as we very well know, has increased. There are rumors that companies from Tunis and Algiers back these gangs to weaken our city-state. Odongo-Mauharim resides between Algeria and Tunisia. Their borders are expanding and closing in on our territory."

The other companymen listened closely. Their intentions were different. The Four Winds company underbosses were mindful that Guyotta's words were just to entrance Nasir and Wakil, especially the young company boss. Nasir and Wakil, however, aware of the Turks' schemes, listened to the list of problems plaguing the city while silently judging the Turks' actions for causing them.

"We have no army to defend our population in a war with either neighbor," continued Guyotta. "Two hundred soldiers are not enough. Plus, their intentions cater toward the Sultan and his chiefs. The Green Army, our strongest soldiers, is so few, numbering twenty elite. The Djenhai kingdom is again at odds with the wandering tribe, the Ogunsanwo-Mashek. The tribe has become increasingly bold with raids. We fear trade routes in that direction. So, we are now cut off from the Djenhai kingdom's resources and the small army they have." Guyotta managed a smile. "There are advantages to our situation, though. We may not have an army, but we do have solidarity among our greatest companies. We are united in ways that other corsair states—"

Nasir interrupted, "We are a city-state. We are a port-city." Nasir then cleared his throat. "Forgive my offense—my interruption. I understand we of Africa-north have been branded the title of a French pirate, the corsair. Some of our enforcers at sea don't mind being called corsair. I respect that. But our city, our region, does not thrive totally on piracy, and I include our brother and sister regencies of Sale, Algiers, Tunis and the others."

"Of course," Guyotta accepted Nasir's words.

"True," spoke the lawyer Aguyan. "Was England branded a pirate state once it employed the services of John Hawkyns and other pirates? No, it was considered a genius strategy. By that time Africa-north had been involved in employing pirates to police and guard the seas for almost a hundred years. John Hawkyns is called an adventurer for his acts. We are branded barbarians. Are any of the European states considered pirates for their barbaric raids on the coast and interior of Africa-west, looking for our brothers and sisters as slaves?" Aguyan nudged Nasir with his shoulder. "Pay no attention to the Regent Master, he's full Turk. Half of your blood runs through me," the lawyer joked producing light laughter from the table's occupants. "I'll translate your civilized words to this *swarmahu*."

Nasir and Wakil were shocked when the Turks around the table erupted in laughter. Even Taran felt too awkward to share in it. The word 'swarmahu' was an extreme offense spat in the face of the growing Turkish and tawny Arab population. Guyotta tapped Nasir on the arm, seeing the young company boss's concern. "It's not a secret what your people say about us foreigners, or our mixed blood. We're not too foreign, though. Not after all these years. Let me remind, Turkey, as with most of Southern Europe, was once considered Africa."

Nasir bobbed his head. "Yes. True. Those days are long gone, for some. But, you really can't offend a man that has power over you."

The laughter crumbled to an awkward silence.

Guyotta continued to chuckle. Again, he tapped Nasir's arm. "There is a hierarchy here. Yes. I am Regent Master. But we are all in the same situation. You must get used to the fact that we are equals."

Wakil steered the situation somewhere else, a common ground. "What is unequal are the acts of servitude the European has engaged in with our African-west people. There are many rumors surrounding the slave trade," spoke Wakil. "I've heard of unimaginable horrors taking place in the European's so-called New World. Dutch and French travelers that stop in our ports tell tales in the taverns."

"That is why re-establishing al-Mari Ifriq will send a message of our strength," said Guyotta. "There is nothing that can be done for the African cursed into slavery. Let your brothers and sisters go. It's a small sacrifice, but a temporary one. We fortify al-Mari Ifriq and we can then consolidate all of the Africa-northern states. Once Africa-north is unified then we spread to the other territories. The Moors can be a great power again, this time in their African homeland."

Everyone looked at Nasir. The Moor removed the parchment for the new trade route. He unraveled the map and placed it on the table. "This parchment shows a new trade route. I must have your word that while I'm establishing this new route—" Guyotta reached for the parchment and slid it into his own view. "—creating a plan to revitalize our old trade routes will take precedence."

Guyotta examined the route that was sketched out on the parchment in front of him. He barely heard Nasir's words but then looked up and answered, "Of course. One new trade route will not do. We have eight routes. This will be our ninth. I believe four new routes in total will do. I want to stimulate trade in the four directions. This will boost the routes we already have. The next trade route should be the south. Our problem is the nomadic tribes, of most concern is the Ogunsanwo-Mashek." Guyotta looked at Taran and called the man to attention. "Taran, you and Nasir, while on your travels into Algeria, will formulate the other three routes. The Four Winds will concentrate on putting together a new annual market and boosting the import and export on the routes established."

"Will The Four Winds lift the taxes and tributes from the routes and merchants?" Nasir asked boldly.

"We will lighten them," assured Hyle. The accountant looked at Taran, Wakil, and the lawyer Aguyan. "We'll need to come to an agreement with the Council of Captains, the merchants, and caravans."

The men nodded toward Hyle. Then Guyotta spoke, "That will convene when Taran and Nasir return." The Regent Master raised an eyebrow. He put his sights on Nasir and leaned close to the young man. "Provisions are ready. Can this route sustain wheels? We have one canopied coach for the caravan and eight caged carts for the cargo—gifts from European sea-merchants. Make use of them, somehow, in this region. You and Taran will ride in the canopy."

Nasir did not know how to answer. "I don't believe the coach would sustain, or at least be comfortable," he addressed the Regent Master's question. "We'll carry the coach as a gift. The iron cages will be fine. This is an old trail, but it checks out. There may be some problems, as it's probably not been well kept. It does pass through the mountain ranges. There are flatlands, even grass. Of course, there are the sands."

"That is fine. We will suit you with two elephants and fat camels for travel," Guyotta announced. "You will be accompanied by fifty mounted men and twenty-five foot soldiers," continued Guyotta. "They will be armed with weapons and skill, should you encounter any problems with bandits or terrain." Nasir nodded in appreciation. "Your journey begins tomorrow morning. Meet here at the palace." Nasir again nodded toward the Regent Master. Guyotta looked at the trade route and commented, "You may have to veer away from this path and head south."

"There are small connection routes for this path," explained Nasir. "I am aware of that much."

Guyotta nodded then smiled at Wakil. "May we drink now?" he asked.

Wakil waved his hand toward the jugs of wine. Guyotta stood up and took a jug of wine and began to pour each of the gentlemen a cup. It was ritualistic, as the Regent Master rounded the table, pouring to a precise measure for each companyman. He ended his journey and poured himself a cup. The other men waited for the Regent Master to lift his cup before taking their own. Guyotta spoke, "The European now makes moves to conquer the world and discover all the secrets she refuses to bestow upon him. The African, the Turk, the Arab, and all the races of Asia make moves simply to survive. No longer, gentlemen. The corruption of fat chiefs that keep us from uniting stops today with this plan."

The men waited for Guyotta to take the first sip, then saluted him with their cups and started to drink. Guyotta adjourned the meeting after one small cup of wine. The companymen stood up and Nasir was again showered with gentlemen hugs and respectful bows for his new status as company boss. There was no more mention of his father. The Four Winds wiped away Sa'ad's memory just as quick as they had assassinated him. Nasir was their puppet now.

Guyotta, along with Taran, escorted Nasir and Wakil from the palace. The Regent Master instructed Taran to get rest for the journey that began at sunrise, to which Taran commanded his servants and guards to escort him home. Wakil and Nasir's entourage was assembled. The two men extended cordial goodbyes to the Regent Master and then, along with Taran and his servants and guards, made their way from the palace.

Nasir did not enjoy Taran's company. He heard the land baron ask Wakil to speak with him in private and the lawyer obliged. Taran made no attempt to speak to Nasir, with the exception of a goodbye as he and Wakil turned onto a different street toward Wakil's house. Awa and Tegu guarded Nasir as he made his way to the company house to help his brother.

The two senior companymen, maneuvering their small entourage through al-Mari Ifirq's morning traffic, arrived at Wakil's house and left their servants and guards outside as they continued into Wakil's private quarters. Sanura, the assassin disguised as Wakil's servant girl, was summoned and commanded to bring refreshments and light morning snacks consisting of fruits, nuts, and boiled eggs. Wakil took a seat on one of his fine cushions while Taran paced the room. Wakil raised an eyebrow, and after a time, asked in a trenchant voice, "Is there something on your mind?" The lawyer then joked, "Use your words, young child."

Taran stopped. There was a look of contempt on his face. Wakil did not back down. He acted as if his friendship with Taran was still intact, his friendly, yet teasing smile, never leaving. Sanura returned with the refreshments ordered and then left the room after pouring two cups of water. Wakil continued to aim his teasing gaze at Taran. The other huffed and continued to pace. Wakil then lost his smile and stood up. He stepped to Taran, blocking the baron's back-and-forth path. "Our friend is dead!" hissed Wakil. *"Sa'ad!"* He held his voice back so as not to sound too accusing. *"Great Sa'ad, may God have mercy on his soul.* His son is terrified, and vicious pirates and gangsters surround us. Al-Mari Ifriq, and all of Odongo-Mauharim, faces a potential crumble. Our neighbors, friendly to our face, are already calculating what they will divide among one another when this region collapses, and you pace in silence!"

Taran could see the intensity in Wakil's eyes. He flinched from the lawyer's gaze, as if a force projected from Wakil's eyes and pushed him. Taran stuttered with his words. Wakil took a forceful step forward. Taran straightened up instantly upon Wakil's approach. The baron's lip trembled. "There is no hope for al-Mari Ifriq," said Taran in a very low voice. "All of Odongo-Mauharim is doomed." Wakil reacted toward Taran with a curious eye. Taran continued. First he turned his back and then he spoke over his shoulder, "Aguyan does much to stop the military presence of the Empire." He turned back to Wakil and explained, "His brother has gained a strong voice among the Ottoman chiefs." Taran took time to swallow, the gesture coming off nervous. "There are large treasuries under the palace. Four vaults. All the tributes go there. Like dragons, the four heads sit on gold. The Ottoman chiefs have not seen full tribute in years. They are furious. Al-Mari-Ifriq is in extreme debt. The Four Winds have three months to show profit. The companies will be reduced. The land and its resources will be drained. The Four Winds' heads will disappear. It will be the citizens that have to deal with the Ottoman wrath."

"But, Aguyan's brother—"

"Can only do so much," finished Taran. "He was able to negotiate three months. They plan to evacuate. Aguyan's brother will share in their profits." Taran sighed thinking about Aguyan's promise that he and his family was included in the evacuation. But Taran could not trust Aguyan's word. Again, the land baron was forced to play both sides and then favor the winning party. "Guyotta let slip a truth at this morning's meeting. Nasir will find out quickly that al-Mari Ifriq has very much turned into a brutal corsair state. Even Sa'ad wasn't so prideful. He knew not all the story, but he knew that much. I know he was waiting for a moment to strike."

Wakil's look became more curious. He stated in a careful tone, "Did they kill him?"

Taran shook his head. "I don't know," he lied. "The Four Winds and I waited that night for Sa'ad. I was nervous. I thought The Four Winds would finally kill me. I thought I was there as a guarantee, a title I've quietly branded for myself these past fifteen years or so." Taran laughed with a sad tone. Feigning remorse, he said, "Sa'ad never showed. We all know the rest."

Wakil knew he was lying. The lawyer's heart burned, feeling blood pump through his body as if it were a hot wind conjured from the desert. He was both angry and sad for Taran. But he would play the land baron as if their friendship never existed. "So this restructure is all a ruse."

"To some degree," said Taran. "Guyotta will create a surplus revenue. He will begin to give full tributes to the Empire. By the time their ships are on the horizon, The Four Winds will be gone. We, al-Mari Ifriq's indigenous population, will then battle for control. The Ottoman army will subdue us and we will become a military state under the Empire's total control."

Wakil was not going to share any plans with Taran. The lawyer placed his hands on Taran's shoulders and expressed, "Nasir and I will do all in our power to make the Sa'ood Company the most prominent. We will force the other companies to look to us when The Four Winds leave, and the Empire arrives."

Taran shook his head and insisted, "No. The Four Winds must die! Aguyan already plots Guyotta's death. They are not united."

"Then let them quarrel," said Wakil. "Let them burn one another."

Taran continued to argue. "But once an eastern trade route is established, they will use it to extract their treasuries. We must strike before they move their monies."

Wakil disagreed only as a lie. "Nasir is young. He has absolutely no experience with being a wartime company boss. I will not submit our friend's son to such an ordeal." Wakil lifted a stern finger to Taran's face. "We will wait. We will have patience. We will be prosperous for the benefit of al-Mari Ifriq. That's how Sa'ad would have played all this."

Taran did not agree with Wakil's last statement. For the first time Taran had wished that Sa'ad was still alive. He would've made war with The Four Winds. In that instant, the baron decided to concentrate all his verbal skill on Nasir. He would begin his manipulation tomorrow while he journeyed with Nasir through the new trade route.

The two men exhaled and shared the refreshments brought to them. Taran then dismissed himself to prepare for his travels with Nasir, mostly concentrating on how he would manipulate the young man. He could not confess the killers of Nasir's father, though that would work best.

He could not even admit that The Four Winds marked the young company boss for death. Taran would have to answer for having knowledge of such information. Taran had to play upon the supposed actions Sa'ad would take if alive, and how Nasir should do the same to honor his father. But while Taran plotted the next day's manipulation, Wakil called upon his son, Jabari, once the land baron left house. He asked his son to bring Nasir to him. Wakil knew Taran's next move was to manipulate the young Moor. The lawyer needed to warn Nasir and report everything Taran had told him.

Chapter Seven

Desert sand congregated with jagged rocks and mountainous regions to form vicious cabals shaped from terra formations that lay miles away from al-Mari Ifriq. The rough landscape contrasted with its own pristine sparkle. The midday sun stretched out its light and created a diamond-like glint on the jagged rocks and rough terrain. Taran and Nasir's caravan, presented as a gift by Regent Master Guyotta Sahin-el Bey, had little trouble navigating through the perilous terrain. An old, carved path eased travel through the rugged territory. Roberto's suggested pathway was, however, not without its obstacles. The trail had sunken areas, gravelly sections, and patches of thick sand sprinkled throughout. The camelmen and foot soldiers periodically stopped the caravan and removed the obstacles on the path, smoothing the ground again and making it fit for travel.

The caravan looked more like an army than a cavalcade that was en route for trade. The caravan was a motley crew of African Moors and Turks. Camelmen, armed with spears and cloaked with hoods and wraps, led the procession. Foot soldiers, equipped with muskets and strapped with pistols and sheathed short swords, followed close behind the camelmen, never showing signs of fatigue for the last six hours of travel. They were given time to rest, and of course, there were the menial duties of helping smooth the trail. The foot soldiers were cloaked with burnoose, shading them from the noonday sun. Soldiers walked in a horseshoe formation around the elephants carrying the main carriage occupied by Taran and Nasir. The carriage's windows were draped with fabrics that shaded the two companymen. Other foot soldiers flanked the nine, empty iron-bar carriages that would be used to transport the plundered slaves and goods the caravan was en route to recover.

Behind the elephant carrying the companymen was the brown, wooden carriage to be presented as a gift. Soldiers kept it afloat in the sands, guiding the vehicle forward. It was shaped like a headless, giant insect, with wheels substituting for legs. What would have been the insect's thorax, the area of the body lying between the head and the abdomen, was an intricately carved piece of wood that jutted out like a tongue and attached to the strong, leather harness that was pulled by two Arabian steeds. The cloaked Moorish riders kept in position a canopy that was attached to the harness and served to keep the horses shaded. The carriage's cabin was shaped like the abdomen of a queen bee. Behind the carriage was another elephant, carrying Taran and Nasir's servants.

Taran and Nasir sat comfortably inside the mounted carriage, its compartment large and relaxing. Nasir sat facing the direction of travel. Taran was opposite him. The young company boss brushed aside the curtain that covered the window, keeping an eye on travel.

"We have twelve more hours to go," teased Taran. "That does not include rest."

Nasir exhaled. He and Taran had not exchanged many words since pulling away from al-Mari Ifriq. Nasir preferred the silence, but he was on guard. He was aware that Taran was biding time to find the perfect words to draw him into committing murder against The Four Winds Company and the Regent Master that led them. Nasir already made plans, however, which also included eliminating Taran for traitorous acts against his father and al-Mari Ifriq. Nasir had to bite his lip to keep his anger from showing. But he raised an inquisitive eyebrow as he thought about exactly how Taran, the heads of The Four Winds, and the Regent Master, were going to be executed. Nasir had a little less than three months to plan and few allies to trust.

"We should keep our eyes open for a group of frontier raiders called the al-Jasi Nzambi," Taran scoffed. "Roberto would love them. They believe in much the same, dark and disturbing spiritual elements he goes on and on about. They claim right to Moorish ancestry."

"Are they Moors?" Nasir asked putting his eye on Taran.

"They claim to be direct descendants of al-Andalusian Moors," Taran said sitting back. He shifted his weight to get comfortable and said in a disgusted tone, "I don't care for nationalities or claims to heritage within the people of Africa." Taran lifted his hand to stop the young company boss from responding. He added, continuing in a sincere tone, "Now, I understand greatly the need to separate ourselves from intruders, conquerors, and usurpers. But to me, all the people of Africa have claim to every great dynasty or rulers within our bloodline. There is no need to be specific. Was al-Andalusia any greater than Kush, Abyssinia, Nubia, or Egypt? Or even the great kingdoms that stand with us now? Many of our western brothers traded within the Americas for centuries. It's a 'new world' only to Europeans."

Nasir took his hand away from the curtain, letting it again guard them from the outside. Nasir leaned forward and asked Taran, "But you seem to doubt these people's claim."

Taran exhaled. He looked down, fixed his tunic and then put his eyes back on the young man in front of him. "It's not their claims. It is the extent to which they go to make them. They are at war with the people we trade with." He exhaled again and continued, "Now, yes, the people we trade with are not Moors. They are not Africans. They are Turks mixed with the tawny Arab's blood. They run a corsair-state."

"Is their corsair-state fair to these people?" Nasir asked with a little force in his voice.

"The Turks of al-Mari Ifriq run a fair state," answered Taran

"That was not my question," Nasir said sharply.

"I don't know the al-Jasi's story," Taran admitted. "Word is they are bandits, plundering the wealth of al-Gherab, the state to where we travel now. Others say that the al-Jasi are trying to build a state of their own. It's said that resources are robbed from them by al-Gherab's Governor, Al-Kasim Askari." Taran put his hands together. "I fear our dealings with al-Gherab and its governor will bring the war to us. This route could be in danger."

"Al-Mari Ifriq is too far to be touched by these skirmishes," Nasir countered.

Taran smiled at the young company boss's naiveté, and he shook a finger at him. "Governor Askari has done al-Mari Ifriq a favor. He will want one done in return. I'm sure he'll ask for weapons or even militia to help put down the al-Jasi's insurgence." Taran waved a hand. "Then what will happen next? The al-Jasi will ally with the Ogunsanwo-Mashek. They will concentrate their attacks on al-Mari Ifriq."

Nasir chuckled, "Impossible."

"And why?" asked Taran.

"Because the Ogunsanwo-Mashek battle with the Djenhai Kingdom," Nasir stated as if the answer was obvious. "It is an ancient war based on principles. That war has never touched al-Mari Ifriq, even with our ties to the Djenhai kingdom."

"Trade routes have been sacked and completely compromised," reminded Taran.

Nasir argued, "Many nomadic tribes roam that area. The plunder of those routes could have been—"

"Each of those wandering tribes are factions of the Ogunsanwo-Mashek," Taran interrupted. Nasir went silent. Outside came a call from the caravan leaders about entering grasslands. Nasir peeked out of the window at the scenery and then put his attention back on Taran. The baron continued, "What I mean to say, Company Boss, is that I do not trust the moves made by Guyotta Sahin-el Bey and The Four Winds."

Taran's lips made the slightest turn upwards. Nasir paused, inspecting the baron's movements. He took only a second to inspect Taran. The baron sat back, the small glimmer of a smile, and any hint that the gesture existed, had been erased from his visage. Nasir had been on his guard, but the baron's tactics were well organized, causing Nasir to be drawn into an exchange that could lead to a slip. Nasir was now aware of Taran's scheme. The young Moor chose his words carefully.

"It's expected," Nasir finally spoke. "Your distrust for the Regent Master and his ruling Turkish company," he stated further, noticing Taran's perplexed look. "I understand. We're all cautious." Nasir leaned forward. "I didn't only inherit my father's company." Nasir decided to appeal to emotions Taran did not have by stating, "And there's also the predicament you've found yourself in with them. They have made your daughter's bathhouse a brothel. It's put you at odds inside your family. I have taken this into consideration." Nasir knew that Taran did not care for his daughter's circumstances. He actually pushed for it to please the heads of The Four Winds. "I claim your daughter as my sister. Maurice and Fusan I claim as my brothers. We find ourselves in an interesting situation."

"Interesting?" Taran wondered allowed. He did not mean to speak his thought, but his reflex was like a hiccup.

"This morning, the Regent Master and Army Official Tous Zeki, explained to me that the Empire is reaping too many benefits from our hard work. It was something Guyotta mentioned in passing when we first met at his palace. The tributes paid to the Ottomans dry al-Mari Ifriq into a financial desert." Nasir squinted his eyes, contemplating. "It was peculiar to see two Turks speak of their Empire as if separate from it." He blinked his perplexed expression from his face and said to Taran, "I must have clearly shown my disconcert because Companyman Zeki explained that there are ambitions to expand al-Mari Ifriq's power to Asia and the New World. Again, Guyotta hinted at a notion earlier, but there were no details. The Regent Master looked so proud as his Army Official explained to me the plans of *The Four Corners*. They actually want to separate from the Ottoman chiefs and the Turkish Empire. My father always feared a fight of such magnitude would leave al-Mari Ifriq desolate." He locked an open eye on Taran, closing the other. Nasir shook his finger and smiled slyly. "But that's where things get interesting. We'll let this many-headed dragon fight itself. We'll play both sides."

That was not the plan.

Taran, however, was none-the-wiser. Nasir could see the baron wanting to protest the notion. He did not allow Taran a chance to offer a rebuttal. Nasir ordered, "I want you to gather as much information as possible. Stay close to The Four Winds. Let us know their movements."

Taran's demeanor changed. He no longer looked ready to dispute the young Moor's moves. He decided that he could use his assigned task to buy time to truly manipulate Nasir into a physical attack. The ambassador did not rule out confessing the heads of The Four Winds as the architects behind his father's death. The timing in disclosing the information had to be right. Taran could reveal that he stumbled upon the information during his assigned duties to watch the Turkish company. Taran also did not want to reveal The Four Winds' true intentions. Wakil might have informed Nasir, but Taran could not be sure. Nasir was aware, however, the company boss did not want to reveal how much information he possessed.

Taran conceded to Nasir's plan, believing it naïve but finding a way to manipulate the situation. He bowed his head and respected his company boss's wishes. The carriage's ride became even. The traveled path was smoother in the stretch of land covered by African grass. Nasir ordered a foot soldier, whose proximity to the carriage was close, to keep an eye out for bandits. He and Taran conversed about a proper time for the caravan to rest again. Both Nasir and Taran inspected a parchment that had sketched upon it the trail they now traversed. They were still half a day's travel away. The two concluded that it would be easier to press forward, rest for several hours, and then continue until nightfall rather than take rest and continue travel in the morning.

The caravan pushed on for three more hours before pitching a rest site. The soldiers took turns guarding while others rested or enjoyed rations. Awa and Tegu tended to Nasir, while Taran's servant addressed the ambassador's needs. Nasir did not have time to steal with either Awa or Tegu, to question the two covert assassins about anything they learned from Taran's servant. The two men played their parts as servants and no words were exchanged between them and Nasir, save commands for refreshments and rations.

The materials used to pitch the site were quickly gathered, and the caravan continued its pace toward al-Gherab. There were now nine more hours of travel. It was seven in the evening. The sun returned to the horizon, sinking on the opposite side from which it was birthed. Nasir and Taran wanted the caravan to push another four hours before a night's rest. Both camelmen and foot soldiers became more alert at night. The grassland faded back into dust and sand, and small mountain ranges began to rise up around them as the caravan traveled further. They broke from the path they followed, heading south onto another trail that came close to al-Gherab. The possibility of night stalkers, animal and bandit alike, kept the caravan and its company leaders' senses heightened.

The night was disturbed only by an occasional growl, howl, and rustling that produced no predators. The wind was mostly responsible for all the noises. The night rest lasted for only three hours. The caravan continued to travel just as the sun climbed over the horizon. The night wind ceased into the day's desert haze. Al-Gherab climbed out of the distance. The cavalry lead announced the caravan's final approach to the city. Nasir was relieved. He hoped Governor Askari would have a fine suite to accommodate him. He also hoped the room would be a separate quarters from Taran's. He wanted desperately to know if Tegu or Awa gathered any information from Taran's servant.

"What's al-Kasim Askari's title?" asked Nasir to Taran. "Is he Regent Master? Emir? Pasha? Bey?" Titles were a large problem for the corsair states of North Africa. There was no set hierarchy. Rulers chose titles based upon what the population responded to.

"He is considered governor," Taran answered. "He is to be addressed al-Kasim Askari Pasha at all times," explained Taran.

"I have to call him by his full name followed by his title?" Nasir said disgusted. "I'm going to call him Malik. Simple."

"Guyotta said that al-Kasim carries an air of European sophistication," Taran said in a voice that did not understand what the phrase truly meant.

"So, he's a refined savage," Nasir hissed.

"Al-Kasim considers *bey* a low title," Taran explained. "He finds it tribal."

"He will address me as company boss," Nasir said angrily. "We get the plundered cargo and we leave tomorrow morning."

"Al-Kasim may take that as some offense," Taran warned.

"He'll understand," Nasir said in an assertive tone. "We have live cargo to transport. This is not a vacation."

Travel stopped. Nasir took a peek through the curtain. Al-Kasim Askari Pasha's city army blocked the caravan's path. The Commanding Officer was at the front of the army. He was clad in dark brown robes, a black turban, and a long beard. His skin was light yellow. He introduced himself politely, stating his name as Baha al Din. The caravan lead returned a polite bow. Baha asked for the company boss, after respectfully announcing that al-Kasim Askari Pasha was expecting their arrival. The caravan lead bowed again. He dismounted and strode over to Nasir and Taran's elephant.

"You are company boss," said Taran as Nasir moved the curtain back. "I follow your lead," continued Taran, a smile that could be construed as taunting beamed from his visage.

Nasir did not take the time to be offended. The elephant's handlers guided the beast to lower. Nasir felt his stomach drop. He never became accustomed to a traveling animal's sudden, downward movements. The caravan lead approached the carriage's side and looked up, waiting for Nasir to reveal himself. Nasir moved the curtain back and smiled. The soldier announced the arrival of Baha al Din and al-Gherab's army. Nasir asked if the commanding officer wished to speak to him. The soldier faced Baha al Din and asked, "Do you wish to speak with Company Boss Nasir ibn Sa'ad al-Din Sa'ood?"

"If it would not displease the Company Boss, Representative of the Guyotta Regency." Baha al Din's accent was thick. Nasir barely understood the language he used. It was an amalgam of regional dialect mixed with Turkish and Arabic. Nasir understood enough, however. He knew al-Kasim Askari Pasha's accent would be much the same.

Nasir stepped from the carriage, guided by handlers and soldiers. He walked over to the army official, who dismounted out of respect, making sure not to elevate himself over a higher authority. He bowed at Nasir's presence and kissed his fingers, making Nasir a little uncomfortable. Baha al Din introduced himself to Nasir, adding to Nasir's name the title of *bey* instead of company boss. "Word of your father's death ails al-Kasim Askari Pasha's heart. We grieve for you." He spoke an encouraging Mohammedan phrase and bowed again.

"Thank you," said Nasir. He struggled with Baha al Din's accent but managed to decipher the words spoken to him. "It will be a pleasure to conduct this business. Please, lead us to your glorious city." Baha al Din bowed again. Nasir returned the gesture and then returned to his transport. "Their Army Official is no older than me," he informed Taran as he slipped inside assisted by handlers and caravan troops. "He looks older with that beard. He's either a very skilled and experienced soldier…or he's not, no in between. That's something to keep in mind, should we ever find ourselves at odds with al-Gherab."

The ride jerked to life, lifting and moving forward. Nasir held tight, relaxed, and then kept a gaze on the city through a small window behind Taran. The first contrasting element Nasir noticed about al-Gherab were the many mosques placed about the city. Their domes rising over the other elements, however, did not shadow the palace at the far side of the city. Baha al Din's soldiers led the trade caravan around the city to a southern entrance that was located closer to the palace.

The city was larger than al-Mari Ifriq, but less care was taken for its interior. The houses, apartment complexes, and buildings were constructed of a soft, burnished mud-brick element, rather than the hard stone of al-Mari Ifriq's housing. The city looked war torn, though no heavy conflict ever penetrated the city walls. This was all because of a lack of care in architecture and craft. Even the palace was dull. The courtyard was bare of any real design. There was no fountain, and the garden was not kept well. The courtyard, however, was very large. The courtyard's potential for growth and design was magnificent. Al-Kasim Askari Pasha waited at the front of the palace. His three wives, ten guards, eight personal servants, and twenty-seven maidens surrounded him. His servants were mostly African Moors, as was one of his wives.

Baha al Din led the procession of troops and caravan through the city gates and then through the palace gates. The riders from each regime moved to the lower left corner of the courtyard. The soldiers on foot moved to the lower right of the courtyard. Nasir and Taran's transports, followed by the nine, empty iron bar cages, pulled up to al-Kasim Askari Pasha.

Two male servants from al-Kasim Askari Pasha's entourage approached the caravan. Handlers lowered both elephants. Al-Kasim Askari Pasha's two servants stood at attention, waiting to receive the company boss and ambassador. The drapery was pushed aside, and out stepped Taran. Handlers and soldiers assisted the ambassador from the carriage. Taran's servant came from the rear elephant's carriage and took his master's side. Nasir was next to exit the mounted carriage. Tegu and Awa joined him, exiting their transport at the same moment. Al-Kasim Askari Pasha clapped his hands and stepped forward. He was dressed in a tight black robe, red sashes around his waist. A dark purple turban crowned his head, and he wore a long, thick mustache above his upper lip. He had the sharp features of a Turk, and the yellow-brown skin of a tawny Arab.

Al-Kasim Askari Pasha took Nasir into a great embrace and kissed his cheeks. A Mohammedan greeting followed the affectionate gesture, and then condolences for Sa'ad al Din Sa'ood. Nasir bowed, greeting al-Kasim Askari Pasha by full name and title.

"I am so glad you arrived," said al-Kasim Askari Pasha with a pompous air. His refined speech actually made it easier for Nasir to understand him. He enunciated each syllable with an air of pseudo-intellect.

"This is the beginning of a great venture. I have extended a favor to your Regent Master, and now I give praises that a favor can be extended back."

Nasir smiled, but inside he stirred. It was not because what Taran said came to fruition, but the fact that Taran may have already been aware that this was an exchange for a favor. Taran was smart. But Nasir did not take his bait completely. If both played the fool, their dialogues, which had ulterior motives, would run in circles and reveal nothing to the other. That scenario played to Nasir's favor.

"Did you face any trouble from bandit-tribes on your travels?" asked al-Kasim Askari Pasha.

"No, al-Kasim Askari Pasha," Nasir answered finding it ridiculous to state the Pasha's full name and title.

"The al-Jasi Nzambi have made trade nearly impossible." al-Kasim Askari Pasha grimaced. "They are black as the devil. They are bandits that make war with al-Gherab. They make war to the north of us. We seek relief in our alliance with al-Mari Ifriq. But, that is a discussion for myself and Regent Master Guyotta Sahin-el Bey."

Nasir's smile remained unnaturally glued to his face. "Understandable. We took an alternative route to get here. We moved south before the trail we followed took us north of your city. But we were cautious."

"I can see," said al-Kasim Askari Pasha in a voice that reflected that he was impressed with the caravan guard. The pasha turned and introduced his entourage. He showed Nasir his wives, servants, and maidens. "My nephew leads the army. You have met him. Baha al Din will escort your nine cages to the area where the cargo is being held. Your troops will stay in a guest barracks. Do you wish to inspect the cargo now or after you rest and freshen up?"

"We are due for a rest," informed Nasir. "A good rest."

Taran took Nasir's side and greeted al-Kasim Askari Pasha. Several maidens and servants attended to Taran, Nasir, and their personal servants. The maidens and servants spoke cordially to Tegu, Awa, and Taran's servant. They asked about their masters' luggage, and the three servants escorted two stewards to several cases strapped to the carriage.

"Come," said the Pasha. "Refreshments await in the dining hall. He turned and made a signal to Baha al Din with a wave of a finger. The army official began to gather the entire caravan, minus Nasir and Taran's carriage, to lead them to the city's guest barracks. Taran and Nasir followed al-Kasim Askari Pasha, and his entourage, inside the palace.

The palace interior was a sparkling wonder, at least the first, large room. Smoothed walls, some carved out with bookcases filled with tomes, were garnished with illustrious tapestries, woven from orange and dark-brown fabrics. Paintings of Spanish and Turkish countrysides lined the walls, with unlit torches—not in use because of the brilliance of the sun flowing from the large window at the top of the ceiling. Two sets of winding stairs, opposite one another, and separated by three columns, led to a second floor. A small, well-kept garden existed in the middle of the first chamber, and at each cardinal point was a door leading to a hallway attached to other palace chambers.

Al-Kasim Askari Pasha's wives, along with several maidens, were dismissed upstairs. The remaining servants and maidens escorted Taran, Nasir, their servants, and al-Kasim Askari Pasha to a marvelous banquet area. The room was down a corridor, through the left door of the first chamber. It was illuminated much like the first chamber, daylight raining down through a window placed above. Wooden tables that were filled with various foods and drink occupied the room. Musicians filled the room with their music. The maidens surrounding the gentlemen journeyed to the front of the room and started to dance in a free flowing style.

Al-Kasim Askari Pasha turned to Nasir and Taran with a proud smile. "Welcome." He held out his hands and demanded, "Please, eat. Your rooms are being prepared. How long is your stay?"

"We leave in the morning," said Nasir, his eyes taking in the sight. "We are not trying to be rude."

"Of course not," commented al-Kasim Askari Pasha. "I understand. There is business I wish for you to take back to your Regent Master. The quicker, the better."

Nasir nodded.

"Eat well," said al-Kasim Askari Pasha. "Rest when your rooms are ready. We will travel to your cargo some time after noon."

Nasir and Taran thanked al-Kasim Askari Pasha. The two men stepped forward and started to indulge in the flavors of food, wine, and entertainment. Two hours passed before the two men were escorted upstairs. Their rooms were simple. There was a nice view of the city at the front from the window. There was a large, soft bed that was colonized with pillows, and most important to Nasir the room was separate from Taran. But Tegu and Awa had no information to report. Taran's servant did not say much. He either knew his place well, or knew much information that could not be shared. Tegu suggested assassinating Taran's servant, smuggling a spy to service Taran's needs. Nasir contemplated the suggestion and said he would counsel with Wakil to find if the move would be prudent.

Tegu and Awa were taken to a separate quarters designated for servants while Nasir was granted three hours of rest. Nasir reflected on al-Kasim Askari Pasha, noting his black Moorish servants. He internalized how the servitude reflected al-Kasim Askari Pasha's true opinions of the black Moors. Nasir also thought about the pasha's comments on the al-Jasi. He wondered if this was once their city, or homeland at least. Were the al-Jasi truly bandits, or were they freedom fighters? Nasir did not contemplate long. He passed into a light, relaxing sleep.

The light nap replenished Nasir and he awoke refreshed. He was treated to a bath by three maidens and presented with new garments, a gift from al-Kasim Askari Pasha. Taran was treated the same. None of the clothes they brought with them were used, save their undergarments.

Taran and Nasir met al-Kasim Askari Pasha in the front area of the palace. Their servants surrounded them. Al-Kasim Askari Pasha, surrounded by guards, and flanked by his nephew Baha al Din, escorted Taran and Nasir to the carriage they were presenting as a gift.

"You will follow us," said al-Kasim Askari Pasha after thanking Nasir for the complimentary carriage. His voice was less cheerful. Business was now his tone. "We will take you to your cargo." A caravan waited beyond the palace gates. "Should we all share the ride? Our servants will ride separately."

Nasir contemplated his options. If alone with Taran, the ambassador would gloat, as if his deduction of al-Kasim Askari Pasha's proposition for a favor-in-return had not come from insight already received—most likely through counsel with The Four Winds. However, accompanying al-Kasim Askari Pasha would allow him to gather more insight to al-Gherab's war with the al-Jasi.

Nasir decided to make things interesting. He turned to Taran and commanded, "Follow us to the cargo. I will accompany the good al-Kasim Askari Pasha in his new ride. Stay with the servants in the other carriage." Nasir decided to separate the two snakes. He smiled on the inside knowing that Taran would be tossing and turning over what he would learn from al-Kasim Askari Pasha.

But Taran did not show any signs of displeasure. He bowed his head like a gentleman and walked to the carriage with his servant. Tegu and Awa were commanded by Nasir to ride with Taran. Nasir looked back to al-Kasim Askari Pasha and joined him inside the gifted vehicle. The two men made themselves comfortable, and al-Kasim Askari Pasha yelled through the drapery for Baha al Din to lead the way.

"A company from the north plundered this cargo for your Regent Master," informed al-Kasim Askari Pasha as the ride began. His words came with a hint of sadness in his voice. The Pasha sighed. "I only held the cargo for him. I hope that is enough for Guyotta Sahin-el Bey to grant me a favor."

"And what is that favor," asked Nasir.

"Weaponry. Militia. I need a good army to double mine. I need to crush the unrest in the north." al-Kasim Askari Pasha took a deep breath. "I have risked my life to hold this cargo for your Regent Master." al-Kasim Askari Pasha struggled to keep his voice from sounding frustrated. Nasir considered the Pasha's actions a ploy to coax the next question from him, which Nasir obliged to ask.

"How have you risked your life?"

Al-Kasim Askari Pasha did not hesitate to explain. "I trade slaves with the Portuguese. I have made deals with African kingdoms that are civilized by Mohammed's law, to extract slaves from troublesome, tribal factions or heathen city-states. Aiding-and-abetting pirate companies that have sacked Portuguese vessels, is a crime against my partners in trade."

"With no offense, al-Kasim Askari Pasha, but you are a grown man that can think and make decisions for himself. So, why did you aide-and-abet a corsair-state?"

If al-Kasim Askari Pasha took offense, he did not show it. He smiled warmly and explained, "I aide-and-abet my Turkish brethren, and those who follow Mohammedan Law. This is a family thing, Nasir. I make money with the Portuguese and French, yes. But there is a deeper, more spiritual matter. And I won't let them come prancing in here with their bloated, foreign flags trying to change things."

Not too much, thought the Moorish company boss. Al-Kasim Askari Pasha didn't mind the Portuguese and the French enslaving the African and changing and lightening the face of the continent and all her regions.

"Guyotta is aware of my favor," continued al-Kasim Askari Pasha. "But, the weaponry and militia might be too much for al-Mari Ifriq to spare."

"The two of you will work something out," assured Nasir, closing the matter. The conversation then steered to the subject of Nasir's father and Nasir's feelings on running the company. Nasir was cautious with his answers. He simply stated that he hoped to be as excellent a company boss as his father before him.

The carriage ceased travel. Al-Kasim Askari Pasha brushed the drapery of the compartment aside and held out a hand for Nasir to exit.

Nasir followed the command and stepped out onto the dusty city streets. Citizens cramped the roads. The traffic was overwhelming, making what little room it could for the Pasha's caravan. All of the citizens were Turkish or Arabic immigrants. The only African Moors that could be seen were Taran, Nasir, their servants, and the servants of al-Kasim Askari Pasha, or local slaves.

The traffic parted with al-Kasim Askari Pasha's presence. Citizens bowed their heads and extended smiles to their Pasha. There was small applause and light verbal praise for al-Kasim Askari Pasha. The Pasha waved to his people while guiding Taran and Nasir into a large storage house.

Al-Kasim Askari Pasha's servants opened the door to the large storage area that was guarded by local police. Natural light flooded the dark, humid room. The captives were clothed well and had been bathed. Meals were served to them, but they were chained and living in hard conditions. The rugged floor of the storage facility was their bed. Thin linens were given as blankets. The captives were only taken care of because al-Kasim Askari Pasha did not want to upset Guyotta Sahin-el Bey. The merchandise had to be kept well.

"These are just the slaves found aboard the vessel," al-Kasim Askari Pasha clarified. "An added bonus to the amount of riches aboard the ship. There are precious gems and stones, spices, wine, other goods for your Regent Master to sort out. There are two crates of silver."

Taran acknowledged the Pasha's comments.

Nasir continued to look around the room at the African slaves.

Al-Kasim Askari Pasha backed away. He allowed for the two al-Mari Ifriq representatives to inspect the captives. Nasir and Taran stepped inside and carefully walked around the captives who sat on the floor, staring at the arrival of the two black, Moorish gentlemen. The sun's light barely touched the corner of the room, but it rest there nonetheless. It was in the far left corner where both Taran and Nasir's interest in the captives became piqued. Both men recognized the chiseled physique of the Moorish revolutionary named Ameer Las El-Behar.

Taran had not seen Behar since two or three years before Rashaad al-Hammon's death. The revolutionary was one of the greatest strategists the *Alliance* had ever known. But they could not fully employ the renegade's service. Behar's heart was set on liberating Spain, or for Moors to re-gain a political force within the country. Sa'ad didn't agree with Behar's decision, but he supplied him with two ships and several carts of weaponry. Sa'ad was sad to see Behar leave for Spain. The rebel was a great loss for Sa'ad's alliance. But his withdrawal from company service allowed Taran and Rashaad to move forward with plans to side with the encroaching Turks. Ironic that now he would use Behar to help him cut ties with the very Turks he had sided with. Self-preservation was such a viscid business.

Nasir too recognized the revolutionary named Ameer Las El-Behar. The rebel was older now, but Nasir knew it was he. Behar used to stir Nasir's imagination with stories of high sea adventure and swordplay that was both factual and romantic to a little boy's ears. Sa'ad thought Behar's stories were too brutal for his son to hear. But the stories were permitted, and Nasir went wild trying to conjure the image of each scene. Nasir remembered that his father always respected Behar, and he thought that the adventurer's insight could be used in taking down The Four Winds. Nasir figured that Taran might have recognized the revolutionary as well, if he certainly did through faint, childhood memories.

Behar tried to look inconspicuous, which only made him stand out more to the Moorish companymen. Nasir decided to act first rather than give Taran the advantage. He clenched his teeth and cursed. Taran was quickly alerted to Nasir's demeanor. Nasir turned his back to the captives. Taran stepped to him quickly. "What is wrong?"

"Don't you see?" said Nasir in a quiet hiss.

"See what?" Taran asked looking back to the captives and scanning the room.

"It's him!" Nasir said forcefully. "Ameer Las El-Behar. I know it to be him. My memory is faint, but I know."

"I did recognize him," said Taran in a hesitant voice.

Nasir looked deep into Taran's eyes. "That man betrayed my father." Nasir looked over his shoulder, throwing a sharp eye at the rebel captain. His intense gaze returned to Taran. "He would hold me close as a child, entertain me with stories, and all the time he was reaching for a knife to stab my father."

"But how?" Taran questioned.

"My father implicated him in the sacking of trade ships and routes," explained Nasir. "This led to Maurice and Fusan's father being murdered. This led to the Turks taking over. And of course, I hang over this foul man the death of my father. All these events lead to that fateful murder."

Nasir could see that Taran wanted to disagree. He struggled with protesting Nasir's claims. The Ambassador asked, "How do you—"

"My father told me," Nasir lied with great conviction. "He would say that it was no coincidence that company trade routes were sacked after

Behar disappeared. He and my father disagreed with investing energy into Spain. My father blamed him for the sacked ships, at least being the instrument. The deed done most likely to fuel this fiend's personal revolution in Spain."

Al-Kasim Askari Pasha walked back into the entrance to check on the two companymen. Nasir and Taran looked up simultaneously and beamed false smiles. Al-Kasim Askari Pasha returned a smile, bowed at the neck, and walked away to give the Moors their privacy for discussion.

Nasir leaned close to Taran and said with a burning gaze, "I want that man in my service so that I may slave him to death. I will work him to bleed his feet and fingers."

Taran's jaw trembled. He was convinced by Nasir's ploy. The young man radiated with anger and hatred, and Taran knew there was no diverting the young company boss's intentions.

"I…I will see to it…that it is done." Taran's voice quivered. Nasir was so intense that Taran committed to a promise he had no idea how he would keep, negotiating the terms with The Four Winds' heads.

Nasir exhaled. His intense eyes relaxed, and so did Taran. The young Moor smiled. "Good. You see to it." The company boss's cocky smile hid other intentions. "Good al-Kasim Askari Pasha," Nasir called for the lord-Governor while still looking at Taran. Al-Kasim Askari Pasha came into view. "We're satisfied with this catch. Take us to the other merchandise."

"Yes," spoke al-Kasim Askari Pasha politely.

Taran and Nasir were taken to another area of the storage house. The crates filled with goods, silver, spices, and precious gems and stones were examined. Nasir did not care for the material prizes. His prize had already been discovered. He feigned interest, reacting pleased at the sight of the numerous crates and the materials they carried. He complimented al-Kasim Askari Pasha for holding plundered wares. Nasir became anxious. But it would be a long time before he had time alone, and even longer before he was alone with Ameer Las El-Behar.

Al-Kasim Askari Pasha held a celebration when they returned to the palace. The celebration went until after sundown. Nasir retired to his assigned quarters, servants dismissed. Tired and alone in the dark of his room, overwhelmed by delight for revenge, anger against the traitorous Taran, and hatred for his circumstances, Nasir lowered his knees to the floor, and with head and arms atop the bed, started to weep.

Chapter Eight

Night and day were equally dark to the captives held inside the storage house. There were glimmers of light that had the audacity to peek from underneath the doorway. But the flood of outside traffic shaded the experience too often to be continuous. Ameer Las El-Behar and his four lieutenants huddled close together, hugging the far corner of the cramped area. Each of the Moorish rebels had to admit there was better treatment among the Arabs and Turks than with the Spanish captors, save the possibility of being turned into eunuchs. Of course, for Behar and his lieutenants at least, they were no longer held captive for crimes of conspiracy against a ruling monarchy.

However, no more than thirty-minutes ago all of the captives realized why they were being treated so well. Two Moorish gentlemen, one old, the other young, had come to inspect them as merchandise. Their time for being treated well had come to an end. Their time as slaves was just beginning. None of the captives wanted to guess how they would be treated once in service to the African Moors. Behar, however, was very optimistic. He had plans for rebellion even before the Portuguese vessel was attacked. He continued to hold onto his plans of rebellion even after the Portuguese slavers were slain by North African pirates. Behar was centered on his plans to free himself, his four lieutenants, and the other African captives, even while being treated well—save the living conditions. Slavery was slavery, regardless of the master served.

But Behar's plans for rebellion were quelled with the presence of the two Moorish companymen. He dared to postulate what type of treatment would be received once subjugated to the two Moors that inspected the captives. He recognized Taran Zaher. The Companyman was older, more weathered with time, but so too was Behar. He wondered if the baron recognized him as well. Behar did not find the younger Moor familiar. But Taran Zaher was all he needed. He would bargain for a role inside the *Sa'ood Alliance,* the Moorish company he walked away from more than twenty years ago. He would bargain for the lives of his lieutenants and even better conditions for the other African captives.

"We are safe," Behar whispered to his crew.

"How can you be so sure?" asked Bo Yusuf. "They will make us slaves, no different than serving in the colonies, perhaps more harsh. The Arab continues to disrupt African rule. Their admixture into our blood makes them believe they can claim true Moor."

"I know one of the gentlemen that came to inspect us," Behar said with a hiss to silence the fiery Bo Yusuf. The lieutenant backed down out of respect, and because of Behar's glorious news. "I will bargain for all of us to serve in a Moorish company. The company is in a small city named al-Mari Ifriq." Behar put his back against the wall and exhaled relief. He rolled his eyes and spoke, "A good life is ahead of us. A steady life, anyway." He panned around him as if he could see his crew through the room's pitch-black atmosphere. "You can join the company or return home."

Behar's young lieutenants were conflicted with emotions that sided with staying, leaving, and being finished with a life of rebellion. Anything the Moorish rebels did after today—if Behar's negotiations reversed their predicament—would relax them until life's end. The great conflict for the lieutenants would be to learn how to calm the fight that still fluxed through them.

"Yessir," al-Jeheuty said softly.

"I don't want any of you young men to celebrate yet," announced Behar. "Al-Jeheuty, Ojodo your families are close. But embrace not their image yet. Bo Yusuf, do not feel that a simple life waves a white flag in the face of the rebellion we led. A warrior can swing an instrument to till the land for produce just as good as any sword used to till the battlefield. As well, Rahmis, your kingdom can stretch until the horizon, or just be a simple garden." Each lieutenant nodded in the direction of the captain's voice. "The fight is over; it is behind us. A new life is ahead. All praises to whatever god you choose."

"There still needs to be negotiations," reminded al-Jeheuty, meaning no disrespect.

"Of course," said Behar with a smile that none of his crew could see. "I too am caught between caution and an early celebration. But I believe we'll be alright." Behar sighed, thinking about Taran and Sa'ad. "I also hope I can bury old feelings with my associates in the company."

Their voices carried to the other captives. The dialect the rebels used had a heavy accent, but was discernable to the other African captives. They too participated in a small, joyous emotion deep inside them. But only the future knew what lay ahead as it remained wrapped inside the present.

Behar passed the time by relaying stories of the *Sa'ood Alliance* and its leaders. He remarked that they were revolutionaries of a different sort. Their strategy was less about short, spontaneous bursts of physical war and more about intellectual, corporate designs. The *Alliance*'s moves were like advances in chess. Behar's lieutenants, especially al-Jeheuty, were entranced in thoughts of becoming company bosses or masters.

The captives became aware of the night when the storage area's door opened again. The moon's light painted a bright coat of white light inside the dark facility. Behar hoped to get another glimpse of Taran, but it was only Arab-Turkish soldiers that walked inside to feed the captives. The captives drifted into sleep not too long after their meal. Bo Yusuf, al-Jeheuty, Ojodo, and Rahmis eased their minds to sleep by envisioning themselves as companymen.

Thunder drew the captives from sleep. Their eyes opened to a bright, burning sun and a day filled with haze. The thunderous sound emanated from the storage area's door slamming back, opened by a great force. Nasir, legs apart, arms behind his back, stood menacingly in the opened area.

"Round them up," he barked.

Servants and soldiers—some issued by al-Kasim Askari Pasha—forced the captives to their knees, supplied their arms and legs with new shackles, and started to load them into the nine empty cages from Nasir and Taran's caravan. Behar and his lieutenants were dragged in a manner no less rough than the other captives.

It was early morning. The roads were bare of pedestrian travel. The captives were moved into the tight cages one-by-one. Crates carrying the other plundered goods were strapped to the top of the mobile iron bar cages.

Nasir snapped his fingers as Behar came into his sight. "This one with me. Now." His voice was intense, cutting. The dreams of an easier life were suddenly questioned as Nasir's belligerent manner shook the hopes of all the captives. "*He comes with me!*" Nasir repeated the order. He stepped into Behar's view and asked in a cold voice, "Do you understand my speech?"

"Yessir," Behar stated firmly.

Bo Yusuf, al-Jeheuty, Ojodo, and Rahmis could see their captain's interaction with the young companyman. Their teeth were clenched. Their emotions were ablaze. The fight they wanted to leave in Spain quickly embraced them again. But their tongues and bodies remained still from aggressive movement. This was for the sake of their captain. The four lieutenants were dragged to separate cages. Their eyes kept Behar in sight.

"You will address me as either company boss or company *master*," snapped Nasir. "Is that understood?"

"Yes, Company…Master," Behar replied in a humble voice.

Al-Jeheuty and Bo Yusuf, despite having been in separate cages, kept one another in sight. They locked eyes and then made hand gestures to slit Nasir's neck for the insolence displayed toward their captain. Their signals went unnoticed.

"Throw him into the carriage," Nasir ordered. "He will ride with me back to al-Mari Ifriq."

Awa lugged the burly Moorish rebel into Nasir's carriage.

"Taran," yelled Nasir. The elder Moor made himself present quickly. "You ride with the servants now and on return."

"Yes," Taran said politely. But he needed to say more. "I understand your…feelings toward this man, but I beg you to relax."

Nasir took a deep breath. "I will try," he said, continuing to play his part well.

Taran bowed at the neck and stepped away. Nasir coolly walked to his carriage, pushed the drapery aside, and stepped in. Awa and Tegu already occupied their compartment. Nasir took another look out through the drapery and commanded, "Let us go."

The caravan started up.

Baha al Din led the Moorish cavalcade to the very spot he met them, on the outskirts of al-Gherab. The rest of their caravan was waiting. The two massive elephants stood tall. The handlers guided the beasts to sit. Taran and the servants exited from their coach and then were hoisted into one transport. Behar was shoved into another. The army official gave his sentiments to Nasir before the young company boss climbed into the carriage atop his transport. Nasir gave his regards to al-Kasim Askari Pasha. Baha al Din said he would pass Nasir's regards on to his uncle. The two bowed their heads and Nasir gave a command to pull off. He made himself comfortable, took a peek through the drapery after the ride moved forward, and then he relaxed.

Behar said not a word. He barely moved. He examined the young Moor, whose relaxed state contrasted greatly with his rough manner. Nasir removed a jug of water. Even with two cups also removed, Behar did not feel the second was for him. He believed the young company boss would taunt him by drinking from both. But Nasir filled both cups and presented Behar with one.

"Please, drink." Nasir's sincerity was so strong that it almost wiped clean Behar's memory of the young company boss's earlier demeanor. Behar hesitated. He again believed this was all a trick. He contemplated the odds. Behar knew he could easily kill the young man in front of him. He could wrap his chains around his neck and snap it, instead of allowing him to choke. But the young Moor's caravan troops would take him out. He would die. His lieutenants would die. They would protest as Behar was executed before them, and then they too would join his fate.

Behar had to play along with this young man's indignation until he was positioned to speak with Taran and negotiate better terms. But, Nasir presented the cup closer to Behar, and very sincerely spoke, "I insist, Ameer Las El-Behar."

Behar took the cup. He was in awe as his full name was also presented to him. He took a small sip, keeping his eyes on Nasir at all times. Nasir sat back, eyes starting to water. His lower lip trembled and he looked away from the old, burly Moorish captain.

"Company Master—"

Nasir waved a hand toward Behar. The rebel captain backed away.

"My name is Nasir," he said, finally looking at Behar. Nasir's voice trembled. He sniffed back his tears, leaned close and spoke, "My name…is Nasir ibn Sa'ad al-Din Sa'ood."

The name was recognizable to Behar. He remembered sharing the story of his travels and adventures with a young boy, son of Sa'ad al-Din Sa'ood. Nasir. Behar inspected the young man before him. He saw the face of the boy he knew, still inside the matured man.

"I used to bounce you on my knee, young man, and excite your imagination with my stories." Nasir nodded at Behar's revelation. "You would love those stories so much." Nasir nodded again. "So, it begs the question, why do you hate me so much now?"

Nasir's instant smile burst into a short laugh. He wiped his runny nose and watery eyes. He sniffed away his overwhelmed emotion and chuckled more. "I apologize for my behavior, *A-sir*."

Behar smiled warmly. "*A-sir?* You embarrass me. I am no knight. I'm a wanted scoundrel, branded so by the Spanish Crown." He took another sip. "I recognized Taran Zaher, but not you. You do take after your mother. Has your father retired from his *Alliance?*"

Nasir bit his lip and dropped his head. His emotions flooded him again. He looked to Behar and spoke, "My father was murdered." Behar's look became intense. "Al-Mari Ifriq has been under Turkish control for the last twenty years—the entire regency of Odongo-Mauharim. The Sa'ood Company barely exists. The Turkish rulers, who call their company The Four Winds, killed my father just days ago. Taran Zaher—that phallus suckler—conspires with them." Nasir divulged the entire story to Behar. Their roles had been reversed. Behar became the captivated audience while

Nasir relayed the intriguing tale of al-Mari Ifriq's past twenty years.

Behar sat back, his mouth hanging open.

"You have led great rebellions," said Nasir in a very low whisper. "I need your help, sir, and the help of any men still in your company, so that I may slay the heads of The Four Winds and restore al-Mari Ifriq to glory. I want to make real my father's dream."

Behar contemplated the circumstances. He raised a single eyebrow at Nasir. "I used to bounce you on my knee. Now I want to throw you over it and give you a great chastising for putting me in this predicament." Behar's laugh sounded like a sigh. "Four of my lieutenants reside in your cages."

"They will be placed in my service," Nasir assured. "Present to me their names."

Behar exhaled, this time it was clearly a sigh. "I will." He leaned close to Nasir and said, "You do realize that my revolution in Spain failed miserably?" Behar presented the statement with a warm, fatherly smile.

Nasir lifted his cup of water. "Here's to a second chance."

Behar knocked his cup against Nasir's and added to the declaration, "And to a dream for a life of peace…deferred." Behar took a large gulp of water, swallowing the cup's entire contents, and wishing there was something inside that was stronger than water.

Chapter Nine

Traveling back to al-Mari Ifriq could not have gone slower. The time, in reality, passed no differently than when traveling to the Algerian interior. Nasir was just anxious. Behar relaxed the young Moor by spinning numerous tales about his rebellion's exploits. He also noted how sadly the rebellion ended. Nasir returned to his rough role as a slave driver while on their first rest. He dragged Behar to the rations line and pushed him to eat with the rest of the captives.

Bo Yusuf, al-Jeheuty, Ojodo, and Rahmis scowled at the spectacle. The four lieutenants' emotions burned at the sight of their beloved captain pushed around like an unruly animal. To them, the young company boss was making an example of the strongest captive. They figured that the governor of the city they had come from informed Nasir about which captive seemed most like the leader. Nasir was now putting that information to use. The lieutenants were completely unaware of Nasir's ruse, and that Behar was now a part of the company boss's gambit.

Behar was able to steal time while lining up for rations. Al-Jeheuty took his side and questioned, "Can you survive long enough to negotiate with this Taran Zaher fellow? The company boss continues to make an example out of you in such a violent nature. How has the god treated you, high atop his kingdom?"

"With water and fresh bread," Behar whispered, a smile on his face.

Al-Jeheuty was perplexed. His expression hid nothing.

Behar explained, "I'm okay. *We'll* be okay. The company boss is the son of a friend." Behar tried to keep his voice low. "The elder Moor—the man I was familiar with, Taran—is a traitor. He helped engineer my friend's death, this young Moor's father." He looked around as he and al-Jeheuty stepped away from the ration's line. He spoke again, voice low. "Turks rule the regency we are being taken to. Their company is called The Four Winds. There are four heads. They are bleeding the city of revenue. The Ottomans are sending in officials to conduct an audit. The Turkish rulers will be gone by then, and the Empire will take their anger out on the Moorish citizens."

Al-Jeheuty's brow rose, as he was intrigued by the situation. "So his treatment of you is a ruse?" He suppressed a smile. He looked over his shoulder and spotted Nasir and Taran conducting a conversation away from the rest of the caravan. He put his gaze back to Behar as he shoved a handful of steamed vegetables into his mouth. "So, we are mercenaries now?"

"No," said Behar. "We have one more act of revolution to commit. Then we will be companymen. We will help restore peace in the city—"

Nasir, seemingly coming from out of nowhere, suddenly shoved Behar. The captain's plate of food dropped onto the earth floor. "Do you plot revolution, dog?" Nasir screamed. "Perhaps you would like to ride with the filth."

Al-Jeheuty was speechless. He wanted to strike Nasir, though he understood that this was all play. The company boss was acting his part too well, according to the lieutenant. Nasir stared at al-Jeheuty with great intensity. "What do you look at?"

"Nothing," answered al-Jeheuty, a hint of an insult in his tone.

Nasir grabbed the rebel's chin and shook. "You address me as *nothing?* You are looking at a company boss!" Nasir let go.

Al-Jeheuty suppressed the feeling begging him to strike Nasir. "I apologize, Company Boss."

Nasir looked over at Behar. He grabbed the captain by the arm and pushed him in the direction of the resting transport. "Back with you. You will eat what I give you."

Behar understood there was probably a better meal in the carriage than the steamed vegetables, bread, and slice of meat served on the ration's line. So did al-Jeheuty. The lieutenant now wanted to strike Behar and Nasir alike. But, he went back to enjoy his meal. He stepped away from the conflict and found Bo Yusuf, Rahmis, and Ojodo.

"I'll kill him," Bo Yusuf said immediately upon al-Jeheuty's arrival. But the fiery Moor cooled his temperament when he noticed al-Jeheuty's demeanor did not match his. He lifted an eyebrow when he noticed a slight grin issued by al-Jeheuty. His fellow lieutenant walked away from the group, Bo Yusuf and the others followed. Clearly al-Jeheuty had news he did not want picked up by the other captives, or the caravan soldiers. "Speak," commanded Bo Yusuf when they were huddled far enough away to not look too conspicuous. The group stood at the side of one of the caravan cages.

Al-Jeheuty fed himself while keeping a teasing smile on his face. He then started to explain the circumstances in a language that sounded like numbers being recited. It was a code the rebels learned to speak, taught to them by Behar. "The young company boss's behavior is a ruse. He is the son of Behar's friend, and he plays to trick the one named Taran Zaher. The company boss wants us to kill the Turks that rule over the regency we are being taken to. The Turks killed this young company boss's father, and the man named Taran Zaher helped them. They are also robbing the regency of money. The Ottoman chiefs are angry that revenue has not been given to the Empire. They are about to make themselves present. The regency will become a police state. The Empire will brutalize the Moors. The four Turks that rule presently will disappear before the Empire anchors at port."

"The revolution continues," Bo Yusuf commented, almost sounding relieved.

"Our prize, gentlemen," al-Jeheuty started to emphasize as his grin left his visage, replaced by complete stern sincerity, "will be the title of *companymen*."

Ojodo raised a massive hand. "Wait," his voice reverberated with great bass, though a whisper. "We are to kill four Turkish heads, one traitor, turn back an Empire's audit that has the potential to become very violent, and reorganize a city's political and economic infrastructure?"

Al-Jeheuty did not flinch as he responded with great conviction, "Yes."

Ojodo contemplated. "Oh. For a second I thought this was going to be difficult," he responded in a sarcastic, monotone voice.

The four rebels finished their meals, inching their way back into a circle of captives. They were provided a single cup of water to drink, and once finished, their wooden plates and cups were snatched from them by caravan troops. All of the captives were dragged back to their cages. The four rebels were separated again.

The caravan stopped for rest twice more, and each time Behar would steal a moment with al-Jeheuty and relay more news. Al-Jeheuty would then repeat the information to the other rebel lieutenants. Behar instructed al-Jeheuty to hand out duties to the other lieutenants. Al-Jeheuty, in coded language, instructed the business savvy Rahmis to develop an economic plan for the city, and not shy away from corsair politics.

"This is a company, after all," al-Jeheuty joked to the princely Moor.

To the Moorish titan Ojodo went the duty of connecting with his maritime family for legitimate and illegal trade on the Mediterranean. To Bo Yusuf went the duty for developing clandestine politics to deal with other company bosses. The plan to assassinate the four Turks would be plotted with Behar and the young company boss named Nasir.

The next two rest points did not employ the tactics of being too rough with Behar. The rebel lieutenants guessed that their captain might have advised the young company boss that the hijinks may be too much. The next two rest sites went without incident. Behar was put inside one of the iron cages after the last stop. The luxury ride was over.

The caravan pulled into al-Mari Ifriq two hours after sunrise. Army Official Tous Zeki greeted the cavalcade at the city outskirts. The Green Army escorted the returning party to the city palace where Guyotta Sahin-el Bey awaited their arrival. The other heads of the Four Winds and Wakil al-Hakam waited with him.

Nasir and Taran stepped from their transports and bowed in Guyotta's presence. The Regent Master beamed a wide smile, like a proud father witnessing his son mature. Guyotta's smile enraged Nasir, but the company boss remained calm.

"How was the journey?" asked the Regent Master.

"Pleasant," answered Nasir. Taran nodded his head in agreement. "None of the cargo is damaged. All of the captives are well," Nasir reported.

Guyotta pursed his lips and sighed. "You may split the live cargo among the other companies. We are more interested in the goods. We are trying to boost our markets. We hope to buy time with the precious metals and gems. The Empire will have them for tribute, though I would like to add them to al-Mari Ifriq's treasury."

Nasir doubted the Regent Master's proposed intentions for the plundered wealth, but he was delighted that negotiations would not be necessary for Behar and his lieutenants to be placed in his service. He did not trust Taran with the job of coaxing the four heads into allowing the placement of the specific bodies into his employment. Guyotta only asked for a head count of the captives. The labor was to be divided equally among the companies, and Guyotta was to receive a report from each company on their new labor count.

Nasir presented Guyotta Sahin-el Bey with a parchment, a declaration of favor scribed by al-Kasim Askari Pasha. Guyotta unfolded the parchment and perused the writing. The Regent Master sighed again. He handed the document to Aguyan and said, "See how we can get around this favor. Al-Mari Ifriq does not have troops to spare."

"We may be able to ally al-Gherab with the Djenhai," Taran suggested. "The al-Jasi and the Ogunsanwo-Mashek could be smothered in one fell swoop. It would open up the southern routes that we wish to establish."

"Excellent," complimented Guyotta. He said to Aguyan, "Send word to al-Gherab that we will meet with al-Kasim in a week's time. He will come here." Aguyan took the document to peruse later. Guyotta returned his gaze to Nasir and spoke, "My men will take the carts of plunder. You may store the live cargo where you wish. Document dividing them among the other companies," reminded the Regent Master. "You are dismissed Nasir, Taran."

Wakil stepped to Nasir and greeted the young man with a warm embrace, and with the respectful acknowledgement of Nasir's title. It was then that Hyle Tecer called for Taran. "There are tax matters to discuss." He turned to Wakil and said, "I will inform al-Taran of all we have spoken about."

"Yes," addressed Wakil. "The three of us will counsel tomorrow."

"Afternoon," Hyle specified.

Wakil nodded his head. Taran exchanged a greeting with the lawyer and then stepped to Hyle. He would use this time to inform Guyotta and the rest about Nasir's destructive behavior toward Behar. However, it would prove to no avail. Taran would be disappointed some time from now when Guyotta advised he would allow the behavior to persist to keep the young company boss occupied, and the anger over his father's death directed at someone other than he.

In the background, the caravan disassembled. Caravan guards worked with Green Army soldiers to breakdown the train of vehicles, paying closer attention to the plunder favored most by the Regent Master. The captives were released from the nine cages and chained together in one line. Nasir was stripped of the transports granted to him by Guyotta Sahin-el Bey, but he was given a carriage to ride through the city. He climbed into the vehicle. The compartment was only large enough for he and Wakil. Awa and Tegu walked alongside the carriage. Guyotta granted eight troops from the caravan to help escort the train of captives to the Sa'ood company house.

While traveling through the city, Nasir spoke to Wakil about his trip, Taran's deceitfulness, his stay at al-Gherab, and al-Kasim Askari Pasha. He asked for Roberto Hamaat's whereabouts, and Wakil answered that the occult assassin was waiting for them at the company house. Nasir then presented a preview on the consequences of his travels. There was no sly smile or excited voice, however. Nasir spoke plainly. There was a hint of anger in his voice.

"I have a surprise for us all," his voice trembled with

determination. He leaned forward, enveloping Wakil's hand with both of his. "The Regent Master let slip a great treasure." He let go of Wakil and sat back. He cupped his face with his hand and sighed, "I am exhausted with how I had to keep Taran's grimy hands from this prize. I belong in a theater," he laughed lightly with his joke. Nasir finally smiled.

Wakil's interest piqued, but the lawyer was more concerned for his friend's son. Nasir indeed look exhausted. Though Wakil heard the company boss admit to being so, the lawyer figured that it was not just from *'keeping Taran's grimy hands from some prize'* but also from travel to al-Gherab, the first diplomatic situation—no doubt accompanied by a night of celebration with loud music, drink, and maidens—minding his behavior among other officials, keeping company with Taran, and the return.

"Your brother has been running the daily operations remarkably," Wakil reported.

"I knew he would," said Nasir as he relaxed. "I told him to run the company as is…while we handle the more aggressive side of the business."

"So he knows?" Wakil questioned.

"He suspects. He asked. I neither completely confirmed, nor completely denied." Nasir presented a stern look. "But he knows his place."

The train arrived at the company house. Nasir held out a hand for the elder to proceed first. "Age before beauty, huh?" Wakil joked.

"Or shit before shovel," Nasir retorted.

The lawyer burst out laughing. "I will ponder that and find a retort. My quick wit has simmered down with age. It only works in courts of law."

"Greatly proving your first sentiment," Nasir continued, following right behind Wakil. He stepped out of the carriage and marveled at the familiar sight of al-Mari Ifriq's docks. Zakiy charged from around the storage house and embraced his older brother, almost tackling Nasir to the ground.

"My brother has returned!" Zakiy shouted. "The traveling man has come back—" the younger Sa'ood brother's voice trailed away when he noticed the line of chained men. "—A slaver…" He looked at his brother with concern.

Nasir raised a hand. "Relax. These are new laborers for the companies. They will see a wage given to them. We have the money." He turned to the line of chained captives and shouted, "These men are to be treated well." He looked at the caravan guards and dismissed them back to Guyotta. The troops retreated to the city palace after leaving the keys to the chains that attached the captives to one another. Nasir gave the keys to Tegu. When the caravan guards were far in the distance, Nasir looked back to the captives and yelled, "When you hear your name, step forward. You will be employed in my personal services." Nasir panned the men before him and called, "Ameer Las El-Behar."

Wakil's heart thundered. He felt a cool wind embrace him. The venerable lawyer's eyes went wide and his mouth was agape. Behar stepped forward on command. Tegu unlocked the rebel captain from the rest of the line of chained men. Behar stepped toward Nasir. Wakil did not stir. He regained his composure, inspecting the burly revolutionary. Behar was older, but he looked as chiseled and ready for war as any young upstart. This must have been the prize Nasir was referring to. Wakil sent a prayer to his friend Sa'ad. *Your son, Sa'ad, has already done the impossible. Oh, forgive me my friend as I express that Nasir has done what you could not. He has succeeded where you had failed. Your son, as you already know, watching from Allah's kingdom, has employed the services of Ameer Las El-Behar, the great strategist. It must have been all those stories Behar fed him as a child. And you thought them too violent. Oh, I confess. So did I.*

Nasir's voice carried all the way into the window of the Sa'ood company house. The sound of the name *Ameer Las El-Behar* alerted Roberto Hamaat. The stocky rogue jumped from his chair and peeked outside the window. His eyes noticed Behar's frame, but the rebel captain's back was to him. He could not see his face. Roberto wondered if that was truly he. He hoped so. After all, Roberto was owed money for three soldiers. And maybe, Roberto would also be a little happy to see his fellow scoundrel and friend.

Nasir continued, "Ojodo Yerodin." The Moorish titan stepped forward, was unlocked, and stood next to Behar. "Bo Yusuf ibn Tachfin al-Dume." The rebel warrior was released from the chain and marched up to Ojodo's side. "Rahmis Husani." The princely rebel lieutenant walked to his fellow rebels with the grace of a noble. His chains did not deter his regal step. "And al-Jeheuty Anhur Has." The negotiator kept a challenging stare on Nasir as Tegu undid his line shackles. Neither of them blinked, even as al-Jeheuty stepped forward. Nasir turned to his brother and commanded, "See that these other men are taken care of. Place them in the labor areas. Make sure they are given good rest and food. Alert the other bosses about the new labor. We will hold council on this matter with the other bosses in three days. This will give these men time to rest." He turned to Behar and the others. "With me. Follow."

Zakiy attended to his job. He called for the captives to follow him. Nasir led his party to the company house. Roberto Hamaat anxiously waited upstairs. He heard the men downstairs in the open storage area.

Next, the assassin heard the troupe climbing the stairs to the council room he occupied. Roberto's eyes scanned each of the people that passed through the door. The assassin walked up to Wakil and gave him a respectful Mohammedan greeting. Wakil beamed a sly smile. The lawyer's smile confirmed Roberto's suspicions, but he needed to see the presence of the rebel captain for himself.

Roberto congratulated Nasir on his return. Then filed in the soldier Roberto wished to see. Ameer Las El-Behar walked into the room. He walked behind Tegu and Awa. The two men parted, allowing the rebel captain to step forward and present himself. Behar and his four lieutenants' shackles clanked against the stone floor. Roberto acknowledged the rebel captain as if he had been gone for just several days rather than decades.

"I'm glad you're wearing chains," Roberto said stepping back and pointing a finger at Behar. "It saves me the trouble of arresting you. You owe me money and three soldiers."

Behar looked from Wakil to Roberto. "Of course the scoundrel keeps tabs." Behar walked over to Roberto and patted the assassin's belly. "It doesn't seem like the money I owe you has affected your meal schedule."

Roberto chuckled. He slammed his hands onto Behar's cheeks and shook the captain's head. The impact of Roberto's hands jarred Behar, but he understood the assassin's playful, yet rough, gesture. "You sonava bitch!" Roberto hollered with a wide smile. "The sea hasn't drowned you yet?" he asked his old friend, the rebel captain. "It's shape as a beautiful mermaid has not seduced you?"

"Rumors," laughed Behar.

Roberto walked back to the table near the window. There were wine jugs laid out, but only three cups. Nasir asked Awa to seek out more. The elder guard nodded and disappeared to find more cups. Tegu was commanded to unlock the rebels' shackles. Roberto poured a cup of wine and lifted it for a toast.

"Mistress Ilindia and I did a ritual last night," announced the occult assassin. "Your presence is the proof of the ritual's great work. You see, now? That's that ritual, you see. That's that Mother Goddess—that powerful, *feminine* energy. Ask me if a holy ghost can do that."

Wakil chuckled lightly. "I prayed to Allah last night. Perhaps it was *His* doing." There was a sly smile and an expression that conveyed an excellent chess move just played.

Roberto was not silent on the matter. Ever the metaphysical occultist, the answer was there. "Well that's the feminine and the masculine spirits coming together and giving us these results as their child." Wakil and Behar raised an eyebrow to the assassin. Al-Jeheuty noted that he agreed, which prompted Roberto to continue his spiritual case. He stepped toward Wakil and insisted, "That's what these so-called religions are missing. The feminine. We have that Greek and Roman form of worship. Men on men." Wakil laughed again, and Roberto insisted, "Wait now, good man. Let's look at the science. When man and woman come together—physically, sexually—there is life. That's power! Take that to a spiritual level. Good man, I'm tellin' you to tap into that."

Wakil rolled his eyes and chuckled. "You pirates need a *stable* God."

"Well, I'm a Mohammedan," proclaimed Rahmis. "I believe in any tenants that declare a man can have up to four wives." Wakil did not take the joke from the young upstart well, but he kept his disdain to a simple glare, like a father silently chastising a son. Behar shared the same look to the princely lieutenant. This was no way to introduce their unit to the veteran companymen. Rahmis was quick to observe his joke had a lukewarm reception and hid his words until called for.

Nasir offered the five rebels a seat. He turned to Roberto Hamaat and Wakil al-Hakam and announced, "My father's partners-in-company, I present to you the return of a man whom my father tried desperately to employ. This is Ameer Las El-Behar. Twenty or more years ago, this Moor, with rebellion and retaliation in his heart, turned from company employment, with no ill feelings, and decided to plot against the Spanish Crown. He sought revenge for century long atrocities committed by the white Spaniards against the Blackamoors. Al-Mari Ifriq, all of Odongo-Mauharim, faces potential atrocities. Though I hold authority of company boss, I ask your permission to grant Ameer Las El-Behar, and his surviving lieutenants, employment."

Wakil and Roberto looked at one another and smiled. They rolled their eyes in a playful manner and pretended to silently ponder the matter with the exchange of facial gestures. Then Roberto spoke, "We no longer hate him, and all his debts are forgiven."

"I want that in writing," Behar noted.

Awa returned with more cups for wine.

Everyone indulged, including Wakil.

Behar formally introduced his small crew to Roberto, Wakil, and Nasir. Al-Jeheuty greeted Nasir with title. The company boss waved the title aside. "But with no jest," al-Jeheuty protested with a humorous tone, "We are in the presence of Nasir ibn Sa'ad al-Din Sa'ood, the greatest actor the theater has *never* seen." Nasir smiled shyly and sincerely asked for the other captives to dismiss his earlier actions. "My goodness, man. You need to hold your head up." Al-Jeheuty turned to Wakil and Roberto and stated, "You should have seen him. He was rough. He cut our captain down to size. He had Bo Yusuf and I signaling with our hands to act against him. He was close to death. And to think his act was all a ruse. This man deserves the stage in a theater just as much as he deserves to lead this company." Al-Jeheuty took a sip of wine. The room around him chuckled.

"And what was with that stare down after I called your name?" asked Nasir.

"I wasn't too sure you understood I was on the list," the negotiator confessed. "I thought you were making another point."

"Oh, you were scared," Nasir grinned.

"To death," al-Jeheuty confessed as he took another sip.

Nasir waited for the light laughter to simmer before moving to more important matters. He began, "Al-Gherab is at war with a group of nomadic, African Moors. They are called the al-Jasi Nzambi. Have you heard of these people, Roberto?" The assassin shook his head, no. "Taran made mention that they hold the same spiritual outlook as you. Occult. I'm not sure if the Turkish and Arab population of al-Gherab usurped the urban center from the al-Jasi nation or of any other excuse that has the two states at war. But I believe they can be used as allies."

"I'll send an envoy to speak with them," stated Roberto. "Or go myself with several members from my clan. We'll find the motive of their strikes, and see if they can be an ally."

"Is it okay to present them with supplies," al-Jeheuty asked, his voice sounding reluctant. "If their battle is over resources, then we should provide for them. We don't want their war to escalate." He was unsure when he used Roberto's name, out of respect of the occult assassin's age, and because he was not sure if 'Roberto' was his name. But, al-Jeheuty continued, "...Roberto's...people—" Nasir gave a nod to confirm Roberto's name as correct. "—can move the commodities secretly. That will buy us enough time to deal with al-Kasim Askari Pasha. We will support them if their cause is just."

"Of course it's just," Bo Yusuf snapped. "It's against colonizers."

Al-Jeheuty raised a hand to calm his friend. "The allies we create will give our enemies less of a reason to attack. If we are allied with bandits that can't be tamed, that reflects on us. But I'm sure their cause is just."

"We should find out their reasons for attacking al-Gherab," Behar interjected.

"I'm sure it has something to do with al-Kasim Askari Pasha in business with Portuguese slavers," Nasir commented. "The Pasha provides African slaves for the Portuguese. He uses a silk tongue to coerce African kingdoms against nomadic nations. He works exclusively with African kingdoms that have accepted Mohammedanism."

"That bastard," Wakil cursed.

"We begin sending supplies when that is confirmed as the al-Jasi's cause," said al-Jeheuty. "And regardless, we will eliminate al-Kasim Askari Pasha." Bo Yusuf nodded his head in approval.

"What about our governors?" Nasir asked. "We can make no moves until we deal with them. We have three months."

"We will proceed according to *their* plans," Behar stated. "Let them know not a thing. We study their movements."

"We're on that," said Roberto.

Wakil reiterated The Four Winds' plans to establish four directions of trade and then leave once an eastern trade route is established. Behar noted that the heads' greed could be their ally.

"Let them know our economic plans," suggested the rebel captain. "We will give them a plan to generate revenue. It will be our true economic plan for al-Mari Ifriq." He looked to Rahmis and asked, "Has one been formulated?"

Rahmis nodded his head. "We will keep the entire maritime plan to ourselves. I don't believe the Turkish heads will want to cause a stir by hijacking Spanish and Portuguese vessels sailing the Mediterranean."

"If it makes money, they won't care," said Nasir.

Rahmis nodded. "Consolidate the city's Moorish corsairs into a Council of Captains. Offer protection to Asian, Turkish, Arab, Dutch, and even French trade ships—legal or otherwise."

"French," questioned Nasir. Wakil and Roberto held the same disbelief on their faces.

Rahmis shook his head. "Al-Jeheuty believes we can do it. I believe in his word." Rahmis and al-Jeheuty nodded toward one another. Rahmis then continued with business. "All ships that dock in port shall give a ten percent tribute of their cargo in coin." Rahmis asked Nasir, "Do you have corsair allies?"

The company boss answered, "Yes. A man named Hieremias Sunwil has dedicated his service to my company. He is the best."

"Can he create a tight Council of Captains?" Rahmis continued to inquire.

"One is already established," Nasir informed.

"However," began Wakil, "The Four Winds are increasing taxes on the Council."

Rahmis brushed the notion aside. "That will not matter. Have Captain Sunwil increase his acts of piracy against the Dutch and French," Rahmis advised. "We will scare the nations into our protection. We'll put out word that even Africa-north is under attack. Let word be passed that this city's companies have come together to form a protection ring for trade ships of any nation. We then offer our service, and most importantly, our price."

Al-Jeheuty spoke up. "I'll push for French interests to seek our help," he said in a confident, but not non-challenging tone. "My brother has dealings with them." The rebel lieutenant's last statement was expressed in a frustrated tone. He hadn't left his family on a good note. He and his brother were not seeing eye-to-eye when it came to his brother's evangelical business with the French and Arabs.

"Do you believe protecting Dutch ships is in our best interest?" asked Bo Yusuf with a raised eyebrow. "Their ships carry live cargo from Africa, brought to the Americas for slavery."

"No different than the French," Behar said calmly. "We can only do so much for our African people. All nations have their hands dirty with this African slave trade, but we must worry about this particular room in the house before we clean the others."

No more was said on the matter.

"We will also give the European nations' ships bogus warrants," Rahmis remarked. "We will allow combat in our waters. Of course, by that time the very Moorish captains and crews that have been hitting the other nations will then be protecting them. Our clients will be none-the-wiser."

"I will bring in my family's maritime company—both legal and piratical—to help with trade on the sea," announced Ojodo.

"And I will continue to supply you with trade routes to present to The Four Winds," Roberto assured Nasir.

Nasir nodded.

"Our revenue will also increase internally," continued Rahmis. "We will build more inns for the city, and more taverns with entertainment. Gambling. Maidens. We will control it all, a percentage of earnings brought back into the city's revenue."

Roberto glanced over at Wakil. "Does the pious lawyer agree?"

"All for the sake of the city," Wakil said reluctantly. "It's nothing that does not already persist. But control must be strict."

"We promise," Rahmis insisted, sounding apologetic for his earlier insolence toward the lawyer's faith.

"I will introduce you to the al-Hammon brothers, Maurice and Fusan," said Nasir. "They control a very entertaining tavern named *The al-Hammon Palace*."

Al-Jeheuty and Rahmis nodded. "The city should be more inviting as it becomes a rest area for all maritime travelers," al-Jeheuty continued. "Unfortunately, the city will have to negotiate a loan from the Regent Master to bankroll all of this."

Nasir sighed.

"Don't worry, Nasir," al-Jeheuty spoke comfortingly. "Enlist me as one of your personal servants. We will work on subtle signals, gestures for you to negotiate around any disapproval from these Turkish heads. You will know when to be more aggressive and when to let these snakes be."

Al-Jeheuty's words re-ignited the young company boss's confidence. He looked at each of the faces surrounding him and then announced a conclusion to his father's era. "This is the last time the Sa'ood Alliance convenes." Nasir watched Wakil and Roberto. They cocked their heads to the side, interests piqued. The elder companymens' eyes squinted as if to examine the invisible words from Nasir's mouth. "This Regency will be given a new name," Nasir continued. "It will be given new leadership. Wakil, I elect you as governor. I want your conscience to guide the law, not your Mohammedan faith. We cannot force God's complicated law on people, especially in a corsair-state. But we can make things civil." The lawyer agreed by nodding his head. Nasir looked at Roberto and restored him with the title of police captain. "You will carry the law created by Wakil and Behar." He put a hand on his chest. "I will continue with duties for the Sa'ad Company. Ship building. Loaning. Repairing. Docking." He then turned his attention to Behar and the four rebel lieutenants. "You, Captain—to you I bestow the title of *Beylerbey*, Chief-Boss of all Chiefs. The other company bosses will not argue."

Behar was reluctant, but accepted the title. He chuckled lightly and said, "My reputation is not that renown in al-Mari Ifriq. But we shall see." Behar tapped his finger on the table and continued, "This will remain the primary company, however." Behar's voice rang with authority. "When The Four Winds are eliminated, we will offer most of their hoarded treasures to the Ottoman chiefs as tributes. That will keep the Empire at bay. Our resources for revenue will increase. We will establish Odongo-Mauharim as an independent state."

"We will need to negotiate with the kingdom to the south," exclaimed Wakil.

"Then it will be done," Behar acknowledged. "Killing the Turkish heads is our first priority." Behar pointed to each man in a single, fluid motion. "This group is the beginning of a new alliance, much like young Nasir declared. We will be more than a business. We will be more than a company. This venture will be treated like a family, an organized family. We will be a *maehfil.*" Behar stood up and poured wine into each of the men's cups. "We serve no religion. We show respect to you, Wakil, and to anyone who carries a personal faith. We show respect to all nations allied with us. But we serve no nation. We are all that in one. We will call this motley crew—this company made of so many parts—something magnificent. We shall be mythic in nature. Our flag, our crest, our coat-of-arms will don a creature that personifies this family. We will continue to be like the griffin. We are *The Griffin Company*. We will grow to be the Griffin Regency. Odongo-Mauharim will become a true state, and then when history tells our tale, we will be the Griffin Dynasty."

They raised their cups and drank.

Behar walked over to Nasir and placed a hand on his shoulder. "Taran does not die with the heads of The Four Winds." He massaged the company boss's shoulder. "This may pain you. But we need him alive. He must use his voice to soothe the Ottoman chiefs. He will be our international voice, as is his current role. He dies when all ties to the Empire are severed, and we become a true, independent nation."

Nasir agreed to the Beylerbey's suggestion. He bowed his head at the neck and then offered a suggestion. "Tegu suggested to place a mark on Taran's servant, whereby then we would sneak in our own to keep close tabs on him."

"I agree," said Behar letting go of Nasir. "We'll pick a random night. Have it done before Guyotta and his company are taken down." The newly announced Chief-Boss of all Chiefs then tasked his lieutenants. Rahmis and al-Jeheuty were to continue work on the business proposal to present to Guyotta and the other Four Winds heads. Al-Jeheuty also had the task of coaching Nasir on hand gestures and eye signals for when Nasir was in counsel with the heads of The Four Winds. Bo Yusuf was commanded to convene with Captain Hieremias Sunwil and Roberto Hamaat to form a plan for piracy at sea, and to form an attack to eliminate Guyotta and the other heads. Nasir suggested assigning Ojodo to work alongside Zakiy. Ojodo was also granted leave, to coax his family to setup a base of operations at the city port.

The sun might have set on the *Sa'ood Alliance*, but Sa'ad al-Din Sa'ood's spirit remained, and Nasir imagined his father smiling down on him. The young company boss returned to his home. Al-Jeheuty followed, disguised as Nasir's new servant. Nasir embraced his mother affectionately. Afya recognized her son's newfound happiness and confidence. She took close notice of his demeanor, but made no mention of it. Afya was happy for the first time since her husband's death.

Nasir was calm, even in the face of the task ahead of him.

A new company was formed for the purpose of bringing an old dream into a reality. The dream of Nasir's father, and the founding black Moors of al-Mari Ifriq, was closer. All the newly formed Griffin Company had to do now was kill four of the most powerful men in the regency.

Chapter Ten

Nasir invited al-Jeheuty to share in his morning ritual. Nasir had not seen the sun rise in days. He explained to al-Jeheuty the significance of the ritual, his father taking him to the shores every morning. Nasir said that he was a little more than ten when he started following his father to watch the day begin. Al-Jeheuty appreciated the sight. Nasir went on to say that watching the day begin, listening to the starting sounds of the city, made him understand timing and precision. Al-Jeheuty respected that. He told Nasir that he too studied behavior in much the same way. It helped with negotiations.

Zakiy did not accompany the two men. Nasir's brother was busy working with Ojodo Yerodin, sorting out dock tasks for the company house. The newly acquired help needed to be separated from the other workers. The new labor was given an early meal and rest for the day. Zakiy was also tasking messengers with delivering news to the other company bosses about the additional laborers.

Nasir visited the company house after his morning ritual to meet with Wakil, Behar, Roberto, and the other two lieutenants. There was a quick exchange of words before Nasir and al-Jeheuty departed, Tegu and Awa with them. Nasir's party traveled to an outdoor café. Tegu and Awa stood behind Nasir while he sat. Al-Jeheuty stood on the other side of the table, awaiting command. Nasir granted him permission to sit. This was all for the surrounding patrons. Al-Jeheuty could not look like an equal to Nasir. The young company boss even made it a point to speak loud when he commanded al-Jeheuty to sit close. "You are newly serviced to me," he said. "I want to know your life. I want to know the young man who serves my company." Al-Jeheuty moved closer to Nasir, next to him. "Was that too much?" Nasir asked in a whisper.

Al-Jeheuty shook his head, no. He had a smile on his face. "What do you wish to know of me, Company Boss?" he asked, voice equally loud.

"Your life before now," answered Nasir.

The conversation then turned clandestine. Al-Jeheuty's voice was low, as was his head to keep onlookers believing his humble status to Nasir. Al-Jeheuty expressed how impressed he was with Nasir when he spoke to Wakil, Roberto, and Behar, handing out titles and tasks. "They are humble men," said al-Jeheuty. "Their egos did not inflate. Have the same conviction when explaining your plan to Guyotta about increasing the revenue. You have been through a lot. I understand you are emotionally exhausted. Concentrate on the fact that you have a way of making people believe in you. Make The Four Winds go along with your plans. Don't worry, they'll have to follow your commands."

"Even when I make request for monies?" Nasir asked, eyebrow raised.

"They'll give you whatever you want in order to shut you up," explained al-Jeheuty. "Any friction would shake their plans. We can't get too greedy, though. You must ask for a reasonable loan. We'll work out the details with Rahmis and your lawyer."

"Wakil," Nasir provided.

"Yes. Wakil," al-Jeheuty repeated, committing the counselor's name to memory. "The two of them, Rahmis and Wakil, can estimate the cost of building a new market for the city. I do want to push the envelope on some issues."

"How?" Nasir asked a little worried.

"I want you to convince Sahin-el Bey and his heads that the plan can succeed so well, they actually prefer to stay and reap the benefits." He took a moment to look Nasir in the eye. "We need them distracted from their plans to escape. I want you to bow to the Regent Master and bestow upon him the title of Beylerbey *Neggur*."

Nasir couldn't help but laugh. "What makes you think he cares about such a title?" Nasir had to catch the volume in his voice. "He is the Beylerbey already. Not privately, like your captain. He is Beylerbey publicly. Adding Neggur does nothing."

Al-Jeheuty grinned. "Neggur is a title sought after since Alexander the Great tried his best to burrow into ancient African temples and be ordained as part of our ancient priesthoods. The Ptolemy line was the same. This fight has manipulated both the Christian and Mohammedan faiths. Now the Romans and the Turks battle over hosting religion's legitimate See. Rome has proposed their Vatican. The Turks control the Hagia Sophia. We give a tawny Turk that title, and we give him the case for the true papacy. We ordain Guyotta. We play into his ego. We become Sylvester to his Constantine."

Nasir smirked. "You're vicious."

"Trust me, great Company Boss," al-Jeheuty began. "This will slow The Four Winds' ambition."

Nasir pondered the negotiator's words. He asked, "And if they show no interest?"

"We speed up *our* ambitions," countered al-Jeheuty. "And we calm the Winds."

Nasir agreed with a nod of his head. He called Awa and Tegu to fetch wine, bread, and cheese for he and al-Jeheuty. They returned quickly, Awa pouring wine for the two gentlemen. But al-Jeheuty's time to rejoice was quickly interrupted. His eyes looked up, and the sight before him locked the rest of his movements, save his heart's beat. The beauty of Nasir's morning ritual dulled in comparison to this new sight. The joyous feeling of watching the flow of true Moors in the streets of al-Mari Ifriq was negated. The passersby disappeared with the presence of a wondrous, feminine image.

The woman's skin was black and smooth. It was as if midnight defied the sun's brilliance, daring to shine brighter than the sun before the heavenly body resigned to set. The woman was shapely, voluptuous. Her beige dress, billowing off her like a light, visible breeze, accentuated her curves. The sun brought out an invisible design woven into the fabric of her garments. With close inspection, a shimmer of gold embroidery, lightly knit into the dress, was illuminated by the sun's touch.

A dark wrap covered the young woman's short, coiled hair. She wore around her upper body a black cloak that had gold trim and gold embroidered designs. On her feet there were tan shoes, a shade darker than her dress. Her ears were adorned with large gold loops.

The woman was staring directly at al-Jeheuty, wearing a smile. She was intensely focused on the young Moor, who felt swallowed by the woman's large, dark brown eyes that were decorated by sharp-lined, well-manicured eyebrows. Al-Jeheuty tried to lower his gaze away from the young Moorish woman. The heat of her eyes sent chills through him, but he could not look away. Nasir called his name, but al-Jeheuty didn't move. Then the company boss snapped his fingers to grab al-Jeheuty's attention. The rebel lieutenant remained still, fixated on the approaching maiden. Nasir aimed his eyes in the direction of al-Jeheuty's gaze. Nasir was then stirred by the presence of the young woman approaching, but it was because he knew her. He jumped from his seat and embraced Mehit al-Tarqiyya Zaher, who did her best to keep her eyes on al-Jeheuty. The lieutenant looked away and became respectable once it was revealed that his company boss knew the young woman.

"Mehit," greeted Nasir.

Al-Jeheuty took note of the woman's name. This name he would remember.

"Nasir," Mehit said with surprise. "My father said your trip was prosperous."

Nasir shook his head. "Yes. Indeed."

Mehit backed away and looked down at al-Jeheuty. "And who is this young man?" she asked with flirtatious curiosity.

"He is my new servant," Nasir answered in a mocking tone intended to tease al-Jeheuty. "Our trip's bounty included goods, silver, precious stones, and live cargo. *Al-Jeheuty Anhur Has* was among the live cargo."

"Slaves?" Mehit questioned.

"Good slaves too," Nasir continued. "Africans. Moors. They will live a better life here than in the American colonies where they were intended to serve. At least here, a young man like al-Jeheuty Anhur Has— educated at Sankore—has the ability to rise in company status."

Mehit kept her eyes on al-Jeheuty. He did not speak or stir. Mehit questioned, "Intended for servitude in the American colonies?"

"Yes," Nasir answered, teasing tone still intact. "As educated as al-Jeheuty Anhur Has may be, it did not stop him from dealing with riffraff. He helped lead an unsuccessful rebellion against the Spanish Crown. He's lucky his head is still attached to his shoulders."

Mehit raised a curious eyebrow. "A rebel?" she said in a low voice, intrigued. She turned to Nasir and asked, "And how do you know such a man would not rebel against you." Her voice was teasing.

"I no longer care for that life, *mora*," al-Jeheuty answered, drawing Mehit's eyes back to him. "All I wish is for a good job, which the Company Boss has given me, a good life, and to see my family again."

"A wife and child?" Mehit interrogated.

Al-Jeheuty blushed. "No, *mora*. My mother, father, and twin brother." Al-Jeheuty looked at Nasir, feigning a concerned expression. He stood up and took Nasir's side as he asked in a humble voice, "Did I speak out of turn, Company Boss?"

Nasir put a hand on al-Jeheuty's shoulder. "No. Who better to answer such a question?"

Mehit's gaze passed between Tegu, Awa, al-Jeheuty, and then back to Nasir. She addressed, "Well, Nasir, you have many servants. May I borrow this one later?"

Both Nasir and al-Jeheuty gave Mehit the same perplexed look.

Mehit turned her attention to al-Jeheuty. She then spoke commands sharply, as if Nasir had already granted permission. "I own a bathhouse, just several blocks from here. Several crates filled with new furnishings, decorative items, and scented burnings were delivered the other day. I have no help unloading them." She turned to Nasir and said with a downcast voice, "You know how my father refuses to help me with my place." Mehit then became angry. "Aludra now services Hyle Tecer. The young girl…is not the same." Mehit held back tears, though her eyes shimmered. "Your brother could not spare anyone. I understand. He was putting your company back on track and meeting with corsair captains and company bosses. I just wanted to see if everything was in order, and if a man—or men—could be spared."

"Yes, *mora*," Nasir said taking her hand in his. "Al-Jeheuty and three others will join you. There was a giant among the live cargo." Nasir curled his arms humorously, and he pushed out his chest. "His name is Ojodo. I will send the men to help you in one hour."

"Thank you," Mehit said with a quick bend in her knee and a bow at the neck, her hands together like in a prayer. She turned to al-Jeheuty and finished in a flirtatious tone, "I will be waiting." She turned and disappeared into the flow of traffic down the street.

Nasir and al-Jeheuty returned to their chairs. Nasir leaned close to al-Jeheuty's ear and whispered, "Her name is Mehit al-Tarqiyya—"

"She is beautiful," al-Jeheuty said dreamily.

"—*Zaher*," Nasir finished, his tone heedful.

"Name sounds familiar," al-Jeheuty quipped. He raised an eyebrow at Nasir and asked, "Taran's niece?"

"No," said Nasir.

"Younger cousin?"

Nasir shook his head and again said, "No."

"Daughter?"

"Yes," answered Nasir.

Al-Jeheuty sighed. Though his guesses were wishful thinking and playful, he knew immediately upon hearing Mehit's surname her relationship to Taran Zaher. He commented, "Well, that news felt like cold water."

Nasir then patted al-Jeheuty on the back. "Let's carry on with business. The matter you are trying to press is very dangerous, al-Jeheuty." Nasir sighed. "But I fear Mehit's stubbornness rather than your ambitions, though I'm sure the two will meet somewhere in the middle. I haven't seen her smile like that in months."

Al-Jeheuty playfully fixed his garments. "Be honest, Company Boss, you've never seen her smile like that at a man. Ever." He fixed his hair and grinned. To make sure he was not stepping into his fellow Moor's territory, al-Jeheuty asked, "You don't wish to court the young woman?"

Nasir shook his head, no. "Mehit is like a sister to me."

"*Like* a sister," al-Jeheuty emphasized. "But *not* a sister."

"However, she *is* Taran's daughter." Nasir's voice was stern. "Dodge every pursuit." The company boss smiled and leaned close to say, "And when you visit her window at night—when your rebellious hide stows away behind my back—you make sure neither I nor Taran find out."

Al-Jeheuty blushed again. "Yes, Company Boss."

Nasir stood up. "Let's walk. Maybe if we keep moving, we can keep out of trouble."

Al-Jeheuty followed Nasir. The two continued forward, Tegu and Awa in drag. Tegu snatched the bottle of wine while Awa held the cups. Al-Jeheuty spoke to Nasir about hand gestures and eye movements to look for when next dealing with the heads of The Four Winds. Al-Jeheuty revealed signals that would instruct Nasir to back away from the topic, or to press the issue further. Other signals were made, subtle, to show that someone was bluffing, or to use a strong argument. In return for the lesson, Nasir paid al-Jeheuty with information about Mehit al-Tarqiyya Zaher. Al-Jeheuty became disgusted when he was informed that Taran was forcing his daughter to have the women of her salon service the governing Turks' desires. Mehit's bathhouse was slowly being turned into a brothel. Taran was turning his daughter into a Madame of Ill Repute.

Al-Jeheuty, Ojodo, and two other laborers were sent to help Mehit later that afternoon. Ojodo performed most of the heavy labor. Al-Jeheuty and the two other laborers removed ornaments and other furnishings from storage crates and set them up where Mehit commanded. The enormous Moor, Ojodo, helped rearrange the larger furnishings. Ojodo did his job with a smile, recounting romanticized tales to the young ladies of the salon. Ojodo was not glaringly boastful with his stories. He captivated his audience as he weaved his tales into an intricate lattice of life-lessons learned, humor, and honor—even in the tales of piracy and deceit.

Al-Jeheuty and Mehit interacted only with quick, shy glances toward one another. But the two kept each other in view, holding long looks when they believed the other was not aware. Mehit's few words toward al-Jeheuty came in commands, remaining professional. Ojodo playfully exposed the two by announcing one of his stories as, "*A tale of romance between a Moorish pirate and a noble Moor's daughter.*" Ojodo's call to narrative came when he (and the others in the bathhouse) noticed al-Jeheuty and Mehit flinch when catching each other's eyes for what seemed like the hundredth time in an hour's span. The women chuckled lightly, and even al-Jeheuty and Mehit found the witticism humorous. It was also inspirational. Al-Jeheuty and Mehit stole a few minutes to disappear and speak to one another.

But even their escape was professional. Mehit called for al-Jeheuty to bring several scented burnings to a salon area in the back. Mehit started conversation by politely asking al-Jeheuty what he studied at the university. Al-Jeheuty answered, "World Studies." He was smiling, thankful to be interacting with Mehit. His life had changed from where he was several days ago, let alone within the last several years of his life, fighting, rebelling, and being an outlaw. Al-Jeheuty concluded his tale by saying, "Then, of course, I used my great education in diplomacy in an attempt to bring down the Spanish Crown with extremely violent means." Al-Jeheuty lifted his shoulders. "I guess talking doesn't always work."

Mehit chuckled. "How did you get into that?"

"That's a good question, *mora*." Al-Jeheuty lifted his eyebrows. "I jumped from job to job after my studies were over. I got into a lot of mischievous behavior. Met my captain while running from the law. Just wanted to have fun. I went a little too far."

"Does your family think you're dead?" Mehit asked.

Al-Jeheuty again lifted his shoulders. "I'm not sure. I've asked Company Boss Nasir for permission to leave." Mehit sighed. The title did not fit Nasir, knowing how he had earned it. Al-Jeheuty did not take notice of Mehit's behavior and scoffed, "They probably would be none-too-proud with my actions. I come from a family of lawyers, diplomats, and businessmen."

"Ah," Mehit said, interested in al-Jeheuty's sentiments. "Then you and I suffer the same problem." Al-Jeheuty looked at Mehit curiously. "My father does not approve of my salon," the woman explained. "This bathhouse was supposed to help fund my studies at the University, which in turn was supposed to make me respectable." Mehit smiled lovingly as she continued to decorate. "But this place is me. My business. I love doing this. I am the governess here. What would an education under the laws of religion provide me but a husband that believes in my complete servitude unto him."

Al-Jeheuty lifted an eyebrow. He then remembered what Nasir told him about Taran trying to use Mehit's bathhouse as a brothel for the Turks. It was at that moment when Hyle Tecer and five Turkish soldiers from The Four Winds entered the bathhouse. He stood in the room's doorway and signaled for Mehit with a polite smile. Al-Jeheuty noticed Mehit's expression. Her visage flowed from irritated to professional in a quick wave. She feigned a smile and stepped toward the Turkish accountant. She bowed respectfully and kept her head low as he spoke to her with a pompous air. Hyle threw a sharp look at al-Jeheuty, who quickly stood up straight in a servant's manner. Al-Jeheuty listened closely as Hyle asked for several women to be assigned to the soldiers. Mehit bowed respectful. Her mouth was shut, teeth clenched out of frustration. She gained composure long enough to tell Companyman Tecer that she would gather all her girls for his soldiers to choose from. Tecer patted Mehit on the head. "Thank you little girl," he said. "And of course, bring Aludra."

"Yes," Mehit said, her voice straining to be polite.

"We'll be in the front," said Hyle. He rubbed Mehit's cheek, patted her shoulder and then turned away to wait the selection for he and his soldiers.

Mehit turned back to al-Jeheuty. She was humiliated. Al-Jeheuty said nothing to her. Mehit's demeanor reverted to a professional manner. Al-Jeheuty received nothing more from Mehit's voice, save sharp commands. He, Ojodo, and the other laborers were finished and dismissed before the selection began. Hyle locked the door behind the servants as they left. Nasir, Awa, and Tegu waited outside. The company boss noticed the disgusted look on al-Jeheuty's face.

"Come," Nasir said sharply, continuing to play his part as a slave-driving company boss. Al-Jeheuty was silent. He could only concentrate on words he spoke to Mehit earlier. *Talking doesn't always work.* Nasir shot him an icy look that cooled al-Jeheuty's heated temperament. The lieutenant tried to signal the company boss about the situation brewing within Mehit's bathhouse. But signals were not needed. Nasir understood al-Jeheuty's emotional constitution and the cause of it. That was still no excuse for al-Jeheuty to continue to wear a scowl on his face. Nasir needed al-Jeheuty to be like stone, and continue to play the part of a servant, detached from the environment around him. Al-Jeheuty needed to look as if he was ready to serve his environment, not jump into battle with it.

Nasir made a quick gesture with his hands, signaling for the lieutenant to fix his face. The party passed through the city streets, out of the gates, and toward the company house. Al-Jeheuty tried to remove the image of Mehit's girls being taken advantage of. He even had visions of Mehit being used for the pleasure of that fat Turk and the Turkish soldiers he brought with him.

Al-Jeheuty was burdened by these thoughts for the rest of the day. He was able to bury his emotions only when conversing at the company house with Behar, Nasir, and the others about strikes against The Four

Winds. Behar approved of al-Jeheuty's plans to feed Guyotta's ego. Wakil relayed that The Four Winds wanted a meeting held, one day a week, to discuss plans to re-build al-Mari Ifriq. The first of these meetings was scheduled for the afternoon. Roberto noted aloud that this was the first sign of a pattern. Nasir commented that Hyle Tecer had a midday ritual.

"He visits the bathhouse of Taran Zaher's daughter." Nasir noticed al-Jeheuty flinch. "Taran has forced his daughter to turn her bathhouse—once exclusive for women—into a brothel for use by The Four Winds."

Behar reflected on the information and said, "If this ritual takes place every day at midday—"

"We don't know for certain," Nasir interrupted the rebel captain. "I only know of two occasions, including today."

"I'll get confirmation tonight," said al-Jeheuty. He looked at Roberto and stated, "This fat man—Hyle Tecer is it? He fancies one specific girl there. Here name is Aludra. I hear she is quite distraught. Have your mistress take her place. Slit his throat. Have his phallus removed. Not in that order."

Everyone but Nasir was perplexed at the angry emotion resonating from al-Jeheuty's tone. Behar broke the awkward silence. "Well, we know where The Four Winds' leaders will be once a week. We know where one of the heads is at midday. They must be executed separately."

"We can work around the one with the midday ritual," said Bo Yusuf. "I'm sure the meeting is catered to this lech's needs. If we attack on the day scheduled for a meeting, we'll know that at midday one will be occupied at a bathhouse. At that time, I'm sure Guyotta will be in his palace waiting for Nasir's arrival."

Roberto scoffed. "The son-of-a-bitch is arrogant, too. He feels no one would dare attack him. His guards are not prepared for an attack by The Seventy-Two Points of the Universe. My spies, slipped among Guyotta's servants, have counted the palace guards. There is only thirty-three total, inside and out. The Turkish army is too busy guarding the walls of the city."

Despite Roberto's confidence, Wakil insisted, "We'll need all the members of your clan. This must be extremely covert. Your soldiers must be at their best."

Roberto nodded.

Bo Yusuf then reminded, "We have to make sure the other two heads are separated as well."

Behar lit several lamps as the sun made its descent. "Keep close watch on the heads' whereabouts before each meeting. Watch close over the next several weeks," he said.

Nasir named the other two targets. "Aguyan Ozan and Tous Zeki."

Al-Jeheuty poured himself a cup of water and started to drink. "What are their jobs," he asked after swallowing a sip.

"Aguyan is the lawyer," Nasir answered. "My brother tells me he has come through over the past three days." The company boss looked at Wakil to confirm. The lawyer nodded affirmatively.

"What was his purpose here?" al-Jeheuty continued his interrogation.

"He's been interested in the cargo coming through our company, and the ships that dock," the company boss answered. "I have no idea why. I'll find out in a meeting."

"Be careful when questioning The Four Winds," reminded Wakil.

Al-Jeheuty stood up. "We'll use it against him. Establish an audit of the Sa'ood Company. The audit should be scheduled before the meeting. Midday."

"Suggest it, don't insist," advised Behar.

Al-Jeheuty nodded with the captain's counsel. "Their lawyer can check cargo," the negotiator continued. "And their accountant, should we happen to miss him at the bathhouse. The two of them can examine the number of ship repairs and loans your company has made. Cargo too. The Four Winds will feel in control with that knowledge, especially before a meeting. They'll be comfortable believing that there is no way to lie to them about what is and what is not going on."

Rahmis presented a written proposal to Nasir. It consisted of business propositions for a market, a new maritime trade partner, protection revenue, tribute taxes for docked corsairs, and the income for two new trade routes. Roberto presented to Nasir sketches for two new trade paths.

"Ojodo," Nasir called, "Your family's business? You're sure they'll join?"

Ojodo nodded. "Absolutely. My uncle and Behar are good friends. I just need permission for leave."

"You will travel with my brother," Nasir ordered. "I will run the company duties. You can leave tomorrow night. You will be fitted with provisions for travel. I'll meet with you and my brother in the morning." Ojodo nodded. Nasir steered the discussion to their next target. "Next is the Army Official, Tous Zeki."

"He's trying to burrow his way into the Council of Captains," Wakil informed. "The next move, for The Four Winds, is to take control of all the captains. They will start by increasing the taxes."

"That's good," Nasir expressed. "We can have Captain Sunwil watch Zeki's moves. We'll inform the captain of our plans. I trust him. We can attack on a day with an audit. Each head can be slain. The attack can be blamed on bandits that received word of large trains of gold coming from the city. The timing must be perfect, like the rise of a new day at the shore of al-Mari Ifriq."

Everyone agreed.

"Are all matters settled," Behar asked. Everyone nodded after looking at one another to confirm agreement. Behar stood up and addressed, "I will gather the bosses of the other companies on the day of revolution. They will come under us. They will agree to this." He stepped forward and continued, "However, until that day, Nasir will work to consolidate the companies. You will smile, laugh, and drink with these men. Little-by-little, you will let them know the politics. Let them bring it up. Fan flames of their curiosity. They are going to know who to side with. They'll know you're close. They'll be conversational with you. Act as if you are not concerned, even with all the impending politics. They will believe you know something. They will admire that, even the more hardheaded bosses." Behar waved a hand. "Adjourned."

The house dispersed into teams. Behar went with Wakil. Ojodo and Bo Yusuf went to find Zakiy. Rahmis paired with Roberto, journeying to *The al-Hammon Palace*. Al-Jeheuty went with Nasir and the servant-guards Tegu and Awa. But al-Jeheuty separated from Nasir when he noticed Mehit at the docks. He politely asked Nasir for permission to leave, and when he received Nasir's consent, he made his way to her. Nasir did not let al-Jeheuty leave without a clever command to escort the young woman back to the city. Al-Jeheuty winked appreciatively at Nasir and approached Mehit. The woman's eyes were fixed to the heavens, the darkening sky. Mehit heard al-Jeheuty's footsteps. She imagined that it was the young man approaching her. She indulged her imagination and said, "I wish I had your nerve, al-Jeheuty."

The young Moor was taken by surprise. He wondered how Mehit could have known it was he approaching. *Perhaps*, he thought, *she wanted it to be him. Or maybe, it was just a woman's magic.* Al-Jeheuty was content either way. He stood at attention next to the young woman and stayed silent. Mehit did not look at al-Jeheuty, but his image was in her head.

"I wish I could rebel," Mehit continued.

Al-Jeheuty dared to say, "You have been brave enough, *mora*. You have your own business, a woman in a corsair-state. You don't go to study just to be a man's wife. You defy an entire religion's God." He crossed his arms and added, "I was only running from the law."

"Nasir is brave," Mehit said, showing little concern for al-Jeheuty's words. "He runs his father's business. His father died days ago, killed by bandits. Has he told you?" al-Jeheuty answered, yes. Mehit sighed. "But he and his brother Zakiy continue with company duties. I know they want to breakdown, but they go on. I want to fight like that, but I can't. I can't hold my anger, but I can't cut anyone with it either. I can't free myself. I feel like I'm feeding young girls to sharks."

"Do they come everyday?" al-Jeheuty asked.

Mehit nodded her head. "Yes. Midday."

Al-Jeheuty took note of the information. "You mentioned a specific girl that is preyed on. Aludra?"

"Yes." Mehit's eyes watered. As strong a woman as she carried herself, she felt powerless, again.

Al-Jeheuty wanted to tell Mehit everything, but he remained silent on the matter of revolution. "Well, *mora*, I will rise through the ranks of Nasir's company. I will seek a high political position, and I'll wipe this city clean of oppression."

Mehit smiled warmly at the young man's sentiment. "You'll be years too late," she said to him. Her tears and sorrowful manner returned quickly. "In the meantime, I have to wonder how to hold a revolution in my father's mind so as to change it. How can I get myself to hate him as he deserves to be hated?"

Mehit finally turned toward Al-Jeheuty, tears in her eyes. Her dark flesh absorbed the sun's dying glow and its reflection rippled like a desert campfire. The woman looked divine. Al-Jeheuty took a quick glance to see if others spied he and Mehit. He did not reach to touch her, though he wanted to embrace her, comfort her. Mehit longed for the same, but she understood al-Jeheuty as a servant. To her, he was not a free man. He could not touch her, let alone hold her the way she longed for.

Al-Jeheuty simply bowed his head in a gracious manner. "I will be here, this time, every day," he told the Moorish woman. "If you wish to speak, I will listen. My ear will be as much a servant to the words from your lips as the rest of me serves my company boss."

"I hope not all of you is dedicated to him," she said, sniffing back tears and illuminating with a flirtatious smile. Mehit stepped closer to al-Jeheuty.

He made a bold move toward Mehit and whispered, "You are beautiful, *mora*. You are a breath of fresh air after all I've been through. I hope I can advance my status in this company and city so that I may promote my lips to serve you as well as my ears…and eyes." Mehit tingled with the words al-Jeheuty spoke. The young man stepped back from her, bowed again and said humbly, "If I may present such an offer."

Mehit chuckled again. "We shall see, gentle-moor." Her words were all that al-Jeheuty could hope for.

Al-Jeheuty crossed his arms and said, "Well, Company Boss Nasir has given me command to escort you back to the city before dark."

Mehit wiped away the remnants of her tears. She waved her arm toward the gated city and said, "Lead the way."

Al-Jeheuty turned and started his way up, Mehit two steps behind him. The two passed the time by speaking about growing up in Moorish cities that were slowly changing into a state of foreign control. Al-Jeheuty confessed that with all his travels he was looking forward to settling down. Mehit wanted to experience more travel, but was not going to live anywhere but al-Mari Ifriq. She expressed that with all the city's troubles, it was still her home.

There were too many people around for al-Jeheuty to sneak a light kiss. He also did not want to overstep his bounds. But he believed that he could pull off a maneuver so sly that his brother-in-arms Rahmis would've been proud. He thought better of it and made no move. Mehit's father was not seen when the two arrived at Mehit's house. The two saluted one another gracefully, and Mehit then disappeared inside. Al-Jeheuty turned to walk away and was quickly greeted by Tegu and Awa.

"I saw Tegu several blocks back," al-Jeheuty remarked.

"I'm still teaching him," quipped the elder assassin, Awa.

The three started walking up the street. "Where's Nasir," al-Jeheuty asked.

"Back at his house," Awa answered. "We have been called to the servant quarters. Come."

Al-Jeheuty wanted to look back at Mehit's house. But he kept his eyes forward. All he would have seen, had he looked back, was Taran's black silhouette standing at the second floor window, candlelight burning intensely behind him. The land baron held an inquisitive gaze, narrowing on the departing gentleman who had just escorted his daughter home.

Chapter Eleven

Guyotta Sahin-el Bey raised a single, curious eyebrow. He looked over the parchments that had been submitted to him by the young company boss Nasir ibn Sa'ad al-Din Sa'ood. The young man had first explained the written proposition before handing the parchments to the Regent Master. Guyotta's mouth curled into a sly smile, admiring the words in front of him. Nasir and the Moorish lawyer Wakil al-Hakam inspired Guyotta's admiration. The two were impressive. Nasir had much of his father in him. Hopefully he did not have too much of his father's intelligence. Guyotta believed that it would be a shame to assassinate Nasir as well. At the very least, it would be a shame to assassinate him earlier than planned.

Guyotta's eyebrow and smile were the first signs of life and interest that he showed in the entire meeting. He was like a stone statue up until now. Guyotta's stiffened manner rattled Nasir at first. The company boss gave a slight look to al-Jeheuty who stood against the far wall next to two other Moorish servants. Al-Jeheuty moved his eyes slightly, giving Nasir a sign not to worry and keep pushing the subject. The lieutenant knew that Guyotta's unflinching behavior was purposeful. The Regent Master did not want to showcase his admiration for Nasir, the proposal, and Wakil. But Guyotta's recent movements exposed his true disposition. Nasir relaxed, but did not show it. He asked the Regent Master for permission to stand. The permission was granted. Nasir paced the room.

"The Empire bleeds all revenue generated by our trade routes and market," Nasir continued. "You have expressed many times about becoming an independent state, Regent Master. You would need a greater title than Bey. Al-Mari Ifriq could be the capital of a great state, a united Odongo-Mauharim. This would nullify your title as *Regent Master*. Any title connected to the Mohammedan religion could be usurped or imitated by a successor looking to assassinate you. The Turks lay claim to *Dey* and *Bey*, regardless of how far back the titles can be traced. You have the title of *Beylerbey*, but there needs to be more."

Guyotta sat up straight. He watched Nasir with focused curiosity. It was not just Nasir's words that captivated the Regent Master, but also the company boss's demeanor. Nasir transformed into the companyman his father had been.

Nasir made his way around the table and then added coolly, "What about *adding* to your title?" Nasir, Wakil, and al-Jeheuty noticed Guyotta lean close. His interest was completely piqued. Taran too was crippled with intrigue. "*Neggur*," Nasir exhaled in a haunting whisper.

The simple word grabbed Guyotta and forced his chest out. It made him feel like a titan in a single breath. He gasped. Aguyan grimaced. The expression was as quick as a flash of lightning. The lawyer's teeth clenched. He relaxed himself and just waited for the Regent Master's answer, much like everyone in the room.

Guyotta's reaction was interesting. His laughter was small breaths, and then bubbled into an uncontrollable fit. Nasir froze. Wakil and Taran were still. The other heads chuckled along with the Regent Master, forced as the lawyer Aguyan's laughter was.

Guyotta stood up. He slammed the table with both fists and shook a finger at Nasir. "Have you gone mad?" Guyotta said with a wide smile and a loud voice. He calmed his laughter and walked toward Nasir with small, exaggerated steps. "Are you an Egyptian priest? Do you have blood claim to Nubia or Abyssinia? You're going to bestow upon me a title you have no authority to give?" Guyotta slapped his hands against Nasir's cheeks and pushed. "I love you like my son. With no offense to your father, who, by the way, would be proud of your ambition." Guyotta's tone was sincerely excited.

Aguyan felt ill trying to keep up with the Regent Master's pleased spirit. The muscles in his cheek started to burn as he struggled to keep his smile. His throat started to dry as he tried to maintain his laughter and chuckle. He didn't know if his fellow companymen were as sincere. He figured that invisible strings attached to Guyotta pulled at their emotions.

Guyotta turned to Wakil and Taran and asked, "Do you concur with this title?"

"We do," answered Wakil, speaking for himself and Taran.

"And the rest of the company bosses?" Guyotta inquired.

"We are in talks with them," informed Wakil. "We are preparing the proposition. We know we will position your title with the understanding of separating from the Empire. However, we must have strict assurance from The Four Winds, and you our Regent Master, that taxes will be lightened."

Guyotta turned to Hyle. "Have you and Taran come to an agreement about the taxes?"

Hyle nodded. "Yes we have," answered the fat accountant. He

looked at Wakil and said with a smile, "We will discuss them with you after this meeting. Let us hope we can come to agreeable terms."

Wakil returned his attention to the Regent Master.

Guyotta slapped his hands together. "Then I will have Aguyan draw up the work to approve all of the points from your proposal." Guyotta chuckled. "I agree to the loan. A stronger market must be created. We shall test your new trade routes. We will begin the protection of sea merchants, traders, and corsairs. We will begin the deceit of the European nations by attacking their ships." He addressed his Army Official. "Spearhead the expeditions with the Council of Captains." The Regent Master laughed at Nasir. "And you said this was not a corsair-state." He laughed harder. "Black Moors have no bounds to their hypocrisy." Nasir just smiled at the comment. Guyotta returned to his seat, as did Nasir. "An audit will happen every two weeks, midweek, midday. We will hold a meeting every week. Again, midday."

Everyone nodded.

"To your duties then," Guyotta commanded. He waved his hand, dismissing everyone in the room. Wakil, Hyle, and Taran stood, bowed at the neck toward Guyotta, and then left to hold their own council. Nasir, bowed to Guyotta, and left with his servants. Tous was next to leave. Guyotta tapped his fingers on the table and signaled for Aguyan to stay seated. He exhaled after palace servants escorted everyone out of the room.

Aguyan sat and waited for Guyotta to speak. He knew that the Regent Master was taken with the addition of *Neggur* to the title of Beylerbey. It made Aguyan sick. The four heads had a plan. Al-Mari Ifriq was to provide them a secure future. All its riches were supposed to feed them more than the Empire ever could. It was almost dry. Its people were on the verge of battling one another instead of pointing weapons toward them. Guyotta had plans to disappear from the Empire, fleeing into Asia Minor.

The plans, however, always conflicted with Guyotta's ambitions to gain power within the Empire. Aguyan and his brother al-Rinak had a plan to eliminate the rubbery-minded Regent Master. Guyotta was scheduled to die some time after The Four Winds assassinated Company Boss Nasir and his lawyer Wakil. Taran was next. The Ghanem Company would take the fall for al-Mari Ifriq. Aguyan believed that Guyotta could live if he just stayed with their plan. Now, nothing could spare him, so Aguyan thought.

Guyotta had his thoughts too. He focused on the addition to the title of Beylerbey. *Neggur*, the appropriate title for they who were referred to as Pharaohs. It was also the title of high priests or priestesses. Alexander III of Macedon, after conquering Egypt, wished to be ordained within the priesthood as *Neggur*. The priests boldly refused. The priests' audacity came with the understanding that they were well protected by warriors from Nubia. Should the priesthood be attacked, Nuba warriors would be quick to react. Some historians believed that Alexander dared to fight Nubia, but was defeated. Other historians insist he was too afraid to step foot near the ancient kingdom, knowing it could mean certain death. Regardless, Alexander died without gaining full acceptance to the Egyptian priesthood, or any major title. The Ptolemaic line, beginning with Ptolemy I, Lagi, called Soter, inherited the task.

The priesthood compromised with Ptolemy's ambitions, bestowing upon him a new philosophy that catered to him and the foreign population flowing into Egypt. Though he was not ordained into the Egyptian mystery system, he was presented with a new god, made in his image. The god's name was Serapis. He was a combination of Osiris and Apis. The foreigners had a priesthood of their own. The newly fashioned Order of Serapis was not accepted by the Egyptians, but was respected. This did not suffice the foreign rulers. Temples were closed. Scrolls moved, re-written, or burned. New libraries were built to honor and house the doctrines dedicated to Serapis. Priests and Priestesses who upheld ancient traditions were either killed or forced to worship in their homes, their temples subjugated or closed. Quarrels ensued. The priesthood was then split in two factions: those who recognized the Order of Serapis as a legitimate order, and those who refused to recognize the Order's legitimacy, the Melchite Coptic priests and the Exterior Coptic Community, respectively.

The Ptolemy line continued to assert its power. Rituals, philosophies, and mythologies were usurped from other Orders to make Serapis authentic. Temples were closed and reopened with ancient imagery supplanted by carvings and statues of Serapis lining the walls, hallways, and sacred chambers. The priesthood became more divided than ever over the foreign assertion. The ancient lands of Africa, once hailed as great learning centers, became wrought with discord, with martyrs on both sides of the priesthood. The philosophical and religious strife would permeate and even shape Christianity, Mohammedanism, and Judaism. No doctrines were safe. The human and spiritual nature of religious 'saviors' would come into question. Constantine would try to alleviate the conflict with donations, trying to buy his way into the Exterior Coptic community, a debated historical fact. Constantine wanted to be blessed with title, and baptized within the priesthood. He too was not accepted. No title was given. Constantine could only dream of being an Ecclesiastical Neggur. Even the story of conquering in the sign of his newly accepted religion was nothing more than a propagated legend for Christianity to push. Constantine's acceptance of any philosophy was based solely on political gain, the power to rule mass amounts of real estate, and the population.

When it seemed as if the debates, the controversies, and small scrimmages could get no worse, then stepped forward a man named Arius. He declared, with a strong statement, that all contemporary saviors were spawned from the debate of Serapis, and that they were nothing more than man-made, created creatures. The debates that had been raging for centuries went further than just going back to square one. Councils were convened. Banishments were made. Divine triads were constructed, using ancient trinities and doctrines as a template. But there were only more divisions made, and no one with a title to rule them. Everyone scrambled to have their saviors titled the Logos, the Logos Incarnate, part of a Homoousian Creed (one with the substance of The Father), and labeled the Kristos.

Dispute would continue. Turkey was at the center of all the councils. Divisions in spirituality were mangled with argument over a human and divine nature of a savior. New philosophies would rise in Arabia and spread to Spain. Emperor Justinian I, and his wife Theodora, would construct the Hagia Sophia in the interim. The wondrous church housed all of the doctrines related to the centuries long debate. It also housed ancient doctrines that held the keys to spirituality. This was considered by most as the true See of religion. Rome countered with the Vatican. Real estate wars, disguised as crusades, and veiled under the Christian and Mohammedan religion, would take place. Now Europe possessed knowledge of what they called 'The New World'. The last known Eden was in Christian hands. Carried there as slaves, were the descendants of the African priesthood. Rome could confiscate out of Africa and Arabia what was left of the true spiritual doctrines.

But no one had the title yet. No one was a true Ecclesiastical Neggur. Now, a young Company Boss and his team, within a desperate attempt to strengthen a region, granted Guyotta the title and power to declare the true nature of spirituality and true religion using a title sought after for centuries.

Aguyan watched his Regent Master closely. There was a relieved expression on his face, as if he had just ended an intense argument and come out the victor. Guyotta cupped his hands together. He leaned back in his chair and exhaled, "To achieve what Alexander, his bastard Ptolemaic line, and Constantine could not."

Aguyan cleared his throat and thought, *You die in a month, you delusional man.*

But the lawyer's thoughts were curbed when Guyotta declared, "I will take this back to Turkey. I will become part of the main state, rather than a province that pays tributes. I will lead the Empire over all its chiefs. The current Sultan, Ibrahim, is insane. The rumors are that he is mad. They are looking for new leadership. He is not stable, and worse yet, newly come into power. I will take his title and so much more. The council and state are looking for stability." He aimed a finger and stern eye at Aguyan, "And you will rule al-Mari Ifriq. It stays. I will clear the debt. We will alleviate pressure by giving a portion of what we sit on. The tribute will come from my portion, if there is any argument."

Interesting, Aguyan thought.

"We will stay on course of plan, otherwise." Guyotta sat up straight. His demeanor was now business. "We'll take Nasir's plans. We'll give him a month or two to prove that it works. We use it. We kill the boy, we kill his lawyer, and keep Taran just to govern the people."

"I plan on marking Taran as well," explained Aguyan. "I will bring my brother in. He has a way with people."

"The Regency will be yours to govern," proposed Guyotta. "Make it a Republic if you wish. Make it a state. I will support you."

Aguyan then relaxed. His treachery diffused.

Guyotta was not an idiot. He considered Hyle would be better left in charge of al-Mari Ifriq as a controlled state in an Empire under Guyotta's control. Aguyan would be marked in the next three months. His brother, al-Rinak, would follow in his footsteps just for safe measure.

Guyotta was no fool.

Chapter Twelve

The cleanliness of *The al-Hammon Palace* tavern was made possible through the efforts of the princely businessman, and ex-rebel, Rahmis Husani. Behar's lieutenant used his princely charms to befriend the notorious pirate Fusan al-Hammon and his ornery brother Maurice. Rahmis started to frequent the taverns nightly, escorted by Roberto Hamaat and several assassins. *The Palace* was bawdy, disorderly in its presentation. The music was rough, and the patrons were drunken marauders and corsairs. Both tawny and black Arabs and Turks, the occasional Moorish citizen, Asian, French, Italian, and Dutch seamen populated the alehouse. All were privateers in one form or another.

A few drinks of wine or beer relaxed the men long enough to forget their ethnic, racial, and nationalistic rivalries. A few drinks more made all the anger return. There was at least one fight a night. The fisticuffs were brutal, and too often turned from honorable hand-to-hand to a hidden knife or small pistol drawn. It was no place for a cultured woman, save if she were dragged into the backroom bound and gagged, where most of the captured Euro-Christian women were held before joining the harem of The Four Winds. The *al-Hammon* was not short on whoring. The night featured erotic dance that turned into far more for the patron with the highest bid for the female dancer. Some of the male pirates used the sexually pungent backrooms for one another, with no female in presence.

Rahmis quickly realized why Captain Sunwil, a man he had met weeks earlier in a meeting between he, Behar, Wakil, Nasir, and al-Jeheuty, refused to step foot inside the tavern. Rahmis promised the captain that the reputation of the *al-Hammon* would change, given time. Captain Sunwil's Chief Officer, Ras Ali, despised the *al-Hammon* more than Captain Sunwil himself. But there were parts of Captain Sunwil's crew that were fond of the tavern. *The Palace* was a place to wind down, despite the raunchy, violent, and dangerous behavior that persisted. Tobal Lessman, Captain Sunwil's Boatswain, and Yan 'Blackey' Nuh, the Quartermaster, were such crewmembers. They were given a curfew, however, which they respected.

Ironically, Maurice al-Hammon was not too thrilled with the uncontrolled activities circulating through his bar. Fusan, however, reveled in the debauchery. He considered the atmosphere as exciting as life on the sea. Rahmis looked to Maurice's disposition as a way in, to turn the tavern around to a more respectable, if not more controlled, setting. Nothing had to be sacrificed. The band could remain, but its players need not be as drunk as the audience it entertained. The women need not be raped captives, but gifts provided from The Four Winds' harem. The alcohol could remain, but added security would regulate the violence it brought about. Rahmis propositioned that the gambling be made the forefront, cards and chess tournaments, coupled with dice throws and dominoes. Maurice loved the idea. Fusan was far less enthused. How could he relax in a place that did not have the potential to turn violent? But Fusan was quickly distracted. The Four Winds and the Sa'ood Company put out a secret order to attack European trade vessels in the Mediterranean. Fusan was on call, the order given in person by Tous Zeki, the Army Official who had been placed over the Council of Captains. Captain Sunwil was also on call, but he understood the entire extent of the plan. The meeting between he and the secretly established Griffin Company let him in on the plan's arc to eliminate The Four Winds' rule.

Two weeks time from the order, trade vessels, both legitimate and illegal, sought the Guyotta Regency for protection of its ships. There was one problem, however. Fusan. His brutality was unmatched and was impossible to tame. His repulsive exploits only increased against ships and their crews while at sea. The Mediterranean marauder focused all his energy into pirate debauchery as Rahmis and Maurice restructured the *al-Hammon* into a less violent den of ill repute. Fusan did not cease his attacks, much like the other captains, once protection was paid for.

Fusan was burning captains, torturing the crews of enemy ships, and raping anything with two legs. Guyotta sent a stern warning to Maurice that if his brother's acts were not calmed, *The Palace* would be taken from them, and then their lives. Rahmis and Maurice created another distraction. A fighting tournament was implemented. Fusan not only joined, but also managed.

Rahmis then connected the *al-Hammon* to other interests, mainly inns. The seafarers needed a place to rest. *Al-Hammon*'s backrooms were too busy entertaining games and sexual exploit. Small inns were created at the docks with *The Palace's* newly generated revenue. Inns within the city's interior were made partners with the al-Hammon brothers. Rahmis saw some coin, but he gave it to Behar as tribute. Behar promised the young prince that once the Turks were removed, he would see more money for his work.

The *al-Hammon Palace* became a more respectable place. Even Captain Sunwil and Chief Officer Ras Ali frequented the tavern. The interior was no longer dark and moody, loud and violent. It was festive. Jokes, laughter, and drink filled the air. Women danced and collected the coin tossed toward them. The band stayed in rhythm, and most importantly, on stage instead of jumping into fights. The patrons were able to keep national prejudices to a minimum. All debts were settled through dice, dominoes, cards, or chess. The larger disputes were taken to the fighting ring.

A tight friendship was formed between Rahmis Husani and Maurice al-Hammon. But there was a strain. Maurice was always brooding, and though Rahmis understood Maurice shared a history and friendship with Nasir, he seldom wanted to be in presence with the company boss. Rahmis did not persist to ask either side what the matter was between them. Rahmis believed he would find no answer with Nasir. Maurice's temperament seemed one-sided too.

Today, though, the *al-Hammon Palace* was the setting for a meeting between Wakil al-Hakam and Taran Zaher. Though the bar functioned as a café in the daytime, it was now host to these two important men. Wakil and Taran were now routinely engaged inside *The Palace* the day before an audit.

The *al-Hammon* was completely empty, save these two men and their small entourages. The sun brightened the bar, acting like a spotlight for the two parties seated in the center of the main room. Wakil and Taran sat opposite one another. Ojodo and Rahmis, dressed in the fashionable manner of Moorish merchants, stood on either side of the lawyer. Guyotta's company soldiers flanked Taran. Awa stood at the baron's side, having been made Taran's personal servant within the last two weeks.

Resting on the table was a small plate of refreshments. Each man had a glass of water. Between them was a chessboard, all pieces lined and made ready for play. "May we speak freely?" asked Wakil.

"Of course," Taran assured.

"How do we play," Wakil inquired about the particular rules they were to play under. The lawyer took some fruit from his plate and started to eat.

"In the Mad Manner," Taran answered. He adjusted himself in his seat and made the first move. "I never thought it was a good move for Guyotta to support al-Kasim Askari Pasha." He moved his middle pawn two spaces forward.

"Their war with the al-Jasi has potential to come to our Regency, whether ignored or clandestinely engaged," said Wakil. "At least we will be prepared for it. But the support does not come without its conditions." Wakil matched Taran's move. Two pawns faced one another. Small moves, with no harm done. Wakil thought about Taran's next move and calculated against it. He also thought about the circumstances surrounding al-Kasim Askari Pasha, the city of al-Gherab, and the war against the African Moors called the al-Jasi.

Weeks earlier, on Griffin Company orders, Roberto Hamaat left al-Mari Ifriq to meet with the al-Jasi nation and find out the circumstances of their scrimmages with al-Gherab. Six assassins from his clan accompanied him. Roberto learned that al-Kasim Askari Pasha's armies lay waste to the urban center from which the al-Jasi originated. Al-Kasim Askari Pasha was supplying European slavers with the remaining population of the urban center, making an incredible profit. The al-Jasi claimed that the Pasha's plans were to usurp all land from the true African Moors, aiding Europeans in the African slave trade. The defeated urban center lay on the other side of al-Gherab. The al-Jasi were making moves to take back their land and resurrect their culture. Al-Kasim Askari Pasha dealt with a neighboring African kingdom that functioned under Mohammedan Law, in a manner thought more traditional than the defeated Moorish kingdom. This African kingdom was assisting the Pasha with enslaving other kingdoms and peoples. They had no idea that once the al-Jasi was defeated, and the inhabitants of Moors were dried from the urban center, they would become the new target for slavery.

Roberto sent back word by way of one of his guards, a Sun. Roberto assured the al-Jasi that aide would be sent to them, but no aggressive moves could be made toward al-Gherab. The al-Jasi leaders agreed.

Al-Kasim Askari Pasha traveled by caravan to al-Mari Ifriq to meet with Guyotta at the same time Roberto's Sun delivered the news to the Griffin Company. Groundwork was quickly laid to manipulate the troublesome alliance between the Pasha and The Four Winds. Guyotta consulted with Nasir about al-Kasim Askari Pasha's personality. Nasir, with help from al-Jeheuty, told the Regent Master to give al-Kasim Askari Pasha as little as possible, and under certain conditions. Guyotta allowed the Pasha to have weapons on the condition they were used for defense, not attack. The Pasha reluctantly agreed.

Five ambassadors were sent to oversee the proper use of al-Gherab's armament. One of them was Ojodo's uncle. His name was Eibib Oba, an African Moor that controlled several shipyards in Tunis. Ojodo had earlier journeyed to see his family, and he negotiated to partner their maritime business with the Griffin Company. Ojodo's uncle agreed, loving the opportunity to work with Behar again. Great revenue was brought to al-

Mari Ifriq when Eibib arrived. Guyotta trusted the merchant-smuggler's judgment, and with the coaxing of Nasir, promoted him to ambassador along with four Turks. Guyotta made the move in an effort to curb the revenue that was being earned, most of which circulated through Nasir's company, and only little was given as tribute. But with Ojodo in charge, not much changed.

Taran didn't agree with Guyotta's move. He cleared his throat thinking about Guyotta's silly advance. He then concentrated on his moves against Wakil in the game of chess that was at hand. He moved his knight and took a pawn. Wakil countered by putting another pawn in play.

"Do you like your new servant?" Wakil asked.

Taran grimaced. Awa was good, but too old. Taran blamed al-Jeheuty for his former servant's death. He even made the accusation that al-Jeheuty killed the servant himself. The indictment was not too far off. Al-Jeheuty gave the order, but did not slit the servant's throat. Awa was the perpetrator. The servant had been marked beforehand. Taran simply gave the Griffin Company the opportunity.

Taran did not approve of his daughter being escorted by al-Jeheuty. He did not like the pairing ever since he witnessed the two share a light kiss two days after he saw al-Jeheuty escort his daughter home for the first time. Taran argued with his daughter that she needed a proper escort while Hyle and The Four Winds' soldiers were occupying her business. Mehit retorted that al-Jeheuty was escorting her by orders of Nasir. But Taran had the last word. He assigned his servant to escort Mehit to and from her bathhouse. He gave Nasir a strong warning to keep al-Jeheuty from his daughter. This gave the Griffin Company ample opportunity to carry out their mark, a plan formed within the company long before. Al-Jeheuty gave the order for the execution. Taran's servant was found on the street with his neck open. Nasir granted Awa to Taran, and the baron accepted. Al-Jeheuty and Mehit met secretly every night, chaperoned by Awa. The elder assassin's true purpose, to spy on The Four Winds through Taran, turned up no information. Taran was suspicious of Awa. Not much information was exchanged in his presence.

Taran's thoughts, reflecting back on the entire incident, allowed his mind to slip away from the game. Wakil moved his queen. Taran retreated his knight. Wakil moved his second pawn to take the first pawn Taran put in play. Taran moved his knight again. The two didn't talk. Both were completely focused on the game. Wakil retreated his queen. He moved his knight when Taran's bishop was put in play. Wakil took another pawn, forcing Taran to move his queen. The move cost Wakil another pawn.

Taran attempted small talk with the lawyer, trying to force Wakil to reveal Sa'ood Company plans. Wakil gave little information. He focused more on the game than on the conversation. He sacrificed a knight to take Taran's bishop by queen. Taran put a knight in play, but Wakil's bishop quickly took it.

"How are the Turkish chiefs back in the Empire?" Wakil inquired, turning the questions of company business on Taran.

"They've been relaxed," answered Taran. "Guyotta delivered a great sum of money to them as tribute. They see things picking up. Guyotta has not revealed his newly earned title." Taran's rook eliminated a pawn. "But the tribute has given him newfound respect. They are considering strengthening his regional powers. I believe all of Odongo-Mauharim will legally be under their protectorate."

Wakil put his knight in play. Taran eased his rook further up the board by one square. Wakil slid his rook to the right, facing Taran's identical piece. The two rooks were separated by one square. Taran moved his rook up and removed Wakil's rook from the game. It was a play that led to the elimination of Taran's rook by way of Wakil's king.

"Behar is treated well," Wakil informed. "Nasir has lessened his abuse. Behar is used as extreme manual labor, however."

Taran grinned. "Who would've thought that Sa'ad's son would be so tortuous?" He moved his pawn, taking another pawn from Wakil. Wakil retreated his queen. Pawns and knights were put in play. No killing strikes were made. Taran became cautious with the placement of his queen. He moved her away. Wakil advanced his queen. Taran then made a strong forward move with his queen, and Wakil moved his king toward her. Taran backed away. Wakil advanced his bishop.

The two men took sips of water. They stared at the chessboard, calculating moves.

Their queens faced one another. Wakil moved his queen away, advancing far into Taran's territory. Taran chased Wakil's queen with his own, and stood several rows from Wakil's advance. Wakil just moved his king and waited for Taran's next move. The land baron moved his queen again. Wakil refrained from smiling as he executed Taran's queen with his own, but he was still lost. Taran moved his knight to take Wakil's queen.

The lawyer contemplated.

Both men advanced their bishops.

Wakil moved his king to safety and watched Taran play the rook. Wakil countered with his bishop. Taran pushed his knight. Small defensive plays defined the two men's next set of moves. No one lost a piece. Wakil and Taran wanted their defensive moves to look offensive, to make the other slip. It came down to Taran's knight, which was lost to Wakil's bishop, but quickly avenged by the rook. The offensive moves regained momentum. Wakil became careful, with fewer pieces on the board. Several intelligent moves forced Taran to advance his king. But Wakil remained cautious. He lost a pawn, but was able to keep his knight and rook in Taran's territory, forcing Taran to find safe spots for his king. Wakil needed to take Taran's rook. His focus on the rook made him leave his knight open to Taran's bishop.

Wakil was down to three pieces. He had his king, pawn, and rook. Everything else had been taken. Taran then took Wakil's remaining pawn. Two pieces was all Wakil had left. Then one. Then check. Taran smiled. Victorious. Wakil clapped for his friend and shook his hand. He congratulated Taran for winning a splendid game. Taran was now up by one when it came to chess wins. Wakil respected Taran's mastery of the game.

The two men stood up and gave one another a hug. There was always a good game the day before an audit. The servants bowed to the opposing masters, and then Wakil left the tavern. Taran and his entourage remained.

"You let him win," smiled Rahmis.

Wakil shook his head. He admitted, "No. Taran is just very cunning. Sometimes there is no better enemy than a friend. But enough philosophy, we prepare for tomorrow's audits. Everything must be precise."

Ojodo hated audits. Aguyan was always agitated when he came to inspect the docks and the company house. The Moorish titan knew tomorrow would be no different. Nothing ever pleased the accountant, and he was very rude to Ojodo's uncle and other company workers. Aguyan was always fiery, even though the companies and the Regency were turning a profit. Every two weeks was the same. This would be the fourth audit, with a surprise visit that came the week after the second. Aguyan and Guyotta were trying to keep the companies on guard. There would be no cheating with numbers. All business was to be recorded honestly. Ojodo felt his stomach turn. He was going to lose sleep. He still didn't have it as bad as Nasir. The company boss had to meet with The Four Winds once a week. Ojodo knew that he wasn't the only one anxious for the day when the Moors once again ruled al-Mari Ifriq.

Chapter Thirteen

Guyotta Sahin-el Bey was completely lost in thought. He stood on his balcony and gazed out past the maze-like hedges planted and groomed in the rear courtyard of his palace. His thoughts were thousands of miles beyond the horizon, causing him to miss the sudden disappearance of on-duty palace guards walking the perimeter. Shadows rustled the hedges and reached for Guyotta's sentries, pulling them into oblivion. Guyotta's thoughts were so fixed on the recent news of al-Kasim Askari Pasha's assassination, which also included the political execution of four of five al-Mari Ifriq ambassadors assigned to al-Gherab—the fifth taken captive—that he missed the scene of his guards' appearing to be swallowed up by the hedges they journeyed through.

Guyotta did not know whether to enjoy the Pasha's death or consider it a bad omen. Nothing was clear on the circumstances. The al-Jasi Nzambi were implicated in the attack, but there was no evidence supporting the nomadic, Moorish tribe as the assassins. The weapons that were used and left behind were too advanced for the uncultivated al-Jasi people. Bombs were used. The most advanced muskets and finely crafted blades were employed.

Guyotta thought the only thing resembling something tribal was the swift manner in which the attack was carried out. But even then the attack was too calculated for the al-Jasi. Guyotta also considered that al-Kasim Askari Pasha's brother-in-law was behind the killing. He was now in charge of al-Gherab, and he was not pursuing a swift act of vengeance against the al-Jasi. Under The Four Winds' conditions, al-Gherab was permitted to use the weapons granted to them against the nomadic tribe should the city be attacked. The absence of a move against the al-Jasi had nothing to do with honoring the conditions put forth by The Four Winds. But Guyotta only had his suspicions, which also included a strike by disguised European forces.

Al-Kasim Askari Pasha was dealing with the Portuguese and French. He provided African slaves to the two nations. In the last month he was not honoring their agreement. The attack may have been a retaliation, staged to look like another African nation, regency, or tribe, was responsible. The European was a remarkable strategist on fanning the flames to cause infighting, considered Guyotta.

Guyotta then sighed as his thoughts yielded to pleas made by Aguyan. Al-Mari Ifriq had to be abandoned. Guyotta's dreams of becoming a great statesman inside the Empire had to be left behind. He never revealed his newly acquired title to the Ottoman chiefs. He feared they would never respect the title, and it would cause an uproar that he had no time to deal with. He just wanted his position as *Neggur* to be accepted on revelation. But he knew it would cause a revival of century-long feuds and councils. Guyotta would let his dreams go. He would inform Aguyan after the day's meeting and audit that the original plan should be taken up once again. It was time for Company Boss Nasir ibn Sa'ad al-Din Sa'ood to reunite with his father.

A servant knocked on Guyotta's door. The Regent Master turned from the balcony, walked inside his private quarters and called for the servant to enter. The doors opened and the servant informed Guyotta that Nasir had arrived, waiting in the council chamber on the first floor. Guyotta thanked the man and allowed the servant to escort him to the room where Nasir waited. The Regent Master was taken off guard when he saw that Nasir was alone, save his close servant al-Jeheuty Anhur Has. The lawyer Wakil al-Hakam and Taran Zaher were nowhere to be found. The fact that the two Moors were dressed equally also caught Guyotta by surprise.

The two young Moors were dressed in fine black suits, the coats of which were sewn with gold-colored buttons. Black turbans adorned their heads. Both young men bowed at the neck toward the Regent Master. Guyotta apologized that the other company heads had not yet arrived. Nasir retorted that Wakil and Taran would also be late, but that business should commence before their arrival. Guyotta was shaken again. Nasir's voice commanded such authority that it rattled Guyotta like an unexpected roll of thunder.

Guyotta took a seat. Nasir joined him at the table. Al-Jeheuty presented the Regent Master with a parchment and then stood in the corner behind Guyotta. The Regent Master opened the parchment and inspected the eastern trade route etched on its face. Guyotta smiled. He was now relieved. The plan to shuffle all of The Four Winds' tributes to Asia could now take place. Nasir would be dead in two weeks. The Regent Master jumped from his seat and happily charged the young Company Boss who stood to meet him. Guyotta threw his arms around Nasir and kissed his cheeks. He said a thankful prayer aloud and then both he and Nasir returned to their seats. *This will be a great meeting. This will be a day long remembered.* Guyotta clapped his hands together and sat back, proud.

The Regent Master's life came to an end with the flash of al-

Jeheuty's pistol.

The shot entered the back of Guyotta's head, tearing through the bundled fabrics of his turban. Guyotta's face smacked the table in front of him, landing atop the opened parchment. The rebel lieutenant shot the Regent Master with a second pistol, at close range, through the back of the neck. Al-Jeheuty put both pistols on the table, removed a dagger, and shoved it into Guyotta's back. Al-Jeheuty, finished with the deed, took a seat next to Nasir.

Two days ago.

The morning breeze was suddenly intruded on and colonized by the sun's hazy and humid offspring. The air became thick, and traffic inside al-Gherab was sluggish in its response to the morning atmosphere. Even Al-Kasim Askari Pasha moved slowly. His servants kept a quick step in their movements as they dressed and groomed their Pasha, but they too moved at a slower pace than normal.

This was not how al-Kasim Askari Pasha wanted to start his travels, though he hoped the sluggish atmosphere actually slowed the travel between al-Gherab and al-Mari Ifriq. He was not looking forward to his meeting with Guyotta Sahin-el Bey. Al-Gherab was losing earnings. It had been at a ceasefire with the al-Jasi tribe. The remnants of the Moorish urban center had abandoned their city of origin. Al-Kasim Askari Pasha's scouts noticed the disappearing population within the urban center coincided with the increase of the al-Jasi population. Trains of black Moors were being led out en masse, joining the ranks of their people that lay north of al-Gherab. Al-Kasim Askari Pasha lost money with every departing refugee. He could no longer turn a profit from slave trading.

He needed a war.

He needed an excuse.

Al-Kasim Askari Pasha's merchandise was not missing.

It just moved to another area.

Al-Kasim Askari Pasha was going to push for the use of the weaponry that The Four Winds had given him. His argument would be that his government was noticing an increase in al-Jasi activity at the northern borders. Al-Kasim Askari Pasha was ready to argue just cause in striking first with his weaponry before the al-Jasi made a strike with their growing numbers. He wanted to explain this to The Four Winds. Presenting his ambitions were the only thing that inspired him to make the grueling journey to al-Mari Ifriq.

Five al-Mari Ifriq ambassadors resided in al-Gherab. They waited for the Pasha just outside the palace gates. Each of them was aware of al-Kasim Askari Pasha's push to use Guyotta's granted weapons. The ambassadors were uneasy. War had the potential to erupt between al-Gherab and al-Mari Ifriq if these talks did not end well. Al-Kasim Askari Pasha was weary too. He did not want to waste time squaring off with Guyotta's troops, or lose an ally. This was about money. War was just a necessity.

Al-Kasim Askari Pasha, primped and ready, stepped away from his servants and out of his dressing room. Personal travel assistants and eleven guards quickly flanked him as he left the dressing room. The Pasha's wives, maidens, palace servants, and brother-in-law met him in the palace's grand hall. Al-Kasim Askari Pasha was kissed and wished safe travel. He reminded his brother-in-law of specific governing duties while away, and then the pasha walked from the palace interior and out into the front courtyard. The five al-Mari Ifriq ambassadors waited patiently. Eibib Oba was one of the ambassadors. Ojodo's uncle was tall and dark, with thin straight locks draping past his shoulders. Eibib's visage had a thick mustache and groomed beard. His face was triangular, with sharp features and an aquiline nose. He wore the long, flowing robes of a politician, which were a far cry from the merchant rags he was fond of. He bowed toward the Pasha, as did the other ambassadors.

Al-Kasim Askari Pasha greeted the ambassadors warmly. He shook each of their hands and waved for them to walk beyond the palace gates to their curtained coaches. All the elected statesmen moved out of the courtyard and onto the main road that acted as a wide alleyway. The most expensive houses and apartment complexes were on either side of the road leading from the palace.

The five ambassadors waited for al-Kasim Askari Pasha to slip into his coach. Eibib quickly inspected the Pasha's ride. His eyes went straight to the rear axels, catching a glimpse of two hard, leather-seamed sacks, three inches in circumference. The leather-seamed sacks dangled from two strings that wrapped around the back axel and extended to the front axel.

Eibib moved away from al-Kasim Askari Pasha's carriage. He took a quick glance up at the city rooftops and then, with two of the Turkish ambassadors from al-Mari Ifriq, entered a second carriage. The other two ambassadors accompanied al-Kasim Askari Pasha. Eibib took a deep breath.

Camelmen and foot soldiers moved into formation. Al-Kasim Askari Pasha's carriage moved forward to carry him to the northside of town. He would greet the cheers of his people before exiting the city and substituting his transport with four wheels for one with four legs.

The carriage jerked to life. The movement of the front axel caused the attached strings to wrap around. The leather-seamed balls rotated along the back axel, being caught on the underside of the carriage compartment. Something broke from each of the leather-seamed balls, and dropped onto the road. There was a flicker, a spark.

Eibib took another deep breath. The Moorish Ambassador exhaled and held onto the carriage's door just before Al-Kasim Askari Pasha's vehicle flashed violently, the leather-seamed bombs strapped underneath exploding wildly. The force of the erupting gunpowder launched the coach high into the air, flipping it over. The carriage crashed onto the strong, Arabian steeds attached to it, crushing riders, mounts, and the burning bodies of the Pasha and two al-Mari Ifriq ambassadors inside.

Men, masked and robed, appeared on several apartment rooftops. The men aimed muskets toward the traveling entourage and opened fire. A salvo of bullets ripped through the unsuspecting troops. Camelmen, camels, and foot soldiers dropped to the road, dead or severely wounded. Some of the Pasha's soldiers ducked into houses or apartment complexes to escape the barrage of bullets. The Pasha's guards tried to return pistol fire, but their aim was wild.

Eibib and the remaining ambassadors sat still. They were too nervous to move.

There was screaming outside.

Flames from the burning carriage whipped at the air.

Musket fire cracked like lightning, and then the shots started to cease.

The curtain was ripped from the carriage. Eight robed and masked men stood outside. The men were equipped with muskets and short swords. The closest man grabbed Eibib and hauled him from the vehicle. He tossed the merchant-made-ambassador into the grip of two other masked men. Three soldiers removed pistols and fired into the Turkish ambassadors' chests. The first man jumped into the carriage, removed a dagger, and stabbed each ambassador twice in their abdomens, assuring the ambassadors' deaths. The man reached into his robe and removed two leather-seamed sacks. He tore off the tops and dropped them. He darted from the carriage just as a spark erupted from the bombs. He joined his fellow attackers in an alley, Eibib their captive.

The second carriage burst into fire.

The remaining soldiers from the caravan stepped out from hiding.

Fires raged in the middle of the road. Burning flesh perfumed the humid air.

The soldiers inspected the damage.

No attacker was found. The only evidence of their appearance was the damage lying in the middle of the street. Their attackers' weapons were left behind. Muskets and swords were left on rooftops where the attackers had struck. Pistols, daggers, and more muskets lay in alleyways. The mark was a success. The troops were enraged at their failure to protect their city's leader against the attack.

Now.

Mehit al-Tarqiyya's bathhouse was impressive. The money Mehit generated went back into the architecture of the establishment. The property was now two stories, and no longer had the feel of a storage house, from which it was redesigned. The second floor, which surrounded and overlooked a long rectangular courtyard, accommodated private quarters, exclusive rooms used for pampering the women patrons. The rooms were designated for massage, cleanses, facials, and hair treatments.

Each room was decorated with flora and fauna, hosting exotic, wild plants that snaked up the walls from their pots. Imported caged birds whistled and hummed, and female musicians strummed sweet music from stringed instruments. The rooms were also adorned with long cushions for massage, and elaborate chairs that made each woman patron feel like a queen serviced in her own fantastical sovereignty. Incense burners lay on shelves, smoking and populating the rooms with heavenly sweet and spicy fragrances. Sconces lined the walls in each room. Some of the rooms were purposefully designed without a window. Lit candles shimmered brightly, illuminating the windowless rooms in a cinnamon-orange colored aura that relaxed each of Mehit's clients, and made them feel as if they were levitating or floating on a heavenly cloud.

Columns holding up arched areas created the hallway for the second floor that overlooked the courtyard below. At the far end of the hallway were three diamond-shaped, stained-glass windows. Light poured into the multicolored windows, bathing the interior with a rainbow of celestial design and radiance. The midday sun also crashed in from above. The roof had a large glass opening, to which the sun's light could be invited to illuminate the courtyard.

In the courtyard was a running fountain that had an incense bass and a tiled floor with intricate orange, brown, blue, and white patterns. The tile was cut out in a large circular pattern going around the running fountain and surrounding soil, where budding up from the earth was blossoming, scented flowers and wild grass. The fountain was connected to a timed mechanism that allowed the water to flow when the greenery was in need of watering. The first floor was also where the large, steaming bathrooms could be found. There was also a kitchen built into the bathhouse, to serve the patrons any food ordered.

Hyle Tecer, the paunchy and lecherous accountant from The Four Winds Company, was the only stain that marked such a perfect picture. Five guards accompanied Hyle. Mehit's business was shutdown an hour before the accountant and his entourage arrived. The place was emptied of the women patrons—for whom it was built exclusively—and Mehit and her staff worked diligently to prepare the place for the bookkeeper's arrival.

Hyle and his company people would only stay for two hours. It was the worst two hours Mehit's business experienced. The serene ambiance was grossly disturbed with sounds of haughty, drunken laughter and singing. Ale and acrid wines attacked the aroma of fresh juices. Rooms were left with filth, food, and sour smells. Women screamed or wept as Hyle and his soldiers had their way with them. Mehit's dream was so quick to become a nightmare. Hyle's two-hour presence took three hours to clean.

Today, the young executive woman was more embarrassed by the circumstances. Roberto Hamaat's mistress, Ilindia Kali, a woman she greatly respected for her knowledge in women's care, and superb dancing and entertaining abilities, had finally come to visit and inspect Mehit's business. Mehit wanted so much for Mistress Kali to examine her practice, but not today. However, when Ilindia Kali expressed interest, Mehit could not turn her away. She was a beautifully aged woman whose looks and perfect physical design could smother a woman half her age, and she possessed a smile that—though it relaxed Mehit's worries—seemed naïve to the affect Hyle's presence would have on the day's activities. Mehit tried to warn her about Hyle's advances. Ilindia assured Mehit there would be no problems, she even volunteered to dance for the companyman, training Hyle's favorite, Aludra, two days before his arrival. Mehit was nervous. Roberto Hamaat was rumored to be the leader of a gang, continuing to police the city with his own form of justice, long after being dismissed from the duty of Chief Officer. Should his mistress be mistreated, Mehit feared the potential violence that would follow.

Mehit greeted Hyle and his entourage at the courtyard. She welcomed the accountant with all the skill and grace that her abilities as a hostess could muster. Being in the presence of the accountant, and restraining from breaking down and crying—or even from breaking down into a violent rage against the companyman—took so much energy from

Mehit. She bowed respectfully toward Hyle. The accountant smiled warmly and patted Mehit on the head. He looked around at the finished interior of her bathhouse and inhaled the swirling, natural fragrances in the air.

"Magnificent," Hyle exclaimed.

Mehit thanked him. The maidens surrounding Mehit courteously removed Hyle and his party of any heavy equipment. They kept their swords, however. Muskets and heavy coats were removed. Mehit motioned for Hyle and his soldiers to follow her to the largest steam-room. Mehit opened the doors to a splendid room. Heat had not been applied to the room as of yet. Ilindia and Aludra occupied the open area, waiting to perform for the companyman and the soldiers. A female guitarist waited patiently for her cue to begin playing. All three women wore thin, shimmering veils and blue dresses woven from a light fabric that created the illusion that the women were clothed in a heavenly fog.

Hyle was immediately drawn to Ilindia's physique. Her hips curved and sloped in such an illustrious and hypnotic manner, even when still. Her movement, when walking, was so rhythmic, she seemed to always be in dance. Mehit guided the accountant and soldiers to a bench on the opposite end of the room, sat them down, and wished them well with their entertainment. Servants brought wine and glasses to Hyle and his party. Mehit bowed toward the men and left the room. The door closed. The sunlight illuminated the entire room through the window. Mehit's heart raced. She believed that Ilindia did not know what she was stepping into. Ilindia would never return, her skills forever out of reach. Mehit pushed the thought away. She went to the kitchen to oversee the accountant's meal.

The performance began with magic, according to the Four Winds official. Hyle thought that Ilindia must have used the moment where Mehit dismissed herself to lie out a long purple rug, for he had not seen the action, though clearly it had been performed. She and Aludra stood side-by-side on the purple carpet. "Remember what I taught you, child," said Ilindia.

Aludra nodded her head. The two women jumped into their routine, undulating and oscillating sensuously. Hyle gasped. He always had an eye for Mistress Kali. She was wonderful. Her movement was like fire and water, waves and flame swirling together. Her body was like a tongue licking his senses. But his attention was quickly diverted to Aludra as Ilindia stepped back and let the young woman take the forefront.

Hyle was infatuated all over again. He gasped as Aludra twirled. He tried to take a sip of his glass of wine. His hands trembled, most of the wine ending up on his robes than in his mouth. Hyle's body quivered as Aludra twirled more and more. The ecstasy the woman stirred inside Hyle choked the accountant. He could not wait to grab the young woman and devour her like a well-cooked meal. His eyes, for an instant, spotted Ilindia. What he would love to do with those hips. Roberto's mistress knew how to move. He would not care of the consequences of Roberto's actions after ravaging Ilindia. The Satanic thug no longer held power, Hyle thought to himself. Roberto was no longer Police Chief. Hyle's attention was focused on Ilindia. She must have taught Aludra, thought the accountant. Hyle planned to go back and forth between the two. He would even invite the female guitarist to join them.

The lecherous accountant observed Aludra again. She danced closer and closer, twirling around and around. She was bewitching, magnetic. Aludra was so enticing that Hyle did not see the sly movement of the sharp dagger removed from her sleeve, even as it gleamed in the sunlight. When Hyle did notice the dagger, he thought it part of the routine. He joked to his soldiers that he loved a woman with fight. The accountant was so aloof, the heavy sips of wine starting to take effect, he failed to consider Aludra's stab in his direction as an attack. He was quite aware, however, when he felt the dagger enter his groin. His eyes went wide! His mouth opened to scream, but Aludra was swift in removing the dagger and slicing its blade across the fat, lecherous man's neck.

Hyle's body dropped onto the purple carpet, bleeding. The soldiers quickly sobered. Ilindia, still dancing, tossed small daggers at them. The guitarist did the same, continuing her music without missing a single note. The five soldiers dropped, piling dead near Hyle's corpse.

The two women finished their dance and faced one another. The music stopped. Ilindia removed Aludra's veil. She took the dagger from the weeping young woman and asked, "Are you alright, child?"

Aludra threw her arms around Ilindia and addressed, "Yes, Mistress Ilindia Kali." Aludra's tears stopped.

Ilindia held Aludra close, like a mother holding her child. Aludra was going to make a wonderful addition to The Seventy-Two Points of the Universe.

Aguyan's voice sounded like a cannon blast, quickly capturing the attention of the laborers working diligently within the Sa'ood Company storage house. Aguyan was furious. His mounting impatience was with a fellow companyman rather than the low-class workers he was about to take his frustrations out on. Hyle Tecer was late, as usual. Aguyan knew the lecherous accountant was going to be drunk whenever he did show up. He would have to keep a close eye on the count, making sure everything was precise.

Aguyan called for another check on the time. Ojodo jumped to attention and answered the irate lawyer. The Moorish titan figured the lawyer would dare not say much to him. Aguyan knew Ojodo as Ambassador Eibib's nephew, though, according to the lawyer, the merchant-turned-ambassador had been kidnapped days earlier. Ojodo was also confident in his size to cool Aguyan's temperament. Aguyan did relax, but when he spoke it was rough. He asked to inspect the week's shipments before Hyle arrived. Ojodo bowed at the neck. He and Rahmis took the lawyer's side and walked him through several rooms inside the large storage space. Aguyan commanded his eight guards to stay outside and watch for Hyle Tecer's approach.

Aguyan kept close count of the crates. Each wooden container was opened on command. Aguyan made a mental note of each prize: spices, gems, precious stones, goods, wines, and cloths. The lawyer then barked an order to see the items ready for export. Ojodo and Rahmis hesitated, giving one another a look that was none-too-inconspicuous. Aguyan tapped his foot and yelled his command again. Ojodo stepped forward, confessing that not much export was leaving the warehouse. Rahmis included that there was also more import to explore. Aguyan did not care. He insisted on seeing what little export was being shipped. The two men bowed and promptly led Aguyan to a small room with only four boxes. Aguyan shook his head. "This will have to be noted," he spoke to the two men. He sighed and took a step forward to inspect the contents.

It was then that Roberto Hamaat made his entrance. The bulky assassin called to Aguyan, as respectfully as possible. The lawyer pivoted, scowling as he faced the assassin. Roberto walked forward and pleaded, "I've paid an excellent sum for an old friend's company to help me out. Company Boss Nasir is getting rid of some items for me."

Aguyan's lip curled into a fiendish smile. "Should the law not see these contents?" The lawyer chuckled. "Hashish is illegal. Your coven knows better."

Roberto looked genuinely offended. He stood straight and proclaimed, "My circle doesn't use such a drug for our rituals." However, for recreational use was a different matter.

"So the whispers are true," Aguyan taunted. "Is your clan as deadly as they say?"

"I lead a group of people that study a deep form of ancient, spiritual science," Roberto retorted.

"We shall see." Aguyan turned toward Ojodo and commanded the giant to open the first large crate. "This is evidence, Reverend Hamaat. Don't move. My guards are right outside. Companyman Hyle Tecer will arrive soon with an armed entourage. Then we will take you to Tous Zeki. Our Army Official has been waiting a long time to catch you, Minister Hamaat." Ojodo opened the first crate. Aguyan peered inside and found nothing. He sneered and returned to his former disposition. "The next," he shouted to Ojodo. The large Moor opened the second box. Aguyan looked inside. His heart stopped, and his eyes went wide with horror.

Army Official Tous Zeki lay inside. His body was riddled with bullets and stab wounds. The site grabbed Aguyan by the collar and shook him like a treacherous cutpurse looking for spare coin. Aguyan gasped in quick breaths. His body trembled. His mind started to race. Aguyan tried to center on any thought just so the room would cease to spin. He focused on a motive for Tous Zeki's slaying, and on a time when the captain of the Green Army might have been slain. Tous was supposed to meet with Captain Sunwil this morning at the lodge outside the city. The wounds looked fresh. Aguyan silently accused Roberto Hamaat of the deed. He played out the scenario of Roberto's 'satanic' gang ambushing the Army Official and his soldiers right outside the city. The lawyer's judgment, however, was completely inaccurate.

Captain Sunwil and soldiers from his crew were the assassins.

Aguyan turned to face Roberto. The old assassin reacted quickly, removing a small knife and slamming it through the right side of Aguyan's neck. The tip of the blade passed through the lawyer's throat and broke through to the other side. Roberto, in the same swift motion, closed the lawyer's agape mouth, shut his eyes, and pushed him into an empty wooden crate.

Ojodo sealed the box.

Roberto asked if his mistress had brought the body of Hyle Tecer. Rahmis acknowledged that she had. The accountant was resting in one of the three large wooden crates. The portly assassin then informed the two men that Aguyan's soldiers had been dispatched. "We'll all meet here when this is finished. Bo Yusuf should be back with your uncle soon." Roberto opened the crate furthest from the right. It was empty. "Al-Jeheuty and Company Boss Nasir are conducting a final meeting with *former* Regent Master Guyotta Sahin. I'll see how that has concluded. My soldiers are already securing the palace perimeter."

Nasir ibn Sa'ad al-Din Sa'ood, company boss, sat with his hands on the table, fingers gripped around one another. He trembled with anger as he looked at Guyotta's dead body. His eyes watered. Al-Jeheuty palmed his friend's arm and consoled him. "It's over, and it's also just started."

Roberto Hamaat opened the door and informed the two men that the palace had been cleared. It was safe for Nasir to leave. Tegu joined Roberto to clean the council room and remove Guyotta's corpse. Al-Jeheuty escorted Nasir to a group of Roberto's assassins, and then the company boss was safely led home. Nasir greeted his mother and brother with open arms. Al-Jeheuty was dismissed. He ran to find Mehit. He was going to explain Mistress Kali's true intentions, and that her bathhouse, Aludra, and all the women who had been accosted, were now free. Roberto had already informed the young woman, however, when the assassin collected the body of Hyle Tecer and his soldiers.

Wakil, joined by Behar, counseled with Taran. The lawyer introduced the captain as the new Regent Master, and as the Beylerbey Neggur. Taran was made privy to the deaths of the city's governors. Wakil explained to Taran that Nasir lied to make Taran's actions with The Four Winds genuine. Taran accepted the explanation, feeling Nasir had acted no different than his father. However, the Moorish land baron instantly became nervous about his own life. His anxiety simmered down when it was explained that he was needed to help negotiate with the Turks. Of course, he was not aware that he was marked to die afterwards.

The company bosses from Ahangar and Ghanem met later that day at the Sa'ood company house with Behar, Wakil, Taran, and Nasir. Leaders from minor companies filtered through, bestowing presents at Behar's feet and kisses to his hand. He was now their chief boss, the governor-general. The Beylerbey. Guyotta's devilish reign with The Four Winds had come to an end. The Griffin Company won its first major battle.

Al-Mari Ifriq could breathe again and reach for the coastline.

Chapter Fourteen

Five sturdy merchant ships anchored in the Turkish harbor just as the sun locked into its highest position in the sky. The ships and the sun were like gears inside a mechanism, their movements acting as if dependent on one another. The small fleet's presence was imperial, captivating the Turkish citizens that stood in awe at the giant, magnificent wooden structures. The ships looked like floating cities from a distance. They carried an impressive ambiance that gave the illusion they were far greater in size than was the reality, though they were truly grand. The rhythms in which they rocked and coasted over the horizon, was part of the effect. Now docked, the five ships were like massive towers.

Hieremias Sunwil, the tall, imposing Blackamoor Captain, stepped out onto the deck of the middle ship. He was cloaked in a long black cape, brown baggy pants, a dark-green shirt, and a beige wrap encircling his head. A rapier was sheathed at his side. A dagger strapped to his belt, and musket worn on his back. Chief Officer Ras Ali, the bulky sun-colored Moor with short, curly hair, was close behind him. Two trumpeters flanked the officials. The two musicians walked past their captain and faced opposite directions. They blared a triumphant arrival on command of their captain.

Then opened the belly of the two outer ships stationed at either end of the fleet. A wide plank extended from the opened mouths of the ships, sliding with a smooth mechanical grace. Music sounded just as the planks slammed against the docks. Drums bombarded the air like cannon fire. The beat of the drums captured the rhythm of the Turkish citizens' hearts, and beat against their chests. More horns sounded, coming from two musical bands that disembarked from both ships. The music was festive, mixed with a declarative and militaristic sound. The musical Moors marched while playing songs inspired by Ottoman pieces, paying homage to the Turkish chiefs and sultanate. There were twenty-seven pieces that made the band. There were eight large drums, five kettledrums, ten bugles, two trumpets, and two pairs of cymbals. The large drums were called *davuls*, and they were played with the fingers. The kettledrums were named *nakkare*. The Moorish musicians reinvented the powerful euphonic rhythms of the Ottoman Janissary corps', strongly accented meter music.

This was meant with no disrespect, and was not perceived as such.

Mounted steeds followed the marching band. The train of horses dragged elaborately decorated wheeled cases that were encrusted with jewels on their colorful exterior design. The trunks held massive amounts of gold and silver coins, jewels, clothing, and spices. The two inner ships opened up and dropped plank. Moorish soldiers and officials stepped out from either ship, on cue of the cavalry's exit. Nasir, decked in expensive robes, stepped from the left ship. He was surrounded by a tidal wave of al-Jasi soldiers. From the right ship stepped forth Jabari al-Hakam. He too was escorted by a flock of soldiers consisting of al-Jasi Moors. Wakil's son had recently taken on his father's responsibilities within the Griffin Company, in addition to sitting on the judicial council that governed al-Mari Ifriq. Wakil currently saw to the duties that accompanied his new role as regional governor.

Laith al-Hakam, Wakil's eldest son, returned to al-Mari Ifriq with his family. Laith left the city when he was old enough, despising the rule of the Turks. He had not left on good terms with his father, either. Laith al-Hakam was enraged that men as strong and as rough as his father, Sa'ad, and Taran did nothing to stop the Turkish incursion. He returned, however, proud, and lending his skills as an accountant to manage the money flowing within al-Mari Ifriq's stable economy. He also managed the loans given out by the Governor and Beylerbey. He first asked for his father's forgiveness, which Wakil graciously extended. He also admitted, now being older, and as a father and husband, he understood why direct war was not always a viable option for even the toughest of men.

A fleet of steeds, dragging wheeled trunks filled with precious items, followed the exit of the two officials. Then the middle ship opened. The music's rhythm quickened, calling attention to the arrival of the new Chief Boss of al-Mari Ifriq. Beylerbey Ameer Las El-Behar's entourage shuffled into the flow of the Moorish parade. There were numerous servants, guards, dancing harem girls, and captured European Christian slaves. Taran walked onto the plank, followed by another sea of soldiers. In the middle of the mass of soldiers was Beylerbey Ameer Las El-Behar. He was not hoisted inside a canopied carriage, lifted by servants or elephant. Beylerbey Ameer Las El-Behar walked inside the protection of soldiers. The Turkish citizens bubbled over one another to gaze at the man referred to as *The Iron Moor*. Behar was what the citizens had expected. Visually, he was a venerable and tough, rugged General wrapped in the noble robes of a king or statesmen. He looked dangerous and honorable, an admirable mix. Behar was part of the mystery and rumor surrounding the disappearance of Guyotta Sahin-el Bey and the other three Turkish heads of The Four

Winds. The beige, brown, and even a small population of black Turks that welcomed the foreign troupe looked to find answers by simply gazing upon the mysterious Moors.

Word spread rapidly throughout Odongo-Mauharim in the months following the death of The Four Winds' heads. No one knew what to believe. Al-Mari Ifriq and surrounding territory was renamed *The Griffin Regency*. The declaration made by new rulers, most specifically the Beylerbey named Ameer Las El-Behar. The disappearance of The Four Winds, and former Regent Master Guyotta Sahin-el Bey, was shrouded in mystery, rumor, and conspiracy theory.

The consensus, however, was that the Turkish heads of The Four Winds were killed by desert marauders while they secretly moved hordes of gold, silver, and precious gems through an eastern trade route. The death of The Four Winds exposed company and government corruption. The tight grip Guyotta held on al-Mari Ifriq, bleeding the city dry, was not the greatest news of deceit, however. The harsh taxing laws that deteriorated al-Mari Ifriq's social and economic infrastructure were also not the most rattling news of duplicity. The four large treasuries, hoarding every ounce of tax money, contraband, and plundered booty that was hidden underneath the palace, was what left people in awe. None of this money was being sent as tribute to the ruling chiefs and sultanate in Turkey.

The Four Winds' defiance shocked every tribe, small state, and kingdom residing inside Odongo-Mauharim, and even those outside its borders. The citizens of al-Mari Ifriq, the Djenhai kingdom, and nomadic tribes that received word of the news, were worried about receiving the punishment of their former rulers' behavior. So much wealth was hoarded that it could have been split up among the entire region of Odongo-Mauharim, paid for tribute, and given to Sale, Tunis, and Algiers, with a generous amount left over for other corsair-states to profit.

The story of The Four Winds' treachery reached across the sea into European states. France, the Netherlands, Spain, Portugal, Italy, and other surrounding European nations were talking. The states receiving paid protection from al-Mari Ifriq's corsair ships declined further services out of fear of war. Mediterranean trade routes had been abandoned for arduous and old-fashioned passages on land. The sea became active with brutal corsairs and privateers sorting out ethnic and nationalist disputes on the Mediterranean. The fear gripping the European nations came from understanding that the news of The Four Winds' death bounced all the way to the ruling courts of the Turkish chiefs who were furious and ready to take swift action.

The crookedness of The Four Winds did not shake the Turkish chiefs. The chiefs' blood boiled from the persistent rumors of rebellion and assassination that sprang up after the disappearance of The Four Winds. The rumors were loud and vocal among the faraway ruling Turks, and were allowed to fester for two years as Ameer Las El-Behar, the ruling Beylerbey, steered the city away from the brink of economic and social collapse. Al-Mari Ifriq's current rulers were protected from the troubles stirring within the Ottoman Empire and their new Sultan, Ibriham I, an eccentric ruler secretly dubbed *The Mad Sultan.*

However, an army in search of the truth behind the disappearance of The Four Winds' company officials was prepared to take hold of al-Mari Ifriq. Company Boss Feroz Aunun docked in Turkish waters and held council with the chiefs and sultanate before any such action could be taken. The chiefs' anger was quelled. The army was called off.

Feroz returned to al-Mari Ifriq with a message for its new rulers. The message called for al-Mari Ifriq's current Beylerbey, Ameer Las El-Behar, Taran Zaher, and Company Boss Nasir al-Din Sa'ood's presence in Turkey. None of the men felt easy about the meeting. Jabari al-Hakam, on Behar's orders, accompanied the three men.

Behar's lieutenants were instructed to remain in al-Mari Ifriq and attend to assigned tasks. Al-Jeheuty was given permission to leave the city to seek his family in Morocco. The company lieutenant's twin brother, Aatif Anhur Has, had business ties with the French. The Griffin Company wanted to curb French intrusion, controlling the nation's growing activities along Africa-west and Africa-north. Al-Jeheuty's intensions also were to bring French coin back into al-Mari Ifriq's economy. Hopefully the French could be persuaded to travel its old trade routes while under the protection of the Griffin Regency. Ojodo continued his duties at the docks, assisting his uncle and Zakiy Sa'ood. Rahmis teamed with Roberto Hamaat, introducing law in the city and its ports. Bo Yusuf helped Captain Sunwil reorganize the Council of Captains and create a brilliant naval army, overseen by him in the captain's absence.

Currently, Hieremias Sunwil watched the march of al-Mari Ifriq's ruling Moors strut through the Turkish streets. The Turkish citizens received them well. The captain believed that Sultan Ibriham would do the same. However, there was a plan concocted for immediate escape, had this all been a trap. There were more troops hidden in the belly of each ship. Roberto Hamaat's assassins were hidden among the personal guards, harem girls, servants, and musicians marching in the street. Cannons were at the ready to provide a shield if the ships needed to make a quick disembark.

Ras Ali stepped away from the deck to oversee the backup plan, if needed.

Company Boss Nasir ibn Sa'ad al-Din Sa'ood admired the marvelous Turkish city and its citizens that resonated in varying shades and colors. The city was steeped in domed citadels and towering structures that blended elegantly to the open sky above. Nasir was relaxed, smiling and waving to the welcoming citizens. This was not the war he expected. None of the officials expected this. Only Taran continued to shake. His eyes scanned the crowd, looking for any of the official divan or statesmen positioned in the Sultan's cabinet. More specifically, Taran looked for Aguyan's brother, al-Rinak Ozan. But al-Rinak was not the official that met the grand parade, steering them to the domed palace at the far end of the city.

The impressive parade broke in half. Some of the soldiers and musicians returned to the five ships, while the others continued forward. The palace gates opened to an elaborate courtyard. Fountains and natural springs sparkled brilliantly. The spouting water reflected the sun's rays and cast the illusion that the fountains and springs were filled with wine. There were large trees bearing fruits, and gardeners harvesting the bounty. Arches and columns lined a paved pathway to the palace opening. Councilmen waiting for Beylerbey Ameer Las El-Behar and his entourage currently blocked the pathway. Al-Rinak Ozan was among the Sultan's divan council members waiting for the parade of Moors.

Taran spotted him immediately.

Al-Rinak was in his late forties, and he was darker in color than his brother Aguyan. The two men were, in truth, only half brothers. Al-Rinak's father was a black Turk. His mother was Soudanese. The Statesman had an odd silvery, metallic tone that resonated in his flesh. His face was rectangular, much like his hulking frame that supported wide shoulders. He had sharp facial features, aquiline, allowing many to incorrectly conclude that he was a very dark-skinned Turk. Al-Rinak's tight curly hair was hidden beneath a white turban, and his face was beset in a white hood that his turban wrapped around.

Al-Rinak closely inspected the Beylerbey's arrival. He spotted each of the high officials among the parade, guessing correctly that Behar was the Beylerbey. Behar's position among the entourage, centered, and his fine robes and age gave him away. Nasir and Jabari dressed as officials, but al-Rinak was not interested in their specific roles. He assessed the young officials and then moved his gaze to spot Taran. Al-Rinak smiled slyly at the sight of the Moorish Commissioner of Foreign Affairs. The black Turk had plans to isolate Taran. Al-Mari Ifriq's Commissioner of Foreign Affairs was the key to finding out the truth about his brother's death.

Statesman Sinan Demir greeted the cavalcade upon its entrance. The other councilmen gathered in a horseshoe formation behind him. Behar's entourage parted, allowing the Beylerbey to step forward. Sinan respectfully bowed in Behar's presence, and the Statesman addressed him by his title and full name. Behar cordially bowed back, greeting the Statesman in the Turkish language, which impressed Sinan. He spoke about being honored by Behar's presence and waved a hand toward the palace entrance.

Behar waved the comment aside and spoke through a jovial chuckle, "I'm sure the Sultan and his state are more honored by the booty I bring him." Sinan and the other statesmen politely returned a chuckle. Behar followed his jest with an apology and confession. "I am excited to be here. I am thrilled to be conducting a civil meeting. A pall smothers our homeland. Al-Mari Ifriq, and all of Odongo-Mauharim, shakes with fear at the possibility of an occupied police state or a great war."

The officials were separated from the tribute-laden trunks and the musicians. Only personal servants and guards enclosed Nasir, Jabari, Taran, and Behar. The rest of the entourage was escorted to waiting chambers. Sinan and the other statesmen understood that the Christian slaves and trunks of goods were gifts of tribute. The remaining statesmen introduced themselves, and Behar expressed his deepest condolences to al-Rinak on the loss of his brother Aguyan. Behar knew, under counsel with Wakil, that Taran and al-Rinak had ties to one another.

Sinan then steered the conversation back to Behar's last comments about the Turkish army occupying al-Mari Ifriq under a police state. "I can assure you that nothing of such nature can be expected," Sinan said humbly as he escorted Behar's remaining fleet into the luxurious palace, leading then to a large banquet chamber. "I will be the representative for these affairs. Sultan Ibriham is reorganizing his administrative cabinet. His introduction to the position of Sultan has been…trying. His assigned duties are taking him around the country." Behar's expression melted into concern. Sinan believed that the Beylerbey was offended and quickly assured him, "A decision on the affairs of al-Mari Ifriq has been made." Sinan's confidence in leading the affairs quickly dissolved. He turned to al-Rinak, who stepped up to answer the concerns painted on Behar's visage.

Al-Rinak put a hand against his chest and said, "I have lost too much in al-Mari Ifriq." Al-Rinak's voice was raspy, sounding like the strange mix of five voices echoing eerily through an ice tunnel. "The disturbance of raiders striking my brother and his partners pains me. I know too that my brother was distressed by the corruption he witnessed Guyotta Sahin-el Bey commit. I received letters the last month of his rule. There were plans to arrest Guyotta once the treasury was emptied and shipped," al-Rinak lied. "He had to be caught in the act. Tragic. Plus, this misfortune comes at a time when our country, politically, is overwhelmed." He stepped to Behar and said in a gentle voice, "Al-Mari Ifriq is granted a state of semi-independence."

"Semi-independence?" questioned Taran.

Behar saw his musicians take the stage along with the Turkish band. Dancing women and servant girls and boys entered the banquet chamber. The Beylerbey paid closer attention to al-Rinak and Taran, making sure no subtle gestures or signals were exchanged.

"We hold a company there," said al-Rinak. "We wish to oversee our company without asserting any power into local politics. Our nation's rightful earning is what concerns us."

Behar shot a glance to Jabari al-Hakam. The Beylerbey was upset. Al-Rinak took notice that Behar was rattled, but he also observed that the Chief Boss was well prepared with soldiers of law, word, and sword surrounding him. He knew to whom to turn. Al-Rinak deduced that Behar's greatest strategy was to know his resources.

The young law bearer stepped forward, but before he spoke Behar lifted an authoritative hand and commanded, "I understand that this banquet, and all the festivities that it hosts, are to welcome us from such a long travel by sea. However, business seems to be at the forefront of all our minds. Let this be an after party celebration."

The authority in Behar's voice demanded respect. Within the instant the command was suggested, Sinan and al-Rinak bowed at the request, and then fulfilled it by leading all the officials to a grand, circular council room that had pillars creating a circle within a circle. One statesman stayed behind, attending to the musicians, servant boys and girls, and dancing women.

Large chairs with cushions provided seating. Sinan commanded two servants to fetch refreshments and water. The statesman then seated the four Moorish officials, and he, al-Rinak, and the other Turkish council members took seats. Behar looked at Jabari and waved his hand for the young lawyer to speak. "The Ghanem Company, to which I am sure you are referring—" the councilmen nodded affirmatively, "—is under strict law of al-Mari Ifriq. The company's current head, Feroz Aunun, has stated that he will give full control of the company to the Djenhai kingdom should anything happen to him. Your direct involvement would be a conflict of interest."

"Was the Empire's continued claim in Ghanem discussed with Feroz prior to our visit?" asked Behar.

Sinan smiled and admitted, "No, but we feel that our proposition is fair considering the amount of money we have lost in our investment in al-Mari Ifriq."

"We have returned a great deal of wealth to you and your Sultan," insisted Behar.

Sinan smiled again and cleared his throat. "We don't believe that makes up for the loss. Not every slice of bread stolen from us has been returned, nor do we expect such. But what this comes down to is that al-Mari Ifriq has committed great offense in the eyes of its protectorate."

Behar sat up straight. His demeanor lost all the jovial cadences he displayed earlier. Sinan remained motionless, fearing Behar would call for a sudden attack to wipe out all of the Turkish officials in the room. Al-Rinak did not let Behar's manner affect him this time. He would not diffuse his assertiveness, though he did not wish to match Behar's emphatic behavior.

Behar's eyes locked onto Sinan so heavy the statesman felt as if the Beylerbey had placed a tight grip around his neck. Behar cleared his throat and spoke with intense conviction, "The offenses committed to this state were committed in al-Mari Ifriq. Yes. I agree to that. However, the offenses were not committed *by* al-Mari Ifriq. At the risk of committing an offense to the Turkish state at present, may I remind you the offense came from your own chiefs that were bleeding both your state *and* the citizens of al-Mari Ifriq? Conspirators have been rounded up and executed for the deaths of the heads of The Four Winds Company. And I say this next statement with no slight to the Turkish council before me, but I am being something that your own people were not to you. Courteous."

Silence.

Servants entered the room and poured each official a cup of water.

The servants were quickly dismissed after leaving a plate of refreshments.

Taran decided to speak as an attempt to reduce tension. He put his cup down and said, "How long do you feel a withdrawal of Turkish forces will take? There are, after all, troops still occupying al-Mari Ifriq. They seem to be waiting for an order. They hold a civil form of disobedience. They respect the new leadership in the city. But they will not take orders to leave from anyone but a Turkish official."

Al-Rinak lifted a hand, stopping Sinan who was about to speak. "I will arrive in three months from your departure. Feroz informed me that your city needs more time to recover. I will withdraw the remaining troops over a month's time after I arrive, even while overseeing business inside the Ghanem Company. I would like to enforce the fact that we do have investments within that maritime business. The Turkish Sultanate relinquishes control and protectorate status over al-Mari Ifriq, but—and with no disrespect to you Beylerbey Ameer—we cannot relinquish all of what continues to bring in revenue. We will abide by your city's rules. We will not interfere in affairs, nor ask for any voice or say in local government."

Behar was still. He said calmly, "Feroz has a voice in affairs. However, he is considered a citizen. The decisions he makes effects the city."

"And the Persians who own a company do not return revenue back to their homeland," Taran interrupted, much to the chagrin of the Beylerbey. "Nor will the French."

The last comment made Behar furious. He now considered it a mistake to leave Taran alive. Nasir too re-imagined the attack on The Four Winds heads, conjuring up wishful images of Taran being silenced as well. Behar cursed himself. The governing Sultanate, his chiefs, and divan were not as stable as many believed. The power that threatened al-Mari Ifriq was in complete disarray. The Griffin Company could have done without Taran's voice. Behar considered his next objective, killing Taran and placing al-Jeheuty as Commissioner of Foreign Affairs.

"The French?" questioned Sinan. The other officials looked just as perplexed, save al-Rinak, who looked slightly perturbed. His annoyance was a ruse, however. Taran was communicating to him plans for the Griffin Company and regency. Al-Rinak was actually most joyous. His suspicions now had some confirmation. These Moors had a hand in his brother's death.

"The French are making bold hits on corsair-states," spoke Behar, trying to calm his anger at Taran. "They have become very destructive on their push to intrude on African-north affairs. We are making a strategic move to invite them in and curb the attacks before they reach al-Mari Ifriq. We hope to gain allies from other states in the process. By subduing the attacks we can all keep a fair coin in our purse." Behar took a deep breath and steered the conversation back to the Ghanem Company. "The French will have no voice either. And, as I was saying, if Feroz was to bow down or an unfortunate circumstance take shape, power will be transferred to the Djenhai kingdom. The Turkish state will be like a silent partner." Behar's tone was quiet but threatening.

Al-Rinak wanted to smile. The Turkish state would be silent as the Beylerbey called for. Al-Rinak had plans to make a lot of noise, however. He believed the rumors that whispered tales of revolution against his brother Aguyan and Guyotta Sahin-El Bey. Turkish ambassadors were killed. A Moorish ambassador kidnapped, with ransom paid. An Arab Pasha from a partnered corsair-state was assassinated. No Moor was scathed. And conveniently, these Moors took power. Al-Rinak may have shared lineage and blood with these Moors by way of his mother from Africa, and the blackness of his father, but they were not his family. Aguyan and he had plans to take al-Mari Ifriq. These Moors interfered. Money. Power. Family. That was al-Rinak's prayer that put him to sleep every night. But, fifteen years of plotting and speaking his sacred prayer were washed away in several months. This was the very reason al-Rinak was not a religious man.

Al-Rinak took a sip of water. "Our current Sultan is insane," he confessed, much to Sinan's surprise. Al-Rinak chuckled. "We're trying to hide the fact, surrounding that half-Greek bastard with the correct divan. People believe that our nation is absolutely no threat because of Sultan Ibriham. So, please, give us five coins from your rich stock, Beylerbey. A state that once threatened to burn your city to ash, is now bowing humbly before your presence. I ask for enough of a voice to shield us from our enemies."

Everyone looked at Behar, who answered, "Your voice will count after your troops have been withdrawn, and it can be made void by either the dominant voice of the company boss or the ruling Djenhai official."

"Great," Sinan said as if exhaling. "We shall stay informed through Taran, your Commissioner of Foreign Affairs. We elect al-Rinak as our Ambassador of Company Affairs in Africa-north."

"Oh, I hate that," said Behar with a slight smile. "He sure knows how to speak." The officials laughed, and they were unaware that Behar included Taran in his sentiments. "I should've brought my great negotiator, al-Jeheuty Anhur Has."

Sinan stood up. "Well, bad for you that he was not here, and bad for him to miss this celebration. Come." The Moors and Turks rose from their seats. Sinan suggested that Behar and his entourage be escorted to their private chambers, and encouraged they primp themselves before returning to the banquet hall. Behar agreed. He, Nasir, Jabari, and Taran needed time to rest before entering into a loud celebration with wine, food, song, dance, and extravagant display. Palace servants took each of the Moorish officials to private guest chambers. Taran waited anxiously for al-Rinak to meet him. He needed to know what the Turkish council-member was thinking. Did al-Rinak suspect that the Moors he now counseled with were involved in his brother's death? If so, was retaliation planned? And most of all, if al-Rinak believed any of this, and if retaliation was planned, Taran needed to assure the black Turkish official that he was completely innocent in the death of the heads of The Four Winds.

But while Taran paced in his private guest quarters, al-Rinak attended to the other Turkish officials, conferring with Sinan that the negotiations with the Moorish officials had gone well. Al-Rinak did not communicate with Taran until two hours before the ceremony. He sent a note expressing that their time to counsel would come soon. The note also revealed that al-Rinak believed Behar had eyes watching Taran closely. An attempt to speak to him would endanger any plans al-Rinak possessed. The note was hidden inside a formal invitation that marked the new time of the ceremony. Behar, Nasir, and Jabari had each received an invitation. This move would cover suspicions that any contact was made between Taran and al-Rinak, or any of the Turkish councilmen.

Behar and the other Moorish officials, along with their personal servants, were summoned an hour after sundown. A palace servant arrived at their door, as stated in their invitations. Behar converged with Nasir, Jabari, and Taran while being escorted from the second floor guest chambers. The Moorish entourage was led from the second floor back to the banquet hall. The Moorish and Turkish band blazed the hall with music as the officials entered through the large doors. The dancing girls gyrated and twisted elegantly in rhythm of the music. The company of Moors was greeted by Sinan, al-Rinak, and the other Turkish statesmen. Nasir and Jabari, young and with spirit, stepped into the festivities in order to capture a young woman for the night.

Behar stayed close to Taran, keeping al-Rinak from stealing a moment alone with the land baron. The councilman stayed close too, so as not to allow Behar a moment to chastise Taran for speaking about company plans. He had an eye watching Behar's chambers. The Beylerbey did not exit his guest room. Al-Rinak knew that he had not scolded Taran as of yet. He probably was waiting for their departure, so as not to make a scene while on foreign soil.

The three men joked and laughed as if friends. Underneath the laughter rotated the gears and machinations of murder to gain ground or cover tracks. But the faux-jovial festivities could not last forever.

Al-Rinak made a move, simply calling a servant to summon his mistress, Melusina Augyal. She entered the room and quickly captured the attention of all the men that were present. The young French-Turkish beauty had long, black hair. She was slender and sensual; her features were very striking. The young winsome woman was light solidified in the flesh. Her skin gleamed like the moon when resonating against a clear, celestial night. Al-Rinak introduced his lover and called for drinks. Melusina disappeared and returned later with three cups filled with an imported French wine.

Behar's drink was drugged. The drink was so sweet to the taste that Behar did not mind having a second. Though Behar was careful not to get carried away, he did not know he had been given a tainted cup. The dissolved powder took its effect within thirty minutes.

A dizzying sensation slowly crawled over Behar, like a spider ensnaring its prey. Behar complimented al-Rinak that the wine was too much even for him. He took a seat and asked for water, which he received quickly. Nasir and Jabari took time to attend to their Beylerbey, but Behar waved them away and back to their festivities. "Too much drink for my head to handle at the moment." The water only stirred the drug in his system. Sleepiness was the next sense Behar perceived. Eventually, both his personal servants and palace servants took Behar to his guest quarters. Nasir and Jabari continued to frolic with the dancing girls. There was no complete need to worry. Awa stayed close to Taran, even following his master's movements as he slipped into a corner with al-Rinak. The councilman, with a sly smile, called for Taran to come to his quarters for counsel. Taran instructed Awa to follow.

Awa was surprised when he was not told to wait outside while al-Rinak and Taran counseled. Melusina stayed close to al-Rinak, acting as more a servant than lover. But the young woman was al-Rinak's diabolical angel. Al-Rinak took another sip and instructed his lover, "Prepare a third cup. This is too much not to share, even among servants." Melusina prepared a third cup and offered it to Awa. The disguised assassin refused. "Ah. It is too much to ignore. Your lord will not protest, will you Taran?"

Taran smiled warmly. "We've traveled too far. Let us loosen up. Even our Chief Boss lay drunk, probably with a woman in either arm. Drink Awa."

The old assassin took the offered drink and then took a sip. Awa said a final occult prayer just as the drink slipped down his throat. The small sip turned into a giant gulp. *Here's to the light of life, and the beauty of the dark beyond*, thought the assassin, *to the Great Mother*.

Awa's drink was tainted with a lethal dose. The poison was not immediate. The invisible grip that attacked Awa's heart was not even that painful because of his training. The old Moor's throat constricted. He wanted to scream at Taran that the Griffin Company was aware of his betrayal. He wanted to scream that Taran was marked for death. He could've fought against the constricting, but Awa was too loyal to the Griffin Company. Why would he actually reveal company secrets?

Awa slumped to his death, his vision blurry then black.

Al-Rinak kissed Melusina deeply. The young French-Turkish woman pulled away and smiled at al-Rinak. "I am French. I am Turkish. Which part of me do you wish to lay with tonight?"

"Surprise me," whispered al-Rinak. Melusina ducked out of the room. Al-Rinak turned to Taran who was inspecting his cup closely. Al-Rinak stepped next to the land baron. "Where is our servant that was assigned to you?"

"Killed…" Taran answered.

"And then you received this man?" al-Rinak chuckled. He then said in a stern voice, "They do not trust you. Believe my words, you have been marked. I can only guess that your survival most likely depended on business with the Empire. I will do all in my power from stopping them carrying out the mark against you." Al-Rinak looked down at Awa's corpse. "I'll have your 'servant' placed outside your Beylerbey's guest quarters. You will sleep in a chair inside the room. When your Beylerbey wakes in the morning tell him that you watched him carefully the whole night. He will not suspect that we counseled. This old man, that now lies dead before us, well…he simply had an old heart. Poor old fool." Taran put down his cup. "I don't need the details, Taran. Just answer my suspicions. Did these Moors revolt against The Four Winds? Did they kill my brother?" Taran nodded, yes. "This country is dying," said al-Rinak as he rolled his eyes. "The power the Ottomans had is being challenged. I will make my claim on my mother's homeland. Al-Mari Ifriq will see many storms."

Chapter Fifteen

The caravan, grand and majestic with steeds, curtain-draped coaches hoisted atop elephants, marching soldiers, musicians, and cavalry mounted on camels, paraded into Nusurika, a small town located a few miles inside the Moroccan border. The people flocked to get a glimpse of the cavalcade that had been announced by a traveling messenger from Odongo-Mauharim to arrive later this very day. The streets of the small and prosperous town were respectfully cleared of traffic. Behind the awe and excitement, there was still a great deal of mystery surrounding the caravan's appearance. No manner of reason was given for the visit. No name or title of the visitor was released.

There was one among the crowd that had the answer. He watched the caravan with subdued enthusiasm, his eyes taking quick glances at the crowd to judge their excitement level. The Moor, of average height, had brown skin, a thick beard, and wild hair. His clothes blended the style of a businessman and evangelist. This Moor stared at the caravan with an interest as great as the crowd's, though he did not show it. Inside, there was an intense longing that had been aroused by feelings to possess the audience's attention with a caravan just as great. Aatif Anhur Has could not bring himself to be proud of his fraternal twin brother, al-Jeheuty, the distinguished commander of the admired, marching fleet.

Aatif sifted through the crowd, making his way down the street, following the caravan's route to the town square. He managed to get ahead of the caravan, entering the crowded square, where he regrouped with his parents. He whispered to his mother, Jawhara Anhur Has that the caravan was approaching. Sakeen Anhur Has, Aatif's father, stepped forward, raising a curious eye toward the street's horizon. The elder Moor's face, a burnishing amber color, was hidden behind a white bushel of hair from his thick beard, to thick eyebrows, to the thick, domed and curled hairstyle hidden beneath the turban atop his head.

Aatif glanced at his father. His inspection was in the same manner as when he inspected the crowd earlier. Aatif could see that his father was not as impressed as the gathered townsfolk. Sakeen Anhur Has was anxious, and hovering emotionally between the feelings of relief and anger toward his returning son.

Al-Jeheuty was continuously leaving and returning over the last six years. Much time had passed since al-Jeheuty left for the world as a graduated student. Sakeen and Jawhara believed their son was intelligent but without focus, and unfortunately armed with a great deal of mischief coupled with the wrong friends. Al-Jeheuty wanted to travel, to see the world. Sakeen and Jawhara relied on Aatif's business associates for information about their son. Information returned, notifying Sakeen and Jawhara that their son was working a legitimate job with a French company that shipped fruit around the Mediterranean islands. Aatif was unable to find the exact position al-Jeheuty played in the company. He was just a menial worker, however. Then word came that the company had trouble. Many workers voluntarily left. Al-Jeheuty's name was present, and at the forefront of trouble. Sakeen's son came to visit, saying that he was seeking refuge in Spain, joining a militia of Moors. He confessed to his parents that his previous employer was involved with financing routes for the African slave trade, profiting from the ugly ordeal.

Sakeen and Jawhara were furious. Sakeen thought his son should not have gotten involved with idealistic crusades staged by revolutionaries. He did not hold to his son's ideals, believing he should have stayed close to home. Al-Jeheuty left Nusurika an unfocused but brilliant student, according to his parents. He came and went. The last time he visited he was as an outlaw. Now he returned again. His parents thought perhaps he was now a prince.

The soldiers and musicians moved around the square, making way for the three large elephants that carried coaches atop their backs. The beasts' handlers made gentle hand gestures that made the large behemoths bend at the knees and lay flat against the ground. The handlers fed the beasts. The music ceased and the crowd waited in anticipation. Even the town governor was still. Servants placed against the elephants mobile stages that were equipped with stairs. The town provided the stages.

The compartment's curtain opened wide. A woman issued from the carriage. She was dark, beautiful, and curvaceous. Her movement was elegant, royal, and like the soft tides sweeping onto the shores.

Mehit al-Tarqiyya Zaher, dressed in a grand headpiece and exquisite violet, silk dress-robe, received the hand of a servant, and was guided to the front of the mobile stage. The same servant stepped down one stair and announced, "Al-Mari Ifriq presents to the town of Nusurika, an Ambassador of Exchange. Nusurika's former resident. Al-Jeheuty Anhur Has."

The name echoed in each of the citizens' mind. Sakeen and Jawhara could feel the heat of stares suddenly fall upon them. Here returned the son of the town lawyer and his wife, the doctor with her nursery and midwifery business. Sakeen and Jawhara smiled to keep appearances. Al-Jeheuty appeared from the carriage. He was decked in three gold chains, a black suit with billowing pants, gold colored buttons on his tunic, and a blue sash around his waist. His long locks were wrapped in a blue cloth. Al-Jeheuty took Mehit's hand and descended the stage. There was no applause, just curious silence. Al-Jeheuty's face was complete business. He motioned for the town governor and asked for the streets to stay clear as he made his way to his house by steed. The governor complied with the request.

Town guards surrounded al-Jeheuty's family and guided them to their son. Jawhara quickly embraced her son, kissing his cheek. Al-Jeheuty returned the favor to his mother. He introduced Jawhara to Mehit. He turned to his brother, leaned in for an embrace, and said into Aatif's ear, "I've come to counsel with you, my twin." Al-Jeheuty left his brother's embrace and stood before his father.

The elder Anhur Has looked his son up and down, put his eyes on Mehit then returned his gaze to his son. He did not smile. He extended a hand and asked, "Have you become royalty?"

Al-Jeheuty laughed. "Far from it. I'm a businessman, and to some degree, a politician."

"Politics *is* business," said Aatif sharply, but with a smile.

"Political business that should not be conducted in the streets," retorted al-Jeheuty, "We're not thugs." Al-Jeheuty gestured toward the elephant behind him. Jawhara protested. "Ma-ma," al-Jeheuty said trying not to break a cool composure. "Would you prefer a steed?"

"I'd prefer to walk," insisted Jawhara with a nervous chuckle. "It's just a couple blocks. How do you think I got here?"

"*Ma-ma,*" al-Jeheuty said with a boyish smile. Mehit enjoyed the exchange between mother and son. Al-Jeheuty was a soldier, a revolutionary. Mehit could only imagine the acts her man had committed or seen while staging insurrections in Spain. He was a man that made decisions on whether men lived or died, and often got his hands bloody with the murderous deed. Still, al-Jeheuty was not immune to the bickering of his mother. No man was.

Sakeen stepped into the conversation and consoled his wife. "It will be alright, Jawhara."

Jawhara looked at her husband, inspecting him as if he had just gone mad. "It may be alright for *you*. I am *not* traveling on that beast." There was light chuckling coming from the audience of townsfolk.

Sakeen did not show the level of embarrassment he was feeling. He nervously laughed aside his emotions. Sakeen and al-Jeheuty locked eyes and smirked. Al-Jeheuty pointed toward Mehit and said, "She's much the same way. Is this what I have to look forward to?" Sakeen erupted in laughter, but not from his son's gesture, but from Mehit's sharp gaze in his direction.

"You're in trouble now, my son," exclaimed Sakeen as he volleyed laughter from his gut.

Mehit then smirked. The tension between the father and the son had been diffused. Al-Jeheuty looked back at his father and voiced, "I guess no religion can tame the spirit of a woman. So much for the religious law the two of you swears by." Al-Jeheuty pointed to his brother and father.

Sakeen added with laughter, "Men use the Word of God to keep sane in the presence of those who swallowed the apple first."

Then your God is not perfect, thought Jawhara. Her sentiments were echoed in a soft smile and a roll of her eyes at her husband.

"Business," said Aatif, breaking into the enthusiasm.

Al-Jeheuty nodded. He looked at his mother, mocking a child's innocent stare to plead to a parent. Jawhara huffed, smiled, and kissed her boy on the cheek. She yielded and asked, "Which one of these beasts do I jump into?"

Mehit took Jawhara's hand and guided her to the stairs. "This way, Ma-Ma Anhur Has."

Jawhara beamed thankfully at the young woman and started up the stairs. Servants quickly swarmed them. Guards from al-Jeheuty's entourage, coupled with town police, began to disperse the crowd. There was no incident as the gathered townspeople filtered back to their daily lives on command of the two troupes of official soldiers. Three strong steeds were brought to al-Jeheuty. The Ambassador gestured for his father and brother to mount two of the steeds. The gentlemen jumped to their mounts while al-Jeheuty conversed with the town's governor. Aatif inspected his brother's interaction with the governor. He raised an eyebrow as he watched al-Jeheuty receive a firm handshake from the governor. Aatif gave a quick glance to his father. There was a smile on Sakeen's face. Al-Jeheuty's father looked more relieved that his son was fine than prideful in his formidable position.

Al-Jeheuty finished his small talk with the governor, speaking about his troops being stationed outside town before he journeyed back to al-Mari Ifriq. Then came a small joke, prompting the governor to laugh and pat al-Jeheuty's shoulder in a friendly manner. Then he returned to the steed prepared for him and mounted the horse. He watched the elephant handlers guide the beast carrying Mehit and Jawhara, keeping the creature calm and steady as some of the cavalry forces surrounded it. The other elephants, along with the remaining caravan guards and musicians, spirited away to the outskirts of town. Al-Jeheuty led the rest of his entourage down the street to the house he once lived in as a boy.

"Forgive this grand entrance," he explained to his father and brother. "It was the idea of a friend. He is of noble blood, going back to al-Andalusia. I met him in Spain."

"So he too is a revolutionary," questioned Aatif, a sly smile on his face. He looked at their father to see how he reacted to the question. Sakeen did not flinch. He kept his eyes on al-Jeheuty who did not take his brother's verbal bait.

"He is an excellent city host," remarked al-Jeheuty, continuing to speak about Rahmis Husani. "He knows how to make all of the citizens comfortable, and all our visiting travelers feel welcome."

"And what is it that you do, brother?" Aatif asked.

"I negotiate trade and the taxes for trade routes," al-Jeheuty answered quickly. "I'll speak more on that matter when we reach our house. Do you still live at home?" he asked his brother.

"No," Aatif answered. "I live in an apartment complex on the governor's block, located near his residence. The money I've brought to our town has rewarded me the perks of working closely with our local government."

"That's what I wanted to hear," said al-Jeheuty.

"Is that your wife that you've returned with," Sakeen asked his son. His voice was stern.

Al-Jeheuty knew that he would be struck down if Mehit turned out to be his wife. His father would be murderous if no proper ceremony was involved, nor his family invited. Luckily that was not the case. "No, pa-pa," al-Jeheuty coolly answered, as if his worries about his father's potentially rough retaliation had not manifested. "I am still courting her, though a legal union is planned. She is the daughter of al-Mari Ifriq's Commissioner of Foreign Affairs. He's also a landowner." Al-Jeheuty hoped that mentioning Taran's title would help resonate a positive judgment on Mehit. "We are building two massive forts on some of the land he owns. Tall, giant towers equipped with cannons and the best spyglasses to overlook the sea."

Sakeen was impressed, but he had another question. "Will she be your only wife?"

Al-Jeheuty smiled boyishly toward his father and answered, "You know us Anhur Has men. We choose that one special woman that acts as many."

"Sounds like someone doesn't bring in enough coin to care for more than one wife," chuckled Aatif.

"Does Khaira live with you?" al-Jeheuty retorted sharply.

Aatif hesitated. He felt his heart jump with a sharp sting. He exhaled and exclaimed with a forced smile, "She is affianced to a Frenchman. He is a business associate of mine. I introduced the two of them."

Al-Jeheuty heard his brother's words breaking. It was subtle. Aatif was hurt. But al-Jeheuty was caught in the moment. He quickly made his brother's pain the topic of ridicule. "So you don't even have enough coin to keep the possibility of a *first* wife." He regretted his words the moment they were spoken. The jarring, emotional pain that instantly stabbed Aatif, and cut his sharp tongue into silence, also penetrated al-Jeheuty. He did not address the sharp look his father sent him. He also found himself at a stalemate to express regret for his words, feeling that acknowledging his words, even regretfully, would stab his brother even harder. Al-Jeheuty could not take his words back. They had to be swept away and ignored.

Al-Jeheuty's breach of manners silenced his conversation with his father. His thoughts then turned to Mehit and his mother. He hoped the two women were becoming acquainted with one another, and to what would have been to his great enjoyment the two women were getting along wonderfully.

Jawhara and Mehit conversed about one another's business. Jawhara was delighted that Mehit invested in a bathhouse for women. She encouraged the young woman to seek scholarship in medicine and massage therapy. Mehit listened closely as Jawhara enlightened her on how this would certify her business. Jawhara made it a point not to be too preachy while instructing Mehit to seek further education. She also did not want to insult the enormous accomplishment already gained by the young woman. She considered the woman in front of her the very reason why her son was on the right path.

Jawhara was as encouraging as she set out to be. Mehit considered al-Jeheuty's mother a breath of fresh air. She was nothing like al-Jeheuty described. Al-Jeheuty was most dear to Mehit, however, the manner in which he obsessed over the acceptance of his family, and the affect of their flaws on him, took their toll on her. He spoke constantly since they left al-Mari Ifriq about the grand backstory of his childhood. His parents, together, were very demanding. Al-Jeheuty described his father as too bold, hard as stone, and just as hard to impress. He said his mother was just never satisfied. Nothing was good enough.

Al-Jeheuty's intelligence was not fit for simple business. Sakeen and Jawhara understood that about their son, though they did not accept it. Al-Jeheuty felt tremendous scrutiny coming from his mother and father. To al-Jeheuty's belief, his parents close inspection of his strategic intellect revealed to them that he was a blackguard, a charismatic miscreant. Al-Jeheuty considered himself more honorable than just blindly offering his intellect to people he considered unworthy. He believed his parents felt that he could've been a great General commanding a legitimate army. However, there was no army to serve in the small town of Nusurika. Being part of the town police and guard would not suffice. Al-Jeheuty considered some crimes justifiable. He and his father debated at great lengths about such issues. This excited Sakeen, as he believed al-Jeheuty would consider studying law and continue the lawyer line. But al-Jeheuty believed people that became lawyers gave up too much time, reason, self-respect, conscience, and spiritual essence.

Sakeen and Jawhara thought al-Jeheuty would join a military service in a prominent city, their hopes he would become a great General resurrected. But, al-Jeheuty regarded joining an army in the name of God an abuse of a higher power's words. Just cause is what inspired al-Jeheuty's intelligence. If al-Jeheuty were to serve an army, it would be a band of outlaws bent on revolution. If he were to find a business for which his work and intellect could earn a wage, then it would be a corsair-state that would stimulate his strategic, blackguard reasoning. Ameer Las El-Behar's personal war in Spain provided sanctuary for al-Jeheuty from the minor wrongdoings committed against powerful businesses engaged in slave trades and piracy against African states.

Aatif Anhur Has was the complete opposite, according to al-Jeheuty. Mehit was informed that al-Jeheuty's twin used his intellect to please his parents, mostly in the name of making al-Jeheuty look bad. Aatif did not let pass any opportunity to outshine his twin. Aatif was praised, even for the reprehensible act for which al-Jeheuty considered him no longer a brother.

Aatif Anhur Has was an evangelist, both Christian and Mohammedan. His step toward religion was, according to al-Jeheuty, an attempt to appease their parents. Aatif was ordained a Man of God in both faiths. He then set out to spread the *Words* of God to various African kingdoms. But Aatif's benefactor was neither church nor mosque. He worked for the Dutch, the French, and tawny Arabs. Aatif received large sums of money for converting any African nation, kingdom, or tribe to Christianity or Mohammedanism. He received an even greater sum for the nation, kingdom, or tribe's enslavement. His game was simple. He helped tawny Arabs convert African kingdoms to Mohammedanism. These kingdoms would then fall under Arabian jurisdiction and Mohammedan Law. Citizens became slaves. Kings disappeared or renounced their kingship to foreigners. Black queens bore half-Arabian children. The royal bloodline passed through to them. Too young to rule, a tawny Arab would take control of the regency. More and more Africans were swept into slavery.

Converting African kingdoms to Christianity on the command of the Dutch or French resulted in the kingdoms turning against small nomadic nations. The 'wild heathen tribes' were subdued with advanced weaponry provided by either the French or the Dutch. Aatif was the middleman. The Christian African kingdoms would then battle the Mohammedan African kingdoms. Each African kingdom fought for Europe under the banner of Christianity, or fought for the tawny Arab under the banner of Mohammedanism. The losing kingdom, weakened, was enslaved.

Aatif collected coin regardless of which African kingdom prevailed. He received praise for giving a great deal of his wealth back to Nusurika. No one was aware of how Aatif made his money. Aatif was considered a businessman, dealing with the Dutch and French to import supplies to African kingdoms and nomadic nations.

Al-Jeheuty learned of his brother's exploits from a drunken Frenchman while staying in a small French hamlet. The inebriated Frenchman worked for the French company connected to Aatif, and was actually tasked to find al-Jeheuty. His family wanted to know how he was doing. Al-Jeheuty turned the tide. He bought several rounds of beer for the Frenchman, getting him drunk and pulling a great deal of information about Aatif's exploits. Al-Jeheuty wondered how the Frenchman knew to find him at this particular location. Then he realized the Frenchman worked for a business connected to his employer, Phineas Broadwood, a Jewish merchant with a business that imported and exported fruits across the Mediterranean and Europe. It wasn't long before the Frenchman confirmed that Phineas Broadwood was trafficking more than fruit. He also earned coin setting up routes for the purpose of trafficking African slaves.

The story saddened Mehit. Having heard the story multiple times, coupled with al-Jeheuty's worry about his family's response to his return, exhausted her emotionally. For the moment, al-Jeheuty's mother was pleasant company. Jawhara Anhur Has only became rattled when the elephant and coach made unsuspected moves. Both women would laugh during these moments. Mehit was use to the slight jerks, having traveled for several days inside the mounted compartment. Jawhara's smile was refreshing. Her full, red lips resonated brilliantly against her cinnamon colored skin. Mehit could see al-Jeheuty inside his mother's face. Her face too was triangular, more full with age. The two were definitely mother and son. Mehit could also deduce as to why Sakeen fell in love with her. Jawhara's eyes were hypnotic.

Their conversation was then steered to Mehit's relationship with al-Jeheuty. The questions were not too probing, and eventually Jawhara changed the focus of her questions to her son's work. Mehit described al-Jeheuty's duties within the political infrastructure of al-Mari Ifriq as a negotiator, an ambassador. She did not speak about how the city's government was organized. That bit of information would have rattled Jawhara, quickly causing her to understand that her son was involved with a corsair-state. But, she already suspected, considering the news leaking from Odongo-Mauharim and its prominent city, al-Mari Ifriq. Jawhara was even bold enough to ask, "Has there been great turmoil in al-Mari Ifriq? There has been news that its leaders were assassinated two years ago. I had no idea al-Jeheuty was there. We believed he had been killed in Spain." She whispered when she spoke.

"The death of our leaders did shake us as a people," Mehit said comfortingly. "However, their corruption was revealed. They were hoarding tribute money. Al-Mari Ifriq was on the verge of total Ottoman occupation. The governors were killed overseeing an escape route that was used to move vast trains of money from their treasury. This money was not given back to the Ottomans as tribute, and it was not put back into the welfare of the city. Al-Mari Ifriq is being restructured under the guidance of good men like your son. The last two years have been marvelous." Mehit made it a point to refer to al-Jeheuty as a man. She understood that it was hard for mothers to see their sons as such.

Jawhara sat back, relaxed by Mehit's words. Their journey ceased. The waving compartment settled as the elephant came to a stop. There was commotion outside. Mehit understood that it was just the servants and handlers readying the stage and stairs for her and Jawhara to step out on. The elephant lowered, shifting the compartment uncomfortably for Jawhara. She looked through the curtain to get a better view. She watched as the servants and handlers prepared the stairs and landing area. Two servants scaled the stage and then came to the coach, moving the curtain aside. They extended a hand to either woman and graciously helped them out of the coach, down the stairs, and to the street.

Jawhara cautiously walked away from the elephant, relieved that she was no longer being totted upon the beast's back. Al-Jeheuty dismounted from his steed and waited for Mehit to take her place two steps behind him as he walked inside his old home. Sakeen and Aatif followed. The servants and handlers steered the elephant and steeds to the outskirts of town where the rest of the caravan lay.

The Anhur Has home was an estate that opened to a small hallway, leading to a dining area. In the dining are was a door to a courtyard. Beyond the courtyard was a kitchen area and servant quarters. To the right were stairs leading to the second of three floors. Upstairs were three bedrooms. Al-Jeheuty and Aatif's bedroom had been converted to guest rooms. To the left of the entrance was a well decorated seating area; a room used to host guests and conversation. Sakeen Anhur Has' private study lay beyond a curtain. The keeper of the house, Saleema Thurayya, immediately greeted the party. She was a dark, venerable Moorish woman, and she was Jawhara's mother. Al-Jeheuty was very exited to see his grandmother, throwing his arms around her. He introduced Saleema to Mehit. "This is my grandma-ma. She is my mother's mother. This is a surprise."

Saleema was old, but there was a great deal of life in her. Mehit greeted her warmly, and the elder complimented her beauty. Saleema looked at al-Jeheuty and said, "Boy has got midnight in his life." She was referring to Mehit's dark tone. "That's what a good Moorish man needs. You got the whole universe's magic with this one."

"This from a woman that married a man as light as the desert," laughed al-Jeheuty.

"Bless him," Saleema spoke. "He was no tawny Moor. He was dark Africa, true. His heart was midnight and his skin was sunshine."

"That reminds me," began al-Jeheuty. "The Chief of the Guard, Roberto Hamaat. Grandma-ma, you would have wonderful conversations with him on magic and the black universe." He wiggled his fingers and made the sounds of a haunting ghost.

"I hear you make hell in Spain," Saleema continued as they all shuffled into the living room. "How have you earned such a royal suit?"

"I negotiate trade, grandma-ma," al-Jeheuty answered as he and Mehit removed their headpieces. "I've settled in Odongo-Mauharim in the city of al-Mari Ifriq." Al-Jeheuty and Mehit took seat on a large cushion. Sakeen and Jawhara placed themselves on the sofa, and Aatif sat in a large imported, Spanish chair.

Saleema was impressed, but expressed she had to return to the kitchen. "I hope you like lamb and vegetables, Mehit, because that's what I'm cooking."

Mehit laughed lightly at Saleema's assertiveness. "I don't mind at all, grandma-ma."

"I'll be back with some refreshments." Saleema left the room.

Al-Jeheuty looked at his parents and asked, "When did grandma-ma begin living here?"

"Three years ago," Jawhara answered. "She was staying with your uncle's family. She came here to relax. She decided to stay and help around the house. You know your uncle's kids are still young, running around. It's too much for her. It's quiet here. And she does not want to travel down to Mali to be with your other uncle and aunt. She does fine to keep the house while your father and I do our duties. She even helps me with midwife duties."

"Why are you so surprised," Aatif commented watching closely his brother's reaction. "Do you believe time stops when you leave? Or are you surprised because you come and go so frequently you forget when six years passes?"

Al-Jeheuty waved the comment away with a sly smile. "Is this revenge for the comment I made about Khaira?"

"Boys..." Sakeen growled threateningly.

Aatif just smiled. "Tell us more about your exploits running a corsair-state, as such are the politics in al-Mari Ifriq. Did your failed revolution in Spain turn its attention to the Ottoman leaders in the Odongo-Mauharim Regency?"

"Boys!" hollered Sakeen.

Silence.

Saleema entered the room with a tray of refreshments, bread, cheese, fruit, cups, and a jug of juice. She laid the tray on a table in the center of the room. Saleema left to attend to the final details of the meal she was preparing. Al-Jeheuty rose, walked to the table, and prepared a cup of juice for Mehit. He turned and presented the cup to the woman. He took a small plate from off the tray and scooped up different portions of refreshments, prepared a cup of juice for himself, and returned to the cushion. He took a sip and stared at his brother, there was a smile on his face. Aatif returned the smile and asked, "So tell us more about this corsair-state."

"Al-Mari Ifriq is a city that was unfortunately plagued with bad leadership," al-Jeheuty said nonchalantly. "I was lucky to escape Spain before another great slaughter of Moorish rebels occurred. My commander, three good friends, and myself joined a merchant company in al-Mari Ifriq. We are legit. The company's owner is the son of a friend of my commander. I presented my education; he invited me in as a negotiator. I helped restructure business to create revenue. The heads of the region were actually excited. Our plans brought them more money too. They died before they could enjoy the money, however. They were trying to make a break with all of the city's wealth."

Sakeen asked, "Are there suspects?"

"Members of a group of bandits have been rounded up. Supposedly they got word from a palace servant with loose lips. He spoke of the load of treasure being shipped through an eastern trade route. We don't believe they knew that the heads of the region would be personally overseeing that shipment on that day." Mehit watched al-Jeheuty tell the fabrication with such ease. She too almost believed the story, had she not been privy to the truth. "It's been scary," al-Jeheuty continued. "We've had to restructure the city's politics, get the trust of the citizens back, and quell the anger of the Ottomans."

"Do you believe there will be a fight to keep the city away from the Empire's hold?" Jawhara asked.

"The new Regent Master, along with the Commissioner of *Foreign Affairs*—Mehit's father—is on Ottoman soil conferencing with Turkish councilmen and state officials. I've heard that the Empire is adjusting to a new Sultan."

Sakeen smiled. He stood up, poured a drink for himself and took seat. He lifted his cup and said to his son, "I wish this was something with more strength than juice. I never thought I'd hear you speak on such politics, or be involved in them. We'll have something more fermented for dinner. But this is to you, my son, al-Jeheuty. To your success."

Al-Jeheuty lifted his cup toward his father. The two took a heavy gulp. Mehit smiled, relieved. She could only imagine the excitement al-Jeheuty was feeling. His father had accepted him. Al-Jeheuty lifted from the cushion, reached for Mehit, and lifted her to stand. "I'm going to show Mehit around the block. She can experience where I grew up. We'll return for the meal."

Al-Jeheuty and Mehit were excused. Sakeen, Jawhara, and Aatif walked the couple to the door. Al-Jeheuty stepped outside with Mehit and started down the road, pointing out alleyways and lots where he and Aatif played, schemed, and ran through the best and worst times growing up. Mehit expressed carefully that there was not as much tension between al-

Jeheuty and his parents as he had feared.

"My parents always wished the best for me," said al-Jeheuty, sounding apologetic. "I may have done things that, to them, appeared dangerous. But through all that, I wear the garments of a nobleman."

"Appear dangerous? Your exploits have been *completely* dangerous," Mehit made clear. "The stories of al-Mari Ifriq do scare your mother," Mehit revealed. "But, I gave her an appropriate story. She feels a little more relaxed. Your mother seemed to take a liking to me. She was suggesting I further my education to help my business."

"I can tell she's very excited about you," al-Jeheuty said with a smile. "She probably feels that you provide a solid foundation to keep me focused and grounded. She's right. Unfortunately, I offended my brother when making our way to the house. He tried to cut me with a comment. I retaliated and cut too deep with mine."

"Is that why he acts like an ass," Mehit said with a heavily disgusted tone in her voice. "He continuously asserts that al-Mari Ifriq is a corsair-state."

"My parents are smart," said al-Jeheuty. "Al-Mari Ifriq is the talk of the world right now because of what's happened in the passed two years."

"That's not the point," Mehit insisted. "There exists turmoil and strife throughout Africa. Your brother has an agenda to put you into a particular frame that your parents can scowl at like some indecent painting."

"Well, I came here to do business with him," al-Jeheuty reminded. "Hopefully that will please his ego, knowing that I need his help." Mehit rolled her eyes and scoffed. "Don't let my sibling rivalry become your fight," al-Jeheuty told her. "Though I do appreciate the support."

The couple spent more time walking through al-Jeheuty's old neighborhood. Al-Jeheuty narrated the tour, pointing out areas where childhood scenarios played out. They made their way back to the house half an hour later. Dinner was served upon return. Candles in chandeliers and oil lamps were lit. Saleema joined the meal as Sakeen Anhur Has made a toast with the proper fermented beverage. The Anhur Has family drank to al-Jeheuty's health.

The conversation at dinner was not marred by al-Jeheuty and Aatif's trite sibling rivalry. The two were very cordial to one another, which al-Jeheuty was quite thankful for. He guessed that his father may have reprimanded Aatif while he and Mehit walked the neighborhood. But that particular thought was not the truth. Regardless, al-Jeheuty did not care. Peace was all that mattered. He was also hoping it was an opportunity for he and his brother to talk business. He was pleasantly surprised when his brother asked to be excused so that the two of them could talk privately.

The dinner was finished. Mehit volunteered to help clean the dining area. Saleema accepted. Sakeen disappeared to his study to work on a town case. Jawhara went to check on a client to see how the newborn was coming along. Al-Jeheuty and Aatif stowed away to the second floor, residing in the space that was once Aatif's bedroom. Al-Jeheuty sat at a desk that faced the street at the front of the house. The sun's light flickered below the horizon. Aatif ignited a lamp hanging on the wall. Al-Jeheuty lit the lamp resting on the desk. Aatif shut the door. He turned back to his brother with a sly, proud smile on his face. "So," said al-Jeheuty's twin. "What does the pirate-son need from me?"

Al-Jeheuty rolled his eyes. "Our parents are not here, Aatif. You can accomplish nothing with such accusations. You may get me angry, however."

"I'm just teasing you, al-Jeheuty," Aatif laughed.

Al-Jeheuty again rolled his eyes as he scoffed, "I don't have time for this. We're not twelve." He stood up abruptly and made his way to the door. "It doesn't matter. I'll find someone else that can get me what I need from the French."

Aatif blocked his brother's way. Al-Jeheuty was surprised to look up and see his brother's face covered in anger. He stepped back. Aatif's eyes watered. "Do you really believe I was setting out to embarrass you in front of our parents?" Al-Jeheuty didn't answer his brother's question. Aatif stepped forward as al-Jeheuty rested back on the chair. "I *need* you to be a pirate. I *need* al-Mari Ifriq to be a corsair-state. I *need* to know that you have the power to command people to kill."

Aatif's determination was overwhelming.

"Brother, I…" Al-Jeheuty's voice trailed off.

"*And,* I need that more than you need my contacts with French businessmen to re-establish protected trade routes." Aatif noticed the brief flicker of surprise that appeared on al-Jeheuty's face. Aatif exhaled. His next words were spoken in a calmer manner. "Simon Beaumont, a powerful merchant, is trying to take French trade back to the Mediterranean. Land has become too cumbersome, time consuming, expensive, and dangerous. He deals with goods—legal and contraband. He does not deal with slavery, which I know you'd like to hear." Al-Jeheuty nodded his head slightly. "But even with his power, he is having a great deal of trouble convincing French nobles to trust the sea again. They only wish to cross the Atlantic." Aatif raised an eyebrow and a single finger before voicing, "Trust that the conspiracy theories that linger in the wake of al-Mari Ifriq's regent leaders' demise are believed far greater than any story about bandits having taken them down." Al-Jeheuty stayed completely silent, which said more to Aatif than a confession. Aatif even believed he witnessed a hint of a sly smile run across his brother's face. "What stops the French, and all the other European states, is the possible war at sea with the Ottomans. They believe the Empire will strike al-Mari Ifriq for the offense of killing their ambassadors."

"That is being settled at this very moment," al-Jeheuty said. "But, as much of a voice as I have, I cannot order the death of French nobles. I could not give such an order. I would not give such an order even if I was Regent Master. The French have been hitting Africa-north very hard as of late. It seems like they are on suicide missions. Many Moors, Arabs, and Turks are killed by these wild attacks. They are just as wild as the *razzias* the corsair-states run on coastal European towns."

"I would never ask you to engage in such a risky affair," Aatif assured. He took two, slow steps back, and then turned away from his brother. Aatif locked his hands behind his back and turned his head to speak, "Simon Beaumont and I have a common problem. That problem's name is Emile Raulf. He's a businessman. He profits from the lack of trade routes in the Mediterranean. And though his caravans are at times hit by bandits or find trouble with terrain, he makes a great deal of money. He blocks Simon Beaumont from putting trust back in sea trade. He also adds a great deal of friction to the growing fire of concern about Barbary war in the Mediterranean." He twirled around and confessed cryptically his disdain for Emile Raulf. "I don't admire his affinity for African Moorish women. One in particular, especially."

Al-Jeheuty blinked with surprise. "Khaira."

Aatif again looked hurt. He trembled when he walked. His words broke just the same. "Emile believes that he is entitled to everything. He takes what he wants. She's not even being prepared for marriage. She's his mistress. He offered me ten percent of his trade earnings…and he promised to leave Nusurika alone, not marked for enslavement. Khaira is a willing participant." Aatif cleared his throat. He let out a laugh that sounded like a sigh. "That isn't the big problem. This is not just about my ego over a woman. Not completely."

Al-Jeheuty was intrigued.

Aatif continued. "When Khaira gives birth, her child will not have an ounce of French blood. It will be all Moor. All Africa. All black." Aatif smiled guiltily. "Her and I have kept in touch." The two brothers spoke in unison—*"Literally."*

Al-Jeheuty lifted his shoulders and joked, "I don't know whether to curse you out or congratulate you."

"Just help me." Aatif knelt down in front of his brother and looked up at him. "You take Emile Raulf, and you will accomplish a trifecta. I get my fiancée and unborn child back. Simon Beaumont can re-establish trade by sea. You get to profit from the routes."

"And so do you," Al-Jeheuty said with stern authority. "You will cease with the evangelizing. Understood?" Aatif nodded. "You earn money from this. Work your angle with Simon Beaumont. I'll return to al-Mari Ifriq and work on marking Emile Raulf." The twins shook hands, finalizing their deal. Their handshake turned into a heartfelt hug.

Al-Jeheuty and his caravan marched away from Nusurika two days later, the rest of his stay having been tremendously cordial and pleasant between he and his family. The travel back to al-Mari Ifriq lasted three days. Al-Jeheuty and Mehit were welcomed home with a party hosted by Rahmis. Al-Jeheuty conveyed the news to his brothers-in-arms, Ojodo, Bo Yusuf, and Rahmis. Roberto Hamaat was summoned, and the mark against Emile Raulf was assigned.

Chapter Sixteen

The al-Hammon Palace vibrated with laughter, song, music, and tales. Rahmis Husani glided through the tavern beaming a smile at every patron. He overlooked the gambling and gaming activities, stopping to congratulate winners and wishing more luck to the runners-up. Chess, cards, and dice were used to settle national, ethnic, racial, or just piratical pride. Sea battles were often settled on land with a game. The true winners were the women working the *Psalace*, however. Most of the earned coin was tossed their way as they engaged in erotic dance and even more erotic favors in the backrooms. Drink enhanced the raucous clamor, but no man dared to step out of line with the city guards in attendance. *The al-Hammon Palace* was a new place.

Semi-respectable.

There was no way to completely stomp out the indelicate behavior of men who lived wild by land and sea. Behaviors typically demonstrated when attending a tavern could not be completely tamed, but the more violent and deadly drunken acts were curbed at *The al-Hammon Palace.*

Rahmis now had co-ownership of *The al-Hammon*, investing a large sum of his game earnings back into the tavern. This was his court, this princely Moor. The *Palace* was just one of his kingdoms, however. Rahmis was able to charismatically muscle his way into being the proprietor of three other places, a tavern and two inns. One inn was for weary maritime travelers. It was named *The Mermaid.* The second catered to the citizens of al-Mari Ifriq, especially the romantics and lovers. The inn was named *The Royal Highness*, and it was built to reflect the image of an al-Andalusian palace.

Rahmis' tavern was a sophisticated and civilized dive. It too hosted games, wine, dance, and musical entertainment, though it was never a lascivious place. *The Siren's Call*, as the tavern was named, hosted the greater gambling tournaments. Rahmis allowed Ojodo to host a night of poetry and sublime storytelling. *The Siren's Call* harkened back to the al-Andalusian nights, where gathered in the town square were the average citizen and noble aristocrat to express their poetry. The tavern was for the more upscale citizens of al-Mari Ifriq. It hosted the various company bosses, traveling traders, lawmakers, governors, the Beylerbey himself, and the average citizen who did not want to be caught up in the rambunctious activities of *The al-Hammon Palace*. The tavern also entertained private parties, one of which was thrown three nights ago, welcoming the return of al-Jeheuty Anhur Has from his hometown in Morocco.

Al-Jeheuty presently stole a few more hours with the woman he courted, the lovely Mehit al-Tarqiyya Zaher. The two lovers occupied *The Royal Highness Inn*. Mehit's father, Taran Zaher, was due to arrive later in the night, most likely an hour before dawn. He, Nasir al-Din Sa'ood, Jabari al-Hakam, and Beylerbey Ameer Las El-Behar were returning from Turkey. Rahmis allowed al-Jeheuty access to the finest suite *The Royal Highness* had to offer. Mehit might have been from a strict Mohammedan family, but no religion could halt the curiosity of a young man and young woman.

The primary stakeholders in *The al-Hammon Palace*, Maurice and Fusan al-Hammon, watched their patrons from a corner table that was shrouded in darkness. A single, jarred candle, situated atop their table, illuminated the corner. Its light made shadows of Maurice and Fusan, and the two lovely ladies who accompanied them.

The main attraction was the center table. Most of the patrons gathered around the card game that was currently in play. Rahmis kept his watchful gaze primarily on this table. It was becoming volatile. Ojodo and a European *renegado* named Kyler Piett traded playful, verbal jabs. Each man, while handling his cards against the other players, tried to see who could tell the bawdiest tale or joke. Bo Yusuf, also seated at the table and engaged in cards, did not appreciate Kyler Piett's presence. Kyler was a fourth stakeholder in *The al-Hammon Palace*, and a European convert to Mohammedanism. His conversion was in name only; he was far from a practicing Mohammedan. His partnership with the al-Hammon brothers was muted for the purpose of allowing him to participate in gaming. But his affiliation with the al-Hammon brothers, and investment in the *Palace*, did not earn him any form of favoritism. He lost just as much as he won. It was fair, which Kyler appreciated.

Kyler, though he was a renegado, had connections to Dutch merchants that made trade by sea. Al-Jeheuty allowed Kyler claim to *The al-Hammon Palace* on one condition: He wanted Kyler's connections to Dutch merchants. He also believed that Captain Piett would tame Fusan's reprehensible acts made at sea. Unfortunately, Kyler encouraged Fusan's pirating. The two even teamed up for several expeditions. Kyler and Fusan were as violent as any tempestuous sea storm.

Bo Yusuf did not like Kyler Piett. He still had not produced the Dutch traders, though the captain claimed to carry the message to his contacts about the offered protection on trade routes over the Mediterranean. The sea was still quiet with Dutch activity.

Kyler was producing even more tension at the moment. His humorous and raunchy tales consisted mostly of lewd triumphs on Moorish women. Bo Yusuf had enough when Kyler spoke, "All the brown races have phenomenal bitches." He waved his hand across the table, making a face. He then combed his blonde curls with his hand and carried on, "But there is nothing like the taste of a black, African cunt."

Bo Yusuf felt as if someone shook him violently. He spoke in a voice that showed he was clearly rattled. He asked as calmly as possible, "Is that why you would steal them from our towns back in al-Andalusian times?"

Kyler ignored Bo Yusuf's manner. He knew his words affected Bo Yusuf. Kyler had word that the Army Official did not like him. He took a sip of his liquor and continued to laugh. He went into his pocket and pulled out several coins. "I will not use these to toss into the pot," said Kyler. He called for his servant and dropped the coins into his hands. "Find me the blackest bitch to lay with." He pushed his verbal luck too far when he turned to Bo Yusuf and spoke with a sly smile, "Perhaps we'll have a pup your color, you tawny looking Moor."

Kyler was suddenly lying on the floor, unconscious. There were scars scratched onto the side of his face. Blood mixed with purple colored liquid. Shards of glass from the bottle broken across the renegado's head were clumped against his temple and outlining his head on the floor. Bo Yusuf stood over Kyler Piett, the neck of the broken bottle in his grip.

The music stopped abruptly.

The patrons were still.

Ojodo checked Kyler's body, finding him alive.

Rahmis hurried over to Bo Yusuf, arriving seconds ahead of an irate Fusan. Bo Yusuf's focus was on the heavy, Moorish pirate. He pointed the jagged edges of the broken bottle in his grip and asked, "I can use what's left on you."

Fusan's eyes went wide, his face showing his anger boiling. Rahmis put a hand on Bo Yusuf's shoulder and raised his other hand at the incoming Fusan. "Relax. Relax." Ojodo stood up, making his presence as imposing as possible. Ojodo was bigger than Fusan, but the burly pirate was far more ferocious. Rahmis looked at Ojodo and motioned for him to continue to look after the unconscious Piett. "Sit, Fusan. Sit. I'll take care of this." Rahmis watched nervously as Fusan backed away slowly. He turned and waved to a guard that was stationed at the door. The *Palace* guard rushed over to Rahmis and the tavern stakeholder pushed Bo Yusuf into his grip. "We'll get Kyler some care. Take this one home. His night is over." Bo Yusuf and Rahmis exchanged looks.

Bo Yusuf tossed the jagged bottleneck onto the table and walked from the tavern into the cool, North African night. The *al-Hammon Palace* guard walked Bo Yusuf to his entourage of servants and guards that lay outside the tavern. Bo Yusuf assured the tavern guard he would be fine from here, and to return to his duties at the tavern. It was in the middle of this exchange when an excited dockworker charged toward Bo Yusuf. The Army Official's personal guards, and the tavern guard, quickly made a barricade against the incoming young man. Bo Yusuf recognized the dockworker and moved his guards aside. He stepped to the worker and put a hand on his shoulder. "Catch your breath, Dakarai. Catch your breath."

The young Moor stood up straight, inhaling and exhaling deeply. He took a final breath and then reported, "A ship approaches. Galley class."

Bo Yusuf showed no concern. He was relieved. The ship was from Behar's fleet, most likely carrying a message that Beylerbey Ameer Las El-Behar was no more than an hour away. "Good. Return to the docks. Monitor the ship and allow it to land."

"Yessir." Dakarai bowed. He stood up straight and headed down the road to return to the docks beyond the city gates. Bo Yusuf gave another order for the tavern guard to return to *The al-Hammon Palace*. He commanded his personal guards and servants to follow him to *The Royal Highness*. Al-Jeheuty had to be alerted. The inn lay several blocks from the *Palace*. Bo Yusuf and his entourage approached the block. He cursed under his breath when he recognized two of Rahmis' guards posted outside the inn. He instructed his entourage to wait out front while he went inside. The innkeeper greeted Bo Yusuf and announced, "Maser Husani has already come. He speaks with Lord Anhur Has at present."

Bo Yusuf thanked the innkeeper, managing to hold a smile in place. The Army Official was anything but happy. He knew Rahmis was conversing with al-Jeheuty about his actions at the tavern. Rahmis must have filed out of the rear entrance of the tavern and made his way to the inn while Bo Yusuf was busy gathering his entourage and speaking with Dakarai. Bo Yusuf took a deep breath as he walked down the hall where al-Jeheuty's room lay. Rahmis was already conversing with al-Jeheuty in the hall. The two men aimed heated gazes at Bo Yusuf as he approached them. Al-Jeheuty, dressed in an open beige robe with no shirt, dark billowing pants and curled slippers, shook his head with disgust.

"What are you doing, Bo Yusuf?" he whined.

"He deserved it," the other said. He looked al-Jeheuty up and down and commented, "And what are you doing looking like the main character from one of Ojodo's romance tales?"

The comment drew a small chuckle from Rahmis. "He's finally taking my advice on how not to look like a scoundrel," said the princely Moor.

Al-Jeheuty turned and expressed, "I'm on your side, remember?" He looked back to Bo Yusuf and said, "He may have deserved it, but you know better. I'm not even concerned about losing his Dutch contacts. I don't want the citizens believing you're a hotheaded Army Official. We just rid al-Mari Ifriq of its dictators. You will receive penalty for this."

"Fine," agreed Bo Yusuf, his face contorted. "But I don't want Piett to feel comfortable that he's somehow protected from consequence because of his potential contacts—that he has yet to provide, might I add. I put him in his place. He's lucky it was on the floor. I could've made it six feet deeper." He looked at Rahmis and asked, "Where is he now?"

"The infirmary," Rahmis answered, annoyed. "He'll be alright."

"His lover was quite upset," Bo Yusuf joked, though held a serious tone.

"Hey. Watch it." Rahmis fired.

"What?" Bo Yusuf defended. "He and Fusan consort at sea. Their behavior should be checked. They don't know how to just plunder and leave. They have to make a scene, leave an impression. Goodness. If they want to make such a name for themselves they need to sail out to the Caribbean where pirates are the talk of the town. We're trying to keep secrets here."

Al-Jeheuty flapped his lips. "Everyone knows al-Mari Ifriq is a corsair-state. We're just trying to run a respectable one. Hopefully create a government that looks legit in the eyes of the world. Unfortunately, this is how governments are run."

"Not in Africa. Not by the Moors," Bo Yusuf commented. He saw smiles drawn on his friends' faces. "Which reminds me. The party is over. Behar's messenger galley was seen approaching the docks. It hasn't reached yet. But I suspect we have no more than an hour before Sunwil's fleet docks with our Beylerbey."

"Damnit," said al-Jeheuty. "Let's get everything together. Rahmis, shut down the tavern for the night. Gather Maurice and Fusan. Get them ready. I want all entourages together, down at the docks. Bo Yusuf, find Roberto and Governor al-Hakam."

The two bowed toward al-Jeheuty and rushed to fulfill his orders. Al-Jeheuty returned to the extravagant room granted to he and Mehit by Rahmis Husani. Mehit lay asleep, sprawled out comfortably in the bed. Al-Jeheuty walked to the side of the bed and gently laid his hands on her shoulders. Mehit stirred from her light sleep. "Come, *mora*," al-Jeheuty affectionately called. "Wake. Your father is returning in an hour. We should meet he and Beylerbey Behar at the docks. We have an hour to prepare."

Mehit whined a little as she stretched and lifted herself from her comfortable position. She kissed al-Jeheuty, sleepiness possessing her eyes. She sat up in the bed, her back against the headboard. "So your time as a king has come to an end. You are a prince again."

Al-Jeheuty chuckled and kissed Mehit on the cheek. He pulled away and sighed. "And until I am really your husband we have to go back to living in separate quarters." He leaned close to Mehit and began to playfully assault her, mostly tickling her. "Or there will be great scandal in al-Mari Ifriq." Mehit fought back with her own playful barrage of assaults and tickling. The two simmered down and rose from the bed to prepare for the arrival of Beylerbey Behar and Taran Zaher. They used the tavern's facilities to freshen up, and were ready in less than thirty minutes. Rahmis, Bo Yusuf, Ojodo, and the al-Hammon brothers greeted the couple upon exit of *The Royal Highness* inn.

"Sister, you look very proper," spoke Maurice, a teasing smile on his face. Fusan appeared as if he wanted to ravage Mehit on the spot. They were, after all, not sister and brother by blood. "Don't worry," added Maurice. "Your father will never know." He wanted to add the sentiment, *how much of whore you are*. But Maurice kept quiet. Fusan, however, decided to express that their silence would come only if Mehit gave service to he and Maurice. The others looked disgusted. Al-Jeheuty was offended, to which Fusan barked that his comment was just a joke.

The incident was brushed aside, but noted. Al-Jeheuty ordered the troupe to the dock. He whispered to Bo Yusuf, "Why didn't you knock *him* out?" Bo Yusuf explained that he was about to before Rahmis split up the fight. "Remind me to penalize Rahmis as well," al-Jeheuty concluded.

Bo Yusuf scoffed. "You mean I'm *actually* going to receive penalty for the incident?"

"Yes," al-Jeheuty replied sounding apologetic. "We don't need Captain Piett stirring up the citizens that our new Moorish regime is just as bullying as the previous Turkish regime. Some of our citizens are Turks and tawny Arabs. We want them to feel comfortable. I know they don't feel easy. They have to be assured that the tension in al-Mari Ifriq was between the city and its leaders, not between Moors and the Turks, or the Moors and foreigners." Al-Jeheuty then added, "Better I than Behar."

Bo Yusuf exhaled and whined, "What's my punishment?"

Al-Jeheuty informed, "Half of your earnings will finance Kyler's expeditions."

"What?" Bo Yusuf hissed.

"Expeditions that serve only the purpose of bringing the Dutch our proposal." Al-Jeheuty fixed his robes. "If the proposal does not go through, we will take Kyler's claim of *The al-Hammon Palace*." Al-Jeheuty made sure his voice did not carry, though Maurice and Fusan were many steps ahead of them.

The officials trekked through the streets, making their way to the city gates. The guards opened the gates upon the officials' arrival. Al-Jeheuty and the others continued to the docks, grouping with Governor Wakil al-Hakam, his eldest son and Chief Accountant Laith al-Hakam, Chief of the Guard Roberto Hamaat, Zakiy al-Din Sa'ood, Feroz Aunun, Isaiah Iraj, and their personal guards and servants. The five men greeted al-Jeheuty and the rest with hugs and handshakes. Also at the dock were the few workers keeping lookout, and the docked crew of the galley that was reported earlier. Al-Jeheuty and Bo Yusuf greeted each member of the crew. The leader announced the rest of the fleet's arrival.

They waited quietly, but not long. A fleet of five large merchant ships appeared over the black horizon, flickering like ghostly shadows against the night sky. The waiting crowd started to clap as the ships came closer and then finally docked. No musicians marched free with music, nor dancers paced out in rhythm. There was no parade. Behar appeared on the deck of the middle ship and looked down to roaring applause. The revolutionary-turned-Beylerbey smiled at his lieutenants. He waved and then disappeared from the deck, stepping down the boarding plank.

Nasir, Jabari, and Taran emerged with Behar. The four men greeted the waiting party. Zakiy welcomed his older brother home with a great embrace. Wakil pulled Jabari close to him and congratulated him on his first major outing. Laith joined in the celebration. Behar took Roberto aside and regretfully informed the assassin leader of Awa's passing, explaining the aged assassin passed from sudden heart failure. "His body is in the hull of the ship, wrapped. I asked Captain Sunwil to deliver the body to you, though you may have access to Awa tonight."

Roberto gave a signal to the men and women of his party. He instructed them to find Awa's body inside the ship. Roberto's outfit walked into the ship, returning moments later with the wrapped body of the old, distinguished assassin and spy. Roberto joined the members of his clan. He whispered to Behar before departing, "Your package was has been waiting for you."

"I'll hurry," said Behar.

The crowd stayed silent as Roberto and his crew walked away, Awa's wrapped body held up above their heads in honor. Everyone watched closely. Taran watched amazed. Al-Rinak guessed correctly. Roberto and his company disappeared into the night. They traveled away from al-Mari Ifriq's city gates.

The reunion continued, dispersing the somber mood. Behar studied al-Jeheuty like a proud father. He patted his second-in-command on the arm and smiled wide. His gaze then turned to Mehit. She was giving Taran a polite embrace. Her eye caught the Beylerbey and her smile became more warm and sincere. Al-Jeheuty noticed Behar stiffen in Mehit's presence, and it was not the first time. He was timid, becoming overly cordial. His demeanor was like a shy boy in the presence of a crush. Behar put his hands together and bowed politely to Mehit. He then nervously stepped forward and presented her with a hug and kiss on the cheek.

"You certainly found a lovely woman," spoke Behar to al-Jeheuty. Al-Jeheuty simply bowed and smiled in appreciation of Behar's comments. Taran stepped to Mehit's side as if he was shielding his daughter from a predator. Behar stepped back, almost shameful. He hid his face in a shadow, but continued to smile. "You and your wife produce such wonderful children," he told Taran.

Taran bowed his head and said, "Thank you, Beylerbey."

Behar turned to the others and continued business, "Tomorrow we will all converse. Business will convene at noon. I don't mean to sleep in, but I am tired." He turned and addressed Taran with an authoritative voice. "See your daughter home. Al-Jeheuty, come with me. Rahmis, Bo Yusuf to the palace as well. You three will put together all reports. All company chiefs, Fusan, Maurice, Zakiy, Ojodo, organize all details of your exploits. Feroz, assemble all small company bosses. Isaiah, deliver to me reports on all city merchants and smiths. I want this done by the end of this week, Feroz. Isaiah, next week, deliver to me the merchants' reports. Laith, we will delve into al-Mari Ifriq's finances once the seasonal reports are delivered. I come with good news. We are free of the Turks." The surrounding people applauded. "Not completely," admitted Behar as he fanned his hands to simmer down the crowd's excitement. "They still have to remove their troops. Feroz, I bring unfortunate news that Ghanem will still deliver tribute to the Ottoman Empire. They do hold investment in

Ghanem."

"I foresaw as much happening," the black Turk said with a grimace. "How long will this continue?"

"You and I will conference at the end of this week," Behar told him.

"Yes, Beylerbey," Feroz acknowledged, sounding defeated.

Behar wanted to assure him that things would be better, that he was already thinking of a plan to loosen the Ottoman grip on Feroz's company. But he did not trust Taran. Behar wanted to keep as much information from Taran as possible. He was also suspicious of Awa's sudden passing. He believed somehow Taran was behind it. Awa might have been old, but the assassin was in great physical shape. Though, even Behar knew aging had a way of presenting unexpected problems.

The large group split into small factions once inside the city gates. Mehit and al-Jeheuty exchanged words and a simple kiss before separating. The al-Hammon brothers parted with their foster family. Fusan and Maurice knew that Taran would want to converse with them. Taran promised his foster sons news from al-Rinak. The Moorish Ambassador had much to tell the two brothers. Feroz and Isaiah returned to their homes, as did Wakil and his sons. Nasir and Zakiy did the same. Nasir could not wait to see his mother again. Afya was still awake, waiting for her son's return. Ojodo held conference with Nasir and Zakiy before the two departed. They arranged a time to come together and organize the company reports Behar demanded.

Behar and his outfit made their way to the palace. He explained to his young lieutenants that he had received plenty rest on his voyage, but there were private matters to attend to. No one questioned the Beylerbey. They each suspected the same thing. Behar was very fond of his harem, though it only consisted of five women. The Beylerbey dismissed the guards and servants once inside the palace. He wanted to converse with his lieutenants in private, mostly al-Jeheuty. The others were dismissed, Behar reiterating his orders made to them at the dock before they walked away.

"France?" Behar asked al-Jeheuty once the two were alone.

"My brother's contacts will come through," answered al-Jeheuty. "We do have a favor asked of us. Roberto's people are on it. A man named Emile Raulf has been marked. This will please our contact. His name is Simon Beaumont. Silencing Emile Raulf will give Beaumont a stronger voice to re-establish trade at sea."

"Good. The quicker we can bring France into the fold, the quicker we can mark and silence Taran. I do not trust him." The two stopped outside Behar's private quarters. The Beylerbey looked at al-Jeheuty and sighed. "He opened his mouth about company secrets while we held conference with the Turkish statesmen." Al-Jeheuty conveyed disbelief before Behar continued. "His loose lips led to a statesman giving a great argument to keep hold of Ghanem. The statesman was al-Rinak Ozan, Aguyan's brother."

"Yes. Yes. I know the lawyer has a brother in the Empire's cabinet," al-Jeheuty remarked.

"Wakil warned me to keep Taran and al-Rinak apart," Behar stated. "The only time they may have had a chance to speak alone was when I was given some very strong wine. It knocked me out." Behar grit his teeth and cursed. "I suspect it was made to be strong. I could not refuse the drink, though I had my suspicions about it. When I awoke, Taran was in my room. He said he'd been watching me since I passed out. For all I know they could have been bold enough to speak over my unconscious body."

Al-Jeheuty asked, "Did Nasir or Jabari see anything while you were unconscious?"

Behar shook his head. "As the wine was getting to me, I waved them away. I assured them I had just become too ambitious with my drink. They went back to the festivities. Awa was suspiciously dead outside my room, where Taran told him to stay guard." He balled his hand into a fist. "Careless." He looked back to al-Jeheuty and declared, "Once Taran is dead we will then mark al-Rinak. We will sever our ties to the Empire. You will be our Commissioner of Foreign Affairs." Al-Jeheuty nodded reluctantly. He felt honored, but he also felt overwhelmed by the title. He would make Behar proud nonetheless. The Beylerbey slapped al-Jeheuty on the arm. "Were your parents proud when you returned?"

"Yes, very much so. But I didn't get out of being al-Mari Ifriq's king-apparent completely unscathed." Al-Jeheuty noticed Behar's eyebrow raised and he disclosed, "Bo Yusuf had an incident tonight at *The al-Hammon Palace*. He may have struck Captain Piett."

"May have?" Behar said in a voice demanding clarity.

"Knocked the hell out of him," al-Jeheuty clarified. "He's in the infirmary, but stable." Behar began to grumble and huff. "I have dealt with the situation. Bo Yusuf will be penalized. I've issued his punishment. His earnings will finance Piett's expeditions that will be in our favor."

Behar's mood cooled. He nodded his head and said, "Good. Good. Get some rest al-Jeheuty. Dream of your lovely wife-to-be," he advised.

Al-Jeheuty laughed. "I feel that you may do the same. What was with your exchange with *my* Mehit?"

Behar presented a humble smile. "She reminds me of someone. That's all. It is very innocent. I apologize."

Al-Jeheuty raised an eyebrow, but kept his smile. He bowed and then retired to bed.

Behar watched his second-in-command walk away before he stepped inside his room. The room was already lit, illuminating the fine colors of brown, red, and orange spread around the room. There were gold and red bed sheets, fine dark wooden furniture, and orange liquid swirling inside clear bottles. Behar's focus was on the large, curved basket placed at the foot of his bed. Behar sat upon a chair and stared at the basket with a wide smile. He started to sing, reciting an old Moorish song about the beauty of the sea seducing a Moorish pirate. He sang as best he could, keeping his voice from cracking. But producing a sweet voice was not Behar's intentions. He was simply being playful. The top of the basket popped up, and raised from its interior, a beautiful woman whose skin resonated the mixed colors of burnished gold and brown.

She had full lips, and her hair was fashioned in short twists that outlined her head like a bowl. The tips of her twists were accented with gold highlights. The woman was dressed in a red and gold tunic made from silk, and a long blue dress that tightly hugged the curves in her hips. Around her neck was a gold necklace with five large pendants at the front. Her snake-like movements caused her elaborate gold bangles to jingle rhythmically, but not with much noise. Her dance steps were perfect. No one would guess that this woman was fifty years of age. Roberto and Behar continuously joked that the women they were fond of retained such a youthful quality to them.

The woman danced free from the basket and continued her sensual movements, catching Behar and holding him and his smile with her hips and sultry stare. She finished her dance by pulling Behar from his seat and taking him into her arms. They kissed passionately. The woman felt as if she was going to magically fly away. Behar's kiss was uplifting. He devoured her not just with his mouth, but also with his hands. He moved them along the woman's curves then hugged her tighter, kissing her even more deeply. They pulled away from one another to catch a breath, foreheads together.

The woman was happy Behar returned to her. She considered him dead, a casualty of his foolish revolution in Spain. His return to al-Mari Ifriq stirred both her passion and anger at him. The two met infrequently while he served under Company Boss Nasir. Their affair blossomed more when Behar suddenly and surprisingly was announced as Odongo-Mauharim's new Regent Master. Al-Mari Ifriq, once their Turkish leaders were lost to them, looked to this legendary Moor for guidance. He took the challenge. His first powerful move was to bring this woman closer to him. Their meetings became more frequent, and more dangerous. Alimah Zaher could not let her husband Taran know. And for Behar, she was also the primary reason he wanted to eliminate him.

"Do you think Taran will be looking for you?" Behar asked Alimah.

"No," she answered. "I have been here for the last two days. My daughter believes I left for Tunisia to visit my mother. Roberto has been bringing me food. I will 'return' tomorrow evening."

Behar smiled at Alimah's cleverness. He walked away from her and sat on the bed. He sighed, "I always feel like Mehit knows. When I see her I just become flustered. Tonight, al-Jeheuty noticed my behavior. I hid my face in the shadows. Taran appeared to—"

"He doesn't know or suspect," Alimah interjected.

"But the way he's treated Mehit throughout her life," Behar pleaded in a whisper.

Alimah repeated, "He doesn't know or suspect."

Behar exhaled again and smiled. He waved his hand and said, "I still looked away when addressing the both of them, especially as they stood together. Your husband is very intelligent. I don't want him noticing how much Mehit and I resemble one another." He shook his head and confessed, "Sometimes I would like to shake him when I see the two of them argue. My complex believes he knows Mehit is not his child. I want to grab him and scream, *'Do not speak to my daughter with that tone of voice.'"* Behar laughed, but there was sadness behind his delighted emotion. "My daughter…"

Alimah put her arms around Behar, and then placed his head on her bosom. Behar smiled. He then became devious. He stood up and tossed Alimah on the bed. "And *you* are mine as well." He tossed his robes and shirt away, wearing no more than his pants.

Alimah played along. She cowered in the bed, crawling away from Behar. "Oh, no. *You pirate!* My father would never allow a marriage between his daughter and a scoundrel such as you. He has my marriage arranged to a respectable boy ready to inherit great land."

"You speak the truth wench," Behar hissed as he crawled on top of her. "But you love the excitement a pirate gives you." They smiled at one another and dived into a passionate dance.

Chapter Seventeen

Behar ordered the lodge that lay on the outskirts of the city torn down. The order was given months after the disappearance of the heads of The Four Winds Company. The material was re-used and mixed with new medium to build Behar's council house. It was constructed a short distance from the main company houses resting at the docks. Behar jokingly referred to his council house as *Behar's Big Mouth*. No one else dared to refer to the council chamber in such a manner, though they laughed when Behar made his joke. It was respect for their Beylerbey that made the others refrain from indulging in the joke, not fear.

The council house's interior consisted of two rooms. There was a small kitchen, where servants prepared meals for officials in attendance. The large, main room hosted Behar's council. The room's walls were bare. The large open space was filled with a set of cushioned chairs arranged in a horseshoe pattern around a circular canopied bed. Behar currently occupied the bed. Two servant girls attended to him, primping his clothes and lighting incense to fragrance the room. Both were young and beautiful. One was Turkish, the other an African Moorish girl. He had no interest in either of them, especially after his wonderful nights with Alimah Zaher. Behar rescheduled his meeting with the other officials, delaying counsel for two days. He maintained he needed rest. Truthfully, he spent more time with Alimah. She too delayed her 'return' from Tunisia by two days. Roberto Hamaat smuggled food into Behar's private chambers. Al-Jeheuty continued his duties as acting chief, working closely with Governor Wakil al-Hakam.

Behar counseled with al-Jeheuty privately, Alimah hidden inside the large basket or in the closet when the young lieutenant made appearances. Behar would give his input on city matters and subjects needing further discussion. Al-Jeheuty would return to Governor al-Hakam with the information, leaving Behar to continue his 'rest'. Behar returned to his duties two days later. Alimah returned to her husband, professing a return from Tunisia. She greeted Taran enthusiastically, glowing with a wide smile. Taran embraced his wife lovingly, completely unaware of her deceit. He never knew of the relationship his wife had with Behar before their arranged marriage. Alimah's father never presented his disdain for Ameer

Las El-Behar to anyone but Alimah. The arrangement was made and fulfilled. Taran never heard anything about a previous affair with the now reigning Beylerbey.

The front door to the council house was left open. Four guards were stationed at the entry. Two guards on the inside, and two guards stationed outside. The only thing they could not stop from entering was the sun's bright stroll through the front door. The morning light also crawled through the four windows placed on each wall. The guards pivoted and bowed their heads as Roberto Hamaat stepped in the doorway. The Chief of the Guard announced the arrival of Governor al-Hakam, Jabari and Laith al-Hakam, Company Boss Nasir Sa'ood, and Council Officials al-Jeheuty, Rahmis Husani, Ojodo Yerodin, and Bo Yusuf al-Dume.

Behar shooed his servants away, calling for an order of morning meals to be prepared. He stood up from his bed and greeted the men as they entered. He shook Wakil's hand and bowed respectfully. "Pasha al-Hakam." Neither man truly cared for the formality. Their friendship was too strong. Behar greeted the rest of the men just the same. The officials waited for their Beylerbey to lead them to the center of the room. The officials took seat. Behar sat at the edge of his bed, legs folded under him. There was a moment of silence before Wakil and Roberto, respectively, offered prayers that represented their faiths. Behar joked that if there were any Jews or Christians among the gathered men that also wished to give a prayer. The Beylerbey continued joking by asking Wakil and Roberto if they were blessing the proceedings or silently engaged in a philosophical debate. The officials chuckled.

Behar pushed aside the moment with a smile and continued business. "Farm production. What is our status?" Behar looked to al-Jeheuty for the answer.

Al-Jeheuty stood up. He peered down at the parchments in his hand and then addressed the Beylerbey, "Production has doubled since the past year. Our farmers are enjoying the city's stability. The first year was a struggle, as you know. Our farmers' production started to balance out early in the growing season. The crops are now at a wonderful surplus. The rain has been a blessing. Cereals and rice are plentiful. Olive trees are in bloom. Olive oil production is up. Our coffee import from Africa-east is no longer needed. We've been able to cultivate the bean here. I know Rahmis and you will enjoy that information, but who doesn't like a little coffee?" Al-Jeheuty moved on. "Fruits are in abundance. We have watermelon and coconut imports from Africa-south. We're receiving bananas from Africa-east. Our orchards are overflowing with grapes, pears, oranges, dates, apricots, and lemons. We no longer have to depend on Asian imports, though we still have close ties to Asian partners—corsairs and merchants alike. They are continuing to deliver the apple. Fruit merchants have docked in our waters delivering us the plum and the cherry. We're working on cultivating those fruits here. We do have a variety of homegrown nuts." Al-Jeheuty joked, "Anyone else getting hungry?"

Behar chuckled. "Vegetable crops?" asked the Beylerbey.

"From Isaiah's reports," Al-Jeheuty looked again at the parchments, "the farms are at full capacity for onions, an assortment of peppers, cucumbers, and eggplants. We have imports of carrots and tomatoes. Again, for the foreign crops, we're working on becoming independent of imports. We have perfected celery thanks to African-easterners setting up farmership in al-Mari Ifriq. Africa-west provides us with okra-bamyah."

"Spices?" the Beylerbey inquired.

"Salt mines are producing," answered al-Jeheuty. "We have garlic. Cinnamon is coming in through our eastern routes. Africa-west is supplying us with hilbeh, ginger, and cloves. Ethiops are bringing in peppercorn from Madagascar. Of course, there's caraway, coriander, cumin, and we have mint and honey for our teas imported from Africa-south and Asia."

"And the meat markets?" the Beylerbey demanded.

Al-Jeheuty responded, "Fish is plenty, all types, domestic and imported. We have guinefowl, and chicken being farmed. Lamb. We have sheep for wool. The production of milk from cows and goats is growing. Both animals are in enough abundance for meat."

Behar was impressed. "That's fantastic." He took a breath and then moved to another subject. "Let us deal with our religious population. Al-Mari Ifriq's total population has increased since new rule has been announced. Immigrants, black, brown, and white, have flocked to our city seeking some form of refuge. People hear that Moors have power, and so with that, tolerance must have gained new ground. This must be curbed, to an extent. I have no problems with the al-Jasi. They have adapted well. They are Moors. They are black. They are African. I'm talking of a greater foreign population, the lighter shades. This foreign population cannot supersede the indigenous man and woman who reside in al-Mari Ifriq. I still do welcome all aspects of foreign blood and religious thought. I am, and will continue to be, a very tolerant man. Therefore, I will be a tolerant Beylerbey.

"I call for two more mosques to be built. The Mohammedan way of life is the dominant faith in Africa-north. I cannot ignore that. Our very

Governor follows the ways of Mohammed. I respect you greatly Wakil. Odongo-Mauharim, however, is not a Mohammedan state. The Djenhai kingdom is of two natures. So shall be the main city. The nomadic tribes practice fractured forms of more ancient and complex philosophies. Why try and force all of Odongo-Mauharim to see through one eye when it has many? We Moors often forgot that, being a little too religiously overzealous against our African brethren in the past.

"I do stress, however, there can be no church or synagogue built. The Jew and the Christian that have migrated here are European. They are white. The swarthy Jew and Ethiop Jew—the original stock—are scattered about Africa and greater Arabia. The white Jew and the white Christian seek refuge from their own people. The Protestant Movement has shaken Christianity within Europe. I say again, people think that Moors have gained power, so they seek refuge among us. We had a good record and relationship with tolerance. But considering that these Jews and Christians are not of the original stock, I do not wish to give Europeans a place to congregate and ultimately plot. No church. No synagogue. Religion falls by the wayside when the European believes he holds an advantage to conquer a dark-skinned race."

"Unless he feels he can conquer those dark-skinned people with that particular religion," spoke Bo Yusuf.

Behar pointed to the Army Official and commented, "Take note of that. I think every religious man can say *amen* to those words." After a short round of murmurs expressing agreement, Behar continued. "I do believe that this is an advantage for the Jew or Christian. Instead of listening to one man interpret the scriptures for them, they can read on their own and decide for themselves what God has said through their particular philosophy or faith. The same goes for the Ethiop or swarthy Jew or Christian, should they find solace in al-Mari Ifriq. They'll understand. There are churches and synagogues built outside of the Djenhai kingdom. They can make pilgrimage there."

"What if the European Jew or Christian find that disagreeable?" asked al-Jeheuty.

Behar took a deep breath. "Then we cordially remind them that this is a port city. There are ships that leave here every hour. May they leave no article of clothing behind." Behar lifted a finger and said, "On the same note, Wakil and I have agreed that foreigners can own land. They will pay double tax, much like foreign business owners. We have already decided that no foreigner can be an elected official, and all refugees will pay a protection tribute that is factored into their taxes, should any refugee wish to remain a resident.”

“Has there been a decision on foreigners having a council?” asked Jabari.

Behar looked to Wakil for the answer. The governor stated, “I will allow foreigners to have a council. There can be no more than five members on foreign councils. Each council must have two Moorish officials presiding over the meeting. The head of each council will present their disputes to these officials, and the heads will also accompany the Moorish officials in presenting their population’s issues to myself or a representative of my cabinet.”

Behar nodded in approval. He turned to Rahmis and Roberto, calling for them. The two straightened respectfully, giving their Beylerbey complete attention. “How are the infirmaries? What are we doing to increase the doctors in al-Mari Ifriq? And what is happening with seasonal wear?”

Everyone took an interest, looking at Rahmis and Roberto with a curious eye when finding out the duty of seasonal dress was assigned to them. Roberto stepped forward to address the first issue. “Our five infirmaries are fine, the two largest functions at top level and capacity. Our smaller infirmaries might need expanding. We’ve seen an increase of twenty doctors come to al-Mari Ifriq. Eight are from the Djenhai kingdom, sent by orders of the King. I guess that shows we’re on good relations with the interior kingdom.”

“Relations that need to be strengthened,” Behar insisted, looking at Bo Yusuf and al-Jeheuty. “And strengthened without upsetting the Ogunsanwo-Mashek people.”

“Their incursions have lessened since al-Mari Ifriq has been reclaimed by the Moors,” reported al-Jeheuty. “Relations need to be strengthened between the Ogunsanwo-Mashek and Djenhai people. I understand their fight has been for hundreds of years, obviously far longer than we have taken rule. But, I figured we pulled off a miracle by taking the regency. Why not pull off the impossible by bringing peace to these two people?”

Roberto chuckled. “Wakil and I will pray to our respective gods to push that miracle along.”

Their morning meals were served to them. Behar took quick bites before moving on with business. “Al-Jeheuty and Bo Yusuf,” he called to attention. “I send the two of you as delegates to the interior kingdom. A safe route has been established. A guide from Roberto’s clan will lead your caravan. Your caravan will be small. There’s no need for a large, fancy impression. This trip is strictly business, not to assert power." The two officials nodded, understanding their orders. "Company Boss Aunun will join you." He turned back to Roberto and addressed the matters of the infirmaries. "Our finances are stable. The treasury is far from empty. I will meet with Feroz and all company bosses, including you Nasir, by week's end. Rahmis, you will join as well." The princely Moor's duties now included helping keep the city's financial records alongside Laith al-Hakam. He too bowed in acknowledgment of the Beylerbey's request. "We will check our purse to see how much can be given to expand the infirmaries. Now, let us deal with seasonal dress."

All eyes went to Rahmis as he stepped forward. "Relax," he said waving his hand at his fellow officials. "I might be in charge of women's undergarments, but you'll not find me wearing them."

"At least not before three shots of a good hard drink," al-Jeheuty interjected humorously.

"It takes more hits than that, negotiator," retorted Rahmis. "I can hold my liquor, unlike you." The officials roared, slapping hands in appreciation of the jibes al-Jeheuty and Rahmis exchanged. Rahmis waved his hands downward, trying to smother the noise made by the officials. "Wait. Wait. I cannot offend my good Moor too much. I need his help on this." He turned to al-Jeheuty and said, "I know that Mehit's mother is a seamstress, correct?" Al-Jeheuty nodded. "Good. Is she with business?"

"Small," answered al-Jeheuty. He groaned. "Taran keeps her on a short leash. Mehit tells me that her mother wishes to branch out."

"I'll speak with Taran," Behar assured, fixing the cuffs of his sleeves. He looked at Rahmis and spoke, "I know where this is going. I think this will be a great success. We can preview a succeeding season's dress within the current season. We'll create a showcase. Vendors, tailors, and seamstresses can demonstrate their styles, like the days of al-Andalusia."

"Where is Taran," asked Nasir, annoyance in his voice.

"I heard his wife returned from Tunisia yesterday evening," Behar answered. "This morning, I sent word that he has two days off." Behar raised an eyebrow as he surveyed the officials in front of him. "This gives us time to plot how he should be marked. Roberto." The assassin nodded his head and then went about dismissing all servants from the council house. The servants, at present, resided in the kitchen area. Roberto called for them and shuffled them outside. The guards shut the door once the servants were dismissed. They were permitted to stay, being men from Roberto's clan.

Behar continued speaking when Roberto finished his duty. "Hindsight is always more clear," said the Beylerbey. "Taran should have been snuffed with The Four Winds. But, we believed that he would be needed to quell the tension between the Empire and our city. The Empire is not as threatening as we believed. They have their own problems. We are of no concern. They want a little revenue from an investment here in al-Mari Ifriq. That is fine and fair. We can give that up. Carefully, however. The Ghanem Company controls the smaller bosses. We can make bet that al-Rinak—now, we are all aware of whom I speak?" The officials shook their heads as acknowledgment. "Good. Let us consider that he wants complete control of Ghanem. Let us consider that he plots to take Djenhai's portion of control. That's fine. We take away Taran, we take away a great advantage that he holds."

"What is our timetable for Taran's dismissal?" Nasir asked.

"When all of the Empire's troops have been removed from al-Mari Ifriq." Behar looked at Nasir with an expression that his next statement needed to be understood without protest. "That may take months."

Nasir did not take the hint, but he was cordial to the Beylerbey when he asked, "May Taran's mark be handled during the Empire's withdrawal? It may seem more random than occurring directly after their departure."

Behar smiled warmly. "Roberto will plot both scenarios."

Nasir said appreciatively, "Thank you, Beylerbey."

Behar exhaled. "The matter is resolved. Roberto, you have your mission to plot. Rahmis, I want you also to attend my meeting with Isaiah and the merchants. I know the Griffin Company has claim in several inns and taverns, but I want our company to get more of the café and coffee house revenue. And look for more games to bring into the fold. People are engaging in illegal game in alleyways and the back of small cafes."

There was rustling on the exterior side of the door that stopped the meeting. The two guards took a defensive stance, swords drawn. They turned to Roberto for further instructions. He waved his hand forward, signaling for them to open the door. One guard sheathed his weapon and removed his pistol, thumbing back the hammer. He stood at the side of the entrance, while the other guard slowly opened the door. A young Turkish messenger lay on the other side, the second set of guards surrounding him. "What is this kid's business?" the answering guard asked his fellow clansmen.

"He carries a message for Lord Anhur Has," the guard stated. "The message comes from Isaiah Iraj, Company Boss of Ahangar."

The guard signaled the other to holster his pistol. The second guard loosened the pistol's hammer back to a safe position and slid the weapon through his belt. The first guard turned and announced, "A young boy carries a message for Lord Anhur Has from Company Boss Isaiah Iraj."

Everyone looked at al-Jeheuty. He was as perplexed as his fellow officials. He looked at Behar for an answer. The Beylerbey lifted his shoulders and aimed a hand toward the door. Al-Jeheuty called back, "Permit him entrance." The teenage Turkish boy entered the council house. Al-Jeheuty put up his hand and commanded that the boy come no further. "Give your message."

The boy stopped, standing straight. He reported, "Master Isaiah would have come to give this message himself, but he is busy at the docks with Second Company Boss Zakiy Sa'ood. Four ships have anchored. The visitor is a man you know. He was in contact with Master Isaiah during your departure." The young messenger was very professional, but clearly nervous. "I do not know the corsair's identity, just that he is a Persian and—"

Al-Jeheuty jumped to his feet, exciting everyone. Had he not been a city official, the guards would have taken him down, considering his actions as threatening. The wide smile that immediately lit up al-Jeheuty's face smothered the guards' defensive movement, though no one's interest reversed. Al-Jeheuty tossed off his robe, revealing his light brown pants, black boots, silk white shirt and black vest. He apologized to Behar and said he would return shortly. His words needed a second thought from the Beylerbey. They first sounded like one unintelligible phrase as al-Jeheuty rushed from the council house and ran toward the docks.

Al-Jeheuty saw Zakiy Sa'ood in the distance catering to seaman. Isaiah Iraj conversed with their captain. Al-Jeheuty squinted, focusing on the young, Persian captain talking with Isaiah. He almost tripped as he increased his speed. The Persian captain noticed his balancing act and turned toward al-Jeheuty. The two of them screamed at one another, two friends united. Captain Hesam Gandarewa was light brown in tone and possessed black hair that was as straight as an arrow. He had a very boyish face and a charming smile that bestowed upon him a deceptively innocent quality. Hesam was a rogue of the sea nonetheless.

"You damned water-demon!" al-Jeheuty hollered.

Hesam slapped al-Jeheuty's shoulder. "I considered you dead until this bastard tells me you're a city official. I needed sanctuary several days ago from the law at sea. I figured al-Mari Ifriq could adopt me for some time, considering no one dares to be associated with it.”

“He came while you were away,” Isaiah said with a smile. “This was supposed to be a surprise. I apologize if there has been any offense Lord—”

“Enough,” al-Jeheuty smacked the air, swatting Isaiah’s words away. “All that *‘Lord Anhur Has’* talk. We’ve been drunk at the taverns too many times together for such formality to exist, *Company Boss* Iraj. Now that’s a real title. Company Boss. It sounds like someone with power. It sounds like someone you’d like to have on your side in a tavern brawl.”

The three men burst out laughing. “Please,” said Hesam through chuckles. “A Lord is a title religious people praise. And a city official is good to befriend when you need to get out of the legal troubles a tavern brawl can bring, among other things. Ah, and look at you,” spoke Hesam. “A Lord *and* City Official. From revolutionary to politician.”

Al-Jeheuty pointed at his friend and said, “Now that’s a true revolution, changing the self.”

“And goddamned philosopher,” Hesam added happily. The Persian pirate cleared his throat and revealed, “I come baring gifts, *Lord Anhur Has*.” He turned around and pointed to the four ships docked at port. “Two merchant class ships. The first is a Spanish Treasure Galleon. It was heading to the Caribbean. It’s slow, which I took advantage of.” Hesam smiled slyly remembering his adventure commandeering the vessel. “But it has a very wide turn. It can hold a maximum cargo of one hundred and forty tons, with room for over one hundred and fifty crewmen. It has a cannon capacity of forty, holding twenty-five at the moment. The second ship is a Spanish Trade Galleon. The ship has the same speed and turn as the Treasure Ship. Its cargo hold is one hundred and twenty tons, with one hundred crewmen at its maximum. It is equipped to its cannon capacity, mounted with twenty guns. In the belly of each Galleon there rests the finest goods and coin I can present as tribute.”

Al-Jeheuty stood in amazement. He then inspected the ships at the docks and raised an eyebrow. “That seems like more than a tribute.”

“Well, the ships are nowhere near filled to capacity with tribute,” Hesam confessed. “The ships are tribute too.”

Al-Jeheuty nodded. “I caught that. What of the other two ships?”

“Warship class,” Hesam answered. “Frigates.” He turned to al-Jeheuty and winked as he stated, “Compliments of the British.”

“I’ll send a letter,” al-Jeheuty joked.

Hesam chuckled lightly and then explained the layout of the ships. “They have great speed, with a wide turn. Their cargo capacity is eighty tons, with the ability to hold two hundred crewmen. Both are fitted with thirty guns, and there is booty in them as well," Hesam informed.

Al-Jeheuty crossed his arms, looking at his friend with a serious eye. "Well your voyages with the notorious pirate Cid Meier are no doubt the foundation for your knowledge of ships. Your independent voyages most likely solidified that knowledge." He stepped closer to Hesam. "But I can't shake the feeling that this is less tribute in honor and more a payment for task."

Hesam lost his sly smile. He took a breath and said, "I need to speak with your Pasha, Bey, or Dey." Hesam grasped at titles while trying to interpret al-Jeheuty's still expression. Al-Jeheuty finally smiled, pulling his friend close and aiming his thumb at the council house. He explained to Hesam that he was in a meeting with al-Mari Ifriq's Beylerbey, Ameer Las El-Behar. Hesam recognized the name, delighted to hear it. "Do you think he would speak with me?"

"Of course. I will present you. You'll have to leave your weapons with the guards," Al-Jeheuty notified. "You don't sound like a pirate. It's hard to believe you're the scourge of the waters I've heard so much about. I kept my ears to the sea. I started to believe that it was another Persian with your name."

"I'm a gentleman and humble when need be," explained Hesam. "And a sonava bitch when I *have* to be."

Al-Jeheuty grinned. "Well, you *sonava bitch*, leave your weapons here."

Isaiah's servants stripped Hesam of his weapons, a sword, a dagger and two pistols. The pirate commented that he felt naked without his arms. Al-Jeheuty commanded Isaiah jokingly to find the worth of Hesam's weapons and trade them for their value. He then escorted his friend to the council house, retelling the events that led he and Behar to al-Mari Ifriq. Hesam asked if there was any coincidence between Moorish revolutionaries entering the city and the disappearance of corrupt Turkish officials.

Al-Jeheuty replied, wording his response carefully, "So as not to make you a co-conspirator, I will answer you with a 'yes'. It's all just a coincidence."

Al-Jeheuty advised Hesam to wait outside while he proposed to Behar to permit the pirate entrance. He walked into the council house just as Behar finished scolding Bo Yusuf for his behavior against Captain Piett. Behar's chastising was fatherly, expressing to Bo Yusuf that he knew better. Bo Yusuf apologized and then, like the other officials in the room, put his eyes on al-Jeheuty's entrance. Al-Jeheuty bowed as he stepped forward. He stopped in front of Behar and asked permission for his friend's entrance. He explained Hesam's arrival and that the young pirate brought a great tribute. Intrigued, Behar allowed Hesam entrance. Al-Jeheuty motioned for the guards to bring the pirate inside. Hesam cautiously walked forward, the guards escorting him to where Behar rested. The young Persian kissed the Beylerbey's hands and then stepped back, putting both knees to the floor. Behar permitted Hesam to rise. Hesam stood.

"I hear you bring great tribute," said Behar. Hesam simply nodded his head. "There has been no greater tribute that you have brought me, Captain Gandarewa, than your friend al-Jeheuty. I sit on edge to think about what you present to me now."

"No more than an opportunity, Beylerbey," Hesam said humbly. He once again recounted the statistics of the four ships he docked at port. Behar's face was still, but underneath he was very impressed with the bounty from the young corsair's campaigns at sea. "They are more pay for task than tribute," Hesam clarified.

"And what is this task you would have me complete," asked Behar. The tone in his voice was unmistakable. He considered Hesam bold for tasking a chief boss.

Hesam spoke to Behar, but addressed everyone. His charm quickly returned. "Lord Anhur Has and I worked for a man named Phineas Broadwood. He was a Jew. German. He managed a company that shipped fruit throughout the Mediterranean. When it was discovered that he also invested in the African slave trade, Lord Anhur Has walked away, finding a job maintaining records for a weapons company in France. Phineas Broadwood never liked Lord Anhur Has. He did not like any Moor, for that matter. Ironically, he learned all he knew about trade from a Moor—a Moor he made work for him. He didn't like me either, considering me having black blood.

"He paid Lord Anhur Has and other Moors, a wage that was just enough to keep us coming back. When Lord Anhur Has left, it was a silent revolution. I know that—and forgive me for addressing my friend common—*al-Jeheuty* meant nothing of the leave. But it inspired the best of Phineas Broadwood's workers to leave as well. Now, yes. Lord Anhur Has and I did sabotage some of the trading vessels that Phineas Broadwood sold to slave traders, but he knew nothing of it—I'm sure. But he continued to scream about Lord Anhur Has being a thief and a spy for the black nation. That is when I helped Lord Anhur Has seek refuge with you, Beylerbey Behar."

"So, has Phineas Broadwood reared his ugly head," asked Behar waiting for the task to be presented in the corsair's words. Behar was not an impatient man, though his voice had weight enough to prod Hesam to state the proposition.

"No. My career as a Privateer began when I took Phineas Broadwood's contact books, or rather stole information from them. With Captain Cid Meier I sacked trade routes, whether they transported goods, coin, or live cargo. I spared one contact in the books. An Italian named Azzolino Bidonare. He is called The Squid for the simple reason that when he takes hold of something, he does not let it go. I have been in business with him since leaving Captain Meier. I helped The Squid take control of a hashish ring that goes from Morocco to Asia Minor. He also controls an opium trade. He has not given me my proper share of either trade." Hesam turned serious. "I understand that smoke and ingestion of plant is a delicate issue in the more faith-based states of Africa-north. I believe if regulated, there can be a great deal of revenue."

Behar sat back, contemplating. He turned to Wakil and Jabari. The younger al-Hakam said nothing, only looking to his father for judgment. Wakil groaned and grimaced. "Drink is one thing," said the pious governor. "I don't know about smoke. There is a definite no on opium. I will not budge to that." He exhaled. "Hashish? I can't say. What is your word, Beylerbey?"

"No to opium," Behar yielded, his head bent low. "Your word is law. But, hear me, Wakil. The boy has a point. We can regulate the hashish to cafés, not the taverns or game rooms." Wakil continued to groan. Behar pressed, "Regulate it to age. Put a tax on it. We can manage its distribution within al-Mari Ifriq's walls. It's here anyway. Let's not pretend it isn't. And to the European nations that are craving both opium and hashish, we will supply them." Behar waited for Wakil's answer.

The governor threw up his hands dramatically and sighed, "I concur."

Behar turned his attention back to Hesam. "Captain Gandarewa, you will control our trade in hashish and opium. We will put together an outfit for you. You will command three ships and a caravan. The hashish can come through al-Mari Ifriq. The opium goes to the European states. If an ounce finds its way inside al-Mari Ifriq, there will be great consequences. Is that understood?"

"Greatly, Beylerbey." Hesam thanked Behar, kissing his hands again. "The Squid resides in Tunis," informed the Persian Captain.

Behar expressed his gratitude for the information and assured the Persian pirate, "The Squid is marked." Behar declared, "Calamari for everyone." He started to chuckle. "*Mon Calamari,*" Behar repeated as his chuckle grew into great laughter. "*Mon Calamari.*" His laughter continued, drawing in the other officials. "*Mon Calamari.*" He laughed harder. His laughter simmered down, and he sighed his last few guffaws away. "Roberto," he called for the assassin. "Put Admiral Akbar on him."

Chapter Eighteen

Azzolino Bidonare gave strict orders that no one was to disturb his meeting at the café. Azzolino kept his anger at a minimum when the café owner's son disregarded his wishes and entered the backroom, disturbing his meeting with three Arabs, two Moors, and a second Italian man named Ricardo Donato. His anger was harder to keep stable when he realized that the young man stood in the doorway with another. This new guest was a Moor with an oval-shaped head, dark reddish-brown skin, and large, bulging eyes. He wore white pants, a white sleeveless shirt, and flat shoes.

The Moor surveyed the scene, looking closely at his fellow Moors sitting on either side of Azzolino. The three Arabs and Italian man stood, leaning over the circular table. Azzolino, with an opened book in front of him, looked up in surprise. He sat back, a look of annoyance on his face. The men did not stir, save their eyes being drawn to the open door as the sun's light overpowered the flickering flame cast from the lamp. The gathered men waited for Azzolino's move.

"What is this?" asked Azzolino. He slapped his leg and sighed. "I called for no disturbance."

The boy bowed and apologized. "This is Burhan, a messenger," said the teenage boy. "He has traveled far to bring you news about a plot against you." The Moor named Burhan bowed at the neck toward Azzolino. The Italian reluctantly waved Burhan closer. The café owner's son was dismissed. Azzolino snapped his fingers toward the Moor on his right. The man jumped from his seat and held it out for Burhan to take his place.

"Thank you," Burhan said in a humble voice as he sat down.

"Get up," sneered Azzolino. Burhan stood. "Search him," Azzolino commanded. One of the Arabs ran his hands around Burhan and reported nothing. Burhan was told to sit again. Azzolino leaned close to the Moor and asked, "You know of a strike against me?" Burhan eyed quickly each man surrounding him. He shifted in his seat and then looked Azzolino in the eyes nervously. "Where are you from?" Azzolino asked.

"Libya," Burhan answered, his voice far more firm than its initial tone. The Moor's posture became confident. "I have news, Captain. For a price."

Azzolino leaned away from Burhan. An intimidating grin appeared on his face as he asked, "Which do you believe to come quicker? A strike against me or a strike against you?" Burhan started to stir. Azzolino shook his hand. "Sit still. Sit still. There's information we need to exchange." Azzolino smiled and added, "For coin, of course. I am a fair man. How much can your purse hold?"

"Thirty pieces of silver," Burhan joked. He removed two medium sized leather bags strapped to his belt, and he tossed them to the table. "Fill these with jewels and coin." Azzolino put his palm on the bags and slid them to the Moor sitting next to him. He turned back to Burhan and gestured for him to speak. Burhan asked, "You are Azzolino Bidonare, yes?" Azzolino nodded. Burhan whispered his next question. "You deal in opium and hashish, yes?" Again, Azzolino nodded. "I am a contact for your partner, Hesam Gandarewa. You have swindled your partner from his commission. That is what I have heard."

"That whelp has the nerve," Azzolino said to no one in particular.

"Two of your shipments have not been delivered," Burhan informed. "Captain Gandarewa has re-routed them to al-Mari Ifriq. He seeks the Beylerbey's permission to have you marked, and then have that mark carried out."

Azzolino grimaced. "He dares not."

"Oh, he does dare, Signore Bidonare. He spoke his plan while in Libya," Burhan explained. "He was angry. He was drunk. He decided to keep the cargo and present it to the new Beylerbey. His ships also carry other bounty as tribute." Burhan paused for effect. He watched closely Azzolino's manner. "Filling the sacks with coin and jewels does not concern me. I wish to take Hesam Gandarewa's portion of the trade. I'll take his cut, or less if I have to. I am not greedy. I would be most thankful."

The Italian drug lord sighed. He reflected that Hesam Gandarewa would be such a hurtful loss. He was a young, promising privateer. "People always want more," Azzolino murmured.

Burhan leaned forward. "That is not the bad news, Captain," the messenger continued.

Azzolino's eyes went wide with wonder. "There's worse news?" he questioned. He moved closer to Burhan. "What is that?"

"An assassin has already been sent," Burhan answered. "He is called Admiral Akbar. He carries a message from your brother Brizio."

Azzolino became perplexed. His confusion was displayed clearly on his face. "My brother? Brizio? A message?" Azzolino's expression melted into anger that he could not control. "My brother died a year ago!" he yelled. Azzolino struck the table. "Gandarewa said he was hit by pistol fire when they boarded a vessel." He grabbed Burhan by the collar and shook him. "Do you mean to tell me that Gandarewa was more responsible than a random shot fired?"

"I don't know," said Burhan trembling. "That is the bad news." The Moor reached down his pants, grabbing a dagger sheathed and strapped to his bare leg. He removed the weapon and stabbed Azzolino through the temple. "You'll have to go to hell and counsel with your brother on the matter to find out!" The blade broke through Azzolino's skull, slicing into his brain and killing him instantly.

Ricardo Donato jumped back, reaching for the handle of his pistol that was tucked into his belt. The Arab that had earlier searched Burhan removed a pistol. He fired a bullet into Ricardo Donato's back. The Italian landed on top of the table. The Arab pulled Ricardo's pistol from his person and shot him again, this time in the head, guaranteeing his death.

Burhan 'The Admiral' Akbar stood up and wiped his bloody hand on Azzolino's clothes. He shook the Arab's hand and thanked him for his assistance. The Arab was a new member of Hesam Gandarewa's crew, and he had arrived three days ahead of Burhan. Akbar asked the remaining Arab and Moors, "Do you wish to earn coin in a new outfit?" The men nervously answered with an affirmative nod of their heads. "Your first assignment is to clean the café's backroom. Rid this pleasant place of these corpses. Any coin on their person is to be given to the café's owner.
Tomorrow we journey to al-Mari Ifriq."

Chapter Nineteen

Beylerbey Ameer Las El-Behar made an abrupt change in plans. Al-Jeheuty Anhur Has and Bo Yusuf al-Dume were no longer being dispatched as envoys to Odongo-Mauharim's interior kingdom. Much was going well for al-Mari Ifriq. Trade and revenue were in great abundance. The earnings were put into city projects. Taran Zaher and Governor Wakil al-Hakam had plans to introduce seasonal markets. This feat struggled for a decade to be reinstated. Behar sent al-Jeheuty and Bo Yusuf to Algiers and Tunis. Company Boss Feroz Aunun continued the campaign to the Djenhai kingdom in their stead. Al-Jeheuty and Bo Yusuf, traveling by sea with Ras Ali as captain of his own ship, appealed to Algiers and Tunis' leaders to curb piracy at sea. Written proposition was being sent to these corsair-states to join in the revenue shared from protecting particular trade routes, and dubiously marking others.

Tunis was considered an easier sell on the proposition. Odongo-Mauharim may have been neither Tunisia nor Algeria, but the small patch of land was considered Tunisia's sister state. Tunisians affectionately referred to Odongo-Mauharim as *The Pollux to its Castor*, in reference to the Greek twins Pollux and Castor, the constellation Gemini. This was an odd nickname for Odongo-Mauharim, considering that the region was several times smaller than the Tunisian nation. More accurately, Tunisians denoted Odongo-Mauharim as *Al-Ras al-Tau-am al-Mu'akhar*, translated as *The Head of the Second Twin*. Residents of Odongo-Mauharim returned the warmth by calling Tunisia *Al-Ras al-Taum al-Muqadim, The Head of the Foremost Twin*.

Al-Jeheuty used this information to his advantage when negotiating with Tunis' leaders. Though he would be disturbed to find few true Moors in power. Africa-north was becoming a blend of light-brown Turk, tawny Arab, and black African blood. The mixed population was retaining the title of Moor, however. The black Moor was either in servitude or pushed to the south, closer to Africa-central. Algiers would prove to be no different in its population's makeup. Al-Jeheuty would figure that as long as they referred to one another as Moor, honor, love, and respect could be paid as tribute. Bo Yusuf thought otherwise, maintaining a heightened state of caution.

Small internal struggles surfaced in al-Mari Ifriq while al-Jeheuty, Bo Yusuf, and Feroz Aunun were on assignment, but it was nothing that

Behar could not handle. Fusan al-Hammon's exploits at sea raged greater than any fire on land. His campaigns made pious men and women believe that the waters of the world would be stirred up again like the floods witnessed by Noah. Captain Piett assisted Fusan's exploits. No longer interested with just managing fights on land, or even partaking in them, Fusan returned to the sea with Captain Piett looking to loot trade ships to increase income.

Fusan's engagements interfered with Captain Gandarewa's drug trade, assisted by Ojodo's uncle, Eibib Oba. Hesam appealed to Behar to carry out an issued mark on Fusan. The Persian's appeal was considered. Behar had taken great offense to words Fusan dared to speak in his presence. The Beylerbey tried to warn the burly, Moorish Corsair that his actions at sea were hurting relations that needed to be re-established. Spoke Fusan to the Beylerbey, *"I need not the law of a Turk or the law of a Franc to tell me what ships to mark for plunder. I will mark any ship that carries my interest. Be wary. I have expensive tastes."*

But Behar did not flinch. When Fusan left his presence he said to his audience of Captain Gandarewa and Captain Sunwil, *"He has expensive tastes? Then we'll cut his tongue out."* Captain Sunwil was then ordered to have Fusan's ships marked. The attacks were crippling. Maurice was enraged, counseling his brother that they now stood alone from the Beylerbey's protection. With four of his five warships sunk, Fusan took his brother's trade ships to complete his fleet. Slow and poorly armed, the ships were sunk as well. The greater insult to the maritime injury came when Hesam— on orders of the Beylerbey—attacked the piratic merchant, Carlos LaFregona. Captain LaFregona was the largest importer of the *al-Hammon Palace*'s liquor and beer. One ship was struck. The entire crew was taken hostage; there were no casualties. Hesam and Captain Sunwil negotiated with LaFregona to cease all imports into the *al-Hammon Palace* until further notice. *The al-Hammon's* fermented well ran dry.

Maurice pleaded with Behar for new ships when he was finally granted an audience with the Beylerbey. Behar assigned Maurice to work closely with Nasir's company, taking the company boss's ships on loan. Maurice was furious by this turn of events, and sulking in his brother's presence only brought taunts from Fusan. *"You still harbor anger? His pa-pa killed our pa-pa. I weep. We carried out a mark on his father. Why are you still angry?"* Fusan expressed these words while feigning tears, teasing Maurice. *"Drown your sorrows in drink, rugrat. Or be like ma-ma and drown your sorrows in the waters."*

Further changes were made. Behar allowed the al-Hammon brothers control of two trade routes to keep the two men busy. Behar was aware of their father's treachery against al-Mari Ifriq, the information revealed to him by Wakil. Behar was also told to keep such information away from Nasir's ears, which the Beylerbey disagreed, but honored.

One of the al-Hammon trade routes brought goods to their tavern and inn. The second trade route was assigned for Fusan to police, and for him to protect other trade vessels at sea. The job of policing the sea routes cooled Fusan's piracy, though he was an abusive cop. Captain LaFregona's crew was released, and his trade was again welcomed into the *al-Hammon* tavern.

Al-Jeheuty and Bo Yusuf returned from their mission just as the events involving the al-Hammon brothers settled down. Nasir presented the political gossip once the two officials disembarked from their ship and were safe to talk of such matters within the palace walls. The two envoys were also made aware that Feroz Aunun had returned from Djenhai.

It was sundown. The palace servants started to light the hallways and entryways to the refurnished and redecorated Moorish palace. Bo Yusuf and al-Jeheuty were thankful to hear that not only was Behar able to quell the al-Hammon brothers, but he was also able to situate them within a venture that would keep their behaviors in check, especially Fusan.

Nasir carried two letters. He informed al-Jeheuty that the letters were marked 'urgent'. The two letters had come by courier. One letter was French. The second letter was scribed in Turkish. Nasir presented both to al-Jeheuty, keeping what looked like a thick book tucked underneath his arm. Al-Jeheuty invited Bo Yusuf and Nasir into his private quarters. He took the letters to his desk and lay them down. He lit two lamps and took seat at his writing table. Nasir dropped the book upon the desk, the heavy piece of literature slamming hard against the top of al-Jeheuty's writing table. The book caught al-Jeheuty's attention, to which he addressed Nasir, "What is this?"

"I was curious myself," stated Nasir. "I looked it over an hour before you arrived. It's a declaration from the Dutch. I have a small understanding of their language, but enough of one to know they've refused our terms."

Al-Jeheuty was perplexed. His confusion was not inspired by the Dutch's answer to the Griffin Regency's proposal, but rather by the heavy volume of paper bound together to declare a simple answer as 'no'. Al-Jeheuty took the book and opened it, thumbing through pages and perusing the composition. He looked at Nasir and Bo Yusuf and asked, "It took them over a hundred pages to say 'no'?" He stated with a perplexed tone, "This is a book! All this here says, 'no'?" he asked again for clarification.

"Yes," Nasir replied quickly.

Al-Jeheuty narrowed his eyes at Nasir. His face returned to normal as he waved his hand and spoke, "I'm not even going to get into that banter." He pointed to the book and asked in a rhetorical manner, "Why does it take over a hundred pages to say 'no'?" Nasir thought about the question, disregarding its rhetorical fashion. "Never mind. Let us indulge in an exercise." An extremely sarcastic smile appeared on al-Jeheuty's face as he defined the terms of the exercise. "Ask me if I would like your ships to protect my goods *whilst* my trade ships follow route through your territory. Go on."

Nasir chuckled slightly and then asked in a monotone voice, "Would you like my ships to protect your goods—" he looked at Bo Yusuf who was covering his mouth and doing his best not to burst into laughter, "—*whilst* your trade ships follow route through my territory?"

Al-Jeheuty answered in a very professional manner, "No thank you. I don't believe it would be in our nation's best interest at the present time." He raised his shoulders. "You see? Short, to the point." He flipped through the pages and scoffed, "This is an insult to my intelligence. They wave articles, maritime laws, and policies in my face as if I'm ignorant of them. They could have saved the extra paper—*and time*—simplifying all of this by scribing on a small piece of parchment the words *'Fuck you'!*" Al-Jeheuty relaxed. He turned to Bo Yusuf and ordered, "Inform Captain Sunwil, and the riffraff of the sea, that the Dutch do not have our protection. Hit them hardest at their slave ports in Africa-west. They want us for servitude but not for business. Send word to Sale to handle that. We will take ten percent of the spoils from the actions performed on our coast. Sale can keep the live cargo. Let me run this through Behar first, of course." He opened the letter from the French and read through quickly. He smiled and shook the letter in his hand. "We are thanked for carrying out the dismissal of Emile Raulf—" Bo Yusuf and Nasir started to clap. "—*And* Simon Beaumont will dock his ship in al-Mari Ifriq in one week. Good news to report to Behar." He folded the letter and opened the correspondence sent from the Turks. An eyebrow angled sharply, the other raised. He poked his cheek out with his tongue and made the noise, "Huh."

"*Huh?*" repeated Nasir. "What's 'huh'? 'Huh' is never good. I've never seen anyone 'huh' something good."

Bo Yusuf raised his hand. "I've said 'huh' to something good," the Moorish rogue said with a smile.

Nasir put his hands on his hips. "When?"

"I was fifteen. An older woman—she was thirty, I believe—

disrobed in my presence.”

Nasir and al-Jeheuty put their eyes on Bo Yusuf, poked their cheeks out with their tongues and stated contemplatively, *“Huh?”*

“See,” Bo Yusuf said pointing his finger toward each of them. “That’s the same thing I said before she made me a man.”

“Well, Nasir is right,” declared al-Jeheuty. “This ‘huh’ is not good.” He stood up, taking both letters. “Let’s take all of this to Behar. Leave the novel for me to cuddle up to and read before I sleep.” He turned to Bo Yusuf and communicated, “Congratulations. You now have stock in *The al-Hammon Palace*. Captain Piett’s expeditions did not provide what we hoped. You will take his share. That will recoup the losses you’ve incurred financing his expeditions to the Netherlands.” Bo Yusuf felt vindicated. He humbly thanked al-Jeheuty, feeling the need to state that Captain Piett would not like the decision made. Al-Jeheuty reminded the Moorish nationalist that Captain Piett was aware of the risks that failing negotiations incurred.

The three headed to the door and opened it to find Behar accompanied by Roberto Hamaat and two servants making their way through the hall. The two parties looked at one another with surprise. “Al-Jeheuty, Bo Yusuf. It was reported that you had returned. Your missions?”

“Successful,” al-Jeheuty answered triumphantly. “We brought written document to prove it. They are in my travel bag. But there are more pressing matters. Should we step into my quarters or follow you to yours?”

Behar waved the three men back to al-Jeheuty’s room. “We can counsel here.” The servants were told to wait outside. Behar and Roberto followed the three men into al-Jeheuty’s quarters. The party returned to the desk. Al-Jeheuty allowed Behar to sit at his writing table. He presented Behar with the letter from the French. Behar looked through the letter and responded pleasantly to the news.

Al-Jeheuty put his palm on the Dutch response and smiled mockingly while saying, “This intense epic is the Dutch’s response. They said ‘no’ to our proposal.” Behar was perplexed, looking at the size of the response. “I know,” al-Jeheuty assured. “We’ve already spoken about it. I’ll still review the content.” He then said to Behar in a tone that sounded as if he was asking for permission, “For their rude and arrogant lack of respect I have decided to let the riffraff have their way with them until they decide it will be in their best interest to have us as friends.” Behar agreed. Al-Jeheuty showed the second letter, the one from the Turks.

Behar started to read. He sighed immediately. He looked at al-Jeheuty, and then as much as he tried to resist, his eyes went to Nasir. He looked disheartened. "We may have to delay Taran's mark until the troops are pulled out," he told Nasir.

Nasir rolled his eyes and sighed, "What's the letter say?"

"The letter is from Sinan," said Behar in a surprisingly calm voice. "He will be accompanying al-Rinak. They ask to work closely with Taran while reviewing the Ghanem business. They request that all relations be worked through Taran, especially while pulling out the troops." The Beylerbey took a breath. "I fear they will carry out a mark on our substitute in retaliation for carrying out Taran's mark during the process of getting their troops out. That substitute would be al-Jeheuty. Al-Rinak is playing a move to keep Taran alive. He's smart. He knows—or at least is assessing—that Taran has the potential to be marked and eliminated."

"Let's mark al-Rinak," Bo Yusuf suggested. "We let Taran follow them back to Empire soil and hit the ship on their return. We get them both."

Behar sighed. "The French are coming into the fold. The Dutch will do the same after some convincing. The Empire stands upon whispered rumors that war can breakout between us at any moment. We have to approach this with caution. We don't want to upset our other investors."

Nasir relaxed. He remembered his father's words about actions and their possible repercussions on al-Mari Ifriq. He bowed at the neck toward Behar. "At your word, Beylerbey. I stand ready."

"We will find a way to close all of this, Nasir," Behar promised.

It was clear that Nasir was disappointed. "I know, Beylerbey," the company boss tried to sound assuring. "I know better than anyone here that the timing must be perfect."

Behar stood. The men around him stiffened to attention. Behar waved them at ease and walked to the door. "Al-Jeheuty, I leave you with the duty of reading the Dutch's epic narrative." Al-Jeheuty led the group to the door and saw them out. He informed the Beylerbey and the others that he would leave the palace shortly and make his way to *The Royal Highness* inn. No one questioned why, but they knew al-Jeheuty had a rendezvous scheduled with Mehit. The rendezvous most likely would take place in the morning, when Mehit could sneak away with the excuse of checking on her bathhouse.

Before he shut the door he remembered the documents from Tunis and Algiers that he needed to present to Behar. He found the written agreements in his travel bag and gave them to Behar. The Beylerbey thanked his lieutenant. Al-Jeheuty closed the door behind his guests and returned to his writing table. He opened the Dutch's proposal and started to read the bound document. He became annoyed with every other word. Al-Jeheuty was fluent in the Dutch language, and he believed the tone of the declaration was condescending. He closed the book, stood, and then walked over to his sword that lay sheathed in its scabbard next to his nightstand. He belted the sword to his hip, returned to his writing desk and tucked the Dutch's declaration under his arm. He left his room after putting on his burnoose and hood, and then he extinguished the lights flickering in the room. He exited the palace without guard or servant at his side, traveling quickly to Rahmis' inn where lay waiting was a room already prepared for him.

Al-Jeheuty removed his sword from his belt as he walked inside the room. He sat at the writing desk inside the suite and opened the book, picking up where he left off. Al-Jeheuty's eyes became heavy after reading twenty pages. He made his way to the bed, changed into nightclothes that tavern servants prepared before his arrival, and then stowed into bed. He daydreamed of Mehit until he fell asleep, waking to the sound of her light knocks at the door. It was the morning. Al-Jeheuty rose from the bed and opened the door, finding his African Moorish beauty on the other side. She held a serving tray filled with a morning meal made for two. Al-Jeheuty took the tray from Mehit and let her inside the room. He set the tray down on the table and quickly embraced his wife-to-be.

They kissed.

"How is everything, *A-Sir*," Mehit addressed al-Jeheuty affectionately as their kiss ended.

"Tunis and Algiers went well," he said with a devilish smile, leading Mehit closer to the bed while embraced. "We've received a fond letter from the French about our proposal. Al-Mari Ifriq will host two French officials next week." The official thought carefully of his next words. "The Dutch still need some convincing, but I'm sure they'll come into the fold. How have you been, *mora*?"

Mehit kissed al-Jeheuty's cheek and sighed. Her eyes looked regretful. Al-Jeheuty looked at Mehit with concern. "I've decided to attend a University. There's one in Tunisia that caters to women seeking an education in medicinal practices."

"So my mother's words sold you," al-Jeheuty said.

Mehit nodded, yes. She then informed, "My education will take a year, al-Jeheuty."

"That's of no concern," he assured her. Al-Jeheuty's tone, however, seemed to question Mehit's worries. "Who will watch your bathhouse?" he changed the subject.

"Mistress Kali," Mehit answered.

"It will be well guarded then," remarked al-Jeheuty.

There was more Mehit needed to tell her husband-to-be. "I want to start immediately." Mehit looked as if she was bracing against al-Jeheuty erupting in anger. He did not. She then clarified, "This will delay our wedding."

Al-Jeheuty exhaled. Taran may have been more cordial toward al-Jeheuty since the death of The Four Winds, but he was still adamant at keeping the official and his daughter apart. But Taran conceded, recognizing his daughter's sincere interest in al-Jeheuty, but he believed a wedding would be best once al-Mari Ifriq was politically and economically stable. Taran professed that he did not want a busy official neglecting his daughter. But now, Mehit was volunteering another delay for their union. "Oh. That's not a problem," al-Jeheuty lied. "Is it? You graduate, you marry. The ceremony will be grand."

"I will be living in Tunisia," Mehit continued. "I will be staying with my mother's family."

Al-Jeheuty sighed again. He ran his finger along Mehit's cheek. "You can't escape me. I'll find you," he said playfully. "Just don't let another man charm you."

"I can't," Mehit laughed. "I used you to get in. A woman affianced to a city official has some pull. Especially if that city is the bustling al-Mari Ifriq."

Al-Jeheuty chuckled lightly. "Oh. I'm a means to an end?"

"Yes," she teased.

Al-Jeheuty let Mehit go. He backed away and said to her, "Once we are married I have no intention to make you some kind of servant-wife. If we were to marry tomorrow I would not prevent you from furthering your education. I follow no tenants that would make you an ornament as a display of my power, or try and rule over you. This is not a business deal. I love you."

"I don't prolong getting married for such a reason," Mehit assured al-Jeheuty, though it was a lie. Mehit truly loved al-Jeheuty. She understood that al-Jeheuty truly loved her as well. But she could not trust the growing climate forecasted for women's future. This was not al-Andalusia. This was a corsair-state with Moors desperate to survive. Women's roles in society, especially after Turkish rule, were becoming more and more restricted under the banner of either Mohammedanism or Moors declaring that too many freedoms could be detrimental to survival. All actions needed to be accounted for. Women had a strict role to play, as did the men. Mehit's actions were not inspired by al-Jeheuty, or what Beylerbey Behar had brought to al-Mari Ifriq. Her actions were inspired by observations made while growing up with Taran as her father. She was even witness to Nasir's father making such statements to Nasir's mother, as equal as he treated her. There were activities Afya was barred from simply because she was a woman.

Mehit concluded with a statement that was half true. "Your mother was inspiring, convincing me to further my business and education."

"Good," al-Jeheuty said slyly, embracing Mehit again. "Because your business brings great revenue."

"Oh," Mehit snapped with sass. "So now *I'm* a means to an end."

"Of course," he said while leaning in to kiss her.

Mehit backed away. "Eat your morning meal."

Al-Jeheuty playfully grabbed at Mehit. *"My kiss! I demand it!"*

Mehit playfully fought back. "You're too use to getting what you want," she teased.

"That makes two of us," al-Jeheuty retorted. "We're spoiled."

Mehit calmed her antics and allowed al-Jeheuty to take her in his arms. He put his lips against hers. The two were locked in a passionate debate. Their lips spoke gentle arguments. The sensual rebuttals waving through Mehit's lips could only defend for so long against al-Jeheuty's fervent position and angle. Sakeen Anhur Has would have been doubly proud of his son. Al-Jeheuty would have made an effective lawyer, especially if these were his methods. He gave so much to Mehit, and she tasted so much of his love for her. The negotiator placed an argument so strong against Mehit's lips it forced her to finally confess when she pulled away to take a breath, "I have been scared, al-Jeheuty. I have been scared that you will change when we marry."

"Has my demeanor changed toward you since going from revolutionary to city official, *mora?*" he asked her in an affectionate tone. "I don't seek to control you, just hold you."

"Aww," she mocked him.

"I'm serious," he said to her, the smile on his face contradicting his tone. "I'm also upset." His tone and expression then came together. "You don't have to plot against me, *mora.* I actually believe getting your medicinal studies before we marry is a good idea."

"I'm sorry," she said in a sincere tone.

"I'm going to have to watch you," al-Jeheuty said while pointing at Mehit. "You know you lied to a city official?"

Mehit took a step away from al-Jeheuty. Her movements were

sensual. Her hands rubbed her hips as she backed away from her husband-to-be. "City official, will you take all your mighty power to punish me?"

"I believe you'll benefit more from your punishment than I," al-Jeheuty quipped.

Mehit raised a single eyebrow. "You think?"

Al-Jeheuty crossed his arms and stated, "I think I'm once again a means to an end."

Mehit put her palm against al-Jeheuty's chest. She backed him up to the bed and then made a light push. Al-Jeheuty fell backwards. Mehit crawled atop him before he could adjust to the bed. "Means to an end," she said in a flirtatious breath. "Of course."

Chapter Twenty

Aatif never felt more like a king than now, even during his eight successful years in business. A caravan sent from al-Mari Ifriq arrived in Nusurika to escort him back to the port-city in Odongo-Mauharim. The caravan was not as magnificent as the one his brother marched into town with, but it was elegant in its simplicity.

There were fifteen soldiers that guarded his cavalcade. Four of the fifteen soldiers were mounted atop mighty steeds and camels. They were robed, hooded, and masked with cloths. Each mounted soldier carried with him a sword and musket strapped to his back and a pistol at the waist. The foot soldiers were armed just the same, carrying their muskets rather than having them strapped to their backs. Servants accompanied the train. They guided camels and mules that were loaded with provisions.

Then there was the canopied carriage. The compartment was decorated with soft, illustrious upholstery and pillows. The space was perfumed with a wonderful fragrance of flowers. There was a medium sized trunk built into the compartment's design. Inside were refreshments. The carriage rested atop an elephant.

Aatif's travel was three days long and without incident. His caravan entered al-Mari Ifriq to the sound of trumpets and a gathered crowd of officials. Aatif was taken by complete surprise. Al-Jeheuty appeared inside the coach, pushing aside the drapes and jumping in with a smile. The two brothers greeted one another with a hug, and then al-Jeheuty escorted Aatif from the coach. The two officials exited onto a short stage, the elephant rested in the street. Aatif gazed upon the Beylerbey. Behar was dressed in all black—pants, robes, shirt and vest. His headpiece was lined with purple and red fabric. The other officials were dressed identically to one another. Brown and beige were their colors, the same as al-Jeheuty. Aatif's brother differed only by his vest, black with brass colored buttons. Aatif did not move. He was in awe at the sleek appearance of the Beylerbey and his officials, and the beautiful bustling activity of citizens swarming in the streets.

"They don't look like pirates," Aatif said to al-Jeheuty. His voice's tone melted from surprise to awe. Aatif clarified, "Our fellow Moors over there."

Al-Jeheuty looked at his associates and friends. Beside Beylerbey Ameer Las El-Behar there stood Rahmis Husani, Ojodo Yerodin, Bo Yusuf al-Dume, and Nasir Sa'ood. He asked his brother, "What do they look like?" He was not offended by the fact that his brother may have expected to see a roguish group of thugs presiding over an unruly ghetto.

"They look like governors," Aatif admitted.

Al-Jeheuty patted his brother on the shoulder. "Indeed," he said. He then escorted his brother to the officials and introduced them. Aatif bowed and kissed Behar's hands, acknowledging him as Beylerbey. The group made their way to a local café. Armed guards quickly surrounded them, shielding the Beylerbey and the officials. "You'll never guess who's here," al-Jeheuty spoke once the formal introductions were done, and to keep his brother from feeling uncomfortable in the presence of the armed guards.

Aatif inquired, "Who?"

"Hesam Gandarewa," al-Jeheuty answered. "*Captain* Hesam Gandarewa."

Aatif lifted a finger and shook it as he declared, "Now there's a rogue."

Al-Jeheuty explained to the others, "Hesam's father brought goods to Nusurika from Libya, where Hesam grew up. They lived in Nusurika for three months of the year while Hesam's father was on duty." The other officials nodded with the information. Al-Jeheuty addressed his brother by asking, "How is Khaira?"

"She returned safely," Aatif informed with a thankful tone in voice. For assurance he added, "Thank you. She's doing well. I don't know how—" and then his voice lowered to escape detection, "—the deed was done, but I heard Emile Raulf had an accident of some sort. He was found in the woods, neck broken, his horse traipsing around the woods with a broken leg. No one suspects foul play."

Aludra el-Amin, who was now an initiated Moon, accomplished the deed. She was sent to France weeks ago to carry out the mark against Emile Raulf. She blended in with the street peasants domiciled several miles from the district in which Emile Raulf resided. The well-trained Moon watched Emile's movements, learned his haunts and routines. The Moorish woman followed the businessman to the woods, where he enjoyed a private gallop at the end of his day. This is how the middle-aged Frenchman tried to recapture his youth. It was in the woods where his bewitching assassin revealed herself. She was clothed in a loose dress that teased her viewer of her alluring and slender, dark brown frame. She declared herself lost and in need of assistance. Emile Raulf could not refuse. He dismounted, tying his horse's reins to a tree. He walked over to the beautiful assassin, unaware. Aludra was graceful, her movements quick. She broke his neck and placed his body atop a set of large rocks. The scene Aludra left behind would make the naïve viewer believe Emile Raulf made a fatal attempt to jump the set of rocks with his horse. The Moon proceeded to give the horse an injury too. She wounded the animal by tossing a heavy rock hard against its right hind leg. The bone was crushed on impact. Aludra watched the horse convulse wildly, waiting for the horse to settle from the intense pain. She untied the mount, letting it limp away into the woods. The Moon's next task was to sneak onto Simon Beaumont's premises, leaving in his study an item confiscated from Emile Raulf's body. This was proof that her mission had been accomplished. The item, placed on Simon Beaumont's writing table, was the master key to Emile Raulf's warehouses.

"Simon Beaumont is grateful," continued Aatif. "I received a letter from him, which I'm sure you have as well. He's worked quick to increase trade at sea."

"He'll be here in an hour," informed Behar. "We just received word from his messenger ship."

"This will help bring revenue to your state, Beylerbey?" asked Aatif.

Behar shook his head affirmatively. "Yes," he said. "The Dutch have also come into our fold. They took some convincing, but it didn't take as long as we suspected." Behar eluded to the bombardment of Dutch trade ships, which was ferocious. Behar put Fusan in charge of the hits. The burly corsair was delighted to receive the mission, though he was kept on a short leash. His behavior could not be so fiery that the Dutch decided to make war in the Mediterranean. Sale continued to bombard the Dutch at their slave ports in West Africa, but lessened attacks when the Dutch ravaged the coastline of corsair-states with a massive naval fleet. The Dutch conceded to the Griffin Company in the end, however, paying for the protection of their ships sailing within the Mediterranean—with the exception of those carrying live cargo: African slaves. The Griffin Company continued to mark those ships, and bring the freed Africans into al-Mari Ifriq's population.

The party entered a small café and was quickly greeted by the proprietor. He was grateful to see the Beylerbey and the officials, greeting them all with a respectful bow and a kiss to the hand. The owner led his distinguished guests to a large table that was already prepared with a buffet of morning food. Behar's guards waited outside, surrounding the café's perimeter. The curtains were drawn shut on all but one window. A servant girl came from the back and placed cups and two large jugs on the table. One jug was filled with juice, the other with water. Another trip to the back produced two coffee mugs, one for Behar and the other for Rahmis. The woman disappeared again and returned with plates. Behar thanked the woman. She bowed toward the Beylerbey and apologized for not being adorned with veil. Behar shrugged the young woman's apology away, telling her not to worry. The woman then stole a quick glance at Rahmis and presented a shy smile. She returned to the back of the café.

Nasir nudged the aristocratic Moor with an elbow. "Rumor is you two are close," Nasir teased.

Rahmis protested the accusation. "She is a servant girl. A barmaid. She is fresh out of her teenage years."

"So you have *not* been courting her?" Nasir asked teasingly.

Rahmis cleared his throat and then stated matter-of-factly, "I have shown her around the city, yes. We have met at night. Yes. I have returned her to her family before the hour was late."

"Sounds like courting to me," Ojodo quipped.

Rahmis stirred milk into his coffee. "She has a good education and a very sweet nature. She knows how to please a man with her manner. I have not taken her to bed. I feel that would be taking advantage of her."

"You are a gentleman," al-Jeheuty joked as he filled his plate with food.

Rahmis ignored al-Jeheuty and turned his full attention to Nasir. "I just feel she would do better with, maybe perhaps, your brother. They are closer in age."

"I'm trying to finish an arrangement my father was setting up between my brother and a young woman," Nasir reminded. "The two of them fancy one another, and have for some time." Nasir advised Rahmis, "I would not ignore this woman's good-natured advances, or lead her to believe you have intentions. She is also very pretty."

Nasir did not lie. Fumnyana Maysa was a delicate young woman. She was no more than twenty years of age. Her hair flowed in large, tight curls, outlining her quaint oval face like an ancient Egyptian headpiece. She was dark brown with large doey eyes. Her hips and thighs were seductively fleshy and curvaceous. Her breasts were small, and at the moment she covered herself in a simple, pink maiden's outfit.

"I hope you're not letting your noble and royal blood go to your head," Behar spoke while taking a bite of the food on his plate. "You should all find the proper woman to keep you grounded. Roberto has great lessons on the Divine Mother. I recommend attending the lectures he and his mistress give to their students."

Rahmis refrained from retorting. He felt as if the others looked upon him with a judging eye. He also hoped that Behar did not recommend he continue courting Fumnyana. Rahmis believed her to be simple and without ambition. She confessed one night that she was content with her life.

"Your city's actions secured the proper woman for me," expressed Aatif. "I thank you again, Beylerbey. I also ask a favor to allow my brother leave to attend my wedding."

"Of course," Behar said with a haughty laugh that made Aatif flinch. "When is the special day scheduled?"

Aatif said cautiously, "It's scheduled around my brother's schedule, Beylerbey."

Behar took a sip of coffee. He placed the cup down and shook his head agreeing. "We'll deal with the French today," he declared. "We'll get them set up throughout the week." He looked at al-Jeheuty and said in a warm voice, "Then you will return to Nusurika with your brother. Take Mehit with you." Behar took another sip of coffee and then asked, "When is she scheduled to leave for school?"

"Next month," al-Jeheuty answered. "Several days after al-Rinak and the Djenhai King's daughter arrives," he specified.

Rahmis grinned devilishly as he sipped his coffee. He looked up as everyone went silent. They were observing his change in manner. "The King's daughter," he exhaled. "Now that is an ambitious woman. I am preparing the finest suite for her to stay in. I have planned an excellent catering service. I will have the Princess believe that she has not left the comfort of her kingdom."

Ojodo chuckled. The titan's mighty voice boomed, "I now have a new story to prepare. I will call it *The Noble Woman and the Perpetrator.*" Nasir, Bo Yusuf, and al-Jeheuty joined in on Ojodo's laughter. Behar chided all three of them. The young officials straightened their manner as best they could. Rahmis grit his teeth in frustration. Ojodo said when Behar pressed him, "I apologize, my brother-in-arms."

"Truthfully she will be coming to us under the title of Royal Ambassador, not as a princess," al-Jeheuty reminded, and also breaking the tension. "Does she still qualify?"

"Completely," Rahmis smirked. "She is still a Princess, royal and noble. I've talked to Feroz about her continuously. She participates in company matters and decisions. Feroz reports to her about Ghanem; he sends word to her and the King every month."

"It will be interesting to see al-Rinak's reaction to a woman in power," al-Jeheuty commented.

"It's hard to say," said Behar in a contemplative manner. "I didn't get the feeling that al-Rinak would not accept a woman as a head. I would wager that he does believe that women are weaker than men. At least that's what he tells himself when he decides to manipulate them for his purpose. He seems like a person that must equip himself with an excuse as to why he feeds his selfish ego."

"The trick with someone like that is to force him to be honest in his intentions," said al-Jeheuty.

Behar rested his arms against the table and looked at al-Jeheuty. There was warning in his voice when he spoke, "May you be surrounded by familiar faces if ever a man like al-Rinak is honest with his intentions. If not, that stranger standing next to you is on order to kill you." Behar then returned his attention to his food.

Roberto Hamaat strode into the café and alerted the Beylerbey and the officials that French ships had just been spotted on the horizon. Behar was informed that Governor Wakil and Taran Zaher were already waiting at the docks. The Beylerbey took a moment to finish his coffee and meal, giving his officials time to finish their food too. Behar stood first; the others followed his lead. The Beylerbey instructed Rahmis to pay the café owner. The official responded by calling Fumnyana to the table. He instructed the young woman to retrieve the café's owner. She returned with the man hastily. The owner hoped the Beylerbey and the officials enjoyed their morning meal. Behar assured the man that the food was splendid. Rahmis presented the café's proprietor with a sack of coins, which the owner did not expect to receive. He was surprised, and could not hide the expression from his manner and face. He kissed Behar's hands and bowed to the officials as he spoke his thanks. Behar presented a warm smile and then commanded his entourage to leave the café.

Behar's guards, as they exited the café and coffeehouse, immediately formed a tight perimeter around the Beylerbey and the officials. The party made their way beyond the city gates and to the docks. The small fleet of French barques settled into the Moorish harbor just as the Beylerbey's troupe approached. Simon Beaumont exited to a group of Moors that waited humbly outside his ship. He had shaggy, light brown hair atop his wide head that sported a large nose and an aging face. Simon was approaching his mid-forties, and his physique was starting to slump and thicken with age. He had broad shoulders and carried himself in the manner of importance and nobility, being a successful businessman in France.

A fellow Frenchman named Rene Chaffee walked next to Simon Beaumont. Rene was thirty-five, but still filled with youthful ambition and vigor. He had brown hair that was well groomed, and blue eyes beset in a chiseled, sunken face. The navy-blue capes worn by the French businessmen cast an illusion of them floating on the air as they journeyed down the plank. A troupe of soldiers marched behind them. Taran greeted both men in their native French. He introduced the men to Governor Wakil. He then escorted the Frenchmen to Behar and introduced Simon and Rene to the Beylerbey.

Simon and Rene bowed respectfully toward every official they were introduced to, though Behar did not receive a friendly kiss on the hand from the Frenchmen. Behar was able to overlook the inaction. Bo Yusuf did not. No one dwelled on the matter. Simon relieved the enmity of the moment by greeting Aatif pleasantly, and then he praised the established business between the French and the North African power. He introduced Rene Chaffee as his emissary to al-Mari Ifriq. "He will stay among you, overseeing business," Beaumont informed. "He will send reports to me every two weeks. I will visit once a month, staying a week to supervise all French activities."

Rene thanked Behar for his actions against Emile Raulf, though he did not mention specifically the deed. He simply said, "I praise you Beylerbey, and the state of al-Mari Ifriq, for assuring that no one could halt the progress of civilizing trade at sea. I find it most pleasant to dock in a North African state rather than bombarding it."

"Al-Mari Ifriq is not the state," Taran gently corrected the Frenchman.

Tension resurfaced. Bo Yusuf and Nasir cleared their throats. The offense came in the perception that the French Emissary was insinuating that al-Mari Ifriq was nothing more than an uncivilized corsair-state, governed by pirates, barbarians, and gangsters. Nasir understood very little of the French language, but he understood enough.

Al-Jeheuty put his arm around Rene and shook him playfully. "We are not a state. Yet," he said trying to dismantle the mounting tension. "We're just a port city, standing alone. A *city-state*, yes we are. Odongo-Mauharim—*the region*—we are trying to unify into a nation-state. The Griffin Regency, like the Guyotta Regency before us, stands as a local region or city-state. A true nation-state will be accomplished once we can connect with the Djenhai kingdom in a manner less business and more noble." He hugged the Frenchman tighter. "I am honored at your *compliment* to acknowledge our region as a cohesive state." Al-Jeheuty kept his smile.

He looked at Bo Yusuf and nonchalantly tugged his ear, scratched underneath his eye, and wiped his neck. This was a subtle gesture that Bo Yusuf understood that he now had orders to keep a careful eye and ear on Emissary Chaffee, and if necessary, silence him.

Bo Yusuf nodded in approval.

"Let us show these men where they will conduct business," al-Jeheuty suggested. "Then we will lead you gentlemen to town. There you will see the finest housing complex we have prepared for your stay. Is there a designated emissary for when Monsieur Chaffee wishes to visit his Mother Nation?"

"Yes," Simon answered. He called, "Gautier!" A short young man from the businessman's troupe jumped to attention. Simon presented Gautier Leolin with a proper introduction to the Moorish officials. He bowed and was then dismissed back to his position within the entourage. "Gautier will return to France with me. He will also be kept up-to-date when Rene sends his reports. He will only join your service in substitute for Rene."

The French were led to the Sa'ood company house. The building was renovated to accommodate a third level. The second level was now designated for the French Emissary and his administration. Nasir's quarters were moved to the newly made third level. The officials exited the company house and the tour moved into the city. The French were shown al-Mari Ifriq's various haunts, dives, and elegant districts. The French were then brought to an apartment complex located in the upper class district. Rene and his administration would live among the Moorish officials and affluent citizens of the city. The French were given time to settle in, and then were brought to the city palace for celebration.

Bo Yusuf stole a moment with al-Jeheuty and commented on the earlier exchange given by Emissary Chaffee. Al-Jeheuty relaxed the Moorish nationalist, assuring that eyes would be watching the French closely. "I believe Beaumont is sincere," al-Jeheuty said to Bo Yusuf. "He has the luxury to be, though. He will sit in France and profit off of Chaffee's work."

Nasir stumbled upon the officials' conversation. He kept silent on his feelings toward opening the door to a nation that had continuously bombarded the states of Africa-north. He felt al-Mari Ifriq was being put in great danger, but he did not protest with Behar or Wakil. He had one suggestion to make, however. He told al-Jeheuty, "Keep Taran separate from crucial information. We do not need anything passed on to our French guests."

"I will speak to Behar on that matter," al-Jeheuty affirmed. "I don't think Taran will crawl into bed with the French. His loyalty is to al-Rinak. That will be our greatest worry in the coming weeks."

"I hold my breath," sneered Bo Yusuf.

Al-Jeheuty kept his eyes on the mingling Frenchmen. "I still can't help but believe that the French are here to see how we operate," he disclosed. "We should feel that way about any foreign power that resides among us. Europeans are always wary about the success of the African Moor."

"Does this count for being one of your miracles?" Bo Yusuf teased his friend.

"I did believe that we would be working with the French, but I didn't think they would be our guests." Al-Jeheuty fixed his suit. "I hope the other nations don't see us as cavorting with the enemy. Our talks to Tunis and Algiers went well, though. We should be fine with our brother and sister nations." The official continued to watch the celebration and then announced, "Let us slip back into the festivities. We don't need to look obvious."

The officials meandered back into the celebration, which did not end inside the city palace. Behar disappeared to his private chamber, rendezvousing with Alimah Zaher. The French and Moorish officials moved their function to *The Siren's Call*. Rahmis hosted a casual affair filled with games, light music, and social drink and smoke. It was within these walls that Simon Beaumont declared that Eden and Heaven kissed at the tip of North Africa.

Chapter Twenty-One

Melusina presented her erotic proposition, her bare back facing al-Rinak. The top of her gown lay around her waist. She extended her left arm, turning her head in rhythm with the motion. Her arm rolled out like a line of gunpowder being eaten by sparkling fire. A gold necklace dangled from her hand, wrapped around a finger. With her left arm extended she informed sensuously, "I am French." She extended her right arm in the same manner. Her head turned to the right and she then stated, "I am Turkish." She concluded by asking al-Rinak, "Which part of me do you wish to lay with tonight?"

The black Turk raised an eyebrow. He contemplated and then gave his answer. Melusina twirled around to face him. Her gown slipped from her waist and piled at her feet, leaving her bare body exposed. She stepped away from the garment and straddled the sitting black Turk. Her arms wrapped around him and she began to melt into al-Rinak. He lifted from off the chair, Melusina wrapped around him like a human ornament. He brought her to the bed where he enjoyed the ethnic personality from which he wished to feed. Melusina enjoyed pleasing al-Rinak. Her sexual hunger and moan echoed through the cabin. The haunting erotic sounds plagued the crew every twelve hours since leaving Turkey.

The fleet's messenger boat had been sent an hour ago. The crew now argued as to which man would inform al-Rinak that al-Mari Ifriq was just in sight. The captain decided for five men to announce their approach to land by having them scream and alert the other crewmembers. The men announced in unison. Melusina's moans ceased in a regretful sigh as al-Rinak lifted from off her. It was not too long after that al-Rinak made his way to the deck clothed, primped, and perfumed. His crew formed two separate lines, standing straight and still. Al-Rinak walked coolly, flashing a salute to the mariners and soldiers. No man relaxed as al-Rinak approached the bow of the ship. The captain jumped to al-Rinak's side and informed him that the ship was making its final approach to the African port city.

Al-Rinak became transfixed on the horizon, watching the city grow larger and larger as his fleet made a final approach. Al-Mari Ifriq looked more like a fortress with its company houses, docks, and two large, armed lookout towers stretching across and shielding the city behind it. Looking beyond the obstruction of company houses and towering fortresses only allowed the eyes to gaze upon a magnificent gated facade that wrapped around the city and several acres of fertile land. Few buildings within the walls of the city peaked over the enclosure. Al-Rinak could only see a glimpse of the extravagant palace that lay at the back of al-Mari Ifriq. The city looked radiant, but desperate for a ruler.

The captain's voice was muffled under al-Rinak's private thoughts. The statesman sighed. His brother was no longer a resident of al-Mari Ifriq. His body lay at the bottom of the sea al-Rinak had just crossed. Buried with him were his fellow business partners and former rulers of the city. The statesman narrowed his eyes and spotted a party awaiting his approach. Al-Rinak could make out Ameer Las El-Behar's physical frame, a man given the title Beylerbey for the odious act of murder. The statesman smiled as he thought of the many storms he would bring to al-Mari Ifriq's coast. They would be storms that would wash away the Beylerbey and his troupe.

Al-Rinak stepped away from the bow. His thoughts still had his focus, but the captain's voice became coherent. He asked al-Rinak if a signal should be sent to Statesman Sinan Demir's vessel. Al-Rinak nodded, yes. He called for another crewmember to fetch Melusina. His mistress was brought to him, and al-Rinak traveled to the sturdy, wide, wooden plank to disembark from the docked ship. Al-Rinak's entourage swarmed in formation around him. He stepped from the vessel with Melusina at his side, the army of soldiers and seafarers in tow. His party merged with the party led by Statesman Sinan Demir.

Taran appeared in front of al-Rinak, deceitful smile beaming. Al-Rinak returned the courtesy. Taran brought him to Ameer Las El-Behar. The Beylerbey and he feigned a cordial re-introduction. Al-Rinak showed the Beylerbey enough respect to kiss his hands. He was, of course, on his soil. Then came Ameer Las El-Behar's officials. Al-Rinak kept appearances, his smile warm and charming as he bowed and shook hands.

The official named Bo Yusuf ibn Tachfin al-Dume was silent but not cold. He was very professional, and al-Rinak understood better the young Moor's mannerisms when he was introduced as the city's Army Official. Al-Rinak assessed that Bo Yusuf was calm on the surface but trembling underneath. The Army Official was waiting for the ideal war to strike so he might rush forward to command its waves like the perfect storm at sea. Al-Rinak believed that the young Moor lacked the understanding that nothing could prepare a person more for a situation than being in the situation itself.

Then there was al-Jeheuty Anhur Has. He was far more animated in his greeting toward al-Rinak. It was not that he was enthusiastic, it was just that his smile was wider, his eyes more focused. Behind his cordial manner al-Jeheuty appeared to be evaluating al-Rinak. The black Turk became rattled, but not so much that any emotion surfaced. If ever his fraudulent smile shifted, this negotiator, which al-Rinak had been informed of, would have noticed. Al-Rinak became a little worried when al-Jeheuty decided to grip his hand in gesture, and shake. Al-Jeheuty's grip was tight, both hands embracing al-Rinak's hand. The statesman considered the gesture a challenge, and he decided to concede to the provocation. Al-Rinak gripped his loose hand around al-Jeheuty's hands and equaled the might of the official's grip. The two officials stepped away from one another. Al-Rinak understood that there was always a way to handle a negotiator. Don't give into his demands. Match the negotiator's words with actions. Test him.

Al-Rinak greeted Nasir al-Din Sa'ood. He had already, months ago in Turkey, met the boy that engineered his brother's death. Al-Rinak bowed respectfully. His mood increased when he was introduced to Rahmis Husani. The handsome and pleasant young man briefed al-Rinak of the renowned services al-Mari Ifriq had to offer, and the comfortable housing where he and his guests would stay.

Behar returned to the statesman's side again. He informed al-Rinak on the city's status. Al-Rinak was grateful. This is what he wanted to know, information on the city, finding out where it stood. This was free information for which he neither had to bribe nor manipulate someone to obtain. Behar spoke on the state of the Ghanem Company, and he informed al-Rinak that he, Company Boss Feroz Aunun, and the Djenhai Princess would council and reveal greater details in private. Her caravan was traveling to the city at the moment.

Al-Rinak was also briefed on the French's presence. He was genuinely impressed by the invitation extended to the French state, considering all the brutal attacks made by French ships. The Dutch too had exchanged coin for their ships' protection at sea. Behar and his people achieved what was most likely the impossible. They had calmed the seas, and brought to the immediate world something no one but an African Moor could obtain. These Moors profited from peace at a time where war was a greater tool used to possess silver and gold. And more so, they were able to get the European to believe in such a concept. But al-Rinak was not naïve. He understood that foreign bodies taking an interest in al-Mari Ifriq, settling for peace, was a simple way to move closer to colonizing the land.

Al-Rinak was going to save al-Mari Ifriq from all the naïve optimism plaguing its current rulers. Guyotta Sahin-el Bey was a greedy man, according to al-Rinak. The former Regent Master believed that al-Mari Ifriq was simply a giant purse and treasury. That was why he died, in al-Rinak's opinion. To al-Rinak, and his late brother Aguyan, al-Mari Ifriq was the cornerstone of revolution. It was the active ingredient to unify the surrounding North African states and establish a mighty kingdom that could never be challenged. The statesman hated the knowledge that he would have to, in an attempt to erase the ills from the city, treat her like an abusive lover. Ironically his abusive actions would, to him, prove how much he loved al-Mari Ifriq. He needed her for the purpose of generating a powerful regime the likes of which had not been seen since his Moorish African cousins took Spain.

Al-Rinak was brought into the city, where Governor Wakil al-Hakam waited at the gates with his personal staff. Al-Rinak had last seen Wakil al-Hakam five or more years ago, when he visited al-Mari Ifriq for the last time before his brother's murder. Wakil, to al-Rinak, seemed as aloof as ever. The statesman always wondered how Wakil was ever considered a great lawyer, speaker, and ultimately now, governor of a city. Al-Rinak calculated that Behar and his revolutionaries were the true decision makers. He considered that Wakil was just a figurehead, a face with no true power, not even second to the Beylerbey. Rattling the Governor and shaking him from his high, political chair would not prove to be much of a feat.

From the gates, al-Rinak was guided to the quaint living quarters located near the palace. The area was an illustrious network of pristine and newly constructed apartment complexes. The buildings did not share the rest of the city's rough, weathered, and aged look. Al-Rinak and his retinue were provided rooms and allowed to settle in before the tour continued into the palace and ultimately to the al-Hammon brother's tavern. Most of al-Rinak's personnel stayed within their provided housing. Statesman Sinan, two personal guards and a servant, along with Melusina relaxed with al-Rinak inside *The Al-Hammon Palace.*

It was here that the Turks were introduced to the French Emissary Rene Chaffee. The French businessman's personnel surrounded him. He was cordial to al-Rinak but eager to segregate himself from any further interaction, citing business. Al-Rinak found his presence a foreign concept, but maintained appearances with a pleasant smile and tone of voice. Rene returned to his table, seated with a blonde haired, European man that appeared not to be a part of the French aides. The man was clean, but dressed like a rogue. He was a pirate, and al-Rinak, ever the observer, could see the man keeping a fixed position near Emissary Rene while he interacted with the Turks and Moorish officials. The rogue's gaze flinched only once, catching Bo Yusuf. The look toward the Army Official was for a brief moment, but al-Rinak could easily decipher the disdainful glare. When Rene returned to his table, Bo Yusuf commented that the rogue was Captain Kyler Piett, a *renegado*. Al-Rinak gave no mention of the sharp looks the *renegado* tossed toward Bo Yusuf, but he guessed by the tone in the Army Official's voice that the two did not see eye-to-eye.

Also milling around the tavern were some of the corsairs employed by the state, most notably the Captain of the Corsair Council, Hieremias Sunwil. His Boatswain, Tobal Lessman, his Quartermaster Yan 'Blackey' Nuh, and Chief Officer, Ras Ali joined him at the table. Al-Rinak had the pleasure of briefly meeting Captain Sunwil and his close crew when the Captain transported the Moorish officials to Turkey. Captain Sunwil was a very optimistic fellow, al-Rinak observed. There was clearly friction between Chief Officer Ras Ali and the Quartermaster and Boatswain. Either Captain Sunwil did not notice, or he believed that if he kept a wide smile and a delightful personality, others would not.

It was not too long before Governor Wakil returned to his duties, leaving the tavern. Rahmis politely dismissed himself to prepare for the arrival of the Djenhai's royal ambassador. Behar too excused himself to ready his council house for the scheduled meeting with the Djenhai ambassador, Feroz Aunun, Sinan Demir, and al-Rinak. Al-Jeheuty and Bo Yusuf stayed behind at the tavern, purposefully obstructing Taran and al-Rinak from conversing. The four officials sat back and engaged in small talk. Fusan and Maurice al-Hammon split the conversation. Taran stood and introduced his two adopted sons. Al-Rinak commented that the two boys were continuing to grow into fine young men since last he saw them.

A messenger interrupted the reunion, bringing word the Djenhai caravan was in the distance. Taran suggested that he, al-Jeheuty, and Bo Yusuf leave immediately. He assured al-Rinak that he would send back word once the Djenhai ambassador was accommodated and the meeting in the council house was underway.

The officials made their leave. Fusan casually strolled to the tavern entrance and signaled to Maurice that al-Jeheuty and Bo Yusuf were far from the building. Maurice asked al-Rinak and Melusina to stand. He wished to show the backrooms of the tavern to the black Turk and his mistress. "Should you ever need to rest during the night, we have space here." Maurice escorted both to one of the backrooms, entered after them, and shut the door behind him. Immediately upon the doors' close Maurice said, "I will be the intermediary between you and Taran."

Al-Rinak bobbed his head, less in acknowledgment and more in contemplation. "I will observe closely the undercurrent of all the politics confronting al-Mari Ifriq. I have observed much already," he informed. "Why does that *renegado* and the Army Official have so much disdain for one another?"

"There was a fight months ago," Maurice answered. "Bo Yusuf hit Captain Piett with a bottle, putting the captain in the infirmary. Piett has recovered well. However, greater injury was sustained when his claim in this tavern was stripped from him because he could not produce Dutch interest to seek al-Mari Ifriq for protection at sea. He and Fusan are good friends. They are partners at sea."

"I've heard," said al-Rinak. "A terrible team—in a good way. Has he latched onto the French Emissary?"

"Piett is a *renegado*," continued Maurice. "He is a convert to Mohammedan Law. But he is a European *first*. He finds comfort among a group of his own people, though they are not of the same *national* extraction. They are whites nonetheless."

"And how is the relationship between the French and al-Mari Ifriq?" al-Rinak inquired.

"Between Simon Beaumont and the city officials," started Maurice. "Things are tight. They could not be better. Beaumont's emissary, Rene Chaffee—whom you have met—he does not feel so at ease with rubbing elbows with us blacks. Africa is for investment, especially in its indigenous people. That's his belief, so I'm told."

"And who has told you," asked al-Rinak already having an answer in mind.

Maurice confirmed the statesmen's suspicions when he answered, "Captain Piett."

Al-Rinak smiled, his suspicions correct. "Good. Has he any other information?"

Maurice was enthusiastic. "Emissary Chaffee continues to hint that he answers to more than one benefactor. He may be a French spy."

"I'm sure the Beylerbey is cautious, if not aware." He put a fatherly hand on Maurice's shoulder. "Let us confirm this information. We'll make Emissary Chaffee answer to us as well." Al-Rinak contemplated for a moment. "I think it would be best for me to meet the noblewoman scheduled to appear. Maurice, take me to where she will arrive. I dare not miss a second of observing her manner."

Chapter Twenty-Two

Al-Mari Ifriq's southern wall stared down the march of soldiers parading over the sandy horizon. The train of soldiers scurried like black ants trailing from an anthill. The Djenhai convoy was militaristic in nature, armed with seventy-two soldiers, twenty-five of which rode atop camels that surrounded three enormous elephants fashioned with canopied carriages. The middle carriage hosted Royal Ambassador Yaminah Igdobe Djenhai, Daughter of the Queen of the Second World.

The meaning of the Second World in her mother's title referenced Mohammedanism. The first Djenhai king, who took a beautiful, black Moorish woman as his second bride, and proclaimed himself the *King of Two Worlds*, as he professed Mohammedanism and became an African Ambassador of the Mohammedan Law. The First World was Africa, or more specifically, Nubia, from where the first king, and his people hailed. The first king, and every king of Djenhai thereafter, passed on his state of affairs through two bloodlines. The Queen of the Second World's first son and first daughter would be the Ambassadors to Foreign Trade and Foreign Affairs.

The notion of a Second World—that being Mohammedanism—was becoming more and more obsolete, however. The current African Moors residing in al-Mari Ifriq were increasingly separating faith from politics. The Mohammedan Theocracy of the defunct Four Winds Company and former Regent Master was now part of the many tolerated faiths among the populace. The current Queen of the Second World, Queen A'sharia, worried more and more about her role, and the role her children and descending bloodline would play, as this trend continued. Yaminah Igdobe Djenhai's undertaking in al-Mari Ifriq was to personally gauge how the new Beylerbey and his officials would affect Djenhai's Second World.

And so continued to march the Djenhai caravan in pursuit of business. The Djenhai warriors were cloaked in the custom African robes, wraps, and scarves of their kingdom's military dress. Breastplates made from fine metal protected them, worn over their robes. The army was divided into swordsmen, musket men, and spearmen. Riders leading the caravan held a pole furnished with the kingdom's flag and colors that whipped furiously in the wind.

Al-Jeheuty was transfixed by the military procession. He understood that the Djenhai kingdom was not declaring a show of power. The caravan's heavy armament was for protection against the Ogunsanwo-Mashek, a desert marauding tribe locked in a fiery feud against the Djenhai kingdom. The conflict between the two nations was hundreds of years old, and sadly the feud's reason was lost with time. Border disputes were what either side clung to for motivation. This did not make much sense, however, because the Ogunsanwo-Mashek people were nomadic, though they wandered within a set region of Odongo-Mauharim. Their migrant lifestyle was seasonal, and the Djenhai kingdom's borders did not disturb the Ogunsanwo-Mashek migration. The Djenhai's second king expanded the kingdom's borders in 1275. The third king put protective walls around the large city in 1337, thirteen years before the Ogunsanwo-Mashek arrived as refugees from Africa-east. The fighting between the Ogunsanwo-Mashek and the Djenhai people occurred in the time of Djenhai's fourth king.

Al-Jeheuty feared that the talks between al-Mari Ifriq and the Djenhai Kingdom would stir massive attacks from the nomadic tribe. He demanded Mehit leave for Tunisia before the Djenhai people's arrival. This strict command was for her safety, and Mehit understood the danger, though they had just returned from Nusurika, attending Aatif's wedding. With worries that the antagonistic tribe would perceive al-Mari Ifriq as an enemy aligned with the Djenhai kingdom, all activity coming from the city had the potential to be attacked. Mehit left al-Mari Ifriq a week prior to the Royal Ambassador's arrival. She traveled with her mother, outfitted with several Moons and Suns from Roberto's Seventy-Two Points of the Universe assassin clan. Al-Jeheuty was intrigued by Behar's sudden pleasant mood when Taran announced to him that his wife would be leaving the city to accompany Mehit. Behar explained to al-Jeheuty that with Alimah gone, Taran's control over the garment district would be alleviated long enough for Behar to shift the power to Isaiah's company. The truth, unbeknownst to al-Jeheuty, was that Alimah would return earlier than she had proposed to her husband, and would be snuck into Behar's quarters for the two to spend time together.

The army eased their approach and stopped in front of the officials, Taran and Rahmis, closest to the caravan. Rahmis stood still, but his emotions quietly quivered on the inside. His nervous demeanor oddly translated into a smug smile. He took a deep breath as the second elephant, commanded by soldiers trained as handlers, knelt to the earth floor. Four strong soldiers walked to the side of the elephant. They carried with them a gold colored palanquin, the compartment of which was shaded with a sparkling, light-blue curtain. The brawny soldiers lifted the palanquin to the exact location of Yaminah Igdobe Djenhai's compartment. The woman slipped from the elephant mounted coach to the carried palanquin. Rahmis shifted, trying quickly to get a glance of the Royal Ambassador. The soldiers lowered the carriage to their shoulders, making the ordeal look effortless. They lugged the noble ambassador to the Moorish officials and set the carriage down. Two soldiers moved the curtain aside and Yaminah Igdobe Djenhai stepped out.

The royal ambassador's face was cloaked in a veil that was attached to a bowled, gold colored cap resting atop her head. The cap was tailored to expose her ears and allow her thick, shoulder-length locks to be wrapped up in a bun on either side of her head. The sovereign woman elegantly lifted the veil in a meticulously cultured grace. She drew back the veil in what could only be described as the precise moment. Yaminah revealed her smooth, beautiful, ebony face. The sun resonated off her cheeks, elevating the hidden purple hue lying deep within her flesh. Her amber eyes, though dark, shimmered brightly. Yaminah appraised the audience in front of her. She stepped forward. Every movement made by Yaminah was deliberate, regally erudite. The noble emissary was clothed in a long, dark brown skirt that boasted a mustard colored waistline. Her upper garment possessed long sleeves that matched the colors of her skirt.

The Moorish and Turkish officials bowed in Yaminah's presence. She presented an admirable smile at their gesture. "Rise," she said in a pleasant voice, and in al-Mari Ifriq's common language. Her voice, though low and humble, carried an authoritative sound. The men stood up. Behar walked between Taran and Rahmis. He put his hands together and bowed respectfully toward Yaminah.

Behar spoke in the Djenhai language. He spoke slowly, but his words were well practiced. "Yaminah Igdobe Djenhai, Daughter of the Queen of the Second World. I am Beylerbey Ameer Las El-Behar, and I welcome you to al-Mari Ifriq."

Governor Wakil appeared at Behar's side. He echoed Behar's manner, bowing. He spoke a pleasant, Mohammedan greeting toward Yaminah. She replied to the governor's greeting, her smile bright. Behar introduced Yaminah to the other officials, presenting first Taran, his title, and then Rahmis. "This is Rahmis Husani," said Behar. "He will be responsible for your comfort in our city."

Rahmis and Yaminah exchanged cordial smiles. Rahmis was drawn to the regal ambassador's wide, curious eyes and smile, interpreting

Yaminah's gestures as exclusive to him. The princely city host spoke in his patent deep, rich voice. "Your High Emissary, the treatment you will receive within these walls will make you believe that you have not left the comfort of your home city, but you will experience the exoticism of travel to another land. I can only apologize for the lightheaded side effects that will leave you breathless from your experience in al-Mari Ifriq."

Every sensuous nerve inside Yaminah's body vibrated with the touch of Rahmis' voice and physical presentation. He was a dream made flesh. He was the dream all young African women had. The dream of the dark, regal Afro-Moorish man carved from the black core of the universe itself, and speaking in the deep, rich tone that vibrated from the universe's core, a tone so often echoed by meditating priests. Yaminah pulled from every lesson of her royal schooling to keep still and look unfazed. The greatest lesson she extracted was that on courting, most importantly a man's approach. Yaminah calculated that Rahmis was completely aware of his prowess, and confident in his presentation as well. He was more than just an excellent host. He was an excellent marksman in flirtation. Yaminah kept her composure, even when she discreetly rubbed her knees together, a warm river salivating underneath her skirt.

Behar introduced Yaminah to two other officials. The first was al-Jeheuty Anhur Has, presented as the city's Commissioner of Affairs. "It is a great pleasure to meet you, Royal Emissary," he greeted Yaminah professionally.

"It has been far too long, Lord Anhur Has," she replied to him. "A legitimate, face-to-face discussion between kingdom and city is long overdue." Al-Jeheuty bowed respectfully. Yaminah considered him a warrior with words, waiting to strike with any physical weapon if the situation called for such behavior. Her head automatically turned to the second official even before Behar gave a proper introduction. The Royal ambassador was immediately drawn to the official's presence. Yaminah smiled at him awkwardly, as if she was a simple citizen and he was the royal figure. She froze. The man was introduced to her as the city's Army Official. His name was Bo Yusuf ibn Tachfin al-Dume. He was tall, stretching toward the sun. He looked like he was born from Africa's wild, desert storms. The sands congealed into a physical man.

Bo Yusuf bowed to Yaminah, smiling in a manner none of his colleagues had ever witnessed. The knightly Moor sensed Yaminah's hesitant manner. He moved closer to her and displayed an uncharacteristic form of humor to quell the situation, "I am the Army Official of a city that ironically does not officially have an army." Yaminah chuckled at Bo

Yusuf's words. "I lead what I can. I am also the Minister of Defensive Strategy and the Beylerbey's representative in the Council of Captains."

Behar walked to Yaminah's side. "Strategy will be the focus of our topic on trade with the Djenhai kingdom. We will discuss the southern route, its protection against the Ogunsanwo-Mashek, and the possibilities of meeting with your father, the King, in hopes to establish a true State for Odongo-Mauharim. Bo Yusuf will see to the care of your entourage. There is a barracks built outside the western district."

Bo Yusuf and Yaminah exchanged smiles. The royal emissary turned to her caravan and explained to Behar, "My brother has joined me. He's here to learn about your city, and to learn about the duties of an ambassador. He's only sixteen."

"There is a school in session for young men," stated Behar. "Perhaps he can attend while on his stay."

"That would be excellent, Beylerbey." Yaminah commanded the leaders of each of the guards' units to follow Bo Yusuf. The leaders assigned their top soldiers to escort Yaminah through the city. Assigned to guard Yaminah was a swordsman, a spearman, and a musketman who was also equipped with a short sword. The two other elephants were handled with care, and made to sit at ease while four servants exited from the third elephant's carriage and Yaminah's teenage brother exited the first elephant's carriage. Yaminah introduced her brother to the officials. His name was Asim Igdobe Djenhai. He was a handsome young man that looked eager to put his charm to work, mostly on the female population of al-Mari Ifriq. He was dressed in a green billowing outfit that was outlined with gold designs, and atop his head was a wrap the same color as his suit. Asim was instructed to follow Bo Yusuf while the Army Official helped the Djenhai caravan gather and be led to the barracks.

Yaminah and Bo Yusuf stole one last glance at one another, and beamed a parting smile. Yaminah was escorted through the palace, entering through the rear courtyard, now cleared of its maze of hedges and mirroring the courtyard in the front. Rahmis described the palace's history in great detail, regurgitating every facet of the palace's grand past that he learned from Nasir. Rahmis' historical recount prompted Yaminah to ask if he was born in al-Mari Ifriq. Excited to narrate his past, Rahmis presented his history as a revolutionary in Spain. He also mentioned being under command of Behar, and that al-Jeheuty and Bo Yusuf were also lieutenants. Yaminah responded to Bo Yusuf's name, Rahmis mistaking her interest as a gesture made toward him. She became intrigued that the Army Official had experienced the same history as a revolutionary. Rahmis went on to explain how Behar demanded his lieutenants study their family history, finding his moment to recount to the royal emissary about his noble lineage. Yaminah remarked how remarkable that must have been. She also commented that the city was lucky to adopt such men, especially at a time of turmoil when the former leaders were lost.

Yaminah's tour continued out into the lovely district where visiting nobles and ambassadors were accommodated. Rahmis' rich voice dissected every aspect of al-Mari Ifriq, pointing out the farmlands inside and beyond the walls, and the two, large industrial mints placed in the northeast district that manufactured coin for currency. He was poetic with his speech, elevating the city to the level of a magical kingdom. His voice was warm, but did not caress Yaminah in the same manner as when she first heard it. Now Rahmis' voice was like a gentle song that played in the background while Yaminah thought of the Moorish Army Official, Bo Yusuf ibn Tachfin al-Dume. The royal emissary's tour of the city ceased at the complex of living quarters reserved for her, her personal servants, and assigned guard. Rahmis aided Yaminah in settling within her living quarters. He then left so that she could rest from her travel.

Yaminah was granted several hours to rest before holding council with Beylerbey Behar, Governor Wakil, Commissioners Taran Zaher and al-Jeheuty Anhur Has, Company Boss Feroz Aunun, and the Turkish Officials al-Rinak Ozan and Sinan Demir. Rahmis returned to Yaminah's guest quarters and escorted her and her party to Behar's council house. The sovereign ambassador complimented the staff of the guest quarters and expressed to Rahmis, "You were correct. I feel as if I have not left the walls of the Djenhai palace. Al-Mari Ifriq is truly a home away from home."

"Your compliments are well received," said Rahmis. "I dare not speak out of place with politics, but perhaps this draws us closer to a unified state. Djenhai and al-Mari Ifriq, the kingdom and the capital city of Odongo-Mauharim."

Yaminah nodded politely. "My father would love to see that. We just fear an all out war with the Ogunsanwo-Mashek."

"Again, Royal Emissary," Rahmis began, "I do not wish to speak out of place, but I don't believe such a small tribe could afford a full-scale war."

Yaminah noted how much more interesting the princely Moor was when he let his urbane façade melt away into an engaging personality. She answered Rahmis, "War would rage on the trade routes. It would draw al-Mari Ifriq into a conflict I don't believe it could handle. Not without an official army."

Rahmis inquired, "Is it possible that peace could also rage?"

"There's a trick to that question," Yaminah responded. "If I answer 'no' then I give up on the possibility. If I answer 'yes', I ignore the reality of the situation. Where we stand now is with arms at one another."

Yaminah and her entourage were the last to arrive at the council house. This was deliberate. When the royal ambassador arrived there was an authentic Djenhai carpet leading from the door to the council area. Trumpeters announced Yaminah's arrival, and as the sounds of the trumpets ceased, musicians played a lovely string-piece composed by a famous Djenhai melodist. Yaminah was flattered, bowing in appreciation and beaming a smile toward Wakil and Behar. She tossed a playful, accusing eye at Feroz Aunun, knowing the company boss, and relative, put the Beylerbey and governor up to this. Wakil met Yaminah at the carpet's end and said in an almost apologetic tone, "I hope this is not too overwhelming."

"I feel very welcomed, Governor," Yaminah assured.

"Please, sit," instructed Wakil. "We will have refreshments afterwards. Company Boss Aunun has instructed our cooks to prepare an authentic Djenhai meal."

Wakil led the royal emissary to her seat. She was positioned directly in front of Behar as he sat with his legs crossed atop his bed. Al-Jeheuty and Feroz Aunun sat on either side of her. Taran Zaher sat adjacent to Company Boss Aunun, the Turkish officials sitting on the other side of al-Jeheuty. Wakil took a seat facing them, positioned next to Behar's bed. "Let's begin," stated the governor. "This council comes together over the business of the Ghanem Company. This one company has three great investors. There is a kingdom that built the company. There is an Empire that re-constructed it. There is its company boss that not only runs it, but is connected by blood and nationality to the two investors earlier defined." Wakil scanned the participants. His eyes became fixed on Yaminah, a perplexed look on her visage. "Royal Emissary...?"

Yaminah blinked. Her mouth hung open for a moment as she tried to find the words. "What of its fourth investor?" she asked. "Al-Mari Ifriq. The Beylerbey, and you as the governor?" She waved the question aside before an answer could be provided. "Ghanem, or Marjani as was its original Djenhai name, is the heart of all the companies within this wonderful city's walls. With four chambers connected to it—four interested parties—Ghanem-Marjani is the true four winds of the regency." She looked to every man in the room, specifically the interested parties, and then addressed Wakil and Behar. "Governor and Beylerbey, our unique connections to the company are what makes our separate ventures thrive—though I may not be able to speak firmly for the Turkish Empire. I'm sure they have plenty of investments."

"Which we see as equally important to one another," al-Rinak interjected.

"Yes, Statesman Ozan." Yaminah nodded. "But if I understand the company's role completely," she continued, "then I believe that tributes are shipped to the Empire. Company Boss Aunun receives revenue, and holds the duty of overseeing the minor shipping and trade companies within the city. And the Beylerbey and the Governor are in charge of overseeing that all accounted goods and trade-imports are brought back into the city for al-Mari Ifriq to prosper."

"That is correct," stated Behar.

Yaminah added, "Djenhai sees tribute."

"Is the problem the amount of tribute?" Wakil asked.

"No," the royal emissary assured. "The problem, as we all know, is with the lack of trade. We have much to export to al-Mari Ifriq. We have much to import from the city too. There are exotic goods and trade that al-Mari Ifriq possesses that Djenhai wishes to take part in. We don't ask in a manner that stems from greed, but in a manner that stems from fairness. Our company oversees these goods and trades. We also have product that al-Mari Ifriq could benefit from. My father seeks trade and good relations—balanced relations that may possibly lead to a unified state."

Wakil smiled. "That is what we have sought for so many years," he expressed. "Many years before your birth, and many years before your father was king."

"However, it has only been within the last two years that this relationship has become attainable. But what has stopped us," Yaminah said in an authoritative tone. "Nothing but the extreme ferocity of a barbaric people. The trade routes have become infested with the Ogunsanwo-Mashek; the safer travel routes are not suitable for trade caravans. The activity of the Ogunsanwo-Mashek has lessened since the tragedy of al-Mari Ifriq's former leaders. We, a triad made up of a great Empire, kingdom, and city, dare not disturb the rabid hyenas. But we can't stay our hand much longer."

"Do you call for war, Royal Emissary?" Behar asked. His eyebrow arched in curiosity.

Yaminah responded in a lighter tone, "Absolutely not, Beylerbey. I would not condone a course of action that would threaten my kingdom and its people, even those ready to fight. I simply call for a push to increase trade and relations between kingdom and city."

Al-Jeheuty added, "Would you agree to push for peace talks and negotiations with the Ogunsanwo-Mashek?"

Al-Rinak coolly suggested before Yaminah could answer, "Protecting the trade routes should be the primary concern. I believe I have a solution."

Al-Jeheuty decided to ignore the Turkish statesman. He pressed harder his question, repeating, "Would you agree to push for peace talks and negotiations with the Ogunsanwo-Mashek?"

"I would," Yaminah answered. "But Statesman Ozan is correct. Protecting the trade routes should be the primary concern. I would like to hear the statesman's solution." Al-Rinak leaned forward to speak, his mouth opened to state his proposition. Before he could utter a word he was interrupted by Yaminah's concluding words, "But I would very much like to hear how al-Mari Ifriq plans to bring peace to a war that has raged for hundreds of years. Please, Lord Anhur Has, speak."

Al-Rinak sat back.

Al-Jeheuty first addressed Behar. "I extend my apologize on the outset of the words I'm about to speak. They might touch a sensitive issue." He turned to al-Rinak and spoke, "I set my apology before your feet, Statesman Ozan." Al-Jeheuty watched closely as the statesman raised an eyebrow out of curious reflex. "There have been whispers that The Four Winds, including your brother Aguyan, were assassinated by the current rulers of al-Mari Ifriq, rumors of revolution. I wish to suppress the erroneous claims of the rumors, but exploit what is true about them." Al-Rinak was more enthralled by the young official's words rather than offended. He permitted al-Jeheuty to speak further. Al-Jeheuty addressed Wakil and Behar, they too anticipating al-Jeheuty's plan. "We fan not the rumors of revolution, but the sincerity of myself, our current Beylerbey, the Army Official, the city host, and lead dock worker, as Moorish revolutionaries from Spain." He turned to Yaminah. "The Djenhai people look upon the Ogunsanwo-Mashek as desert marauders, barbarians. That is fair, considering the hostility. But they may view themselves as revolutionaries. We may gain their ear if al-Mari Ifriq's current rulers, revolutionaries as we are, can be perceived as having only the potential to empathize with their cause. They will talk to us. We will have them talk to you."

Everyone looked at Yaminah. The royal ambassador smiled as if seduced by the words of a remarkable poet. "Even if Djenhai wanted peace, I don't believe the Ogunsanwo-Mashek would agree to meet. They may even see Djenhai's move toward peace as a trap—that has been used in the past. Your plan has great potential, though." Al-Jeheuty bowed his head at Yaminah. "I must still consider protecting our trade routes." She looked to al-Rinak. "Statesman Ozan."

"I would like to volunteer the Turkish troops that still reside in al-Mari Ifriq," al-Rinak proposed. "There are a little more than two-hundred troops. We can put them to use." Behar boiled, but he did not allow his emotions to stir on the surface, however. Al-Rinak supplied an apologetic expression and proclaimed, "This will be temporary, of course. The troops are scheduled for leave. I can arrange for the Empire to extend their stay for these specific services until al-Mari Ifriq can build an official standing army, or peaceful terms are met with the Ogunsanwo-Mashek. I only ask that half of the army reside in al-Mari Ifriq, and half the army reside within Djenhai. One contingent protects the caravan one way; the other contingent of troops protects the caravan on its return. This will insure that each leg of travel will have fully rested soldiers on guard."

Yaminah agreed. Al-Rinak smiled on the inside. He knew the young woman's status as royal emissary could not hide her nature as a woman. According to al-Rinak, Yaminah was like all women, wanting the assurance of security, protection. Even when dealing with the young, handsome male officials of al-Mari Ifriq, al-Rinak noticed the royal ambassador seemed to favor the one with the sword over the one with the elegant speech and noble demeanor. Had her father been in attendance, al-Rinak would have proposed the army as a showcase of power, because, according to the Turkish Statesman, all great men of importance needed to be recognized for their strength. Al-Rinak could now rest easy knowing that he had a standing army at his command. There was no protest from the Beylerbey or the governor. Both men bestowed their blessing in the matter and adjourned the council. Behar stood from his bed and shook the hands of each official, bowing courteously toward Yaminah.

"Let me not forget, Beylerbey," expressed Yaminah, "that my father extends an invitation to Djenhai."

"How long will your stay be, royal woman?" Behar asked.

"Three days," the Princess answered.

Behar smiled in a warm manner. "Then I will return to Djenhai with you. Feroz Aunun and Statesman Ozan will accompany me." He looked at the two gentlemen. They nodded, confirming that his orders would be respected and carried out. "Good," said Behar.

"You will enjoy yourself, Beylerbey," Feroz expressed. "Djenhai is an otherworldly kingdom. It harkens back to the days of ancient African kingdoms."

"You'll need the vacation," said Wakil with a round of laughter. "Tomorrow we are due in court. Jabari, several other lawyers, and citizens will be presenting cases. There are over one-hundred disputes."

Behar sighed. Nothing was more boring than court. He called for al-Jeheuty and ordered, "Counsel with Bo Yusuf and Captain Sunwil about putting together an outfit of fifty or more soldiers to guard trade by land. No one from Roberto's outfit may join. That is our police." He walked away from the other officials, al-Jeheuty keeping close as Behar whispered low, "Have this be a secret matter. I don't want other nations, states, or—"

"Wandering tribes," al-Jeheuty finished.

"Correct," applauded Behar. Their conversation moved outside as the other officials were brought Djenhai-inspired refreshments and meals. Wakil dismissed himself and joined al-Jeheuty and Behar as the Beylerbey continued, "I do not want anyone believing that we are arming ourselves for the purpose of setting out and conquering, especially as we have brought peace for the past two years." Behar briefed Wakil on the subject matter discussed.

"Yes," said Wakil. "Many would perceive that we were trying to lull the other states to sleep with promises of peace while we prepare for war."

"I'll keep the word within the Council of Captains," assured al-Jeheuty. "The al-Jasi's warrior-class is continually looking to join and serve in an established al-Mari Ifriq army. We've regulated them to galley ships to hijack marked trade vessels. I don't feel it would be in our best interest for them to join a caravan guard. I just have a bad feeling about the possible setbacks of the al-Jasi and Ogunsanwo-Mashek clashing."

"And we will see clashing before there are any moves toward peace talks," Behar stated firmly.

"But we may use the al-Jasi's story as a way to take steps toward much needed peace talks with the Ogunsanwo-Mashek," suggested Wakil. "If the Ogunsanwo-Mashek see that we have assimilated a nomadic nation into the city, that would be further proof of our sincerity for peace."

"Talking with al-Mari Ifriq is one thing, talking with people they have been at war with for hundreds of years is another," Behar said in a skeptical tone.

"Whatever gets us closer to talking with the Ogunsanwo-Mashek nation," Wakil affirmed. "We'll increase the number of caravan guards by continuing to draw from the supply of soldiers not on duty with corsairs or trade captains. We have to quickly establish an official guard for trades by land. We must not allow al-Rinak control of a Turkish army inside our walls, or inside the walls of the Djenhai kingdom."

All three men agreed, and then stepped back into the council house to join the festivities. The affair did not last long. Al-Rinak and Sinan retired first, stating that a long travel by sea had exhausted them. Feroz Aunun departed next, Yaminah following him to his company house to examine work and official papers. There, Yaminah reunited with her brother, who had been escorted around by Bo Yusuf. Asim helped to overlook papers, studying the duties of a company boss along with his sister. He stayed with Feroz Aunun even as Bo Yusuf escorted Yaminah and her entourage to their housing.

Yaminah revealed that Rahmis mentioned being brothers-in-arms with Bo Yusuf while they lived in Spain. Bo Yusuf confirmed and expounded on the stories. Yaminah asked what did he learn of his bloodline, and the Moorish Army Official answered that he was connected to a line of knights and soldiers. He revealed to her that his father taught him their family history at an early age. Bo Yusuf brushed aside the awkward feeling he often felt when he was opening up to someone; he spoke honestly, clearly, and with confidence.

It was not long before Rahmis joined their party. His mouth hammered into the conversation and never slowed down. Yaminah and Bo Yusuf exchanged quaint smiles at one another as Rahmis' voice played like gentle music in the background.

Chapter Twenty-Three

Bo Yusuf's smile lasted for a week. It started the day after he spent a pleasant evening with Yaminah Igdobe Djenhai and had not faded since. He reminisced about their walk through al-Mari Ifriq's streets, escaping a party held in honor of strengthening the union between al-Mari Ifriq and the Djenhai kingdom, a step in the direction of a nation-state, a government with a traditional monarchy. Their escape took them through the winding streets and avenues of al-Mari Ifriq, Bo Yusuf pointing to the areas torn by old feuds and hostility. The former revolutionary admitted to Yaminah, *"I may not have walked these city streets in those times, but I have lived a life that can relate to its damage."*

Yaminah responded to Bo Yusuf's words by saying, *"I still fear waking up and seeing Djenhai in flames. The other side of the wall has always been a symbol of the unknown and a symbol of strife."*

The conversation was not bleak, however. Politics, concentrating on nationalism and the birth of a nation-state took front stage. Both were passionate about the ideals of an African state, especially to work against the increasing encroachment of European slavers. Both dazzled one another with their knowledge of the ancient past, al-Andalusia, and ancient philosophical thought. The laughter and lightheartedness seeped into their conversation when Yaminah tried to teach Bo Yusuf words and phrases from the Djenhai language. He in turn tried to teach the royal emissary some of the European languages. She was fluent in the Romance Languages, surprising Bo Yusuf. She continued to jump on him for his mispronunciation of native words and sayings.

They slipped back into the party only to regroup with Yaminah's entourage. That same night, Bo Yusuf escorted Yaminah back to her housing, entourage in tow. Bo Yusuf ended the night with a respectful bow toward the royal emissary and nothing more. The night may have faded, but Bo Yusuf's smile and lighter attitude did not.

The Army Official's smile would only be eclipsed by the Beylerbey's elated emotions, brought on by his wonderful trip to the Djenhai kingdom. When he returned from Djenhai, the Beylerbey claimed, *"My lieutenants, we have been surrounded by war too long. Al-Mari Ifriq is not a ghetto, but there are too many remnants of its war torn past. There is much to repair. It must have a greater sparkle if it is to be the capital of our nation-state. Djenhai is a kingdom that reflects cities only spoken of in legends and mythologies spread around the world."*

Behar informed his council that King Igdobe Djenhai was an exuberant spirit, and looking forward to more talks seeking to unify Odongo-Mauharim. He also reported that he and the king spoke about specific trades, and he stated that King Igdobe allowed him to inspect the best of Djenhai's goods. *"Yaminah spoke highly of her stay,"* Behar also notified. *"She extends a special thanks to the city's host, Rahmis Husani—whom she referred to as the Noble Host."* Rahmis received the compliment with a halfhearted smile. There was no news presented to Bo Yusuf, but the Army Official did not mind. It did not halt his smile, which he carried for several more days. It even garnered Captain Piett's attention. The raucous renegado made passive-aggressive comments critiquing Bo Yusuf's mood. The Army Official retorted just the same. He asked the captain, "How's your head?"

No more was discussed between them.

That is when Bo Yusuf dismissed himself, walking from *The al-Hammon Palace* and into the city streets, sparkling with the reflection of the noonday sun above. He continued up the street, still smiling. He greeted passersby warmly as the citizens bowed to the Army Official out of respect. Bo Yusuf grouped with al-Jeheuty, Ojodo, and Nasir who were on their way to the coffeehouse for a light meal before returning to Nasir's company house. Bo Yusuf joined them, his smile still holding. Al-Jeheuty teased him relentlessly as the men sat down and gave their orders to Fumnyana, the young servant girl.

"You can't wipe that smile away, can you?" probed al-Jeheuty.

Bo Yusuf pointed from across the table, "Make no judgment. I'm still a sonava bitch ready to fight. My father always used to say that to Behar."

Ojodo witnessed Rahmis make his way down the street. "And you may have to fight. Here comes the *Noble Host.*"

Bo Yusuf looked up and watched his brother-in-arms approach the table. Rahmis looked pleasant, but he could not keep his eyes off Bo Yusuf. Fumnyana approached Rahmis immediately. He barely gave her notice as he ordered a cup of coffee. Fumnyana disappeared as quick as she came. Rahmis sat down and patted Bo Yusuf on the back. "Still smiling?" he asked. "Do not wear your smile long. I have received news that Yaminah has requested me to help prepare Djenhai for a celebration that will commemorate the arrival of the first train of goods coming from al-Mari Ifriq." Rahmis looked at the others and notified, "Roberto put together two safe passages that should not upset the Ogunsanwo-Mashek. The routes also do not deviate too far from Djenhai. They should not be cumbersome. They probably will add no more than one or two hours from the normal travel to Djenhai."

Bo Yusuf, despite Rahmis' plea to not become accustomed to smiling, asked his friend, "And once inside the kingdom's walls you plan on showering Yaminah with more of your cultured recounts?"

Rahmis chuckled. "Watch close from al-Mari Ifriq's southern wall. Equip yourself with the finest scope. You will see me sneaking out of her palace window by morning."

"Under the cover of darkness she won't know it's you," Ojodo remarked. Their meals were placed down in front of them. Light music from two Moorish musicians played behind them. "You will be surprised when her aroused tone speaks Bo Yusuf's name."

Rahmis waved the suggestion away as the others at the table laughed lightly. "She will know me by my noble touch. Should trouble arise my brother here will use his fine negotiating skills to initiate my release." He aimed his hand toward al-Jeheuty.

"Brother?" al-Jeheuty exclaimed. "I don't remember us sharing a mother."

"*In arms*, good Moor," Rahmis said as he laughed. "And in spirit."

Ojodo nudged al-Jeheuty and commented, "He'll use that argument too, should his escapades get him thrown in the Djenhai cells. *My brother is an Official of al-Mari Ifriq!*"'

Rahmis said before he took a sip of his drink, "I just might."

Al-Jeheuty waved his hand around and blurted, "Oh hell no you won't." He sat up, smiling and enjoying the moment with his friends. They stole small chances in official meetings to let loose and laugh. Most of their downtime was spent at a tavern among the company of others. Rarely had they the chance to enjoy one another's company without an engagement that pertained to business. "Because when the Djenhai police throw your ass in a cell, and I'm called upon to negotiate your release, this is what I'll say: *'What, Officer? My brother? Oh, no. We definitely had different fathers.'*" The table roared with laughter. "Check this out." Al-Jeheuty pointed to himself and declared, "Sunrise," he pointed to Rahmis and said, "Midnight. No way."

Rahmis took another shot of his coffee, treating the drink as if it was a harder substance. "I could slap the locks off your head, smartass." He laid his cup down and stood. "I have to meet with Behar in the palace. I will be traveling to Djenhai in three days. Don't let this uncivilized place crumble without me."

"We won't," spoke Bo Yusuf. "Not with me on guard."

Fumnyana appeared just as Rahmis straightened himself to leave. He interrupted her before she spoke and then asked that his friends be treated well for the rest of their stay. She brushed his shoulders clean and smiled at him. She put her hands together, bowed at the neck, and stepped away into the back. Rahmis made his leave.

Ojodo watched the servant girl and Rahmis as the two of them left their company. "Rahmis took her to bed," Ojodo reported when the coast was clear. "I overheard him talking to Fusan about it. That's why she's so wrapped around him, at his every command and appearance."

"When did this happen," asked Nasir.

Ojodo again looked over his shoulder to make sure Fumnyana was not around. She was nowhere to be seen. He leaned over the table and whispered, "Not too long after Yaminah left. Supposedly he purchased a gown for Fumnyana. He described the garment as being fit for a princess."

Bo Yusuf reacted with a sour expression on his face. "He used her?"

Ojodo confirmed with a nod of his head as he said, "Taking one woman to be with another on his mind. The maiden is none-the-wiser. And now she hangs at his every command."

"And he still pursues Yaminah?" Nasir whispered.

"Let's not mention the royal emissary anymore in his presence," commanded al-Jeheuty. "I don't know where, or even *if,* there will be a courting between Yaminah and you," he motioned to Bo Yusuf. "But it's quite obvious that she favors you. You also favor her. At the moment Eros has simply just struck the two of you. That could be either good or bad for business."

"You would tie what I feel into business?" Bo Yusuf questioned, his tone carrying a hint that his emotions started to boil.

"With no offense, Bo Yusuf," al-Jeheuty spoke cordially. "You've only known her for a couple days. However, if you begin to court her, both her father *and* Behar will see it as a symbol of al-Mari Ifriq and Djenhai's union. What would happen if the courting went bad? A situation like that could be volatile, especially as we stand on the brink of unifying with the Djenhai kingdom and creating a nation-state. Offend a king only if you have the army to do so."

"Is that an order to stay far from the royal emissary," Bo Yusuf asked, his smile not hiding the frustration in his voice.

"Let her come to you," al-Jeheuty instructed. "That is fair. You don't have to ignore her advances. I'll speak to Rahmis about this as well.

He'll continue to flirt; it's in his nature. But it means nothing. One: he's a host. He should have a form of charm about him. Two: Yaminah favors you, and I think Rahmis knows that." Al-Jeheuty watched Bo Yusuf sigh. The Army Official's smile finally wavered. Al-Jeheuty comforted, "This is our fate. We are city officials." Al-Jeheuty cupped Bo Yusuf's hand and shook it hard as he smiled. "We are reconstructing the glory days of al-Andalusia, Bo Yusuf. Here, in Africa-proper."

"And you have the potential to be a nobleman," Ojodo's voice rumbled. "When you marry Yaminah Igdobe Djenhai," he added.

"Hey!" Bo Yusuf expressed as he raised his hands. "Even I believe that's going too far."

Al-Jeheuty and Ojodo laughed. Nasir added sincerity into the conversation, saying, "You should be honored at the potential to court a woman, an actual courtship too, not one that only lasts a night or a few days."

"The lonely heart speaks," al-Jeheuty jibed.

"If you define lonely as being with a different woman almost every night," Ojodo said in a nonchalant manner.

"And you're one to speak," Nasir reacted to Ojodo's claims. "When your pen is not between empty pages your phallus is between the legs of either imported or domestic flesh."

"You say that as if I don't have a day job," Ojodo retorted. "I understand the confusion, since I do both as if I'm getting paid—and very well might I add." The Moorish titan concluded, "What, or *who*, I do in my spare time is my business." Bo Yusuf and al-Jeheuty hid their faces inside their hands as they laughed at Ojodo's commentary.

"My father was right," continued Nasir. "One of my last conversations with my father was about finding a woman, someone to bring balance to my life. Someone to bring balance to this busy life as a company boss." He looked at al-Jeheuty and confessed, "I envy you. You have Mehit. I'm twenty-nine and I continue to act as if I'm twenty-three. Goodness, even my younger brother marries next month."

"Love can be complicated," al-Jeheuty professed. "Love can be frustrating."

"So you'd give up all you have with Mehit for a simple day's peace and running through a caravan of women?" Nasir asked.

"Never," al-Jeheuty answered.

Nasir grinned. "That's what I thought."

"Well, what about Aludra?" al-Jeheuty suggested. "She's been your language tutor for a year now, has she not? You've pursued nothing with her?"

Nasir rolled his eyes. "Don't get me wrong, brother," he said as the rest of the young men at the table threw up their arms and hollered at him. "She's a lovely girl. I would pursue her, but Hyle Tecer put her through a lot. She's trying to work that out."

"With a blade," Ojodo reminded. "Remember that."

Nasir ignored the titan's comment and continued, "There are awkward moments when she's in the middle of a language lesson. Pauses. We look at one another and smile. I notice her watching me when I'm practicing, and she's not listening to my grammar or pronunciation." Nasir said with a pleasant smile, "Aludra's remarkable with the languages."

"Imagine what else her lips and tongue could do," Ojodo jibed.

Nasir smiled shyly. He then concluded, "But she's also delving deep into Roberto's teachings. She's trying to align herself with that feminine energy he and Ilindia preach about. She says that she's trying to clean herself by bathing in the dark primordial waters, be born anew." Nasir looked at everyone with a frustrated expression. "It's hard to make a fancy move when a woman drops that on you."

The group finished their meals and drink, thanked the proprietor and Fumnyana for the service, and then made their way to the Sa'ood company house. Zakiy Sa'ood charged the four men just as they exited the city gates. He came hastily, from the direction of the Sa'ood docks. He called for his brother as he dashed across the open field. Nasir responded quickly. He quickened his steps and walked ahead of the group. He reached his brother and asked what was the matter.

"A messenger has arrived," Zakiy answered. "He demands to speak with our Governor-General and Governor. Behar and Wakil."

"What does he want with them?" Nasir asked.

"He won't say," Nasir's younger brother answered. "He only declares that he carries a message from an Italian Baron. That's all he'll say. He will not say what the message pertains to, nor will he name the baron. I'm thankful, actually. He only speaks in Italian. I barely understand him."

Al-Jeheuty and the other three officials gathered around Nasir. "What's this of an Italian Baron?" al-Jeheuty asked.

"One has come to our shores—at least his messenger," related Nasir. "Does he at least give *his* name?" he asked his brother.

"Donatello Verola," Zakiy answered, finally catching his breath.

"And what does he want?" al-Jeheuty queried.

"He demands to speak to our governors," Nasir summarized. "The messenger will relay his message to no one but our Beylerbey or governor."

"Take us to him, Zakiy," ordered al-Jeheuty. The younger Sa'ood brother led the way, taking al-Jeheuty and the rest down to the section of the docks that were owned and controlled by his family's company. Anchored there was a small foreign vessel flying two flags, one atop the other. The flags were limp, crinkled with a lack of wind rushing through them to whip and straighten their face, but they were still recognizable. The bottom flag was simply the colors of Italian nobility. It was the top flag that caught the attention of the joining party. The top flag was white, and even in its lame position the print of four, crowned Moorish heads could be seen. Donatello Verola, along with eight men at his service, stood just off the docks, on the shore.

The Sicilian messenger was of average height with a bulky build covered by a ruffled shirt, tight black pants, and a long coat with intricate designs embroidered into its fabric. He had pale brown skin, a square face adorned with a well-groomed patch of hair around his chin and lips, and tight curly hair that draped a little past his ears, dangling from the small cap atop his head. His eight men were dressed as soldiers, coat, pants, boots, sword and pistol strapped to them, each one of them looked around cautiously at the gawking Moorish, Arab, and Turkish workers surrounding them.

Al-Jeheuty's steps quickened toward the Sicilian messenger, pulling out in front of his fellow officials. He flashed a welcoming smile and put his hands out toward Donatello. The messenger smiled back, accepted al-Jeheuty's hand and asked in Italian, "Are you the Governor-General?"

"No," admitted al-Jeheuty, answering Donatello in the same language. "I am his advisor and Commissioner of Affairs."

Donatello shook his head, and then spoke in an apologetic tone, "I cannot speak to you. I can only speak to your Governor-General."

Al-Jeheuty paused in contemplation. He turned around and called for Bo Yusuf and Ojodo. The Army Official and Moorish titan sprinted over. Donatello's guards stiffened as an armed Bo Yusuf approached closer, and as the giant Moor Ojodo stepped toward them. Donatello's heart beat faster as Ojodo's overwhelming presence towered over him. Al-Jeheuty relayed his command in the messenger's language, "Bo Yusuf, find Beylerbey Behar. He is in the palace. Ojodo, seek out Governor Wakil." The two bowed, turned, and carried out their orders, returning to the city gates. Al-Jeheuty looked back to Donatello with a wide smile. "Now, you will have an audience with our city leaders. That's guaranteed. My fellow officials will prepare your stage. I, however, need to do my part. When I present you, I must announce your mission—more than just the fact that you carry a message."

Donatello leaned close and whispered, "I do not want war with you."

Al-Jeheuty held back in asking if the Italian Baron's message was a declaration of war. He chose his words carefully. Keeping his smile, al-Jeheuty asked, "No war need be made on the messenger."

Donatello took a deep breath and confessed, "I bring a message from Baron Agusto Ghislanzoni." He said in an even more hushed voice, "He calls for the head of Captain Hesam Gandarewa, for the offense of—"

Al-Jeheuty stopped Donatello by raising a hand. "That is enough. You may present the rest to our leaders." Donatello relaxed and stood up straight as al-Jeheuty contemplated what offenses his friend Hesam Gandarewa could have committed. The offense, al-Jeheuty thought to himself, was most likely a ghost coming back to haunt his friend. At least he hoped that Gandarewa had not done anything while under the employment of al-Mari Ifriq. Behar would not hesitate to hand Gandarewa over to the Italian Baron. Even worse, al-Jeheuty would have no power to stop the Beylerbey—no case to argue. "Come with me," al-Jeheuty commanded. "Leave four of your guards to tend to your boat. You can trust us to care for your vessel, but too many armed men in the palace might sound an alarm."

"Understood," Donatello said. He turned and split his guard in two camps. He, and his four assigned soldiers, grouped with al-Jeheuty and made their way to the city gates. Nasir was commanded to tend to his company along with Zakiy before al-Jeheuty led the messenger and the four soldiers away.

There was little said between the two, al-Jeheuty and Donatello Verola. As they walked through the city streets, and came closer to the palace, al-Jeheuty asked how far off the baron's fleet was. "We were ahead of them by several hours, I believe. I will send my vessel back to hail him that all is safe. The baron wanted to be assured that his approach did not stir arms against him."

Al-Jeheuty only responded with a smile. He was anxious to learn of Hesam's offense. If no offense was committed under al-Mari Ifriq's banner, then al-Jeheuty believed he might have an argument. The Moorish official also wondered about the messenger's anxiety. The man appeared to be anxious about events beyond present politics. The silence continued as al-Jeheuty led the men into the palace. There were small moments of chatter when al-Jeheuty pointed out various aspects of the palace's interior. Bo Yusuf approached al-Jeheuty before the official stepped into Behar's public quarters. Rahmis was by the Army Official's side, looking considerably less happy. Al-Jeheuty ignored his friend's demeanor, and in their native language he asked Bo Yusuf, "Is the Beylerbey busy?"

"No," Bo Yusuf answered. His demeanor too appeared not to be centered on the situation at hand. "He has been informed of the messenger's arrival, and the urgency. His schedule has been cleared for the day. Governor Wakil has arrived too." Al-Jeheuty sensed an excited tone to Bo Yusuf's words.

"Everything all right?" al-Jeheuty was forced to ask.

Bo Yusuf fought against his intruding smile as he said, "We'll speak later. The situation at hand needs attending."

"Very much so," al-Jeheuty expressed in a serious tone. "I was able to extract part of the message that our messenger holds. It appears that our very own Captain Hesam Gandarewa has committed an offense against the Italian Baron named Agusto Ghislanzoni. Is Roberto inside?"

"No," Bo Yusuf answered. "I saw him lounging with his mistress, comfortably, while I was at *The al-Hammon Palace*. He may still be there."

"Let's hope. Rahmis," al-Jeheuty called the man over. "Find Roberto Hamaat. He most likely lounges at *The al-Hammon Palace*. Simply ask him if he knows anything about a Baron Agusto Ghislanzoni."

Rahmis nodded his head and quickly walked away to carry out al-Jeheuty's orders. His strides were forceful, almost pushing his way through the palace servants and even past al-Jeheuty and Bo Yusuf.

"What has him tied up?" al-Jeheuty inquired.

"The same thing that has me hiding a smile," Bo Yusuf answered, his smile creeping through his straight-faced manner. "I've been asked to lead the first trade caravan into Djenhai. Yaminah called for me personally. I was just informed. I have to meet with the Turkish commander. He will lead the army on regular occasions. But for now, let us tend to these matters."

Al-Jeheuty thanked his friend and then turned to address Donatello and his guards in their language. "Our leaders are waiting for you, Signore Verola." Bo Yusuf moved aside, taking drag behind an Italian guard while al-Jeheuty led the men through the door and into Behar's public chamber.

The chamber room was a wide and long area filled with marble columns and exquisite tapestries stitched from the finest fabrics. Behar and Wakil sat at the far side of the room, perched atop a long upholstered piece of furniture, servant girls surrounding them. Al-Jeheuty led the men to the feet of the Beylerbey and governor. Both men were very imposing, even when smiling and laughing. The two were like aged gods, their powerful presence never before seen by Donatello, not even in his Baron. Donatello felt inclined to drop to both knees in the Beylerbey and the governor's presence. The Sicilian's guards dropped to both knees as well. Al-Jeheuty and Bo Yusuf quickly removed the stunned look on their faces. Behar and Wakil simultaneously asked the men to rise.

Al-Jeheuty stepped forward and presented, "This is Signore Donatello Verola. He brings to our city a disturbing message from the man he represents, Baron Agusto Ghislanzoni. The message concerns an offense made against the baron by Captain Hesam Gandarewa."

Behar looked disturbed. He put his eyes on Donatello as if trying to draw the answer from the gaze aimed at him. "What offense is this," he asked in a voice straining to remain calm.

Donatello took a step forward and answered, "As stated, I carry an urgent message from Baron Agusto Ghislanzoni. The baron demands the head of Captain Hesam Gandarewa for offenses made against him."

"And what are these offenses?" Wakil asked.

"Captain Hesam Gandarewa has been charged for the murder of one of the baron's business associates," Donatello informed.

Al-Jeheuty, Bo Yusuf, Behar, and Wakil all shared a quick glance at one another. They did not need to ask the name of the business associate, they already knew the answer. Al-Jeheuty quickly wondered if he could bargain his friend's life out of this particular situation, but he did not dwell on the matter long before Behar asked the associates name for confirmation.

The Sicilian messenger answered, "Azzolino Bidonare."

Behar relaxed. He managed to smile and responded, "The Squid." The Beylerbey started to chuckle. "As I have been told about this man, his exploits are not as noble as your Baron's title. I'm not so sure that I can be swayed to hand over one of my most valued captains. How far off is your Baron?"

"I am three hours ahead of him," Donatello replied. "I am to send word that I have arranged an audience for him to negotiate terms for Captain Gandarewa's release into our custody."

Behar kept his cool smile. "Captain Gandarewa is on a two-day expedition. I cannot hand over what I do not claim. But to be fair to your Baron, I will send word to Captain Gandarewa for an early return. Then we shall all speak fairly at court. Al-Jeheuty, come to me." The official stepped to the Beylerbey's side. He leaned close to Behar as the Beylerbey relayed in their common language, "I can do nothing to save your friend if he was aware of this Italian Baron backing Azzolino Bidonare."

"I understand," al-Jeheuty whispered back.

"It would be a great shame," Behar commented. "Your friend, with more years experience, could rival Captain Sunwil. I would suggest—to save his ass—that he deny knowing the connection, though he would still answer to my anger."

Al-Jeheuty took a peek over his shoulder. Donatello looked anxious, trying his best to decode the words of the conversing Moors, though he had no understanding of the Afro-Arabic language they spoke. Al-Jeheuty put his attention back to Behar and said, "I have a feeling he didn't know. I'll get word to him that he must return. He'd be in al-Mari Ifriq by tomorrow night if we send word now."

"Have Isaiah make the move," the Beylerbey recommended.

"Yes, Behar," al-Jeheuty acknowledged. He turned around and walked back to the Sicilian messenger and his guards. "I will have word sent to Captain Gandarewa," he said in Italian. "He would not arrive until tomorrow night. You and your baron would have to spend time in our city. We will host you in our finest housing district."

Donatello nodded his head. "I will send word to the baron. I will remain here with two guards."

Al-Jeheuty walked past Donatello and his soldiers and casually ordered, "Come. We'll prepare your stay." Al-Jeheuty waved to Bo Yusuf to follow, and his fellow official again took drag behind the Italian guards. Al-Jeheuty led the troupe out of the palace and to the housing complex for visiting officials. Donatello and the guards were given quaint accommodations, and chambers were reserved for the baron and his incoming party. The Sicilian messenger and his soldiers were then taken back to the docks to join the other Italian guards. Donatello assigned a leader among his guards and set all but two out to sea to carry a message to Baron Agusto Ghislanzoni that he was granted a warm admission into al-Mari Ifriq.

Donatello commanded the rest of his men to stay at the docks and watch for the baron's approaching ship. He humbly asked for a meal for both he and his remaining guards. Al-Jeheuty assured that Donatello and his guards would receive sustenance. First, al-Jeheuty ordered Bo Yusuf to inform Isaiah of the present matters, and then have the company boss send a messenger-vessel to catch up with Captain Gandarewa, ordering him to return. Bo Yusuf left immediately to carry out the task. Al-Jeheuty politely asked Donatello to relieve his soldiers of duty, and for all of them to follow al-Jeheuty to the council house. Donatello relayed al-Jeheuty's wishes to the guards and asked them to follow. Once the party arrived at the council house, al-Jeheuty instructed the servants to prepare a meal. Al-Jeheuty invited the men to have a seat. He gave a courteous bow and then dismissed himself from the council house. The Moorish guards at the door kept a close eye on the foreign men occupying the house.

Al-Jeheuty made his way to the Ahangar company house. Roberto Hamaat intercepted him. The official asked the assassin clan leader, "Do you have any information on—"

"Baron Agusto Ghislanzoni," Roberto finished. "Got a cargo's hold of dirt on him. He's whispered about by some of the more ambitious privateers. He's known as *Muro di Ferro*. Translation: *The Iron Wall*. He's a modern-day Charles the Fifth," he continued. "One-hundred years ago, Charles the Fifth of Spain safeguarded the Mediterranean island of Sardinia from 'Barbary' raids. He did this by fortifying the island's coasts with a network of lookout towers. Our Baron Agusto Ghislanzoni has done the same with southern Sicily. He's Northern Italian, considers himself above the 'peasants' of Sicily. He rules a small village that's a remnant of Moorish occupation. It's located in western Sicily."

"If he despises the Sicilians why does he live there?" inquired al-Jeheuty.

"He may own land there," Roberto guessed. "I don't know. But he has a noble title. I'm sure your visiting friend may have an answer. The baron has been in power for a little more than a decade. Al-Mari Ifriq's exploits never really crossed him, though some of the regular privateers have."

Al-Jeheuty looked back at the council house. "I'll see what the Sicilian knows," he expressed. "I'll have to separate him from his assigned guards." He looked back to Roberto and asked, "Have you brought this information to Behar?"

Roberto shook his head. "Yes. He told me I'd find you here."

"I'm going to extract more information about the baron," al-Jeheuty informed. "Wait for me at the Ahangar company house. Bo Yusuf and Isaiah are there now." Roberto nodded his head and walked away. Al-Jeheuty returned to the council house where he entertained al-Mari Ifriq's new guests, dining on a wonderfully prepared meal. Al-Jeheuty kept far from politics. He inquired about the coastal town they were from. Donatello informed that the village was named Crocifissa, located on the far west of the island, south of the city of Trapani. The messenger then revealed information al-Jeheuty desired. Baron Agusto Ghislanzoni took control of the region because the revolts, famine, and plagues ravishing Trapani sent refugees to flock into the already overcrowded region of

Crocifissa.

"Baron Agusto is Vatican appointed," Donatello said as if providing a warning. "He is backed by all the money of the Church." One of the two guards flashed a grimace and then cleared his throat, a signal for Donatello to cease speaking. Donatello looked at the guard and said in a stern voice, "This is information that our hosts will be privy to soon enough. My job is to deliver a message, and emphasize its importance." The messenger returned his attention to al-Jeheuty and said, "Baron Agusto has been an excellent head residing over us." He again addressed his guards, "Have you both finished your meals?" he asked. The guards responded affirmatively. "Then leave us," Donatello commanded in a powerful, authoritative voice. "Return to the docks, post up, and observe the sea for our baron."

"Guards," al-Jeheuty called for the men at the door. "Escort these two gentlemen back to the Sa'ood docks." The guards bowed and set about on their duty.

Donatello and al-Jeheuty waited in silence before the messenger spoke, "I am a man of Christ. Jesus Christ is my Lord and Savior. Call me naïve if you must, but that is what I strongly believe. I do not believe in defiling His image, or making war with it. I do believe in making war to defend my Lord and Savior, however." Donatello paused from his cryptic speech. He took a breath and continued, "The Moors were kings in Sicily. They were great rulers," he patronized. "Ports were enlarged. Architecture, language, art, agriculture, all improved under the direction of the Moors. The food. The spices. There was hydraulic engineering. Nations have come and gone, none have equaled the glory of the Moors."

"You patronize me for a reason, Signore Verola," said al-Jeheuty, prompting Donatello to arrive at a conclusion.

"Azzolino Bidonare's death is an excuse," the Sicilian messenger relayed sharply. "The baron is backed by the Vatican. This is reconnaissance. This is a secret crusade, and all the politics of religion play significant parts, though unseen."

"Are you saying that this is a situation we cannot win, even if we handover Captain Gandarewa?" al-Jeheuty asked.

"This is the true Moors' last stand," continued Donatello. "The world is closing in on you. You will join your fellow blacks in slavery in America or be enslaved in your homeland. The peace you've brought to the Mediterranean has disrupted European interests in creating a New World Order. The European states may squabble among one another, but there is one sentiment they can agree on: no black nation will rise again. Odongo-

Mauharim threatens that possibility."

"Why do you tell me this, Signore Verola?" asked al-Jeheuty entirely perplexed.

"I believe Christ would want peace," the Sicilian said in a stern voice, his statement a declaration. "The death of Azzolino Bidonare, and losing the narcotics trade—and most importantly the revenue earned from the trade—has hurt the baron's pride, but he is on orders to watch the blacks of North Africa. How much are the blacks here worth? Trust that more than Italy uses the baron as a pair of eyes."

"What other white face walks into Africa?" asked al-Jeheuty.

"Baron Agusto Ghislanzoni has several benefactors," Donatello reiterated. "I am only privy to Rome."

"Does he speak of others?" probed al-Jeheuty.

"Yes," answered Donatello. "He does not name them, and it's no ruse." The messenger sighed. "I don't wish to offend you, Lord Anhur Has, but while you enjoy the fruits of your labor, while you watch your city flourish, there are plans to wipe it from history and bury it deep below the sands of Africa." He leaned close and relayed, "The French too are here to observe you. They don't conspire with the baron, however."

"We suspect one spy among the French," al-Jeheuty admitted. "We treat this person carefully." He adjusted himself while sitting, fixed his robes and then reiterated, "I'm still at a complete loss as to why you're speaking to me in such a manner. Why would you give me such warning, or any warning at all for that matter? Is it the hint of the color of Africa in your skin," al-Jeheuty teased.

Donatello chuckled. "We are all mixed children. The baron claims French and Spanish blood. The Vatican uses that. Religion is made political. The more European states they have control of, the better—regardless of the squabbles. What better way to control the states than with men whose blood represents them all." He paused, thinking. "I do believe they expect my betrayal. A touch of Moorish blood spices my veins." He then stated in a serious tone, "I just don't agree with politics that…I cannot speak about at present. You will get a clearer picture when the baron arrives. Trust me. I will tell you, however, that Captain Gandarewa does not have to be handed over. The baron is on orders to establish relations with your city. Give him part of the trade's revenue. Put his nephew, and myself, in charge."

"The Beylerbey will not allow anymore foreign powers to populate our city," al-Jeheuty expressed.

"I understand that there is a port in Libya that Captain Gandarewa uses," Donatello quickly retorted. "Myself and the baron's nephew will operate from there. The baron will be most pleased with that option."

Al-Jeheuty said nothing. He stared at Donatello, his gaze locked on the messenger's forehead, trying to extract any information that lay behind Donatello's brow and deep within his head. Al-Jeheuty discerned that the Sicilian was more than a simple messenger.

The Moorish Official stood up. He signaled Donatello to do the same, and then he escorted the messenger back to the docks. Al-Jeheuty excused himself and returned to Behar to relay all of the information that Donatello had given him. Behar internalized the information. He and Wakil became anxious to know the Sicilian messenger's true motives. All three men deduced that Signore Verola's intentions would not harm al-Mari Ifriq, but they wondered if the city would benefit from them.

Behar advised al-Jeheuty to return to the docks and watch for the baron's approach. Al-Jeheuty carried out the order. There were no words exchanged between he and Donatello Verola that pertained to the present politics. They did not stay at the docks the entire time, Donatello and his guards rested inside the Sa'ood company house, the guards taking shifts. It was within the Sa'ood Company House that Nasir became acquainted with the Sicilian messenger. Nasir took the moment to practice his knowledge of the Romance Languages, conversing in Italian with Donatello Verola. Company Boss Isaiah Iraj visited to inform Donatello that a messenger vessel had been sent to intercept Captain Gandarewa on his expedition. Donatello was informed again that Hesam Gandarewa would not return until the following night.

There were two more watch shifts, several rounds of cards, and another meal before Baron Agusto Ghislanzoni's fleet of three ships, including Donatello's returning ship, was spotted on the horizon. The sun had two more hours left in its stay. Al-Jeheuty, Bo Yusuf, Roberto Hamaat, and Company Boss Iraj joined Donatello in welcoming the small, inbound Italian fleet. Donatello stood at the head of the group to meet the baron as he disembarked from his ship.

Baron Agusto Ghislanzoni was a man of average build and height, wearing spectacles on an angular nose attached to a paunch, olive colored face. Light brown and gray hairs were combed over his brow, in thinning, aged strands. He was dressed royally, wearing satin doublets and breeches. He was adorned in a long, dark cloak that had a high collar decorated with lavish, laced scallops. He donned plain, black shoes and walked with an imperious sway in his step.

Baron Agusto's nephew, Giovanni Ghislanzoni-Verdi, a handsome young man of just twenty years, walked at the baron's left side. He was dressed in the attire of a nobleman, a lesser version of the outfit displayed by the baron. Giovanni was poised to inherit his uncle's title and enterprise. Both his parents had succumbed to the hardships of rebellion and plague that sickened western Sicily. His father was shot and killed at the onset of a riot. His mother passed from disease just three months later, giving up on life after the death of her husband. The baron, having no children of his own, took his young nephew under his tutelage, prepping Giovanni with a fine education should any unfortunate circumstances befall Baron Agusto. Everything had been planned properly for Giovanni's life, even down to the woman he was to marry, which was a fine business opportunity.

Signore Michele Solera, the baron's advisor, flanked him on the right side. He was dressed in brown, gold-trimmed breeches and doublet, white stockings and brown shoes. He was only two years older than the baron but looked much more aged. Time had scratched many wrinkles into his oval face. His head had a neatly combed patch of black and gray hair, thin with age but not as receding as the baron's. His eyes were dark brown, almost black, small, round, and penetrating.

Donatello quickly greeted the three men before the rest of the entourage could disembark. He politely greeted Signore Solera first, then the young Giovanni, and lastly the baron himself. He guided the Italian triad to the Moorish officials. From behind them came an impressive entourage that consisted of fifteen African slaves. Guiding the slaves was a young, dark and slender Ethiop slave-girl. She was nineteen years of age, clothed in a long shroud; her hood down, allowing her long black, braided hair to flow past her shoulders, draping elegantly over her bosom. Though she was slender, she possessed an enticing and curvaceous feminine frame. She moved like the flickering flame of a candle as she led the procession of slaves. Her black skin irradiated with a haunting amber glow. It was as if all the rays of the sun that her flesh encapsulated sang in a harmonious, vibrating gleam.

The rest of the Italian entourage consisted of guards and servants.

Donatello introduced the baron, his nephew, and advisor to al-Jeheuty and the other Moorish officials. The baron did not participate in the introduction. His eyes surveyed the workers and the host of piratical characters that were also disembarking from expeditions. He scoffed at the sight, the rogues of the sea collecting their visiting papers, paying to use the Moorish docks, and being escorted into al-Mari Ifriq. Donatello turned the Moorish officials' attention to the Ethiop woman. He brought her forward and presented her name. "This is Adaeze."

The baron interrupted the Sicilian messenger's introduction by stating firmly, "She is our *Regina di Schiavi.*" He then emphasized in the common Afro-Arabic language, "She is our Queen of Slaves." The baron looked at Isaiah and asked, "Is this Persian the Captain Gandarewa that I seek?"

"No," answered al-Jeheuty. The official became relieved. His suspicions had been confirmed. The baron and his friend Hesam had no prior knowledge of one another. At least the baron had never seen Hesam Gandarewa. Al-Jeheuty now had to gamble that his friend had never heard of the Italian Baron.

The baron said sharply, "I am here to see your Governor-General. The Persian in question will be the focus."

"Yes, yes. Of course," said al-Jeheuty. "This way." He gave quick glances to the other officials around him. Nasir and Bo Yusuf looked the most disgusted. Roberto and Isaiah broke away from the group, gathered several workers from the docks, and stopped the flow of visiting captains trying to make their way to the city gates. The baron split his party, some of the guards staying to attend the docks. All traffic was cleared for the baron's party to be led into the city, through the streets heading to the palace, and into Behar's public quarters. The governor and the Beylerbey stood up as the Italian baron's entourage entered their public chamber. Taran had joined them, standing at the base of the stairs leading to the two leaders' divan.

Behar opened his arms wide. "Baron," he proclaimed. "I have waited for you. Chairs have been prepared for you," he informed pointing to the set of chairs stationed in front of him. "We shall not sit upon our high seats," Behar continued as he and Wakil stepped down several stairs. "I will look at you as an equal in this court."

Al-Jeheuty introduced the Beylerbey and the governor to the baron. All three bowed politely. The official made an inconspicuous gesture toward Behar, signaling that their suspicions concerning the relationship between Hesam Gandarewa and Baron Agusto proved to be true.

"I hope your courts are civil, Governors," said the baron in a pompous tone.

"This is a public chamber, but we are holding a private court," explained Wakil. "Please, sit," insisted the governor. He turned to several servants and ordered, "Drinks. Refreshments. Please."

The baron and his entourage of officials, including Donatello, took seat. The African slaves, the Ethiop slave-girl that was 'queen' over them, and the baron's guards continued to stand. Behar and Wakil sat facing the baron and his people. Al-Jeheuty, Taran, Bo Yusuf, and Nasir stood behind their seated leaders. Behar began the proceedings by stating in Italian, "I have been informed of your request, Baron Agusto. I cannot comply—even with threat of war."

The baron, though impressed that the Beylerbey understood his language, huffed as he rolled his eyes. "This is a city of rogues," he commented as if his visit was a waste of time.

There was a moment of tense silence, which not even Behar's sly smile could relieve. His smile, it could be said, added to the tension, and so did the words he chose as a retort. For he retorted, "You are correct, Baron Agusto. This *is* a city of rogues. We are rogue enough to not allow any foreign power that believes it has a divine right by pale birth to bully us, and we are well organized. There is a boss for every district of our city. Each boss controls captains and merchants of the sea. Every captain controls soldiers; well-informed men that at sea give orders to officers, or rather, enforcers of our laws that govern and protect the waters—barbaric as you may perceive these laws because of the color and heritage of those who created them. Our enforcers protect greater associates that bring in large sums of revenue. And of every associate, of every enforcer, of every soldier, captain, and chief of districts, *I* am *their* chief. So if only offense continues to spill from your mouth, you may leave this court that I have so graciously brought together in *your* honor to give you my ear and time, and you may then return to Sicily and tell all your Sicilian brothers how we Moors run North Africa. Or rather, maybe, you can remind them that it was our barbaric, roguish laws that once governed your island to the ironic point of civilizing its inhabitants. From black Carthaginian all the way down to the even blacker Moor. You see, good Baron, you may run around this place but you do not *run* this place. You have my permission to relay that message to your boss, the Vatican. For *you* are merely an enforcer for the European Church."

Baron Agusto simply chuckled. "Organized?" he challenged. "You scoff at the High See of Rome, yet you pattern yourself after the society of ancient Rome and its organization. You corsairs are no better than the bullying, Roman gangsters that ran the trade routes for grain and wheat."

"Don't fool yourself," retorted Behar. "Rome was never *that* organized."

The baron fell silent.

Behar stared intensely at the Italian nobleman.

Bo Yusuf and al-Jeheuty scanned the room, calculating the position of each of the baron's guards. The two of them separately contemplated strategies for defense against the possibility of pistol and swordplay erupting in the chamber. The two officials, separately in thought, deduced that Taran was expendable. They also considered that the Italian guards might have been equally anxious and pensive within the still silence.

Donatello's heart started to race.

Baron Agusto laughed lightly, and then erupted into large guffaws. He and Behar stood up, locked hands and embraced one another chest-to-chest. Behar smiled wide. The two men returned to their seats. "You are a sonava bitch, Governor-General Ameer Las El-Behar. I like you."

"*Beylerbey*," Behar corrected.

"Yes, *Beylerbey*," the baron stood corrected. "I do have to express that an offense was committed against me. Revenue was stolen from me. You are a man of honor. You understand business."

Behar nodded his head. "I do, Baron Agusto. I do. I am indeed a man of honor." He shook his finger and continued, "But I am not convinced that Captain Gandarewa set out to make an offense toward you." Behar then surprised everyone by admitting, "We carried out the mark on Azzolino Bidonare in favor of Captain Gandarewa because of an offense committed by the Squid—as I believe Bidonare was nicknamed. As his moniker hinted at, he would not let go of all the revenue owed to Captain Gandarewa. I'm sure you too were not receiving a full share. Signore Bidonare was known as the Squid for a reason, and deceiving a man of your stature would have given him quite a rush. I don't believe Captain Gandarewa knew of your ties to the Squid. If he had, we would have consulted you. I'm sure we would be in the same situation—sharing control over a narcotics trade."

The baron's surprise over Behar's confession dissipated. His attention centered on the proposal concealed within the Beylerbey's words. "Are you suggesting a partnership?"

"It would guarantee your safe passage home," enlightened Behar nonchalantly. "You will receive more than double the revenue Bidonare declared to you, and I get to keep my good captain. War is so unnecessary. It would also stop you from making the mistake of declaring war in my court, within my city walls."

Behar smiled.

The baron smiled as well. He started to laugh again, getting up and meeting Behar on his feet. The Beylerbey rose, and the two embraced again. "You made two mistakes, Beylerbey. One: I am not here on orders of the Vatican," the baron clarified. "This is a personal matter pertaining to outside affairs and interests that I deal with. Second: I am not Sicilian. I am a pure Italian." He lightened his laugh, and aimed a hand at Donatello. "My messenger is from the Island. He also shares your dirty blood."

"I knew I liked him for a reason. He's a good man. Come," said Behar. "Bring your company. We have prepared a great stay for you. You will be housed far from the rogues of the city. The meal my servants have been preparing will be delivered to your quarters. Tomorrow night, we shall hold court again. Captain Gandarewa will be in attendance, as well as several others who help with the trade. Governor Wakil will finalize the deal. He will make it all legal." Behar then joked. "As much as a narcotics trade can be legal."

Wakil permitted the seated members of the court to rise. Al-Jeheuty and the other Moorish officials followed the procession out of the public chamber. The baron, his African slaves, Italian servants and guards, were taken to their housing. Al-Jeheuty invited the baron and his people to *The Siren's Call* tavern. He promised that the tavern was more sophisticated than the haunts occupied by the city's 'visiting rogues'. The baron declined, but extended leave for Donatello, his nephew, and his advisor. Giovanni and Signore Solera declined as well, retiring to their visiting quarters for the night. The African slaves were placed with the other Moorish servants. Adaeze joined them.

Bo Yusuf was assigned to keep a close eye on the Italian guards. Members of Roberto's clan joined him. Donatello, al-Jeheuty, and Nasir continued to *The Siren's Call*. They were given a private room. A brilliant glow radiated from a flickering, crystal chandelier of candles. A bottle of wine and three cups were delivered to them. Ice crushed into milk lay on the table in small cups. Juices squeezed from fruit flavored the delicious treat. Donatello perked up and grabbed a cup and spoon. "Iced cream," he said like a happy child. "Our priests and nuns make this treat for children. It's made from the recipes left behind by the Moors." He started to eat. Donatello looked at the wine and joked, "There is no need to get me drunk. I will give you more information." He poured himself a drink after tasting two spoonfuls of ice cream. "Don't believe the baron's words when he says that he is not here in the interest of the Vatican. He is. But, as my word is always true, was that not easy, the meeting?"

"Yes," said al-Jeheuty waiting for the Sicilian to finish with the bottle of wine so that he may partake in a cup. Donatello, however, was courteous enough to pour the wine for the Moorish official and the Moorish company boss. Both thanked the messenger. Before al-Jeheuty took a sip he requested, "Tell me about Adaeze, the Queen of Slaves."

Donatello took a heavy gulp of his drink as the men sat down. He shook his head, wiped his lips, and returned his cup to the table. "The topic of interest fills in the blanks of my earlier silence." Donatello smiled. "My mother's family is a part of a tight organization. My mother has passed. Bless her. I have gone into the family business, helping my uncle. We have a strict code of silence that we call *omerta*. We try and control the trades within Sicily, keeping its total control out of the hands of the powers that try and rule our island. We are just as organized in our hierarchy as the corsair companies of North Africa. We extend protection, and we direct trade. Azzolino was an associate of ours that our enterprise introduced to Baron Agusto to boost our village's dying economy," Donatello clarified. "We also like to choose the legitimate rulers of Sicily. As of now, we do not favor Baron Agusto. His kind is like the European Jew, constantly fucking their way into bloodlines to claim legitimacy. Yes, legitimacy through forced intimacy." Donatello laughed at his joke. The two Moors remained silent, wondering how all of this pertained to the so-called Queen of Slaves. Nasir kept up with the Sicilian's dialect, his language lessons with Aludra paying off.

Al-Jeheuty decided to ask, "And what is Adaeze's role in the baron's plans."

"He was showcasing his power to you," said Donatello. "He brought in African slaves as a message. It was to show you how serious business can be, and your possible fate if you do not comply."

"Or his future plans for us," al-Jeheuty suggested.

"Most definitely," the Sicilian agreed. "But he is acclimating the Cushite slave-girl to her home continent. That is why being part of the Libyan leg of the trade, close to the Soudan—Cush—must be part of your Beylerbey and governor's deal. He needs to feel as if he is closer to his goal of marrying into African nobility." Donatello saw the two Moors in front of him flinch. "Rome has made a great investment in Adaeze. She was stolen long ago with many other Ethiop men, women, and children. Nobility was the target."

"She's a noblewoman?" Nasir said in a surprised tone, his response in Italian simplistic.

Donatello specified, "She's a princess. Soudanese. Cushite. Nubian. Ethiopia proper. She has been groomed to marry the baron's nephew. She's even allowed an education, as well as being kept a virgin until her day of marriage. He courts her now. She has been somewhat reluctant in his courting. He too is tripping over his feet." Donatello took another sip of wine. "Adaeze's nobility will be revealed to her after their union. She will return to her land and take the crown, even if war is needed to do so."

"What does the Vatican stand to gain?" asked al-Jeheuty.

Donatello said as if obvious, "Claim to a holy land. Cush and all her treasures. The Vatican could then claim ultimate legitimacy to Christianity. It would possess the cornerstone of Eden, and the possible location of the Ark of the Covenant."

"I was under the impression that the Templars already ran away with the item," al-Jeheuty countered. "Or is it true that there is more than one ark, the Templars confiscating an ark that didn't hold God's Commandments to Moses, but great architectural plans? I find it odd that when the claim was made—as I've seen in my studies—that Europe's architecture went through a sudden change. Even the sciences increased."

Donatello smiled, chin tucked to his chest. "So many theories, legends, and myths run through the pious world." He made a low chuckle. "This is chess made real; the greatest crusade lies in the bloodline of this black woman. Adaeze is a good friend. I have watched her grow into a wonderful, young woman. I don't wish to see her defiled by such politics. She should know her heritage in all its beauty, but not by this deception. She is made to govern the slaves as a form of practice of governing her own kind."

There was silence. Al-Jeheuty contemplated everything Donatello was telling him. He thought of another point. "Cush does not exist…anymore. The Wisdom Keepers of the civilization also approach Christianity and its tenants in a far different way than the European Church."

"They are targeted for elimination," Donatello said as a sigh. "As usual."

"Why can't your organization eliminate the baron?" Nasir inquired as best he could in the Italian language. "Why ask for our help?"

"We're a proud people," Donatello answered. "We see the baron's presence as foreign rule. My family, part of a larger organization, has done its best to keep foreigners from our shores. Sicily for the Sicilians. That is an ideal that has not been recognized for hundreds of years. Without stirring offense, I believe that it would be best if the blacks were held responsible, without a close tie to your company and city. Let me entice you by saying I would be in your debt. I would owe you a favor. Besides, the baron is not our only tie to the Vatican. We have spies among them. They are associates that allow our organization to continue business without any dire legal ramifications." He took another sip. "Have we a deal? I don't care how long it takes."

"It's a deal," al-Jeheuty accepted.

Donatello took a breath. He played with his fingers, inspecting them close and asking without looking up, "What do you call your companies?" He looked up. "There are whispers that there is a more distinct name. I've heard a word that means 'union' or 'unify' in its *Latin Romance* translation."

"Our operation is called a *maehfil*," al-Jeheuty answered. "A union."

Donatello chuckled. "We are not so different," he said as he lifted his cup to toast to their secret union and plans. The two Moors did the same. All three men stood up. "*Salud.*" Donatello toasted and then took a sip.

The men sat down and enjoyed their ice cream.

Chapter Twenty-Four

No enemy or nation ever rattled Captain Hesam Gandarewa. He always remained focused even when his crew was outnumbered by a rival's crew or by the crew of a marked ship. The heavy, rocking movements of his ship at sea, mixed with the sounds of pistol and cannon fire, men screaming, and swords rattling against one another, satiated him like a well-prepared meal. The adventure and danger of the sea excited him. However, the days of plunder and adventurous campaigns at sea were quiet now that Hesam Gandarewa had a legitimate job of overseeing a trade route. The trade was illegal. The job was legitimate only because a powerful authority funded it.

There still was the thrill of conducting the trade of narcotics by land and sea and under the noses of other states. The intrigue of paying off officials to conduct business, or even marking and eliminating the officials that threatened to expose the trade, and also eliminating competitive narcotics traders was satisfying. Hesam never knew until now the appreciable power that was brought and felt by simply ordering the death of another man. Locking ships, swords, and eyes with an opponent had so many emotions rolled into it that the moment could not be fully appreciated, even when surviving the ordeal. Meeting with corrupt officials, handing them sacks of money to turn a blind eye to business, and whispering to a crewmember the orders to carry out a mark on a rival or a hardass official that would not budge on their principles, made Hesam feel kingly. This was the kind of authority that made people whisper about him with a sense of fear and respect. Hesam found his reputation spreading quicker, and respect toward him increasing.

It was the rumors about the identity of his backers, the new officials of al-Mari Ifriq, that made people cower. There was still a great air of mystery surrounding the new officials of the city. The greatest subject of talk was about their pasts, that they were Moorish revolutionaries that escaped Spain. Al-Mari Ifriq's new officials were also admired for their ability to bring peace among some of the corsair-states, and the ability to bargain with European states that were considered enemies of Africa-north.

It was this power wielded these new officials that made Hesam nervous at this very moment, sitting alone in the private quarters of his friend al-Jeheuty Anhur Has—one of the officials of the city and a childhood friend. Hesam once stated that it would be great to have a city official as a friend. He was not so sure, now. Captain Gandarewa had been ordered to return to al-Mari Ifriq by orders of his benefactors, the Beylerbey Ameer Las El-Behar and the Governor Wakil al-Hakam. Two days earlier, a messenger vessel caught up to his ship, struck al-Mari Ifriq's colors, and boarded to deliver the news that an Italian baron was calling for his head. He was relieved when the messenger explained that al-Jeheuty was working hard to battle the accusations. A court session was scheduled when Hesam returned to the city.

Hesam arrived, but the Italians were gone.

Company Boss Isaiah Iraj did not greet the captain when he disembarked.

Captain Gandarewa was arrested when he returned, but he was fortunately not taken to any cell. He was escorted to the palace and brought to his friend's private quarters where he was instructed to wait, and had been waiting for an hour. Al-Jeheuty had not made an appearance, increasing Hesam's nervous demeanor. When the Moorish official walked through the door of his private quarters, it did not settle the captain's nerves. Al-Jeheuty said nothing. He did not even look in Hesam's direction, and Hesam did not dare speak unless spoken to. He watched his friend open a cabinet and remove a bottle of wine and two glasses. Al-Jeheuty walked over to the table seating Hesam, placed the two glasses down, opened the bottle of wine, and poured its contents into both glasses. He moved one glass in front of Hesam, sliding it like a chess piece. He lifted the other glass and took a sip. Hesam nervously tasted his drink, first giving a quick smell to the contents. His nose did not detect poison, and neither did his tongue. The glass was clean.

Al-Jeheuty sat down and sighed. "I know you were expecting to hold court with the Italian baron and his troupe." Hesam nodded, saying nothing. "You are aware that the Italians have left." Hesam nodded again. "Eibib Oba will oversee the hashish and opium trade. This is not a punishment against you, my friend," al-Jeheuty assured. "Behar, Wakil, and I understand that you had no prior knowledge of Azzolino Bidonare's connection to this Baron Agusto Ghislanzoni. Behar was angry at first, but he was still not ready to hand over one of his best captains. He wanted you to deny any knowledge of Azzolino and the baron's connection, had you truly known of them." Al-Jeheuty shook his finger and smiled, "That did not free you from Behar's wrath. He had a punishment in mind for you."

Hesam cracked a slight smile. His nerves did not ease. He started to wonder if this was how he made others feel when he sat them down to conference on affairs, as the people he consulted with knew quite well that an order to kill them hang in the balance. Al-Jeheuty continued, "I suspected that you did not know of the baron. Behar was able to draw that information out of Baron Agusto. Surprised us all. Behar actually admitted that we carried out the mark on the Squid."

Gandarewa blurted out, "Tell the Beylerbey that I am most grateful."

Al-Jeheuty lifted his hand to calm his friend's outburst. Hesam regained his composure. "He knows. At least he understands that there should be a debt of gratitude. We are now, however, sharing the trade with Baron Agusto. Naturally. It's only fair. We will not miss the revenue, considering how much money passes through the trade. But," and he took another sip, "we averted terrible circumstances with the Italians. There was almost war here in al-Mari Ifriq, and not because of the ordeal concerning you. This was another circumstance that occurred just hours after we settled a peaceful court meeting. Two of the baron's guards were arrested, suspects of a terrible crime. They were in the wrong place at the very wrong time. It caused an uproar."

Hesam was drawn in, intrigued. He watched al-Jeheuty closely as the official paused to grit his teeth and ball his fist in anger. Hesam did not move. He did not take another sip, though he felt more wine would settle him.

Al-Jeheuty continued. "Bo Yusuf, and some of Roberto's outfit, were assigned to keep an eye on the baron's entourage. These two Italian guards slipped away to check on the baron's ships docked in Sa'ood ports. The two guards were arrested soon after, they being in the proximity of the crime. The baron was outraged. Behar was the same." Al-Jeheuty sighed. "I met with the baron's messenger—there are politics about him that I will fill you in on later. The messenger and I concluded that the guards would not have done such an act. I counseled with Behar and Wakil, and we concluded the same. To ease the matter, Behar, Wakil, and Baron Agusto met privately and shaped the new agreement for share in the trade. The Italians then left so that tension would be relieved. Al-Mari Ifriq had been locked-down for over five hours, exhausting what little soldiers and police that we have." He sighed again. "There still remains a mystery. Roberto, Bo Yusuf, and myself are conducting a private investigation." He took his drink and stood up. "For now, I drink to you, Hesam Gandarewa, Company Boss of Ahangar." Al-Jeheuty sipped his drink and returned his glass to the table.

Hesam's glass dangled under his lip in his trembling hand. He could not bring himself to raise the glass any further to take a sip. He knew instantly that he had not mistaken the title of company boss bestowed upon him.

Al-Jeheuty then clarified, "Isaiah Iraj was murdered a night ago. His body was found inside his company house, drenched with blood. The murder weapon, a cleaver, was left behind. It belonged to the cooks boarded on the Italian ships. Someone confiscated it. There were deep gashes on the back of Iraj's neck and down his spine. We can deduce that he was attacked from behind. We know that he had just finished collecting taxes from the local merchants in al-Mari Ifriq's northern district. The money was not found. Isaiah was murdered while we held court, perhaps after we convened. No one saw him after he returned from the district, save when his body was discovered."

Hesam gulped the last of his drink, taking a hard shot. He reached for the wine bottle and poured another glass for himself. "No suspecting an eye for an eye?" he asked al-Jeheuty.

"No," the official answered. "Stand. Come. Take the wine and your glass."

Hesam stood up and followed al-Jeheuty from the palace, exiting out of the rear entry. Wakil and Bo Yusuf met the two men in the rear garden and courtyard. Behar joined them several minutes later, Nasir and Feroz at his side. Each man held an empty glass that Al-Jeheuty poured wine into. Behar tipped his glass, spilling a small amount of the contents to the garden floor. "For Isaiah," said the Beylerbey. The other men poured a small amount of wine from their glasses. Behar lifted his glass and proclaimed, "To Hesam Gandarewa. Company Boss of Ahangar."

The men tossed back their drinks.

Behar motioned for Hesam to follow him back into the palace. There was a great deal of business for him to discuss with the new company boss. Hesam, in the morning, would meet with the Ahangar associates and learn the machinations of the company business.

Isaiah Iraj's body would be returned to his homeland.

Chapter Twenty-Five

Isaiah Iraj's murder remained a mystery even six months after it occured. Al-Jeheuty's secret investigation, conducted with Roberto Hamaat and Bo Yusuf ibn Tachfin al-Dume, revealed nothing. Casual conversation was started to see if anyone within al-Mari Ifriq's walls knew about the incident. Conversations revealed that all patrons of the taverns, legal and illegal seafarers alike, were rattled and saddened by the event. Isaiah was still young, even at thirty-five, and he was such a noble man; survived by two wives, a four-year old son, and twin daughters that were ten years of age. His family, with the help of close associates to the Ahangar Company, and Roberto Hamaat, brought his body back to his homeland. There was also given a treasury so large in sum that a few whispers dared to suspect his wives of the deed.

But that notion was swept aside out of respect for the dead.

However, Emissary Rene Chaffee and Turkish official al-Rinak Ozan were outraged by the incident. Calming both men proved difficult, but not impossible. No tension between the Turkish Empire and the French nation was wanted. Emissary Chaffee declared that the streets of al-Mari Ifriq were not safe for companymen. He did not bite his tongue on his suspicions of Italian involvement. The French, including businessman Simon Beaumont, expressed concerns directed at al-Mari Ifriq's leaders' involvement with the Italians, especially under such sanguinary circumstances. Emissary Chaffee propelled the notion that the Italians took the life of one of the Moors' chiefs in retaliation for an Italian associate. Nothing was going to stop the association between the Moors and the Italians, however. Baron Agusto's outfit had already settled within Libya, and all the suspicion surrounding their possible involvement with Company Boss Iraj's murder dissolved before they left al-Mari Ifriq's ports.

Al-Rinak proposed more troops patrolling the city streets, brought in from the Empire, no less. He broadcast that al-Mari Ifriq's local police were just a small faction, and though crime was very low, it was not enough to discourage the more bold and brave criminals. Behar acknowledged al-Rinak's concerns, but he did mention, with no disrespect for the dead, that Isaiah Iraj was working late without his guards, overseeing a large sum of money. The crime was not considered premeditated. The official statement released to the public was that thugs carried out the mark on Company Boss Iraj. The governor and Beylerbey deduced that Isaiah was the unfortunate victim of a spur-of-the-moment robbery, and they expressed that the culprits may have fled the city after the crime was committed. The Moorish officials conducted a public investigation of the ships that left port on the night of Isaiah's murder, and the ships that departed the following morning. The investigation pulled up nothing, but al-Jeheuty, Bo Yusuf, and Roberto Hamaat had a private investigation where everyone was a suspect, including the French Emissary and Turkish officials.

Speculation was rampant, but in low whispers. The fervor sparked by Isaiah Iraj's death quieted within weeks, though talk occurred in the taverns. The fervor was quelled not just out of respect for the surviving family, but also because of the excitement and celebration of the established trade between Djenhai and al-Mari Ifriq.

Bo Yusuf ibn Tachfin al-Dume successfully led the first caravan, taking charge of the Turkish soldiers. Like the Beylerbey before him, Bo Yusuf was impressed by Djenhai's pristine structure and architectural design. He spoke more about the kingdom's beauty than he did his courting of Yaminah Igdobe Djenhai, meeting the King and the rest of the royal family, and the great celebration held within the city upon their arrival. That entire event was arranged and delightfully executed by Rahmis Husani.

The celebration was short-lived, however. Light skirmishes with the Ogunsanwo-Mashek occurred just two months into the trading venture. The casualties sustained by the nomadic nation were not calculated, but a good number of kills were made. There were no casualties for the Turkish army or the merchants handling the trade. The confiscated goods included foodstuffs, weapons, spices, and fabrics. Forms of currency were left alone.

Al-Jeheuty, still in search of his miracle, continued to push for peace talks between the Ogunsanwo-Mashek and the Djenhai people by allowing word that al-Mari Ifriq was run by great revolutionaries, sympathizers looking to speak with the nomadic desert people. Taran Zaher and Wakil al-Hakam both agreed that al-Jeheuty's move toward peace was futile, both men having known nothing but conflict existing between Djenhai and the Ogunsanwo-Mashek. Al-Jeheuty requested an early morning meeting between he, Taran Zaher, Governor Wakil, Beylerbey Ameer Las El-Behar, Statesman al-Rinak, and Bo Yusuf ibn Tachfin al-Dume. The meeting was held at dawn.

Taran Zaher rose from his bed just before dawn. He was washed, perfumed, clothed, and completely primped before he gathered his entourage of personal servants and increased security, and strolled from his home to the council house that lay beyond the city gates. Taran had become increasingly annoyed with al-Jeheuty's attempts at forcing two nations, clearly determined to destroy one another, into peace. The Ambassador did not know who was more stubborn: al-Jeheuty or the Ogunsanwo-Mashek and Djenhai. But the young negotiator continued to stress that the conflict between the two nations was now affecting al-Mari Ifriq's process to make Odongo-Mauharim a unified nation-state. His speech was peculiar in the previous meeting, noting that the Ogunsanwo-Mashek were mainly pilfering supplies. He declared that the nomadic nation was in need of assistance, not war. He also made mention that casualties were suffered by the Ogunsanwo-Mashek, but not from either Turkish soldiers or trade-merchants within the caravan. Al-Rinak made a rebuttal that it was only because of the Turkish soldiers' successful attempt to retrieve stolen goods that the Ogunsanwo-Mashek suffered casualties. The Turkish statesman also pointed out that the southern trade routes were not as safe as the Moors initially considered. That was when Behar stated in his nonchalant manner, *"If you fear for the safety of your Turkish soldiers, perhaps you should return them to the Empire."*

Al-Rinak said nothing. His silence opened up an opportunity for Bo Yusuf and the Beylerbey to introduce a new proposal. Every district boss would hold an open recruitment for an al-Mari Ifriq army. There would be a mandatory enlistment for all eighteen-year old males, with two years of required service. They would also study a trade of their choice while serving and training. Al-Jeheuty declared that he would continue to campaign for peace talks while the transition from Turkish soldiers to al-Mari Ifriq soldiers took place.

That was two weeks ago.

Al-Rinak had not communicated much to Taran in that time. The Turkish statesman had not stirred up much for the Moorish rulers of al-Mari Ifriq. He spent most of his time at the Ghanem company house and inside the tavern, plotting with Maurice and Fusan. They too kept much from Taran. He was upset by that notion, considering he was like a father to them.

Taran was upset with the black Turk too. There was very little al-Rinak shared with him overall, believing the less Taran knew the better. But it was becoming increasingly harder for Taran to find excuses to keep the Turkish army within the city, as well as having al-Rinak sit in on council meetings. Taran's thoughts started to get the best of him as he made his way past the city gates and toward the council house. He was frustrated. His two sons plotted in secret with a third father figure. His daughter was off to school, and standing ready to marry a man of whom he did not approve. Worse yet, al-Jeheuty was a man he plotted against and had plans to eliminate. Taran's wife was also becoming more distant, working later within her business as Head Seamstress and helping lead the garment district. Taran would have objected to such behavior, but the revenue generated was worth the break in his wife's more traditional roles. But when his wife was not busy, and had a spare moment, she continuously visited her family in Tunisia, and their daughter too.

Thinking of all this made the frustration return.

His party was moving closer to the council house.

Taran did not want to listen to al-Jeheuty's rants about peace, or al-Rinak's sly, underhanded commentary. He did not feel like watching the two play verbal chess, and then watch Behar mediate the game. He was getting old and impatient.

Taran took a deep breath to calm down.

It was within the instant he expelled his breath that he heard the silence in the calm morning air disturbed by a simple popping noise. One of his guards dropped to the earth, a hole in his throat, blood spilling from the guard's open wound and mouth. A second pop accompanied the first. Taran felt a sharp pain in his right shoulder. His arm burned as if it was on fire. A third pop. Something punched and pierced Taran's stomach. He fell down, his body wracked with intense pain.

Taran's guards reacted, lifting their pistols or thin, long-barreled muskets. The guards formed a perimeter around Taran's fallen body. Several servants tended to Taran, his other servants ducked low within the perimeter of guards. From around the city walls came a high-pitched squeal. Mounted, cloaked soldiers, with their faces wrapped with cloth, and their chests covered in light armor, appeared from out of the dust kicked up by the hooves of their camels. They aimed muskets and fired in succession. Cylindrical pellets tore through Taran's guards, leveling some of the armed defenders. A bullet broke into a servant's skull, dropping her dead. Another servant was shot in the chest. From one of the watchtowers came two armed and cloaked men. A mounted man tossed the reins of a bare camel to them. Both men dropped their muskets as they charged the animal. The man in the lead grabbed the camel's reins and leapt onto the camel's back. The second man was able to catapult himself onto the animal's rear, grabbing the rider tightly around the waist.

Behar, Wakil, and al-Jeheuty rushed from the council house. Pistol fire polluted the morning air. Al-Jeheuty rushed the Governor and Beylerbey back inside. He strapped on his sword and snatched a Dutch

Blunderbuss located at the side of the door. Armed, al-Jeheuty marched into the foray with two guards at his side. Bo Yusuf charged from the open city gates, guards close behind him. He drew two pistols and fired at the attackers. Bo Yusuf's first shot crashed into the chestplate of an attacker; his second shot bore through a mounted attacker's underarm. The man bucked forward but managed to keep his balance and his grip on the camel's reins. The city guards fired their pistols. More attackers were wounded, but did not slip from their mounts. Nasir came from his company house, choosing a dire moment to investigate the disorder. A mounted attacker tossed a small throwing knife at the company boss, hitting Nasir in the arm. Nasir bent back with the blade's impact. He slammed against the side of his company house, and slumped down slowly. Another knife was tossed at Nasir. The blade punctured the lower-right side of his abdomen. He winced and clutched his second wound.

Two small iron spheres, packed with gunpowder and slow burning wicks, were tossed through the Sa'ood company house's windows.

The bombs exploded!

Nasir's body was pushed from the wall, and he fell face first onto the gravelly sand.

The attacking riders continued forward. Three more iron spheres were tossed toward the second watchtower. The base exploded, rocking the foundation. Four more iron-sphere bombs crippled the tower, but the structure did not fall apart. The attackers disappeared around the far corner of the city wall.

Al-Jeheuty rushed to Nasir's aid. The company boss was breathing and conscious, groaning from the assault made against him. Bo Yusuf joined al-Jeheuty, standing over his fellow official and Nasir. Al-Jeheuty turned his head to inspect the bloody scene. Guards and officials writhed on the ground, puddles of blood underneath them. There were cries of confusion coming from over the city gates. There were dead that lay covered with debris, and there was smoke filling the morning air. Al-Jeheuty cursed the sight. The Moorish official was still bent on declaring peace, even through the smoky declaration of war left behind by the Ogunsanwo-Mashek warriors.

Guards and soldiers spilled from the opened city gates. Roberto Hamaat led the charge. Bo Yusuf rushed to the occult-assassin's side. Roberto ordered the Army Official to group with and lead the guards that were trying to get control of the panicked crowd. Al-Jeheuty called for Roberto to send guards to gather the wounded. Soldiers swarmed around Nasir, Taran, and the wounded servants and guards. Other troops flocked inside the Sa'ood company house, helping put out fires, assisting the wounded, and gathering the dead.

The French suffered both wounded and dead. Three men—two Arabs and a Moor—were found dead inside the undisturbed watchtower, stabbed numerous times with their throats slit. The council house was not disturbed. Behar and Wakil rested safely inside, personal guards at the ready. Roberto and his troops were allowed entry. He presented the details of the Ogunsanwo-Mashek attack. Behar and Wakil frowned. Wakil ordered for al-Jeheuty and Bo Yusuf to make an appearance after the two officials handled all matters of assisting with the wounded and dead. He also called for all officials to be brought to the council house.

Roberto and his soldiers returned to the scene, helping al-Jeheuty and Bo Yusuf. Both Taran and Nasir were taken to the palace infirmaries to recover. Zakiy went to inform his mother of Nasir's condition. Al-Jeheuty ordered him to go to the palace afterwards.

The wounded guards were taken to the barracks' infirmaries in the city's western district. Al-Jeheuty ordered Bo Yusuf to round up all company bosses. Feroz Aunun and Hesam Gandarewa were quickly accounted for. The company bosses kept safe inside their company houses during the attack. Statesmen Sinan and al-Rinak were found at *The al-Hammon Palace*, al-Rinak resting inside a backroom with Melusina. The woman was primping al-Rinak for his meeting with the Moorish officials. The two men were ordered to the council house immediately.

Emissary Chaffee resided inside the Sa'ood company house, and he was feared dead or wounded. The businessman was irate, but otherwise fine, his clothes slightly tattered and seared. The attack left four Frenchmen dead. One was a servant. One was an accountant, and two were guards. Several more were wounded, and Rene refused to have his men taken to the barracks to be looked after. Al-Jeheuty calmed the French businessman and was able to sway him from his position. Chaffee was then ordered to the council house.

Two hours passed before al-Jeheuty and Bo Yusuf, along with Roberto Hamaat, reported back to the governor and the Beylerbey. Wakil and Behar dismissed all servants and guards. The perimeter of the council house was covered.

Everyone took a deep breath.

"We will address the citizens," declared Behar, speaking for he and Wakil. "We will inform them of the entire extent of the attack, and the extent of the attack's damage. We will also confirm that the Ogunsanwo-Mashek are suspected as being responsible—"

"Suspected?" cried Emissary Chaffee. "Do you believe another group of savages have caused this damage? This is war, Beylerbey," said Emissary Chaffee in a condescending tone.

"When will al-Mari Ifriq receive French forces to assist in fighting?" asked Behar.

The emissary made a perplexed expression. He stuttered, "I have no authority to initiate such an—"

"Then please do not feel as if you have the authority to either speak *for* me, lead *my* city into war, or decide against whom we will fight." Behar's voice was thunderous.

Al-Rinak stepped forward. "Beylerbey, you are not still trying to seek peaceful means as a solution? Al-Mari Ifriq and her citizens must be protected and feel safe."

"That is why all trade with Djenhai will be come to a stop," Behar informed. "The next train is not due for two weeks. Al-Jeheuty, Bo Yusuf, and Roberto," he called. The three men stepped forward. "I want you to watch the Ogunsanwo-Mashek's movements. Watch them from afar. You three understand the necessity of stealth. Report back in a week. Statesman Ozan," al-Rinak stepped forward, surprised that his name was called. "We will need the might of the Turkish troops here. I want a blockade protecting the southern wall. When we learn the Ogunsanwo-Mashek's activities, we will have the Turkish troops stationed in Djenhai mount an attack on them. They will be joined by your troops guarding the southern wall. We will smother them."

Al-Rinak bowed at the neck. "Yes, Beylerbey."

"I cannot allow that," said Statesman Sinan Demir. "The Empire has interests in al-Mari Ifriq. However, because of the recent restructure to the Ottoman state, our troops cannot be exhausted, nor can they be used without full permission of the Sultan. Not in this capacity anyway. The Empire patiently waits for al-Rinak and myself to return the troops. Using them as we do may also be considered an offense." Sinan turned to al-Rinak and addressed, "I also do not want to be responsible for drawing the Empire into an incident of this nature."

"We would be acting in the Empire's best interests and protecting a great investment," al-Rinak responded visibly irritated at Sinan.

Sinan did not retort. He turned to the governor and the Beylerbey and said, "I'm sure we could come to a deal for al-Mari Ifriq to purchase the remaining troops." The statesman let too much of a smile come through in his words.

Behar was furious. "Men are bleeding," he said in a low, angry voice. "Men are dead. And you dare see the potential for profit?"

"Beylerbey," Sinan stammered. "I was just proposing that, if monies were exchanged, it would diffuse the potential for any offense made toward the Empire. May I remind you—with no offense to your grand city—that you do not have a real army?"

Behar thought for just a second. He stated, "There will be no purchase of troops from the Ottoman Empire. You will hail your country and ask permission to continue to use the Turkish troops as they operate. If the Empire feels compelled to remove their troops from our situation, they will leave immediately. We will seek help from Algiers and Tunis."

Al-Rinak fixed his face and erased any signs of the intense anger writhing inside of him. But he still boiled. Sinan had just given the Beylerbey the means to remove their army from his city, a feat that would prove difficult for the two statesmen considering the army was owned by the two gentlemen, already purchased from the Ottoman Empire. Ottoman interest in al-Mari Ifriq did not exist. This was a power move for the two statesmen who now held very little say among the Ottoman council. Their intent was to manipulate the Moorish officials into believing there still existed a threat of a return to Turkish rule. But the Sultan's advisors had no time for trivial matters such as al-Mari Ifriq. Al-Rinak and Sinan were backed by other powers in Turkey, influential men that had more power among the officials than the Sultan himself.

Al-Rinak decided to mark Statesman Sinan Demir for his lack of intelligence. The plan to eliminate Sinan was formulated as the buffoon stumbled over his words. Al-Rinak decided to put his plans in motion. He addressed Wakil and Behar. "Allow my fellow statesman to return to our country. He will submit your request to the Empire."

Behar and Wakil looked at Sinan for an answer. "I will leave immediately," he said to the two city leaders. "Tomorrow," he said hastily. "No. Nightfall," he corrected. "Keep your plans to watch the Ogunsanwo-Mashek. If I return with news that the remaining Turkish troops are permitted to engage, then we will move ahead with the plans."

Behar turned to Rene Chaffee. "Notify Simon Beaumont. Tell him that the French suffered casualties on African soil. Assure him that the matter is being dealt with."

The French emissary scoffed a little. He did not want to upset the Beylerbey. He was, however, grateful to leave al-Mari Ifriq for a small amount of time to bring the news to Simon Beaumont. He would also report the news to his more covert benefactor.

The council was dismissed. The foreign officials were instructed to return to their houses. There would be official guards located outside their housing complex, and they would be escorted everywhere. It was all for their protection. Behar sent a message to Ojodo Yerodin. He was put in charge of preparing Statesman Sinan and Emissary Chaffee's ships for departure.

Behar and Wakil adjourned to a private chamber in the palace. Al-Jeheuty, Bo Yusuf, and Roberto Hamaat were summoned to the room to receive further instructions for their scouting expedition. Behar turned to the three men. He aimed his finger at them and said in a severe manner, "Find their chief. Engage them. I want answers. Is that understood?" The three men simply nodded. "Announce our address to the citizens, and then be on your way."

The three men nodded again and left the room. Wakil took a deep breath and then told Behar, "I will find my wife and sons. They need to know I'm all right, and about what has happened. I will meet you in the city square for our announcement to the public." Behar simply shook his head as Wakil exited the room. The Beylerbey took a deep breath. He waited for several minutes before he decided to leave and find where Taran Zaher was being attended. Alimah Zaher had already arrived. She was waiting outside the room where Taran was being treated. She wept, her tears collecting against her veil. Her servants were dismissed as Behar approached. The mature and beautiful woman stood up and tossed her arms around the Beylerbey. She started to cry harder, gripping Behar's robes tightly, tugging at them. "Don't let him die, Beylerbey. Don't let my husband be killed. Give mercy. I know what you plan to do. He cannot die like this."

Behar could not believe Alimah was weeping for Taran. She did not love him. He was not even the father of her eldest daughter. The Beylerbey sighed as he started to understand. Despite the arrangement in marriage, despite an initial lack of love, and despite the insecurity Taran wielded through doctrines of faith that kept Alimah bound to him because she was a woman, somewhere deep within Alimah was a desire to hold onto Taran Zaher. Behar considered that Alimah could not let go of Taran. He thought it was possibly because of the guilt knowing she would profit from his death. She would then be Queen alongside him as King.

Behar took another breath. He stepped away from Alimah as she continued to beg him that her husband receive the best care. Her words were sincere, every syllable like a knife tearing into Behar. He wanted to grab her and shake her while yelling, *"You don't even love him! It's me! It's always been me!"* But the Beylerbey did not stir in the woman's direction. He stepped inside the room where Taran was being assisted for his wounds.

The official was unconscious, a drug flowing through his body helping him sleep past the operation of removing the small, cylindrical projectiles and stitching the wounds. The lead doctor looked up and locked eyes with the Beylerbey. The doctor's name was Essien. He was in his mid-thirties, and he was one of the best doctors in the palace. He was also one of Roberto Hamaat's recruits. Essien was as skilled at taking lives as he was at saving them.

Behar looked back to the weeping Alimah.

He loved her so much.

The Beylerbey returned his gaze to Essien and made a signal to save Taran's life. "Beylerbey," said the doctor. "I will give your official the best care. We have removed the projectiles. He has lost a fair amount of blood. There is still the chance he may catch a life-threatening fever." Essien was giving Behar assurance.

The Beylerbey brushed the warning aside. "See him through any complications," Behar instructed. Essien bowed at the neck. He and the nurses returned to attending to Taran. Behar walked back to Alimah. She grabbed the Beylerbey's arm and kissed his hands, acting as if she was an ordinary citizen to him. Alimah stood up. "Thank you, Beylerbey," she said to Behar. "My husband cannot go like this. Not like this." Alimah continued to cry.

Behar consoled her. "He will survive. He's old, but stubborn." He wanted to add the fact that he personally believed that neither Heaven nor Hell wished to have Taran's company. The Beylerbey did add, whispering into the mature, beautiful woman's ear, "Your husband will curse our presence for some time."

"Behar," Alimah said in an extremely low tone. She did not want anyone to hear her addressing the Beylerbey common, though there was nothing but continuous rushing through palace corridors as servants, doctors, and nurses scurried to attend to the wounded. Behar turned away from her. "Bey—Behar. He suffers. His spirit would be in agony. His spirit would not see rest; he would watch us. He would be vengeful when I went to the other side."

Behar spun around. His anger was unmistakable. He grabbed Alimah's arm and rushed her into a nearby, empty room. He shut the door and yelled at her, "You believe such nonsense, yet you don't believe that my power extends beyond this physical world. I would protect you in the next world even as I remained physical in this one." Behar's expression proved his belief in his words.

Alimah became frightened by the intense conviction in Behar's tone. She sniffed away her tears, gaining a small moment to rebuttal, "You are such a hateful man! Taran is innocent. He never knew of us. He did not come between us. That was my father's arrangement. Taran—*my husband*—in his present state, does not deserve to be taken advantage of, especially not because of a small glimmer of emotion we carry for one another, which has only become lust."

Behar, pointing to the room where Taran resided, hissed in a low angry voice, "That man turned *my* daughter into a pimp. He should die for that alone. I would understand his action if he had the slightest bit of knowledge that Mehit was *not* his daughter. But he did so under the belief that she is his child. You really believe he gives a damn about you, or even his real daughter that he sold off to an aged, Turkish official? Should I continue to speak and explain your husband's practices within business and politics?" Alimah lifted her hand, turning her head away. "Of course not," said Behar in reaction to Alimah's displayed behavior. "It's easier to make the decisions without the full scope of reality to contend with."

Alimah responded angrily, "Then tell your doctors to kill him!"

"Without your consent? Yes, leave it up to me to make your decision," Behar replied. "Let me take your responsibility from you. The consequences of which would have you transfer to me all the anger you hold for your beloved husband. All the guilt you would feel for being happy and rid of this odious man, would churn out nothing but anger in my direction. Go ahead. Let me have you take out all the hate you possess for him on me. How dare I make you happy." Behar said to no one in particular, "Why is it that women continue to live their lives through easy choices rather than taking responsibility? You would rather have veils tossed over you, nooses thrown around your necks, chains at your ankles and wrists, whips lashing your backs, and fire cackling at your feet while tied to stakes, than castrating the men that use corrupted forms of politics and faith to control you." He bent down again and whispered low into Alimah's ear, "The day you decide to sever the *Devil's* penis, instead of bargaining with the fourteen pieces of the *proper* black Osiris, and assemble that broken, black god to help protect you—or be at your side in battle—is the day no doctrine or word of a corrupt man will hold you down, or stop you from being happy. Stop hating the man you love, and stop loving the man you hate." He calmed his demeanor and said, "Do you really believe I've held you all these nights under the pretext of lust? When I was in Spain, as I watched men die in the bloodiest of fashions, you were my only thought, Alimah. I worried that you would never know my fate should I fall in battle. Ironically, thoughts of me died inside you long ago."

"I couldn't think of you, Behar," Alimah said as her voice cracked with sadness. "I couldn't. Dreaming of you would have killed me."

He gently lifted her veil. "You need to wake up from that notion. This isn't a hope to capture my youth. I hold the woman I have always loved. It may give us a rush, but it is more than that. You may feel as if you're getting back at Taran, and your father, while we sneak nights with one another. Our time together may make you feel youthful, but that's all a cover. You don't want to admit you love me because you're so afraid of being attached to the very essence you rebel against, and that is a man. But you have to stop generalizing. You have to start understanding that you are angry with your father and your husband, and their pursuit of using you as a symbol for status. I love you, and I want you to rule by my side." Behar exhaled. He stood up straight. "I understand that this is not the right time. Al-Mari Ifriq will be locked-down. No unofficial travel is permitted. I will have word sent to Mehit about Taran's condition. Your husband will be fine. I allow you to remain miserable, if that's what makes you happy."

The Beylerbey turned, opened the door, and walked from the room. There was a statement he had to make to the citizens of al-Mari Ifriq.

Chapter Twenty-Six

Odongo-Mauharim was a hidden paradise, reflecting the ancient look of North Africa during the time of the Roman period. The region was mostly desert, a burning, dune sea where the Saharan dragon breathed its fiery sands into the small territory. But there were small patches of mountain ranges on the outskirts of Odongo-Mauharim. The region also possessed uncultivated, pre-desert land that either melted back into the sands, or gave way to jagged terrain and gravelly paths that grew into mountain ranges that acted as natural deterrents for enemy nations. Odongo-Mauharim severed this mountain range, the Atlas Mountains, in two halves, and the mountain range formed natural borders between it, Algeria, and Tunisia. Small paths had been carved out to lead into the adjacent nations.

Al-Mari Ifriq, a city built upon the northern most pre-desert land, had the potential to be as much a prosperous piece of land as it had in the Roman Era. The continuous strife is all that kept the city from a great destiny, and with it, all of Odongo-Mauharim. The hourglass shaped region, with sand flowing through the middle, mountains at its side, small patches of pre-desert land in its interior, is where roamed the nomadic tribes in accordance to the land's seasonal fertility.

Al-Jeheuty Anhur Has, Bo Yusuf ibn Tachfin al-Dume, and Roberto Hamaat searched within the desert region for the nomadic tribe, the Ogunsanwo-Mashek. The men were mounted on camels, and they were armed for survival. Muskets were strapped to their backs. Pistols were tucked through the belts wrapping their waists. Daggers were sheathed at their hip. Swords dangled in decorated scabbards at their waist-side. Provisions, bagged inside sacks, hung from their camels. Tools lay inside pockets on the mounts' leather harnesses. Their search took them southeast, closer to the open border between Odongo-Mauharim and Tunisia, just south of the mountain range.

No words had been exchanged since the beginning of their journey, almost two hours ago. Each man concentrated on a separate aspect of the mission. Roberto focused on the strategy of a possible offensive attack. Bo Yusuf centered on a possible strategy for defense. Al-Jeheuty plotted to use the right words to keep the three men out of any confrontation. No one believed that any of their strategies were impossible, though the situation appeared to be three against an entire nation of warriors. The greater task was to find and question the chief. The three men would, before engaging, watch the Ogunsanwo-Mashek from a distance. Once the tribe's movements where studied, an attack would begin.

This was a difficult and dangerous mission. The three men, of course, were not alone. A faction of Roberto's clan traveled close enough for the officials to be kept in sight. The hidden reinforcements only numbered five. It would be enough, so the officials believed. The Ogunsanwo-Mashek were masters of the land. This was their arena. The three officials were already being watched closely, and not by the protective eyes of Roberto's soldiers. Roberto's troupe had already been subdued. The Ogunsanwo-Mashek warriors were now poised to strike the unsuspecting Moorish officials.

An arrow was fired from a distant sand dune. The sharp projectile hit Bo Yusuf's mount, striking the animal's left eye and breaking into the camel's brain, killing the creature instantly. Bo Yusuf held the reins tight as the beast toppled over. The Moorish official rolled away from the weight of the animal, and then took cover behind the camel's fallen carcass. Neither al-Jeheuty, nor Roberto Hamaat, had time to react. Two Ogunsanwo-Mashek warriors emerged from the sands. The desert raiders were armed with swords, which they quickly swung, cutting the necks of al-Jeheuty and Roberto Hamaat's mounts.

Al-Jeheuty smacked the ground, but quickly recovered to reach for the blunderbuss strapped to his dead mount. The Ogunsanwo-Mashek warriors stopped him, their swords pointed toward he and Roberto. The occult-assassin's right shoulder had popped from its socket. Roberto stayed strong, reaching for a hidden throwing knife. Roberto did nothing more than reach for the knife. He stayed his hand even as an Ogunsanwo-Mashek warrior placed the tip of his sword to Roberto's neck. Someone yelled from the direction of the first attack. Three warriors came from over the sand dune. The middle warrior held a musket, aimed at al-Jeheuty and the two other officials. The flanking men aimed bows locked with arrows that were drawn back at the ready.

The three Moorish officials held their breath as Ogunsanwo-Mashek warriors surrounded them. The man holding the musket stepped closer. Four more warriors approached from behind. All the men were dressed identically, save the man aiming the musket. The colors of the clothes were the same, gray-blue. The warriors were clothed with baggy pants, tan boots, and long, flowing shirts. The warrior with the musket had a long fitting coat, like the kind worn by clergy. All of the men were masked and wore headwraps, their blue-black skin only previewed through a small, uncovered, rectangular shaped opening. Their dark, exposed eyes watched the Moorish officials intensely. Each man was fashioned with breastplate armor.

The man with the musket shouted something to the three Moorish officials. None of the officials understood the language. The man yelled again, this time louder. The officials did not move. He yelled a third time, and al-Jeheuty understood that the Ogunsanwo-Mashek warrior was repeating the same phrase in different languages, trying to see which the Moors spoke. Al-Jeheuty replied, "I do not understand."

"Identify yourselves," spoke the warrior.

"We are officials from al-Mari Ifriq," al-Jeheuty responded. "We seek the Chief of the Ogunsanwo-Mashek." He stood up slowly, arms raised. "We received your message. Much damage has been done. We're looking to settle before more damage occurs. There is no need for war."

"War will be made with any supporters or consorts of Djenhai," the warrior stated. "Throw off your weapons," he commanded.

The Moorish officials tossed away their daggers, swords, and muskets. The weapons were quickly gathered by the other Ogunsanwo-Mashek. Roberto kept his hidden throwing knives. The assassin winced in pain. His shoulder throbbed. He dropped to one knee, clutching his shoulder. Bo Yusuf made a move toward him but was stopped by an Ogunsanwo-Mashek warrior.

"Back away," said the warrior with the musket. He called another warrior and spoke in his native tongue. The swordsman sheathed his weapon and approached Roberto. He put his hands on the assassin's arm and shoulder then popped the dislocated limb back into place.

Roberto screamed!

The initial shock of pain exploded through every nerve in his aging body, his shoulder the epicenter of the blast. The assassin used an old technique to absorb the pain, quieting the inceptive, fiery sting in his shoulder. Roberto controlled his breathing, and he was able to stand on his feet. He thanked the Ogunsanwo-Mashek warrior, not knowing if his language was understood. The words were not, but the sentiment resonated.

Al-Jeheuty and Bo Yusuf shared a quick look at one another. The warrior with the musket started to chuckle. "We have caught a great prize today. Even our gods smile on you. We cannot send you to hell today."

"I'm grateful that you've postponed the trip," al-Jeheuty quipped.

"But why such a destructive display against our city, and such hospitality now?"

"I did not lead an attack against your city today," relayed the warrior. "It might've been led by two of my fellow warriors. They are far more militant than I. They are extremely impatient. Our leader has given us strict orders. I follow these orders for the same reason I don't send you to hell." He finally lowered the weapon. "If we were to kill you now, a combined fleet consisting of Djenhai and Moorish troops would wipe us all out." He handed the weapon to the warrior next to him. The man relaxed his bow, placed his arrow back inside his quiver, and then took the weapon. The unarmed Ogunsanwo-Mashek warrior stepped toward al-Jeheuty, lowered his mask, and extended a hand. "My name is Balde-Sih."

Al-Jeheuty did not hesitate to shake Balde's hand. He introduced himself and his associates. "There are others with us," confessed al-Jeheuty.

"Subdued," Balde said. "They are unharmed. This is our land, Moorish refugee. All the terrain is ours to manipulate. We tell the sun when to make a shadow for us to hide. No man or woman can sneak around these parts unless well trained in our arts." He turned to the warriors and commanded in their native tongue to bind the three Moors. "You will see our chief, but you will see him under conditions of capture." Balde then said in a sincere voice, "We will let you go. We need you to survive to tell the tale."

The officials were bound tightly. A long rope was wrapped around their necks, connecting the three officials to one another. Their mounts were stripped of provisions, legs tied, and carried back to the Ogunsanwo-Mashek camp for food. The officials' weapons were collected, confiscated as war trophies.

The trek was long but not arduous. The three captives were reunited with the five members of Roberto's outfit. Two of them were females, to which Balde made the comment was the reason why the troupe was so easily suppressed. The Moons in Roberto's group wanted to retort with a toss of the small throwing knives still on their person. The binding that the captives found themselves in was poor, especially for two well-trained revolutionaries, five assassins, and one master assassin. A display of skill was not the goal, however, though neither was being captured by the Ogunsanwo-Mashek. The desert warriors caught the officials and their support by surprise. If luck was a god or goddess, only he or she needed to be praised for the officials still being alive. Regardless, they would receive audience with the Ogunsanwo-Mashek chief.

The Ogunsanwo-Mashek's camp lay on a pre-desert region, several miles from the Tunisian border. The captive officials were impressed with the sight. It was a settlement that mirrored the quaint scenes of magical desert life orated from enchanting bedtime stories. Domed houses supported by compact millet stalk pillars populated the land. Canopied carriages, once mounted to elephants, and most likely seized from traveling caravans, were refurbished into different types of stores.

Men and women wore long, colorful, and elegant flowing robes that were either decorated with ancient signs and symbols, or just moderately embellished by stitch. Some men and women walked with little clothing, their bodies covered with short cloth and fabrics. Every man and woman was adorned with necklaces, anklets, nose rings, or earrings. Some jewelry was made of beads, bone, and some were fashioned from precious metals. The sight was far more peaceful than what was allowed to gestate inside the politics and minds of the Moorish officials.

Balde-Sih raised his hand and yelled to the Ogunsanwo-Mashek population. The men and women turned to the incoming warriors and yelled for their return. Balde turned to a fellow warrior and stated in their native language, "Release the negotiator. Put the rest in the cage."

The man set about his task, liberating al-Jeheuty from the rope that wrapped around his neck. Al-Jeheuty was brought to Balde, his wrists still bound. The other captives were taken away, placed inside a confiscated cage that was stolen from a Djenhai caravan that once contained animals for trade. Balde ushered al-Jeheuty to the largest and most decorated domed house. The Ogunsanwo-Mashek chief lay inside.

The interior of the domed house was furnished with commandeered treasures. The house was a treasury, where all the wealth, taken or handmade by native hands, swirled around a beautifully carved throne. The chair was sculpted from the finest wood, etched in gold with ancient symbols, and encrusted with precious gems and stones. Adjacent to the throne was an equally beautiful long seat that was carved from wood, also embroidered with symbols and encrusted with gems and precious stones. A purple blanket lay across the seat.

The throne was empty.

The long seat was empty.

The far right corner of the house was boxed off with walls that were not high enough to touch the ceiling. Water poured into the boxed area from an open hole in the ceiling. Al-Jeheuty raised an eyebrow at the ingenuity. He also wondered where the water was originating from, and how the water flowed up and then down into the house. He could see the head of a woman bathing from behind the walls. His eyes turned back to the throne. The Ogunsanwo-Mashek chief stood behind the sovereign chair. Al-Jeheuty wondered when the man made his entrance. The Moorish official was also shocked to see that the chief was a young man in his mid-twenties.

The chief was dark and tall, boasting a slender yet muscular frame. He looked like a shaft of black lightning, his black flesh gleaming. The chief's torso was bare of shirt, but he wore a black, gold, and silver sash drawn over his shoulder and across his chest. He was clothed in dark, billowing pants that had purple stripes lining the legs. He had shoes to match. Atop his head were five locks, the middle lock dyed silver. Four braided strands of hair surrounded the locks. The rest of his head was shaved.

Balde bowed his head at the neck. The warrior looked up and aimed a hand toward his chief. "This is our Chief. Mazigh-Lumumba Ogunsanwo, *Descendant of HIM of Nine That Was a King.*" Al-Jeheuty bowed in presence. Balde stepped forward as Mazigh walked from around his throne. "This is al-Jeheuty," reported Balde. "He is a Moorish official from al-Mari Ifriq."

Mazigh smiled and asked al-Jeheuty, "Are you here to arrest me? Perhaps your city's army is prepared to do what those cowardly Djenhai cannot. I'm impressed. An actual representative of al-Mari Ifriq's new governing body is in my presence. Are you one of the great revolutionaries? There are rumors that you slay the former rulers. Foreigners."

Al-Jeheuty surprised the chief by confessing, "Yes. We killed the heads of The Four Winds. We killed the Turkish rulers. Myself, three other revolutionaries, led by my General and current Beylerbey of al-Mari Ifriq, teamed with a young company boss, plotted and revolted against the former, Turkish rulers. We killed their soldiers. We shot and stabbed them. We killed their associates in other cities. We killed an Algerian Pasha. We killed their associates at sea, and we killed their associates from, and on, foreign soil. We threw their bodies into wooden boxes, and buried them at sea. We blamed their deaths on bandits. No one is the wiser, or so I continue to think."

Mazigh was moved by al-Jeheuty's intensity. The Moorish official's eyes glistened with tears, but no stream snaked down his face. "Why do you confess such deeds as if they were sins?" He walked closer. "Do you know why your revolutionary deed is not completely suppressed by the concocted story of bandits? The fabrication is not believed because among all of Africa the truth of your revolution gives hope. No nation, nomadic or fixed, wishes to cooperate with the tale of bandits slaying the foreigners, because so much hope exists that we may all do the same." Mazigh then asked, "Are you alone?"

"Two fellow officials were detained along with me," al-Jeheuty answered. "And some soldiers."

"Have them freed," commanded Mazigh to Balde. "Prepare meals for them. Have them bathed in the water-houses. Ready our people. We will hold a ceremony tonight, entertain our guests in our 'savage' customs." Mazigh chuckled as he said, "They have said, since the days of Usar, that the blacks always find a reason to hold a festivity." Balde removed al-Jeheuty's bindings and then disappeared. Mazigh put his arm around the Moorish official and guided him outside. "Let us give my wife privacy. We have much to discuss." The chieftess stepped from her shower just as the men exited the house.

Mazigh walked al-Jeheuty through the settlement. The Moorish official spoke carefully when he asked, "We have a great problem, Chief Mazigh-Lumumba. Al-Mari Ifriq was attacked this morning by a rogue group of Ogunsanwo-Mashek warriors."

"Nonsense," replied the chief.

Al-Jeheuty continued, "The attack has left our city crippled. Officials, foreign and domestic, suffered casualties. Two Moorish officials were critically wounded; one of them was my friend. My party is on orders to capture you and bring you before our city's leaders." He took a breath and added, "Balde informed me there has been no order to engage al-Mari Ifriq, but he said there are militants among you."

Mazigh stopped walking. He greeted several passersby as they bowed in the presence of their chief. He then returned his attention to al-Jeheuty. "Balde speaks about two of my warriors. Chwezi, *Keeper of the Five Percent of Knowledge*. He is a remarkable thinker. A great strategist that thinks through probability calculated with a supreme and more spiritual form of mathematics. He is innocent, as is the second warrior Balde references. Gu-Gurzil. He is a fiery man. His very presence resonates with battle; he vibrates with an aura of war. But, like I said, he too is innocent. These men, and the small units they control, have been guarding this settlement all day. That is my sincere word. Which, of course, presents a greater problem than you may imagine. A devil, sly enough to wear our robes, left your city in flames. We do not want war with your damn city, even as you consort with our enemy the Djenhai."

Al-Jeheuty exhaled. "I have not been treated in a manner that would hint that your people just attacked my city."

Mazigh admitted, "We have been responsible for the attacks on some of your trade caravans going in and out of Djenhai. But we have been cautious not to stir too much war. We have robbed you of supplies, foodstuffs, and weapons. When word spread that African Moors took al-Mari Ifriq there was great rejoice. Our nation made trade with early rulers of the city. Al-Mari Ifriq was very young. But attention turned to Djenhai, an enemy of our nation. Djenhai declared claim in al-Mari Ifriq. The union between the city and kingdom was considered more gainful. We were hurt when again recently al-Mari Ifriq turned its attention to Djenhai and overlooked our nation. History repeated itself. And word is that you also congregate with whites, slavers no less."

"We do not mingle with slavers," al-Jeheuty defended.

"You dance with their cousins," Mazigh pressed. "That is the same. You drink and break bread with whites that have not yet found reason enough to dip into the gainful practice of crushing the blacks of Africa. I say again, that is the same. But that is not the reason we planned a crushing, quick hit on the next train leaving Djenhai. That act would have been retaliation."

"Retaliation for what?" asked al-Jeheuty.

"There was a strike made against our settlement," answered Mazigh. "The soldiers guarding your train engaged a unit of my warriors who retreated to our settlement. They were followed. Women and children were killed. We were enraged. Chwezi and Gu-Gurzil wanted to rush your city. I calmed their anger. I felt that something was not right. The warriors that were not able to retreat were found stripped of their clothes and weapons." Mazigh added with a concerned expression, "I understand that there is more than blacks that populate your city."

Al-Jeheuty looked around the settlement. He returned his gaze to Mazigh and said, "Move your people. Do not engage any more trade caravans. I will note your defense for your warriors. I will submit that to my Beylerbey and governor. But it's your word against eye witness accounts from wounded officials and workers of the city, not to mention my own eyes."

Mazigh shook his head and said regretfully, "I can't move our settlement far. We move according to the seasons. There are few patches of non-desert land that is suitable for living during this time of year."

"We will bring you supplies," al-Jeheuty assured. "This will be our secret."

"Can you truly arrange that?" Mazigh asked in disbelief.

"Yes," al-Jeheuty answered with a confident tone. "We've done it before with other nomadic nations."

Mazigh patted the Moor on the shoulder. "I will hold a ceremony tonight that will induct you into our nation." He smiled slyly. "This is not because I like you. I will ordain you as blood to us so that if you fall back on your word, then we will spill that same blood."

"There is a mystery to solve, good Chief," al-Jeheuty reminded. "Should evidence show that you have lied, should evidence surface that your people led a bold and bloody attack on al-Mari Ifriq, then you will have to deal with soldiers coming here again and going after your women and children, and they will approach from that horizon." Al-Jeheuty pointed to the northwest direction. "Until then, we are brothers-in-arms." The two men embraced. Mazigh led al-Jeheuty to where Bo Yusuf, Roberto Hamaat, and the others were being held. The detained officials and assassins had already been released. Mazigh and Balde left the Moors to congregate among themselves. Al-Jeheuty informed Bo Yusuf and Roberto Hamaat about the conversation he had with Chief Mazigh-Lumumba Ogunsanwo.

The Moors mingled among the Ogunsanwo-Mashek people. Not everyone knew the Moors' language. Conversation was very limited. The people understood that strangers were among them, but word was spread that the visit was friendly. Mazigh and Balde introduced the Moorish officials and assassin-soldiers to Chwezi and Gu-Gurzil. Chwezi was short with a triangular, shaved head. Gu-Gurzil was tall, with bushy hair and intense eyes. Not much in the way of words was exchanged, but everyone managed to be pleasant. Al-Jeheuty, Bo Yusuf, and Roberto Hamaat secluded themselves again trying to figure out the hospitable demeanor of a group of desert marauders that just attacked their city.

The three officials had no answers by the time the sun went down. Mazigh gathered all three officials, along with Roberto's soldiers, and brought them into the circle of festivities. Drums and stringed instruments filled the night. A circle of dance was formed; onlookers clapped to the rhythm of the music and cheered the dancers. Lamb, beef, and camel meat were served with tomatoes, peppers, and onions. Milk, mixed with pounded goat cheese and dates, was provided as beverage. There was also water available. The visiting Moors were thankful. Mazigh took a seat next to al-Jeheuty. "Lovely, is it not? Lovely, considering how much of a barbaric people we are." Al-Jeheuty did not comment. Mazigh continued, "I say these words not to conform to what the Djenhai think about us—or even the people of al-Mari Ifriq. I speak about the reality of what this nation has degenerated to." Al-Jeheuty braced himself for a confession. But what he was told was far more disturbing and sorrowful. "Africa has fallen apart.

The whites and their tawny conspirators divide and conqueror us. Some of the whites believe that this process of divide is a newly forged plan, but the Ogunsanwo-Mashek are living proof that this has been the white's aspiration since we blacks gave birth to them. Our nation's origins attest to that." He took a sip of his drink. "The Djenhai plot to have us enslaved. That is why our nomadic movements have been more varying. Djenhai's King has not informed you of those plans, has he?"

Al-Jeheuty shook his head slowly.

Mazigh smiled cynically. "We wouldn't have known either, had we not extracted the information from a Djenhai soldier." He rolled his eyes as he wiped away the cynical attitude that was beginning to come over him. His face and emotions became stern and he told al-Jeheuty, "My father used to tell me—as I'm sure you too are aware—but a lot of these nomadic nations are refugees from conquered kingdoms. In ancient times, before a student entered into their field of study, they would venture out from the urban centers and into small communities that trained the student to observe life from nature's point-of-view."

"Yes, I'm aware," responded al-Jeheuty. "*The Nature Walk*. If a man or woman was to study architecture, the student would then have to study the way nature, and all Her creatures, would build from resources. If a student were studying to be a warrior, they would have to study the way nature defended and killed in order to protect Herself, and understand the repercussions of taking a life. If a student were to study medicine, they would have to know all the aspects of life and death. A student looking to become a teacher would observe how all aspects of nature would give lessons. A student ready to study law would observe nature's judgments, fair and just." He looked around at the open area. "Here is where we would come. Of course, the land was far more plentiful in those days."

"Yes," said Mazigh, pointing to al-Jeheuty. "We would begin to understand the esoteric sciences behind the myths we studied. Gods and Goddesses were mathematical astro-physical-biological equations, positions of the sun, moon, and stars. The interaction of the Gods and Goddesses were chemical equations. The spiritual, mental, and physical sciences were locked inside our stories. And we would study our aspects of life here in communities no different from the Ogunsanwo-Mashek. Then the student would return to the urban center and attend the universities to become the mathematician, or the lawyer, doctor, artisan, teacher, and so on." He put his cup down and explained. "I say all this to note that many of these nomadic nations are descendants of students cut off from urban centers that are now conquered by the whites or their tawny conspirators. We are descendants of students that do not have the entire lesson, and the masters have either been conquered or turned against us.

"We have been divided and conquered, and so, there has been a great deterioration in thought. Myths are believed as real. Spirits, Gods, Goddesses, and the alchemy of inner energy are a spook's tale. Chwezi, a few others, and myself fight with the elder priests constantly. They know we are right," Mazigh said, cynicism entering his tone. "But keeping the people afraid rather than informed creates authoritative power." He shook his head and shrugged. "Roles that were commonplace in urban centers for men and women have been given only to the men. Women are reduced to particular labors deemed fit for them. Now we squabble over hints of power, wandering in a wilderness with no direction. Our ways are becoming more and more harsh. Women are subdued, subjugated by rules meant to keep them from harm; men battle for supremacy. I had to separate from two wives because they plotted against my chief-wife. Other women that have gained power treat the women under them like slaves. Women's egos have increased because of subjugation. They have become disrespectful toward the men. This has bred great abuse, and further subjugation to keep the women's egos in check. Violent deaths occur too often. This I have to deal with." Mazigh sighed. "I have become chief too young. Perhaps we can have more visitors, so that we might feign civility."

"Not much is different in al-Mari Ifriq," al-Jeheuty consoled. "We fight over different faiths, societal roles for men and women. It only looks civilized because we wear fine suits."

Mazigh and al-Jeheuty laughed.

"I would rather the Ogunsanwo-Mashek be there," expressed Mazigh. "We have come across other nomadic nations that have warned us of great trickery among our own people." Mazigh clarified, "A black, compensated by a white, will wander into a nation and feign friendship. The black will lead the nation to a so-called safe haven. Once there, the nation is enslaved. Whites, armed with great weapons, subdue the nation and take them away. Other nomadic nations are resorting to scarring to identify one another. They disfigure themselves to appear too feeble for slavery. They have incorporated these acts into their rituals and mythology, justifying these deeds through the words of their Gods. I believe this necessity for survival will, in time, become a dysfunction too. The nations will forget the reasons for these acts, continue to do them, and force them upon women and children. I do not want my nation to resort to that." The chief suddenly put his attention on the dancers and said excitedly, "This is where I become silent."

Then he watched intensely as his wife walked out of the darkness and toward the fire. She was magnificent, and in control of every masculine eye attending the gathering, the eyes of the male, Moorish visitors also following her. If Africa had a physical frame, chieftess Nugaymath-Famien Mazigh Ogunsanwo would be that corporeal chassis. She wore little clothing, her hips and buttocks flowing wide from the fabric worn around her waist. Her breasts were cupped in gold bowls. Nugaymath was crowned with long, black braids; her body was adorned with anklets, large hoop earrings, and medallions. She started to dance. Her movements were erotic. She spun, twirled her hips, and straightened her arms, then pulled them back in to embrace herself.

"This is a dance that symbolizes creation," whispered Mazigh, proud of his wife. "This is the moment the dark mother-spirit is impregnated by the dark father-spirit, and she gives birth to their physical children: the stars, the suns, moons, and all planets in the heavens."

The sight overwhelmed Roberto. He looked for any woman among the Ogunsanwo-Mashek people that could speak his language so that he may ask for lessons to bring back to his mistress. His mission was in vain, however.

The dance was hypnotic. Two women joined the Chieftess, flanking her. Two men joined the women, close. Nugaymath danced alone, her eyes fixed on her husband in the crowd. Her smile was for him. She seemed to bring light to the fire.

"My wife is a great archer," Mazigh told al-Jeheuty. "She trains our bowmen. I admire that you have female warriors among you. Because of our instability, our women are not allowed to enter combat. But, they train for defense." Mazigh grit his teeth and said, "There was much controversy when I chose her for my chief-wife. She is ten years my senior. Younger women are being taken as brides by far older men. Nugaymath is beautiful, with all of Africa wrapped up inside her. Mature. She has given me two daughters and a son, which are two daughters and a son more than those vile creatures I separated myself from had ever given me. Nugaymath supported me when my father passed. She is of noble Ogunsanwo-Mashek blood, born of the warrior class, a reason why she was not wed until so late. Her father was a captain at my father's command. She helped me re-organize my people. She is a great Queen." Mazigh laughed and said, "You can thank her for successful raids against caravans. Or hate her." He then scoffed. "Some of my people think me weak because I choose only one wife. We, like so many other nomadic nations, have taken on some form of poly-marital ritual for the benefit of protecting our women, or if the population between man and woman is not equal. But like so many ways born out of necessity and circumstance, that too has degenerated into a symbol of power. A man is measured by the women he holds as wives, children born, or a woman measured by the men she commands as husbands."

The dance finished.

The visiting Moors started to clap, but quickly ceased their actions as they witnessed the Ogunsanwo-Mashek remained silent. The onlookers stood up, the visiting Moors copied their actions. The Ogunsanwo-Mashek bowed to their chieftess and the dancers, then returned to their seated positions. Mazigh jumped up and walked to his wife. They gave one another a warm embrace. Mazigh escorted Nugaymath over to al-Jeheuty and the other visiting Moors. He introduced his chieftess. Everyone bowed respectfully. Roberto dared to ask, "Can that dance be taught to outsiders?"

Al-Jeheuty pointed and said with a smile, "This one likes Africa's ancient arts."

"In time," replied Nugaymath. "Perhaps we may initiate your women one day. It is a sacred dance, but we are all of Africa."

Mazigh called for his wife's decorative throne and asked for her to have a seat. A robe was brought to the chieftess and she put it around her as she took a seat. Mazigh stood alone inside the circle. He waited for all in attendance to take a seat before addressing his audience. "We stand inside the alchemy of a magical operation. This is an initiation of a new aeon. We are the ingredients for this change. Officials from al-Mari Ifriq have opened their arms to us. We here initiate them into our nation. The day of seclusion, secrecy, living through dated traditional roles, and a life of pilfering is over. Peace has come to the Ogunsanwo-Mashek."

Chwezi and Gu-Gurzil gave one another a look. Their skepticism etched clear on their faces. Gu-Gurzil leaned toward Chwezi and whispered, "Eh, these are no Wisdom or Peace Keepers." Chwezi agreed with him. "They consort with the Djenhai. We keep our plans, right?" Chwezi nodded his head again.

"If these Moorish officials are to be initiated into our nation," continued Mazigh, "then they must know where our story begins. Let us tell of the magical operation where time began its countdown to birth the Ogunsanwo-Mashek nation. I speak now of the *Tale of the Nine Black Bastards*—"

"—*One a King*," the men in the audience concluded in unison.

Mazigh took a breath. He looked around at his people, and then he spoke in a storyteller's mesmeric voice. "I tell the tale in the language of our guests, forgive me. We have all heard the story. You will know, if you do not understand the language, because the story resides in your heart." Mazigh paused and then spoke again, this time in the language of the Moorish guests. Some of his people understood, some did not. "Hundreds upon hundreds upon hundreds of years ago, and thousands of years before that, in the days of Usar, past the borders of the ancient University nation of Egypt, when Mesopotamia was Eastern Abyssinia, there was a great kingdom ruled by blacks. Hundreds of years later—and thousands too—the face of the land changed. There was great turmoil. There was war with Tamahu tribes, whites. Tawny races took the kingdoms of Mesopotamia, and they created war among each other. This war removed Mesopotamia from Africa. Some of the tawny races called upon Africa to send soldiers to quell disputes. Africa answered. Some of the wars were stopped. The African soldiers did not return home; the soldiers created settlements among the Mesopotamian kingdoms.

"As time continued, some yearned for Africa-proper. There was one settlement that sent out its best nine warriors to scout ahead for a trail to follow home. They searched for a trail that did not cross the path of any Mesopotamian kingdom. It seemed like the trickster-gods of that era had swindled the Fates when the Nine came across a war-tattered Mesopotamian kingdom. Captured, the Nine were brought before the king and recognized as African descendants that were allies for an opposing kingdom. The Nine were thrown into prison for their crimes—a war hundreds of years in the past.

"Excellent in the art of escape, the Nine put their skills to use and broke through the walls of their prison, tunneling into a series of shafts that led into the kingdom's treasury. Gold coins, with an ancient African symbol, were scattered inside the treasury. The same symbol lined the walls. This same symbol was tattooed on one of the Nine. In awe at the sight, the warrior recalled his family emblem and crest. The symbol was given to all family members to remember Africa-proper. It is then that the eldest of the warriors declared, *'We are not going home. We are home.'* They were bastards no longer.

"This war-torn, Mesopotamian kingdom was once an African kingdom, and the descendant of the proper kings lay among the Nine. The warriors declared they would kill the king and take the throne. Legend recalls the warriors, instead of escaping, marched into the king's throne room. They held the gold coins and declared the kingdom rightfully theirs. Showcasing the symbol of the coins that adorned the walls of the palace, and the warrior with the tattoo, the Nine hurled insults toward the king.

The Fates had their own tricks for the trickster-gods. The current king was a tyrant; his people prayed for his removal. Their prayers were answered.

"The king's ego was not insulted, rather intrigued. He challenged the Nine to a contest. The warriors were to be bound and blindfolded, placed in different sections of the city. He declared that if the Nine could make it to the throne room again, getting past guards, palace and sewer traps, city police, and ultimately take his head, they could claim the throne as the rightful heirs. The Nine, bound, blindfolded and separated into different sections of the city, escaped their bindings and re-grouped, all while evading and slaying guards. The warrior-outlaws devised a plan. Eight would stay behind. One would alert their settlement that still waited for their word. The Eight split into four teams of two, covering four sections of the city. The Eight converged on the castle, fighting past traps and city guards. Each warrior held tight to a gold coin with the ancient African symbol. In their heart, the lion began to roar. Among them was the proper king.

"Stealth was their greatest weapon. Shadows were their greatest cover. Standing before the castle, bloody and fueled by the smell of the fight and dreams of conquest, the Eight stood. Hundreds of guards gathered at the castle, ready to strike. Behind the guards came the roaring sound of reinforcements from their settlement, the eldest of the Nine leading them.

"The castle was taken. The king was beheaded. The kingdom was reclaimed. But that does not end our story. Unfortunately, the kingdom did not stand long. A tawny Mesopotamian kingdom, six generations later, marched through and conquered the black kingdom. The nobles fled with the royal army, running back into Africa. Some warriors stayed behind to fight. There was promise of return by the nobles and royal army, but there was never word. A group of over a hundred men and women made a long journey into Africa to find the nobles. They eventually settled here and became the Ogunsanwo-Mashek. Though we are truthfully descendants of the kingdom's abandoned warriors, we claim the whole story, because that *is* our story. That is our glory." Mazigh saw the look of overwhelming wonder on the Moorish visitors' faces. He smiled and added in a very humble voice, "At least, that is what I have been told." He repeated the sentiment in both languages.

There was light laughter.

Mazigh then declared to the Moorish visitors, "We welcome you among our nation."

Al-Jeheuty stood up and he and Mazigh embraced.

The Moors had journeyed into Ogunsanwo-Mashek territory with a mission to capture its Chief and find answers to an attack made upon them. Instead, they became honorary citizens of the Ogunsanwo-Mashek nation. Al-Jeheuty was distressed. He understood, as politics so often proved true, that one could not be a friend to everybody. He was cautious of future conflict. He, as well as Bo Yusuf, still considered that Chwezi and Gu-Gurzil had gone rogue, and could do so again.

The Moors stayed among the Ogunsanwo-Mashek people for another three days. They were fitted with camels and provisions; their weapons were returned to them. Al-Jeheuty left with a warning, telling Chief Mazigh not to make any movements without consulting either him or one of the Moorish officials present. He assured the chief that his nation would be given supplies, and Mazigh assured that he would keep an eye on Chwezi and Gu-Gurzil.

Roberto and his outfit went their separate way before returning to al-Mari Ifriq. Bo Yusuf and al-Jeheuty entered the city without welcome, their mission having been of a covert nature. They returned to the palace and learned quickly that Nasir was recovering well, Taran too. Al-Jeheuty and Bo Yusuf relayed to their two leaders everything they witnessed while among the Ogunsanwo-Mashek nation. Wakil and Behar cited that al-Jeheuty was indeed a miracle worker. Peace was now a contender against war. But there was much to be done, especially with the knowledge that King Igdobe of Djenhai planned to capture the Ogunsanwo-Mashek people and sell them to European or tawny Arab slavers. Al-Jeheuty and Bo Yusuf were informed that al-Mari Ifriq was no longer on emergency lockdown. Statesman Sinan had left for Turkey seeking a decision on the Turkish soldiers' use. Behar and Wakil did not expect news for a while.

The two officials were dismissed, both instructed to get rest. Al-Jeheuty was greeted by a pleasant surprise on his return to his chambers. His wife-to-be, Mehit al-Tarqiyya Zaher, stood in the palace corridors waiting for him. She was looking as beautiful as ever. Al-Jeheuty rushed to his wife-to-be and embraced her. She returned his affection, passionately wrapping her arms around him. "I returned when I received news about my father." She held him tighter. "I was so worried about you. They told me that you had gone to confront the Ogunsanwo-Mashek. I dragged it out of Behar and Wakil."

Al-Jeheuty chuckled. "Not even a man such as Behar can fight back a woman." He kissed her cheek and divulged in a whisper, "The Ogunsanwo-Mashek made us honorary members of their nation." Mehit looked at him with a surprised expression. "It's possible that rogues among them attacked us. There is still an investigation. Their chief is a great man. He's surprisingly young, younger than I even. But he is very mature. He hopes for peace. They are a people formed from circumstance and condition."

Mehit smiled slyly. "My goodness. Your miracle comes to light more and more."

Al-Jeheuty rolled his eyes. "Tell me about it." He walked with Mehit to his private quarters and entered the room. Al-Jeheuty lit lamps for light and continued to speak. "Behar and Wakil said the same thing. I'm a miracle worker."

"You're a *hard* worker," Mehit added. "I have news too," she said. She sat on the edge of al-Jeheuty's bed and told him, "I'm not returning to Tunisia. Rahmis tells me that Djenhai has a School of Medicine for women." She slapped her forehead and laughed. "And stupid me. All this time, I could have also been training under Mistress Ilindia." She looked at al-Jeheuty, beaming a coy smile. "I know you're happy."

"Of course," blurted al-Jeheuty. He walked to the bed and kissed Mehit on the forehead. "You'll be closer. You'll be among a friendly nation. And you said that you didn't much care for that place anyway."

Mehit scoffed. "If I wasn't too old, then it was because I was unwed. I was treated like an outcast, and I was top of my class. It was a woman's school controlled by the laws of men. We were to dress a particular way at particular times. We had to keep our heads low in the presence of a man. And much of Tunisia has changed. There is not a true Moor in sight, at least not with any real power. You saw when you came to visit."

"Ah," al-Jeheuty replied. "And the best thing about your enforced code of dress was removing it to see what lay underneath."

"You did more than *see* what was underneath," Mehit teased. She reversed al-Jeheuty's incoming motion to kiss her by putting a finger against his lips and pushing him back. "Which brings me to my *next* subject, which focuses on the consequences of the last time we got together—a month ago when you visited. Or did I come here?" She thought about it and then wiped away the debate she was having with her memory. "We have to get married in a month's time. Maybe quicker." Al-Jeheuty, lips still pursed, blinked his eyes rapidly. Mehit placed her hand gently against her belly. "Before I start showing."

Al-Jeheuty realized instantly.

His lips started to quiver. Tears grappled his eyes, some too weak to hold on, let go and fell down his cheek. He breathed rapidly with joy and disbelief. He knelt down before Mehit and wrapped his arms around her waist, placing his head against her stomach. Mehit smiled. She ran her fingers through his locks.

"Yes, good Moor. You will be a father. I will be a mother." Al-Jeheuty looked at Mehit with inquisitive eyes. She answered his unspoken question. "I was told at the school, which I'm sure gave those young *harem* brides more fodder against me. But," then she relaxed, "Ilindia confirmed yesterday."

"Which means Roberto will know," said al-Jeheuty.

"Women know how to keep secrets," Mehit retorted in a coy manner. "Trust me."

Al-Jeheuty gave her a hard look. "What does that mean?" He stood over Mehit and leaned close to her. "The child *is* mine?"

Mehit's face contorted. "Please. I am not the Whore of Babylon."

Al-Jeheuty raised an eyebrow and quipped, "I've seen you perform. You do a wonderful imitation. You at least went to the same school she did."

Mehit laughed flirtatiously, "I *perform*—if that's what we're calling it—only for you, good Moor."

Al-Jeheuty gave Mehit a deep kiss. He tried to force her back against the bed but she resisted and stood up. "I have to return to my mother. She cares for my father. We are taking temporary residence in the palace." She kissed her husband-to-be on the cheek. "I will return later, *Papa Lion*. We will discuss our wedding plans."

Al-Jeheuty smiled at Mehit as she stood in the doorway, beaming at him seductively. "Yes, *Mama Lion*," he said to her.

Mehit disappeared. Al-Jeheuty kept his eyes and his smile on her as she left. He took a deep breath and then lay upon the bed. He did not know what to strategize first, his wedding or politics. He chose a third option.

Fatherhood.

Chapter Twenty-Seven

Al-Jeheuty Anhur Has and Mehit al-Tarqiyya Zaher were wed in a grand, festive ceremony that lasted over a period of seven days. Rahmis Husani helped Mehit and al-Jeheuty plan the majestic affair. The celebration was so grand that all of al-Mari Ifriq participated. Al-Jeheuty considered the weeks spent planning the magnificent event no different than strict negotiations with foreign powers, or even the citizens of al-Mari Ifriq.

The negotiations were between he and his wife-to-be—if they could be called negotiations. Al-Jeheuty would simply nod, smile, and agree with all of the suggestions from his wife-to-be. Mehit was not too much offended, though she would have liked for al-Jeheuty to voice more of an opinion on the wedding proceedings, fabrics, garments, and meals. But it was the Moorish official's smile that calmed her. She would make a suggestion for the after party music, refreshments, or garment colors, and al-Jeheuty, her husband-to-be, would simply smile and nod, saying, *"If that is what you wish, mora."* It would melt her heart every time.

Annoyingly, al-Jeheuty would turn to Rahmis for translation if he did not understand Mehit's fabric or particular food suggestions. This is the only time 'negotiations' tended to be difficult, and where Mehit would tend to be a little irritated. Al-Jeheuty would tease her by turning to Rahmis and asking, *"Could you please translate? My understanding of excited-wife-to-be-can't-wait-for-the-wedding language is very basic. She seems to be using terminology more advanced than my basic tongue."* He would say this while sitting in his chair with his legs crossed, pretending as if the scene before him were a conference with an international leader.

But Mehit found solace in consulting with her mother and Ilindia. Al-Jeheuty introduced a third woman with whom Mehit could plan the wedding. She was an expert at weddings. At the very least, she was married and had gone through the ceremony before. Al-Jeheuty escorted Mehit's sister into the palace one afternoon. Neither Mehit nor her mother had seen Fadheela Zaher in almost nine years. Mehit and her mother were overjoyed. Taran, still recovering from fevers brought on by his wounds, was delighted to see his youngest daughter. Mehit quickly noticed the three children in presence. Mehit's eyes widened at the fact that she was an aunt to two boys and a girl. Alimah and Taran greeted their grandchildren, introduced by Fadheela.

Al-Jeheuty explained that he and al-Rinak worked together to locate Fadheela's husband. The Turkish nobleman, now dying of old age, and preparing to marry Fadheela off to his youngest brother, was an old friend of al-Rinak and Aguyan. He resided in a small parish in Turkey. Al-Rinak, having left al-Mari Ifriq to further the stalled negotiations for the use of the Turkish soldiers within al-Mari Ifriq, located the nobleman and urged him to permit Fadheela to attend her sister's wedding. She was allowed. Savas, Fadheela's husband and nobleman, could not attend because of his health. Her husband's younger brother, Firat—the man set to be her new husband—supervised Fadheela.

Mehit was too excited to have the politics of her sister's life ruin the moment. She put her arms around al-Jeheuty and thanked him for such a wonderful gift. But there was more to come. Mehit, her sister, her mother, Ilindia Kali, and a host of other intimate female friends gathered a week before the wedding and prepared cakes, sweetmeats, and other refreshments for the coming festivities. Mehit and her close female companions assembled one night at her bathhouse. Musicians played light music that filtered throughout Mehit's establishment. There was much rejoice as the women shared secrets, affairs, memories, and laugher. Mehit became a patron at her own business. Her staff and close friends pampered her. She was washed to symbolize the cleansing of all past ills. She was primped and perfumed to symbolize becoming new. Mehit retired to her private quarters at the back of the bathhouse, on the second floor, just as the sun came up. Her friends rested below, continuing to enjoy the refreshments and each other's company.

The women all fell into slumber just two hours after dawn. They were awakened by music coming from outside. Mehit sprang from her bed and opened the window. She looked down and watched as al-Jeheuty, and his friends, perform a wild ritualistic dance for her. Roberto Hamaat, under Mehit's window, slaughtered a goat and cooked the animal's meat. Al-Jeheuty and his friends, including Roberto Hamaat, were stripped down to just their pants. The men were bare-chested, ancient symbols carefully painted across their body in intricate designs. The men were joined by some of Mehit's friends. Al-Jeheuty danced without a partner. Mehit smiled down on him. The door to her chamber opened. Mehit's sister, mother, and close friends walked inside, chanting with candles in hand. Ilindia Kali followed them. She carried with her a decorated haik. She tossed the large silk garment around Mehit and escorted her to the bathhouse's lower level.

Mehit's family and friends followed, all the time chanting their emotive song.

Mehit was taken to a private room. No one followed. Her friends and family sang outside the room, the door closed. The sun provided light. Ilindia sat Mehit down in the center of the room. The elder woman commenced to decorate Mehit's arms and hands with an intricate, painted pattern of occult symbols of ancient African origin. Mehit looked around the room. Ilindia recalled that the Turkish accountant Hyle Tecer was slain in this very room. Mehit had not forgotten. The music that played outside the bathhouse had long faded away, Al-Jeheuty and his troupe having retreated. The soulful and powerful singing from the Moorish maidens—Mehit's sister, mother, and friends—penetrated through the door. The voices harmonized, clear like crystal.

Mehit had forgotten how powerful her sister's voice was, but another voice took lead as the rest of the women's voices stayed chanting in the background. It was Fumnyana Maysa, the young woman courted by Rahmis Husani. Her voice was riveting as she sang a fervent ballad so passionate that it drove Mehit to tears. The singing stopped. The design was finished. Ilindia proceeded to cut Mehit's hair, shaping her tight curls into a low crown. Mehit was led home when the process was finished.

Private affairs for the bride-to-be continued over the following days. Mehit was presented with presents and marriage advice. Ilindia reapplied her designs that were beginning to fade on Mehit. Women danced and musicians played. Al-Jeheuty's family entered town, and his mother and sister-by-law joined the feminine festivities. Mehit's mother, and her soon-to-be mother-by-law, met with her one at a time to present advice on married life. Jawhara, al-Jeheuty's mother, imparted wisdom to Mehit on how to work around a husband's expectations of a woman. "Do not disrespect your husband's authority, or become as deceptive as Eve in the Garden, or as cunning as the snake that seduced her, " Jawhara said to Mehit. "But let him understand that marriage is a union, not servitude. Love him, as you do. Respect him, as you do. Receive the same in return."

Mehit assured Jawhara that she would not have to be so crafty with al-Jeheuty. She proclaimed that al-Jeheuty was a noble man, a man of great honor. "And those are but some of many traits that have held my attention to your son, and made me fall in love with him," Mehit assured.

Jawhara did not want to push the fact that though love was a strong adhesive to keep two souls together, marriage was a union of business. Mehit would come into that understanding soon enough. Jawhara accepted Mehit's statements. She did not want to push too much on the bride-to-be. The young woman was excited, and Jawhara did not want to smother that excitement. She admired and liked Mehit. She did not want to stain a relationship with a woman that would be around for a long time. Jawhara then left Mehit's room.

Alimah entered the room shortly after. She stood at the door, eyeing her daughter as the sun's light created a golden aura that blanketed Mehit while she sat with the window at her back. Her eyes glowed like stars against her black, heavenly body. Mehit presented a shy smile. She almost turned her head away from her mother, but she remained still. Alimah approached her daughter, sitting down next to her. She said nothing for a long moment and then asked Mehit if she loved al-Jeheuty. Mehit answered, "Yes."

"That love will be tested," Alimah said to her daughter. "But you know that. When it does, however, remember that you do love him. Do not let your ego get in the way of petty things. If he is violent toward you, which I do not believe Lord Al-Jeheuty Anhur Has will be, then your uncle will be notified." She patted her daughter on the shoulder. Mehit enveloped her mother's hand. She placed her cheek against it.

"I love him," Mehit said aloud. "Like you love pa-pa."

Alimah considered Mehit's words. She exhaled and said, "Yes. I truly love your father." She tilted her daughter's head to look at Mehit eye-to-eye. "Believe me when I say this. Your father approves of this marriage." Mehit shook her head, acknowledging her mother's statement. Alimah rubbed her daughter's cheek. "Your *father* approves, Mehit. He approves." Mehit smiled wide. Alimah concluded, "Al-Jeheuty's garments have been prepared. They will be delivered to him today."

Al-Jeheuty was too going through pre-wedding rituals. It started after serenading Mehit with music and dance, beginning when his family arrived. Al-Jeheuty retired to his private quarters within the palace. His grandmother prepared for him a grand meal, on which al-Jeheuty dined while wearing a white burnoose, his hood drawn over his head. Ilindia joined the bridegroom. She painted an intricate design on his finger, and using blue paint, an ancient symbol behind his left ear that was to protect from evil. The night continued with al-Jeheuty joining his friends at *The Siren's Call*. The evening was not too improper, though scantily clad women entertained the gentlemen with dance. Wine was served and stories of life were recalled. Al-Jeheuty sought marriage advice from his brother and Zakiy Sa'ood. Both men joked that al-Jeheuty would have an easier time governing the citizens than a wife.

Al-Jeheuty's pre-wedding ritual continued several days later; he was taken to a local bathhouse. He too was washed for the symbolic reason of cleansing past woes. His cleansing included a proper shave and hair grooming, which Rahmis Husani personally provided. Music played softly in the background as servants attended to al-Jeheuty. He was fitted to his wedding garments. Al-Jeheuty's father and brother, Taran, Behar, Nasir and Zakiy, Hesam, Bo Yusuf, Rahmis, and Ojodo joined him as he slipped into his clothes. The men tossed coins at al-Jeheuty's feet. "For a picnic," declared Behar. "And to pay for the musicians and Rahmis' shave."

Another, more tame night, was spent at *The Siren's Call*.

Al-Jeheuty remained in one of the backrooms. Each of his friends came to him, one at a time, and they gave their blessing and advice. Then came the elders. Taran was the first elder to speak. The ambassador entered the backroom as if sneaking inside. He was more animated than in recent weeks, his body recovering remarkably well from the wounds and fevers received. Al-Jeheuty joked with Taran, as he recovered, that he was now a war veteran. The land baron seemed to be as full of spirit as ever, overseeing the creation of a large fortress outside the city gates, and the reconstruction of both towers. Al-Jeheuty was impressed with Taran's initiative, but it was this encounter that intrigued him.

Both men were cautious of one another, though neither man knew the other had marked them for death. Both were aware of the complications of executing such a task, however. Mehit lay in the middle of the deleterious politics involving the two men. The dilemma both men faced was in finding a way to execute the other without losing favor with Mehit. There was also the complication of al-Jeheuty potentially being taken out by the Turkish Statesman al-Rinak in retaliation for Taran's death, and having the Statesman sway the Empire to no longer favor their former North African province.

For now, al-Jeheuty greeted Taran with a warm smile, bow of the neck, and a firm handshake. The two men sat down. Al-Jeheuty did not move while Taran spoke. "My daughter is very rebellious," he said with a peculiar fatherly smile and tone. "Tradition, and a woman's place and duty alongside her man are not her strong points. Mehit is untamable. Her *passions* and pursuits may go against your wishes. Keep a close eye on her. She will, however, serve you well as something like a Queen. Whatever it is the two of you govern—household, children—she will be there to add her voice, order, balance, harmony, and justice. You could not have picked a finer woman to assist you to rule." Taran placed his hand on al-Jeheuty's shoulder. He chuckled and stated, "She will be your *only* wife." He started to laugh harder. "Mehit will not stand for another woman to invade her space. You will be more her husband than she will be your wife." He brushed aside his laughter and concluded. "I know more than anyone that al-Mari Ifriq is entering uncertain times. Protect this city. Keep my daughter safe. You are more than just a citizen of al-Mari Ifriq. You are as much a governor as Wakil or Behar. I am glad that you will be among my family, son." Taran's concluding statement sounded completely sincere, but it did little to wipe away his earlier, more condescending comments.

Taran stood up, bowed at the neck, and left the room.

Sakeen Anhur Has walked in soon after. He stood tall like a mythic figure. The cloth of his garments, white like clouds, enhanced his celestial stature. Sakeen took a seat next to his son, brandishing a wide smile, two cups of wine, one of which he handed to his son. He made a toast to his son and then took a sip from his cup. "There is not much advice I can give, al-Jeheuty. I believe you will know what to do when the situation arises in your marriage—any difficult situation. Mehit is a fine woman, though. She reminds me of your mother. She is very strong-willed, independent, but don't let that frighten you, my son. These qualities do not mean she does not love you as a man, or respect your word, even if she challenges it. She will be your greatest audience and advisor. They say that a man should only seek the advice of his greatest friends, after that, then his wife. And that is only on the condition that his friends' advice fails him or seems inconclusive. I don't believe in such things. Mehit, like every wife, will know you so well—perhaps too well. Confide in her." Sakeen chuckled nervously. "After all, the great decisions you have to make, being an ambassador, well, you confide in your friends first anyway. Most of the cabinet you serve in is made up of your friends. But, should any decision you make trouble you, talk to your wife. Be careful, however. She may not understand the full scope of your city's politics."

"A *corsair-state*," al-Jeheuty interrupted sharply.

Sakeen smiled warmly at his son's conclusive words. "No, my son. No. I speak about the politics of a city that stands in the midst of a crucial moment in Africa's history. This is a city governed by just and honorable men, but surrounded by politics so dangerous, your city, with the wrong decision made, could go from being in the midst of history, to simply being a part of history—long in the past and only a memory for romantic storytellers. Women can be aloof to the burden we as men carry in our relentless efforts to keep them safe. While they examine every potential house, on every street, trying to decide a place to live, they are unaware that we examine every man that passes by—a potential thug no matter how fine they are dressed. I'm a lawyer, al-Jeheuty, and I am greatly aware of that burden. Your brother is a businessman and he is aware. In fact, I may not know all the details, but I'm sure the two of you discussed covert ways of procuring his wife from that Frenchman." Sakeen lifted his hand. "I do not need to know the details on how that was done. In the end, you have a lovely niece. I can see in your brother's eyes that all of his worries about protecting his wife have been transferred to his daughter." He patted his son on the back. "I cannot even imagine the burden you carry. A wrong decision in politics concerning this city could end up at your front door, carrying torches, weapons of all sort, and calling for your head. That is why I have little advice for you, other than this. Enjoy every moment of peace with your wife. At all times, keep peace with her." He smiled and then joked, "It's easiest if you just agree with her. Remember these two words: *Yes, dear.*"

Al-Jeheuty laughed.

Sakeen stood up and started to back away, all the time keeping an eye on his son. "You have engaged in events that people only read about or experience in staged dramas. You have remained as solid as a rock." Sakeen balled his fist and then pointed to his son. "I am proud of you, al-Jeheuty." Al-Jeheuty stood up to hug his father, but Sakeen lifted a hand and waved his son to sit again. "Later. Your second father wishes to speak to you." He was speaking about Behar.

Al-Jeheuty shook his head. "Behar is a man that helped me focus on the lessons you gave me. He is a man that I do respect. He is a great general and captain. I am his soldier and advisor. But I only have one father. You are my father, and I am your son." Al-Jeheuty stood up and he and his father embraced. Sakeen backed away from his son, patting him on the shoulder as he stepped away. He opened the door and was quickly met by Behar's presence. The two greeted one another joyfully.

"How did the Oedipus anecdote go?" Behar asked Sakeen. "Did he find it amusing?"

Sakeen huffed. "I didn't even get the chance to recall it. Let it wait—"

"No, absolutely not," insisted Behar in a good-natured manner. "Sakeen this entire city is my household. I demand it." Sakeen rolled his eyes playfully, sipping from his cup again. "Well, go. Sit," Behar ordered. "Or there will be a scandal when I have one of my best officials, and his father, arrested." The two were jovial toward one another. Al-Jeheuty marveled at the sight of the two men. It was like observing two, great and mythological gods from different cultures cross folkloric worlds and meet in an unbelievable tale.

Al-Jeheuty and Sakeen turned around and returned to their seats. Behar stood behind them. Al-Jeheuty was perplexed about the meaning of the Oedipus anecdote that his father was going to recount. He had heard of the Greek story of Oedipus, taught to him from the points-of-view of various educations. In mythology, Oedipus was the son of Jocasta and Laius, King of Thebes. An Oracle told Laius that his own son would slay him. Oedipus was thus abandoned in a land beyond Thebes, but he was saved and raised by a Shepard. Oedipus returned to Thebes as a grown man, answered the riddle of the Sphinx, and unknowingly killed his father and married his mother. Oedipus, upon discovering where his life had led him, violently stabbed his eyes in a fit of madness. His mother-wife hanged herself.

Al-Jeheuty raised his eyebrow, wondering what to anticipate from his father. Sakeen leaned close to his son, hands gripped together and a smile on his face. He looked back at Behar. The two men shared light laughter before Sakeen returned his gaze to his son and asked, "You have heard of the Oedipus story?" Al-Jeheuty nodded his head slowly. "There are many interpretations of what the story could mean. The story was popularized in Greece. People have thrown all types of nonsense to what the story could mean; it has been as perplexing as the Sphinx's riddle."

"I do like the theory regarding the personality of the sly, conquering foreigner," Behar interjected. "They seek to kill their father—the king—and they wish to sleep with their mother, burying their seed into the queen to claim legitimacy through a child."

Sakeen dropped his head in mocking shame. He looked at al-Jeheuty and pointed over his shoulder at Behar. "*He* gave you focus on *my* lessons." When asked by Behar if he did not agree, Sakeen replied, "I must yield and give praises to that particular notion. But this has been a tale men have told before the Greeks came—again, it was just popularized by the white Greeks. But, the story is a tragic comedy."

Al-Jeheuty replied sarcastically, "Yes. I can see how a man unwittingly killing his father, marrying his mother, and going insane to the point of gouging his eyes out would draw an audience to uncontrollable fits of laughter."

Sakeen slapped his son's knee. "No. No. Listen. You will ultimately become me. You will kill me off—"

"And marry ma-ma?" asked al-Jeheuty in a confused tone.

"This is all symbolism, al-Jeheuty," Sakeen pleaded in a light, fatherly tone.

"I know, pa-pa," al-Jeheuty admitted. "I'm just dragging you along."

"I'll drag you along," Sakeen warned playfully. He wiped the situation away and continued. "You will replace me. That is what killing the father is about. Whether you like it or not, one day you will awake and see me in the looking glass, where of course, your reflection should be. You will kill me whether you like it or not. Better yet, you will become me. Then of course, there is Mehit. She will be just like your mother. She will nag you. She will baby you—even though you are a man. She will constantly bicker—" Behar tried to smother his laughter with the palm of his hand. Sakeen spoke more. "You have not escaped that feminine attitude that tears at every man—that *hangs* over him. The mystery of women, the riddle of the Sphinx, is never truly answered. And if you are blind to that fact," he started to make stabbing motions at his eyes, "then you will be driven insane."

Behar looked over Sakeen's shoulder and lifted his cup of wine, "And even through all that you will continue to love her," the Beylerbey added as he started to laugh, smothered only by his sips of wine.

Sakeen patted his son on the knee again. "I said the same to Aatif on his wedding day. I will leave you with that." He stood up, offered Behar his seat, and then left the room. Behar sat down, shaking his head and taking more sips from his cup. "I never heard that before," he commented. "Your father is a good man."

"He knows how to brighten his charisma at the right time," al-Jeheuty noted. "He is a lawyer, after all."

"Very much where you and your brother gather your skills," Behar noted. "If only you could find that nurturing aspect your mother encompasses. But, I see your future through your father. I know what you will become long after I'm gone."

"Behar…" al-Jeheuty said in a stern voice.

"I can't live forever," the Beylerbey said matter-of-factly. He put his cup down. "I know Taran rambled about something. I hope he was more coherent than offensive. I suspect that your father imparted some form of wise words to you, his son. That is why I will not say much." Behar became silent, nervous. He rolled his hands into one another. He took a deep breath. "I, instead, have more of a confession to make." He sat forward, looking directly across at al-Jeheuty. "I used to live in al-Mari Ifriq.

I was a captain, of sorts. I helped commandeer ships for the local bosses and chiefs. Sa'ad wanted me to join his company."

"I know," said al-Jeheuty.

Behar shook his head. "You *don't* know everything, Lieutenant." He took another deep breath. "I was involved with Alimah—your bride's mother." Al-Jeheuty barely let out an acknowledging statement when Behar continued. "Her father did not approve. I was too much of a pirate to be courting his daughter; never mind the fact that I could provide for her, and I treated her with all the chivalry and elegance of a gentleman. But, I do understand. My profession was nothing that a man of his stature could brag about. I was a corsair. Alimah was then arranged to marry a young landowner and businessman. Our own, wonderful Taran Zaher; he was from a very distinguished family. It was not the reason I left al-Mari Ifriq, but it was good motivation." He cleared his throat and then looked at al-Jeheuty with a very guilty expression. "Alimah and I have…caught up on old times, and have been involved with one another since before we calmed The Four Winds. Roberto has been sneaking her into my room at strategic times when she was not due at home. Wakil knows. Our pious governor turns a blind eye."

Al-Jeheuty's eyes widened with disbelief. He coughed up laughter and admitted in a whisper, "That might be better than carrying out Taran's mark."

Behar's tone turned serious. "Alimah and I have had tensions as of late—but we're working through it. I'm contemplating Taran's mark. How it can be done, but…that's my worries. There's more," Behar said with a forewarning tone. The guilty expression on his face was substituted with a stern look and an equally stern declaration. "I want you to understand this. Even if Taran does not approve of your marriage to Mehit, it does not necessarily mean that her *father* does not approve of your union."

It only took al-Jeheuty the blink of an eye to decode the hidden message within the hint Behar presented. His mouth trembled as he tried to speak.

Behar interrupted al-Jeheuty's muted stutter. "Alimah was pregnant at the time of her wedding," he explained. "She was not showing, yet. Much like Mehit now." He smiled. "You don't think your rushed wedding would not raise her mother's eyebrow? She's plotted the same thing before. Your courtship has been years, and then this sudden jump to marriage. Alimah talked to Mehit about it. At least the child is yours. When it came to Alimah's rushed wedding on the other hand, well…" The Beylerbey took another deep breath. "Taran does not know that Mehit is not his daughter;

Mehit does not know that I am her father. It is the reason why I always shied away from your bride-to-be. I did not want Taran to see our resemblance. Mehit will know in time." He stood up and commanded al-Jeheuty to do the same. He put his hands on al-Jeheuty's shoulders and announced proudly, "Al-Jeheuty Anhur Has, I approve of your marriage with my daughter. I am honored to have you as my son-by-law. *Spiritual* law."

Al-Jeheuty nodded. He decided that no one would know the news he just learned. Mehit would be the first to know. The other lieutenants, his friends, would remain blind.

Behar led al-Jeheuty to the door. "Come," he ordered. "Let us return. Roberto and Wakil have been prodding me to tell you. I told them this would be the appropriate time. I have not confided in Alimah that I would do this." The two exited the room and rejoined the pre-wedding ritual in the entertainment area of *The Siren's Call.*

Then came the grand day.

Mehit was dressed in a shimmering pink gown that flowed like water when she moved. Her elaborate headdress was blue, a pink scarf flowing from the mounted headpiece. Her veil was violet. Her shoes were sky blue, symbolic of an angel walking across the morning sky. Handmaidens, female friends and relatives, and soldiers on horseback surrounded the bride. Her journey started at the city's main gate. The celebrating citizens were now calm. This early morning, a noblewoman and city official were joining in a holy union.

Mehit's entourage merged with al-Jeheuty's entourage in the city square. Al-Jeheuty's troupe approached from the east. The bridegroom was decked in long robes, brown and beige, with a long cape. His turban was the same color, black and gold stripes running through the design. The two entourages flowed as one, walking toward the castle. A group of musicians followed them, playing festive wedding music all the way to the palace.

They walked into the palace's public chamber. The chamber was converted into a grand auditorium for the wedding. Most of the two entourages dissipated, not even entering into the ceremony. Mehit and al-Jeheuty walked to the front. There stood Wakil and Roberto, each with a different book of faith in their hands. Wakil, as governor, spoke first. He spoke from his pious, Mohammedan heart, blessed the union of the two people before him, and then declared the marriage legitimate. Roberto spoke second. He spoke from the heart of his philosophies and ancient teachings. He blessed al-Jeheuty and Mehit's union and deferred back to

Wakil to again call for the union to be complete and recognized by the power of the city-state.

The festivities began shortly after. There was a great feast, wine, laughter, music, song, and dance. Great compliments were extended to the bride and groom. Mehit and al-Jeheuty received words of advice, compliments, and blessings from friends—some of which had too much wine in their systems. The two danced several rituals together, with family members and friends.

Roberto secluded al-Jeheuty in a corner, a book held in his hands, presented as a gift. He first asked before handing over the book, "Are you a Mohammedan?"

"No," answered al-Jeheuty. He put his hand on his chest and declared, "I am a spiritual man but—"

"That's fine," Roberto quickly interrupted. "Are you a Christian? Jew? Or follow any faith that enforces particular inhibitions."

Al-Jeheuty answered, "No. I have self-control over most things. Everything in moderation. Roberto, you know me. Why all the quest—"

Roberto waved al-Jeheuty's words away, seeming impatient. "That's fine. Same questions apply to your new wife."

"No," al-Jeheuty answered again. "She comes from a family that observes Mohammedan Law but—"

Roberto presented the book and demanded, "That's fine. Take this book for your wedding night."

Al-Jeheuty looked down at the small book in Roberto's hands. He chuckled. "Roberto, I am far from a virgin. Mehit and I have practiced many times for this special night. We haven't been very chaste in our courtship."

"Take the book," Roberto insisted. "Good Moor, that book has information in there that will have the both of you calling on every god, goddess, spirit, and all mighty deity known to man. And you might create some new spiritual names. Trust me."

Al-Jeheuty chuckled and took the book from Roberto. He thanked the man and pocketed the tome of erotic lessons. Then Behar called everyone to gather around. He waved al-Jeheuty close, putting his arm around him. "I just have this sweet gift to give," he told the gathered people. "Chapter twenty-four, verse five of Deuteronomy states: *When a man is newly wed, he need not go out on a military expedition, nor shall any public duty be imposed on him. He shall be exempt for one year for the sake of his family, to bring joy to the wife he has married.*" He shook al-Jeheuty hard as he laughed. "I cannot give you a full year, al-Jeheuty, but you have at least a month to enjoy what is known in the proper Arabic language as *shahr el 'assal.* I bid you a good journey to the sweet moon; go to the *honeymoon.* Enjoy your time."

The after party ceremony moved outside the city gates to a large company house. The bride and groom, along with their guests, discovered that the company house's equally large front room was converted into a stage. Ojodo presented the newlywed couple with a play he had produced, written, and directed. The actors were various men and women from around town, some were even dockworkers that yearned for a life on the stage. The production was flawless. The performances were immaculate, moving. It was a love story about a clever trickster that rescued a lovely woman from the clutches of two gods that battled over her, and forced her to choose one of them. Town citizens were permitted entrance into the company house to view Ojodo's production. The play ended and received joyous, standing applause.

Behar greeted Ojodo after the play. The Beylerbey whispered compliments into the Moorish titan's ear. He also wanted to discuss later Ojodo's future as a playwright. But attention was turned back to al-Jeheuty and Mehit. The city official congratulated his friend on a tremendous effort, calling his writing spectacular. He joked with Ojodo by handing him a spear, making him put on a turban, and then declaring, "A Sheik-Spear."

Ojodo retorted, "Bah! British bards make tragic figures of us Moors."

The party did not cease when the sun disappeared. The affair moved back to the palace, but soon after Mehit and al-Jeheuty retired to *The Royal Highness Inn.* A beautiful room had been prepared for them. They held one another while in bed, stripped of the heavier aspects of their garments. A plate of food rested on the bed but was only picked at lightly. The two kissed gently. Al-Jeheuty rubbed his wife's belly and talked to the child inside. Mehit stroked her husband's locks. Al-Jeheuty and Mehit explored the book Roberto had given them. They were too tired to try any of the dynamic and acrobatic sexual maneuvers depicted. But the two teased one another with kisses. They declared that heavier moves would come after the birth of their child, but the lighter moves displayed in the book would be put into practice while on their wedding holiday.

Husband and wife watched the sun come up. This was a new day. Al-Jeheuty and Mehit al-Tarqiyya Zaher Anhur Has had become new to one another. They were a union. Married. Beyond the horizon lay challenges ready to test every angle of their love. But nothing was more challenging at the moment than keeping their eyes open.

The two of them quickly fell to sleep, smiles frozen on their faces, and holding one another tightly.

Chapter Twenty-Eight

He went from captain to company boss. Hesam Gandarewa slipped into the command of the Ahangar Company with such a natural grace that many believed this was the obvious next step for the young man. Hesam was unwittingly rehearsing, and by the Fates being fitted for, this new chapter in his life by way of his last days as a captain-at-sea, and as an overseer of an illegal narcotics trade. The position of overseer lessened Hesam's engagements by sword and pistol, and fixed Hesam into an arena of sly and sharp words used in negotiations. The pistol and the sword were reserved for more covert situations. The weapons were never guided by Hesam's hands, but used by soldiers guided by the Persian's command. Hesam realized quickly that the correct use of the right words could earn more money than over a hundred campaigns at sea.

The business of rearing a company was no different, save there were no incidents of commanding a soldier to kill anyone being resilient against negotiations. Hesam was now in charge of all the trade, traders, and merchants vending within al-Mari Ifriq. He learned quickly the matter of keeping all the businesses organized, and how and when to collect the taxes from their revenue. Hesam lightened his salary, already having a considerable amount of wealth that was made from his campaigns at sea and overseeing the narcotics trade. He did not lead an extravagant lifestyle. Much of the life he led with women, wine, music, and dining, now came free because of his status. He was given servants and inherited the help already enlisted with the company. Lightening his salary lessened the tax on merchants and traders. It increased the wages for his hired help. Hesam did make money, however, through connecting his former sea units with the Griffin Regency and the Griffin Company, earning revenue from their exploits at sea. Most of his former crew fell under Captain Hieremias Sunwil's leadership. Many of his crew had already followed the captain on several exploits. Hesam did employ the services of three of his closest guards from his former crew.

Hesam valued greatly his new position in life.

But all of this came at a sorrowful price, showcasing the immeasurable cruelty of the Fates that equaled their immeasurable generosity. Hesam Gandarewa inherited the Persian company after the former company boss, Isaiah Iraj, was murdered. He was a good friend and business associate. The unlawful killing came without hint or preview, and was coupled with Hesam's quick promotion. He was neither suspected of the crime, nor allowed involvement in its investigation. Hesam's childhood friend, Al-Jeheuty Anhur Has, along with several other city officials, was coordinating a private investigation. The public was given a plausible motive and official summary of the company boss's murder, but further investigation was being conducted.

Hesam decided to honor his friend's memory by erecting an extraordinary trader's market and naming the site *Iraj Trade-Market*. The site was built on the eastern side of the city, canopied with large tents. Hesam used his connections at sea to spread the word that the great trade market of al-Mari Ifriq was being reconstructed. He worked closely with Governor Wakil al-Hakam and Taran Zaher in establishing the market, created one month after Hesam took charge of the Ahangar Company. Merchants traveled across Africa to help boost the Trade-Market's productivity.

Hesam, Taran, al-Jeheuty, and Nasir scouted the new merchants and goods that flocked to the market, which showcased specific goods and merchants based on season. The *Iraj Trade-Market* was a success, only hindered by the brutal attack administered by the nomadic, militant nation of the Ogunsanwo-Mashek. The attack did not touch the Trade-Market site, but it called for an immediate reconstruction around the market's locality. Taran, after recovering from his wounds, engineered plans to construct a massive wall around the market. Trade was halted for several weeks while the construction took place. There was still a large canopied area that lay outside the enclosure. The interior was decorated with bright marbled walls painted with intricate designs. There was stylish tiled flooring and an open roof to provide light. Vendors renting space were provided shelving to display their goods, and they were given large containers for storage.

The market was set to re-open two weeks after al-Jeheuty and Mehit al-Tarqiyya returned from their wedding holiday. In the interim, Hesam received a grand tribute from Beylerbey Ameer Las El-Behar. An elaborate party at *The Siren's Call* was thrown in honor of Company Boss Gandarewa. Behar, Wakil, and Taran Zaher attended the engagement to personally extend their gratitude to Hesam for assisting in the reconstruction of al-Mari Ifriq's open trade-market. The men did not stay long, however. Behar and Taran Zaher were leaving in the morning, accompanied by Feroz Aunun and the Turkish Statesman al-Rinak Ozan. The men were headed to Djenhai. Behar announced their departure at the affair honoring Hesam.

"Djenhai will take part in the new open market," spoke the city's Beylerbey. "Our trade routes have been re-opened. They will bring their trade back to al-Mari Ifriq, and we will begin exporting to Djenhai the goods they seek." Hesam was again congratulated for helping make all of this possible. Behar added, "He took the dream of reconstructing an open market-place and brought to life something far greater. Al-Mari Ifriq is now blessed with a continuous open trade-market rather than hosting two large markets a year."

But as much as Hesam was given thanks, he was once again kept in the dark about greater details. He would have cared very little for the greater politics surrounding the Beylerbey and the other officials' visit to Djenhai, had he even suspected. On the other hand, Governor Wakil and Beylerbey Behar would have rather been in Hesam's position. Talks with Djenhai would begin a day after the Beylerbey arrived in the kingdom. The dialogue between al-Mari Ifriq officials and the Djenhai King had nothing to do with trade or attendance at the open market. The talks would center on how war with the Ogunsanwo-Mashek would be conducted.

Behar was ready to argue peace, introducing al-Jeheuty's council with the nation's chief. Al-Rinak was ready to argue against peace. He was preparing to elevate the war with the Ogunsanwo-Mashek by introducing the terms of elimination he had been discussing with King Igdobe since his small, Turkish army began guarding the trade caravans to and from Djenhai.

Slavery.

Al-Rinak already had French, Dutch, and Turkish investors. He just needed King Igdobe to say yes.

Hesam continued to party, blind to the true purpose of his leaders' journey to Djenhai. Behar envied Hesam greatly.

Chapter Twenty-Nine

The Djenhai kingdom, enclosed inside a mighty, defensive wall, was a living mathematical equation. The architecture flowed like waves, representing two worlds, two cultures, all made under Djenhai. The kingdom's interior was multilingual in its presentation, speaking in the traditions of Mohammedan architecture and the architecture of ancient Africa.

Sun-baked mud bricks, mixed with mud-based mortar and plaster, sculpted the smooth design of holy edifices, towers placed at every corner of the city's wall, residential housing, industrial locales, and commercial sectors. Coral stone tiles bathed building interiors. The buildings used for a more political purpose, including the grand palace situated at the heart of the kingdom, were constructed from imported limestone.

Djenhai offered its praises to the Mohammedan faith while stretching its arms heavenward to the celestial gods and goddesses of the past. All the spiritual tribute could not, however, make the current delegations any easier. Beylerbey Ameer Las El-Behar, Company Boss Feroz Aunun, Ambassador Taran Zaher, and Turkish Statesman al-Rinak Ozan entered the Djenhai walls a day before the proceedings. Their entourage was not too heavy, and it was mostly fitted with soldiers to protect the officials on their travel. The officials were greeted in grand style with an impressive parade that guided them into the city. The citizens believed that the celebration marked Djenhai's participation in al-Mari Ifriq's open market, drawing closer the day that all of Odongo-Mauharim was united as an African state with a traditional monarchy.

The parade was a façade, however. The authentic significance for the visit from al-Mari Ifriq's officials was to initiate talks on how to engage the nomadic Ogunsanwo-Mashek people. The glorious mood that surrounded the Djenhai people and officials from both the northern city and the southern kingdom dissipated the next morning, three hours after dawn, inside a small conference area within the Djenhai palace. The palace's pristine glimmer, with the sun brightening its front hall laced with carpets woven from African fabrics, columns lined with authentic gold, finely carved furnishings that sparkled with encrusted precious gems, and the glow of silver and gold statues of former kings and queens could not brighten the mood in the conference room.

King Igdobe hosted the meeting. His advisor and younger brother, Munashe, accompanied him, as well as his wife, Halima, Queen of the First World, and his daughter Princess Yaminah. The King and his entourage entered several minutes after the al-Mari Ifriq officials were settled in. The city officials stood up and bowed their heads. King Igdobe waved a single hand, motioning for his guests to sit. He sighed as he sat down. His brother and his Queen sat on either side of him. Yaminah sat next to the Queen of the First World.

King Igdobe was brown skinned, with a square face, short hair, and a light beard. Though he was usually joyful and with a smile, the politics of the day did not allow his famous glow and beam to show through. His brother, Munashe, the only sibling to assist him in politics, had dark brown skin, sharp eyebrows like a hawk, and a patch of hair lining his lip and chin. His face resembled a British Bulldog. He possessed aged wisdom-lines, making him look as if he had a permanent scowl on his face. Munashe was the worrier between he and his brother. Though he was three years younger than Igdobe, he looked far older.

King Igdobe sighed for a second time. He looked up and spotted Behar. The Beylerbey was calm, though his eyes conveyed a sad look. He was empathetic toward the King, which made Igdobe straighten himself. Yaminah and Halima blessed the proceedings with an ancient prayer and a Mohammedan prayer.

King Igdobe looked at the Beylerbey after the blessings were bestowed. He added spiritual words, and then he addressed, "The conflict between the Ogunsanwo-Mashek and our kingdom has reigned for hundreds of years. They have always been small skirmishes, even when the damage has been great on both sides. They hit us. We hit them. Al-Mari Ifriq has always been neutral. Al-Mari Ifriq has always expressed an agenda to unite Odongo-Mauharim, to connect with Djenhai and create a recognized African state with a traditional monarchy. Not many African states are united the way Odongo-Mauharim has the potential to be. We stand ready to further that agenda. The Ogunsanwo-Mashek people stand in opposition to that notion. So, it is with great sorrow, that I call to elevate the engagement of the Ogunsanwo-Mashek. However, I cannot comply with my declaration before having the consent of Beylerbey Ameer Las El-Behar, and our Turkish partner-in-company, Statesman al-Rinak Ozan."

The Beylerbey cleared his throat. He straightened his clothes and then made a rebuttal after being permitted to speak. "Drawing closer to creating a legitimate state has brought unwanted attention to our recent trade activities. The Ogunsanwo-Mashek people, feeling threatened, have sacked caravans along our trade routes. Statesman Ozan and his Turkish troops have thwarted their attacks many times. A little more than a month ago, al-Mari Ifriq—our beloved city—felt the brunt of the Ogunsanwo-Mashek's wrath. There were casualties; there were great injuries. My immediate reaction was to hunt down and slaughter the people responsible. I sent three ambassadors, guarded by an elite group of soldiers, to watch the Ogunsanwo-Mashek's movements, learn their nomadic routines. My ambassadors engaged the nation, talking with their chief."

Everyone looked at Behar with surprise.

"Why was I not notified?" asked Taran. He quickly changed his tonality. "I mean no disrespect, Beylerbey. Please, pardon my interruption. I understand that I was a part of the injured. I was recovering. But after my recovery, I should have been updated on any dealings with nations outside of our city. I was informed the dispatched ambassadors only observed the tribe from afar."

"I forgive you," said Behar with a smile. "And you have a right to be upset, but I needed this operation to be silent. I dispatched al-Jeheuty, Bo Yusuf, and Roberto to engage the Ogunsanwo-Mashek." He then addressed King Igdobe. "My ambassadors' mission was to capture and question the nation's chief. The Ogunsanwo-Mashek reversed the circumstances, and the nation's warriors apprehended my ambassadors. Al-Jeheuty, my negotiator, spoke with the nation's chief. His name is Mazigh, I believe. A young man, from what I've been told." King Igdobe flinched as the chief's name was uttered. The Queen cupped the King's forearm with her hand. Behar continued, "We have not spoken with their nation since."

King Igdobe was baffled by the news that Behar presented. An impressed emotion struggled to surface, however there was a faint smile resonating through the King's wide open mouth. "What did these talks bring?"

"The Ogunsanwo-Mashek admitted to the raids made on our trade caravans," said Behar. "Mazigh, the chief, he spoke about great troubles that plague his nation's way of life. There are power struggles among them. He confessed that it might have been a separate faction of extremists that made the attack against al-Mari Ifriq. I do believe that if you held out a hand of peace, he would accept it, embrace it."

King Igdobe pondered the thought.

Peace.

The King looked at the Queen of the First World. She was an elegant woman, dark, with a pretty oval-shaped face, and a low patch of hair twisted into coils. Her slender eyes were bright with life, hiding the fact that she struggled with her health. What attacked her body for so long was beginning to slow her down, now that she was nearing fifty. It brought great complications in conceiving a child. She only bared one son for her King, but he was an able man, ready to assume the position of king should he be called upon. The Prince, at this very moment, was receiving an education that prepared him for kingly duties. Igdobe would have rather turned to his son Kemnebi than his first wife and Queen. This was not because Halima was not able. She was a very capable Queen. She was very dependable for her insight on order and justice within the kingdom. But she needed rest. These stressful matters would not help her health. Though, bringing in his inexperienced son would not help matters much either.

Halima lifted her shoulders. "My instinct is not to trust the Ogunsanwo-Mashek. Their chief might be sincere, but even if there exists only a small pocket of militants among them, they would need to be dealt with."

Munashe interjected, "It's possible their chief condemns their actions only when he's confronted by them." He turned to Behar and addressed, "I believe your ambassadors were not slain because the chief didn't want an army trudging through his nation's temporary site. Your officials were allowed to live to bring a message. The Ogunsanwo-Mashek have peculiar ways in seeking peace, using a brutal strike to get your city's attention. I don't believe the chief expected such a quick response to his nation's strike. He was greeted with the possibility of being extinguished in a war by two nations positioned on either side of his people. These people are desperate." He looked at al-Rinak and said, "We have been pondering your solution, the King and I. I believe we need to satiate the whites' appetite for black slaves before they decide to choose all of us."

Al-Rinak nodded. It was his turn to speak. "Peace is idealistic not realistic. I too do not want war. Our combined strengths, al-Mari Ifriq, Djenhai, and the Turkish troops that we have at loan—all praises to the Empire—would crush this tribal nation. But we would sustain losses. Our city and kingdom are stationary. This tribal nation is nomadic. While we send out a party to fight them, they have already fired upon our homes, burning the city and kingdom we care so much about. Gathering this tribe, handing them over to European interest, would not only bring tremendous revenue to both city-state and kingdom-state, but it would avert a long-term war, and it will avert the European states that are avarice in their pursuit to enslave the blacks. At least, it will draw their attention away from the more civilized nations residing within Odongo-Mauharim."

Behar asked al-Rinak, "Do you consider yourself black? You most certainly are. But you are also a Turk. You are part of an Empire that is situated within the European states. You serve a nation that has become tawny in its color. I ask this because I want to know if you could carry the burden of sending your people to the colonies."

Al-Rinak feigned appreciating the Beylerbey's words. "I understand, Beylerbey. First, I would like to remind the council that the Empire is situated in an area once considered Africa. The Empire is also very far removed from European interests. Christianity backs Europe's agenda. The law and faith of Mohammad backs the Empire's agenda, and even holds the proper tenants of Christianity that are stored within the Hagia Sophia. This separates the Empire from white Europe." He took a breath. "Yes. I am a black. That does not stop me from being a realist to the times. I want peace. That peace can be obtained by removing a belligerent element that is a danger to all of us." Al-Rinak addressed King Igdobe. "I have French and Dutch investors bidding on the tribe. Turkish backers too. They are willing to outfit al-Mari Ifriq and Djenhai with weapons. There will be minor skirmishes. It's only natural. I don't believe this tribe will volunteer their services to the American colonies." Al-Rinak said as a slight, "Besides, the hypocrisy of speaking about slavery when Euro-Christians are brought through al-Mari Ifriq in droves and made slaves."

"Washed, cleaned, provided good care, and sold *back* to European nations," Behar countered.

"*Or* sold as concubines and servants to Mohammedan or corsair-states," al-Rinak added. "And black slavery is happening all around us in the various African states. Tawny Arabs and tawny Turks, from official to farmer, are using the African as servants. This is nothing new."

Silence.

King Igdobe gazed back and forth between Behar and al-Rinak. He contemplated each of their proposals. He looked to his advisors and asked for their input. Munashe spoke first. "I agree with al-Rinak. We face minimal engagement, generate revenue for our kingdom, and solve our problem with little stress."

Then the Queen of the First World spoke. "I am intrigued with the idea of meeting the Ogunsanwo-Mashek's chief and chieftess. I am curious about the idea of engaging the Ogunsanwo-Mashek with words, which might lead to peace."

Yaminah felt overwhelmed. She spoke honestly, "I am being fitted for a role in business. I may also be stepping into a future that has Odongo-Mauharim united as a state. My first instinct is to protect our investment and interest in that future. I don't believe the Ogunsanwo-Mashek can be trusted, but I don't know about shipping our problem to another world."

It came back to King Igdobe. This was his decision to make. His gaze fell on al-Rinak. "Keep your investors close." Al-Rinak smiled. King Igdobe continued, "Bring them in through the Ghanem-Marjani Company. Company Boss Aunun, handle the matters closely with Statesman Ozan." He turned to the Beylerbey. "We will host talks with the Ogunsanwo-Mashek. We will present their nation with an ultimatum. The chief will hand over his militants, or he will hand over all his people." He looked at all the delegates. "This is fair. This is just."

Behar's heart sank. He bowed in unison with his fellow officials. He did not agree with forcing the Ogunsanwo-Mashek into the action of handing over its warrior class, sentencing them to servitude, and ultimately disarming the nation. Al-Rinak also disagreed, but he said nothing. European investors wanted strong blacks for slaves, but they were not looking for a warrior class. Warrior class men and women were harder to control. The warrior class possessed the will to fight back. Al-Rinak needed a small war with the Ogunsanwo-Mashek in order to weaken its strongest men and women. His European buyers were more interested in the working class blacks, agriculturalists. They were not even interested in artisans— freethinkers as artisans could be.

However, both Behar and al-Rinak silently concluded this was going to be the best outcome in these discussions. The officials agreed to continue talks at the Open Market. Behar kept his opinion close. Al-Rinak remained silent too. Both continued to smile for the three days that they and the other officials remained in Djenhai. When Behar returned home he briefed Wakil, Bo Yusuf, and Roberto on the Djenhai council. Behar ordered Roberto to find the Ogunsanwo-Mashek and brief Chief Mazigh on what had been discussed. He sent with Roberto a direct order for the young chief.

Chief Mazigh was to allow no movement within his nation. It proved difficult, but the Chief kept Gu-Gurzil and Chwezi close. The two men had plans of their own, which called for kidnapping King Igdobe.

Chapter Thirty

Al-Jeheuty and Mehit al-Tarqiyya Anhur Has were delighted to be home. They had seen so much in their travels, overwhelmed by the desert sands, grasslands, outposts, ancient sites, and even snowy mountains, but al-Mari Ifriq was never more warm and inviting. The newlywed couple had accomplished an extensive amount of travel, staying nights, and continuing to explore the various sceneries their home continent had to offer. Ships and caravans were their transport across the Mediterranean and through East Africa.

Al-Jeheuty and Mehit arrived in al-Mari Ifriq a month and three days after they left. It was the afternoon, and they surprised everyone. Al-Jeheuty was eager to know of the current politics, but Behar told him to rest one more day. The Beylerbey briefed al-Jeheuty on Hesam's plans for the Open Market, scheduled within the coming weeks. Behar mentioned the conference held in Djenhai, but did not discuss the meeting's details. He did say that al-Mari Ifriq and Djenhai were closer in their pursuit to unify Odongo-Mauharim. But to change the subject, Behar informed al-Jeheuty of a letter from his father delivered the week after he left for his wedding holiday.

The newlyweds retired to al-Jeheuty's quarters after a small gathering with close friends and family. Both of them found it strange that Mehit could now withdraw to al-Jeheuty's palace quarters without suspicion of pre-marital affairs, or sneaking Mehit around. This room was now her quarters too, unless the couple decided to move to a housing complex. Mehit already scoped the blocks she preferred to live on, taking al-Jeheuty along just to agree with her. He did not mind. He could live anywhere with her. Not only could they afford most of the housing they scoped but Behar would provide monies for purchase if need be.

Mehit lit the lamps around the room, providing light. She then started to change into her nightclothes already residing in the room, once secretly stowed among al-Jeheuty's clothes. The clothes they took on travel were delivered to servants to wash. Al-Jeheuty immediately went to his writing table and found the letter addressed to him. He opened and started to read. Mehit witnessed her husband give a curious look to the door. He turned around, shook his head, and continued with the letter. She approached him cautiously, seeing his mood grow sullen. She put her hands on his shoulders and asked, "Is everything okay?" Al-Jeheuty groaned. He inhaled dramatically and tossed the letter to the table. "Al-Jeheuty," Mehit voiced. Al-Jeheuty cupped his wife's hands, rubbing them for comfort. "What did the letter say?" she asked.

Al-Jeheuty just groaned again, but he eventually answered, "My brother left for the Americas. A Frenchman visited him just as my family arrived home. He was waiting for them. My father gave his name. Traont Coutelier. He was there specifically for my brother. He had a large—*and well armed, according to my father*—entourage with him. The way my father writes it, our town looked besieged. My brother said it was business. He was gone the next day. Some French troops stayed behind." Al-Jeheuty grew angrier, but he covered his emotion well. "I've heard that it takes six weeks to travel to the Americas. I've also heard it could be up to three months to travel from the coast of Africa-west to the Americas." He took a breath. "I don't mean to be prejudice, but I wonder if *this* Frenchman has any connections to our French associates."

"Put your worries aside, al-Jeheuty," Mehit recommended in a sweet voice. She kissed al-Jeheuty on the back of the neck, and then rubbed her cheek against his. "Come to bed."

Al-Jeheuty managed to smile. He stood up and danced his wife over to the bed and laid her down. He crawled into bed and started to rub her pregnant belly, now three months full. Mehit took great care of herself while traveling. One of her close servants was a student of Ilindia. She wore wider gowns to hide her pregnancy, though most everyone knew of her state, save Taran and al-Jeheuty's family. Her belly was not too full, but she was cautious to hide what showed. The two of them had discussed names for a boy or a girl while on travel. Nothing was finalized, but the two were greatly excited about being parents. The same conversations about parenthood were stirred up as they lay in bed, and continued as al-Jeheuty left the bed to change into nightclothes. There was only a brief intermission where the conversation turned to places to live within al-Mari Ifriq.

But Mehit, exhausted from travel, fell sleep. Al-Jeheuty carefully removed himself from Mehit's embrace without waking her, and he extinguished the flickering lights in the room. His mind went back to the business between his brother and the Frenchman, and the travel to the Americas. But not even his thoughts could fight against his exhausted state. He had been moving around so much since returning home that he did not feel his weariness until now. He pondered a few more reasons behind his brother's sudden voyage to the Americas before going into a deep sleep.

The Moorish official awoke to Mehit gently shaking him from slumber. She informed him that Bo Yusuf was at the door. Al-Jeheuty shook the remaining, groggy sleep from his head and made his way to the door. He welcomed his Bo Yusuf inside. The Army Official became reserved around Mehit. The woman saw this immediately and she dismissed herself from the room, but not before teasing the two gentlemen that she would *'allow the boys to catch up on political gossip.'*

Bo Yusuf began to brief Al-Jeheuty on the Djenhai conference. The two sat at al-Jeheuty's writing table. Bo Yusuf first stated that Behar gave orders to bring al-Jeheuty up-to-date on all matters. He continued, "Al-Rinak is pushing for the enslavement of the Ogunsanwo-Mashek. Behar revealed that we had been dispatched to engage the nation, and he spoke about our talks with Chief Mazigh, also revealing that he may not have ordered the attacks on al-Mari Ifriq, but that it may have come from extremists among the nation. Behar said the King and Queen's eyes lit up; they seemed impressed and hopeful. But they were still unconvinced that a mutual peace could be achieved. Al-Rinak used that uncertainty to his advantage. He declared that he already had European investors, French and Dutch—most likely speaking with our associates among those nations, offering them a deal they'd been waiting to jump at. The King weighed both options. He mediated his choices." Bo Yusuf saw al-Jeheuty's eyebrows raise, curious. "King Igdobe will talk to the Ogunsanwo-Mashek. He will offer them an ultimatum. Either the militants can be carted off to the Americas, or their entire nation can."

Al-Jeheuty sat back, exhaling. "Did al-Rinak reveal the names of his investors?" Bo Yusuf shook his head no and asked why. "I received a letter from my father," answered al-Jeheuty as he reached back, took the letter, and handed it to his friend. "The letter states that my brother went to the Americas with a Frenchman. This was no more than a day after he arrived home from my wedding. The Frenchman's name is Traont Coutelier."

"We have a meeting in an hour," Bo Yusuf notified. "I'll put in a request that Emissary Chaffee attend. I'll run that by Behar first." Bo Yusuf stood up. Al-Jeheuty did the same. "Let me get to work." The two walked to the door. "What a way to be welcomed home, huh?"

"I'd have it no other way," al-Jeheuty joked. "I will be ready soon."

Bo Yusuf turned and asked, "How's Mehit coming along," he waved his hand out, curving over his stomach.

Al-Jeheuty chuckled. "She's coming fine."

Bo Yusuf lifted his shoulders and explained, "Good to hear."

Bo Yusuf left on that lighter note. Al-Jeheuty prepared himself. Mehit returned to the room. She relayed that she was going to her bathhouse to check on its business, and that she needed to speak with Ilindia. She also asked her husband if Bo Yusuf had any answers to the situation involving Aatif, the Frenchman, and the voyage to the Americas. Al-Jeheuty told her no, but that he might have answers after the meeting he was about to attend. The two of them washed separately, dressed together, were fitted with palace servants and guards, and then left the palace in separate directions.

Answers were provided to al-Jeheuty when the meeting at the council house opened. Rene Chaffee was in attendance, and al-Jeheuty questioned the French business ambassador. Rene denied knowing a man named Traont Coutelier. Al-Jeheuty quickly, and nonchalantly, responded, "You're lying." There was a hint of a threat to Rene's life, extremely subtle in al-Jeheuty's tone. But the Frenchman picked up on al-Jeheuty's warning. Rene asked for the name again and al-Jeheuty repeated. Chaffee laughed and then corrected al-Jeheuty on the name's pronunciation.

"Yes. Yes. I know him," Rene confessed. "He is very interested in the Ogunsanwo-Mashek. He is bidding against the Dutch. He came to al-Mari Ifriq, and I introduced him to al-Rinak. We are trying to solve a problem that plagues your city. A problem that wounded good men and cost me lives."

Al-Jeheuty nodded in agreement. He asked, "Why has he taken my brother to the Americas?"

Chaffee smiled nervously. "Your brother knows Traont. He has dealt with him before. Traont was a friend of Emile Raulf. He works with Monsieur Beaumont. So as not to be outbid by the Dutch for these slaves, we have taken one of your people to the Americas, to show the fertile land the slaves will live on and care for—in the interest of the French, of course."

Al-Jeheuty was satisfied. Chaffee was dismissed before talks centered on the Djenhai conference. Not much more was discussed at the council, and after the meeting al-Jeheuty wrote a letter to his father that Aatif's voyage was legitimate business. Al-Jeheuty did not reveal his disdain for the actions taken by the French. He took the letter to a courier and then attended a private meeting between he and Behar. The Beylerbey expressed that he feared war was imminent.

Behar told his ambassador, "I sent Roberto to talk with Chief Mazigh. I sent warning of King Igdobe's terms, which only call for war as a response. I had Roberto tell them to not make a move, stay hidden." Al-

Jeheuty agreed with his Beylerbey. "The Ogunsanwo-Mashek will not agree to the terms, getting rid of their warrior class—no proud people would," Behar continued. "Even if they should agree, the French or the Dutch will be furious that they would receive a restless warrior class. We will all be slaughtered and courted to the Americas as compensation. We should be cautious. That's probably what al-Rinak is looking for."

Al-Jeheuty managed a sly smile. "Al-Rinak spoke of two investors: the French and the Dutch. He did not, however, mention the Italians. I will call upon the Sicilian, under the nose of the baron." Behar warned al-Jeheuty to be careful. The official expressed to his Beylerbey that he just wanted to make sure that al-Mari Ifriq still had a dependable ally.

Behar then confessed surprising news, "Ojodo has been coming to me and requesting a leave. He is planning to continue his studies, traveling east. I am making arrangements for his departure."

"When?" al-Jeheuty asked. His face was covered in a mix of surprise and sadness.

"Sometime after the Open Market festival," the Beylerbey answered. "He wants to use his study to perfect his writing and performances."

Al-Jeheuty chuckled. "We live an adventure, and he wants to write and direct fictitious ones."

Behar said in a stern voice, "Ojodo approached me privately. Say nothing to him on the matter. He's struggling with his decision. He doesn't want us to think that he's abandoning us. He will announce his departure after all of his personal business is settled."

"Of course," al-Jeheuty assured. "I am sad, though. But we all must follow our hearts."

The two of them conversed on local politics and then al-Jeheuty left the Beylerbey's presence. He spoke with Hesam days later, asking if the company boss still had connections within the hashish trade. Al-Jeheuty wanted word sent to Donatello Verola, a simple message sent in the form of a question. *"Are we still friends?"* A message returned two days before the Open Market. *"Why of course, good Moor. The trade goes well, as you know."* Al-Jeheuty was relieved. He only needed two fingers to count his allies.

Al-Jeheuty had been welcomed home by dangerous politics.

Chapter Thirty-One

King Igdobe Djenhai's caravan arrived a day before the Open Market, A'sharia, the Queen of the Second World, traveled with him. Their two daughters, eldest Princess Yaminah, and youngest Princess Sabah, and their only son, Asim, accompanied them on the journey. Munashe, the King's brother and close advisor, also attended the trip to al-Mari Ifriq, as talks concerning the war with the Ogunsanwo-Mashek were ready to continue. The Queen of the First world remained in Djenhai, ruling the people in the King's absence. The caravan was furnished with a garrison of one hundred men. The musicians, dancers, and acrobats that led the caravan toward the southern gate of al-Mari Ifriq eclipsed the Djenhai soldiers, however. Governor Wakil, Beylerbey Ameer Las El-Behar, and the city officials and company bosses greeted King Igdobe's caravan.

The King introduced A'sharia Igdobe-Djenhai to the governor and officials that had not the pleasure of meeting the Queen of the Second World. Though she was referred to as Igdobe's second wife, this was only in reference to being Queen of the Second World, and not in reference to the chronology in which he married either wife. Igdobe married A'sharia first.

A'sharia was dark with a wide face, large eyes that boasted long lashes, and she was plump with age, but far from overweight or obese. Her body, nearing fifty, kept more weight than it shed. She looked lovely, buxom, especially in her elegant black and purple robes and headdress to match. Large, gold earrings dangled from her ears. Her veil was lowered, showcasing her lovely smile. A'sharia, wise in the Mohammedan faith and law, carried herself with the grace of her royal title, and she was very self-aware of her presence. One could imagine that A'sharia would have carried herself with all the importance of the world even if she did not have the title of Queen.

The Djenhai entertainment joined the festive people in the streets of al-Mari Ifriq as King Igdobe and his Queen and daughters were provided grand lodging in palace suites tailored to their tastes. Bo Yusuf paid a respectful visit to Yaminah, staying in the doorway at all times. The Army Official became nervous when King Igdobe walked by to check on his daughter. The King was in a joyous mood, delighted to see Bo Yusuf. King

Igdobe asked Bo Yusuf if he could hold a private meeting with the governor and Beylerbey. "I want you to attend too," King Igdobe instructed. Bo Yusuf bowed his head at the request, a smile on his face. The Army Official assured the King that word would be sent by servant when the Beylerbey and governor were ready to speak. King Igdobe said with a smile, "I will be waiting in my room."

The King did not wait long, after helping his daughter settle in and returning to his room, he had just enough time to tell A'sharia that he would be holding council with the Beylerbey and governor before a palace servant knocked and announced through the door, "I am here to escort King Igdobe Djenhai to the Beylerbey's palace council chambers."

King Igdobe opened the door. He bowed to the Moorish gentleman standing in the hallway and informed that he was ready. He first kissed his wife on the cheek and then followed the servant through the palace hallways into a small council chamber.

Behar and Wakil waited patiently inside, sitting at a round table that held refreshments. Bo Yusuf was in attendance, as called for by the King. All three men stood up and bowed to the African King. Igdobe waved them at ease and said with a smile, "Please, dispense with the formalities. I'm in your kingdom now. Where shall I sit?" Behar pointed to an empty chair. King Igdobe made his way to the free space. He gave another greeting to Governor Wakil, expressing, "I am so honored to finally meet you, Governor. Aside from the curses and insults thrown at you, Beylerbey Behar says that you are a most honorable man." Everyone laughed. Igdobe took a seat. "I jest."

"I hope," said Wakil as he coughed through laughter.

"I do. I do," King Igdobe assured. The two men then greeted one another with Mohammedan salutations. There was a wide smile on the King's face as he looked at everyone and said, "Forgive me. I'm excited. This Open Market does not just symbolize al-Mari Ifriq's growing economy. It also marks the day that kingdom and city-state became one—at least the day that Djenhai and al-Mari Ifriq take bold steps to become a unified state. I brought a tribute to your city in the sum of one hundred soldiers. This will increase the city's army. I know that you are strained. I've received word that a program to enlist young men has started, but consider this a boost."

"We are most welcome, King Igdobe," Wakil said excitedly.

The King lifted a finger and said in a stern voice, "There is one condition, however. The soldiers I give to you must bow their heads, and raise their swords at the command of Bo Yusuf Ibn Tachfin al-Dume, their army General." The King smiled slyly. He looked at Bo Yusuf and continued, "These men are at your command."

Bo Yusuf was overjoyed, but remained professionally calm. "I will use this power to protect al-Mari Ifriq," said the Army Official. "And overall, I will serve the Odongo-Mauharim state with pride."

King Igdobe nodded. He lifted his finger again, and said in a stern voice, "Again, there are conditions." And then the King became very sincere. "Djenhai and al-Mari Ifriq will be unified as one. There will be an official Odongo-Mauharim state. It will be a great empire. The Djenhai and Griffin Dynasty will not make history, they will make a future. However, Bo Yusuf, I would like to arrange a union between you and my daughter Yaminah. Marriage," the King clarified with a smile.

Bo Yusuf's heart rose. His jaw dropped, trembling as he struggled to lift it back into place. He put his hand on his chest, his face brightening with a smile. "You are the King. I am at your command. But, but Yaminah...?"

"Shhhh," said King Igdobe. "Quiet. If you listen closely, she is talking about you right now. She does not let up." Wakil and Behar laughed lightly. "Yaminah and I have spoken. She is excited about having you as a husband. You will be known as Company Prince. Maybe we can break tradition and give you the title of Prince of the State."

Bo Yusuf started to breathe heavy. "A Prince? A nobleman." His voice was low, in disbelief. His jaw started to tremble again. Then his jaw clenched. Bo Yusuf's eyes started to water. He cleared his throat and stood up. Behar followed him, standing close behind him. Bo Yusuf dropped his face into his hands and started to cry. He sniffed, pulled his hands away, put them on his hips and said, "We fought so much in Spain. I have achieved my father's dream here in Africa. Now, I have the ability to become the father I lost." He turned around, hugged Behar, let go, and then approached King Igdobe. The man stood and embraced his future son-in-law.

The King then ordered the Army Official to visit Yaminah in her room, calling for the two to discuss the future, but not to get too close. Bo Yusuf, before leaving, bowed to the officials in the room and charged out to speak with Yaminah. The King stated to Wakil that Djenhai and al-Mari Ifriq laws should be compared, reviewed, and fixed to compliment one another. Wakil agreed, saying the high judges and lawyers of both courts should be brought together to oversee the task. The King suggested the council on law convene after the Ogunsanwo-Mashek had been dealt with.

Very little time was spent on political talk. The meeting adjourned, and King Igdobe retreated back to his palace suite.

Bo Yusuf spoke only a few minutes with Yaminah before she suggested to him that he should gather his friends and tell them the news. Yaminah wanted to seek her mother's counsel. Bo Yusuf respected Yaminah's request. The two of them never dropped their smiles. They gave one another a small kiss on the lips, and then Bo Yusuf exited Yaminah's quarters. He had an elated kick in his step. The Army Official rounded up his friends, finding al-Jeheuty and Rahmis conversing in the palace's front courtyard about King Igdobe's stay, and Ojodo and Nasir at the Sa'ood company house attending close to business. It was within the company house that Bo Yusuf stole a bottle of wine from an unoccupied room on the second-floor, and secluded his friends within a small room on the third-floor.

Bo Yusuf opened the bottle of wine and asked Nasir if there were cups stored anywhere. Nasir pulled cups from a cupboard and passed them out. Bo Yusuf poured each man a drink. His friends and fellow Moors were perplexed by Bo Yusuf's light mood. He joked that he could kiss each of them, to which they chuckled lightly, but with a nervous twinge in their laughter. He asked for each man to grab their cups and stand. He then explained, "We have been revolutionaries, unsuccessful and successful. We have been slaves, outlaws. We have become companymen ruling a corsair-state through legal and illegal means. We will now be noblemen, each of us at this table. King Igdobe has made a step in the direction of unifying the al-Mari Ifriq city-state and the Djenhai kingdom by giving tribute in the sum of one hundred soldiers, which will give al-Mari Ifriq a standing army. He has requested that these soldiers be under my command. I their General."

Everyone prematurely congratulated Bo Yusuf and knocked cups to end the toast.

But Bo Yusuf had more news.

"Wait, wait, wait," he said to his friends, a smile wide on his face. "There is more." He waited for his gathered compatriots to relax. "King Igdobe is arranging a marriage between myself and his daughter, Yaminah. I will hold the title of Company Prince, having stake in the Ghanem Company, and helping Yaminah—and her brother when he is old enough—make decisions on company business."

No one moved. Their excitement kept them frozen. Rahmis spoke after taking a hard gulp from his cup. He stretched his neck as the wine coursed down his throat. He sighed, "Congratulations. A descendant of sell-swords, now a nobleman by marriage." It was not the most complimentary statement, and Bo Yusuf could feel a taste of bitterness in his brother-in-arms' statement. The Army Official was ready to lay down his cup and attack Rahmis for insulting the honor of the warrior bloodline that he was descended from.

Al-Jeheuty attacked first, however. He jumped at Bo Yusuf and threw his arms around his friend. "My man," he yelled excitedly. The action prompted Nasir and Ojodo to crowd Bo Yusuf and scream their congratulations just as loud. Rahmis finished his wine in another large gulp, placing his cup on the table. He started to clap obnoxiously, which ceased the excitement surrounding Bo Yusuf.

"I have prepared many beds for Princess Yaminah," he said. "But you—you sly devil—you get to lie in them with her." He walked to his friend and put his arms around him. He stepped away and said with a smile, "You will feel as I feel every day. Noble." He started to laugh and again hugged his friend. "I am happy for you." He backed away. "Let us have more wine."

Bo Yusuf stayed silent, not responding to Rahmis' subtly (and perhaps not so subtly) offensive congratulatory words. But he remained civil. He enjoyed the company of al-Jeheuty, Nasir, and Ojodo. He asked of al-Jeheuty, "What do I do, *married-man?*"

Al-Jeheuty poured more wine into his cup. "You're asking me? I've been at marriage for just a few months. I have no idea. My father gave me great advice, though. Just remember the words *'Yes dear'*. Oh, and let me expound on the Oedipus myth." Al-Jeheuty went on to explain his father's humorous interpretation of the Oedipus mythology, drawing laughter from everyone at the table. An hour passed before each man resigned to his daily duties, but they regrouped by the day's end, huddling in the palace's rear courtyard. Wakil, Behar, Yaminah and her royal family, as well as Roberto, Taran, Alimah, and Mehit joined in a private celebration. Rahmis was noticeably absent, which angered Behar. Al-Jeheuty calmed the Beylerbey in a private corner of the courtyard, assuring Behar that he would speak to Rahmis and deal with the matter.

The noblemoor was at the moment having a drink in *The al-Hammon Palace*, keeping to himself at a corner table. Word already spread throughout the city about the marriage between Bo Yusuf and Princess Yaminah. There were whispers that the wedding would symbolize the union between the city and Djenhai, a final push to create all of Odongo-Mauharim into a state. Some citizens whispered concerns that the move would bring more enemies to their region. Tunisia and Algeria could turn on them, seeing Odongo-Mauharim becoming too powerful. There was concern about another attack made by the Ogunsanwo-Mashek. Other citizens worried about the Ottomans. The Turks had not completely loosened their grip on the city-state, from the citizens' point-of-view. An army of Turks still occupied al-Mari Ifriq, though under orders to be used strictly for protecting trade caravans on their way to Djenhai.

Regardless of concerns, al-Mari Ifriq was joyous. That same joy carried over into the first day's festivities of the Open Market, a successful event that witnessed vendors from all over Africa gather to display their goods and products. Acrobats, magicians and illusionists entertained the crowds. Ojodo put on another play. King Igdobe, Governor Wakil, and Beylerbey Ameer Las El-Behar announced to the citizens what they had already been gossiping about. Al-Mari Ifriq and Djenhai were taking steps to unify. The wedding between Army Official Bo Yusuf and Princess Yaminah was one of them.

Extensive trade carried on through the day. Vendors were scoped. Goods were inspected. Revenue was generated. The Open Market was analyzed. City officials publicly thanked Hesam Gandarewa. The festive climate carried into the Open Market's second day, where much of the first day's activities were repeated. But the joyous mood did not accompany the city officials inside the council house where they gathered with King Igdobe, his brother Munashe, and his daughter to discuss further the politics of war. Al-Jeheuty introduced a rebuttal to the King's proposition. "I don't wish to offend you, King Igdobe, but there are great risks with your ultimatum. Your proposition to the Ogunsanwo-Mashek nation will anger them; it puts them in a no-win situation. It forces the Ogunsanwo-Mashek to disarm, an order made by an enemy nation. There is also a problem with handing warriors over to slavers. They will fight back. The warriors will be too proud to become slaves—not to mention stirred by anger for how their own nation sold them out. It would also bring the European nation with the winning bid back to our shores with warships."

"I take no offense," the King said to al-Jeheuty. "The slaves will be taken to Africa-west, as I understand it—shipped to the Americas. We will devise a plan for them to make the journey. We will have our European contacts subdue them on their journey there. Our investors do not have to be informed they are taking in a warrior-class, and I believe this solves the problems within the Ogunsanwo-Mashek. They do not have to give their entire warrior-class, just the militants, which I'm sure runs through various classes among the Ogunsanwo-Mashek, not just the warriors."

"They are a small tribe," said al-Rinak. "The more militant-minded among them would not make a number to gain sufficient revenue."

"I too push for minimal engagement that leads to the enslavement of the entire nation," said Munashe. "It would solve *our* problem entirely. If we get rid of a few troublemakers now, there will be more in place in due time. We would also be providing our European investors with variety. I don't believe, no matter how strong the warrior class are, that our investors don't want women and younger workers to put to use in the colonies." He smiled. "But I listen to my brother, the King."

"I want to speak with Chief Mazigh," King Igdobe said looking at Behar and al-Jeheuty. "Can the meeting be arranged?" He added as a bonus, "You may even inform the chief of our talks, and the ultimatum."

Behar looked to al-Jeheuty. The young negotiator sighed. "Myself and Bo Yusuf will approach the Ogunsanwo-Mashek after the Open Market festival." Al-Jeheuty then lied, "It will take some time to track down the nomadic nation. We will notify Djenhai. We will not stall on this effort."

The council was then adjourned. Only the King was satisfied with the meeting's outcome. Neither Behar nor al-Rinak cared for the circumstances in which King Igdobe was placing all of them. Al-Jeheuty believed changing the King's mind lay with Bo Yusuf, but he was not ready to play that particular hand. He even kept his idea from Behar. The tension created in the meeting did not spill into the festivities. Al-Jeheuty and the other officials, as well as King Igdobe and his royal family, used the festivities to ease the friction generated in the meeting.

Bo Yusuf, on the sixth day of the festival, was given a proper introduction to the Djenhai unit that he was set to command. It was early in the morning, two hours after the sun had come up, and just minutes before the Open Market would begin for the day. The newly appointed General greeted the unit's former commander. The unit was stationed in the western barracks. Bo Yusuf mingled with the men for a small time.

Al-Jeheuty and Taran Zaher, at the same moment, escorted Rene Chaffee and his entourage to the docks. He was scheduled to leave for France. His holiday had arrived. Monsieur Gautier Leolin's messenger galley had already landed. Gautier's ship was due at any moment. Rene Chaffee was as anxious as ever to leave al-Mari Ifriq. He could not wait to return to France.

Governor Wakil al-Hakam, Company Boss Feroz Aunun, Company Boss Hesam Gandarewa, Beylerbey Ameer Las El-Behar, and King Igdobe Djenhai watched the start of the day's Open Market. Bo Yusuf arrived after the market opened, courting Princess Yaminah. The Princess' brother Asim was close behind, filtering through the crowd with friends made in the city. The Queen of the Second World stayed in bed, opting to come to the market festival in the afternoon.

Gautier Leolin's ship arrived an hour after its messenger galley. Al-Jeheuty liked Gautier. He was easier to work with than Chaffee, happy to work the business. The only problem with Gautier was he wanted too much to explore the other regions of Africa. Like a child, he would scurry out of the city's boundaries and get lost, accompanied by few guards or even none.

Gautier came from his ship, entourage in tow. Chaffee greeted him, relieved that he had arrived to take his place. The emissary ordered his party to board and ready his personal ship. He discussed the most recent developments in business with Gautier and the Moorish officials.

Slavery was omitted.

Gautier reported that four trade ships would be en route to al-Mari Ifriq in three weeks, and the ships would need escorting to Cyprus. Three more ships would launch from France at the same time, heading for Sale and steered by privateers employed by the French. They would need escorting to the Caribbean. Al-Jeheuty and Taran took note, assuring Gautier they would contact their associates in Sale and equip the privateers with protection.

The men watched Rene board his ship and sale away.

Rene's ship disappeared over the horizon.

Al-Jeheuty, Taran, and Gautier turned to head into the city.

An explosion tossed all three men forward!

Al-Jeheuty slammed against the beach. He turned around and witnessed a docked ship fire at Gautier's docked ship. The side of Gautier's ship broke into fiery splinters and large, sharp, broken planks that struck the docks and beach. The opposing, docked ship fired twice more before the ship opened and five robed and masked riders wearing metal chest plates, rushed onto the docks and rode to the west.

Al-Jeheuty jumped to his feet, helping Taran up. Gautier received attention from his men. Al-Jeheuty screamed to Taran and Gautier, "Get into the company house, now. No questions. All of you." There was another explosion. The roaring sound came from the direction of the Open Market. Al-Jeheuty rushed to the Ghanem company house stables, untied a steed, and rode in the direction of the Open Market. He saw chaos, fire, crying, and smoke.

There was screaming.

Gunfire.

Company Boss Feroz Aunun was dead, struck by a bullet through the throat. Bo Yusuf, standing next to the company boss at the time he was struck, covered Princess Yaminah and threw her to the ground, laying over her as the bedlam ensued. A squad of robed, masked riders terrorized the festival, shooting policing guards, cutting down citizens. Princess Yaminah looked up and witnessed three riders fire pistols into her father's chest.

King Igdobe bucked with each bullet. He dropped to the ground dead.

Yaminah screamed.

Bo Yusuf tried to cover the Princess' eyes from the sight, but it was too late. She saw everything. The three riders galloped away. Other attackers tossed more explosives into the market. The air suffered from debris and thick smoke, which Wakil, while laying on his back, swallowed and inhaled. He coughed wildly, spurts of blood in his wheezing. He turned onto his stomach and coughed more, vomiting blood and fragments stuck in his throat. He got to his knees and started to stand when another blast forced him back down. Wakil stayed low. He crawled from the burning Market Place. The riding attackers were gone. The governor tried to stand but he was too week. Palace guards surrounded him and helped him to his feet. Al-Jeheuty jumped from his steed and ran to Wakil's side.

"I'll be fine," assured Wakil.

"Get him to the palace infirmary," al-Jeheuty ordered the guards. They acknowledged. Screaming alerted al-Jeheuty. He turned to see Yaminah crying over her father's body. Bo Yusuf and several Djenhai servants tried to drag the Princess away. Yaminah continued to scream. Djenhai servants and alerted royal guards lifted the King's body. Al-Rinak's Turkish guards rounded the citizens back into the city, trying to keep order. Al-Jeheuty noticed Feroz Aunun on the ground. The company boss was dead. Another female's voice broke through the crowd, screaming. It was Alimah. Al-Jeheuty ran in the direction of her voice. He knew that she and Mehit were making their way to the festival. He cut his way through the crowds of people and smoke.

Al-Jeheuty found Alimah and Mehit. He froze on sight of the two women as if ice penetrated the African atmosphere and locked al-Jeheuty in place. He watched, his mouth agape in disbelief, both Mehit and Alimah, stationed near a palanquin, cried over Ameer Las El-Behar. The Beylerbey was on his back. Al-Jeheuty screamed for assistance, breaking the freeze the scene had over him. Al-Jeheuty darted over to Behar and saw eight bullets had struck the Beylerbey in the chest. There were more bullets in his back, unseen by al-Jeheuty. Behar's robes were torn and drenched with blood.

"They killed him first," screamed Alimah. "Four men. He shoved Mehit into the palanquin for cover. They shot him then. He threw himself over me to protect me. They shot him again. Cowards. They shot him in the back. They killed him first."

Al-Jeheuty screamed again, calling for assistance. Guards rushed him. They lifted Behar's body and placed him inside the palanquin. The guards carted the box to the city's southern gate. Al-Jeheuty, Mehit, and Alimah followed the guards through the gate and into the palace. The palanquin was taken to Behar's private quarters. The Beylerbey's body was gently placed on the bed. Al-Jeheuty instructed Alimah to take Mehit to their private quarters and lay her down and relax her. "Get several nurses. Have them check to see if any trauma has effected our child." Though Mehit felt fine, no shortness of breath or lightheadedness, she obeyed her husband's orders, allowing her mother to escort her to their private quarters. Al-Jeheuty asked the guards to find Rahmis Husani, Ojodo Yerodin, Bo Yusuf al-Dume, Nasir Sa'ood, Governor Wakil, and Roberto Hamaat and bring them to the Beylerbey's chambers. The men jumped to action immediately.

The Moorish official stood over Behar's body. The Beylerbey's bullet torn clothes and body contrasted with his peaceful face. Death only bothered the living, thought al-Jeheuty. Minutes continued to pass. Al-Jeheuty was still alone. He stared at Behar's lifeless body. His jaw tightened like a vice, anger coursing through him. He balled his fists. His vision blurred as his eyes watered and his rage piqued.

Al-Jeheuty was in charge of life unborn, life existing, and life newly extinguished.

Wakil entered, coughing wildly. He informed al-Jeheuty that palace correspondents informed him that Turkish troops were in pursuit of the fleeing attackers. He coughed through every word, cleared his throat, and relaxed. He limped to a chair facing Behar's body, and he sat down. Al-Jeheuty pulled a chair next to the governor and the two men watched Behar's motionless body while saying nothing and thinking everything. It was always an odd site to see someone still, without breath. It always felt like at any moment the body would make a profound noise as it awoke and gasped for air.

There was no such moment.

The other men al-Jeheuty called for slowly entered Behar's room minutes apart from one another. Each of Behar's young lieutenants broke into angry tears on site of his body. Al-Jeheuty stood up and joined them. Wakil's voice, weak and rasping from the pollution in his throat, cut into the mourning lieutenants. The governor said a heartfelt Mohammedan prayer over Behar's body.

Roberto closed the door.

The lieutenants and Nasir bowed their heads as Wakil continued his prayer. "May life continue in your honor; may life continue with your title." He then asked, "What shall we do, Beylerbey? What are your orders?" He stood from his chair. "I do not address this question to the spirit of our dearly departed. I address you, al-Jeheuty. So, might I ask again? What shall we do, Beylerbey al-Jeheuty Anhur Has? What are your orders?"

Roberto said a parting prayer to Behar's body. The officials straightened their demeanor and greeted al-Jeheuty as their new Beylerbey, kisses to the hand and bows toward him. Al-Jeheuty wanted to command the others to stop. He wanted to tell them their gestures were ridiculous, if not premature. There needed to be a time for mourning their fallen captain. But the officials, as well as al-Jeheuty, knew that business needed to be handled.

Al-Jeheuty continued to stare in disbelief at Behar's body. Roberto turned to al-Jeheuty and greeted him the same and then said, "Chief of all Chiefs, the departed blesses you to make war with his killers."

Chapter Thirty-Two

This was Ameer Las El-Behar, the son of two Moorish political idealists and philosophers. He was born in Sale, Morocco and raised throughout the world. He followed the ideals of his mother and father and turned their words into actions, gaining a sense of national pride for the Moor and the rich history of Africa. He was a captain-at-sea, a corsair, an outlaw branded militant revolutionary, a teacher and surrogate father to many, and he was a Chief of all Chiefs for al-Mari Ifriq. He was to this date one of the greatest leaders the city had ever possessed. Ameer Las El-Behar was a King. That was his life.

This was his funeral service.

Every official attended Behar's services, including the royal family, and the entire Council of Captains. A surviving brother and two sisters were in attendance. Three of eight El-Behar children remained. The former Beylerbey was entombed with former company boss Sa'ad al-Din Sa'ood. Citizens watched the ceremony from afar. Nasir al-Din Sa'ood, his brother Zakiy, and his mother Afya, struggled with the memory of Sa'ad's burial service, returning to the company tomb to attend the funeral of Ameer Las El-Behar. The entire affair reflected the father and husband's burial, every ritual performed, prayer spoken, and offering made. Behar's lieutenants offered silent prayers to the man that was their Captain, General, Beylerbey, and teacher.

Al-Jeheuty Anhur Has was publicly ordained the new Beylerbey by Governor Wakil al-Hakam. The ceremony took place in the city square after Behar's burial. Al-Jeheuty pleaded with Wakil a day earlier to take the title, having one of his sons step in as governor. Al-Jeheuty believed he was too angry to assume the responsibility, but Wakil did not comply. After al-Jeheuty's inauguration, the new Beylerbey and the other officials attended the Djenhai family's departure. The royal family carried with them the body of King Igdobe and Company Boss Feroz Aunun, both to be buried in noble soil.

Feroz Aunun's family, one wife, three sons, and one daughter, followed with them. None of his sons were educated in business. One was an architect. One a soldier serving in Tunis. The third was a Mohammedan teacher. His daughter was a doctor that treated children. They would not inherit the company, but monies would be provided for them. Feroz's wife would take up housing in Djenhai, close to her noble family.

Bo Yusuf's unit departed with the royal family. The former unit's commander assured they would return to the city with Princess Yaminah and King Kemnebi to discuss military action against the Ogunsanwo-Mashek, and for Bo Yusuf to again assume command. Al-Rinak expressed that he would visit Djenhai in a week's time. Before leaving, Munashe deferred all company power to al-Rinak. The black Turk accepted humbly.

Al-Rinak created a passion for war within two hours of assuming acting company boss. His Turkish soldiers roamed the streets, helping keep al-Mari Ifriq on lockdown. Al-Rinak's actions inspired the citizens to favor war, and the people turned to Beylerbey Anhur Has and Governor Wakil to execute the hostile initiative. Each day the fervor grew worse, al-Rinak's voice grew louder among the citizens, and each day birthed an entirely new set of disruption for Beylerbey Anhur Has.

The young chief boss could not express his anger. When he did, he looked erratic. When he remained silent, he lost ground. Taran mediated the chaos, which was not always the best way to calm al-Jeheuty and his cabinet of administrators. The disarray fueled furious politics from other corners of al-Mari Ifriq. The Council of Captains represented by Hieremias Sunwil, called for greater spending toward them, a lessening of taxes on their revenue and captured booty. The merchants followed the path of the hired corsairs and captains. The citizens were next, coupled with their calls for war against the Ogunsanwo-Mashek.

It was day four of al-Jeheuty's rule as Beylerbey.

He sat in the council house. It was early in the morning. He was alone, save servants and cooks. Outside waited his wife, Roberto Hamaat, Governor Wakil, Nasir al-Din Sa'ood, and al-Jeheuty's fellow revolutionaries, his newly inherited lieutenants and city officials. Seven people waited to speak with him outside. Al-Jeheuty felt like a mob resided beyond the door.

He didn't know where to begin.

He was forced to see his wife first when she walked through the door. Al-Jeheuty stood up and turned his back to Mehit. He walked away and said coldly, "Did I call for you?" Mehit took long, quick strides toward al-Jeheuty, stopping inches from his back. "Do you have a request too?" he pressed. "One that I would need to fulfill, lest great consequences befall me at your hand?" Mehit said nothing. Al-Jeheuty turned to face her, his face blazing with anger. "Do you come to ask for swift, simple answers to methodical, complicated matters?" His eyes started to water. "Everyone is exhaling their grief for Ameer Las El-Behar as if free from a man they feared. Now they can speak what was on their minds, and I feel every breath of complaint they have been choking on all this time. *Day four,*" he emphasized. "Do you understand that the citizens believe me weaker than Behar? I have inherited all the complaints they covered with smile and praise."

Mehit took a deep breath and then said to her husband, "Behar was venerable, yes. He was older, familiar to the elder citizens, war-torn, and aged with wisdom. He was a father figure to *seventy*-year old men. Yes. The people are scared, al-Jeheuty. They have lost their father. They want answers. Unfortunately for you, Behar's physical presence and voice made the people feel safe. But trust my words, husband, they observed all manners of difficulty handled by you and the other Griffin lieutenants. Behar's sons."

"*Bah!* They want easy answers," al-Jeheuty hissed. "They want the Ogunsanwo-Mashek dead, but no man reaches for sword or pistol to create an army to find them. No man wishes to separate their emotions from a chaotic situation and see that the Ogunsanwo-Mashek are not behind this tragedy." He grabbed Mehit roughly by her arms and drew her close. "And let your lips never speak those words." He let her go and exhaled.

Mehit yelled at him, "You want people to understand but you're not willing to speak the truth."

"The consequences of speaking the truth would have European nations' warships, united under the condition of killing the last vestige of Moors, sailing over the watery horizon and laying waste to this city." He lowered his voice, but his emotions were still elevated. "The consequences of speaking the truth would have us at arms against the Djenhai kingdom. They would be outraged at us for siding with a nation at war with them, even if uniting with the Ogunsanwo-Mashek leads to the death of the true conspirators behind this plot."

"Kill them," Mehit said like a strict order. "Kill every last one of them!" she screamed. "Kill them and let them know that the Gods of Africa-north will cast down those who come from the North. So declares Beylerbey Al-Jeheuty Anhur Has, so declares his wife, Mehit al-Tarqiyya Anhur Has." Mehit's emotions boiled over inside her, spilling out in tears and angry words. "So declares the great, Moorish revolutionaries from Spain, born of Africa, and the greater Governor al-Hakam. Tell them that we will fulfill the destination concerning them." Al-Jeheuty immediately embraced his wife. "*You tell them,*" she continued to scream. "*You tell them!*" She pounded al-Jeheuty's chest while still in his embrace.

Al-Jeheuty spoke softly, having great concern for nothing but his wife. "I will, *mora*. I will."

Mehit stepped away from her husband and slapped him. Al-Jeheuty buckled with his wife's attack. "*You selfish bastard!* Don't believe that you're the only one mourning for Behar. There are three other Griffin lieutenants that were just as close—if not closer. And if the four of you cannot find ground to straighten al-Mari Ifriq, so help me, I will castrate all four of you and toss your testicles to those who will choose to properly use them and be men. You are *Moors.* You are as black as the Gods in the sky and as black as the ink used to describe them to bring validity to all religions. I challenge you to be their reflection." She jumped forward and kissed al-Jeheuty deeply. Frustration, love, and passion rushed from Mehit's lips and through al-Jeheuty's body. She backed away from her husband, panting. She turned and walked from the council house.

Al-Jeheuty trembled as he watched his wife leave his presence. He gained his composure by taking a seat on one of the large cushions near the bed. He then called through the council house's open, swinging door, "Nasir."

The Sa'ood company boss walked inside. He closed the door and stepped toward al-Jeheuty. The company boss called for wine. A servant delivered a bottle and two cups, laying the delivery at al-Jeheuty's feet. Nasir took the cushion opposite the Beylerbey and poured wine into both cups while exhaling a heavy sigh. Al-Jeheuty grabbed his cup and took a sip. "My father and Behar expressed to me how strong Mehit would be as a wife. They were right." Another sip. "There are things she doesn't quite understand, ordering blindly without comprehending the full consequence of action and reaction." He explained, "She has ordered me to kill anyone responsible for the attacks on al-Mari Ifriq, but she has done so without understanding the emotional and physical consequences." Another sip, rather a large gulp ingesting much of the wine in his cup. The Beylerbey exhaled.

Nasir nodded his head. He said gently, while pouring more wine for his boss, "*Let us sit upon the ground and tell sad stories of the death of kings.*" He smiled and drank. "I have one. It's a story, not about a king, but a story about my grandfather, an accountant. When I confronted my father about becoming a companyman he told me this story about my grandfather. My father said to me that he watched my grandfather closely. All my father ever saw him do was shake hands and make people smile. When people were upset, my grandfather would ease them. When people were confused, he would ease them. One day, when my father was around the age of eleven, he saw something different in the interaction between my grandfather and the men he made business with—one particular man, anyway.

"My father saw my grandfather shake hands with this new businessman who, according to my father, looked very wealthy. He was from Libya, a swarmahu man. My grandfather entertained this wealthy man for a week or two. He made him feel comfortable. Then the man disappeared. My father witnessed a local company boss visit my grandfather, and he started to see things clearer. My father started to see a pattern. Businessman would visit. My grandfather entertained them for a week or two. Businessman would disappear. A company boss would celebrate with my grandfather. My father admits that he did not know which businessmen were marked and executed, or which businessmen just simply returned home after business, but there was a clue. My grandfather would seclude himself directly after a company boss visit. Maybe it was guilt." He paused to take a sip from his cup. "My point, Beylerbey…"

"You don't know how strange that title sounds being addressed to me," said al-Jeheuty in a low voice.

"Strange to you, maybe," Nasir replied. "But I believe I've taken more orders from you than I ever took from Behar—with no disrespect to the former chief. I'm sure much of his orders came through you, but…it sounds right to me. The title fits you appropriately, but I understand. I was the same way when people began to call me company boss and company master." He waved the sentiment away and continued on his previous thought, "Anyway…my point is that my *grandmother* always gave my grandfather his space to deal with business, especially with his ritual of seclusion. *My* mother was more involved. She had to be. Al-Mari Ifriq became an extremely seedy, corsair-state. My father was involved in all of its politics. Chiefs, bosses, and gangsters. They all wanted a cut of the businesses left behind by the company bosses my grandfather worked for. The chief boss died. My father's business was partnered with the old man. My father thought he could unify the man's partners, but they proved to be as stubborn as his enemies. My father killed a lot of men. He killed men with his own hands, and he had men killed through Roberto and other loyal soldiers. My mother, though she gave no counsel, consoled my father. But he secluded himself too, and always with a bottle of wine. I saw the decisions made by my father deteriorate him. He stopped his alcoholic ritual when his best friend was murdered, Maurice and Fusan's father. It was a couple of months before the Turks took over. I was six."

"So, Mehit will be with me every step of the way?" al-Jeheuty asked for clarification. "She will be surprised when we near the step that executes the mark on Taran, her father."

"No," Nasir answered. "She won't even see it. She will give you one fiery command such as she has, because the spirit of the original, black goddess resides in her—"

"Okay, *Roberto*," al-Jeheuty interrupted as he took a sip of wine to cover his smile.

"I'm serious, al-Jeheuty," Nasir pleaded. "Mehit has in her the power of the black goddess. She is wise. She is passionate, powerful. She is vengeful. She will give you the order to bring balance to al-Mari Ifriq. It's not in her nature as the goddess to care about how you do it. She wants it done, and it will get done. I don't care how any faith is being twisted. The woman is the supreme ruler. She knows how to keep balance in her home, even when dealing with the erratic behavior of us men, unable to simmer down our emotions. Your goddess has given you the order, and you will follow it the way *you* know how it needs to be executed. These corsair politics began long ago. They stop with us." He raised his cup and said before he drank, "After one last volley of cannon and pistol fire, and after one last great clash of swords. Men. We're always comparing phalluses, huh. Which can *shoot* further, and which can cut the *deepest*."

Al-Jeheuty finally laughed. He then promoted Nasir by saying, "I want you to be my Commissioner of Foreign Affairs. Taran is out. I will put him in charge of urban planning. We will continue to build and expand the city. Most of it is his family's land anyway." He looked at Nasir and explained more, "Zakiy will be Company Boss. All I really need is for you to improve your fluency in the Romance Languages. Italian, specifically. I will command Aludra to drive it down your throat."

Nasir conceded to the promotion and the Beylerbey's orders. "I love al-Mari Ifriq," he said after a moment. "But I am not blind by my attachment. I am my father's son. I understand business. I am not so emotionally invested that I have become bankrupt to sights unseen. That has allowed me to survive being a witness to death, survive a plot calling for my death, and succeed in a plot where I have marked great men for death. That being said—as I thank you for the promotion—may I ask to give my opinion of politics?" Al-Jeheuty allowed Nasir to take advantage of the new title. "Thank you," Nasir said respectfully. He continued, "I know our talks with the Ogunsanwo-Mashek revealed a plot formed by their radicals to kidnap King Igdobe, but the actions we've witnessed are too extreme. Even the radicals among them were not bold or stupid enough to make a move where they would risk their people's total annihilation from our forces and Djenhai forces." Nasir shook his head. "No," he said. "So, let me say that even I can see that no Ogunsanwo-Mashek warrior ever fired a shot toward us. The hostile politics we find ourselves in are descended from the same politics we have always been involved in. So, do you have a plan, Beylerbey al-Jeheuty Anhur Has? Do you have a plan to kill the man responsible for this?"

"No," al-Jeheuty confessed. "But I will box him in. I'll accomplish this by killing every man that has conspired to help al-Rinak Ozan attack al-Mari Ifriq. His actions have killed our beloved leaders and placed the blame on an innocent nation. He's clever. Al-Rinak has brought all of us residing in Odongo-Mauharim to the brink of war and enslavement." Al-Jeheuty finished his drink and called for a servant. A man came from the kitchen and asked for command. "Allow the other officials entrance, please. Then, with the other servants and cooks, after you have prepared a fine meal, leave the council house. Thank you."

The servant bowed and explained that a grand meal had already been prepared for the Beylerbey and his officials. Al-Jeheuty offered his thanks, and the servant rushed to the door and called for the other officials to enter. The men entered slowly, looking nervous at what to expect from the new Beylerbey. Al-Jeheuty did have a concerned look on his visage, misinterpreted by the Moorish officials as anger, but the Beylerbey only noticing Wakil's absence. Al-Jeheuty jumped up and asked, "Where is Governor Wakil?" He started to become worried. He too misinterpreted their concerned looks as looks of remorse.

Roberto explained, "He wasn't feeling well. He was coughing hard again. He went for rest."

Al-Jeheuty put his hand on his chest and expressed a relieving sigh. "I thought, maybe, he was claimed by what ails him."

"He'll be fine," said Roberto as he approached the young Beylerbey. He put his hand on al-Jeheuty's shoulder and asked with concern in his eyes, "How are *you* doing?"

Al-Jeheuty confessed, "I'm terrified, but let's sit." He addressed the other men. "All of us. Let us converse." The men took separate cushions. Al-Jeheuty took the edge of the bed, Behar's former place. He waited patiently as servants carefully placed a grand, morning meal in front of he and the officials. The servants then left the council house as ordered. Roberto notified that several members from his outfit guarded the door. Al-Jeheuty nodded to his officials and then spoke, "What we discuss is not to be discussed by anyone unless authorized by me. Is that understood?"

The officials nodded. "The people do not want an investigation into the attacks made on al-Mari Ifriq, but I do. They want swift vengeance. I want clear answers. I'm assigning each of you a task. I am reworking our cabinet. I have just made Nasir my Commissioner of Foreign Affairs. I will inform Taran that he is to help expand the city's boundaries. I will also allow him to remain close to politics concerning Statesman Ozan. I want both of them to feel comfortable with the change I've made. Zakiy will become company boss of the Sa'ood Company. Are there any objections?" There were none. "Rahmis, I want you to helm another festival and a tournament of games. I want the citizens distracted. I would also like you to work close with Taran in his city planning."

Rahmis confirmed with a nod.

Al-Jeheuty continued. "Ojodo, continue to help Zakiy, but there is something that I need from the Sa'ood Company. Bring me the logbooks for the days following the first and second attack. Also, I want Captain Sunwil brought to me. I know he's been requesting an audience with me."

Ojodo nodded at the Beylerbey. There was a slight hesitation in his movement, and al-Jeheuty understood why. Politics and tragedy were keeping the dramatist from pursuing his travels to the east and studying all manner of philosophy and old literature. Al-Jeheuty decided to discuss the matter later in a private counsel between he and Ojodo.

The Beylerbey turned to Bo Yusuf and said, "The decisions I'm making might cause friction with the Djenhai people. I don't want to rush into war against the Ogunsanwo-Mashek. I know Djenhai is probably gathering arms as we speak. Al-Rinak has pushed for enslavement of the entire Ogunsanwo-Mashek nation. He will continue to push his agenda. I want you to curb his influence on Yaminah. She is emotionally distraught at the present time. Her ability to make a clear decision cannot be trusted. This also goes for her brother, the apparent heir. Igdobe's brother and advisor, Munashe's ability to make a clear decision, is also in question. We might find ourselves at odds with the Djenhai. Until matters are investigated and resolved, she, or anyone in her kingdom, cannot be trusted, especially with Statesman Ozan in their ear. We must view the Djenhai as slavers, considering they've entertained the idea of handing their enemies to the European."

Bo Yusuf retorted, "You're speaking about the woman I'm set to marry. You're speaking about the woman I love."

Al-Jeheuty became stiff with anger. There came from Bo Yusuf, a man now his lieutenant-at-command, the audacity to stand up to his word. He wanted to strike him. He wanted to grab Bo Yusuf and scream how dare he question his judgment and word. His hands curled into the mattress he rested on. The rage inside him rushed to the surface, but only revealed itself as a relieving, exhaled breath. Al-Jeheuty replied in an authoritative voice, "I'm speaking about a woman that has the potential to become your enemy, and when you see her on the battlefield, you better prepare yourself to address her as such." He lifted his hand, ceasing Bo Yusuf from speaking back to him. "I am asking you to protect her from al-Rinak's words so we can prevent such a circumstance. He's put himself in a situation where he can control the actions of a kingdom, a kingdom mourning the death of their king, and the death of a cousin-by-marriage."

Bo Yusuf relaxed.

Al-Jeheuty asked, "Can this be done?" Bo Yusuf nodded, yes. The Beylerbey ordered the Army Official, "Leave for Djenhai ahead of al-Rinak. If you go with him, you won't come back. Roberto," al-Jeheuty called. "Have him escorted by your people. I also want you to call every member of your clan to al-Mari Ifriq. Anyone on business faraway, we need them here. Also, visit the Ogunsanwo-Mashek. Tell them to hide. We will ship goods to them. They are not to roam while these politics continue to heat up."

"Understood," said Roberto.

"To work," al-Jeheuty commanded. "Ojodo, I need those books *five minutes ago*. And get me Captain Sunwil. Is he in port?"

"Ports opened up yesterday after the city was opened up," relayed the titan. "Captain Sunwil has not left."

"Find him," al-Jeheuty ordered. "I demand his presence. At the same time, I want those logbooks."

Ojodo bowed at the neck. "Yes, Beylerbey."

"Roberto, Bo Yusuf, prepare for your leave," al-Jeheuty continued to command. "Nasir, I need you to stay here. Rahmis, find Taran. Inform him that I will counsel with him soon." Everyone bowed to the Beylerbey and went about their tasks. "Roberto," al-Jeheuty called. The assassin stopped and turned to al-Jeheuty. "An update on Wakil's health." Roberto acknowledged and then left the council house with the others. Al-Jeheuty's eyes swept the grand meal in front of him. No one ate. No one drank. He smiled at the sight.

Nasir asked, "What are you thinking about, al-Jeheuty?"

"My wife. Life." He shook his head and then focused on present matters.

Nasir walked over to the buffet and decided to take some food. He scooped the food into his mouth, chewed, and swallowed. "You didn't bring up al-Rinak's possible involvement. Don't you trust your revolutionary brothers?"

"Absolutely," al-Jeheuty said. "There's just a slight problem, which resides in all of their contacts. I need them like stone. Bo Yusuf might, in a moment of weakness, say something to Princess Yaminah. Rahmis deals with the locals. Ojodo will leave soon. They all know what's coming. They know appropriate marks will be executed. This is not the first time we've had to do this. We've plotted before. We know the procedure. They lay in wait to execute the marks when I point. Good men. That's why I had all you bastards a part of my wedding."

Nasir looked at al-Jeheuty with a perplexed expression. "Ojodo is leaving?"

Al-Jeheuty shook his head. "Yes. He was discussing leaving with Behar. He wants to study the world. He wants to learn more, if that's possible with all Behar shoved down our throats and made us research. He wants his studies to make him a great Moorish playwright. He hasn't brought his request to me, yet. I'll approach him soon."

The guards outside the council house opened the main entrance and announced Ojodo's return. The Moorish colossus walked into the council house carrying four large logbooks and escorting Captain Hieremias Sunwil. Ojodo presented the logbooks to al-Jeheuty and bowed to him. He placed the logbooks on the floor in front of the Beylerbey. The Beylerbey thanked Ojodo and then asked Hieremias to take a seat. Ojodo was dismissed, but not before al-Jeheuty explained that he wanted a private meeting with him later. Ojodo bowed, exited, and then returned to the docks.

Al-Jeheuty observed Captain Sunwil. The Moorish corsair was tall, even when sitting. The guards confiscated his weapons before he entered, but he was still an imposing figure, even as his visage expressed a very humble look.

"I have heard the request from the Council of Captains," said al-Jeheuty. "I will discuss with Bo Yusuf, Hesam Gandarewa, and Laith al-Hakam if such a request may be granted. I believe we have lost the wind on generosity, but we will converse to see if taxes may be alleviated slightly."

"Thank you, Beylerbey," Hieremias expressed.

Al-Jeheuty had a request too. "You are chief-captain, Hieremias," he told the Captain. "I request that you relax the hysterics created on the council. Tell them their Beylerbey is doing everything possible to alleviate economic stress. I am fully aware that the captains-at-sea engage in a dangerous job. They should be well rewarded."

"Thank you, Beylerbey," the captain repeated. He continued to look humble, almost nervous. His eyes struggled to meet the young Beylerbey, and al-Jeheuty took note of the captain's behavior.

"That is not why I requested your presence," al-Jeheuty informed. "And I'm sure that is not the reason you requested an audience with me." The captain's anxiousness ceased. He sat up straight, attentive. His demeanor returned to the familiar Captain Hieremias Sunwil that made rival captains tremble with the whisper of his name. To al-Jeheuty, Captain Sunwil's sudden change in posture made him appear to be a man prepared to accept the consequences placed on him. "Your ship, while docked, fired its cannons at another docked ship. Where was your crew at the time of the incident?"

Captain Sunwil knew this was the reason he was brought before the new Beylerbey. This was the same reason he requested an audience with his chief boss. The Beylerbey was right about that. "My crew was spread throughout the city, on morning rest," the captain explained. "My Chief Officer, Ras Ali, follows a morning schedule to check all of our docked ships and report to me. He didn't make it there that particular morning. I found him passed out in the alleyway near my lodge, not too far from his own. It was minutes before the attack. I went outside to wait for his arrival and word on our ship's condition. I heard the explosions at the docks, dragged him inside, and, after placing Ras Ali in my bed, I made my way to the city gates. I was not permitted through. At this moment I still had no idea that it was my ship used for the attack at the docks. I was furious, my anger aimed at Ras Ali. I was under the impression that he had engaged in festival activities too hard the previous night. I was wrong."

"Wrong?" al-Jeheuty questioned.

"Ras Ali has been suffering from an intense fever," Captain Sunwil answered. "He's conscious, but he's not altogether lucid. He's been coughing hard and vomiting steadily."

"He was poisoned," al-Jeheuty concluded.

"I believe so," said the Captain. "Someone left him for dead. He did his best to make his way to my lodge. I have no idea how long he'd been in front of my place." Anger crawled on Hieremias' face.

Al-Jeheuty inspected the captain's visage, reading the lines in his flesh, etched by his anger, as if it was a note personally written for him. The captain's anger was not addressed to the Beylerbey, however. Al-Jeheuty read deeper and quickly interpreted that notion. Captain Sunwil's anger was directed elsewhere. Al-Jeheuty stood up from his bed and took a seat next to Captain Sunwil. He asked, "Where is your Chief Officer now, because he might be in extreme danger."

"My crew's physician is with him," Hieremias informed. "They're at my lodge. Ras Ali is recovering well, but is still sick. I have not informed my crew of these matters."

Al-Jeheuty looked at Nasir and commanded, "Have Ras Ali and the physician moved to the palace infirmary right now." Nasir nodded. He made his way to the door and exited the council house. Al-Jeheuty addressed the captain by asking, "Does Chief Officer Ras Ali carry out his checks alone?"

"No," the captain answered. He looked away from the Beylerbey, concentrated on his anger.

Al-Jeheuty continued, "If Chief Officer Ras Ali was too debilitated to carry out his check, then who would have done so in his stead?"

"The same people that help him with the check," Captain Sunwil said as his lips quivered with anger. "My Boatswain, Tobal Lessman, and my Quartermaster, Yan Nuh."

"Where are they?" al-Jeheuty asked.

"I haven't seen them lately. They reported to me about one of our ships assisting in the attack at the docks. I have not heard from them since."

"Did they ask about Chief Officer Ras Ali?"

"No."

Al-Jeheuty stood up and sat back on the bed. He looked sternly at Captain Sunwil, and the captain looked back at him. Hieremias' expression was eased of anger. "I need you close, Captain Sunwil. I am relaying politics to you that even my top officials are not directly aware of. I have targeted Statesman al-Rinak Ozan as the prime suspect in the attacks against al-Mari Ifriq. He attacked us using accomplices. Your boatswain and quartermaster might be a part of his group of conspirators. From what I've heard you speak, Captain Sunwil, I have deduced that Chief Officer Ras Ali was the victim of an attempted mark so these other men who know your ship well could stow aboard and create a distraction. While all eyes looked in the direction of the loud, exploding sounds, al-Rinak's soldiers, disguised as Ogunsanwo-Mashek warriors, could carry out marks on Company Boss Feroz Aunun, King Igdobe Djenhai, and our beloved Beylerbey, Ameer Las El-Behar."

Captain Sunwil's anger returned. "I offer my regret for having these men in my services, Beylerbey Anhur Has. I will find them and bring them to you. You may give them justice."

Al-Jeheuty shook his head. "Find them. Make them feel at ease. Do not reveal the state of Ras Ali. Look concerned. Act as if you have not seen your chief officer in some time. The consequences of this will be that no member of your crew shall take on an expedition at sea. We will wait for Statesman Ozan to leave for Djenhai. Then we will question these traitors. We will extract from them other conspirators and continue on our path to justice."

Captain Sunwil stood up straight. He then bowed respectfully to the chief boss. "Yes, Beylerbey Anhur Has. I am at your service." The Captain returned to his seat, and he and al-Jeheuty spoke about strategies to corner the traitors among his crew. The talk ended when Nasir returned to the council house, relaying to both parties that Chief Officer Ras Ali was taken to the palace infirmaries. He was doing well, resting. Al-Jeheuty ordered Captain Sunwil to conduct a search for his boatswain and quartermaster. "Yes, Beylerbey," said the Captain. He jumped to his feet, bowed to both officials, and then left the council house to complete his directive.

Al-Jeheuty bent down and lifted one of the logbooks from off the ground and put them on the bed. He grabbed the others, one-by-one, and then waved Nasir over to him. He opened one book, which was marked with entries dated around the first attack on al-Mari Ifriq. He flipped through and asked Nasir to look in another logbook for the dates surrounding the second attack. "What are we looking for?" asked Nasir.

"A pattern," said al-Jeheuty. "I want to cross-reference arrivals and departures within the days preceding and following the attacks." He scanned intensely. "Chief Mazigh said to me that a strike was made against their settlement. It came from the caravan guards. It was the Turkish army, most likely on al-Rinak's orders. Chief Mazigh said soldiers from his nation were stripped of their clothes and weapons."

"An authentic disguise," Nasir concluded.

"Chief Mazigh said the same," al-Jeheuty remarked as he continued to search through the logbook's pages. "He was under the belief that, oh— how did he put it?" Al-Jeheuty looked up, thinking. Then he remembered the chief's words. *"A devil, sly enough to wear our robes, left your city in flames."* He returned his gaze to the logbook. "Whomever entered the city may have left legitimately so as not to arouse suspicion. They would then make the journey back by land, dressed as Ogunsanwo-Mashek warriors. I'm going back two weeks prior to the first attack. Are you there for the second attack?"

"Yes," said Nasir.

"Let's start reading the names of the captains that departed the city," al-Jeheuty suggested.

The two started to read aloud, one after the other. No names matched for the first or second day. However, the two of them came across two familiar names when reading further in the logbooks.

Two captains.

Fusan al-Hammon.

Kyler Piett.

Both departed on the same ship leaving for Tunis. The recent logbook showed the two captains had not yet returned to the city. The earlier logbook noted the two men and their crew returned a full week after the attacks. Al-Jeheuty could see the hurt growing on Nasir's face. Fusan was a fiery spirit that even challenged Behar on occasion, but the volatile corsair was a childhood friend. Al-Jeheuty spoke, "Let's not jump too quickly to conclusions. The log states they were traveling the routes assigned for them to protect. It may just be a coincidence."

Both men admitted silently that it was too much of a coincidence, the same names appearing within the incidents of attacks. Both men were absent from the city. Neither captain witnessed either of the attacks. There also was the peculiar aspect of Captain Piett signing the log when his personal ship stayed in port, and he was just accompanying Fusan on an errand. There was no need to sign the log. Perhaps it was habit. Al-Jeheuty shook his head, almost breaking into a chuckle. It seemed to him that sometimes, in a person's rush to cover his or her tracks, they exposed themselves completely. He commanded Nasir not to question Maurice. Nasir remembered al-Jeheuty's earlier words. He did not want to be kept from information. He agreed not to bring the matter to his friend Maurice. The two of them exited the council house to return the logbooks to the docks and company house.

Chapter Thirty-Three

Bo Yusuf was gone. He left for Djenhai ahead of al-Rinak. Roberto Hamaat was gone too. He left to find the Ogunsanwo-Mashek and deliver a warning for the nomadic nation to stay hidden. Al-Jeheuty watched over al-Mari Ifriq. The days were quiet. Al-Jeheuty and Mehit spent time perusing the different districts and areas. The newly married couple lived in the city palace, which Mehit did not care for. She admired the artistry and the dedication to detail found within the city's architecture, especially the buildings residing within the upscale districts. But there was also an admirable, artistic simplicity to the humble, family homes throughout the city. Mehit would have preferred the homes' modest architecture to even the fanciful aspects of the palace.

The sun dipped a little past the horizon. The sky became a blend of various hazy reds, dark blues, and their mix of bleeding purple. Al-Jeheuty guided Mehit away from the district they journeyed through, their guards following close. "I have business—rather, politics—to attend to, *mora*." He turned toward her, ceased walking, and then said to his wife, "I'm working on bringing peace to al-Mari Ifriq." They continued walking, stopping at the entry of the palace courtyard.

Mehit gave al-Jeheuty a hug. She smiled, though not confidently. She was worried about her husband's emotional state as he tried to handle the extreme stress of politics and war. "Don't be too long, al-Jeheuty," she said.

"I won't, *mora*," he assured her. "I'm going to see al-Rinak and his troops as they leave for Djenhai."

"Why would they wait until nightfall to leave?" Mehit groaned. "It's dangerous, especially with the Ogunsanwo-Mashek wandering the pathway."

"They'll be safe," al-Jeheuty said. "The nation chooses to rest at night. They'd actually be in greater danger traveling in the daylight." He kissed his wife on the forehead and split the guards escorting the two of them. Two men escorted Mehit to the palace. Three guards stayed with al-Jeheuty. He walked away and made the long journey across the city, exiting through the new eastern gate, walking out into the empty Open Market.

The canopy was occupied by al-Rinak's troops, suiting up and preparing for their journey.

The unit's commander greeted al-Jeheuty as the Beylerbey approached with his entourage. His name was Sükh Koray. He was Turkish, mixed with Mongolian blood by way of his mother. He was two years older than al-Jeheuty, beige in color, with long, straight black hair that hung past his shoulders. Sükh was slightly taller than the Beylerbey, and he was equipped with sword and pistol. He stepped to al-Jeheuty with a pleasant smile and hailed, "Beylerbey Anhur Has." He bowed. "What may I do for you?"

Al-Jeheuty saluted the Turkish soldier and then surveyed the scene before answering. He looked at the commander and replied, "I come to see Statesman Ozan and Ambassador Zaher off. Governor Wakil is still recovering. He bids a safe travel."

"The night will conceal us," Sükh pledged. "We'll send a messenger back to note we have completed our journey. Of course, some of our soldiers will remain on duty in the city. Al-Rinak is giving their orders now. I do hope, Beylerbey, that should any trouble find its way to the city, our Turkish command will not be taken off guard."

Al-Jeheuty smiled at Commander Koray and extended solace. "We were all taken by surprise, Commander Koray. I have bared witness to your unit's training and practice sessions. You are impressive warriors. You should be very proud."

The Commander flashed a proud smile. He stepped closer to al-Jeheuty, close enough to make the Beylerbey's guards shift forward in case the Turkish Commander decided to strike the Beylerbey. "We will serve the city well. We will protect all of Odongo-Mauharim, while al-Mari Ifriq does not have the means to provide." The commander stepped back, his smile remaining. "I've heard about your skills with a sword, Beylerbey. I say without offense that perhaps one day we can put those skills to a test, a friendly test; a gentlemen's competition." His pompous smile melted into a chuckle.

Al-Jeheuty quipped with a stern, authoritative expression, "I can only guess at how marvelous a display it would be, considering how you're already *testing* my patience." The Beylerbey stepped to the commander. Sükh lost his smile. "Bring me Statesman Ozan and Ambassador Zaher."

Sükh bowed. "Yes, Beylerbey." He turned around and made his way under the canopy, returning quickly with al-Rinak and Taran. "The officials you requested, Beylerbey." Sükh bowed again and walked away from the group of officials.

Al-Rinak and Taran embraced al-Jeheuty, saluted, and greeted him under his new title as Beylerbey. "How long will you be gone?" al-Jeheuty asked.

"Just a week," al-Rinak answered. "We will return with word on how Djenhai's politics have been restructured."

Taran assured, "There will also be a discussion on engaging the Ogunsanwo-Mashek. Capturing them for European slavers, or a crushing war, are the only options we have."

"Both Dutch and French investors have split the bid," al-Rinak said in a delighted tone. "We will split the capture among them. We will generate substantial revenue from this venture. My Turkish backers will assist for a fee."

"And when I return," concluded Taran, "I will immediately attend to my new duties of expanding the city. Our population is booming."

Al-Rinak walked up to al-Jeheuty and placed his hands on the Beylerbey's shoulders. He said, feigning sincerity, "We'll deal with the citizens when I return. It's a shame they don't consider you the Beylerbey. They want a leader that looks hardened, like Behar. They want a leader that looks strong. They want a leader with experience, one that doesn't look weak, or scared—in comparison to Behar. You are not Behar, al-Jeheuty. You shouldn't have to be. We'll change all that. We will show the citizens your strength."

Al-Jeheuty simply bowed his neck, controlling the instinct to strike al-Rinak for his insolence. He bid the two officials safe travel and then walked with them to their caravan. The officials and their Turkish guard traveled south over the horizon. Al-Jeheuty watched the light and the Turkish convoy disappear. The Beylerbey returned to the palace and dismissed his guards. He entered his bedroom and changed for the night. He conversed pleasantly with Mehit, the two of them sitting at the writing table. He confessed to her that she was correct when telling him that he needed to engage the circumstances with a clear head, and he ultimately apologized for his behavior and choice of words. Mehit apologized for her temperament too. Al-Jeheuty accepted. She was still unaware about who specifically had to die because of the larger scale of politics. Taran.

A knock disturbed their conversation just as they were ready to retire. Al-Jeheuty said to Mehit to stay still. He did not like her quick, rushed movements while she was pregnant. Al-Jeheuty opened the door just enough to see the physician on the other side. His heart started to race as he thought of Wakil's health. The Moorish doctor reported, "Chief

Officer Ras Ali is doing very well. He would like to see you. I hope I am not disturbing anything. I know that you wanted all manner of updates. I didn't believe it was too late."

Al-Jeheuty smiled and waved the palace physician's concerns away. "It's fine," said the Beylerbey. "I will see him. Let me put my wife to bed." The doctor bowed at the neck. Al-Jeheuty closed the door and turned to Mehit. He walked to his wife and held out his hand. "I have more politics, *mora*. Come. To bed." He lifted her up and took her to the bed.

Mehit commented, "It's not as if I'm in the last days of pregnancy, al-Jeheuty. I can move around just fine on my own."

"I know," he said with a smile. "It's just in my nature to protect you." He then added, "Keep Aludra with you at all times when traveling at night, and when I'm not with you."

"I need her at the bathhouse most of the time," Mehit protested. "She's my best interpreter for my foreign patrons, and an amazing masseuse."

"*Mora.* She's your personal guard," the Beylerbey reminded. "Business can come later."

"Fine," Mehit yielded as she got into bed. Al-Jeheuty kissed his wife and then extinguished the lights in the room. He walked into the hall and journeyed with the doctor to the room where Ras Ali was recovering. The chief officer lay in bed, sitting up and waiting for the Beylerbey's arrival. His eyes widened when al-Jeheuty entered the room and he realized the Beylerbey was dressed in nightclothes. "My full apology for waking you, Beylerbey. I didn't mean to disturb you with my request."

Al-Jeheuty waved his hand and assured, "I had not yet turned in, Chief Officer. It's fine. I'm glad to hear that you're coming around. I don't know what was used against you, but you have a will made of sterner stuff."

"Thank you," Ras Ali said. "I have a private request." His eyes slowly floated toward the physician, then returned to al-Jeheuty.

Al-Jeheuty turned to the doctor and said, "Please, allow us some privacy, physician." The doctor exited the room. The Beylerbey looked at Ras Ali and asked, "What do you request from your Beylerbey?"

"I have been recovering well over the past days," Ras Ali notified. "I can walk again. I can move properly. I can keep my food and drink in my stomach. I don't feel so fatigued."

"Good," al-Jeheuty said with a smile.

Ras Ali continued, speaking in a quick manner. "I have been exercising my body, walking the halls as you have seen on occasion."

"Yes," al-Jeheuty acknowledged.

Ras Ali paused. He lifted his arm and said, "I have mostly been exercising bending my index finger." He executed the action and explained, "I want to know that I can…squeeze a trigger." Al-Jeheuty straightened as the Chief Officer continued. "I've also been practicing thrusts with my arm. Jabbing motions." He stabbed the air, as if bringing a knife down into someone's back. He stopped and took a breath. "Beylerbey, I request to be present in the meeting against these traitors."

"Your request is granted," said al-Jeheuty. "In fact, your presence is required. Captain Sunwil, Ambassador Nasir, and myself are meeting with these turncoat agents tomorrow afternoon. I was going to allow you rest and notify you in the morning. So, will you be ready?"

Ras Ali took another deep breath. "Yes. Thank you, Beylerbey. I never liked those two. Always sneaky. Cowardly opportunists." He cleared his throat. "That is all I have disturbed you for."

Al-Jeheuty saluted the chief officer, and Ras Ali saluted the Beylerbey in return. Al-Jeheuty returned to his room to rest for the night. He awoke to a new day. It was the first day marking his strike against al-Rinak and his conspirators. He primped and changed into his political suit and robes. He spoke to Mehit before she started her day at the bathhouse, and then he met Chief Officer Ras Ali in the room where he was recovering. The Beylerbey gave Ras Ali time to get together. He had servants bring in a meal so that the two could dine on breakfast. Ras Ali was grateful and honored. He commented, "I'm forty-two years old. I've never felt more like a kid."

The Beylerbey and chief officer talked briefly about the business ahead of them. The conversation then turned social. Al-Jeheuty was impressed with Ras Ali's vast knowledge of mythology and array of stories, fairytales, legends, and fables.

Captain Hieremias Sunwil, at that same moment, walked toward *The Siren's Call* with his boatswain and quartermaster. His boatswain walked on his right. Tobal Lessman was a short man with a muscular build, a bald, oval head, a spattering of facial hair that was beginning to grey, and brown skin. Quartermaster Yan Nuh walked on the captain's left. Yan Nuh was known as 'Blackey' for his deep, dark skin. He had wide, bulging eyes that made him look as if he was constantly nervous, or very alert. But he professed that he was a very calm and collected person, always believing that he could read people very well.

The captain caught up with the two crew-officials two days prior. He sent out a call for his crew to gather for an expedition. Most of his crew received the call, twenty of them gathering at his lodge. His crew-officials showed after Captain Sunwil turned the others away, telling them to find the rest of the crew, and spread the word they would be leaving in four days' time. He continued to direct crewmembers in this way even after the Boatswain and Quartermaster showed up.

Captain Sunwil greeted his crew-officials with relief and a wide smile. He set a meeting for today, where they now walked into *The Siren's Call*. The tavern was empty. Rahmis Husani was absent, leaving Captain Sunwil the keys on order of Beylerbey Anhur Has. Hieremias told his crew-officials, "Rahmis left me the key. I didn't want to hold this meeting at *The Palace*. People don't need to be in our business."

The place was clean, but prepared for their arrival. Stools and sitting cushions surrounded a bottle of wine that sat atop a low table. Captain Sunwil closed the door after his officials entered, commanding his men to have a seat. He did not lock the door. He turned around and joined the two men to share the bottle of wine.

"I thought Rahmis was going to open this place to serve morning meal," Tobal commented holding out his cup for wine.

Captain Sunwil poured wine for his boatswain. "He's made an investment in a café. I believe the woman he's courting works there. He's connected the investment to the Griffin Company."

Tobal scoffed. "Our officials are corrupt, possessing a company to filter all manner of coin from every business in the city."

"It all goes to building the city," Hieremias defended.

Yan rolled his eyes. "Be honest, Captain. The city officials' Griffin Company is an impediment for anyone looking to become a boss of a company. It's to scare off anyone with a real business plan to make money." He added sarcastically, "All well-earned coin to the heads." He rolled his eyes again. "It's a web. It's dishonest. The charity aspect of the company is a front. That's why I made a notion among the Council of Captains to demand less taxes."

Hieremias kept his anger down. He knocked back a hard swallow of wine. "Where is Ras Ali?" he asked.

Tobal and Yan said nothing. They exchanged quick looks to one another. Yan answered, "I haven't seen him since a day before the attack."

Hieremias cleared his throat. "I want to get as far from the city as possible. I have fought with Beylerbey Anhur Has to leave. He has not inquired too much about the use of our ship's guns used by the Ogunsanwo-Mashek." The captain sighed. "Ras Ali was sent to check on the ship. There was the attack. He has not returned."

"Do you think he's dead?" Tobal asked in a low voice.

"I suspect the Ogunsanwo-Mashek killed him while he was on inspection, but I have not found a body. That gives me some hope." He made a face. "What happened to the two of you that morning?"

There was another split second glance shared between Tobal and Yan. The captain pretended not to notice, again. Yan spoke, "We caroused hard at *The Palace* the previous night. The two of us were passed out. Maurice put us in the back. I suspect Ras Ali probably looked for us at our lodges. He probably didn't have the patience—you know him. He probably went ahead alone." Yan's tone sounded unconcerned for the missing chief officer. He added, "We should do a private investigation. Just to be sure. I'd just hate to count out a man as tough as Ras Ali."

"Of course," said Captain Sunwil quickly. "That's why I already started a private investigation. Despite our bumping of heads, I've been working close with Beylerbey Anhur Has and Ambassador Sa'ood."

The door opened.

Tobal and Yan looked over Captain Sunwil's shoulders.

Al-Jeheuty entered the tavern flanked by Ambassador Nasir Sa'ood and Chief Officer Ras Ali. Tobal and Yan's eyes went straight to Ras Ali. Both of them jumped up and ran toward one of the tavern's backrooms to find an exit. Tegu and Rahmis appeared from the tavern's kitchen. Rahmis reminded Tobal of how well trained a soldier he was by grabbing the fleeing boatswain, wrapping his arm around his back, and slamming his face into the wall. Tobal's nose crumbled inward, crushed. Blood spurt instantly, pumping like water through a spout. Rahmis shoved the boatswain in the direction of where he previously sat. Yan was more reserved. He stepped back, cautiously, keeping his eye on Tegu.

The two crew-officials returned to their seat.

Captain Sunwil removed a handkerchief and tossed it to Tobal. The boatswain accepted the piece of fabric and covered his bleeding nose. Al-Jeheuty ordered Rahmis to close the shutters and curtains. Tegu prepared a round table for the entire party gathered inside the tavern. The Beylerbey, ambassador, and chief officer took a seat at the prepared table. Tobal, Yan, and Captain Sunwil joined them.

"Hands flat on the table," al-Jeheuty instructed. Tobal put one hand flat on the table as commanded. His other hand continued to manage the handkerchief cupped over his broken and bleeding nose. Yan put both his hands on the table, flat. "Normally," al-Jeheuty began. "Normally you would've been brought to me. You would have been escorted to my court. My moves, however, must be careful, secretive, so as not to alert other conspirators behind this plot." He looked at Tobal and apologized for the violence aimed at him. "I intend to pardon both of you. I just want answers."

"We have little to offer, Beylerbey," said Yan.

"Little answers may lead to big things," al-Jeheuty said smiling. "Please, don't try to hide anything. Your haste to escape, when you sighted your fellow crew-official, has given me proof enough that you are the two that attempted to murder him by poison. So, don't insult my intelligence. Tell me all the little answers you can provide. I am aware of all manner of politics that are between Chief Officer Ras Ali and the two of you. Though you may not always see eye-to-eye, he does not owe you money. He has never offended your honor publicly. So, what were your motives for poisoning him?"

Yan started to tremble, his hands rattling on the table. He tried to suppress the quivers in his body, but they continued in small quakes at his forearm, and ultimately in his lower jaw. "We were on orders," Yan confessed.

"Yan!" Tobal hissed.

Al-Jeheuty raised a hand at the boatswain and said nonchalantly, "He's doing fine. Let him proceed." He turned to Yan and ordered, "Continue. Tell me whose orders you were following."

"Emissary Chaffee," Yan confessed further. "He answers to another Frenchman. Traont Coutelier, a man connected to many French nobles. He has the French Crown at his command. He is a very powerful and influential man in France. They want the Ogunsanwo-Mashek as slaves. They will stop at nothing. I'm afraid that warships will cinder the city if he doesn't receive them. He ensured a war by engineering the attack. Boatswain Lessman and myself were ordered to fire the cannons and create a distraction on threat of life. I was promised my own company, something I have longed for. Tobal was promised his own ship."

Al-Jeheuty contemplated Yan's story, sitting back in his chair. There was now a new conspirator. Emissary Chaffee. They had already guessed that he was a spy for another power in France, and the name Traont Coutelier had already surfaced. This was the man that took his brother to the Americas. Rene Chaffee disclosed that Traont Coutelier was the investor for the Ogunsanwo-Mashek as slaves. This must have been the reason Rene was anxious to leave the city that day, al-Jeheuty recalled. He knew the attack was coming.

The Beylerbey insisted coolly, "There are many problems with your story." Al-Jeheuty leaned forward again. He asked Captain Sunwil for a dagger, and when he was given the sharp instrument, he put its tip on Yan's right finger. "First, no European foreigner can offer you a company that only your Moorish leader can bestow and give permission for. That tells me, however, your as of yet unnamed malefactor has promised you this glory upon taking control of this city, which means all present officials are marked for death. Also, the French and the Dutch were supposedly bidding for the Ogunsanwo-Mashek. It had been decided between city officials and Djenhai royalty that a push to enslave the Ogunsanwo-Mashek was in order. The only thing we deliberated on further was whether we would take the entire nation, or just the militants within their nation that have declared war on us. These meetings were private. Emissary Chaffee was invited only to *one*. He was there to provide background information on Monsieur Coutelier, and then he was dismissed. This was days before the attack. The politics that you have fabricated could only have happened if there was an extreme worry on the part of the French that the Ogunsanwo-Mashek people would not be captured for enslavement. Emissary Chaffee would have no time to alert Monsieur Coutelier of any backpedaling on the decisions concluded among our city and the Djenhai nation, especially since I am fully aware that Monsieur Coutelier is at this time in the Americas, and has been on travel to the Americas since I was on holiday with my wife." Al-Jeheuty relaxed his voice. He handed the dagger back to Captain Sunwil and lay a gentle hand over Yan's. "I have no doubt these Frenchmen are instruments, links in a chain, and gears within a machine that have brought trouble to our shores. I would just like to know the hand behind these movements."

There was no answer from either crew-official. Yan even ceased to tremble.

Al-Jeheuty sighed. "That is your story then. Jail them. I will relay this information to Statesman Ozan when he returns from Djenhai. He will be most disappointed to know the predicament we are in with the French."

"No," screamed Yan. "No!"

No one moved.

Al-Jeheuty leaned toward him, his face close to Yan's. "Is there more?" Yan nodded his head, yes. Al-Jeheuty leaned back. "Please, validate my suspicions. Are you taking orders from Statesman Ozan? Is that what you fear? Do you fear him reaching through the bars of a cell and getting you?"

"Yan," screamed Tobal. "Say nothing."

Al-Jeheuty looked at Ras Ali and signaled with a nod.

Ras Ali stood from his chair, removed a small, one-shot pistol, and fired into the back of Boatswain Lessman's head. The bullet broke through the back of Tobal's skull, exploded out his broken nose, and lodged into Tobal's hand holding the handkerchief. The boatswain lay sprawled out on the table, as spattered as his blood and cranial flesh. Yan jumped. His body quaked with fear. His left leg became moist and warm with urine. No one touched the dead crew-official's body.

"I can protect you from Statesman Ozan," al-Jeheuty hissed. "I cannot protect you from your fellow crew-official or your captain. Speak!" Al-Jeheuty stood up. He paced around the table, his eyes focused on Yan. "This recent attack is connected to the first attack, is it not?" Yan answered, 'yes', in a trembling voice. "Taran was not aware that he was going to be hit that day, was he?" Yan answered affirmatively again, voice trembling. "It separates him from the attack. Plus, no mounted attacker had a tawny or white look. All were black. There was no Frenchman or Turk among them." Al-Jeheuty stopped. "We have record of Captain Fusan al-Hammon and Captain Piett leaving a week prior to both attacks, returning a week after the attacks. No other captains in our log follow this routine. Is this a coincidence?"

"No," Yan answered. "Fusan led the charge. He and his crew were disguised as Ogunsanwo-Mashek warriors. Statesman Ozan's army stripped tribal warriors of their garb on one occasion while protecting trade. Mistress Melusina fabricated more uniforms. Fusan and Captain Piett traveled to Tunis, docked, and Fusan and his crew attacked from the east under the guise of Ogunsanwo-Mashek warriors. This happened for both attacks. Captain Piett would leave Tunis and travel to Algiers, where Fusan and members of his disguised crew would flee. They would then return to port, appearing innocent of the deed. The second attack came to ensure a push for enslavement and war. Everyone is using everyone. The French. The Dutch. The Turks. Al-Rinak commands a great deal of influence in the Empire, he is at the head of this conspiracy. You can't fight back. You will be ripped apart by the French and the Turkish armies."

Al-Jeheuty stayed silent. He absorbed Yan's confession, solidifying a plan already formulated in a mental outline. He walked over to Yan, bent down, and whispered into his ear, "Where are those disguises, Yan? Give me that evidence and be rewarded for ending a complicated war."

Yan trembled. "I don't know," he said in a sincere voice. "Tobal and I, after rushing from the ship in our disguises, headed west and discarded them before returning to the city. They were burned. Perhaps Captain al-Hammon keeps the disguises in Tunis."

Al-Jeheuty shook his head. "I am an honest man. You will be protected from Statesman Ozan. You will leave tonight, escorted out to sea by your Captain and Chief Officer. You will go to Libya. There you will stay until the dust is settled. Is that understood?"

"Y-yes, Beylerbey," Yan expressed gratefully.

Al-Jeheuty stood up, he called for Captain Sunwil and Chief Officer Ras Ali. Tegu and Nasir kept a close eye on Yan while the Beylerbey conversed with the two gentlemen in a backroom. Al-Jeheuty addressed Ras Ali first. "I promised your former crew-official protection against Statesman Ozan. I also said I could not protect him from either of you. Do with him what you will when you disembark." He turned to Captain Sunwil. "Ojodo is waiting at the docks with two storage crates. Use them to dispose of the bodies. Go to Libya. Find Donatello Verola. He's working the first African leg of the narcotics trade. He is with Eibib Oba. Bring Verola here. When you return, I'll have another task for you."

"Yes, Beylerbey," said the captain. He informed al-Jeheuty, "I learned before you arrived that these are the men responsible for stirring up the Council of Captains."

"Then, on my orders, let him join his fellow traitor. Be on your way, Captain." The three men walked from the backroom, witnessing Rahmis and Tegu cleaning the area of Tobal's body, wrapping him up neatly in a ragged carpet. Yan stayed still, hands remaining on the table, laying flat. Al-Jeheuty walked over to Rahmis and asked, "You can straighten everything up here?"

"Yes," Rahmis said. "Tegu will help."

Al-Jeheuty leaned closer to his friend and lieutenant and said, "Don't speak a word of this to Maurice. Is that understood?" Rahmis nodded his head. "Stay close to your business. There's no need to watch them. We'll deal with Fusan and Piett when we know how to strike their bosses." Rahmis nodded again. Al-Jeheuty nodded in return. He called for Nasir. The ambassador stood up and joined the Beylerbey. "Good day, Yan 'Blackey' Nuh," al-Jeheuty said in a taunting manner.

Yan looked up. His face was still drenched with fear, but his words carried an air of confidence and warning. "He ordered the mark on Company Boss Iraj," he said. Al-Jeheuty and Nasir turned away from the door and looked at Yan. "Al-Rinak. It was a test. He wanted to see how Beylerbey Behar and the Griffin outfit would react. Rene fulfilled the mark. It was his blood oath to the statesman. Al-Rinak got exited when it looked as if a war would break out between you and the Italians."

Al-Jeheuty believed he could see a glimmer of a smile flicker across Yan's face. The Beylerbey simply replied, "Your leg is wet. Good day, Yan 'Blackey' Nuh." There was no reason to say more. The quartermaster would soon join the boatswain. Al-Jeheuty turned around and walked from the tavern with Nasir. They traveled to the palace, al-Jeheuty shaking hands and smiling at passing citizens that offered their pledge to him. Inside the grand structure, al-Jeheuty and Nasir secluded themselves inside al-Jeheuty's bedroom. Nasir took a seat at the writing table. Al-Jeheuty looked around the room for a pitcher of water. There was none. He asked Nasir, "Would you like some water? Let me call for water." He went into the hallway and asked a servant to bring a pitcher of water and two cups. He returned to his quarters, leaving the door open. He removed his robe and exhaled as took a seat across from Nasir.

A female servant brought in the pitcher of water and two cups, laid the objects on the table, poured both gentlemen a cup, and left the room, closing the door behind her. Nasir took his cup and started to drink.

"We are dealing with businessmen, not governments," said al-Jeheuty. "These businessmen have great influence in their governments, but they are *not* their government."

"Al-Rinak is a statesman. He has a significant voice in the Empire," Nasir reminded.

Al-Jeheuty crossed his legs. He contemplated the notion. "We'll deal with him." He smiled in a humble manner. "I'll seek Wakil and Roberto. I'll have them say a prayer. I hope they can translate my intentions into the languages of their pious ideologies."

"You've accomplished a lot, Beylerbey." He laughed in a low voice, "I hear that both their gods are betting on your next miracle."

Al-Jeheuty's eyebrows rose. "Let me then not disappoint the gods." He returned their discussion to business. "We'll handle al-Rinak, in time. It's Traont Coutelier that makes me nervous. The French have ravaged African shores before, al-Mari Ifriq spared, thankfully. The European is not bound by honor or rules when it comes to war. They attack on holy days. They attack children. Al-Rinak has a plan. He stays to it. People have been hurt. People have been killed. I'm sure we're marked." The sentiment made Nasir recollect being attacked. It made him uneasy to believe that the mounted man, robed, masked, and tossing knives into him, might have been the brother of a longtime friend. Al-Jeheuty's voice came back to him. "There has been no straying from the plan," he heard the Beylerbey speak. "The city has never been penetrated and scorched."

"Al-Mari Ifriq is al-Rinak's prize," stated Nasir. "It wouldn't be in his best interest to burn the city. The European objective is to stand proud on the ashes of the darker races. Let's take caution that he has European nations as partners. I'm sure they're lying in wait to enslave his black ass too."

Al-Jeheuty drank more from his cup. Looking away he said, "Lying indeed. Nothing but chaos will reign when every honorable black is dead. Nature might even turn Her back on us." He shook his philosophical thoughts away and returned to the matter at hand. "I can handle Chaffee. We have his substitute, Monsieur Leolin. He's a good man. He's just looking to do business." He placed his cup back on the table. "I'll have Roberto's soldiers shadow his every move, even after all this has been straightened out."

"You'll need Simon Beaumont's approval to carry out Rene's mark," Nasir reminded.

"I'll get it," said al-Jeheuty confidently.

Nasir asked, "How will you execute marks on two of al-Rinak's accomplices without rattling the statesmen and having the Empire on our shores?"

Al-Jeheuty lifted a single eyebrow. "He has his allies. I have mine."

Nasir finished his cup of water and then dismissed himself. He was late meeting Aludra for a tutoring session in the Euro-languages. He was hard at work preparing for his new role as Commissioner of Foreign Affairs. Al-Jeheuty sat in silence, pondering his situation. Mehit entered the room, interrupting his thoughts. Hours had passed. Time's passing alerted al-Jeheuty to the duties the day called for. He had to meet Jabari and Laith, and he had to speak with Wakil, checking on the governor's well-being. Al-Jeheuty moved from his chair to the bed, sitting. Mehit sat next to him. She could see the weight of the world slumping her husband's shoulders. She gently rubbed his cheek and asked, "What's wrong, al-Jeheuty?"

The Beylerbey did not answer his wife immediately. Mehit was patient. Al-Jeheuty wanted to confess that today was the first day in a long time that he watched a man die. He wanted to confess to her that today was a day filled with violent politics that he had not taken part in since the death of The Four Winds. The gunshot's noise still popped in his ear. He could still see Tobal's body driven forward by the impact. His memory recalled Rahmis grabbing Boatswain Lessman and slamming his face into the wall, hard enough to crumble the traitorous Moor's nose. Every ounce of nobility and gentlemanly quality that Rahmis put on display disappeared. The noblemoor became the revolutionary again, quickly, and in a shocking, violent display.

Mehit placed her head on her husband's shoulder and started rubbing his chest.

Al-Jeheuty finally spoke. "I started negotiations today, making a move toward peace." He felt the need to word his ordeal in a safe manner that kept his wife from being shaken by the truth. He recalled Donatello Verola's words about the Sicilian society he served in. He remembered the Sicilian telling him about the code of silence the society honored. Al-Jeheuty figured the Sicilian creed was most likely initiated to avert discovery. The Beylerbey decided to honor a code of silence to protect the ones he loved, but he understood that was not the right thing to do. His wife's words came back to him, *"You want people to understand but you're not willing to speak the truth."* She was, as usual, correct. There were just too many emotions covering al-Jeheuty to allow him to confess the situation's reality. "This is going to be hard, *mora*," he said to her.

Mehit sat up, taking her head from al-Jeheuty's shoulder, and her hand from his chest. She looked at him and said, "You are the bravest man I've ever met. You will endure, good Moor."

Al-Jeheuty smiled at his wife. He kissed her cheek. When he leaned away from her he noticed his wife's pregnant shape. Their child was making visible progress. He focused on the hump in Mehit's belly that hid the growing child inside her. The sight forced Al-Jeheuty to push aside his earlier concerns. He stood up, his face stern. "I'm sorry, Mehit. I have to go to work. I have to find Jabari and Laith al-Hakam."

Mehit followed him. "May I walk with you? I'm returning to the bathhouse."

Al-Jeheuty took Mehit's hand. "I would have it no other way, *mora*. Please, by all means, walk with me."

Chapter Thirty-Four

Three nights ago, Bo Yusuf arrived at the gates of the Djenhai kingdom under a clear, beautiful black sky that resonated shades of deep, cosmic blue rippled by the moon's shouts of quivering brilliance. A Sun and Moon from Roberto's clan flanked him. An initiating, male Star was riding drag. The sands gleamed white, sparkling like diamonds. The sandy dunes, brightened by the moon's rays, made the desert look like a terrestrial cloud.

Their camels approached the walled kingdom. Sixteen guards were gathered at the kingdom's gate. The guards recognized Bo Yusuf and saluted him on arrival. The Army Official asked for permission to enter. The gates were opened for the visiting Moorish Official and his guards.

Five of the exterior guards escorted Bo Yusuf through the kingdom. Mourning songs shined in the night, resonating through the city streets and corners. King Igdobe Djenhai was dead. The people lamented. Mohammedan prayers for the dead were sung as low, haunting dirges, and blended harmoniously with woeful, African burial hymns. Candles lit in the windows of religious temples and mosques, burned in honor of the dead King, and the noble company boss, Feroz Aunun.

The five guards presented Bo Yusuf and his company to the royal palace sentries stationed in front of the palace gates. One Djenhai sentry bowed toward Bo Yusuf. He turned and instructed another to inform the royal family that Lord Yusuf had arrived. The Army Official dismounted from his ride at the sight of a woman's shadow extending out from the palace's candlelit entrance. The Queen of the First World was attached to the shadow. Bo Yusuf slowed his steps, having expected Yaminah. "What're you doing here?" the Queen asked. Before Bo Yusuf could provide an answer she commanded the sentries, "See that his guards are taken care of. Guards, return to your post outside the city walls." She returned her gaze to Bo Yusuf waiting for his answer like a scolding mother.

Bo Yusuf hesitated. He looked at the Queen and offered an apology. "I'm sorry, Queen Halima." He bowed his head. "I was sent on command of Beylerbey Anhur Has. I hope I haven't disturbed your mourning ritual."

"No," the Queen smiled, thinking of Bo Yusuf's feelings. Her smile didn't last long. The Queen regretfully informed Bo Yusuf, "Yaminah is asleep. She's very tired. She hasn't had a good night's rest, and the morning will only bring more duties and meetings for her to attend—for us all to attend." King Kemnebi approached with an entourage of two servants and three guards. "We have guest suites already prepared," Halima continued. "We're expecting Statesman Ozan and Ambassador Zaher by week's end."

Kemnebi, already looking overwhelmed in his role as King, greeted Bo Yusuf. He approached the Army Official and greeted, "I've been briefed on your role, Unit General. I'm glad you've come. I know Yaminah will be excited when she finds out you're here—*after* the meeting, I'm afraid." Bo Yusuf complied, understanding the importance that Yaminah should not be distracted while in royal conference. The young King stated, "It's good that you've come. We would've sent word for you to join Statesman Ozan and Ambassador Zaher. Your presence will be needed in the talks concerning war on the Ogunsanwo-Mashek." Bo Yusuf again nodded in compliance.

Roberto's assassins were escorted away by several palace sentries. Bo Yusuf was led inside the grand, royal house, the interior of which glimmered with faint yellow-orange hues provided by flickering candle lights. Kemnebi and his entourage escorted Bo Yusuf to his guest suite. The Queen of the First World broke from the group after wishing Bo Yusuf and her son well. She then stowed away to her royal quarters for sleep. Servants lit Bo Yusuf's room, providing light. Bo Yusuf removed his sword and pistol, and the two weapons were confiscated from him. He still carried with him a dagger, hidden. He removed his bag, opened it, and pulled free his nightclothes.

Kemnebi said, "Here you'll stay, until called for. The royal council gathers in the morning. We'll call for you by the afternoon when it lets out. Food will be brought to you. A servant will be outside your door at all times to answer your requests." He dismissed his personal servants and closed the door. He addressed Bo Yusuf, his face stern. "I am King. I have found out very quickly that being crowned does not bring omniscience. I don't have all the answers, but I do have my sister and other advisors. Yaminah is completely shaken. Our father died in front of her—you were there. Seeing you will make her happy. A swift answer will also make her happy. Every single Ogunsanwo-Mashek is an enemy of this kingdom. I will do what must be done, without hesitation or mercy. We can then continue with business to form a solid state. You will not be a General in the Djenhai army, Bo Yusuf. You will be my sword. I ask you, only out of concern for my sister, to undertake the duty of washing these people from our world. That is my order. Whether right or wrong, as I am now King, my words and actions are law. You will abide by them, and you will respect them." He added with a sincere smile. "I can handle the citizens and the royal family, for that matter."

Bo Yusuf's acknowledgement was barely audible. "Yes, King Kemnebi."

The royal figure stepped away, bid Bo Yusuf a good night, and exited the guest suite. Bo Yusuf sighed, wondering how he could hunt down the devil that possessed al-Jeheuty to give him the order to sway an entire kingdom from the obvious objective of total revenge. He changed into nightclothes, put out the light, and retired to bed.

Bo Yusuf awoke at the hour of noon. He slept long, having been exhausted from his travels. He stood up from his bed, opened the door, and asked the servant waiting outside his room if he could be escorted to the baths. The servant obliged, waiting for Bo Yusuf to gather his day clothes. Afterward, Bo Yusuf was taken to a private spa, where he washed, dried, put on his clothes, and primped and polished his face and teeth. He tied his locks behind his head and was escorted back to his room by the same servant.

Bo Yusuf met Prince Asim Igdobe-Djenhai while returning to his room. The teenage Prince was delighted to see the Moorish Army Official. The Prince greeted Bo Yusuf with a firm handshake and an unsuspected happy smile. Prince Asim explained that keeping his spirits high would be what his father would want—demand even. "Kemnebi announced that you arrived last night. Yaminah was excited."

"So the royal council has let out?" Bo Yusuf asked.

"Yes. My sister is in her room right now. She's changing. Come." The Prince grabbed Bo Yusuf by the arm and dragged him from his intended destination, leading him through the hallways of the palace and to the closed door of Princess Yaminah's room. Prince Asim beamed a teasing smile at Bo Yusuf. "She's right through those doors," he said in a low, devious voice. He made a motion of drawing a sword and lunging forward. "I've been practicing, Bo Yusuf. You'll have to get through me."

Bo Yusuf smiled at the youth. He grabbed the Prince by the arm. He tangled Asim's limbs behind his back and said with a laugh, "You should not only practice swordplay with a real sword, but also fight with one."

The door to Yaminah's room opened. The Princess stood in the doorway. Bo Yusuf let Asim go, keeping his eyes on the beautiful young

Princess in front of him. Asim bowed playfully toward Bo Yusuf and Yaminah. Neither of them noticed the Prince's gesture. He then disappeared down the hall.

Yaminah looked tired, and she looked the way a woman in mourning for her father should look. The beauty that resonated from Yaminah's demeanor gleamed as bright as the sun spilling through the open window behind her. Bo Yusuf struggled against being consumed by Yaminah's sadness as her emotion presented itself in such a haunting, beautiful manner. He felt the urge to turn away from the overpowering sight. The Princess attempted a smile, but her lips quickly broke into trembling waves. Her eyes bubbled with tears that streaked down her face like watery snakes. Bo Yusuf approached the Princess. She stepped toward him. The two embraced one another. Bo Yusuf's hold tightened as Yaminah continued to cry. "They killed your father too," she sobbed. She backed away from Bo Yusuf and straightened herself, sniffing back her tears. She turned and walked back into her room. Bo Yusuf followed. "There will be swift action," she said with an icy, authoritative voice. "Statesman Ozan will have his slaves. I would prefer the slaves come from the scraps of our war against the Ogunsanwo-Mashek, but I know the Statesman would rather have minimal combat and maximum profit."

"I understand Djenhai's determination," Bo Yusuf said to the Princess. His words were spoken in a nonchalant manner, his tone seeming to separate the politics of al-Mari Ifriq and Djenhai's dire situations.

Yaminah faced Bo Yusuf. She was perplexed at the Army Official's choice of words and the tone in which they were spoken. "Are you saying that al-Mari Ifriq does not share the same determination? We have both lost kings, and a shared noble businessman."

Bo Yusuf chose his words carefully. "Al-Mari Ifriq shares Djenhai's determination. Beylerbey Anhur Has is hurt the situation has come to this, but he understands. There are some problems to our circumstances, however, your Highness."

"Speak," the Princess commanded forcefully.

Bo Yusuf kept his eyes on Yaminah as he moved to the open window. He answered her, not trying to focus on how al-Jeheuty would negotiate such a situation, but on how he understood where war with the Ogunsanwo-Mashek would lead. "We engaged the Ogunsanwo-Mashek, as I'm sure you are aware. We never found them."

Yaminah was confused. "In a meeting we were told that you spoke with their chief."

"We did," Bo Yusuf said. "But *they* found us. We were captured."

"I know. We were told," Yaminah clarified.

"As well, all engagements that have been between the Djenhai and the Ogunsanwo-Mashek have come through hijacked caravans, or the trade routes we've recently established. Through hundreds of years, they have made trouble with your kingdom. Djenhai has only defended itself with walls. There has been no real engagement between the two of you, just small, troublesome skirmishes."

"What are you trying to say, Bo Yusuf?" Yaminah asked in an impatient voice.

"I'm trying to give you a warning," he responded sharply. "You rule the kingdom within these walls. I help govern a city surrounded by a protective wall, rough terrain, mountains, and a sea. The desert is the home of the Ogunsanwo-Mashek. They will have the advantage, especially as a nomadic people. There will be no such thing as 'minimal contact'. Every engagement will ravage both sides, and possibly take mostly Djenhai and Turkish troops."

"We will be supplied weapons by French and Dutch companies," the Princess declared. "They may also provide troops to join in the hunt."

"A perfect opportunity for the European to scope the rest of Africa for profit," Bo Yusuf yelled back. "The Djenhai kingdom, al-Mari Ifriq—all of Odongo-Mauharim. They will not stop until every black has been shipped to the West. We should be cautious."

Yaminah asked in the same impatient voice, "What are you challenging me to do, Bo Yusuf? Should I call for peace after such a terrible act of assassination has been made upon this kingdom? The Djenhai's call for justice is not unreasonable."

Bo Yusuf shook his head. He approached the Princess and gently placed his hands on her shoulders. "Your call for justice is reasonable. It's understandable. I just want you to know there will be no *swift* action. This will be a long drawn out war. It may take years—this conflict, no different than the small attacks Djenhai and the Ogunsanwo-Mashek nation have made on one another. I also don't believe we should seek the help of Europeans. Make a notion in your next royal meeting, or if you like, I'll bring it up when al-Rinak arrives." He kissed Yaminah on the forehead. The Princess smiled.

Bo Yusuf had no other words for the Princess, save those that comforted her, and words that politely asked for a meal. He was starving. They left Yaminah's room, found a servant, and the Princess asked for a meal to be prepared. Bo Yusuf and Yaminah met with the rest of the royal family and ate an afternoon meal with them in company. The royal family was just as fiery as Yaminah when it came to war. Bo Yusuf addressed his same concerns and King Kemnebi took note of them. "That's why I'm glad you'll be a General in our army," said the King. "This conflict might not be over as swiftly as we would all like, but we'll have an advantage with the Turkish soldiers, and having you leading the charge."

Princess Yaminah's spirits remained bright for the rest of the day. Bo Yusuf stayed in her presence. The two of them toured the city, accompanied by a royal entourage. The sight calmed the citizens briefly of their mournful woes. The ride also provided an interlude to Yaminah and Bo Yusuf's worries. They waved to the crowd, the royal couple. The Princess' somber state returned when she left Bo Yusuf's company for the night. She continued mourning the loss of her father while in bed.

The next day presented the same routine. Bo Yusuf waited while Yaminah was secluded in meetings with her uncle, Munashe, Kemnebi, and Queens of the First and Second World. Bo Yusuf mostly entertained Yaminah's younger brother and sister, and he found himself doing nothing more than consoling the Princess when the two spent time together. Bo Yusuf started to believe that his journey to Djenhai would be fruitless. He offered no philosophical words on war, or warnings on al-Rinak's ability to manipulate the emotions running through the kingdom.

There wasn't much for al-Rinak to manipulate once he arrived.

Djenhai's royal council prepared for war.

Revenge.

Al-Rinak continued his push for enslavement. The Djenhai royal council agreed. Bo Yusuf was allowed access to the final meeting that called for war. There wasn't much revealed to him that he had not already ascertained from his conversations with Yaminah. He presented his notion of removing European, military involvement. "We'll take their weapons," proposed Bo Yusuf. "But we will not accept their soldiers."

Al-Rinak agreed without argument, and the royal council followed his lead. Munashe and newly crowned King Kemnebi made official Bo Yusuf's title and command. Afterwards, there was a public ceremony openly declaring war on the Ogunsanwo-Mashek, uniting the Djenhai people under the banner of war. The ceremony introduced Bo Yusuf as a Unit General and as Princess Yaminah's husband-to-be.

Bo Yusuf watched the citizens rally. They were excited and celebrating. Djenhai was on the brink of war, and war was welcomed with song, prayer, and dance. Bo Yusuf hoped that al-Jeheuty had a plan to sway African bloodshed, and keep Africans from selling other Africans to nations of enslavers.

Chapter Thirty-Five

Beylerbey Anhur Has, Nasir Sa'ood, and Rahmis Husani welcomed the Djenhai and Turkish army back to al-Mari Ifriq. There was still left an hour of sunlight. King Kemnebi, Princess Yaminah, and Munashe Igdobe-Djenhai accompanied the armies. Al-Jeheuty greeted the new King by offering his sincere condolences. The Beylerbey informed all the officials that Governor Wakil was still recovering, his sons standing in for their father's duties. Taran hurriedly made his way into the palace, wishing to see Wakil at his bedside. Al-Rinak and the Turkish soldiers made their way to the barracks without escort. Rahmis Husani pleasantly guided the royal family to their guest suites inside the palace. Bo Yusuf commanded the Djenhai soldiers to keep watch at al-Mari Ifriq's southern wall. He assigned shifts to his command, allowing the troops not on duty access to the palace barracks. "I would like to keep them separate from al-Rinak's troops," explained Bo Yusuf after assigning the first shift and while following al-Jeheuty and Nasir into the palace's rear entrance.

The men made their way into a second floor private chamber located at the front of the palace. The chamber was a small room that Nasir recognized was often used by his father and company partners. He smiled at the memories of being on the other side of the door leading to the balcony. He remembered playing with Mehit, Fusan and Maurice, and Laith in the courtyard below while their fathers governed business within this particular room. He made quick glances around the room as his nostalgia increased.

Al-Jeheuty sat with his back to the open door that led to the balcony. Bo Yusuf sat to the right of the Beylerbey. Nasir sat across from al-Jeheuty, lighting the room and closing the main door before taking his seat. He looked at al-Jeheuty, his eyes signaling for business to commence and for the Beylerbey to brief Bo Yusuf on recent politics.

Al-Jeheuty chuckled. "Oh," he said, responding to Nasir's ocular communication. "So you lead this operation now?" Nasir returned a laugh. Bo Yusuf looked at them confused. Al-Jeheuty explained, "He's working on his signaling skills. It's been what, two, three years, and you're still obvious." He looked to Bo Yusuf and said, "I've been given strict orders to inform you about recent developments." The Beylerbey then became serious. He described to Bo Yusuf, "We were able to extract information pertaining to a grand conspiracy. Al-Rinak has been the guiding hand behind all of our troubles. His accomplices range from Business Emissary Rene Chaffee, Captains Kyler Piett and Fusan al-Hammon, Taran Zaher—which we have already suspected—and Boatswain Tobal Lessman and Quartermaster Yan Nuh, crewmembers employed by Captain Sunwil."

"Yan and Tobal were investigated," Nasir clarified. "Both have been eliminated. The two of them confessed to firing the cannons from Captain Sunwil's ship, creating the distraction at the Open Market. Fusan and his crew, disguised as Ogunsanwo-Mashek warriors, attacked the market. Captain Sunwil and Chief Officer Ras Ali are cooperating thoroughly. This group of conspirators was also responsible for the first attack."

Bo Yusuf's heart raced. He suppressed a smile, but he articulated his joy by blurting, "This war can be averted?"

"There are complications," said al-Jeheuty. "Rene Chaffee is connected to a man named Traont Coutelier. From what we've gathered, Coutelier is a sonava bitch. He would love to see the coasts razed and every black that remains in Africa-north enslaved. He supposedly has great influence on the French nobility. If he points, ships will sail."

"A bluff," Bo Yusuf remarked with heavy disbelief.

"That might be true," retorted al-Jeheuty coolly. "We can't take chances, though. For now, I'm seeking approval to mark and execute Rene Chaffee. Simon Beaumont will be here within a week or two. I'm also plotting a tedious scheme to cover our tracks for Traont Coutelier's mark and execution. Our greatest problem, however, is al-Rinak, his influence within the Empire, and the fact that he commands a group of two-hundred soldiers stationed within our city."

"We also can't pick off his accomplices while he watches everything," Nasir added. "I don't believe Tobal Lessman or Yan Nuh will be missed. We can always make al-Rinak believe they're off on an expedition with Captain Sunwil, and more so, they have accomplished their tasks for him. It's his other accomplices that we have to worry about."

"And this war," Bo Yusuf said. "Djenhai has agreed to Ogunsanwo-Mashek enslavement, and the people are hell bent on war. They can't be blamed. They've lost a good king. I don't think King Kemnebi would listen to our conspiracy theories. He believes it is time to end Djenhai's confrontations with a great war."

"And Princess Yaminah…?" al-Jeheuty inquired.

Bo Yusuf sat back. He rubbed his chin, contemplated, and then answered in a sad tone, "I don't know. I don't think so. She's doing what she, of course, believes is correct. Al-Rinak didn't have to say much to manipulate the Djenhai royal family. He's done enough." He put his hand on his chest and said, "I am a General in the Djenhai army, but I don't want war, and I am against slavery—especially enslaving someone that looks like me."

"Don't worry, Bo Yusuf," said al-Jeheuty. "There will be no war. I've already sent word to Chief Mazigh to leave Odongo-Mauharim. They hide just within Tunisia, close to the Atlas Mountains. They've left behind skeletal remains of campsites. You will lead the armies to each of them. I'll give you their locations. The remains follow the path of our expedition to find the Ogunsanwo-Mashek. Just say, *'This is where we were captured;' 'This is where we were taken;'* and *'This is a site we were given the location to.'* That should route any suspicion that you're leading the armies to dead locations."

"I've already warned Yaminah that this will be a long campaign," informed Bo Yusuf. "I've spoken to the entire royal family about how the land is the home of the Ogunsanwo-Mashek. They'll understand, but the charade can't go on forever."

"I know. I have plans." Al-Jeheuty exhaled. He looked to each man and said, "Behar was a great man. He was an excellent Beylerbey. He was my second father, and I loved him so. I understand his fears about bringing war to the city. Nasir, you've told me many times your father worried about the same thing. My father advised me the same. I'll let you know now that we don't have to kill everyone. We just have to kill the right people." He looked at Bo Yusuf and told his brother-in-arms, "This won't look like the battles we fought in Spain. This will be like those small hit-and-run maneuvers. You're still on orders to keep the Princess safe."

"Those are orders I can handle," the General spoke casually.

Al-Jeheuty dismissed the meeting. The men gathered later for a relaxing night of meal and drink at *The Siren's Call.* Ojodo Yerodin, Hesam Gandarewa, Princess Yaminah, King Kemnebi, and Mehit were present for the private party at Rahmis' tavern. Mehit did not stay long, eating her meal and drinking nothing stronger than water. Al-Jeheuty courted her back to the palace. Princess Yaminah and King Kemnebi decided to turn in as well. Both royals wanted to be well rested. The next day marked an important conference that called for war against the Ogunsanwo-Mashek. With the Princess gone, Bo Yusuf decided to retire. He felt uncomfortable to be around Rahmis. The noblemoor's subtle, scathing comments were increasing, though he acted very gentlemanly in the presence of Princess

Yaminah. The rest retired to *The al-Hammon Palace*. Rahmis closed *The Siren's Call* for the night.

While at *The Palace*, Nasir kept a straight face in Fusan's presence, but his mind and heart raced every time he engaged the Moorish corsair. Kyler Piett or al-Rinak's presence didn't bother the ambassador as much. Their behavior was always considered dubious. Nasir was saddened by Fusan's actions of siding with al-Rinak's plans. He defended Fusan against accusations of diabolical behaviors at sea. Fusan's behavior was harder to ignore in recent years, especially when he had to be subdued under Behar's law. Fusan's exploits at sea were tame ever since his conflict with Behar, which made Nasir wonder if Behar's course of chastisement pushed Fusan to join with al-Rinak's plot against the former Beylerbey. Behar was tough in refining both Fusan and Maurice. The two men had not been chastised as hard since their father was alive. Taran was more a babysitter than a second father to them. They did love him, though. But Taran never made an effort to curb their behavior. Maurice's actions calmed when he invested in *The al-Hammon Palace* while Fusan became wilder as a captain of a ship. In recent years even Maurice had become bitter, and extremely distant from Nasir.

Nasir wondered what course Maurice would take when Fusan was exposed. He hoped his childhood friend would open up and relieve himself of the demons that plagued him. Nasir started to feel more uncomfortable as the night progressed. Fusan began to joke about the wounds Nasir received in the first attack, but complimented him on being such a strong man.

"You're too stubborn to die," Fusan expressed while laughing. Nasir excused himself from the party a little while after. He didn't want to seem rattled by the comment. He made his exit with the excuse of being tired and having to attend the conference in the morning.

But the morning conference was not as strenuous as some of the participants believed. The proceedings were held in the council house, and within the first hour everyone agreed on the war with the Ogunsanwo-Mashek, how it would proceed, and its profitable outcome involving slavery. King Kemnebi, Sükh Koray, Bo Yusuf, and Beylerbey al-Jeheuty plotted the course of the war. Nasir added his approval or disapproval with strategies. He would say, "I'm not a commander of a militia, but I would like to have as minimal casualties to our armies as possible."

Al-Jeheuty and Bo Yusuf kept a straight face as Nasir played his part. Al-Rinak remained surprisingly quiet, Commander Koray doing most of the speaking. Princess Yaminah asked for permission to be dismissed, and al-Jeheuty granted the royal ambassador leave. Her personal guards and servants surrounded her and escorted her from the council house, to the city gates, and back to her suite inside the palace.

A young messenger arrived not too long after the Princess' departure. Beylerbey Anhur Has was summoned to the docks, called for by Zakiy Sa'ood. "What does the company boss call me for?" al-Jeheuty asked the Moorish, teenage messenger.

"Captain Hieremias Sunwil's ship has docked," the boy informed. "The Sicilian Donatello Verola is with him. There seems to be urgent news."

Al-Jeheuty continued to keep a straight face, though an anxious feeling swirled inside him. He excused himself stating, "Let me take leave. The war is now in the hands of the Generals and the King. Nasir, keep me informed." Nasir agreed. Al-Jeheuty left with the young messenger, thanking him. He walked from the council house and toward the Sa'ood company house. He dropped three coins into the messenger's hands.

The boy smiled and said, "Thank you, Beylerbey."

Al-Jeheuty dismissed the messenger back to Zakiy's command when they arrived at the company house. He walked into the facility and was greeted by Captain Sunwil and Chief Officer Ras Ali. Donatello Verola stood behind them. "Remain here," al-Jeheuty commanded the two men. "I'll need to speak with the two of you after I meet privately with Signore Verola." He stepped away from the two privateers and, with a wide smile, welcomed Donatello back to al-Mari Ifriq. The Sicilian offered his sympathies for the loss of Behar. Al-Jeheuty thanked him for the sincere gesture. They made their way to the third floor, holding council in one of the upstairs rooms. He asked kindly for Donatello to sit, and he joined the Sicilian at the table. He spoke in Donatello's dialect. "Did Baron Agusto's nephew suspect anything when I pulled you away from your duties in Libya?"

"No," the Sicilian answered. "He figured this was business pertaining to you as the new Beylerbey."

Al-Jeheuty nodded his head. "I believe it's time for us to barter with favors, Donatello Verola. You want the Moors to carry out a mark on Baron Agusto Ghislanzoni, correct? The mark still stands?"

"Yes," Donatello confirmed.

"I have a similar favor to ask of you, Donatello Verola," informed the Beylerbey. "I have marked a Frenchman. His name is Traont Coutelier. I don't wish to have the Moors involved with his execution—not directly. I have carefully planned his eternal rest to coincide with the death of Baron

Agusto Ghislanzoni. Our troubles with these two men will be solved—should you agree."

Donatello did not hesitate. "I agree to these terms." His smile was unmistakable, though he tried to keep it hidden. He could not. "I suspected this might be the reason I was brought here. I also suspect that you have a plan."

Al-Jeheuty did not hesitate. "I will send you back to Sicily with my Commissioner of Foreign Affairs," he told Donatello. "Nasir Sa'ood. You've met him on occasion. The two of you will deliver a message to Baron Agusto. Tell him that al-Mari Ifriq is in need of greater revenue because we are at war with a local nation. In order to raise finances for this war, we will have to take more from the trade that our governments share."

Donatello did not understand how this would lead to Baron Agusto's assassination. A request of such nature would only anger the baron. Donatello wondered if al-Jeheuty was looking for a full-blown war with the baron. Donatello did not agree. He wanted things quiet. "I don't believe he'll agree with that," said the Sicilian.

Al-Jeheuty made a face. "Perhaps not. Regardless, that is the message you will give him. In compensation, I will offer him two hundred black slaves. I will give the baron one hundred and fifty men, twenty-five women, and twenty-five children. He can use them for free labor, or he may begin to invest in the slave trade and make a fair coin." Donatello became more perplexed. "I will then offer two hundred more slaves, split into the same categories. His revenue will be more than recouped. The first two hundred slaves will accompany you and my Commissioner of Foreign Affairs."

Donatello lost focus on Baron Ghislanzoni's mark. The expression on his face mixed perplexity with abhorrence for what the Beylerbey was calling for. "Beylerbey…"

Al-Jeheuty waved his hand downward, as if shooing Donatello's worries away. "I say again, you will be accompanied by these slaves. One hundred and fifty will be strong men." He explained, "Soldiers disguised as servants." He grinned. "What better way, Signore Verola, for me to place an army inside the baron's court? A rebellious bunch, these slaves will be."

A faint smile came to the Sicilian's face, but there was something that kept him from reveling in the Beylerbey's plans. "There will be casualties, al-Jeheuty."

The Beylerbey sighed. "These men are prepared for it. I have spoken to them. We took in a nomadic warrior class years ago. They are called the al-Jasi Nzambi. Their chief and I have plotted this for the past week. It took time to tame these warriors, adjust them to city life, the males among them. Behar was nervous when he finally allowed them employment as the city's watch and police. That job has not sufficed the warrior in them. They have begged to be a part of the official army. This will be their first mission. Trained assassins, from another source, will be among the women. The children, and the untrained women, will need to be tightly guarded. Have them escorted to safety. A woman named Aludra will lead that march. Is that understood?"

Donatello nodded his head. "What about this Traont Coutelier?"

"Yes. Him," al-Jeheuty answered in a contemplative voice. "He's a slaver. Tell the baron about him. Traont will invest good money in the slaves. Monsieur Coutelier is either returning from the Americas, or he is preparing for his return. Let there be a letter sent to him. Ask for his presence. Let him arrive *after* the insurrection. However, let the insurrection be blamed for his death. Everything must be timed precisely."

"When should we begin these plans, Beylerbey Anhur Has?"

"Two weeks," al-Jeheuty answered. "Send word to Baron Agusto. Tell him there are matters we wish to discuss. Let this letter be sent three days before your arrival. Tell him you are on your way. That will quell his urge to seek us out in our court."

Al-Jeheuty dismissed Donatello, thanking him for their partnership. The two men shook hands firmly. It was their word that was now their bond. Al-Jeheuty ordered Donatello to tell Captain Sunwil and Chief Officer Ras Ali that he requested their presence. Donatello bowed toward the Beylerbey and left the room. The captain and his chief officer walked into the room minutes after. Al-Jeheuty welcomed the two men to take a seat. They joined him at the table. "Is the traitor dead?" the Beylerbey asked of Yan Nuh's fate. Hieremias confirmed his former Quartermaster's death. Al-Jeheuty didn't need to hear the details. He spoke more on his plans to take out the rest of the conspirators. "French trade ships will arrive in our port. They need escorting to Cyprus. I want you to hold the ships hostage. There are more trade ships heading to Sale, which also need escorting to the Caribbean. I have sent a message to our contacts in Sale to hold those ships. This will raise Simon Beaumont's eye, but keep Rene's eye level. Simon will seek us out in person to have an answer."

"I don't mean to offend you, Beylerbey," said Captain Sunwil in a concerned voice. "But he may send a messenger."

Al-Jeheuty replied, "Simon Beaumont is a businessman. I'm sure Rene is making minimal contact with him. Simon will be confused when Rene can't be found to return to al-Mari Ifriq, but he'll brush that aside.

Even if Simon sends another man as messenger, he will request to see me in person. I doubt he'll do such a thing. He knows the troubles we've had recently. We've received a condolence letter from him. Simon will come here, ahead of his usual schedule."

"Even at the risk of his life?" Ras Ali questioned. "If there is war within Odongo-Mauharim—"

"He will come," al-Jeheuty said assertively. "My objective is not to raise suspicions between Rene or al-Rinak. Both will believe al-Mari Ifriq's new war is affecting business. Al-Rinak will believe that losing Behar and entering this war has me rattled. He will believe every minute of every trouble that rises." He paused for affect, and then asked, "Are my orders understood?" The two men humbly nodded their heads and said 'yes'. "Good. That is all. Return to your command ship and await further orders."

The two men stood up, bowed their heads again, and then turned to leave the Beylerbey. Captain Sunwil stopped before exiting the door. He turned around and said, "We believe your strategy, Beylerbey. We just want to make sure every detail is covered."

"Thank you, Captain Sunwil," said al-Jeheuty. "Your words and strategies are appreciated."

There was another bow made by the captain and then he exited the room. Al-Jeheuty pondered his recent schemes. His ego was not invested in his plans, but there was no time for change. He didn't worry long before getting up and leaving the company house. He escorted Donatello Verola to *The Royal Highness*, where a room was prepared for the Sicilian's stay. Guards and servants were appointed to him, but Donatello decided to do some things himself. He didn't call for the servants to bring him a meal. Instead, Donatello ventured out to *The Siren's Call*, getting a breath of fresh air in the open space. He returned to his room at the inn to practice the words he would use against the baron.

Al-Jeheuty assisted Jabari and other judges in court cases for the remainder of the day. He made a visit to Wakil's quarters. The governor was doing well as he recouped in bed. He still had some trouble with a heavy cough, though his coughing was not as frequent. Al-Jeheuty didn't stay long, only confiding in the elder his plans to take out al-Rinak and the statesman's conspirators. He had already sought out the governor's blessing days ago.

"Putting al-Rinak down will give us the ability to make al-Mari Ifriq completely independent of the Ottoman's Empire," said Wakil. "We would no longer be under their shadow." The governor smiled. He took al-Jeheuty's hand and said, "Continue with your miracles." His laughter erupted into a set of heavy coughs. "Still the damn smoke. I told Behar to never let that mess in our city," he joked. "I'll be back on my feet by the time you leave. The physician and a servant are helping me exercise. I'm moving well. I'm not getting winded. I'll start to make more public appearances."

Al-Jeheuty made a face and said, "I bet you'll feel a little off every day court is in session."

Wakil chuckled. His wife escorted Roberto into the room. Al-Jeheuty stepped away from the bed. He bowed to both elders, joked for them to say a prayer for his plans, and then left the room. Roberto and Wakil shook hands. "The last of the *Alliance*," said Roberto smiling.

"Taran," Wakil corrected.

"He'll be dead soon," Roberto noted. "Finally. What did that bastard have to say to you last night? He visited, didn't he?"

"Yes," said Wakil adjusting himself, sitting up in bed. "Let's just say, I threw away the wine he brought me." He started to laugh again. There was another round of coughing. "It's not as bad as it was," he told Roberto about his cough. To change the subject he said, "Al-Jeheuty and Nasir are bold. They're bolder than Behar or Sa'ad. They're cunning."

Roberto huffed, "Shit. It's a different time. It's not about a straight fight. It's not about making a point by killing a man. It's about making bold moves. I'm surprised you're so calm in their decision to approach this fight the way they are."

"They're lucky I swallowed a lot of smoke. I've been slowed down." He laughed for only a second, trying to keep his cough under control. He did so by stating, "I want to be there when Taran dies. He's the luckiest man I've *ever* known. I want to see his luck run out." He cleared his throat. "I haven't kept to my faith as tightly as I'd like. Not in these recent years. I've engaged in wine. I've allowed smoke to be legal on the streets. I have continued to be unsuccessful in telling Nasir about his father's actions against Maurice and Fusan's father."

"Why don't you let me handle that?" Roberto asked.

Wakil shook his head. "No. It should come from me. You'll make it sound nonchalant. You'll make it seem like it was business. You'll disregard every aspect of pain it put his father through. I don't want Sa'ad to seem cold."

Roberto smacked his lips. "The boy will understand, Wakil. Maurice and Fusan's father was a traitor."

"Those are his friends," the governor protested. "Nasir will be shaken."

"You don't know that," Roberto insisted. "He'd understand those boys' behavior toward him, toward life. Nasir is emotionally stronger than you give him credit for. He'll know that Taran has used this information to turn Maurice and Fusan into the monsters they are—believe that bastard passed on this information to his best advantage."

"Maurice doesn't act out like Fusan does," Wakil voiced.

"He internalizes it," Roberto explained. "He's more like his father. He's sneaky. I don't doubt that he too is a part of al-Rinak and Taran's conspiracy."

Wakil took a break and relaxed. He said, "Nasir will face them like his father faced Rashaad. He will kill both of them. He will want to handle the feat alone. He will talk to al-Jeheuty, Bo Yusuf, and you just as his father talked to us and swayed us to let him execute Rashaad."

"It will then be over," Roberto said coolly. "Neither Fusan nor Maurice have children to carry the burden of their passing."

"Nasir will pass his burden to his children," Wakil hissed.

"Stop being so dramatic, Governor," Roberto argued playfully. "I beg you."

Wakil rolled his eyes and waved his hand. "You make death sound so simple."

"That's because I study all aspects of life and the life beyond," Roberto clarified. "That's the difference between these contagious faiths everyone seems to cling to, and the understandings that I studied—that *we* Africans studied long ago. I know the whole to the small parts religion has taken from. Everything was already plotted out. These religions have just added confusion to the shit we already figured out."

Wakil chuckled. "All my life I've seen you take orders to mark and execute men."

"And you've said a prayer to your faith every time. You have nothing to worry about, Mohammedan. You are alright in God's eyes." He smiled slyly. "We're all going to look Taran in the eyes, you, God, Goddess, and I."

"I wonder where he'll go after he closes his eyes," the governor pondered.

"Shit," Roberto cursed. "The Devil will look at Taran when he arrives in Hell, he'll hand him a shovel and say, *'Go make a Hell of your own'.*" The two men laughed, Wakil successful in keeping his cough from rising through his laughter.

"I'm also worried about al-Jeheuty," said Wakil. "He's holding up."

"He'll buckle with emotion when all of this is over," Roberto remarked. "If not then, when he holds his child in his arms. He'll get it out. But don't worry about al-Jeheuty. He has a strong company behind him. I'm not worried. The Alliance was made of businessmen forced to be gangsters. These boys are corsair-governors. They'll do just fine with every aspect of this business and forms of politics."

Wakil and Roberto reminisced for another hour. They traded philosophies and traced spiritual concepts to ancient ways in Africa. More so, they traded verbal jabs and jokes. Eshal, Wakil's wife, requested time with her husband as she entered the room and interrupted the conversation between her husband and the assassin. Wakil made no protest. Roberto gave Wakil's wife a gentleman's kiss, to which Wakil tossed one of his pillows at the assassin and screamed, "By law, I'll have your head for cavorting with my wife."

Roberto caught the pillow and lobbed it back at the governor. "No law will ever catch me, save the Law of Death, and I'm waiting to have intercourse between that curvaceous, dark whore and my mistress." He departed with a sincere Mohammedan prayer. Wakil grabbed his wife's arm and pulled her into the bed. There was a sudden strength inside him. Their two sons, Laith and Jabari, interrupted them.

"We won't be long," said Laith. "I'm just bringing word that Zoeya and Mayeeda will be visiting with their families within the next couple of weeks." Wakil and Eshal were instantly excited by the news of their two daughters coming to visit. "I received a letter an hour before we held court."

Jabari stepped back toward the door, grabbing his brother by the collar. "And now we'll leave the two of you to…whatever an old couple does when their grown children aren't around." He started to laugh.

"It's the same thing you do with those tavern girls," Wakil shouted teasingly as his sons exited the room and shut the door. He looked at his wife. "He calls himself a just judge. He needs to find a good wife. He's twenty-three."

"Arrange his marriage, then," Eshal said aiming her husband's gaze toward her. "You know he fancies that shopkeeper's daughter. She's sweet. What's her name? Sahar? Jabari is so shy in front of her." She had to keep from laughing. "It's cute to see Jabari around her."

"All that cool he has when he's hanging around those taverns is totally gone." Wakil smiled. "All that authority he carries in his voice while in court, quelled. It is a bit sweet, God forgive my insult to my boy's manhood."

"Until then, don't worry about him," Eshal said with a flirtatious gleam in her eyes. "You have this old tavern girl to woo and kiss."

"Woman," Wakil barked playfully. "You'll take what little breath I have left." He kissed his wife, pulled away from her and smiled. "What a way to die."

Chapter Thirty-Six

Three days later. Early morning. Ojodo Yerodin walked into the council house, ducking under the archway and squeezing his massive frame through the entry. Al-Jeheuty and Nasir were in the middle of discussing, with Statesman Ozan, the army's first campaign against the Ogunsanwo-Mashek. Bo Yusuf and Sükh Koray had already departed al-Mari Ifriq, leaving the city an hour after dawn. All three men turned and spotted the Moorish titan make his entrance. Al-Jeheuty smiled at the sight of his friend. He turned to Nasir and said, "Ambassador Sa'ood, escort Statesman Ozan to his residence so that he may prepare to make his leave." He turned to al-Rinak and asked, "You're following the King back to Djenhai, yes?"

"No," the black Turk answered. "Only the King is heading back to Djenhai. Yaminah is staying behind to help me run the Ghanem Company. We're seeing the King off, however. Troops from each unit have stayed behind to escort them." All three men made their way to the door, Ojodo moving from their path. "I still don't agree with pulling Taran from his duties just to concentrate on expanding the city. I say this with no intended offense to you, Ambassador Sa'ood."

"Taran will continue his duties," stated the Beylerbey. "I'm just protecting him from any harm should the Ogunsanwo-Mashek make another bold attack on our Open Market. I've made a promise to Mehit to keep her father safe."

"How has the bazaar been operating," asked al-Rinak.

"The attack has not deterred traveling merchants," al-Jeheuty said with a proud smile. "There is still great activity. Have you kept in contact with the French and Dutch investors?"

"They're united in their bid," al-Rinak reminded. "They're looking to make their investment in two months. I received a letter from Rene Chaffee."

"Yes, I heard," said al-Jeheuty as the men stepped outside into the bright day. "Monsieur Leolin notified me that a letter came by sea. I was meaning to speak to you about its arrival."

"Traont Coutelier and your brother have yet to return from the Americas," al-Rinak informed. "Rene believes that Traont will be offended by the lack of French troops used. The African slave trade is a quick process. In. Out. They are not empathetic that our trade with them will be the end result of a war. They've dealt with African states at war with one another. They're used to participating to make sure their profit is grabbed quickly. That was supposed to be the advantage of working with your brother." Al-Rinak paused to inspect his words' affect on al-Jeheuty.

Al-Jeheuty decided to show emotion, instead of keeping a straight face. The Beylerbey grimaced. "Yes. I know. I guess he's gone back to his old ways." He sounded disappointed.

Al-Rinak spoke in a consoling voice. "It's for the better, Beylerbey. The end justifies our means. Much like the reason you are dealing with the Italians, handing them servants in exchange for a greater share of revenue from the shared trade." He addressed Nasir. "Come, Ambassador Sa'ood. Let us seek out the King and his royal entourage."

Nasir's stomach tightened with al-Rinak's sudden transition to hold an authority over both he and the Beylerbey, but the ambassador didn't let his feelings show. He followed al-Rinak after bowing toward al-Jeheuty to show the Beylerbey his respect. Al-Rinak mimicked the gesture and he and Nasir walked away. Al-Jeheuty returned to the council house. Ojodo waited patiently inside, sitting down and indulging in a cup of water and picking from a tray of freshly prepared treats. The Beylerbey joined his friend. He refrained from picking at the treats and simply prepared a cup of water.

Al-Jeheuty stared inside his cup for a while, trying to gather the correct words to approach Ojodo. He then decided to speak firmly about seeking an audience with the Moorish giant. "I wanted to speak with you about your leave. Behar informed me, before he was killed, that you asked for a leave to go east and study. You want to improve your writing." He looked up from his cup and said, "I'm granting you that leave."

Ojodo bowed his head. "Thank you, Beylerbey." He stood up, towering over al-Jeheuty. "I humbly decline."

Al-Jeheuty jumped to his feet and looked up at his brother-in-arms. "Ojodo…"

"I have a request for you, *Beylerbey*." The titan spoke al-Jeheuty's title teasingly, but meant no disrespect. His voice turned sincere as he spoke. "I can't abandon my brothers-in-arms at this time. Not within this atmosphere. That is why I request joining Ambassador Nasir on his journey to Sicily."

"Absolutely not," al-Jeheuty said in a firm, quick voice.

"Then arrest me when I return," Ojodo retorted with an angry snarl.

Al-Jeheuty's face contorted when he asked, "Do you understand what Nasir travels to Sicily for?"

"Yes," Ojodo answered. "I stumbled upon him speaking with two al-Jasi men a week ago." He said sharply, "Answer me this. How is their engagement any different than some of our exploits in Spain?"

Al-Jeheuty did not answer his friend. He argued, "The baron has seen you before. He'd remember you."

"He's seen me at your command," Ojodo argued. "He's seen me work the docks. To him, I'm a slave. It would play into your plan. The baron will think you a desperate leader. It would lower his guard and validate this move of yours."

Al-Jeheuty suddenly looked sad. "Ojodo, there will be casualties. The Griffins have lost Behar. We can't stand to lose another. We can't lose a brother. It's bad enough I'm sending Nasir in there. He is a Griffin now too."

Ojodo shook his head. He turned away, hoping his movement would throw off the angry emotion that covered him, but it did not. He said in his thunderous voice, "England's King argued with the Church, which brought great upheaval to Christianity. All manner of the religion was questioned over a King's decision regarding his marriage. The English King fought the Church on all of the Church's stances. His nation, however, saluted and bowed to the Church's decision calling for every black to be dragged into servitude within the European states, the Great Isles, and all the way to the Americas. His daughter, The Virgin Queen, was a whore for the trade of black flesh as slaves. No black would reside in her court, save the darkest of the dark, plucked from Africa's belly to perform as jesters. The whites have turned the title of *Neggur* into a slur, and bestowed the title of Moor to a tawnier race. The dominant religions have been re-written to help break the people of Africa, justified by a Curse of Ham and Canaan." He turned and faced al-Jeheuty. "How is it possible for a black to be cursed black? He that was black as his father and mother. Black as all of his siblings. The arrogance of the whites, they that had not yet been a thought in creation's head at the time of that story—yet alone molded to a physical form—to cast themselves into our mythology and re-interpret our works." The giant took a breath. "Nasir has expressed to me that a beautiful, black royal figure wears the title of slave while residing in the Italian court. I request, Beylerbey, to assist in the execution of an agent of slavery. I do not want to die a tragic Moor. I will not be cast in the British bard's buffoonish re-creation of the Moor. I have old stories to tell, and I have new stories to write for us."

Al-Jeheuty believed that Behar's spirit resurrected through Ojodo. He could not deny his brother-in-arms the fight. He yielded to Ojodo's request, as much as he hated to. "You'll leave with Nasir and Donatello Verola. I'll have Nasir brief you on every detail of the mission. Talk with the al-Jasi's chief." He stepped closer to his friend and warned, "And should you fall in this staged insurrection, I will find Jesus Christ to resurrect you, just so I can kill you myself. Is that understood?"

Ojodo bowed his head. "Thank you, Beylerbey."

Al-Jeheuty smiled. "Let's close this place and retire to the palace's auditorium for wine and women. Nasir, Donatello, and the al-Jasi chief will accompany us." He thought. "We'll first see King Kemnebi off, then spend the rest of the day lounging to music and the sway of Moorish women's hips."

"Mehit will approve?" Ojodo asked in a sarcastically surprised tone.

"I didn't say I would touch," al-Jeheuty clarified. "Any thoughts that come up I will enact on her after she gives birth."

Ojodo joked, "So for now, you'll enact your thoughts on your right hand. Or is it left?"

Al-Jeheuty laughed loud. He and Ojodo straightened the council house. "I'll have a servant come to bring the remaining treats to the auditorium. Come, warrior-bard. Let's go." Al-Jeheuty asked as they exited the council house, "You do understand that the British bard has been dead for some time?"

Ojodo laughed loud. "Yes, Beylerbey. Yes."

They met Nasir and al-Rinak at the Sa'ood company house. Palace guards and servants surrounded the officials. Al-Jeheuty commanded two of the servants to deliver the food in the council house to the palace. Then, they made their way to the palace, walking through the city gates, through the streets, and to the palace entrance. In the rear courtyard they found the King preparing for his leave, his caravan waiting beyond the opened southern gate. He and Munashe were saying their goodbyes to Princess Yaminah. Al-Jeheuty rushed into the courtyard, "Are you trying to stow away without any goodbyes?"

King Kemnebi turned to the Beylerbey. "I heard you were in a meeting, al-Jeheuty. I didn't want to disturb you."

The Beylerbey and King bowed to one another and then shook hands. "You're welcomed to stay one more day," said al-Jeheuty. He leaned close and whispered, "You may find a wife with the soiree we have planned."

The King laughed off the invitation. "Tempting, but I have to inform our kingdom and the rest of the royal council about the war's status."

"Understandable," al-Jeheuty voiced. He aimed his arm at Yaminah and expressed, "We will take good care of your sister. She will be fit with servants at her command and guards for protection."

Yaminah smiled. "Thank you."

The King informed, "Some personal servants are staying behind. I'm glad to hear about the guards." He kissed his sister on the cheek. "Goodbye, sister. We'll see you in two week's time."

Everyone walked through the southern gate, approached the King's royal caravan, and then saw he and Munashe off to Djenhai. Al-Jeheuty turned to Yaminah and asked the Princess, "What are your plans for the night, Ambassador?"

"I am finally going to relax," she said in a relieving sigh. "Your wife has invited me to the bathhouse."

Al-Jeheuty raised his eyebrows. "Really…?"

Yaminah chuckled. "I can see your naughty thoughts, Beylerbey. Now what would your brother-in-arms Bo Yusuf think?"

"The same thing," al-Jeheuty joked causing the Princess to laugh out loud.

Yaminah rolled her eyes. "Boys. All the noble titles in the world can't seem to civilize you." She kissed the side of al-Jeheuty's face. "Do you know that Bo Yusuf actually had the same reaction?" Her servants surrounded her. She walked into the palace with al-Jeheuty and the other officials. The Beylerbey assigned palace guards to Yaminah and then walked her to the palace's front entrance, al-Rinak and his entourage in tow. Mehit waited patiently at the front of the palace, glowing with pregnancy. Aludra guarded her, dressed as a handmaiden. Mehit greeted Yaminah with a courteous bow. The Princess teased al-Jeheuty by confessing to his wife: "Your husband has offended the Djenhai crown. He's had impure thoughts about our rendezvous at your bathhouse, Mehit."

Al-Jeheuty's face mixed guilt with a smile.

Al-Rinak chuckled and slapped the Beylerbey on the back.

Mehit shook her head and pulled Yaminah closer to her. "Royal sister, don't even worry about this one." She told her husband, "You men make your own party. We women have ours."

"We can have one big party," al-Jeheuty suggested with a sly grin.

Yaminah looked at Mehit and stated, "Do you see this?" she asked playing as if she was offended.

Mehit laughed. She looked at Aludra with a teasing smile and then to her husband. "We may join you," she looked to Aludra again, same teasing smile on her face, "if Ambassador Nasir be there. Correct, Aludra?"

Aludra blushed.

Mehit chuckled teasingly. Al-Jeheuty raised an eyebrow, but before he could inquire, the women and their entourage exited the front courtyard, journeying out into the streets, and toward Mehit's bathhouse. Al-Jeheuty and al-Rinak faced one another. There were no words exchanged for a moment. Then al-Jeheuty asked, "We're having a carousel in the auditorium. There will be a great feast, music, wine, and dance. It will flow into the night. You are invited."

Al-Rinak bowed humbly. "Let me extend my apologies, Beylerbey. I too, like the Princess, will just relax for the night. A war has begun. I would like to take a breath before greater trouble arises. I'm not as young as you anymore, or the other officials. I know my limits."

Al-Jeheuty expressed false regret and watched the statesman leave with an entourage. The Beylerbey returned to the palace, stopping within its halls to ask a servant to fetch Company Boss Gandarewa, Rahmis Husani, Captain Sunwil, Chief Officer Ras Ali, and Donatello Verola. He returned to Nasir and Ojodo who, in the Beylerbey's absence, had summoned Roberto Hamaat and informed him of the festivities. Al-Jeheuty commanded more servants to prepare the auditorium.

Al-Jeheuty's requested company made their way to the palace, Rahmis Husani and the al-Jasi chief absent among them. Rahmis sent a message to the Beylerbey that he would attend the festive banquet after seeing to his businesses. The al-Jasi chief prepared his soldiers for war.

Al-Jeheuty and the other officials partied within an atmosphere of music, dancing women, incense, feast, drink, and heavy gaming. Ras Ali wreaked havoc on his opponents in dominoes, trading off with challengers that bowed out of cards or dice. "I won't even be kind to you, Beylerbey," he teased al-Jeheuty, to which the Chief Boss replied jokingly, "I suppose this is revenge for the tax put on the Council of Captains." Chess was too long of an activity to engage in, and no one touched the two boards brought into the auditorium. The music was ordered to simmer down to a low, relaxing hum. Rahmis entered the festivities later. The officials continued to drink, trade all manner of stories, and gamble. Roberto gave a ritualistic prayer, adding at the end, *"We have men to kill."* The party ended an hour after midnight. Each official was exhausted, and al-Jeheuty slept well into the afternoon.

The next day, Governor Wakil made public appearances, walking slow, but clearly recovering and losing his intense cough. The al-Mari Ifriq streets started to fill with more and more civilian activity since the days of the attack. Rahmis' promotion of the game tournament drew in every gambler traveling by sea and land, and local resident living in the neighborhoods. The local citizens and travelers were aware of the war al-Mari Ifriq engaged in, but the regular, daily activities coupled with the growing fervor for gaming tournaments and the now consistent Open Market, created calming distractions.

The remainder of the week witnessed no engagement with the Ogunsanwo-Mashek. Word was sent by way of a soldier from each unit, Turkish and Djenhai. The two armies were only coming across site remains, all of which were staged by the Ogunsanwo-Mashek on orders of Beylerbey Al-Jeheuty Anhur Has. The nation left behind only enough remains to allow the pursuing armies to continue to roam in circles. Both al-Rinak and al-Jeheuty decided for the armies to continue their pursuit.

At the start of the following week, Captain Sunwil, with an armada of four heavily armed ships and a galley, escorted the arriving French ships to Cyprus. The captain lowered his sails halfway through the journey. His three other ships did the same, which forced the three trade vessels they surrounded to slow their travel. The four ships extended guns toward the three French trade ships, and staged a hostile takeover. "No one move," yelled Captain Sunwil. "This does not have to be an engagement. I am sending my chief officer to board your flagship to speak with your fleet's captain. This is not a hijacking. This is politics." They were going to Libya.

The French traders made no move. No soldier stirred. No order was given. Chief Officer Ras Ali, along with eight Moorish soldiers, boarded one of the longboats, traveled to the French flagship, and assured the fleet's captain that no one would be harmed. The galley ship, in tow of Captain Sunwil's fleet, sailed back to al-Mari Ifriq for the purpose of delivering word to Beylerbey Anhur Has that his move was in play.

Al-Jeheuty met the returning galley at the Sa'ood docks. A second messenger ship delivered news that Beaumont's ships at Sale were being kept in port, unable to leave for the Caribbean. Al-Jeheuty shook away an uneasy thought. He was now in the middle of his secret war, his hunt and strike. The Beylerbey was dragging an ally into the fold. Business Emissary Gautier Leolin requested an audience with the Beylerbey five days later.

It was an hour after noon when Gautier Leolin humbly walked through the council house door. Ambassador Nasir Sa'ood accompanied the meeting. Gautier was alone. He wore a respectful smile, nervousness subtly quivering on his lip. He presented a bow to the two gentlemen. The Beylerbey and ambassador stood up and bowed to Gautier in return. Al-Jeheuty motioned for the business emissary to have a seat. Chairs were brought into the council house to accommodate the Frenchman. The three men took seats, facing one another.

Gautier decided to jump straight into business, though he stuttered with a low voice when he spoke, his head hanging low and his eyes barely looking at the Moorish officials. "There has been—"

"Speak up," al-Jeheuty asked in an exaggerated authoritative voice. He was teasing the timid emissary. "Relax. You're a fine businessman. I don't understand why you're so timorous with these affairs."

Gautier smiled, a sigh of relief exhaled. "I'm here for business, no more," the emissary spoke. "And what I strive to do is be the best businessman between you and Monsieur Beaumont. The last thing I would like is to be at war with your city, especially if I reside on your coast."

Al-Jeheuty became stern, losing his smile. "War?" He leaned toward Gautier. "What would involve you in our war with the Ogunsanwo-Mashek?"

Gautier cleared his throat. His anxious behavior returned. He stuttered, "There are no politics that would thrust myself, or Monsieur Beaumont—whose interests I represent—into the war that you currently are involved in with the nomadic nation, as foe or ally. However, an incident has risen."

"Risen?" Nasir asked, speaking in French.

Gautier nodded. "Yes. Risen. Come about. Cyprus has reported no French ships on its horizon. They have been expected for some time, escorted by your protection. Monsieur Beaumont is a little shaken. Sale is also not allowing our ships to leave port. There is tension being created by these unfortunate circumstances." Al-Jeheuty and Nasir turned to one another, and then returned their attention back to the Frenchman. "Monsieur Beaumont fears your protection has run out. He's sent a letter. He is en route to al-Mari Ifriq. His ship will dock tomorrow morning. He flies ally colors. There is no cause for alarm."

Al-Jeheuty's smile returned. "Absolutely correct, Monsieur Leolin. There is no cause for alarm. I understand Simon Beaumont's concerns. I can assure you that I will provide an answer for him. I do fear, however, that the answer is not simple. There are complicated matters that my city is involved in, matters beyond the circumstances concerning war with the Ogunsanwo-Mashek. I will present Monsieur Beaumont with the information he seeks, but I will need his help to rectify the matters." He lifted his hand. "I can only provide Monsieur Beaumont with these answers, I'm sorry to say. Our meeting will convene at the palace tomorrow when Monsieur Beaumont arrives. Until then, Emissary, return to your duties without worry."

Gautier smiled wide. He was delighted by the Beylerbey's words. All three men stood from their seats. Gautier was escorted outside. He bowed out of respect of the two Moorish officials, smile glued to his visage. He then made his way back to the Sa'ood company house. Al-Jeheuty, keeping his eye on the departing emissary, said to Nasir, "When I get Beaumont's approval, and the problems have been rectified, you'll leave a day later."

The rest of the day proceeded as normal. Politics, law, and business passed the time for the Moorish officials. Al-Jeheuty, late that evening in his private quarters, informed his wife that he would be leaving in several days for business in Libya. He told Mehit, "I won't be long. I have business with our Italian associates working for us there." He kissed Mehit on her bare, pregnant belly while the two lay in bed.

Mehit laughed whimsically. Her bubbly mood continued when she asked, "Can you ask Roberto why he needs to steal Aludra from me for a week's time? She has an assignment in the Soudan. Why so far?"

Al-Jeheuty lifted his shoulders. "Roberto handles contracts outside of our city's affairs. Ilindia will assign you a temporary Moon. How are your lessons coming with Ilindia?"

"She's prepping me well for school." She smiled and exhaled while thinking of her future travels to Djenhai. "I can't wait to visit the interior kingdom." She looked at al-Jeheuty and confessed, "I am a little nervous, traveling while this war is on."

"Ah, it's not really much of a war," al-Jeheuty commented. "We're having trouble tracking down the Ogunsanwo-Mashek."

"That makes me nervous," Mehit said. "The wilderness is their home. They might be watching Bo Yusuf, waiting for a proper moment to strike."

"The armies are well armed," assured al-Jeheuty. "They'll be fine." He rolled onto his stomach and started to twiddle his fingers. "Besides, *mora*, you're not starting classes until a year after our child is born. Do you think our campaign against the Ogunsanwo-Mashek will take that long?"

Mehit just rubbed her bare, pregnant belly. She asked al-Jeheuty, "Boy or girl?"

Al-Jeheuty smiled instantly. "I don't know, *mora*..."

Mehit leaned over her husband. "Come on," she baited. "I know every man yearns for a son that he can raise to be a man."

Al-Jeheuty flapped his lips. "All men *don't* want a constant headache by developing a protection complex when having a little girl to take care of. You think I'm overprotective of *you*? Just wait until we have a little Mehit running around here."

Mehit swiped her hand, as if attacking al-Jeheuty's comment. "Please," she said. "Ask Aludra or Ilindia—or any of the Moons and initiating female Stars—if they need any help protecting themselves."

"Our daughter will be a Moon," al-Jeheuty laughed turning on his back again. "She can protect us when we're old and feeble."

Mehit asked al-Jeheuty in a sincere voice, "Are you okay?"

The Beylerbey gently rubbed his wife's forearm as it lay across his chest. He kissed her wrist and answered, "Absolutely not, *mora*." He beamed a gentle smile at Mehit. "War just isn't easy."

Mehit played with al-Jeheuty's locks. "It must be something like trying to talk to you, all your cryptic banter. Complicated, I guess." She kissed her husband's forehead. "When you're ready to talk to me, al-Jeheuty…"

"I know, beautiful woman. I know." He took a deep breath. "We'll meet in the council house in two month's time. I'll tell you everything. No more secrets."

Mehit snickered. Al-Jeheuty looked at her, perplexed at her actions. She covered her mouth and apologized. "I was just thinking how fat I'll be—" she rubbed her stomach, "—two months from now."

Al-Jeheuty rolled his eyes. "You won't be fat," he groaned. "Besides, men like a woman with a little meat on their bones."

"Oh, do you?" Mehit expressed with a wide-eyed accusing look. "What about all those slender dancers prancing around the taverns and palace halls?"

"We also like variety," al-Jeheuty confessed.

Mehit placed a grip around al-Jeheuty's neck. "I better be all the variety you need."

"Of course, Mehit," he said as he gently moved her grip from his neck and kissed her hand. "Besides, the last thing I need is for you to execute the mark you have on my testicles."

Mehit chuckled, cuddling up closer to al-Jeheuty. "Tell me of an adventure you had in Spain."

Al-Jeheuty cleared his throat. He thought of the various skirmishes and covert missions assigned to he and his brothers-in-arms. He decided to sum up the years he spent in Spain. "Behar made me study. I trained. Many died. The revolution failed. We escaped death. I'm here. The end. Or the beginning, which ever way you'd like to see it."

Mehit punched her husband lightly on the shoulder. "Seriously! Tell me a tale." She touched her belly and looked down. "Tell our child a tale."

Al-Jeheuty suddenly felt as if he had been pushed out onto a large stage, naked and forced to perform. He said shyly, "I'm not Ojodo."

"You don't have to be," Mehit assured in a sweet voice. "Just be al-Jeheuty. It's worked on me very well so far."

Al-Jeheuty looked at Mehit, staring at his wife and ingesting every aspect of her beautiful face. Her words were like a warm blanket. He no longer felt naked on the stage. He sat up. "Let's go further back than Spain," he started to tell his wife and the growing child inside her. "This was a time that Hesam and I sabotaged a slave ship used by our employer."

Chapter Thirty-Seven

Melusina's erotic proposition spilled from her tongue and lips like a haunting melody. Al-Rinak answered her, pushing her up against the side of a building. The two of them were deep inside an alley. It was morning, several hours after dawn. Al-Rinak and Melusina had yet to sleep. The two of them were wide awake, lustful, and intoxicated from spiced wine. Time was lost to them. Long after midnight passed, and sometime after the sun resurrected, the two of them somehow left *The al-Hammon Palace*'s raucous atmosphere and ended up outside in an alleyway, salaciously entangled in one another.

Melusina pulled her lover closer, squeezing him like a sponge and trying to absorb every ounce of his physique. Al-Rinak's passion slowed, something catching his ear. At the open end of the alley, leading out into the street, there came the sound of a marching army. The black Turk pulled away from Melusina and turned toward the commotion. Melusina didn't question her lover's sudden lack of interest in her. She waited patiently, smiling seductively, writhing against al-Rinak's body as he inspected the French entourage led by Simon Beaumont as it passed by. Nasir Sa'ood escorted the French party toward the palace.

Al-Rinak's drunken, euphoric state sobered as he watched the businessman's entourage pass by the alley. Emissary Gautier Leolin was among the marching troupe. Rene Chaffee was nowhere to be seen. Al-Rinak wondered what manner of business brought the French trader to seek an audience with the young Beylerbey. He hoped it was nothing concerning Rene Chaffee, and further hoped that Rene and Kyler Piett were keeping a low profile while sequestered in France. Al-Rinak would seek his answers now that he was sober. Tiredness caught up with him, but he was not dead. He returned his attention to Melusina and dived back into a wild, fervid lust to conquer her, finishing with a quiet calm just as the citizens started to fill the streets and start their day.

Al-Rinak and Melusina straightened their clothes and left the alley. The statesman ordered Melusina to return to their lodging while he returned to *The al-Hammon Palace*. He watched her walk away, her clothes still loose and seductive. She flirted with passersby, which erected a devious smile on the black Turk's face. He walked down the street, made the first left, and continued walking until he returned to *The al-Hammon Palace*. The tavern was calmer than when al-Rinak remembered it last. There were no drunken corsairs or privateers, loud games, music, or dancing women. It was peaceful, sun illuminating the still scene. Al-Rinak entered just as Maurice al-Hammon exited one of the backrooms. Maurice often stayed at *The Palace*, watching over the seedy dive through the night and clearing the patrons out a little before sunrise, taking lodge in a backroom.

Maurice was bare of shirt. His pants were loose. He closed the backroom door, but not before al-Rinak spotted a young Moorish girl still sleeping in his bed. A blanket covered her slender, naked form. Maurice looked up and finally spotted al-Rinak standing in front of him. There was an embarrassed look on his face. Al-Rinak paid no attention to it. He approached Maurice and made the command, "Find your father for me. Tell him I seek an audience with Simon Beaumont. The Frenchman just landed on our shore. Nasir was escorting his party to the palace."

Maurice prepared himself a cup of water at the bar. Al-Rinak stood near him, turning down the cup Maurice was willing to prepare for him. "Your business with the Frenchman," he asked as he took a hard gulp. "Taran will want to know."

Al-Rinak confessed, "I'd like to make sure of what the Frenchman is doing here. I hope it doesn't concern anything dealing with our filthy rat, Rene Chaffee."

"Rahmis confided in me that al-Jeheuty is having a hard time with his new authoritative duties." Maurice rolled his eyes. "I was told the brat has lost some of Simon Beaumont's ships. The cargo was heading to Cyprus. The Beylerbey is trying to keep the news from getting out. Beaumont's sudden appearance? He's probably angry, furious."

Al-Rinak was surprised by the news. Al-Jeheuty had seemed so calm in their meetings. He was grateful, however, that the young Beylerbey was struggling to grasp the reins of responsibility that came with his new title. He said to Maurice, "I need word sent to Rene for his return," al-Rinak informed. "I know he's trying to keep a low profile, but the dust has settled. Traont Coutelier is scheduled to arrive in al-Mari Ifriq any day."

"He's not heading back to France?" Maurice asked.

Al-Rinak shook his head. "No. He's coming straight to al-Mari Ifriq. Rene should be here."

"What about the Dutch slavers?" Maurice inquired further.

Al-Rinak groaned. "That's for Piett to handle and bring to our shores. We meet with them within the next three months. Al-Jeheuty has agreed to meet the Dutch traders face-to-face. Where is your brother?"

"At our house," Maurice answered. "Resting."

"Is he still grounded?" al-Rinak snarled

"Yes," Maurice answered. He finally looked at al-Rinak. "Al-Jeheuty hasn't opened his police route at sea. The captains are in rotation. Fusan's route will supposedly be opened up in two weeks. There's been no trade activity on the route we protect."

Al-Rinak took a moment to contemplate. "That will be fine," he said looking away from Maurice. He became lost in thought again. He said in a low voice, "In two weeks we will have a greater understanding of the war." He turned coolly toward Maurice. "Regardless of the war's progress, we will hold another council in Djenhai. The best scenario would be that captives have been taken, lives lost. Minimal, of course. This would fuel the Ogunsanwo-Mashek's drive to strike. It would give them reason." Al-Rinak sighed. He put his hands on Maurice's shoulders, gently, like a father consoling a son. "I see the Ogunsanwo-Mashek being very bold. They would hit our caravan as we left Djenhai." He shook his head and then stepped away from Maurice. "Yes. It would be devastating. I can see Beylerbey Anhur Has and Ambassador Sa'ood being killed in the strike, possibly General al-Dume as well." He shook his head again. "Yes," he repeated. "Taran and I would have no choice but then to assume authority over the city, helping the ailing governor." He took a breath, and then he patted Maurice on the shoulder. "Find your father. I still need an audience with the Frenchman." Maurice bowed at the neck. Al-Rinak stepped further away from Maurice. "Tell your father that I will be at my lodge." Al-Rinak made a swift turn and exited the tavern, leaving Maurice to his duties.

The Moor stowed to the back of the tavern, returning to his room. He gently woke the sleeping Moorish girl, one of the *al-Hammon*'s dancing barmaids and prostitutes. "You have to head home," he said to her kindly. "I have business to attend to." The young woman entertained her employer's command. Maurice traded his loose pants for an entire business outfit. He furnished himself with a sword and pistol, and then escorted the young woman home. He then set about his task to find Taran Zaher, a feat that proved quick when he stumbled upon one of his foster mother's seamstresses. "He's consoling your mother at her workshop," she said. "Your mother became hysterical and started crying."

Maurice found the information curious. He thanked the woman and followed her information to Alimah's workshop, finding Taran inside. He was taking Alimah from the workshop. There was cloth in her hands. Taran placed Alimah in the care of a female servant and asked that his wife be escorted back to their home. He approached Maurice who watched as

Alimah was led away from her establishment. "She's still shaken by Behar's death," he said. "She blames herself, in an esoteric sort of way. She stitched the suit he was wearing when he was killed. She told our former Beylerbey that it would be her best work. She supplied the sewing of all his garments that week. She came across the outfit he was to wear the day after."

Maurice said nothing on the matter. He simply reported, "Statesman Ozan is looking for you. He seems a little rattled by Simon Beaumont's unexpected arrival. I told him it was nothing. If there is anyone that should be rattled by the Frenchman's presence it would be our Beylerbey. However, Statesman Ozan would like for you to arrange a meeting between he and Simon Beaumont. He wants to request that Rene Chaffee return to al-Mari Ifriq." Maurice saw the perplexed expression quickly wash over Taran. "Traont Coutelier is en route to al-Mari Ifriq, returning from the colonies. He's not stopping in France. He would like Rene Chaffee to be here so that both can speak personally with Beylerbey Anhur Has."

Taran nodded his head, understanding. He asked for Maurice to follow him, and he dismissed all his servants and guards to his house to watch over his wife. The two of them made their way to the palace. They were both permitted entrance on arrival, but were not allowed into the meeting between the Beylerbey and Simon Beaumont. A servant saw to Taran's wishes to disturb the meeting and deliver a message to al-Jeheuty. The servant returned and assured Taran that his request would be honored: Simon Beaumont was willing to speak with Statesman Ozan.

Both Taran and Maurice waited outside the closed meeting. An hour passed before the meeting was adjourned and its participants exited the room. Taran and Maurice stood still, at attention. They noticed that no one looked happy. Al-Jeheuty looked like a boy that had just been scolded by his mother and father. Simon Beaumont could only contain his anger to an expression. He turned to the Beylerbey and said, "I would like my collateral tribute delivered to my ship. I am leaving tonight." He looked at Maurice and Taran. "Which one of you has business with Rene Chaffee?"

Taran stepped forward, a humble smile on his face. He spoke in French, "Monsieur Beaumont, one of our residents, a Turkish statesman, has business with your emissary."

Beaumont looked anything but pleased. He returned his sharp gaze to al-Jeheuty. "Lead me to the company house where we French hold business."

"Yes, Monsieur Beaumont," al-Jeheuty said in an apologetic tone. He turned to Nasir. "Lead Monsieur Beaumont to your company house.

Have your brother bring the storage crates so that we can commence putting together Monsieur Beaumont's tribute." He looked back at Simon Beaumont and reiterated, "I hope you accept our apologies and gifts. We are grateful that this does not halt any business between your trading company and the Griffin Regency."

Simon nodded, but there was no sign of appreciation in his look or demeanor. Nasir began to escort Simon and his party from the palace. Taran and Maurice journeyed from the palace to tell al-Rinak that Simon Beaumont would meet with him. They arrived at his apartment suite and delivered the news. "Simon Beaumont will meet you at the Sa'ood company house," said Taran. He shook his head, and his eye hinted that there were other things on his mind. He expressed, "Al-Jeheuty is having a tough time keeping things straight with the Frenchman. I understand that cargo was lost. Beaumont is none-too-pleased. Tribute is being offered for compensation."

"Al-Jeheuty looked weak," Maurice sneered. "Apologizing to that businessman. Nasir looked no better. His father would be ashamed of him bowing and playing the buffoon for the benefit of a pale nation."

"We will restore the city's image soon enough," said al-Rinak trying to calm Maurice's growing frustration. "I will meet with Beaumont in two hours. I need some rest."

"I'll inform Monsieur Beaumont," said Taran.

Maurice and Taran left al-Rinak's residence. They traveled to the Sa'ood company house and delivered al-Rinak's message to Gautier Leolin. The emissary then passed the message to his benefactor, Simon Beaumont. The businessman was relieved that al-Rinak was not immediately ready to talk with him. There was much that Beaumont needed to wrap his head around, all the politics plaguing al-Mari Ifriq and its new Beylerbey. The statesman kept to his word too, arriving a little more than two hours later. Both men were well rested, and Simon Beaumont even greeted al-Rinak with a cordial smile, bow, and a handshake. Simon Beaumont and al-Rinak chatted privately on the second level, which was reserved for the French traders.

Al-Rinak spoke first. "I have business with one of your emissaries," he said in the French language. "Rene Chaffee. He left for France some time ago. I would express great appreciation for his return."

Simon Beaumont considered al-Rinak's point. "Governments disagree, statesman. Businessmen, who I'm sure you consider yourself, well, we find resolve as long as there is coin. What business do you have with Emissary Chaffee?"

Al-Rinak was reluctant to speak about the slave trading that al-Mari Ifriq was ready to invest in as a result of the war. He also refrained mentioning Traont Coutelier, a man that was becoming more ambitious against his new boss Simon Beaumont. Coutelier had plans for marking Simon Beaumont, splitting his business with Rene Chaffee and jumping into the African slave trade.

"There is a tavern here named *The al-Hammon Palace*," al-Rinak began his lie. "Rene has put some investments into the tavern, and I've fronted monies for him to increase the liquor that comes into the tavern. His first payment is due to me in three days." Al-Rinak spoke in a concerned tone. "I understand that he has asked for an extended leave. I don't believe he's trying to escape his payments. I believe we both just got ahead of ourselves. If he could return for just the time it takes to award me my monies."

Simon Beaumont said in a relaxed manner, "That will not be a problem, though I've had little contact with Emissary Chaffee. I was even looking for him to accompany me on this journey. I couldn't be too upset. He does have a life outside of business, and he is on a holiday. I will find him as quickly as possible, and have him come here immediately." The two men reached across the table and shook hands. They stood up and Beaumont added, "If only other officials in al-Mari Ifriq were as straight forward as you, statesman. Maybe it's just your years of experience."

They walked down the stairs and out of the company house. Beaumont and al-Rinak watched as Sa'ood workers prepared cargo crates and large chests to take to the palace. Horses and donkeys were fashioned for pulling the cargo to and from the palace. Beaumont sighed at the sight.

"One of your Beylerbey's captains led my fleet astray. Cargo was lost. Trade ships were lost. It was an accident at sea. I also have not heard from privateers that left Sale for the Caribbean. I have lost much coin to this incident. Of all the times…" He breathed a heavier sigh. "I'm being compensated, but all the gold and precious gems seems an unfair sum for replacement. Being in Africa makes these neggars so close to wealth. This is of no trouble to your damn Beylerbey. He has no idea what he's lost." He turned to al-Rinak. "I understand that a war has rattled the political structure, but cannot Governor Wakil be more hands on than this young boy?"

"Governor Wakil is recovering," al-Rinak explained. "We're all doing our best to support the new Beylerbey, especially in these times."

Simon nodded his head. "If this happens again, he will lose my contract. I am the only thing that is keeping the French fleet from bombarding the North African coasts. Trust."

"Trusted," al-Rinak noted.

Simon's frustration returned to him. He turned back to the company house and huffed, "Let me get out of this heat." He started toward the door. "I'll see to it that we both meet Rene Chaffee in person, Statesman Ozan."

Businessman Beaumont's tribute was delivered to his ship throughout the rest of the day. Al-Rinak understood the severity of the situation when al-Jeheuty had not come to see the Frenchman off. Nasir handled the departure, continuously apologizing to Simon Beaumont until the French businessman was aboard his ship. The mighty French frigate lifted its anchor and headed northwest, sails raised and pregnant with the wind.

Chapter Thirty-Eight

Night. A coastal village in France. Wind clapped against flimsy housing structures and shoved passing citizens who scrambled to find lodging. The clouds flickered with light. Low rumbles of thunder warned of a heavy rain. The last thing that Rene Chaffee wanted to be was out in the brewing storm, but he had ignored his employer's wishes for the last three hours. Simon Beaumont requested his presence, and Rene was nervous about the matters his boss wished to speak to him about. Beaumont had just returned from al-Mari Ifriq. Supposedly he was frustrated with the loss of cargo that was headed to Cyprus under the Moors' protection. There was also trouble in Sale concerning privateers that were grounded from making their way to the Caribbean.

None of these matters pointed to the ventures in which Rene was investing his time and money in, but he continued to remain cautious. He didn't want to return to al-Mari Ifriq for another month. And so, Rene had been stalling, continuing to indulge himself in tavern activities. He thought he would use the storm as an excuse, but only the wind invaded the town, and though it was strong, no rain accompanied the roaring gusts. He folded the hand he held in the current card game. He took one last sip before standing and excusing himself from the table. Rene bid his fellow card players farewell and left the tavern.

The wind was like a furious brigand. It grabbed any citizen wandering the streets and shook wildly. Rene lowered his shoulders, held tightly to his hat, and pushed through the heavy force, making his way to Beaumont's house. The coastal town was not Simon Beaumont's permanent residence. He lived further north, out into the country. This was where Beaumont commuted for business, overseeing trade ventures.

Rene approached the door of Beaumont's coastal residence. He knocked heavily and a guard opened the door. Rene hollered over the wind, "I've come to see Monsieur Beaumont. I've been called to the residence." The guard opened the door for Rene and then pushed against the wind to close it shut. The guard escorted Rene to Beaumont's office. Simon looked up from his desk, pausing in sorting through papers to welcome Rene inside. He invited his ambassador to have a seat. He moved the papers away from him and removed his spectacles. There was no dramatic pause before beginning talks with Rene. Simon Beaumont spoke immediately. "This happens only once, Rene," he said to his employee. Rene didn't stir. He refrained from commenting, hoping Simon would relay more information. "How many investments do you have in al-Mari Ifriq?"

"Sir, I just wish to make extra coin." There was a significant pause between each word. Rene still had no idea what Simon Beaumont was referring to. If it was about the business of slaves, he didn't seem upset for a man that was outwardly against the practice.

"Don't I pay you enough?" asked Simon. He lifted his hand and stopped Rene from answering. The wind wrapped around the house and screamed like a wild banshee. "That black Turk told me that he's helped you invest in a tavern in al-Mari Ifriq. He's upset that you will miss the first payment. He asked that you return to al-Mari Ifriq within the next several days to give him his payment." He leaned back in his chair. "Or you may present your payment in person tonight. The statesman followed me here. Truthfully, in a move to settle these matters as quickly as possible, I invited him." Rene's eyes went wide. "I hope you haven't brought Turkish trouble to our shores, Rene. I have him waiting on my ship. He's been there for some time. I didn't want to stir anyone up by bringing the Turk on our shores. The coin I make with these Moors, and for the French crown, has been incredible, but I've lost a great deal of respect by working with them. Rectify this problem now. Follow Statesman Ozan back to al-Mari Ifriq, and square away your payment."

Rene stood up quickly. "Yes, Monsieur Beaumont."

Simon followed Rene. "I've had sudden trouble with the Moors of al-Mari Ifriq. I don't wish to have anymore. Is that understood?"

"What trouble has come, Monsieur Beaumont?" Rene inquired, his voice humble.

"The accidents at sea, Rene. You know." Beaumont heaved a sigh. "The Moors' protection is not as great as they boast. I've lost cargo. Please, handle this business while I set these matters straight."

"Yes, Monsieur Beaumont," Rene repeated.

Simon called for one of his guards to escort Rene to his ship and rendezvous with Statesman Ozan. Simon opened the door for both men. The wind pushed its way in furiously. Simon barely braced for the impact, planting himself hard, struggling against the force. A second guard helped, allowing Simon to back away and leave the duty to his ward. Rene and the guard made their exit, the door closed upon their leave. Rene and the guard braved the fierce, warm winds. There was still a low howl of thunder, but rain struggled to tumble from the sky. As they walked, Rene reflected on

Simon's words. There was no debt that needed to be paid to al-Rinak. The emissary believed the Turk expressed these sentiments to Simon Beaumont just to send him a signal. Traont must have arrived in al-Mari Ifriq. Everything had to look official with al-Jeheuty. Rene would have to be present. But before he would return to al-Mari Ifriq, he had word to send to Kyler Piett. The renegado was contacting the Dutch traders interested in the potential slaves coming from Odongo-Mauharim.

Beaumont's guard led Rene to the docks, and he helped the Emissary aboard Simon's flagship. Rene traveled below. The cargo hold looked empty, save for several crates. The ship rocked in the wind, but was well anchored. Rene looked around and called out, "Statesman Ozan." He borrowed the guard's lantern and saw nothing inside the space. Beaumont's guard suggested that the Turk must have wandered elsewhere on the ship, suggesting he may have been in the cabin. The guard stepped away to investigate. Rene released a frustrated sigh. He decided to wait below, and he moved closer to the crates, four of them were open. Rene set the lantern atop one of the unopened storage crates. He heard a creaking sound behind him.

"Statesman Ozan," he said trying to turn around.

A hand palmed the back of Rene's head and quickly smashed his face against one of the closed, wooden crates. Rene's nose burst blood. His legs buckled. The attacks did not cease. Rene's attacker gripped the Frenchman's hair, and dragged his head back to strike his face twice more against the wooden storage box. Rene's nose finally broke, completely crushed. His attacker kicked him in the back of the leg, twisting his ankle. Rene slumped more, his head wobbled and he tried to orient his bodily mechanics. The attacker came to his left. Rene regained slight control over his twirling body. He looked up to get a glimpse of his attacker's face, but his vision was hazy and shadowed. His sight was blinded by swift attacks, punches that bruised his eye, cracked his jaw slightly, and loosened teeth. Rene's lip split, blood dribbled, and finally his attacker grabbed the back of his coat and tossed him to the floor. Rene lay sprawled out, faced down. His attacker granted him no mercy. He stomped on the back of Rene's hand with the heel of his boot, crushing the bones inward. The attacker searched Rene's person and confiscated the businessman of pistol and dagger. Rene was shot in the leg, behind the kneecap, with the confiscated firearm.

Chaffee's body convulsed as if struck by lightning. He coughed, crawling forward. Reality was a blur of blood and disorientation. Every object had a strange, ghostly double vibrating from it. There was a loud ringing in his ears, and he could not tell if the heavy winds were causing the sway of the ship, or if it was just confusion brought on by his battery.

"Hesam," a voice called. "That's enough."

The Persian company boss pursued no further assault on Emissary Chaffee.

The winds calmed to a low whistle.

Al-Jeheuty and three other Moors stepped into Rene's view.

The emissary chuckled.

He was caught.

His life was over.

Hesam remained behind Rene, waiting for the order to give the killing blow. The sight of al-Jeheuty invigorated Rene with enough strength to balance on one knee and arm. He looked at Hesam and spat, "Returned to your piratic roots have you, Persian?" He turned to al-Jeheuty and laughed, his teeth loose, the skin around his left eye beginning to bubble various shades of purple. "What do you want? Answers?"

Al-Jeheuty calmly shook his head, no. "I have all the answers, Monsieur Chaffee. I wouldn't be here if I didn't. You assisted Statesman Ozan in the assassination of black nobles. One, a noble company coss. One, a chief boss. One, a King. We have you for getting your hands dirty, personally, with the death of a Persian company boss." The Beylerbey declared, "You are guilty of crimes against al-Mari Ifriq."

Rene's sinister laugh became deep, almost like a growl. He looked like a sick animal, blood and saliva collecting as foam that thickened from out of his mouth. "You think you're so fucking smart, neggar!" he screamed. "I will haunt this world just to watch the Dutch and French ships burn your precious city to the ground. I will watch as you are carted off to the colonies, along with that tribe of savages. I will watch and laugh as men ravage your wife. Don't think she's safe. Taran has his own daughter marked. They will cut out the child inside her while she is strung upside down, hanging from a tree. Kill me? We have plans for you beyond my death. Traont will see to that. Tell that phallus suckler Simon Beaumont that he's marked. Every bit of his business will be usurped, and it is the French Crown that waits for the day. Tell that to that hypocrite with neggar slaves! Nothing will stop our moves against him. Mark my words, when I go missing there will be hell to pay."

Again, al-Jeheuty calmly shook his head. "Hell no, there won't," he retorted. "And do you know why, *you whore's pig?* Because, according to your mythology, *I* am the Devil himself. So only I hold authority over what debts and taxes will be collected when Hell is to be paid." Al-Jeheuty lifted his hand, revealing the small one-shot pistol held firmly in his grip. He fired the weapon into Rene's skull. The emissary dropped back instantly. He was dead. Al-Jeheuty casually handed his gun to Hesam.

The wind was calm.

Thunder lightly penetrated the night.

Lightning's continuous flicker retreated.

Simon Beaumont entered his ship. Al-Jeheuty walked up to him. The two men shook hands, Simon struggling to loosen his gaze on Rene's dead body. Al-Jeheuty used a single finger to bring the businessman's focus to him. "Be wary, Monsieur Beaumont. You have been marked. Traont is looking to take your enterprise."

"I am sorry for all this, Beylerbey Anhur Has." He nodded toward Rene's corpse. "I apologize for the trouble this man brought while serving under the banner of my business."

"And I apologize for the trouble that I've caused in order to rectify the problem." Al-Jeheuty then assured Simon Beaumont, "When I return to al-Mari Ifriq, word will be sent to Captain Sunwil to continue escorting your cargo to Cyprus. I will send Gautier Leolin to bring the message. My associates in Sale will be informed that your crew can make its way to the Caribbean—with full escort."

"That will be fine, Beylerbey," Simon acknowledged.

"Keep the tribute that I've given you." He smiled and spoke familiar words to Simon Beaumont. "Being in Africa makes us neggars so close to wealth. It's of no trouble to this damn Beylerbey." He chuckled. "I'm sure you were convincing to Statesman Ozan. I'll have Ojodo scribe a part for you in one of his productions."

Simon could not partake of the light mood al-Jeheuty was trying to create. "I'm still uneasy, Beylerbey," he admitted.

"There's no need to be," said al-Jeheuty returning to a more serious tone. "Coutelier might have you marked, but he must operate carefully. He is still under your employment. You are *his* boss. When you speak to him, tell him that Chaffee has gone to Sicily, overseeing a deal with slaves. Days later, present to him this." He gave Simon a tied and folded letter. "It is an invitation to a coastal village named Crocifissa. It's a forgery in Rene's handwriting. Traont will be enticed. He will leave. Our troubles will then be over." He added, "You may find sanctuary in al-Mari Ifriq the day after Coutelier leaves for Sicily."

Simon took a deep breath. "I can give you proper lodging for the night."

"We will do fine here," said al-Jeheuty. "I appreciate your extended hand. We'll clean this mess for you."

Beaumont didn't push the issue any further, but he did offer something the Moor would not refuse. "I'll bring proper meals for you and your men."

"Thank you, again." Al-Jeheuty walked with the businessman to the ship's deck. "A small vessel will dock in the early hours. That will be our transport home."

"I will see you off." Beaumont looked worried. He assured al-Jeheuty, "Do not listen to Rene. I see that all my slaves are paid. Every black has a salary." Al-Jeheuty nodded toward the Frenchman in appreciation, but he noted that despite paying the blacks that worked for him, Simon Beaumont referred to them first as 'slaves'. He would have to keep an eye on the Frenchman. When honest business started to dwindle, there would come a time that even this righteous man might turn to Africa for indigenous investment.

Simon exited the ship with his guard. The Beylerbey returned below where he, Hesam, and the appointed Suns from Roberto's outfit, started to clean the ship of Rene's bloody corpse. Chaffee's body was placed inside a crate, and the wooden packing case was nailed shut. The crate was scheduled for toss into the sea, holes broken into it for water to invade and sink the wooden box.

The life of Emissary Rene Chaffee would be a watery memory.

Chapter Thirty-Nine

Al-Jeheuty's vessel settled into al-Mari Ifriq's ports late in the afternoon. The Beylerbey disembarked from the small commuter ship. Rahmis Husani greeted the Beylerbey with Roberto Hamaat and Governor Wakil. The Suns assigned to protect the Beylerbey reported to Roberto. Al-Jeheuty first spoke to Hesam and told the company boss, "Get some real rest, in a bed. Get a good meal too." He looked at the Suns assigned to protect them and said, "You as well. Roberto, make sure that these men are…" The Beylerbey lost his words. He became fixated on Roberto's sly smile.

The assassin interjected, "My soldiers have been through this before, Beylerbey." Roberto's smile faded quickly. "But, uh, there are other matters at hand." Al-Jeheuty noticed that all eyes were on him. They looked sullen. An intense amount of concern flowed in their expressions. Roberto nodded toward the governor.

Wakil approached al-Jeheuty. "Nasir and the Sicilian have left." He paused and then said, "Traont Coutelier is here. He's been given lodging. He's also calling for Rene Chaffee. Everyone believes that you were in Libya to overlook trade. We've met with him very little. Negotiations have been halted since he was informed about the city's problems, the last attacks made by the…Ogunsanwo-Mashek. He's been silent, out of respect. Al-Rinak had a short counsel with him. That's all."

Al-Jeheuty huffed. "Between the two of them, that's enough." The Beylerbey did not believe Traont Coutelier was a part of al-Rinak's greater conspiracy other than being an outlet for carting the Ogunsanwo-Mashek people into servitude. Clearly, though, there was more news. Al-Jeheuty sensed greater tension beyond Traont's arrival.

The concern that passed between the greeting party's faces did not seem focused on the presence of the French slave trader, nor were they focused on any complicated politics Traont Coutelier's presence might invite into al-Mari Ifriq. Then Wakil said, "Your brother's here." Al-Jeheuty's emotions erupted with surprise. The governor regretfully informed the Beylerbey, "He has a fever. He's been brought to the palace physicians. He's hysterical, Beylerbey." Al-Jeheuty rushed from the docks, the officials close behind him. Wakil matched al-Jeheuty's pace, losing little breath. "The doctors don't know what could be ailing him, Beylerbey. He's sweating, having trouble sleeping. At first, there was belief and fear that he'd picked up something from the Europeans, or something from the Americas. The physicians say there is nothing wrong with him, however."

Al-Jeheuty pulled away from his entourage. Wakil, in his recovering condition, slowed his steps. All that slowed the Beylerbey was his arrival at the city's gate. Even then, the guards opened the gates before al-Jeheuty approached and gave them an order. He nodded in their direction, extending his gratitude, and kept through to the city streets, the city square, and then to the palace. Rahmis and the other officials followed al-Jeheuty, but they were several steps behind in their strides. The officials slowed their steps once inside the palace. Al-Jeheuty merged with Mehit. She found him in the hall and guided the young Beylerbey to where his brother lay. Wakil and Rahmis remained in the hall, stopping two doors down from the room where Aatif was being cared for.

A physician entered the room and approached al-Jeheuty, addressing in a hushed voice, "Beylerbey, your brother shows no signs of a fever. He sweats, but he is not hot. He is hysterical, though. He has trouble sleeping."

Al-Jeheuty moved his eyes from his brother lying in bed to the doctor. "Thank you," he said. The doctor bowed at the neck. He excused himself, and Mehit led him from the room, telling al-Jeheuty that she would be waiting outside. Al-Jeheuty slowly approached the bed. Aatif turned to face him. His brow was drenched with sweat, his lip trembled, but he managed to smile. The beads of sweat that crowned him started to evaporate as his head and emotions cooled at the sight of his brother.

Aatif closed his eyes, shook his head, and sighed through a light chuckle. "Beylerbey Anhur Has. Chief Boss of all Chiefs. My brother has become a king." His chuckle turned to laughter. "Then let me request something from you, my King. I don't need a doctor. I need a priest, or an imam, a rabbi. Any holy man will do."

Al-Jeheuty bent down next to the bed and grabbed his brother's trembling hand. "The doctors say that there is nothing wrong, Aatif. You're not dying."

Aatif shook his head. "I am not, but I am resigned to Hell. I didn't pick up a fever in the Caribbean. I picked up images." Aatif turned away from his brother. His eyes started to water. "I killed all of us. I saw the end of the world, and I helped every last one of these European devils usher it in." He faced al-Jeheuty, trembling. Tears streamed down his face. "Men and women ravaged. Children beaten. All black. The wealth of African kingdoms tortured. Africa, from all her corners, all her people. Moors are we all, but less in this New World. Every black was stripped of his or her robe and headdress, and then adorned with chains. We reeked with the stench of death and waste while disembarking from ships. Death would be an honor than to arrive in Hell. Kings and Queens were beheaded in front of their subjects. Men were removed of their manhood in front of pregnant women. Pregnant women were whipped and beaten to death. The strongest. The meanest. Mothers were boiled in front of children. Children shot for disobedience. There were trees decorated with hung bodies. Stakes adorned with punctured corpses, severed heads. The smell, Al-Jeheuty! I didn't just see this. I heard it! I smelled it! Screams, stench, and even the sight was so thick in the air I could taste it. Obedience is beaten into us. Resistant hearts are murdered. And *then* we are made to till the lands of America should we survive the tortuous gestation inside the womb of the Caribbean. Oh, how the blessed are miscarried. The birthed are born a slave." He gripped al-Jeheuty's single hand with both of his. "I saw a pregnant woman stabbed. She looked like Khaira. Bring my wife to me, please, brother. Check to see if she still lives. My wife. My child. Our parents. Troops continue to occupy Nusurika." He clenched his teeth and closed his eyes out of frustration. "Is this the fate I resigned African people to? Did I toss my brothers and sisters to this fate just to protect my home that now lays occupied with their slavers?" He opened his eyes. "We'll find no solace with the tawny Arab. Their slavery is insidious too. They make eunuchs of us black men, and rape their way into the bloodline of the black queen." Aatif became overrun with hysterics. "Find me a holy man, al-Jeheuty. Find me a holy man!" He slammed his fist into the bed. "A cup of water to let me sleep! A cup of water to let me sleep!" He yelled the phrase over and over, squeezing al-Jeheuty's hand tighter and tighter.

The Beylerbey grabbed his brother's wrist and pulled free his hand. He called over his brother's voice, "Doctor! Doctor!" The physician assigned to Aatif charged into the room. He grabbed a pitcher of water and poured a cup for Aatif who continued to scream. The physician handed the water to Aatif. He violently grabbed the cup from the Moorish doctor and drank heavy. He laid down in the bed, panting and continuing to speak the phrase, "Find me a holy man." He drifted into sleep.

"He'll sleep. The water is mixed with a powerful herb." The doctor looked at al-Jeheuty and said, "That is how your brother has communicated for the last two days."

Al-Jeheuty released a heavy sigh. He thanked the doctor and said, "Continue to watch him." He didn't hear the doctor acknowledge the comment. Al-Jeheuty rushed from the room and paced quickly toward Rahmis, Wakil, Roberto, and Mehit. He had trouble feigning a smile as he reached for his wife and gave her a gentle kiss on the cheek. He made a quick glance toward her pregnant belly. His thoughts flashed into scenes described by his brother. Al-Jeheuty wiped them away, and then looked at Mehit with a quivering smile. "Mehit, I'll be in our quarters soon. I have business to discuss with these three gentlemen." Mehit did not argue, though she could feel the quake and tremble of anger that resonated through her husband's touch. She could feel it as she rubbed his forearms. She nodded her head and then departed down the hall. Al-Jeheuty waited until she turned the corner to address the three officials in a low, threatening voice, "Bring me Traont Coutelier. I will stab that created creature nine times for completion."

Rahmis put up his hands and said comfortingly, "Brother, you have a plan to stick to. Traont will meet his end. I've heard the things your brother has cried out. We all have. He came to the city looking distressed. He couldn't stand up. Traont told us Aatif might've caught a fever. We secluded him here. Your brother started ranting once he trusted that he was no longer in Coutelier's presence."

"Rahmis is correct," said Wakil. "You know the dangers in confronting Coutelier. He's a powerful man. He uses money to influence nobles. He'll have a fleet of French ships burn our city. We already know he's threatening that. He is—"

"He is Icarus!" al-Jeheuty screamed. His voice echoed through the palace halls. Wakil, Roberto, and Rahmis jumped at the sound of al-Jeheuty's furious voice. All three men relaxed, but nervously looked away as al-Jeheuty continued, his body shaking with a vengeful, angry emotion. "Do you hear me? He is Icarus, and I am the sun! Bring him to me, this I command. I will show you what candles, ornaments, and trinkets the wax of his wings will make when melted down by my heat!"

Roberto stepped away from the heated exchange. He came back with a cup of water and offered it to the Beylerbey. Al-Jeheuty drank, gulping down the entire liquid contents. Then he quickly realized his mistake. The cup was the same cup his brother drank from. It was the cup tainted with the medicinal herb that relaxed his brother and placed him in a sleep. Al-Jeheuty immediately became dizzy. He stumbled. Rahmis and Roberto caught the Beylerbey. Al-Jeheuty's eyes, aimed toward his officials, flickered with anger before rolling back. His lids closed unconscious. Rahmis and Roberto dragged their friend to his quarters, Wakil followed. Surprisingly, the door was opened. Mehit waited inside. She jumped as the city officials entered the room carrying her husband's body. She ran toward them, her face drenched with concern.

Wakil embraced Mehit, her eyes glued to her husband as Rahmis and Roberto placed him on the bed. "He's unconscious, Mehit. It was a stupid move," he looked at Roberto with a stern expression, "but it was a necessary one. He's been sedated. He was becoming erratic."

Mehit shook her head. "I could hear him."

Wakil made Mehit look straight at him. "He'll be fine," he assured her. "He's just overwhelmed by his brother's state, and the state of al-Mari Ifriq. He has a lot on his shoulders."

"I know," she said.

Wakil told her, "I have to oversee some business, and then I'll return to check on al-Jeheuty. Stay by his side."

"I will," said Mehit. "The bathhouse is in good hands for the rest of the day."

Wakil called for Rahmis and Roberto to follow him from the room. The two men, after securing al-Jeheuty on the bed, and loosening his sword and pistol, joined Wakil by the door. "It *was* necessary," said Roberto to Wakil, responding to the glaring look the governor continued to drown him with. He apologized to Mehit and said, "Your husband will have my head when he awakes, but understand that I saved him by making this move."

Mehit couldn't help but chuckle, though she was holding back tears. The gentlemen left her presence. She brought a chair to the side of the bed and took a seat. She watched her husband sleep gently. Her servant and temporary Moon knocked on the open door. The woman walked inside and bowed her head. "Mistress Anhur Has. Will you need my services to escort you to the bathhouse?"

"No, R'uza," Mehit responded. "You may retire to your quarters. I will call for your services later."

R'uza eyed al-Jeheuty. "The Beylerbey returned. Is he okay?"

Mehit nodded, yes. She fought the tears from collecting in her eyes. "Yes, R'uza. He's resting. He's very tired. You are dismissed." R'uza bowed again, and then the she exited the room. Mehit looked at her husband and opened his shirt to rub his chest. She started to cry as she gazed upon her husband's unconscious body. She felt the air fill his lungs, his chest rising and falling. She felt his heart pumping. Mehit watched al-Jeheuty sleep. He awoke an hour later, looking around at the environment he occupied. He felt the bed around him, wiping his hand over the mattress and sheets beneath him. He turned to Mehit, and he managed to smile. He even laughed.

Al-Jeheuty said sleepily, "I will call together a legal council to behead Roberto Hamaat." His comment made Mehit chuckle. He took a deep breath. "How's Aatif?"

"I don't know," Mehit said matter-of-factly. "I've been watching over you this entire time. You've been asleep for an hour. Would you like for me to check on your brother?"

Al-Jeheuty kept his smile. "Please, *mora.*"

Mehit stood from her chair and exited the room. Al-Jeheuty felt relaxed. The anger had coursed through him, though his determination remained. He stared at the canopy atop the bed. He felt lighter, relieved of anxiety. There was a sensation surrounding him that made him believe he was floating. Then he wondered what type of medicine was really used to sedate he and his brother.

Al-Jeheuty blinked the thought away. He lifted himself up, sitting on the edge of the bed. He straightened his opened shirt and stood on his feet. His robe lay on the far side of the bed. He reached over, snatched his garment, and wrapped himself inside it. Mehit and Roberto entered as he fashioned his sword around his waist. Al-Jeheuty turned.

Roberto was giving him a look, chin tucked to his chest, eyes up at an angle. "Wakil sent me to fetch you. Facing you is supposed to be my punishment. But, shit, what the hell else was I going to do to get you to calm down?"

Al-Jeheuty struggled to suppress a smile. He approached the aged assassin and patted his shoulders. "You made a bold move in a desperate situation."

"Sounds familiar," Roberto retorted. He then scolded al-Jeheuty. "You are the Beylerbey. I respect your title, but Wakil and I have years on you. When Wakil says to be silent, you close your mouth. My entire life has involved fulfilling marks on powerful men and common men. My point being is that I understand a little something about knowing when and when *not* to strike. I'm sure Behar instilled that in you all those years in Spain."

Al-Jeheuty said humbly, "Yes. I apologize for my behavior." He turned to Mehit and asked, "How's my brother?"

"Still sleeping," she answered.

"I'll see him. Privately." Al-Jeheuty walked out of the room and made his way back to the suite where his brother was recovering. He walked to the side of the bed, bent his knees to the floor, and cupped his brother's hand with his own. He whispered, "I can't break the trade, but I will kill some of its captains. This will be insignificant to the larger picture. Rest easy, Aatif. The man that holds our home hostage, the man that molested your mind with these images, he will burn in Hell. He will burn in Hell with all of the traders and slavers. Their descendants will burn in Hell too, even as they profit from this venture and live as kings and queens in this physical world. If the trade and practice collapse, but profit is still gained, even generations later, anyone who touches the blood monies generated from the labor of the incarcerated, black slave, they too will burn in Hell." He stood up, still holding his brother's hand. "I love you, my brother. I have to leave now. There are men I have to kill." He gently placed his brother's arm on his chest, and he walked from the room, his presence substituted by the nurse and physician attending to Aatif.

Al-Jeheuty met with Roberto in the hall, Mehit at rest in their quarters. "So, what treason will you perform next?" Al-Jeheuty commented playfully. Roberto gave him a quick glance out of the corner of his eye. "My sincerest apologies, Roberto, for my actions. And my sincerest gratitude for yours."

"Well, Beylerbey," Roberto began as they made their way toward the front entrance of the palace. "Let's go meet the phallus suckler whose life you threatened. He's on his way out. Says he would like Monsieur Chaffee to be in attendance. He's going to France to look for him."

"I'll tell Coutelier that he'll do better looking halfway between here and his home country for a sunken, wooden crate." The two men joined the rest of the officials at the docks. Al-Jeheuty shook hands with Traont Coutelier. He was not the devil or piratic slave-trader the Beylerbey envisioned. He was tall, handsome, and mild-mannered—a charm that probably carried him far in business and in the pursuit of women. He had dark, well-groomed hair, a rectangular and chiseled face, thin lips, and small brown eyes. Traont was polite, a wolf in sheep's clothing. He even asked al-Jeheuty about Aatif's condition. Al-Jeheuty simply replied, "Recovering." The Beylerbey cordially conducted the business, escorting the French trader to his flagship. He created a small air of tension when he asked, "When will your troops leave Nusurika? I don't like the way it looks. I feel like my home is being held hostage."

Traont masked himself with charm. He smiled wide, but the gesture looked smug, condescending. "I apologize, Beylerbey. I can tell you honestly that was not my intention. There are only twenty soldiers. That hardly calls for a military occupation."

Al-Jeheuty retorted in a stern voice, "It could be five soldiers, Monsieur Coutelier, and I would still be offended."

Traont's heart skipped, but his nervousness never showed. His smile continued to beam, he believing it to be charismatic. Al-Jeheuty considered it arrogant. Traont yielded to the Beylerbey's demands. "I will call these troops away when I return to France."

"I will see to it myself that they have left," said al-Jeheuty. "You have a week."

Traont bowed. "Yes, Beylerbey."

Al-Jeheuty put on a smile, shook Traont's hand, and said in a more delightful manner, "Thank you, Monsieur Coutelier. Thank you."

Traont turned and boarded his ship. He expressed in a low voice, his back to the Moors, "Desperate Moorish neggars. They will wear chains yet."

Al-Jeheuty and the other officials watched as Traont's ship left the dock and sailed away. Al-Jeheuty put his eyes in the direction where the island of Sicily lay. The fate of al-Mari Ifriq was no longer in the Beylerbey's hands, though his plans extended over the horizon, staging rebellion on a faraway island. All al-Jeheuty could do was hold his breath and pray to whatever deity would listen. He returned to the palace to watch over his brother, and to be with his wife.

Chapter Forty

The stars' reflection, floating on the water below, made it seem as if the lone, Italian trade vessel were hovering through the cosmos, an illusion spoiled by the faint crimson glimmer of dawn's yawning arrival. The Italian trade vessel entered the last hour of travel to Sicily. Nasir, locked inside the ship's cabin, practiced his Italian rigorously with Donatello Verola and Aludra el-Amin. Most of his language came from memorizing a script, which he only understood the basic elements of. Nasir barely slept, but Donatello lifted his confidence by complimenting the Moorish ambassador. Nasir asked Aludra to act as an interpreter for him, but both she and Donatello disagreed. Nasir needed to appear confident and strong when standing before the baron.

"I can memorize a script," Nasir said to Donatello in Italian, stumbling over his words. "But what if the baron likes to argue? He does understand my language. Maybe I can pull him into using my words."

Donatello shook his head and said, "He understands enough to make a quick point, but you know more Italian than he does the Afro-Arabic languages. Remember our conversation, Ambassador Sa'ood. This is a man who will shut up once you stroke his ego. You don't have much to worry about. I admit, at first, I believed your Beylerbey was insane concocting this idea. This does, however, solve both our problems." He patted Nasir's arm. "I will do most of the convincing, anyway. It's the baron's advisor that needs persuading the most. Signore Michele Solera. If he doesn't believe your mission serves Vatican interests, he will plead for Baron Agusto to decline."

Aludra did not wish to hear the politics. She was tired. She stood up and asked to be dismissed, to take her place among the disguised Moors in the cargo hold. Nasir permitted Aludra to leave. He also reflected on Donatello's words, considering the Sicilian's point. The Moorish ambassador asked, cautiously, "What about the Queen of Slaves? Adaeze. Is she truly royalty?"

Donatello nodded affirmatively. "Her noble line ends with her, but she is noble nonetheless. She might have relatives that would rally around her presence and make war to see her hold a crown. The Vatican is hoping."

"Even with a European husband?" Nasir questioned. "Any descendant of Cush that rallies around Adaeze's claim might be a very strict traditionalist. A Cushitic King for a Cushitic Queen."

"Then Vatican armies will support her." Donatello waved Nasir's line of questions away by stating, "Regardless. She will not marry Baron Agusto's nephew. Adaeze will be a free woman."

"And your family will preside over Crocifissa." Nasir raised a curious eyebrow.

Donatello leaned back in his chair and tapped his fingers against the table. "Yes. That is my goal. I'm trying to secure this area for business reasons, family business, and for the well being of Crocifissa." He smiled. "Much like *your* revolution in al-Mari Ifriq." Donatello smiled wider. "You have no idea how much the European studies your people's movements." His laughter cooled. "Your city will have nothing to fear from me. I will honor my word. I will also keep the Vatican away from your shores." Donatello chuckled. "Your speech is flawless when you're not thinking about what to say. Keep your confidence. Get sleep. We'll be nearing Sicilian shores soon."

Nasir stood up and made his way to the bunk bed. He removed his robe and slipped into the bottom bed. He drifted to sleep quickly, but was disturbed too soon to even remember his dreams. Tegu was shaking him lightly, telling him that the Sicilian shores had been reached. Nasir lifted from the bed, groggy, and cursing the motion of the ship's rise and fall on the water. He took his robe, wrapped himself in it, and headed out to the front of the ship.

Crocifissa glimmered like a beehive colonized by fireflies. The nightlights had not yet been extinguished, greeting both the ship's arrival and the arrival of the new day's sun. Nasir took a deep breath. He was amazed to see the Moorish structures that made up the small village, feeling as if he, in another lifetime, left himself a note about where he had been in the past, should he ever forget. He wondered what other notes he left behind while civilizing the world in past ages and lives. Most of the Moorish architecture had been redone to fit the contemporary Sicilian and Italian aesthetic, but the Moorish planning still haunted the settlement.

The ship was carefully steered into a small dock. Tegu, a second guard, and several personal servants, surrounded Nasir. Donatello's entourage joined the Moors. The Sicilian called for his vessel to remain guarded, along with its live cargo. The two parties disembarked from the trade vessel, Donatello's party taking lead. The Sicilian came across Baron Agusto's servants who greeted him with wide smiles that were wiped away by the curiosity of why African Moors had followed him to the shores. Donatello explained that Nasir was an ambassador from al-Mari Ifriq, and he requested an audience with Baron Agusto.

Nasir followed, Tegu and the others in tow. The Sicilian village's day started early. All the citizens' eyes watched the Moors march through their streets. Nasir scoped the small village and wondered how a quick rebellion could take place without civilian casualties. The plan, put together by Bo Yusuf, the al-Jasi chief, and Donatello Verola, called for no violence outside of the baron's court.

The journey ended at the baron's mansion, centered behind the village. The large dwelling house was hidden among a garden of vines and lush greenery that acted as a natural archway leading up to the entrance. Guards, armed with muskets and sabers, swarmed the perimeter. There were armed guards at the entrance, guards walking the wide balconies of the second floor, guards atop the roofs, and guards scattered around the premises. Nasir took note of their placement, trying to keep in his head the patterns of their movements. Donatello was immediately granted entrance, and Nasir's troupe followed close behind, stares continuing to hold the Moorish entourage.

Through the door was a large front hallway where a sequence of doors connected to the rest of the large manor in a spidery chain of smaller hallways and interior rooms. The wide hallway was empty, save a few placed paintings and vases sitting atop well-crafted wooden stools. The floor was checkered like a chessboard, and Nasir felt much like a pawn moved into a dangerous position. He took a breath and re-imagined himself as a bishop; he clearly was not a knight. The Moorish ambassador thought about how Donatello was castling his own king.

A large staircase lay before the party, which Donatello led them past. They continued through a narrow passageway that lay beyond a door on the far side of the large front room. The narrow hall was red, lined with burning sconces placed between more paintings of nobles unfamiliar to Nasir. At the end of the hall was a door. Donatello stopped. He turned and asked for all parties to wait. He disappeared through the door.

Nasir took another breath. He started going through the Italian language. Questions. Answers. Conjugations. He checked his brow. There was no sweat. He was thankful for that. There was no need to check his heart, it boomed loudly in his ear. He was very much alive. His heart, though, skipped when Donatello returned and waved all the men inside. He waited by the door as the parties entered another large room. The area was magnificent and grand, separated and held up by columns. It was the baron's courtroom. A white platform with three stairs lay in the center of the room, a long red carpet, outlined in a golden color, led to the small stage.

Baron Agusto did not occupy the room at the present moment. Nasir scanned the room again, thinking he may have missed the baron's presence. There were servants. His advisor, Signore Michele Solera, and other men dressed in the manner of officials were in attendance.

Donatello separated Nasir from his entourage and brought him to the front of the court. Michele Solera greeted Nasir respectfully. The Moorish ambassador returned the gesture and stood straight. "Baron Agusto was not expecting your arrival so early this morning," explained Michelle. "Court does not begin for another three hours." He put his gaze on Donatello. "You know this, Donatello."

"Yes," the Sicilian said in a humble nature. He bowed his head. "I also understand that early is better than late in the baron's court."

Michele said to Nasir, "I hope you don't mind your wait."

"I'm a patient man," Nasir said confidently in Italian. "But there's no need to wait. You're just as authorized to preside over court as the baron, are you not? I may at least present the concerns of our partnerships, and the concerns of my city-state, to you?"

"Yes," Michele acknowledged. "However, no decision could be made on the matter until the baron arrives. I apologize, Ambassador. I will not let you go hungry. You and your entourage may wait in the dining hall."

Nasir did not mind. He was merely practicing his speech and keeping his confidence afloat. Had his proposition been effective, he would simply have stated the matters of politics and business that brought him to Sicilian shores. He wondered if he could possibly catch up on sleep, but he decided it would be best to stay awake. Donatello escorted Nasir's party to the dining hall where they all took seat at a long, fine and strong wooden table. Nasir told Donatello that any meal would satisfy. The Sicilian disappeared to the kitchen and left Nasir and the other Moors.

No one spoke.

Nasir inspected his surroundings. Every noise caused the Moorish Ambassador to jump and look around. Nasir tried to relax. He considered this venture no different than when he traveled to al-Gherab and met with al-Kasim Askari Pasha. Nasir reminded himself that The Four Winds had him marked for death at that time. He was fighting and negotiating for his life then. His current mission's contact, Baron Agusto, held the mark this time. He was here, along with an army of Moors, to execute the mark.

There should be nothing to fear, save the violent revolution secretly planned for the remainder of his stay.

Donatello returned with cooks hosting an arrangement of breakfast treats. The Sicilian didn't stay long, attending to other matters. Nasir indulged in the grape juice, wishing it were something stronger. He tried a boiled egg with spices sprinkled over it. He drank water to calm his bubbling stomach. He saw that Tegu and the servants also ate very little. He then thought of Ojodo, Nuru, the al-Jasi Chief, Aludra, and all the men and women still packed inside the cargo hold of the trading vessel. Nasir considered Nuru either brave or foolish to allow his people to help host such a risky venture. Truthfully, Nuru was not a chief. He was a General that once served a Moorish Governor in a city long destroyed by al-Kasim Askari Pasha's forces. The al-Jasi Nzambi were the remnants of the urban center. Nasir considered the nation's story in conjunction with the Ogunsanwo-Mashek, and all that al-Jeheuty and Bo Yusuf reported about the people and their Mesopotamian origins.

These stories in Africa were becoming too similar, and not in a positive manner.

Nasir drank another cup of grape juice. He sat quietly and patiently with his entourage. Donatello entered on occasion to attend to the Moors. "All was fine," he assured. Tegu responded, once the Sicilian left their presence, "I wonder if al-Jeheuty sent us here to die." He joked, "Do you have any outstanding debts to the Beylerbey?" He sat back and apologized for his humor. Nasir thanked Tegu for relaxing him, though he did not crack a smile or chuckle. The remaining time passed with the same awkward silence. Donatello joined the Moors again to escort them back to the baron's court.

"Baron Agusto secludes himself in this fortress of a mansion," Donatello whispered the information as he guided Nasir and the others back to the courtroom. "It allows the people to come to him. He gets to know the citizens that have complaints. They do not get to know him, though."

Nasir walked back into the courtroom. Baron Agusto stood at the front of the court. He waved Nasir toward him. He was cordial, offering his sympathies for the tragedy suffered within al-Mari Ifriq's hierarchy.

"Thank you," replied Nasir. "It's this tragedy that has brought forth a series of events that leads me to your village, Baron." He was calm, firm, and confident in his speech. He took control of the conversation by using Baron Agusto's words to segue into his proposition. "Al-Mari Ifriq finds itself at war with a nomadic nation. The Ogunsanwo-Mashek are the people that have struck against us. The politics are not complicated. The Ogunsanwo-Mashek, despite peace talks with them, considered our trade with a kingdom they have been at war with for hundreds of years, threatening. Our best ambassadors struggled to make a triad of peace. The Ogunsanwo-Mashek took the offensive." He tried to catch a breath, slightly nervous when he realized some of his words were Spanish, and some accented with a French sound. His point was coming across however, and the baron was too intrigued to care about proper grammar.

"You know the extent of the damage." Nasir took another pause, this time for affect. "We are now at war. We are set to round up this nation and bring them to justice." He put his head down, humbling himself before he spoke. It was a gesture that was executed for only a second. He looked up, locking eyes with Baron Agusto. "Beylerbey Anhur Has looks to allies for support. For you, Baron Agusto, he has a proposition. He is offering four hundred slaves. African."

The slightest smirk materialized on the baron's lips as he spoke. "You need financing? How much for these slaves?"

Nasir's heart skipped. This was where the debate would kick in. He couldn't afford to stutter or ask the baron to repeat himself. This was not practice. He put more emphasis on his next set of words. He sounded more confident and assertive. "The Beylerbey wishes to take a greater percentage from the trading venture between al-Mari Ifriq and Crocifissa. He considers this an easier exchange." The baron was silent. He looked to his advisor, Michele Solera. Nasir continued, "We have already brought two hundred slaves. There are one hundred and fifty strong men. There are twenty-five women, and there are twenty-five children."

The baron's silence continued. He finally asked, "How long does your Governor-General believe the war will last?"

"Two months," Nasir answered.

Baron Agusto became silent again. He consulted with Michele Solera. The advisor whispered, "We have just started to enjoy the luxury that the revenue has brought us. We have been able to lighten taxes because of this venture. We have also saved our village from financial collapse and bankruptcy. The last thing we need is to go crawling to the Vatican and ask for another loan. Our only import, Baron, is the citizens fleeing Trapani. Our only exports are disease and our dead. We have to be careful on the percentage of take these Moors are asking for."

Baron Agusto agreed. He turned back to Nasir and asked, "What is your Governor-General asking?"

"A twenty-five percent increase in our take," Nasir answered.

The baron shook his head and responded, "Absolutely not."

Nasir stepped forward. He took a quick breath before speaking, hiding it with another swift look to the ground and then returning his gaze to the baron. "Invest these slaves in the trade. You'll make twice the amount in a month's time. You will recoup your loses."

The baron contemplated.

Donatello Verola stepped up beside Nasir. He bowed his neck and asked, "May I have your ear, Baron Agusto?"

"Approach, Donatello," the baron accepted.

Donatello moved closer to the baron. He whispered in his ear, "The slaves might make a great army," he suggested. "They could rally around Adaeze when we introduce her to her noble roots. It would help in the Vatican's cause." He looked back at Nasir, smiled, and then spoke to the baron again. "Investment in the trade is a good notion. I already know a buyer, a Frenchman. However, invest little. Few of the men. Few of the women and children. We retain most for our Queen of Slaves." He put his eyes on Michele Solera. Donatello spoke loud enough for the advisor to hear his words.

Baron Agusto also looked at Michele.

The advisor nodded affirmatively.

The baron clarified, "You believe this would be a good idea?"

"Yes," said the advisor, reluctantly. "Though, we should compromise with the Moors. Increase the amount of slaves. Six hundred. We'll inspect the slaves they have now. I'm sure they can afford such a deal. After all, the live in the land of *our* opportunity."

The three men lifted from counsel. The baron addressed Nasir. "Six hundred slaves. We have a deal. We will inspect the goods that you have brought to my court."

Nasir stayed silent. He feigned frustration, pretending to hide the expression from the baron. He was convincing. The baron suppressed another sly smile. Nasir noticed. The subtle grin reminded the Moorish Ambassador of his father's lessons, subjects on which were the mocking tones and arrogant grins painted on the faces of hardheaded and hard-boiled company bosses. The men that believed they held the winning hand in business, too stubborn to move from a position or point, too arrogant to understand how much they were being played.

Nasir imagined his father standing next to him. Sa'ad appeared. His face was filled with business, projecting a strong gaze at the baron. Nasir ended his façade and spoke, "As a representative of Beylerbey Anhur Has, as an extension of his power and judgment, I decline your offer." The baron's expression quivered. Nasir smiled. It was a humble gesture as he expressed, "Al-Mari Ifriq will offer you, Baron Agusto, one thousand slaves. The amount will be presented to you over the next two months."

Both men bowed toward one another. Sa'ad's image faded as he turned to Nasir and beamed proudly. The baron stepped down from his platform and shook Nasir's hands. "I will have my judges and lawyers draw up a contract. I have other cases to attend to. Until then, bring the slaves to my court. I would like to inspect my property."

Donatello stepped into the conversation. "I will see him back to my trade vessel." He looked at Nasir. "Let us go." He pointed to the other Moors. "Gather your servants."

Nasir made a signal with his hands toward Tegu and the others. The servants formed up around the ambassador, and Donatello led the party of Moors from the mansion. Neither man discussed the proceedings that just concluded. "We'll give you lodging," said Donatello. "My family controls two inns. The baron may ask for you to stay with him. His delusional suspicions cause him to keep people close, and not out of friendship."

The men boarded the ship. Nasir's entourage waited on the docks. He entered the cargo hold and sighed as he beheld the two hundred men, women, and children. Among them was his friend, Ojodo Yerodin. There also was Chief Nuru, the graying elder looking eager to lead his troops into a remarkable battle. Aludra el-Amin, along with eight other Moons, was among the female participants. The African inhabitants were chained and clothed with flimsy garments. Aludra watched Nasir's sorrowful expression closely. She could feel the weight of duty piled on the ambassador. She wished to reach out and execute the burden troubling Nasir, but it was Ojodo that reacted to the ambassador's state. The titan's chuckle rumbled throughout the hold. "Don't look so sad, Ambassador. We're here for the purpose of rebellion. You're not truly selling us away."

Nasir smiled warmly. "I'm here to continue the ruse. Nuru, Ojodo, Aludra and the other Moons. Keep a close look on the guard count. I believe most of this fight will take place within the baron's manor. The baron's nephew remains in Libya. The targets are Baron Agusto and his advisors, most notably, Michele Solera. The advisors live separately from the baron. Donatello Verola and I will conceive a plan to bring them together." He whispered his next line. His voice carried like a ghost, "Our rebellion will be swift. Should any man grope the women, Moons, you are ordered to begin the rebellion with that as your cue. I don't believe that will be a problem, however. I'm sure that would occur should I truly be selling you, and once I left these shores. Besides, Donatello's people will be overseeing your care—if we can call it that." He looked at Ojodo. "Let the production commence, dramatist."

Nasir returned above board. He gave a nod to Donatello Verola. The Sicilian turned and ordered his people, all members of his covert organization. They journeyed into the ship's hold and led the cast of rebels out of the ship's belly. Nasir turned away from the sight. He walked alongside Donatello, leading the procession back to the baron's mansion. The citizens' stares were revitalized. The line of two hundred black bodies were watched all the way until they disappeared into the shrubbery that clouded the path to the mansion's front entrance.

Donatello and Nasir brought the chained blacks to the baron's court. Adaeze was now in attendance. Two black men and six black women surrounded the young Ethiop woman. Nasir considered the sight surreal. Adaeze looked like royalty even while reduced to a slave. She was still clothed in a shroud, much like the day when she visited al-Mari Ifriq. This time, her garments were colored light yellow and orange.

The two hundred men, women, and children filled the court's arena, huddled across the back. The baron, standing in the center of the room, on his platform, scanned the mass of blacks brought before him. His eyes stopped on Ojodo. His mouth dropped. He stepped down from the platform and called for a servant. "Bring that big neggar to me. The big one."

Ojodo became nervous. He hoped his presence had not endangered the overall mission. He was hoping Baron Agusto did not remember him, a dockworker at al-Jeheuty's command, or, possibly, a worker that was often friendly, sharing a joke with the current Beylerbey.

Servants responded quickly to Baron Agusto's orders, but they became timid when approaching Ojodo's enormous physical frame. Donatello's people unlocked Ojodo from the chain link. They furnished the Moorish titan with another pair of shackles, and they passed him to the baron's still timid servants who nervously escorted Ojodo to Baron Agusto. They kept their eye on the giant's movements. Ojodo presented no struggle. He was placed in front of the baron. Agusto bent his neck back to look up. He examined Ojodo, completely in awe of his size. He walked around the Moor quoting, "*The land, through which we have gone to spy it out, is a land that devours its inhabitants, and all the people that we saw in it are of great height. And there we saw the Nephilim, the sons of Anak, who come from the Nephilim, and we seemed to ourselves like grasshoppers, and so we seemed to them.*" Baron Agusto took another breath. "He is a marvelous spectacle." He put his hands on Ojodo, burrowing his hands along Ojodo's physique, around his buttocks, along his back, and under and around his groin. He palmed Ojodo's leg muscles, felt his arms. "Should I keep this black giant for myself, or make a merchant ship's weight in gold for selling him?" He continued to feel Ojodo's physique. "Look at what fallen angels and the daughters of men can create." He caressed Ojodo's thick locks. "Should I castrate your strength like Delilah, or keep you beautiful and angry?"

Ojodo flinched. He tried to remain still throughout the baron's molestation, but he stirred ever so slightly. The greater offense was that Ojodo grumbled. It was low, but the baron's ears caught the noise. It was a grunt, a growl, and a warning brought on by reflex.

"Yes," spoke Baron Agusto in a low whisper. He then regained his composure, remembering he was in attendance of an audience. He backed away from Ojodo and declared, "*Beastly neggar!* You growl? You bare fangs? I am David, you dreadful Goliath." He waved to his guards. "Whips. Bring them. Hit him. Until his knees touch the floor." Servants brought whips to the guards. Ojodo was stripped of his shirt. The giant remained still, Nasir and the other Moors and blacks looked on in horror.

The guards approached Ojodo and commenced to slap his back. Ojodo barely moved, though it felt like wild animals clawed at him. Baron Agusto turned away from the sight and addressed the other captive blacks. "You do not understand my language," he yelled. "But you will understand this. *Cush will submit herself to God.* Psalms sixty-eight, thirty-one." He turned back to Ojodo who, unbeknownst to the baron, understood the Italian language fluently. "Submit!" Baron Agusto screamed to Ojodo as whips ravaged the Moorish titan. *"Submit!"* he screamed again.

Nasir stood still. He made no eye contact to General Nuru or Aludra. He did not want to give a false signal for attack, though this would have made an interesting time for such action. Nasir watched Ojodo closely. The titan didn't face him. Nasir barely saw Ojodo's face in profile. But there was something there in the Moorish goliath. There was something in his eyes. He looked as if he was on a stage. The whips crashed against him, tearing his flesh, and drawing blood. Ojodo buckled. The goliath sunk to his knees, the rest of his body falling forward like the tower of Babel.

Ojodo submitted, forearms against the floor.

Everyone, including Baron Agusto, jumped. Nasir believed he saw the quick glimmer of a smile on Ojodo's face. Nasir understood. This was the dramatist's greatest act. Ojodo lifted his body, still on his knees. He screamed loud. Baron Agusto commanded his guards, "Continue." The soldiers stepped forward, ready to strike again.

"No," a voice shouted. It was Adaeze. She stepped toward the baron. "Please. I ask your court for mercy, Good Man. Baron Agusto Ghislanzoni, I beg." She stood in front of the baron and dropped to her knees. She bowed her head. "Please, my Good Man. Please, Baron."

Agusto rubbed the back of Adaeze's head. With the same hand, and within the same motion, he cupped the young woman's chin. He lifted her head and stroked her cheek with his thumb. "You bow to me, but I am at your command. Do you want him for your *seraglio*?" He chuckled. He called off his guards. He turned his attention back to Adaeze, removing his hand from her face. "You are so beautiful." He wiped his pointer finger along her cheek. He walked to Nasir and thanked him. "You have brought me the most beautiful, black specimens that Africa has to offer. The trade of these slaves will help our economy. We will not miss the revenue we've lost from our trade. You are correct. We might even gain more. Give my greatest thanks to your current Governor-General. We will celebrate tomorrow night." He put his arm around Nasir and led him away. "It has been a long morning. It will be an even longer rest of the day. I have much to attend to. Tonight we rest. Tomorrow we drink." He looked at his servants. "Donatello, round up these neggars. Take them to the shanty houses that reside in the eastern field. We'll keep them there. They are not to mix with Adaeze's stock. Though, if Adaeze wishes to look over the people—and I stress—*by herself* and chaperoned by you, then that is permissible. Let Adaeze wash the big neggar's wounds."

Donatello hurriedly attended to his duties.

Nasir felt naked as he was left alone to humor the baron. He was brought to an elegant suite that was presented as his lodging. Nasir decided to make his stay in the room. His entourage joined him close to an hour later. Tegu and the others carried luggage brought from the trade vessel. Nasir informed Tegu, "Donatello will be here shortly. He'll give you lodging at his family's inn. I'll stay here—" It was then that Donatello knocked on the partially opened door. Nasir allowed his entrance. "Please, lead my party to your family's inn. They can find lodging there?"

"Yes," said Donatello, surprise in his voice. "You won't be joining your people?"

"No," answered Nasir. "I'll stay within the baron's company. I hope there's no offense."

"None," Donatello replied. He said in a low voice, "We should remain cautious as the hour of revolution approaches. All parties must be accounted for."

"I understand," Nasir assured. "Speak with Ojodo. We will attack after tomorrow night's festivities, just as I retire. The night will be our advantage. All parties not involved in the attack will head to your trading vessel."

"Yes," Donatello acknowledged. He did have some concern, and it showed on his face. He asked Nasir, "Would an attack during the festivity not be a more precise time?"

Nasir considered the Sicilian's point. But he maintained, "The height of the party will allow their blood to be excited. The baron and his troupe would be caught off guard, but it would only be a moment before they sober up. We will catch them drunk. The guards might not take a sip, but they will be relaxed because their benefactors will be relaxed."

"I see your point," Donatello conceded. "However, seeing a bloodthirsty mob of slaves will sober up anyone."

Nasir chuckled. "True. I'm going to catch up on rest. See that my servants are cared for."

"I most certainly will, Ambassador," Donatello assured.

The Sicilian led Tegu and the other Moorish servants from Nasir's suite, taking them to a family inn located at the heart of the coastal, Sicilian village. Nasir removed his robes and slipped into the comfortable bed. He quickly went to sleep, his spirit ripped from his body and taken to another world. When Nasir awoke, the sun was partially below the horizon. There was knocking at his door. It was Tegu. Nasir jumped from his bed and opened the door. He was so well rested that there was no grogginess to shake from his head. He was now hungry, however.

"I haven't disturbed you, Ambassador?" asked Tegu.

"Not at all," Nasir affirmed. He invited Tegu inside and closed the doors. "How is your stay?"

"Fine. Signore Donatello wished for me to find you." Tegu chuckled. "Communication was rough. I barely understand him. He barely understands me. Though, he's gotten a better grasp on our language than I his, considering his time in Libya."

"Welcome to my world," Nasir joked.

"Donatello is hosting a dinner for us," Tegu started to think. "I believe he was ordered to do so by the baron. Regardless, Ambassador, there is a feast waiting for us. There are two Italian servants waiting to escort you to the mansion's bath-room."

Nasir gathered a change of clothes and followed Tegu from the room. The baron's provided servants led Nasir to the baths. Tegu waited patiently while the ambassador soaked, washed, dried, and changed his clothes. Nasir emerged fresh and ready for a feast. He followed Tegu downstairs, returning to the dining hall. Donatello and several other Sicilians occupied the room. "Please, Ambassador, sit. Baron Agusto regrets that he could not join us. He is still holding court, and he and his advisors have other political matters to attend."

Nasir indulged the invitation. He viewed the magnificent meal in front of him. His stomach started to rumble. He stepped toward the meal and immediately felt a strong weight against his stomach. The force spread to his chest, holding him in place. Nasir stepped back. The force was simply a guilty feeling of enjoying a large meal while Ojodo and the others played slave for the enjoyment of the baron. Nasir witnessed that Donatello was watching him closely. The Sicilian's expression denoted that he understood what Nasir must have been feeling.

The ambassador took a breath and took another step forward. Nasir figured that if Ojodo and the others had a part to play, so too did he. He took a seat, inviting Tegu to join them. Nasir's other assistants were dining at Donatello's inn. Nasir and Donatello made pleasant conversation. Nasir engaged in stories about al-Mari Ifriq's politics and growing up in the corsair-state. Without giving too much of his family's business away, Donatello entertained Nasir with tales of trade and enterprise. "Again, some of these foreign rulers have marked my family—and the larger Sicilian organization—as pirates no different than the corsair-states. Gangsters. Violent clans." He looked to each entrance in the room before speaking. The men in his presence checked the doors, opening them a small ways, seeing if the area was clear, and then nodding toward Donatello that all was well.

"I consider Baron Agusto a foreigner," Donatello continued. "His blood is from Northern Italy, and he bleeds the blood of Spaniards and Francs. I'm sure a Brit was fucked somewhere in that mix. Solera, he assists him. The Church backs him." He put his hand on his heart. "My beloved Church. She twists faith into politics and shares her bed with anyone." He stood up and took the seat next to Nasir. "And when a Sicilian cares for his homeland, it is considered treason against the foreign ruler. Foreigners who become prominent figures on Sicilian shores give monies to our occupiers; offering tribute to a noble, they are considered a patriot. The Sicilian can do the same, ah, but he is then committing bribery. A Sicilian opens a business, mostly to serve the interests of the Sicilian people that are forgotten amidst politics in our own land—suddenly we are serving self-interest, not the common good. Our businesses are considered rackets. When the Sicilian refuses to be coerced into turning in his or her brother, suddenly we bear false witness in court." He waved a hand and sighed. "The Sicilian has become the new Jew." Donatello threw up his hands wildly. Nasir believed the Sicilian was feeling the wine running through him. "And yes, I admit, because of our situation, we are forced to stoop to ungodly actions."

Nasir quickly took a sip of his drink and said, "Like bringing in Moors to help stage a rebellion."

Donatello shook his finger at Nasir. The Moorish ambassador beamed a sly grin. He humored Donatello. He liked the Sicilian, though Donatello was lying to him. Roberto's spies already put together that Donatello was part of a crime syndicate vying to control trade and other ventures within Sicily. The one thing the Sicilian was truthful about was the fact that his organization was fighting against foreign occupation and corrupt politics, but they were far from righteous revolutionaries. Donatello's syndicate had a tendency to strong-arm the Sicilian population, forcing the citizens to side with their organization over foreign nobility rule.

Donatello continued to shake his finger and smile. He said to Nasir, "The world looks to you, Moor. The world will follow your lead, even when you are slaves." He sat up and leaned on the table with his elbow. "Perhaps you blacks have always been slaves. You have always served the earth." He looked up and said in a euphoric, drunken manner, "The cosmos." He looked at Nasir. "The European. The Greeks. The Romans. You imparted knowledge to us all. *Princes shall come out of Egypt; and Cush shall stretch her arms out to the World.* That is how some have translated Psalms sixty-eight, thirty-one. No longer. There needs to be a justification to put you in chains. You have always served your offspring. Parents are slaves to their children, are they not?"

Nasir considered the point. He also considered that Donatello was just telling him what he wanted to hear. He lifted his cup and said with a smile, "Good wine makes philosophers of us all, Sicilian."

Both men laughed.

The feast continued.

Chapter Forty-One

Ojodo felt searing pain mixed with a cool, healing sensation as Adaeze applied strips of soaked bandages to the deep lacerations covering his back. Adaeze discovered, long ago, among the imported books in the baron's library, a tattered medicinal manuscript, translated into Italian, and originally scribed by the Moors. Adaeze stole the book, keeping it among what little possessions she was allowed to have. The baron discovered the book, but he allowed Adaeze to keep it. *"The remedies in that book are for you blacks. I have no time for them,"* he said to her. She used the book's knowledge, at the present moment, to blend a medicinal element, concocted from crushed flower petals, into the soaked bandages to allow Ojodo's long, narrow cuts to heal without infection.

Ojodo lay flat atop a torn mattress, the downs and straws of which poured from its open sides. His locks hung long to the ground, over his shoulders, and away from the scars on his back. The two of them occupied a shanty house, one of many stationed in the eastern field that lay beyond the mansion. The houses lodged the baron's black servants, also referred to as *Adaeze's Chain.*

Adaeze was given a comfortable lodge that lay closer to the mansion, but she spent much of her time at the shanty houses, or with the baron's nephew, Giovanni Ghislanzoni-Verdi, when he was not away in Africa. The tribute of new black slaves was kept in separate houses from Adaeze's people. Truthfully, the houses were old, broken down barn houses from settlers long ago. Guards swarmed the fields, making it impossible for an escape. Several men and women tried. None succeeded. The offense was punishable by death. The lost black slaves were replaced.

Baron Agusto, for the most part, treated the blacks well. He was a good man to them, so much so that Adaeze referred to him as her 'Good Man'. The baron made sure she and the others were fed, kept clothed, and there were few incidents regarding the women and drunk and overly spirited guards. However, the intensity with which Adaeze's *'Good Man'* called for the African titan to be beaten into submission, was a fury she had never witnessed from him. Baron Agusto had been extremely kind as of late, teaching her much about the Bible and the African land where she came from. It was, according to him, a holy land. Cush, the true Ethiopia.

Baron Agusto called it *The Center of God's World.* His voice, when he spoke of tales of the kingdom, was so filled with passion and romance that Adaeze felt confused as to why her Good Man insisted on a courtship with his nephew when clearly she was starting to fall in love with him.

It took Adaeze the last three years of her young life to understand that sentiment. She was in love with Baron Agusto Ghislanzoni. However, there were new feelings about the baron. These feelings were conjured up immediately as Adaeze witnessed the baron shout orders to break the black titan that lay wounded in front of her. The baron looked mad. He was sadistic, possessed, especially when he fondled the giant. Adaeze substituted her love for Baron Agusto with pity for him, and she also substituted it with suspicion. Those feelings were washed away as she massaged Ojodo's shoulders and tended to his wounds with the medicinally laced bandages.

Ojodo moaned. The medicine soaked inside the bandages tingled his wounds, pricking at his nerves in a cool, pinching manner. He inhaled, making quick, wincing breaths. Adaeze stepped away from Ojodo to light a lamp inside the shanty house. She tended to Ojodo in the back of the barn. The other blacks huddled to the sides.

Adaeze returned to Ojodo. She inspected his massive frame. There came a sensation that felt as if an invisible hand grabbed at her chest, trying to pull her closer to Ojodo's enormous black, muscular body. Adaeze fought against the feeling. It flickered like a spark, a burning sensation that started in her chest then rippled with intensity throughout her body. Her thighs quivered. She caressed Ojodo's left shoulder with her hand. Her touch was more sensual than a soothing massage. To Ojodo, Adaeze's touch negated the war waged within his nerves between the medicinal bandages and his torn flesh.

"The spirit caresses the physical earth," said the Moorish giant.

Adaeze jumped at the sound of Ojodo's voice, though his tone was soft and as gentle as her hand gliding over his shoulder. She didn't understand his words, but she understood his tone. She felt compelled to say, "Legendary titan. I want to know your name. What does our...home...call you? What does Africa call you?"

Ojodo understood her words. He could not respond to her, at least, not in her language. He replied in his native tongue, "Mend my language back together, my flesh, and I will compose a revolution for you, *mora.* I will call it *The Scream of the Princess's Giant.*"

Adaeze smiled warmly when Ojodo reacted to his own sentiment with a chuckle and sly grin. The giant closed his eyes and started to rest. He lay on his stomach, face resting on a cheek, and arms at his side. Adaeze watched Ojodo fall asleep, rubbing his shoulders the entire time. She stood up and left the shanty house, traveling to the small lodge where she resided. Guards followed her, and Adaeze wished they did not. She always laughed to herself when she watched the guards fumble over one another to escort her across the fields or around Crocifissa. This was an occurrence that happened more and more frequently now that Signore Donatello Verola was not around to attend to the duty. He was now off in Libya, a place the baron continuously promised Adaeze she would soon visit.

However, the guards' presence disturbed her thoughts. Their actions to fight playfully over supervising her travel suddenly did not amuse her. She often wondered what made her so special. This particular incident made her believe the guards' reactions were beyond a simple adolescent-like response to her beauty. Adaeze started to believe there was a magnetic exoticism residing in her that made her as much a spectacle and phenomena as the black titan shackled in the baron's court.

Shame and anger clothed Adaeze.

Adaeze looked around her. She started to see the familiar landscape of Crocifissa as a foreign place. The village she grew up in was quickly becoming a stranger to her. She started to feel like a stranger to the land.

The guards following continued to annoy her. She imagined Ojodo's mighty frame breaking through the earth, conjured through magic, and battling the guards surrounding her. Adaeze conjured up the image of Ojodo's locks growing thicker and longer from his head, the snakes of hair acting independently of Ojodo. They reached out and strangled the guards, snapping their necks. Adaeze smiled. She climbed the wooden stairs leading to her lodge's front door, the house being elevated from off the ground. She entered. The house consisted of only three rooms. There was the front room, a private bath, and a room with a table and three chairs. There was an old canopy bed located in the corner of the front room as well as a large cabinet to store her clothes. Adaeze slipped into bed. She thought about Ojodo. She smiled and exhaled. She kept her imaginings innocent. Adaeze was, even in her imagination, intimidated by the titan's physique.

Her thoughts massaged her to sleep.

Adaeze's dreams did not focus on her infatuation. Her sleep consisted of shapes, colors, and scenarios she didn't understand. There were odd voices and familiar voices. She awoke to the sound of knocking at her door. It was late and very dark. Adaeze rose from her bed and permitted Donatello Verola entrance. He had with him a hot meal and a smile. "Signore Verola," she bowed courteously. Donatello gave her a kiss on the cheek. He presented the plate of hot food and Adaeze led him into the table room. She made light for them to see.

Donatello placed the food down and took a seat. "The hour is late."

Adaeze stood straight, hands together, head down. "Was there a duty I overlooked, Signore?"

Donatello shook his head, no. "The blacks are being fed. The tribute is being attended to as well. My family is overseeing the matters. Feel safe. Get rest." He paused. He motioned for Adaeze to take a seat. The young woman sat down, her head still bowed. "Adaeze, look at me." Adaeze lifted her head on command. "Get rest," he repeated. "I want you to attend to all your duties tomorrow. Get the slaves to the men and women they are scheduled to serve. Do not worry about the tribute."

"What about the wounds on the giant?" she asked.

"Inspect them in the morning and throughout the day," said Donatello. "But worry no more. My people will handle this new stock. I will meet with you at this time tomorrow night." That was all he could tell her. Donatello stood up to leave. Adaeze called his name suddenly, and he stopped.

Adaeze took a small breath, and a chance, when she said, "Signore Verola, please push for the Good Man to permit me travel to Libya with you. I would like to visit. I've become curious with all the Biblical tales of…Africa."

Donatello nodded. "Eat, Adaeze." He turned and left the house. Adaeze started to eat the meal brought to her. She felt lonely. The small house expanded. Adaeze felt exposed. Her meal, though good, was not enjoyable. She still ate everything on her plate. She then returned to the front room, removed her clothes, and replaced them with a nightgown. She slipped back into her bed, and then went to sleep. It was easy to fall back into slumber. Her dreams were not much more coherent, but familiar faces appeared.

Adaeze was standing in a desert wasteland. She was naked, but felt very comfortable, as if she were clothed. Massive, decaying cities crumbled in the distance. The baron's nephew, Giovanni Ghislanzoni-Verdi walked toward her, a crumbling city behind him. He sank into the sands with every step he took. He struggled to move forward, reaching out to Adaeze, eyes wide. Giovanni screamed for help. Adaeze backed away from him. He screamed louder as he sank deeper, ultimately devoured by the sands.

Adaeze turned around. The land dropped, substituted by a vast body of water. Baron Agusto appeared at her left, the sun setting behind him. Adaeze ran toward the sea, the baron pursued. She dived into the water, and though she no longer resided above, she could see the scene in her mind of a giant wave rising as a result of her impact against the water. The baron was drenched by the wave, but he was not killed. Below the waters lay the King of the Sea. It was the black titan recently delivered to the baron. He grabbed her arm and his massive frame grew larger, into a true giant. The titan held Adaeze in the palm of his hand. His upper half emerged from the water, looking down at Baron Agusto who stood next to a wooden pole. Tied to the pole was another Adaeze.

Baron Agusto said with remorse, "My father cut your head off. So too shall I." He removed a sword and decapitated the head of the second Adaeze. He lifted it, brandishing it like a weapon. The eyes opened. Yellow lights glowed from the sockets. Adaeze was terrified. The giant was in danger. She stood on the palm of his hand and jumped down to the sandy beach. Her impact against the earth caused the land to shake, and the baron lost his balance. He remained on his feet, the head in his hands aimed at the giant, the eyes still glowing bright yellow. Adaeze grabbed the head from the baron, but it was too late. The giant's massive figure turned to a dull gray color and broke into fourteen pieces. The head dissolved from the baron's grip. He subdued Adaeze, tying her to the pole where her second body lay moments earlier.

The young Moorish ambassador appeared. Adaeze knew his name. It was Nasir Sa'ood. He held in his hands emerald tablets. Adaeze wanted to ask the young man for help, but Nasir spoke first. He presented the tablets and said, "I did not write these. My chief did. I can tell you what they mean." He spoke his next words very casually, as if Adaeze was not tied to a wooden post. He said, "Come with me. This won't take long." The baron grabbed the tablets. The emerald scriptures transfigured into The Holy Bible. He flipped through the pages looking annoyed.

The baron looked distracted. Adaeze pleaded with Nasir, "Please find me seven scorpions. I have to find my husband. I need to put him back together."

Nasir put his hands on Adaeze's shoulders. He beamed a warm smile. "You'll make love to his spirit. You will give birth to him. He's like the sun, always rising and setting."

Adaeze woke up. It was an hour before dawn. Adaeze was accustomed to getting up at such an early hour. Her dreams were forgotten, but the feeling of escape remained. She rose from her bed without grogginess. She changed out of her robe and picked out clothes to wear. Her wardrobe consisted of the same style of garments, different colors. She chose violet, and then exited to find two black maidens to fetch warm water for her bath.

Adaeze entered one of the shanty houses. Two women were already waiting. They bowed their heads and waited for Adaeze to command them for the heated water. Adaeze instructed them, and then afterwards, she journeyed to another shanty house to wake one of the older black men. The Italians called him *Cavallo*, which meant *horse*. His real name was Labaan. He was the overseer for the fourteen black men in service to the baron, which included Labaan. However, Labaan, a thirty-six year old man, was used for entertainment purposes. The baron believed Labaan was the most magnificent sportsmen. He was born in the Soudan, and he traveled to Crocifissa when he was twenty-five. Labaan traveled in hopes to buy back his sister who was stolen as a young girl, and the last surviving family member he had known. Labaan tracked down her last known whereabouts within Crocifissa, but he never found her. Instead, he found Baron Agusto. The baron was impressed with Labaan's physical prowess when he witnessed the young man chase down a thief. Labaan was given a job to oversee slaves given to Baron Agusto as tribute from the Vatican. The baron was already caring for Adaeze. Labaan accepted the job, hoping to find his sister.

However, the baron also raced Labaan against other men. Running. Swimming. He would run solo through intricately designed obstacle courses. He was placed inside fighting matches, and he was undefeated. The only thing that was truly beaten, over the last ten years, was Labaan's spirit. There came word of his sister, two years into serving Baron Agusto. She was dead. Suicide. Before her death she was made a prostitute, because she was found unfit to sell. The twelve-year old girl's leg had been deformed, broken on her handling when taken from Africa. Her leg was poorly cared for. But there was a 'benefactor' that put her to use. Prostitution. At the age of fifteen, Labaan's sister took her life. The baron revealed the information to Labaan, having been acquainted with Labaan's sister's employer and benefactor. The blow was more devastating than any hit taken in a fight.

Labaan helped Baron Agusto maintain the black male slaves.

He resigned his salary.

Currently, he was sleeping in the left corner nearest the door. Adaeze shook him gently. Labaan woke suddenly. He nodded his head, knowing his daily duties were to begin. He did not hesitate, shaking the stupor that was trying to keep him anchored in sleep. Adaeze watched Labaan as he went around waking the other males. She reflected on the fact that he spoke very little. *"I am a sportsman,"* he would say of himself. *"I run. I swim. I fight.*" He would often joke, "*I am earth, water, and I am air. I just would like to find and become my fire.*" But behind his humor was sadness.

Each of the African slaves had a story. Adaeze, who had lived all her life between Italy and Sicily, wondered if she would expand her story. This was her thought every time she approached Labaan and made him rise for duty. Today was no different, though she decided not to ponder long. There was a small story in her life that she wanted to write, and it featured the black titan that had been brought to the Sicilian shores.

With Labaan about his duties, Adaeze left the shanty house, traveled to another, and awoke Chanya, a black slave in her mid-forties. She was referred to as *Afra-Zia*, or *Afrazia*, Aunt Africa. She was the head of the thirteen black women in service to the baron, the number also including her. Chanya, like many of the other blacks serving the baron, was often sad, though Chanya was more tired. However, her spirits had been brighter ever since the slaves visited al-Mari Ifriq. "*The gods and goddesses reside in me now,*" she would say in private to Adaeze. "*All of them. The Jew's God. The Christian's Trinity. And Mohammed's God too. All are now in me. All the gods and goddesses of the cosmos. The primordial spirits, the first gods and goddesses that look like us, they whom we are all born of. I am refreshed. I was home. This whole world used to be my home, now, just Africa. When I die, all these spirits in me will haunt these wicked men.*"

Adaeze did not understand Chanya's talk and newfound energy until she saw the black titan. The soils of al-Mari Ifriq were as foreign to her as Sicily was now. Adaeze wanted to return. She wanted the black titan to be the doorway back to her homeland; she wanted him to be the vessel that carried her across the waters.

Much like with Labaan, Adaeze watched Chanya gather the other black servants, waking them for the day. Six of the thirteen females resided in this particular shanty house; the other slave women were in the shanty house where Adaeze's two servants resided. Adaeze never understood why the women were split into two groups and the men resided as one. She never questioned either, and she pondered the phenomena even less at the moment as she had other matters on her mind.

When Adaeze believed that all would be well without her supervision, she left the shanty house and returned to her lodge to revel in the morning bath. The other slaves had tubs to bathe in too, though not a private one, and they had to take turns between all the men and all the women.

The sun was rising. Morning dawned.

Adaeze entered her slave quarters. The two servants stood outside the bath's room, the tub having been prepared. Adaeze thanked both women and instructed them to find Chanya. The slave women exited Adaeze's lodge, and Adaeze removed her clothes and stepped into her bath. Images of her dream flashed in her head. Nothing was connected. A giant Ojodo held her in the palm of his hand. The baron threatened them. Adaeze washed away the sight of the baron and concentrated on Ojodo. But she didn't imagine long. There were duties to attend to, and Adaeze could not be late.

Adaeze finished her bath. She opened a plug at the bottom, and the water drained into a hole that leaked underneath her lodge, spilling onto a pile of muddy earth. She dried herself, put on perfume gifted to her by the baron's nephew, and returned to the slaves outside. They had all gathered in the men's shanty house. The women prepared a morning meal as the men washed and put on new clothes delivered by Donatello and some of his family members. The Sicilian still remained among the black slaves, and he greeted Adaeze with a kiss on each cheek. Donatello possessed a peculiarly wide smile on his face. "There is much to be done today," he said. Adaeze had no idea what he meant, or why Donatello was so cheery. She could think of nothing special scheduled for the day, save her own matters attending to the giant. "My people will attend to the tribute brought in yesterday by the Moorish ambassador. You will attend to the titan; see that his scars look fine. Baron Agusto does not know what got into him. He never meant to treat such a magnificent piece so poorly." He patted Adaeze's shoulder. "First, get everyone to the mansion. The baron will split their duties for the day. Then, see to the titan. His name is Ojodo."

Adaeze felt as if she met the giant all over again upon hearing his name. The name was like a title. Donatello might as well have said *the king*. Adaeze's face was unmoving, however. She nodded her head, and then Donatello left to see Ojodo and the new tribute. Adaeze joined the other slaves for a bowl of buttered grains and water. The women served the cleaned men, then, after eating, bathed in newly gathered water. Adaeze did not wait long for the women. They cleaned quickly and thoroughly. They dressed and rejoined the male slaves. Grouped, Adaeze led all the black slaves into the baron's mansion.

Italian servants escorted the black slaves to the baron's court. Baron Agusto greeted Adaeze with a charming smile that now appeared devious in Adaeze's eyes. Her people were split apart, taken by officials to citizens demanding the extra labor for the day. The men that handled the racing horses took Labaan. The baron dismissed Adaeze. She had her duties to periodically check on the loaned slaves throughout the day. For now, she made her way to the shanty house holding Ojodo.

Adaeze walked alone, lost in thought, and celebrating that there were no guards accompanying her. She walked slowly, enjoying her solitude. As she walked, she could see Donatello's people filtering through the shanty houses holding the newly arrived slaves. Her steps quickened, hastening her arrival outside of the house that held Ojodo. She stepped inside. Donatello was standing over the black titan. The Sicilian appeared to be speaking to Ojodo, but to Adaeze that would have been impossible, unless Donatello knew Ojodo's language. Perhaps he was speaking to himself, inspecting Ojodo as the black golem continued to lie flat on the tattered mattress.

Donatello looked up and over his shoulder, observing Adaeze's entrance into the shanty barn. He waved her closer and Adaeze approached him. She started to consider that even his kind presence was a disturbance. "I am not a doctor, Adaeze. Come." He guided her closer to Ojodo. "Tend to this one's wounds. I've brought fresh bandages. Your medicinal concoction is still plentiful." He stepped away from the two of them and left the barn.

Adaeze placed her knees against the rug lying next to Ojodo's bed. She felt as if she was at the altar of a god. He turned to her and smiled. She returned the gesture and said his name. "Ojodo." The Moorish titan continued to smile. Adaeze then inspected the bandages. The blood had coagulated and browned. She gently removed the binding material and saw the results of the medicinally soaked bandages. Ojodo's scars were glazed; the blood was dried, scabbing. She crumpled the used bandages, made a pile on her right, and then commenced to prepare new bandages for Ojodo.

"One day I will teach you Italian, giant," she said to him as she soaked a bandage, rinsed it, and placed it over a long scar. "It's a very simple language, really," Adaeze said as she repeated her process of bandaging Ojodo. "I have a wonderful tale to tell you," she continued. "A dream I had." Ojodo almost perked up, but quickly remembered that he was not to understand Adaeze's language. She tried to remember as many details of her dreams as she relayed the odd, fascinating imagery to Ojodo. "You were greater in size—if that's possible. You grew from out of the water, an ocean. I believe we were in Africa. I think I can remember Giovanni Ghislanzoni-Verdi—that's the baron's nephew—being swallowed by the sands. I think the baron was angry with that." She though for a moment, then resumed replacing the bandages. "I don't remember much more. Unfortunately, I'm just a servant, and not very good at telling stories. Well, not at making them interesting, anyways."

"You leave that to me, *mora*," Ojodo said in his native tongue. His voice rolled like low thunder. Adaeze smiled and commented that she believed Ojodo was starting to understand the Italian language.

"I wish I could understand your…tongue. Language." She giggled, embarrassed. "So few of us here can speak an African language. There is one among us that can speak an African language. His name is Labaan. Another, Chanya, she used to be able to speak an African language. She doesn't remember. She hasn't spoken her language since she was ten, when she was brought here. She only has faint memories of Africa." Adaeze sighed. "It's one thing to be taken early, you forget, but…you know what you have been taken from. Worse, other Africans have resigned you to this fate. Our people. Have things deteriorated within Africa? Al-Mari Ifriq seemed to stand tall." She looked at Ojodo and asked in a very low voice, "Do you too wish to kill your benefactor?"

Ojodo made a misstep. His head turned in reaction to Adaeze's words. His eyes shimmered with surprise. Adaeze noticed. Two guards came into the barn, muskets slung over their shoulders. Adaeze slowly turned away from Ojodo and spotted the guards' entrance. They were not a part of Donatello's people. They were the baron's men. Four servants carrying a steaming cauldron of grains followed the two guards. A fifth and sixth servant carried bowls, delivering them to the slaves occupying the shanty barn. Adaeze was given a bowl. A ladle filled with grains was scooped up from the cauldron and dumped into the bowl. Adaeze was provided a spoon and she began to feed Ojodo, blowing on the hot grains and cooling them before placing the food in his mouth. Ojodo was surprised to taste butter and spiced flavorings on the grain.

"Here, Adaeze," said a guard placing a cup of water in her face.

Adaeze took the cup and put it next to her. She continued to feed Ojodo. She gave him the cup of water after several more spoonfuls of grain. The guards and servants stayed and watched the slaves eat. Adaeze was annoyed at their presence. She finished feeding Ojodo and handed the empty bowl and cup back to one of the baron's guards. The same guard handed Adaeze a scroll of paper. She unfolded the note and read which of her people were sent where. "Make sure they're still at their duties come noon," said a guard.

It was the same routine that Adaeze had been through since she was thirteen. She wanted to look at the guard with a sharp look and reply, *"Are you new?"* But she bit her tongue, thanking him for the note. She folded the note and held it close. Adaeze stayed with Ojodo until noon and then left to check on each of the slaves from her stock. She did not engage

Ojodo any further, though she was intrigued at his response to her question, especially since she was addressing him in Italian. The situation stayed with Adaeze as she walked through Crocifissa checking on her people scattered throughout the coastal village.

Adaeze returned to Ojodo's shanty barn at three in the afternoon. Donatello had been through, leaving another set of fresh bandages for Ojodo. Adaeze's medicinal water was running out. She removed Ojodo's bandages and inspected his scars. They were looking fine, her medicine helping his body heal. She motioned for Ojodo to stand up and walk around to stretch his muscles and move his body.

Ojodo was a little stiff from being immobile, but nothing uncomfortable. The scars on his back tingled as he rotated his arms and bent down to stretch. Some of the scabbing cracked and crumbled, but there was no bleeding underneath. He took his position back on the bed after a few moments of stretching and exercising his legs. Four of the baron's guards had muskets aimed at Ojodo the entire time of his activity. Adaeze didn't mind their presence. She worked on Ojodo's new bandages when they left, but she said very little to the black titan. She was skittish that he might have somehow known her language, or figured it out through trickery. The baron warned her that the unholy Devil knew such tricks. Though Adaeze was never permitted to read the Bible, Baron Agusto taught her many lessons from the Holy Scriptures. He warned her of Satan's ability to possess people, or take wondrous shapes and forms to seduce his victims.

Adaeze's thoughts lingered on Baron Agusto. She was conflicted. Images of her dream flickered in her mind, the baron holding a Bible, thumbing through the Book angrily. She remembered lessons on Africa and all the wonders of the land. She also remembered the lesson on the curse of the blacks. She remembered how the blacks were to submit themselves to God to find salvation from their curse. Adaeze made quick, careful glances at Ojodo, each time making direct eye contact. She remembered the way she felt when she first tended to his wounds. She felt intoxicated, drunk, while looking upon this giant man's naked form. But he was not naked. He was bare, though. He had been stripped of his dignity.

Adaeze's eyes became sorrowful. She again ran her hands gently along Ojodo's shoulders. Her touch was soft, endearing. Ojodo smiled, eyes closed. His voice rumbled like the low purr of a large, wild cat. Adaeze concluded that Ojodo was not the Devil in disguise. He was not the embodiment of Satan's trickery. How could he be? Adaeze moved her hand from his massive frame. She sighed. She didn't know what to believe. She grabbed the bowl of medicinal water, its contents almost completely used, and she left the shanty barn, traveling back to her lodge to start another medicinal concoction, and to ponder whom to trust.

Adaeze formed a plan in her mind while she scavenged together the ingredients of the medicinal mixture. As she mixed the contents with another bowl of water, she put together a story to draw Ojodo's attention to her. She would enact her plan at sundown, when the new slaves would be fed. The guards would be on watch, but not for long. She would tend to Ojodo's bandages after the guards left. She would speak to him again, tell him a story, and watch him close for his reaction.

There was only one problem, which produced many questions. If this black giant could actually understand her language, would she inform Baron Agusto? Would she inform Donatello Verola or even her unit of slaves? Or, possibly, would she keep the knowledge to herself, a secret between she and Ojodo, which ultimately would lead to the outcome formulated within the story she put together to help her expose Ojodo?

Adaeze contemplated the ultimate question. Would she use the black giant to help her escape Sicily and journey back to Africa?

Chapter Forty-Two

Adaeze approached the shanty barn carrying a bowl of medicinal water. It was not yet night. There was a purple haze of sunlight that haunted the dim sky. Adaeze was finished with her daily duties of gathering the black slaves handling village services. Her people were given only two hours to rest and eat. Baron Agusto was hosting a celebration, and her people were asked to attend for their services. Drawing nearer to the barn, Adaeze could see that Donatello's people had substituted Baron Agusto's men. Adaeze felt more comfortable with them around. She slipped in and made her way to Ojodo. He was still lying down. Donatello again left new bandages for her. Adaeze went to work quickly. She too had little time.

The black slave girl knelt down beside Ojodo. He welcomed her presence with a warm smile that reflected the flickering light emanating from the lantern stationed near him. "Princess," He greeted in his native Afro-Arabic language. Adaeze smiled in return. She bowed her head at the neck, though Ojodo's word was foreign

"Ojodo," Adaeze said back to him. She started to remove his bandages and again inspected the scars on his back. They looked fine. "Your scars look well, Ojodo," she informed. "There won't be an infection." She spoke casually, as if aware that Ojodo understood her words. "I can smell the aroma of buttered grains, so I take it you have already been fed." She made a quick turn of her head, making sure no guards were in the vicinity. Donatello's people remained outside. Adaeze went back to work on Ojodo. His body magnified by the trick of shadows and the illumination provided by the lantern's glow. Adaeze's attraction also increased, but she ignored the sensations tingling inside her. Though she did say, "You have excited me, Ojodo. Your presence has inspired me." Her eyes then filled with a sorrowful emotion. "You have also made me sad." Ojodo slipped again, reacting to Adaeze's words. But it was just a flinch. Adaeze did not respond to his movement, though she took note of it. "Watching the baron treat you so wickedly, watching him whip you into submission—to your knees. I want to be free from all this." Her words were expressed like a sigh of relief. She started to tear up. "I *hate* Baron Agusto!"

Until now, Adaeze's words and emotions were just an act. But she was caught up in the moment, swallowed by the truth in her words. Ojodo reached for the crying woman, the palm of his hand caressing the side of Adaeze's face. Adaeze took comfort in Ojodo's touch. She wiped her tears aside and leaned closer to Ojodo's face. Her eyes were wild, determined. "I will teach you Italian. I will teach you this language. I *have* to." She whispered softly. "I have plans, Ojodo." She spoke quickly, "I know you don't understand, but I must tell you. Slowly, as you learn, you will comprehend. Some among us might know your language and be able to translate for me, but I cannot risk another's involvement. They might alert Baron Agusto." Ojodo listened closely. His expression made him look perplexed to Adaeze's words. "I will push to have you serve me as a bodyguard. I will demand it. I will then push the baron for me to visit Libya. He continues to talk about such a visit. I will go with Donatello, you as my bodyguard. When we arrive in Africa, we will make our escape. We will kill Giovanni Ghislanzoni-Verdi, the baron's nephew. We will send a message to the baron. We will *not* be slaves."

Ojodo shook his head slowly. "The baron dies tonight, Adaeze," he said in Italian.

Adaeze's heart skipped. She stepped back, almost toppling over her feet. She considered this all a trap. Ojodo grabbed her arm and pulled her closer. He whispered in her ear, continuing to speak in Italian, "You will be free tonight, Adaeze." Adaeze's arm would have trembled if it were not subdued so tightly by Ojodo's massive grip. She struggled to keep her lower jaw closed. She trembled. Ojodo continued to speak. "Signore Verola helps. We plot with him and Ambassador Nasir Sa'ood too. All the slaves that have been brought to Crocifissa are not slaves but warriors. We are an army." He could feel Adaeze trying to pull herself from his grip. "Donatello is here to free Crocifissa from the baron's iron fist." Ojodo put all his sincerity in his eyes and aimed them at Adaeze's frightened stare. "We are here to rescue you…and all the blacks in servitude."

Adaeze relaxed.

Ojodo let go of her arm when he was confident that she could balance on her own. "Donatello has more news for you. He will come and…"

Adaeze jumped forward and threw her arms around Ojodo's neck. "This is not the Devil's trick?" she asked in a soft, hopeful voice.

"That depends on who your god is," Ojodo replied. He could see the other Moors looking at them.

Adaeze backed away. "You can't fight. Not in this condition. Your scars."

"I'll be fine," he assured her. "Cover my scars, sweet woman. Donatello will bring me a new shirt." Adaeze was conflicted with emotions ranging from excitement to fear. She started to replace Ojodo's bandages, speaking very little. "Have you no more words?" Ojodo asked.

Adaeze chuckled. She kept her smile and admitted, "You have no idea how scared I am." Her eyes started to water again, but no tears fell. "And I don't know if I'm scared of this revolution, or if I fear being free."

"That's very brave to admit, *mora*," Ojodo said to Adaeze. "After all, I didn't hear you say you're afraid to die."

"I thought that was a given," Adaeze retorted matter-of-factly. Ojodo laughed, though Adaeze did not mean for her statement to be a joke.

Donatello entered the barn. Adaeze turned, stood, and greeted him. She was finished with Ojodo's bandages. "He's recovering well," Adaeze informed Donatello. "When will the baron start putting these servants to use?"

"The baron is still undecided as to whether he will sell the entire lot or just a few," the Sicilian answered. "Those discussions will take place after the Moorish ambassador leaves Crocifissa." His demeanor changed to a more concerned expression. He put his arm around Adaeze and led her from the barn. "Come, Adaeze. I have some things to tell you." Adaeze felt the urge to peer over her shoulder and back at Ojodo. She resisted. Donatello shuffled her from the shanty barn, and they made their way to Adaeze's lodge. Inside, the young slave girl lit two lanterns and several candles stationed around her house. "Have you eaten yet, Adaeze?" Donatello asked as he took a seat at Adaeze's table.

"No," Adaeze answered.

"I'll bring you something," Donatello assured. He then invited the young woman to sit with him. He moved his seat closer to her and took a deep breath before beginning. "There will be a lot of trouble tonight," Donatello informed.

Adaeze nodded affirmatively. "I know. Ojodo told me," she confessed nervously.

Donatello did not stir with Adaeze's revelation. He sat for a moment, lost in thought. He finally said to Adaeze, "My people will protect you. They will lead you to vessels stationed a good distance from Crocifissa. You will escape on those ships. The Moors will take you to al-Mari Ifriq." He took her hand and confessed, "Baron Agusto Ghislanzoni has been using you, Adaeze. He has arranged for his nephew to marry you. That is why Giovanni courts you without objection from the baron or his court. Once the marriage is complete, you will then discover your noble line that connects to the ancient lands of East Africa. Cush. Nubia. Egypt. The Vatican could then claim African holy lands without war. They would have right. Your birthright. That is the reason why you were taken from your homeland so long ago. Your mother and father were nobles, a King and Queen." He placed both his hands around hers and emphasized, "You are royalty."

Adaeze inspected Donatello as she wore a perplexed expression. "You do this all for me?"

Donatello chuckled. "Don't believe me so noble, Adaeze. I'm killing the baron for personal gain. I will become this city's chief, connect its trade with my family's enterprise, and give it a boost in economy for what we have planned." He put a gentle hand on her knee. "I care for you, Adaeze. But I don't believe you, or your people, fit into the plans we have for Sicily."

"We?" Adaeze questioned.

Donatello patted her knee. "Don't concern yourself with anything more than leaving. Remain here until my people come for you. I have already escorted your people into the mansion. Baron Agusto believes you are tending to his mistake—Ojodo's wounds. He's not expecting you any time soon."

Adaeze started to cry. "Baron Agusto…he *will* die tonight?"

Donatello nodded. "Yes."

The woman's tears overwhelmed her. She exhaled, "Thank you, God."

Donatello embraced Adaeze until she relaxed. He stood up from his seat. "Goodbye, Princess Adaeze." He smiled, turned, and left the house.

Adaeze sat still. Minutes passed before she made a single movement. She turned her head. The house suddenly felt like a prison. Freedom was far more frightening to Adaeze, however. She had her duties and daily routine given to her. Life was simple when being a part of the baron's system. Now, Adaeze felt she would be responsible for so much, starting with understanding the overwhelming greatness that was her history. It was a history that was not attached to the language she currently spoke. Adaeze was clearly not Italian or Sicilian, but that was the country and colony she had been attached to all her life. She would have to think beyond Italy. She would have to think beyond the borders of Sicily. Adaeze would have to understand herself as African. More so, the concept of

Africa would become real, all its facets both beautiful and unpleasant. Anything romanticized would dissolve into reality, even her nobility.

Adaeze was lost in these thoughts for hours. She barely stirred when Donatello returned to leave a plate of food. There was no conversation between them. Donatello respected her silence. Adaeze did not touch her food for a moment. When her stomach gurgled, she responded by plucking small amounts of food from her plate and taking little bites.

Two Sicilians entered Adaeze's lodge. The men were armed with muskets. She pushed her plate away and stood. Adaeze looked around the small house. There was nothing for her to take. The armed Sicilians surrounded her. She was led from the house. A third, armed Sicilian man stood on the stairs, keeping watch. He moved down the stairs as Adaeze and the two other Sicilians came from the house. All three men drew their muskets, aiming their weapons at the dark as they searched for possible movement. They led Adaeze through the fields, further east. Two more armed men and the remainder of her slaves joined them. Chanya was surprisingly accounted for, along with most of the women. Four of the thirteen women were not present. The missing women were also the youngest. Seven of the fourteen men, including Labaan, were absent. They were entertaining Baron Agusto and his guests at the moment. Adaeze prayed for them.

The group continued past the shanty barns. The other Sicilian men, stationed to guard the newly arrived blacks, handed muskets, rapiers, and torches to the African men. Adaeze did not see Ojodo, and was thankful. She did not want to see the giant step into battle, especially considering his wounds. But Adaeze's attention was captured by another phenomena. The women and children from the newly arrived stock of blacks joined them. Nine women, armed with short swords, daggers, and muskets, joined the guard. Adaeze had never seen women look so fierce. The armed black women made her feel more comfortable than the armed Sicilian men. Their walk was elegant, regal, and determined. Their focus made their eyes as much weapons as their swords or the firearms strapped across their shoulders. Adaeze did not speak their language, though they spoke to her with just their presence.

They continued east, until the Sicilian men signaled to make a turn, leading the group south, and then winding back westward. They came upon the shore where many longboats lay. Adaeze and the other blacks were escorted onto the boats and were taken to two vessels that lay anchored far away from the shore. They boarded one of the large ships, and were ushered into the cargo hold. One of the armed women walked around and made sure that everyone was secure. Her name was Aludra. She introduced herself to Adaeze, speaking Italian. "I am honored," responded Adaeze. Aludra smiled back. The woman politely dismissed herself and spoke with a Sicilian man. Adaeze listened to the conversation. Aludra asked to be escorted, along with three of the armed women, back to the baron's mansion. The Sicilian obliged.

Adaeze felt better. As massive in size as her giant Ojodo was, as possibly skilled in combat as he might have been, Adaeze believed he would be well guarded and in good company surrounded by these armed black women. Adaeze sat back. Chanya came to her side, a wide smile on the elder's face. "We're going home, child," she said.

Adaeze nodded her head. "Say a prayer to all the gods and goddesses that reside in you. Let us protect the warriors that now fight for us so they too may go home."

Chanya agreed. "I will." Though she concluded, "But some of them might be called to a greater home. I can't help that."

Adaeze understood. She smiled and said to Chanya, "There is one among them named Ojodo. Ask that his time be extended so he can get to know…our grandchildren."

Chanya chuckled. "Child, I think you just said it best."

The two women closed their eyes, concentrated, and started to pray. The remaining Moons watched them and started to sing. The other African women joined in song. Two languages gathered harmoniously and created one song of prayer and rejoice, a blessing for the warriors already engaged in battle.

Chapter Forty-Three

Nasir calmed his final, awkward laugh at one of Baron Agusto's silly stories. Some parts of the stories were lost on Nasir, his ability to keep up with the spoken language faltered because of the baron's drunken slur and quick speech. The men dined in a second dining room that was stationed at the back of Baron Agusto's mansion. The room had large glass windows and a door that led to a magnificent patio filled with wonderful flora both domestic and imported. The patio overlooked the eastern field, though large, hanging trees obstructed much of the view. Donatello signaled Nasir as he stood behind Baron Agusto. Nasir, while laughing awkwardly, nodded his head toward the Sicilian to affirm. He took one last drink of his wine, having nursed one cup all night, and he stood from the table. "It's late, Baron," he said as he simmered down his laughter. "I have a long journey ahead of me tomorrow." Nasir patted his stomach and continued, "Well, al-Mari Ifriq is not too far away, but I do so hate traveling, whether it be by land or sea. I've been a spoiled, stationary brat all my life. I don't like being away from home."

The baron lifted his drink toward Nasir. "I understand, Ambassador. I will see you again as your city handles its politics." He took a sip and stood up in a drunken manner. "Again, give my best to your Governor-General. I do so hate war, but al-Mari Ifriq's struggles will make me a rich man—even as you take monies from our shared venture." He steadied himself, belched, and then turned to Donatello. "Sicilian!" the baron called. "Take these neggar slaves back to their quarters."

Donatello bowed his head. "Yes, Baron Agusto."

The baron, drunk from wine, grabbed Donatello by the arm and pushed him toward the dining room door. "Now, you Sicilian mongrel. Go. Go." Donatello caught his balance. Baron Agusto yelled further commands, "And only take the men. The women stay here." He turned and chuckled at Michele Solera and his other advisors and judges. He then had another idea. "Donatello, wait. Take the men, but bring back the giant neggar. I want him to perform for me. I want to see his prowess put against four women."

Nasir and Donatello resisted glancing at one another.

The baron continued, addressing Nasir, "Are you so sure you wish to go to bed? My courtroom is about to be a stage for a great performance."

Nasir hid his disgust behind a smile. He put his hand flat on his chest and said, "Perhaps when I return." He walked from the room, Tegu and the rest of his entourage with him. He said to Donatello, "Will you also take my entourage back to your family's inn?"

Baron Agusto turned away from the conversation. Movement from outside caught his eye. Lit torches moved eerily on what appeared to be a black, ominous cloud. He started to wonder how drunk he was. The baron attempted to focus his drunken eyes. None of his movements worked, odd and humorous as they were. He heard someone scream, which alerted the other advisors in the room. *"Stop!"* the voice yelled. *"Stop, you goddamn neggars!"* the voice continued to scream. "Stop, or we will be forced to shoo—"

Musket fire crackled.

Men yelled battle cries.

Baron Agusto and his advisors sobered.

Torches crashed through the large glass windows, followed by more rounds of musket fire. Baron Agusto ducked down, bullets missing him. Michele Solera was hit in his right shoulder, but managed to stay clear of additional rounds. A judge was hit in the jaw and stomach, slamming against the dining table. He was in excruciating pain. A second advisor was struck through his shoulder blade as he turned to dive to the floor.

Guards stormed the room aiming their muskets toward the door. They fired a round of blind gunfire through the window. One yelled, "Baron Agusto. We have a slave revolt in progress. Follow us to safety." A single bullet slammed into the guard's eye. He dropped his musket and buckled over, holding his bleeding eye socket while screaming.

Baron Agusto jumped up and took cover behind his guards. A lantern crashed into the room. The fire, coupled with the torch that was earlier tossed, and the bottles of alcohol, painted the room with a burst of flames. The other Italian officials scattered from the room. The guards dropped their muskets and returned blind pistol fire before scurrying from the room. The door was closed and Baron Agusto, the officials, and the guards dashed through the hallways, trying to make their way to the courtroom where there lay a secret exit in the panels of the floor. The judge that had been wounded in the jaw and stomach limped behind the party. He tripped over his own feet as he struggled to keep up. He smacked the floor and looked up to see if any of his fellow officials would turn to help him. They continued on, their images becoming smaller and smaller in his hazy vision. He put his head down and released a heavy breath as he died.

The baron's party entered a large study. An exit lay on the opposite side of the entrance. Haunting screams of battle could be heard beyond the walls. Baron Agusto commanded, "All neggars are to be killed, including the Moorish ambassador. No neggar can be trusted. Kill them all. Is that understood?"

Solera disagreed, but he worded his concern carefully. "If Ambassador Nasir is slain, Baron Agusto, how would we explain—"

There was a thunderous noise, a terrifying and determined scream. Armed black men crashed through the room. Their weapons were blood soaked. The baron's surrounding guards removed a second set of pistols and fired. Their attacks killed four of the men. Eight more black warriors flooded the room. One grabbed Michele Solera and stabbed the advisor in the neck, killing him. A guard removed his rapier and severed the black warriors hand. In the same swift motion the guard sliced the attacking warrior's neck. The al-Jasi warrior dropped to the floor. The other Italian guards became invigorated with their fellow guard's kill. They removed their swords and engaged the onslaught of black warriors.

Baron Agusto turned around and exited quickly. His remaining judges and advisors followed. One judge was dragged back into the room and stabbed in the chest by an al-Jasi soldier. The rest of the Italian officials increased their speed, following the baron through another set of corridors. The officials stopped inside a conference room that had three closed exits. "Is anyone armed," asked the baron. No one answered positively. The baron looked to each exit. He cursed the size of his mansion and its spidery maze-like layout. It was designed in a manner to keep insurgents from getting to him, confusing anyone that penetrated his residence. Now, he felt just as trapped and as anxious as anyone else. He stepped toward the western exit. He put his hand on the knob and opened the door.

Gunshots!

Three bullets pierced the baron.

Two bullets broke through his stomach. The third bullet cracked his shoulder. Baron Agusto stumbled backward. His legs buckled and he dropped to the floor. He looked up at his killers. The Italian guards, with smoking pistols in their hands, all had their mouths hanging open, trembling with a surprised expression on their faces. The baron screamed, "You idiots killed me." He held his wounds as blood seeped from them. "Carry out this last order of mine. Kill every neggar, all of them. Spare no black." He used his hands to push himself up against the wall. "Go," he winced. "Leave us here. Leave me to die."

The guards closed the door. They turned around and headed back through the mansion's hallways. The door behind them opened. The judges and advisors joined them as they came into the hallway, closing the door behind them. "He's dead," said one of them. "At least he will be. Get us out of here. Forget his orders." Then came intense screaming from the room behind them. It was the baron. Everyone took a moment to imagine a gruesome scene consisting of the black warriors that now made their way into the room they just left, finding the dying Baron.

In reality, the baron was simply screaming out of panic and terror at the site of the Moorish al-Jasi warriors. The black warriors never touched him, having examined the baron's wounds and considering him dead. To attack a dying man was thought dishonorable. They were cruel enough to allow Baron Agusto to suffer in the last moments of his life. However, among them was the slave Labaan. He was armed with pistol and sword. He lifted his firearm and shot the baron dead.

The guards continued, the advisors and judges behind them. "There's a passage within the baron's courtroom that can lead us out of here," said one of the officials. "Get us to the courtroom." Faint war cries continued to plague the uneasy officials. The horrific sounds quieted and increased in sporadic intervals. The guards led the officials to the courtroom. The room was ablaze. Dead bodies from either army populated the burning room. The treacherous flames reached out for them as the door opened. The fiery tentacles lashed at the party, but backed away. One guard was brave enough to peek his head into the room. A giant, black hand came from around the side of the doorway, grabbed his collar, and pulled him inside. Ojodo slammed the guard's head into the wall, crushing every bone in the man's face. He tossed him into a set of flames and reached around for another guard. He broke the man's arm and threw him to the burning stage that lay at the center of the room.

Ojodo stepped into the doorway.

The guards drew their swords, trembling.

Ojodo reached out and snatched the closest guard, removed him of his sword, and lodged the weapon through the guard's abdomen. He flung the body away and stared down the remaining quivering guards. He watched the judges and advisors back away. They all watched as flames writhed around the black titan. "You are the Devil, black neggar!," an advisor screamed. "You are as much a demon as God has cursed you." The official turned his head as more black warriors came from behind. He turned back to watch Ojodo.

The titan slammed the door and lodged the sword through it at an angle, making the blade pierce the door and the side of the wall, locking the party of Italian officials and guards inside. He turned and casually made his way from the courtroom to the connecting hallway that opened up into the grand hallway, and then exited the mansion.

Ojodo could see citizens and more Italian guards heading up the stone path. He darted to his right, traveling around the side of the mansion, making his way through thicket that enclosed the baron's residence in a natural shield. He heard Donatello's voice coming from behind him. The Sicilian was confronting the rush of citizens and guards that were making their way into the mansion. Ojodo could not make out what Donatello was telling the people, though suspected the Sicilian was taking his first steps in taking charge of Crocifissa, informing the people the baron was dead. However, Donatello was not aware of the baron's fate. He only asked the citizens not to participate in the fray, and he commanded the guards to subdue the fire.

"The fire is contained to several rooms, one of them being the courtroom," said Donatello. "We have routed the rebellion," he continued. "There might be more neggars inside, however. Stay alert. My people are tracking them down through the eastern field." Donatello moved inside with the guards. The citizens returned to their homes.

Ojodo made his way to the eastern fields. He teamed with three al-Jasi warriors and two Sicilian men. The party grouped with Nasir, Tegu, and the rest of the ambassador's entourage. "We'll lead you to the ships," spoke one of the Sicilian men. Nasir barely understood his speech, the man's accent on his words thick. But he understood enough and let the man lead.

"Get them!" a voice yelled.

There was gunfire. An al-Jasi warrior was struck through the throat, dying instantly as he hit the ground. One of the Sicilians was hit in the arm. The others ducked down, Tegu throwing Nasir to the ground before being struck by two bullets that would have killed the ambassador. Tegu fell next to Nasir, sprawled, bleeding, and already dead from the bullets in his chest, one fatally striking his heart. Nasir's eyes locked onto his friend and bodyguard.

The Sicilians stood up and waved their arms. "Hold your fire," one shouted toward the encroaching Italian guard. The second Sicilian man counted eight shadows approaching. He repeated the first man's words.

"Hold your fire!" The eight Italian guards came closer. "We have these neggars subdued," he said angrily.

The guards had their pistols drawn, hammers thumbed back and ready. Nasir took his eyes off of Tegu's lifeless body and watched the Italian guards closely. He was nervous, trembling. The guard at the front overlooked the scene. He lifted his pistol and shot the already wounded Sicilian man in the chest. The Sicilian dropped dead. "Keep him covered," he ordered the other men. They aimed their pistols at the second Sicilian man. "You're helping these neggars," declared the Italian. "If these neggars are subdued, why do they still have their weapons in hand?" He stepped on an al-Jasi warrior's hand, forcing the warrior to loosen his grip on the short sword.

"Ridiculous," retorted the Sicilian. "We had them subdued. Two of these men still had a grip on their weapons. So what? They're swords. We have pistols and muskets aimed at them. They're not stupid. Even with numbers, the odds are against them."

"You're all under arrest," informed the guard. "We'll see what the baron says."

The Sicilian nodded. "As you wish."

The guard ordered the Moors to stand. They were confiscated of their weapons, and Nasir was not questioned about his fanciful clothing, or presented as an ambassador. He was just as much a perpetrator as the rest. There was a thought given to executing Ojodo, but the guards' leader decided the baron would rather punish his prize possession. "Your hands up," said the guard leader. "Up. Extend." He motioned with his hands raised. Ojodo and Nasir understood the command. The others did not. The two men lifted their arms high into the air, mimicking the guard leader. Nasir looked at the other Moors and nodded to do the same. They did. The Sicilian was grouped among the arrested.

The guard waved their weapons for the apprehended men to take lead. Nasir and Ojodo moved forward, the rest following them. Ojodo, before turning around, spotted movement. Blurred shadows moved across the field, and though Ojodo could not make out what hint or preview of a form they were made from, he understood there was more than one moon shining in the night. The guards had their pistols and muskets aimed at the backs of their captured prizes. With their gaze focused on their prisoners, none of the men realized the slaying of individual guards by the attacking Moons. The women rolled, stayed low, and jumped up at precise moments to strike with stabs to the chests, and slices to guards' jugulars. The attacks resulted in the execution of the entire guard unit.

Aludra shouted, grabbing the attention of her fellow Moors and the Sicilian. Nasir and the others stopped. They turned around. The al-Jasi warriors and Ojodo removed the slain guards of their weapons. Aludra approached Nasir and addressed, "Ambassador Sa'ood." The fierce woman, holding a curved dagger in each hand, and spattered with the blood of slain guards, bowed in the most cultured and courteous of ways.

Nasir exhaled. He returned the bow and said, "Thank you, beautiful Moon." He put his hand on her shoulder and then started toward Tegu's slain body. "One among your ranks has fallen, a good friend and servant. Tegu."

"No," hissed Aludra as she sheathed her blades.

Nasir and Aludra knelt down and inspected Tegu's body. Nasir looked over his shoulder and called, "Ojodo. Give me your musket. Carry Tegu's body. Roberto's clan will give him a proper burial." Ojodo tossed Nasir his musket and scooped Tegu's body into his arms, cradling him. The titan also carried a sad expression on his face for the slain assassin. But Tegu had died in combat, and protecting his escort. That was an honor instilled in him since the beginning of his training.

Aludra stayed close to Nasir. She said to the ambassador, "I will keep you safe." Nasir thanked her again as the party continued their journey to the longboats waiting for them at the shores. A large unit of al-Jasi warriors met them. They waited for another forty minutes before Donatello arrived with the remaining warriors and escaped slaves, Labaan among them. None of the baron's slaves had been killed. All the women were now accounted for. The seven men that entertained at the baron's party all participated in the battle. Nuru led the remainder of his warriors. Eighty-seven warriors survived the battle. Sixty-three al-Jasi warriors gave their lives to this mission.

Nasir greeted Donatello. The Sicilian had a wide smile on his face. "The baron's guards are few. All have sought my command. The baron and his cabinet have been killed. This mission was a success. This village belongs to my family and our organization. The people will be better. I, and all my associates, will always give a silent thanks to the Moors." He patted Nasir on the shoulder. "Give Beylerbey Anhur Has my regards. Traont Coutelier will be on our shores in days. I will invite him to the mansion and open fire on him."

Nasir shook Donatello's hand and assured the Sicilian that Hesam Gandarewa would send men to dispatch the baron's nephew. Donatello said he would call Giovanni home, and inform him of his uncle's demise. There was no need to carry out a mark on the young man. Nasir agreed with Donatello on the surface, but decided to tell al-Jeheuty to make Giovanni's death look like an accident. There was no need to have a vengeful young Italian running about, gathering soldiers to bring to al-Mari Ifriq's shores.

Nasir then walked to the longboats and boarded one of them. He gave his thanks to Donatello as he and the other Moors departed. He boarded one of the two ships, Aludra at his side. Tegu's body was hoisted up. Ojodo boarded the same ship, spotting Adaeze on the deck waiting for him. She hugged her giant the minute he stepped above. She never looked back to the Sicilian shores as the ships lifted anchor and caught the night's winds. Adaeze walked to the front of the ship, Ojodo following close behind. It was cold on the deck, and Ojodo noticed Adaeze trembling. He walked away to the captain's cabin and swiped a thick blanket from the bed. He returned to Adaeze and placed it around her shoulders.

Adaeze asked Ojodo, "You live in Africa-north, correct? Al-Mari Ifriq?"

"Yes," he answered.

"I have to travel east. I have a history to learn." She looked at Ojodo and smiled up at him. "Will you come with me? Would you still be my bodyguard?"

Ojodo nodded his head. "I was ready to head east before I decided to take part in this mission. I had to convince my chief boss that I could help lead this run."

"Your…chief?" Adaeze said in wonder.

"Yes," Ojodo answered. "He encouraged me to travel east, fulfill my dreams."

Adaeze was intrigued. She tightened the blanket around her and asked, "And what are those dreams, giant Ojodo?"

"I am a dramatist," he said to Adaeze's surprise. "I write plays. I'm trying to write an adventure that would overshadow my life."

"If your life is anything like tonight, that is clearly a difficult task." She turned to face him completely. "You've traveled to an exotic land, been made a slave, led a rebellion, and rescued a Princess."

Ojodo joked, "I'm making up for lost time. It's been a slow year." Adaeze chuckled. Ojodo continued, "For the last three years I've only been a dockworker. But, I'm a very powerful and influential man. I have the city officials in my pocket." Ojodo winked at Adaeze and the two of them shared more laughter. "Seriously, though, there is great knowledge all over Africa. I want to study every word written on its soil. I want to read every book in every library. Until then, Princess, let me share with you a marvelous tale. I call it *How The Giant Met His Princess.*"

The tale Ojodo spun began with his upbringing, which flowed quickly into his years working with his uncle, and then the adventures serving General Ameer Las El-Behar. His tale introduced Adaeze to al-Jeheuty Anhur Has, Rahmis Husani, and Bo Yusuf ibn Tachfin al-Dume. Ojodo recounted their failed revolution in Spain, their arrival in al-Mari Ifriq, the battle of wits they engaged in with The Four Winds, taking the regency, and all the adventures that governing al-Mari Ifriq had brought. There was some information Ojodo was careful not to relay to Adaeze. There was sensitive, government information about strategic strikes being made against a cunning foe that Ojodo kept to himself.

That would be a story for another time, when the grand adventure of political intrigue was finally concluded.

Chapter Forty-Four

The night was clear. The streets of al-Mari Ifriq glimmered with a golden aura from the shimmer of street lanterns. The city's glittering ambience appeared to reflect the celestial world sparkling above. Al-Jeheuty enjoyed al-Mari Ifriq's shining brilliance as he watched from his terrace. He brought a chair to the balcony of an unused palace tower and watched the citizens scurry through the streets while he nursed a glass of wine, the bottle resting next to his chair. The scenery calmed him. This was his escape, something he discovered only two nights ago. He had just finished dinner with his family before escaping to his place of solitude.

Al-Jeheuty's parents, his sister-by-law, and his niece, were brought in from Nusurika. They were greeted at the small Moroccan town by Roberto's clan members, escorted north to a port, and then traveled to al-Mari Ifriq by sea. Aatif perked up the minute their mother, father, and his wife and daughter entered the palace suite where he recovered. He was still in his daze, and remained so. However, he concentrated much harder to stay focused on his present and familiar surroundings rather than the scenes of slavery that continued to haunt him.

Sakeen Anhur Has informed al-Jeheuty that occupying French soldiers were starting to leave Nusurika. Privately, al-Jeheuty communicated with his father about the origins of Aatif's conditions. *"His mind is in a state of perpetual trauma. He's seen terrible things on his visit to the Caribbean. He's doing a lot better since you arrived."*

Al-Jeheuty thought mostly about his brother's condition. He rested easy on Bo Yusuf's campaign into Ogunsanwo-Mashek territory. The nomadic nation would not be found, having migrated to Tunisia. Nasir and Ojodo's affairs in Sicily were troubling to think about, but al-Jeheuty had confidence in every Moor that was sent into the baron's court. The most troubling aspect to the Sicilian affair was that he understood there would be casualties. The young Beylerbey thought himself selfish when he hoped that Ojodo and Nasir would not be among the number. He did not ponder for long periods of time; it was too sad, and built up a mass of anxiety.

Looking out at the city, inhaling a sense of calm, al-Jeheuty focused on ending the war he and the Griffin Company were involved in. He lifted his glass, toasting to the notion of bringing the war to an end, and exposing all of the criminals behind the conspiracy. He took a sip. Behind him came the sound of someone climbing the tower's winding staircase. The footsteps were slow, but not heavy, almost whimsical. It was not al-Jeheuty's father. He listened to the pattern of steps again and deduced that it was his wife. Al-Jeheuty smiled. Mehit walked out onto the tower's balcony, reached out for her husband, and lovingly caressed his shoulder as she walked around him and made her way to the balcony's rail. She held a cup of water in her hand and was dressed in a flowing purple gown and headdress. She took a sip and kept a flirtatious eye on al-Jeheuty. She swallowed and asked, "How is the King of the city?"

The Beylerbey smiled and asked his wife, "Should a woman with child be making such an arduous climb up a flight of stairs?"

Mehit took another sip. "I'm giving our child exercise."

Al-Jeheuty lifted from his chair. He reached for his wife and guided her from the rail to the seat, placing a gentle kiss on her hand. He took her spot on the rail. He lifted his glass and toasted, "A throne for the Queen of the city."

Mehit groaned as she settled her pregnant frame into the seat. She sat back and observed the view. It was remarkable and completely calming. Mehit smiled and said, "Stunning. Can this be *our* escape?"

Al-Jeheuty turned to look out over the city, eyeing the sight that had transfixed his wife. He looked back to Mehit and said, "Absolutely." He pointed at her belly. "Especially when our little Prince or Princess is born."

Mehit placed her hand on her belly and said in a playfully accusing tone, "Al-Jeheuty!" Her smile was as bright as her eyes. "Are you trying to run from the responsibility of being a father?"

Al-Jeheuty shook his head. "No. I just know that our little rugrat will be running around tearing up the place. I'm going to escape up here and drink a lot of wine."

"*Al-Jeheuty!*" Mehit repeated in the same manner.

The Beylerbey laughed as he assured his wife, "I jest, *mora*. I jest."

"Yes, you do." Mehit scowled playfully. "You will bring our children up here too." She added, "This won't be our only child. You will bring our children up here and show them what their father fought for. By that time, this city will be at peace."

Al-Jeheuty bowed at the neck toward his wife. "Yes, my Queen." He sauntered over to Mehit, bent down further, and gave her several loving kisses on the lips. "Your command, my Queen, is higher than mine."

Mehit smiled with every kiss al-Jeheuty planted on her. She could taste the wine flavoring al-Jeheuty's lips. She caressed the side of his face and asked, "And how has my King been feeling lately? Are you okay with your duties?"

Al-Jeheuty stood up. He kept his smile as he answered, "I'm fine. I have accepted my duties. I have a wonderful wife at my side, and I possess a brilliant set of lieutenants that are also my friends. We are, at this very moment, bringing peace to al-Mari Ifriq. I've come to terms that we are at war, but I will fight this war on my terms. It will be over soon."

The smile left Mehit's visage. She asked, "How are your mother and father dealing with your new status? I know they worry about Aatif's condition, but your mother has to be worried about how you inherited your title. I know she struggles with the possibility of that same thing happening to you. If I worry about it as your wife, then she definitely worries about it as your mother."

Al-Jeheuty nodded his head. He looked down at his glass of wine, twirling it and losing his thoughts while staring at it. He exhaled and finally looked at Mehit. "My mother hasn't said much, which says a lot. My father is proud that I lead the city, but he's hurt by the circumstances that allowed me to inherit the title. He liked Behar." Al-Jeheuty then said in a frustrating voice. "I've tried to talk to him about the politics of the city, but he doesn't want to listen."

Mehit's eyes were wide as she blurted out, "Of course not, al-Jeheuty. You hold sensitive information about the political and economic infrastructure of our city. Not everyone around you is a part of your Administrative Cabinet. Even *I* am a civilian to such matters. I don't want to know either—and it's not because I'm dodging any form of responsibility that comes with being privy to the knowledge you possess. Your father and I are not officials."

"What about the problems of me being cryptic?" al-Jeheuty countered, a sly grin on his face as he matched his wife with her own words. "Or how I would like people to understand, but I don't give them the truth?"

"I understand why you do such things," Mehit retorted in a sincere and gentle voice. "You're trying to protect the ones you love."

Al-Jeheuty looked at his wife. He went silent. He thought about how much the politics of al-Mari Ifriq concerned her. Taran, the man Mehit believed was her father, helped manipulate the war, and his diabolical actions shaped the events of the last several years. Taran helped plot the murder of Nasir's father, and Mehit's actual father, Ameer Las El-Behar, the beloved, former Beylerbey.

This was still not an appropriate time for confession. His thoughts lingered on Mehit's words, and then he remembered the advice his father gave to him. Al-Jeheuty smiled and said, "Yes, dear." Mehit stood up, al-Jeheuty assisting his pregnant wife. She guided him back to the seat and took rest across his knees. Mehit put her arm around her husband. The two of them watched the city's lights flicker and illuminate the night.

The Beylerbey and his wife held one another closely.

Chapter Forty-Five

General Bo Yusuf and Commander Sükh Koray entered al-Mari Ifriq to gleeful citizens and trumpeting music. Al-Mari Ifriq's officials greeted the two armies as they marched through the eastern entrance, filing through the Open Market. Beylerbey al-Jeheuty Anhur Has, Governor Wakil al-Hakam, Taran Zaher, Roberto Hamaat, Rahmis Husani, Statesman al-Rinak Ozan, and Princess Yaminah Igdobe Djenhai applauded the military men's return. Princess Yaminah and Bo Yusuf locked eyes. Bo Yusuf witnessed Mehit whisper something into Yaminah's ear. The Princess giggled, and then continued her flirtatious gaze at her husband-to-be.

The armies moved into the city square, the city officials leading them. They stopped to wave at the citizens. Sükh Koray and Bo Yusuf looked at one another, giving a silent question as to who would address the crowd. Commander Koray aimed a hand toward Bo Yusuf and said, "I am a guest in your city, General al-Dume."

Bo Yusuf bowed his neck cordially toward the Turkish commander. He looked at al-Jeheuty and Governor al-Hakam. "There is very little to report. The Ogunsanwo-Mashek have eluded us for weeks. There was no engagement." He said to al-Jeheuty, "I apologize for such little news."

"We celebrate your return, Generals," the Beylerbey assured with a smile. "Let's be thankful that no casualties were sustained within our army." He then commanded, "Turkish troops to the barracks. Djenhai unit, guard the southern wall after a six-hour cool down. Not all of you. You will guard on shifts. General al-Dume, split your command. You and the commander will brief the officials further. Meet us at the council house. Now, to your orders."

The Djenhai and Turkish units continued on through the city. The citizens parted as every class of soldier, mounted and on foot, made their way to the western barracks. Al-Jeheuty kissed Mehit on the cheek. "Attend to your business," Mehit said accepting his kiss. She turned to Yaminah and teased, "Handle your business too, sister." Yaminah slapped Mehit on the shoulder in a playful manner, a wide grin on her face. Mehit, flanked by R'uza, made her way to her bathhouse. Yaminah joined the city officials. They walked to the city gates, passed through them, and arrived at the council house. Taran did not follow the officials. He stayed within the city walls, having new daily duties.

Roberto took control of the guards surrounding the officials, and he commanded them to take a position around the council house's perimeter. Bo Yusuf and Sükh Koray joined the officials after getting their troops settled. Al-Jeheuty and Governor Wakil al-Hakam did not hold the officials long. Bo Yusuf and Sükh Koray gave their statements about the campaign. Bo Yusuf reported, "All of the Ogunsanwo-Mashek's known sites were abandoned. We came across only site remains. I would like to push further to the borders, possibly into Tunisia. We returned to receive the governor and the Beylerbey's approval. We've already been to Djenhai and spoken with King Kemnebi. He approves the notion. Also, our supplies have been dried up."

Al-Jeheuty did not answer Bo Yusuf's request. He instead looked at Sükh Koray and asked, "Did your search go through areas where you were attacked along trade routes?"

Sükh Koray shook his head and answered, "No."

Al-Jeheuty nodded. He looked back to Bo Yusuf and said, "I would feel more comfortable if those areas were swept first. Perhaps we could stage a decoy caravan and draw out the enemy."

Al-Rinak was intrigued by al-Jeheuty's deceptive assertiveness. He took advantage of the scenario al-Jeheuty proposed. "This would bring the war close to Djenhai walls." He stole a glance at the Princess. She looked concerned. Al-Rinak put his eyes back on al-Jeheuty and concluded, "I do believe King Kemnebi should have a say."

Al-Jeheuty turned to Princess Yaminah. She answered, "I was to report back to Djenhai following General al-Dume's return." Yaminah spoke directly to al-Jeheuty. "I request your presence if this is the agenda you intend on pushing."

"We will discuss it with your brother," said al-Jeheuty. "Would it be a problem if we waited for my ambassador to return? He is off attending to affairs helping us secure more financing for the war."

"We will wait for his return," Yaminah acknowledged.

"Don't be too discouraged, Princess Yaminah," said al-Jeheuty. "I expect Ambassador Sa'ood to return later this day, or early tomorrow morning." He put a sly smile and eyes on Bo Yusuf. "To help pass the time, we will honor your husband-to-be, and Commander Sükh Koray, with a wonderful celebration held within the palace's grand hall. The festivities will begin this afternoon at three. That's an hour from now." He turned to Wakil and asked, "Governor, is there more to add to this meeting?"

Wakil shook his head. "No. I don't want to keep everyone long. This meeting is adjourned."

Al-Jeheuty addressed al-Rinak, "Statesman Ozan, will we be honored by your presence at the celebration?"

Al-Rinak nodded. "Yes, indeed, Beylerbey Anhur Has. My mistress and I will attend."

"Grand," retorted al-Jeheuty. Everyone stood up and shuffled through the door. Al-Jeheuty rushed to Bo Yusuf's side, feeling uncomfortable as he came between his friend and Princess Yaminah. He turned to Bo Yusuf, commanding, "Walk with me. There are recent developments that I wish to discuss. I apologize to you and your wife-to-be." He looked at Yaminah and said, "I'm sorry, Princess Yaminah."

Yaminah answered, "I understand, Beylerbey."

Al-Jeheuty returned his attention to Bo Yusuf. "I won't keep you long. I know you would like to see one another."

Yaminah said to Bo Yusuf, "I will be in the palace guest suite." Bo Yusuf acknowledged her statement with a nod, and then watched her walk away in the company of guards and Governor Wakil. He turned to al-Jeheuty and threw his thumb over his shoulder. "Should we just go inside or…"

Al-Jeheuty watched as the others made their way to the city gates. All of the officials at the meeting walked through. The Beylerbey moved forward. "No, let's make our way to the palace. We'll just keep a pace or two behind everyone else." They started walking toward the city gate. Al-Jeheuty said, "I received permission to carry out a mark on Rene Chaffee. Simon Beaumont was very understanding. Rene was confronted. He too confirmed our suspicions. He's at the bottom of the sea, a bullet in his head."

"How's our Sicilian expedition?" the General asked.

Al-Jeheuty exhaled. "I hope all is well. I barely got sleep. Last night was the supposed night for insurrection. It was scheduled within one or two days of landing in Crocifissa. At this moment, Nasir, Chief Nuru, and Ojodo should be en route to al-Mari Ifriq, docking in our harbor later today."

Bo Yusuf exclaimed, "Ojodo is with them?"

Al-Jeheuty nodded his head, a regretful look on his face. "He made a strong argument. I could not deny him the fight." He sighed again. "If he falls in battle, well, despite the fact that he is a dramatist and poet…he too is a Griffin revolutionary. I hold the same sentiment for Chief Nuru and the al-Jasi soldiers. It's Nasir I worry about. I hope I have not put him in harm's way."

Bo Yusuf patted his friend on the shoulders. "He helps run a corsair-state," the General said to al-Jeheuty. "He was in harm's way the moment he was born."

"True," al-Jeheuty replied, unable to find complete comfort with Bo Yusuf's statement. He also informed the Army Official, "My brother returned from the Americas." He stopped walking and put his head down. Bo Yusuf looked concerned. Al-Jeheuty addressed him. "He saw terrible things there, terrible things happening to us Africans. I can't even repeat them. He was traumatized. He's doing better. But, I saw a look in his eyes. All his business decisions appeared to haunt him all at once. And he knows he can't take anything back." He grit his teeth in anger. "My family came to visit. They're leaving tomorrow morning with my brother, returning to Nusurika." He collected his composure and continued on to the city gate. "Traont Coutelier made an appearance. I had to be sedated with medicine to stop from killing him." From the corner of his eyes he could see the surprised expression on Bo Yusuf's face. "It wasn't in front of Coutelier. When I awoke, and gained my composure, I met him. He went back to France to seek Chaffee. He should be on his way to Sicily now to meet his fate."

"And the troops stationed in your hometown?" inquired Bo Yusuf.

"Withdrawn," answered al-Jeheuty. "My father confirmed when he arrived."

"Excellent," Bo Yusuf praised.

The Beylerbey and Army Official passed through the gates. Both men saluted the guards as they walked inside. "Is there more to report in the field?"

Bo Yusuf shook his head. "No. Nothing more than Commander Koray being agitated while on our excursion. He wants a fight. Maybe he feels pressure to produce a fight for al-Rinak's sake. We need to give them something."

"Word will come of Chafee and Coutelier's demise," explained al-Jeheuty. "That will rattle al-Rinak. From there, I will send Nasir to Turkey and ask the great powers to call back their troops. We'll just have to go around the statesman."

Bo Yusuf asked, "How do we cool the tensions between the Djenhai and Ogunsanwo-Mashek?"

"We prove the attack was made by another's hands. We must find those stolen garments. Fusan al-Hammon and Kyler Piett will be arrested," al-Jeheuty answered. "We've examined Fusan's ships. We found nothing. My guess is that Kyler Piett has the Ogunsanwo-Mashek outfits. Al-Rinak will call for his presence, we'll find the evidence stowed aboard his ship, and we'll have them all arrested. They will confess the name of their malefactor."

"You're positive about this?" Bo Yusuf asked trying to hide the doubt in his voice.

Al-Jeheuty shook his head. "Not entirely. However, I am positive that Wakil, you, and I are marked for death. We are all that stand in al-Rinak's way. Ojodo and Rahmis might be marked too. I don't believe Nasir would be. Taran might get rid of him just for good measure, but I am certain about the three of us. There is a lot of killing that needs to be done on their part, and they have to frame the Ogunsanwo-Mashek for all of it. Those stolen garments will come into play again. Our lives depend on finding them."

"Might I make a suggestion, Beylerbey," asked Bo Yusuf in a cordial voice. Al-Jeheuty permitted the General to speak. "Thank you. I suggest our contacts in Tunis be questioned, not on any accusations. Fusan's disguises might be stashed there, since that is where they dock and ride from in their attacks. Or, even worse, possibly in one of the backrooms of *The al-Hammon Palace*."

Al-Jeheuty commended Bo Yusuf's deduction skills. "I will investigate both of those angles."

"Carefully," Bo Yusuf reminded, not trying to sound condescending.

"Of course," al-Jeheuty acknowledged. "I'll have Roberto dispatch clan members to investigate Tunis. We'll check the inventory books for *The al-Hammon Palace*, we'll see if there is a discrepancy. I'll do this once Captain Piett's ship is investigated. We'll have to come up with an excuse."

"You will be investigating Hesam," proposed Bo Yusuf. He leaned close to al-Jeheuty and whispered, "This is the story. As al-Mari Ifriq's finances become strained, you have asked for more tribute from the companies. The first you paid visit to was Ahangar. It will then be 'discovered' that Hesam has been bringing opium into the city, disregarding the conditions set forth by our city's former Beylerbey. It will also be discovered that hashish has found its way into taverns, again breaching the agreement that the narcotic would only be regulated to the cafés."

Al-Jeheuty smiled. "Brilliance," he complimented. "Everything would have to be searched. Al-Rinak will be none-the-wiser. This would make him believe we're becoming more and more powerless without Behar.

Once the investigation is done, and we have our evidence, we can expose him, and quell this so-called war." Al-Jeheuty contemplated and said, "The hypocrisy will be that smoke has been known to be in *The Siren's Call*, but, we have to look desperate. I'll converse with Company Boss Gandarewa before we depart to Djenhai. We'll conduct investigations when we return." Al-Jeheuty and Bo Yusuf entered the palace. They gave one another a friendly embrace before splitting their journey. "Go claim your prize, General," teased al-Jeheuty as Bo Yusuf headed to Princess Yaminah's guest suite.

The Army Official winded his way through the palace corridors and arrived at Yaminah's room. He knocked on the door and the Princess answered immediately, dressed in a revealing pink gown. She pulled Bo Yusuf into her room and shut the door. Yaminah tossed her arms around his neck and kissed him long and deep. She missed him. The longer she kissed him the more she prayed to God to make her stronger in resisting the desert colored Moor in front of her. She pulled away and said to Bo Yusuf, "Take me to bed." There was a smile on her face and a glimmer shining in her eye. She noticed the baffled look on Bo Yusuf's face and declared, "I'm sure you have already 'defiled' me many times in your mind, General al-Dume. Take me to bed. Please me with more than just your tongue."

"Princess…"

Yaminah groaned. "We will still be married, chivalrous knight. You will not insult the royal crown." She nuzzled her nose around his chin. "You will be making your mark on this fertile, royal soil." Bo Yusuf chuckled at the African Princess' sentiment. "Then use your tongue. At the very least."

"That I can comply with," Bo Yusuf said with a sly smile.

Yaminah removed his sword, pistol, and robes. Bo Yusuf lifted Yaminah into his arms and tossed her onto the bed. Yaminah bounced high, a passionate shockwave writhing through her. When her body lay flat against the bed, she looked up and noticed Bo Yusuf was bare of clothes. He crawled over her, lifted her gown, and moved downward, caressing the Princess' thighs with his fingers, kisses, and ultimately the tip of his tongue. Yaminah wanted to scream a pleasurable, electric cry when Bo Yusuf's tongue penetrated her. Her satisfaction escaped in low moans and excited, quick breaths as Bo Yusuf continued to swirl his tongue around and inside her.

Yaminah's body arched and writhed as sybaritic pulses continued to fill her senses, resting on each nerve in her body. She thrust her hips to match Bo Yusuf's rhythm. Her pleasure increased and spilled out in a climatic and thunderous sensual exhale. Yaminah's body continued to shake as Bo Yusuf crawled over her and kissed her gently on the lips. She pushed Bo Yusuf over, placing him on his back. She reached for his phallus and, while still shaking with pleasure, started to stroke it.

Bo Yusuf now felt the stinging pleasure crawl over him as Yaminah handled him with quick, loving strokes. At times she was gentle with him, and at times her grip was tight and her strokes rough. She grinned as she watched how her movements, rough or gentle, controlled Bo Yusuf's erratic, sensual movements. Yaminah turned to watch Bo Yusuf's phallus as she stroked it. Another sensual burn resonated inside her as she anticipated Bo Yusuf's ejaculation. This was the game the two of them played when they had the chance to sneak away and enjoy one another privately. These were very rare, but memorable occasions.

Yaminah moved closer to Bo Yusuf's phallus, she placed her mouth over the tip, looking up at him to see his reaction. Bo Yusuf arched his hips, pushing his phallus further into the Princess' mouth. Yaminah massaged Bo Yusuf with the pressure of her lips and tongue.

But instead of allowing Yaminah to continue until he climaxed, Bo Yusuf gently pulled her away and placed the Princess on her back. He crawled over her and smiled. She reflected his gesture and opened her legs. Bo Yusuf positioned himself between Yaminah and penetrated her with his phallus, breaking through her virginal façade. Yaminah braced herself, initially. Pain coiled through her as she accepted Bo Yusuf. Yaminah grimaced. She placed her hands on his hips, almost pushing him away as the pain continued. The Moorish General relaxed, not forcing himself any further inside the Princess. Yaminah caught her breath. Bo Yusuf gave her a deep, passionate kiss. He started to suck the Princess' neck, and she exhaled. The Princess dug her nails into Bo Yusuf's back as he made his way deeper inside her.

New sensations of sensual quakes sparked through Yaminah's body. She felt filled, made whole by Bo Yusuf's penetration. She put her arms around his neck and pulled him closer. Bo Yusuf continued to penetrate deeper, thrusting. He moved from her embrace and began to suckle her left breast, her nipple hard in his mouth, his tongue swirling over it.

The Princess planned this moment days after Bo Yusuf departed. She confided in Mehit al-Tarqiyya Anhur Has. Al-Jeheuty's wife brought her to Ilindia Kali, and the beautiful, elder woman bestowed onto Yaminah lessons of sexual rhythm and positions that would intensify her pleasure.

She used these lessons to help herself climax twice more, Bo Yusuf feeling every quiver running through her, trembling and vibrating on his phallus as it rested inside her. He pulled free from her and ejaculated. They exhaled and shook wildly, tremors of ecstasy running through them. They rolled onto one side of the large bed and held each other close. Bo Yusuf pulled the sheets over them tightly, and the newlyweds-to-be drifted into slumber.

Chapter Forty-Six

The palace's grand auditorium played host to the roaring sounds of festivities. Music and social chatter rumbled through the large room. Guests participated in dance and games, and al-Jeheuty's family was in attendance. The Beylerbey gave remarks honoring Commander Sükh Koray on the military expedition. The gathered crowd applauded, the music jumped back into play, and al-Jeheuty and Commander Koray mingled with the crowd. Bo Yusuf and Princess Yaminah were noticeably absent. Al-Jeheuty made excuses that the General was still asleep, tired from his long expedition. Many women swarmed the Beylerbey, asking for the General's presence. None of the women were being disrespectful. They understood Bo Yusuf was arranged to marry the Djenhai Princess, but the lovely, Moorish women still wanted to swoon in the presence of the Army Official.

The women stepped away from al-Jeheuty as Commander Koray approached the Beylerbey. The Mongolian-Turk motioned toward the Beylerbey's hat, a Djenhai accessory and present that al-Jeheuty wished to show off when Princess Yaminah arrived. "I do not wish to disrespect you, Beylerbey Anhur Has," stated Sükh Koray. "But I agree with the adage that it is most respectful to remove ones hat in the presence of a lady."

Al-Jeheuty hid his intense annoyance directed at Commander Koray. The Beylerbey cleared his throat and patted the commander on the back, a little harder than normal. "Perhaps when a woman finally decides to hold a conversation with you, you may then honor that sentiment. Until then, in the African culture, we keep hats close to protect our dome. Besides, it's a gift from Princess Yaminah. And on a greater note than that, I'm the Beylerbey."

Both men feigned laughter.

Sükh Koray nodded his head. He took a sip of water from his cup and continued to speak, much to al-Jeheuty's annoyance. "Don't blame General al-Dume for this excursion's loss."

Al-Jeheuty addressed the commander, "I don't intend to."

"Good," said Sükh Koray. "I would instead, if I were you, Beylerbey, praise the ferocity commanded by the two armies. We have the Ogunsanwo-Mashek running scared. They know their days are numbered. An engagement would mean their eradication. My sword will fell many of them. I have studied greatly the precise techniques on swordplay, gathered from the most notable cultures and their scrolls."

"How many times have you seen combat," al-Jeheuty asked.

"Few times," admitted the Commander. "And there have been some skirmishes between the Ogunsanwo-Mashek and Turkish troops."

"On trade routes, yes," al-Jeheuty clarified. "They have not engaged us on the level of a war. Bandits fight different from soldiers. Have your conflicts been up close, or have they been from afar?"

Commander Koray shook a finger. "The Ogunsanwo-Mashek are sneaky. We have traded gunfire. There has been little swordplay, but enough for me to know what I fight against."

Al-Jeheuty considered the Commander's words. "A great teacher once taught me that you learn any form of martial art just to forget it. Once in combat, Commander, you can't recall every lesson learned. You must *become* every lesson you've learned, and quickly be innovative, creative. We learn fighting styles just to make them our own. Your opponent will not follow them." He took a breath. "I've been in skirmishes from here to Spain. I'm alive not because of some skill with a blade, but mostly out of desperation to overwhelm my opponent, and a little luck. And if there's anything I draw on, it's other skills that I have. I incorporate them. I speak well. A sword fight is no different than negotiations. It's a debate between two swordsmen and the gods they serve. Which can give the best argument to their deity to stay alive. I admit that we are but chess pieces on the board, and I hate chess."

Sükh Koray chuckled. "My Beylerbey," he drawled. "The fight we are engaged in is not set faraway in some romantic countryside plagued and stained by war. The horrors of war are closer. They are footsteps from where you stand. I don't believe in superstitions—debates with deities and such. Reality is far more dangerous; its proximity closer."

Al-Jeheuty conceded. He chuckled and lifted his drink. "You need to loosen up, Commander Koray. You're a bit tight. Have a drink that's stronger than water. I'm sure you have keen eyesight. If you look around, there happens to be a party—in your honor no less. Join it." He removed his hat and bowed his head humorously. "I insist."

Bo Yusuf and Princess Yaminah entered at that moment. Al-Jeheuty placed his hat back on, smiled wide, and charged his friend and his friend's wife-to-be. He threw his arm around Bo Yusuf's shoulder and yelled for the crowd and music to simmer down. No one heard him. He walked Bo Yusuf in front of the musicians, screaming for silence the whole walk over. The mingling guests and music stopped and looked at their Beylerbey.

"I won't keep your bodies still for long," al-Jeheuty assured his guests. "I would just like everyone to recognize a great army leader. A wonderful strategist that in time will command a victory over our city's enemies." The crowd applauded Bo Yusuf's presence. Al-Jeheuty pulled Yaminah to the front, resting her by Bo Yusuf's side. "His bride-to-be, Princess Yaminah Igdobe Djenhai. Their union might be symbolic of the union between Djenhai and al-Mari Ifriq. However, I do not want that symbolism, or their arrangement for marriage, to be confused with the sincere love these two have developed for one another."

The crowd clapped lightly, impressed by their Beylerbey's words. Yaminah reached out to al-Jeheuty and kissed the Beylerbey on the cheek. She stepped away, bowed at the neck, and returned to Bo Yusuf's side. Al-Jeheuty made an attempt to command the musicians to continue playing, but Zakiy Sa'ood's sudden presence interrupted him. The company boss burst into the auditorium with a concerned look. He approached al-Jeheuty, merchant robes flowing behind him. He stopped and informed, "Men have come to see you." Al-Jeheuty's festive face melted into an expression matching the out-of-breath company boss. Everyone in the room became nervous. "They docked half an hour ago," Zakiy continued. "They demand to speak with you." He turned toward the doorway and pointed. "I could not stop them from entering the palace."

Al-Jeheuty looked up. Nasir ibn Sa'ad al-Din Sa'ood and Ojodo Yerodin stood in the doorway. There was also a third member rounding out the small party. Aludra el-Amin. Nasir guided the Moon inside the auditorium, hand-in-hand. Al-Jeheuty called for Roberto and Bo Yusuf, and ordered, "Arrest these three. They're revolutionaries. Escort them from my palace," he joked. "Rahmis, reverse all manner of decency and sophistication that helped you decorate every room hosted in all the taverns, cafés, and inns you govern. Create a room reflecting chaos and disorder and such nature, then have these three tossed inside for life." He pointed at Zakiy and said, "This one too, for conspiring to scare the hell out of me."

The crowd laughed, relieved.

Al-Jeheuty commanded the musicians to continue, citing the party had more to celebrate. The festivities continued. The Beylerbey embraced his ambassador, thankful that he was safe. Aludra let go of Nasir and made her way to Mehit. The two women embraced, and Mehit's expression was an excited look of congratulations to Aludra. "Do you still serve my company, Aludra?" Mehit asked.

"Yes, Mistress Zaher Anhur Has," Aludra answered humbly.

"And it will be a company soon," Mehit said excitedly. "I have plans to connect all the bathhouses, male and female. I am also expanding my business into a nursery, and a midwifery company. I will connect them with similar businesses in the city. I've already spoken to my husband about it. He will council with Governor Wakil, Jabari al-Hakam, Princess Yaminah, and Statesman Ozan for approval."

"I will serve you with my skills within those services, Mistress," Aludra said, the tone in her voice unsure.

"However...?" Mehit inquired.

Aludra looked up at Mehit. "Nasir lost Tegu," she whispered. "In Sicily."

"Were you there?" Mehit inquired. "I was told you were on assignment in the Soudan."

Aludra only said, "I returned just as he returned. He told me of Tegu. We have spoken about our feelings, or, rather, I've spoken about mine."

"So, your guard will change?' Mehit questioned. "That's fine, sister," she said embracing Aludra. "R'uza serves me well." Something, however, did not sit right with the information she was presented. Mehit decided to interrogate her husband later.

Within Nasir and al-Jeheuty's reunion, the ambassador whispered a report to his Beylerbey, "The outing was a success. Nuru is getting everyone situated, his warriors, the freed Africans. We've been doing that for the past half hour. I left to come see you." He stepped away from al-Jeheuty.

"Well, let us mingle for now," said the Beylerbey, unable to hold back a relieved smile. "We shouldn't be too obvious. We'll hold counsel later." He turned to Ojodo and shook the Moorish titan's hand. The two gave one another a gentleman's embrace. Ojodo was dressed in a fine suit, removed of his tattered disguise as a slave. "I was worried...about the both of you," al-Jeheuty said in a serious tone.

"We're home," Ojodo assured, a wide smile on his face. "Alive. You can cancel your meeting with Jesus Christ."

Al-Jeheuty ordered the two men to join the festivities, grab a drink, food, and attend a game or two. He made his way to al-Rinak and said to the statesman, "Nasir has returned. Baron Agusto agreed to our demands.

We have financing. With that secured, we can move forward. I'm going to allow Nasir some rest. We'll leave for Djenhai in two days."

"Yes, Beylerbey," al-Rinak nodded. Al-Jeheuty returned to the party. The statesman turned to Melusina and the two gave one another a long look. There was a hint of a smile exchanged between them. The party continued until the evening. Al-Rinak and Melusina took leave, along with a greater part of the invited guests. Mehit and her entourage retired to her bathhouse for a relaxing evening. Bo Yusuf separated from Yaminah after a gentle kiss on her cheek. Yaminah joined Mehit's party, and the Beylerbey's wife whispered in the Princess' ear a teasing sentiment about more than a kiss being shared between Bo Yusuf and Yaminah in their absence.

Nasir, Ojodo, Rahmis, and Bo Yusuf retired to the palace's council chambers. Al-Jeheuty, flanked by Roberto and two Suns, looked for Governor Wakil. He was sharing a moment with his sons, discussing politics and business focused on day-to-day operations. Al-Jeheuty asked the governor if he would join the council he was holding with Nasir, Ojodo, and the rest of the Griffin Company. Wakil declined, humbly. "I trust the moves you boys will make. If you've had my approval so far, you will have my approval always. However, I want a full report of any new developments. We will discuss this tomorrow morning. Tell Nasir and Ojodo that I'm glad they've returned safely." He smiled and patted al-Jeheuty on the shoulder. "I was not holding a festival all day. There was still court." He added with a teasing smile, "Might you want to join us in overseeing these decisions, Beylerbey?"

Al-Jeheuty waved his hand. "Absolutely not. I have an easier job trying to end a war and draw out conspirators involved in a plot marking us all for death."

Wakil laughed hard. "I believe you're correct. But you are due in court tomorrow. We're overseeing a lot of new cases. Plus, when I'm finished here, I will meet with our new residents, the noblewoman and the newly freed Africans."

Al-Jeheuty sighed. "Yes, Governor." The young Beylerbey bowed toward Wakil and left the room with Suns at his side. Roberto stayed behind. Before joining the Griffin heads, al-Jeheuty grouped with Chief Nuru, and he introduced himself to the freed African men and women and Adaeze. He welcomed them to al-Mari Ifriq, speaking Italian. Adaeze thanked the Beylerbey for freeing them. She was startled when al-Jeheuty replied, "You are most welcome, Princess Adaeze." He bowed in her honor.

By now, Adaeze's story was known to each of the black captives. It was a story recounted through Ojodo's poetry, and enjoyed by all of the freed captives that heard it. Adaeze admitted that she felt she already knew al-Jeheuty, telling the Beylerbey about the stories Ojodo would spin of their time in Spain. "I hope he didn't talk about everything," the Beylerbey joked. "Again, I'm glad you're a part of our city, in better hands. I know you're anxious to seek your history in the east, but enjoy your stay, and make yourself comfortable for as long as you wish." He looked at the entire group and said, "I express my words to all of you." Al-Jeheuty then greeted and congratulated the surviving al-Jasi warriors, and the women and children that assisted them. He exited and made his way back to the palace to find his family. His father decided they would stay one more day, Jawhara and Khaira having joined Mehit at her bathhouse. Aatif was still doing fine, having had a wonderful time at the festival held in the palace auditorium. The Beylerbey bid his brother and father a good night, then, with Suns flanking him, walked to the small council room within the palace. He walked through the door, the Suns taking post outside the room. He took a seat, looked at Nasir and demanded, "Casualties? I've met with Chief Nuru, but I didn't get a count. I greeted each of the remaining men, and thanked them for their service."

"There were casualties only among the warriors," reported Nasir. "Bless them. A good many fell. Fifty, maybe sixty warriors." Nasir took a breath. "Tegu fell." He went silent for a moment, searching for a prayer to say to his friend, but he did not know a proper Mohammedan or occult phrase to honor his fallen guard and friend with. He simply just said in his head, *Thank you for your duty, my friend. You gave your life for mine.* "Aludra substituted his service. The Moons will inform Roberto. They have his body wrapped."

Al-Jeheuty nodded. The Beylerbey said, "We give thanks for all life that protects us, and all forces unseen. Of course, we ask to be judged appropriately for the lives we've taken, even under the banner of a righteous kill." He added with a sly smile, "We know the kills were just." The men chuckled. "Rene Chaffee's mark has been carried out."

"Signore Verola informed me that Traont Coutelier was en route to Sicily," Nasir said, al-Jeheuty's news reminding him. "We should receive a letter of his fate soon." He also told the Beylerbey, "Signore Verola has decided to leave the baron's nephew alive. I don't think that would be a good idea. He's been called back to Sicily. I was wondering if he could meet a fate at sea before reaching his homeland. We don't need his vengeful ass at sea."

Al-Jeheuty pointed. "It will be done. I will have one of Hesam's old soldiers take care of the deed. I have to speak with Hesam anyway. I want investigations done on all businessmen connected with al-Rinak. I would like to uncover the disguises used by Fusan and his soldiers. I believe Captain Piett might have them. Bo Yusuf has come up with a plan to investigate the backrooms of *The al-Hammon Palace*, as well as interrogate our contacts in Tunis. We'll surprise everyone with an investigation that turns up evidence that Hesam is breaking his agreement on the narcotics trade. This will give us reason to search all cafés, taverns, and inns." He looked at Rahmis. "We'll conduct these investigations after the new tournaments you've set up."

"I am preparing *The Siren's Call*," Rahmis notified. "We've received overwhelming entries. Brother, my ear is to the streets. The people cannot wait. I believe they welcome this distraction more than us."

Al-Jeheuty slapped his lap. He turned to Ojodo and asked, "Will you remain in al-Mari Ifriq until the end of our story?" He looked at each of the other companymen and imparted, "Our friend, the dramatist, is looking to go east for study. Despite the great adventure that is our lives, he's decided that scribing fictitious stories would—"

"Be more safe," Ojodo concluded to a round of laughter.

"Apparently you had one last adventure in you," al-Jeheuty pointed out.

Ojodo shook his head. "You're correct." He looked at Nasir. Their eyes connected. Ojodo looked unsure of his next statement, uncharacteristically shy. Nasir nodded, urging the Moorish titan to speak. "I will be escorting the noblewoman Adaeze to the east."

Al-Jeheuty beamed. "Es-*courting?*"

Ojodo said shyly, "We shall see, Beylerbey."

Al-Jeheuty looked from Ojodo to Nasir. He looked at the others and stated, "Only these two womanizing bachelors could find time to woo women while staging a revolution." He stood up and bowed toward Ojodo and Nasir. "I commend you both." He said to Nasir, "I warn you, the woman you court knows how to use a knife. Break her heart, she will take your testicles." He took a seat.

Nasir chuckled shyly. "We'll see where this takes us, Beylerbey."

"A noblewoman and a Princess," stated Rahmis. "This company might become civilized yet." The noble Moor's comments drew laughter. Bo Yusuf wondered if Rahmis' comments were to cover any insecurities of not courting a woman of noble blood. He did not dare mention his time with Princess Yaminah.

Al-Jeheuty steered the conversation to a more serious matter before the General's thoughts could become contagious. "I am certain that al-Rinak marks myself, Wakil, and Bo Yusuf for death. I will be cautious and give warning to everyone in attendance. Suns and Moons will be assigned to escort us wherever we go, at all times. Nasir, you and I will be heading to Djenhai to discuss plans for the war. Bo Yusuf has delayed progress, as planned. The General will accompany us. Al-Rinak will be there, as well as Commander Sükh Koray—he is a prick, is he not?"

"You should spend a two week excursion with him," Bo Yusuf noted.

"I'll let that continue to be your job," al-Jeheuty responded. He took a breath before saying, "We are working on more charades to keep the Turkish army roaming in circles, but, as Bo Yusuf continues to remind me, the charades cannot last forever. Our backup plan will consist of Ambassador Nasir heading to Turkey and pleading with the Empire to remove the army. The consequences might have Turkish ships dock in our waters, but hopefully they would be here only to take their troops with them. I also hope that we have evidence of al-Rinak's crimes, and have him removed too."

"That's an awful lot we have to hope for, Beylerbey," said Nasir. "I mean no disrespect," he added.

"A voice of reason should never be seen as disrespectful," al-Jeheuty replied. "I'm looking to arrest Fusan al-Hammon and Kyler Piett. Maybe we can force Taran's hand too. Their words would be more valuable than any of the men we've extinguished. Continue to think. I'm open to ideas. Dismissed." The companymen stood up and shuffled from the room, small talk starting among the men. They separated once in the hall. Al-Jeheuty returned to his quarters, Mehit joining him an hour after midnight. Al-Jeheuty rested at his desk, reading a book, and dressed in night garments. He turned to his wife, a stern look in his eyes.

"R'uza and Aludra accompanied myself, your mother, and your sister-by-law to the palace. Everything is fine, al-Jeheuty. All of us little girls are okay." She rubbed her pregnant belly. "And our child."

Al-Jeheuty laughed at his wife's words. "That was a long relax time after a celebration."

Mehit grinned. "We all stripped down, danced, fondled one another, and suckled each others' naughty parts," she answered sarcastically. "I just watched the more raucous acts, since I'm pregnant and that makes me 'unfit' and 'unclean' to be used in such a manner." She rolled her eyes at the sentiment. "But, I danced naked and did kiss Yaminah and R'uza often," She continued to tease. Mehit leaned on al-Jeheuty, placing her hands on his shoulders. She watched al-Jeheuty as his eyes rolled up in thought, thinking of the very scene his wife described. "Is your mother and sister-by-law a part of your thoughts?" she asked teasingly. Al-Jeheuty returned to reality, a scowl on his face. Mehit took a seat in his lap. She kissed him on the lips. "Yaminah and Bo Yusuf made love, my husband. Ilindia and I prepared her for their ritual."

"Intercourse is a ritual now," al-Jeheuty asked.

"Yes," Mehit exclaimed. "Yaminah has taken steps into womanhood. And Nasir courts Aludra."

"I've been told," al-Jeheuty acknowledged.

Mehit took a moment to scope her husband with inquisitive eyes. "Aludra was not in the Soudan, was she? She was in Sicily with Nasir."

Al-Jeheuty nodded his head. "Yes, *mora*." He stroked her cheek with a finger. "We have been making strikes against the true people behind the war—the conspirators." He paused. Mehit assured al-Jeheuty that he did not have to say anymore, but he responded, "It's fine, *mora*. We helped free African brothers and sisters from bondage, one of them being a noblewoman."

"Adaeze," said Mehit. "I remember you telling me about her. She has a remarkable story."

"She's safe on our shores," al-Jeheuty briefed. "We helped a Sicilian remove Baron Agusto from power. In return, this Sicilian will fulfill a mark on one of this war's conspirators."

Mehit asked a surprising question. "How will you convince the Djenhai that the Ogunsanwo-Mashek are an innocent people, and not behind the attacks that claimed noble men?"

Al-Jeheuty did not flinch with his wife's question. He answered honestly. "We're still counseling," he told her. Mehit's beauty filled all of al-Jeheuty's senses as he ingested her sight with his eyes. He examined her for a long moment, his thoughts centered on Rene Chaffee's warning to him. Taran had marked Mehit for death or enslavement. Al-Jeheuty vowed to stop Taran's plans. He wondered if Taran was intelligent enough to know that Mehit was not his daughter. It did not matter. In time, Mehit would learn the truth. The Beylerbey finally spoke, telling his wife, "I'm traveling to Djenhai, *mora*. If you weren't so close to bearing a child, I would have you come along. My trip is not scheduled for days. I would like Nasir to get sleep. He's coming too. Just as usual, my Queen, you stay safe. Those are my orders."

"I will, *Papa Lion*." She kissed her husband.

Al-Jeheuty rubbed Mehit's belly. He looked at her pregnant hump and said to his unborn child, "Keep your mother safe."

Mehit giggled. "My father believes I'm carrying twins. He says I'm so full for only being a few months with child." She started to laugh harder. "He has to know that I was pregnant before the wedding, a whole month. I think it's easier for him to cope with his excuses. Do you know my mother figured it out?"

"Yes," al-Jeheuty said. Mehit's eyes widened with surprise, her expression questioning how and when al-Jeheuty would have acquired such information from her mother. "Behar told me," he said matter-of-factly. The Beylerbey diverted his wife's growing suspicions by explaining, "I think your mother informed him so as to divert any trouble with a scandal, should Behar have figured out otherwise. I don't understand why," al-Jeheuty fibbed. "Behar served no religion where that would rock the foundation of his belief in me, thinking me any less of a noble and competent advisor."

"Oh," said Mehit, her curiosity quelled. "What was his true reaction? After all, he might not serve any religious law, but he helped govern a city that is primarily a Mohammedan state. The citizens would be in an uproar," Mehit concluded teasingly.

"His reaction to me, *mora?*" al-Jeheuty started to explain. "He just had a sly smile. He knew the skies wouldn't darken and pour fiery blood that would raise the already flooded land through great earthquakes, or whatever judgment religion is pushing now. I'm a responsible man that made pregnant the woman I was affianced to."

Mehit laughed. "Fiery blood, flooded lands, and great earthquakes. That sounds like the process of child birth to me." She leaned into al-Jeheuty and whispered in a flirtatious tone, "Or the sexual climax I experienced upon conception."

"If it happened while I visited you in Tunisia, it most likely occurred in that quick session at night in the back alley." Al-Jeheuty smiled as he reminisced. "Of course, that was one of many moments on that visit."

Mehit smiled guiltily. She said to al-Jeheuty, pressing her forehead against his and gripping his face tightly, "When this child arrives I will ravage you. I have missed you so much, al-Jeheuty." She kissed him deeply, her lips pressed hard against al-Jeheuty's lips. Her tongue flowed through his mouth. Mehit pulled away, passion scrawled on her face. Both of them snuck glances at the book they received as a wedding gift from Roberto Hamaat. While on their wedding holiday, they engaged in several sexual maneuvers showcased in the book, but as Mehit's belly expanded, and her pregnancy increased, they resorted to small, passionate sessions. Al-Jeheuty at times would stimulate her to climax by rubbing his fingers between her legs, but never penetrating. Mehit would stroke her husband to climax, or suckle his phallus for the same result. But there was nothing that could substitute for actual intercourse.

Mehit relaxed herself and rose off of al-Jeheuty. He stood up. He extinguished the lights, and the two of them slipped into bed. He said to his wife, "From simple business woman to company boss."

"So, have I been approved?" Mehit concluded.

"Not as of yet, *mora*." He put his arm around her. "Don't worry. I can't see Jabari or Wakil saying no. If so, al-Mari Ifriq will be in a civil war." They chuckled at the notion. "Continue with your business plans," al-Jeheuty instructed. "You'll have to present them to Jabari and Wakil."

"Yes, Beylerbey," Mehit replied.

Al-Jeheuty laughed. "It sounds like you're ordering me to put pressure on them."

"You're the Governor-General," Mehit said playfully.

"Yes. Of course." Al-Jeheuty rubbed his wife's belly until she drifted into slumber. He held her tight and followed close behind.

Chapter Forty-Seven

Al-Jeheuty met privately with Company Boss Hesam Gandarewa the following day. Their meeting was held in the Ahangar company house, and al-Jeheuty informed the company boss of his plans to legitimately search *The al-Hammon Palace* without raising suspicion. Hesam agreed to the plan. The Beylerbey also asked Company Boss Gandarewa to send word to Libya and have a former soldier execute a mark on Giovanni Ghislanzoni-Verdi. *"Make it look like an accident,"* the Beylerbey advised. Hesam assured his chief boss that he would. Al-Jeheuty left the company house, guards flanking him, and returned to the city to engage in daily operations, watching over court—one of the strenuous activities of the day. Al-Jeheuty actually found amusement in the locals' petty grievances. He reveled in how little they knew about the politics their leaders engaged in to keep them safe. After the first session of court was held, al-Jeheuty saw his family off. The Anhur Has family traveled with eight guards to keep them safe on their way home.

The officials traveling to Djenhai prepared for their trip. Nasir took the day to rest, however. Princess Yaminah spent her time overseeing her travel accessories and clothing packed in trunks, and she made sure all her servants were accounted for. She saw very little of Bo Yusuf. Neither of them was put off by the circumstances, considering they would be traveling back to Djenhai together and in one another's company for the next several days—let alone, married until death did them part. Al-Jeheuty and Governor al-Hakam, later in the day, interviewed the recently freed Africans about their skill-sets that would best serve the city. A physician examined each man and woman after the interviews. All the men and women decided to stay in al-Mari Ifriq. Labaan took a job with Zakiy, substituting for Ojodo's loss. Mehit's mother hired Chanya as a seamstress. The other freed men and women took various jobs within the city, or joined Captains' crews, adjusting to a free life.

The al-Hammon Palace hosted al-Rinak and his conspirators. The tavern was closed for the day. The Turkish Statesman met with the al-Hammon brothers and their foster father, Taran Zaher. Fusan was given his orders to attack.

The burly Moorish pirate groaned, "Al-Jeheuty will open up my route after he returns from Djenhai." He addressed al-Rinak. "Should we postpone the mark on he, Nasir, and General al-Dume?"

Al-Rinak shook his head. "I don't believe we'll have another perfect time to strike them."

Maurice interjected, "They are a tight unit. I see them traveling to and from Djenhai often. Postponing their mark would make them feel safe."

Al-Rinak nodded, impressed by Maurice's reasoning. "I see your point. I only suggest their marks be carried out now based on the first campaign against the Ogunsanwo-Mashek. I imagined there would be some conflict. Koray is on orders to take out General al-Dume during the confusion of any exchange. I might have underestimated the tribal nation's ability to disappear into the desert. We take out these city officials and we bring in Traont Coutelier's French command. I'm still waiting for Rene's presence, but all in time. I will also bring in Kyler's soldiers, under the command of our Dutch bidder, Jacob Burker. We make a great sweep of Odongo-Mauharim, emotions high, all of the tribe's people taken. We suffocate the hysteria within our city walls and Djenhai. Governor Wakil will become ill, silenced silently. Poison. Ojodo Yerodin leaves the city tomorrow. When he returns, his friends will be dead. Rahmis is no threat. He will find solace in comforting Princess Yaminah on Bo Yusuf's death. Roberto Hamaat will be arrested. His clan members rounded up and burned." He turned to Taran and asked, "And your daughter?"

Taran sighed. His eyebrows arched in a sorrowful manner. "It will pain her to have her husband assassinated. But it will not be more painful than what my wife will feel when Mehit is taken by the Ogunsanwo-Mashek."

Al-Rinak put his hand on Taran's arm, comforting him as if the acts against his daughter had already been committed. "Her body will not be found. Your wife will be spared the sight of Mehit's ravaged corpse."

"Thank you," Taran said sincerely. He continued to struggle with his daughter's potential emotions once her husband was silenced. Taran knew he would be unable to rule properly while watching Mehit become rattled by the emotional stress. He came to the decision months ago that he would spare her this anguish. Mehit's life was marked either for slavery or death. His wife's emotional state would be easier to support.

"You're welcome, *Governor*," al-Rinak addressed. He turned to Maurice. "Our strike must be quick. We've stalled long enough, though we have accomplished a lot." He said to Fusan, "I have arranged a vessel to

Turkey. I've spoken to the Beylerbey, yesterday at the auditorium. I told him that I would send word about the extension of the use of the army. You will use that as your way out, Fusan. You and your crew will be disguised among my servants and cabinet members. You'll head to Tunis. Roam the Djenhai area. Watch for our exit. Strike, and let your aim be true."

"Please," Maurice complained. Fusan threw a sharp look to his brother. Surprisingly, the elder al-Hammon brother did not retort. Maurice could commend his brother for his last exercise, all three marks carried out. But Fusan missed Maurice's greater target. Nasir.

There was nothing more exchanged between the brothers.

Al-Rinak continued by dictating, "Hit me if need be." He turned to Taran and joked, "Punishment for my actions against you. It's only fair. Such is life. Just." The sentiment was enough to clear the tension between the two brothers. Al-Rinak dismissed his collaborators, leaving with Fusan and Taran. Maurice stayed behind, preparing the *Palace* for the night's opening.

The day continued without incident, fading into night and the following morning. The Griffin heads gathered to honor Ojodo Yerodin's leave. It was within *The Siren's Call* where Ojodo announced he and Adaeze would be joining General al-Dume, Beylerbey Anhur Has, and Ambassador Sa'ood to Djenhai, leaving for the east after a good stay in the kingdom. Ojodo had not yet been to Djenhai, and he wanted Adaeze to experience the awe of an African kingdom, a glimpse of what she was descended from. The Moorish titan's celebration was only an hour long. The Griffin heads dispersed into daily duties while Ojodo met Adaeze and flocked to the markets, heading to the garment district for Adaeze to purchase outfits for travel. Ojodo purchased the finest, African Moorish apparel for her.

On finishing their daily duties, the Griffin heads assembled at the southern wall with a caravan of troops, a fourth of the Turkish army, and the entire Djenhai unit under Bo Yusuf's command. Servants, camels, steeds, and carriage carrying elephants accompanied them. It was sundown. The city's activities were closing. Governor Wakil al-Hakam, Rahmis Husani, and Taran Zaher bid farewell to the Griffin heads, Statesman al-Rinak Ozan, and Princess Yaminah. Mehit, watching al-Jeheuty's caravan disappear over the darkening horizon, started missing her husband instantly. Aludra, standing next to Mehit, felt the same about Nasir.

The caravan traveled four hours, finally arriving at the gates of the Djenhai kingdom. A messenger had already been sent earlier in the day announcing their arrival. King Kemnebi and the entire royal family greeted the al-Mari Ifriq cavalcade. He praised both General al-Dume and Commander Koray. The King was most excited when his sister greeted him. He put his arms around her and said, "I thought you would be with your husband-to-be when he first showed up. You have been greatly missed."

The Moorish officials exited their rides and pleasantly greeted the King. The rest of their journey continued on individual steeds, the women carried in a large palanquin hoisted by equally large men. King Kemnebi and Prince Asim led the procession to the royal palace. Once there, and on foot, the caravan and troops, overseen by Commander Koray, General al-Dume, and other Djenhai Generals, were escorted to another section of the kingdom. Princess Yaminah and Bo Yusuf stole a quick glance at one another. They exchanged smiles, believing one another quick and unsuspecting, but A'sharia, the Queen of the Second World, noticed their subtle, flirtatious parting.

The officials settled inside the palace, little conversation among them. Princess Yaminah readied herself for bed when someone knocked on her door. She did not believe Bo Yusuf would make such a bold move as inviting himself into her room while inside her kingdom's palace. Not at night, she believed. Not with her mother and royal family so close. But the thought excited her, and hope appeared on her face in the form of a sly smile. She opened the door, her eyes widened with surprise when she saw her mother on the other side. Yaminah invited her mother inside and A'sharia guided her to the bed. The two took a seat on the mattress.

The Queen rubbed her daughter's arm. "General al-Dume took you to bed, didn't he?" she asked gently. Yaminah jumped with her mother's accusation. A'sharia cupped her daughter's wrist and smiled warmly. "No. Don't be ashamed. It's fine, Yaminah. You will marry him, yes?"

Yaminah nodded her head. "Yes, ma-ma."

A'sharia sighed relief. "I don't mean to turn your love into politics and business, but your marriage is important to our side of the Djenhai royal family. I understand the leaders of al-Mari Ifriq do not rule through the Mohammedan Law. That is our world. But we can make a new world. Ambassadors to the Second World will no longer be our titles once Kemnebi finds two brides, but the new focus could be the Odongo-Mauharim nation-state. Kemnebi's role will be reduced to a tradition, as well as his wives. His power would still influence the immediate kingdom, but the real authority will come through al-Mari Ifriq. I know you have a meeting tomorrow morning. Let your voice be strong. Let your voice be in harmony with General al-Dume, your husband-to-be." She kissed her daughter's forehead and felt her belly. "Do you believe you might have conceived?"

Yaminah kept a straight face as she answered, "He pulled…away before…"

A'sharia could see her daughter felt awkward speaking of her experiences with the Moorish General. A'sharia stood up, keeping her smile on her daughter. "In time. I *will* be a grandmother." She walked out of Yaminah's room, closing the door.

The Princess extinguished her light and lay down in bed. She was angry with her mother. Her eyes watered but never produced tears. She thought about her experience with Bo Yusuf, concentrating on his feel, smell, and all the sensations he brought to her. Yaminah relaxed and fell asleep. In the morning, she bathed and was primped by servants before attending the morning meeting with her brother, the Queen of the First World, her uncle Munashe, Beylerbey Anhur Has, General al-Dume, Commander Koray, and Statesman Ozan.

Yaminah said little. Her answers were short, mostly agreeing to the sentiments of Statesman Ozan and her brother. King Kemnebi agreed to sweep the trade routes to find remnants of the Ogunsanwo-Mashek. He admired al-Jeheuty's plan to draw them out. The King added, "We'll take prisoners. Not for slavery, but to find information on the whereabouts to their entire tribe. We'll first sweep the trade routes. They will think we're being confident. We'll reinstate trade. The first caravan will be a decoy." He said to both Bo Yusuf and Sükh Koray, "Take few prisoners. We only need one to talk."

"Yes, King Kemnebi," both men replied.

Kemnebi stood up. He waved his hands for the officials to follow his lead. They stood up. He addressed them, "I have duties to attend to. You all know your way around the city. I know your friend Ojodo is having a good time showing his woman around." He turned to Yaminah. "Sister, you finally have free time with your husband-to-be that doesn't pertain to business. Everyone else, I'll see you throughout your stay. Good day to you."

The King and his advisors left first. The other officials followed, separating into different groups once they left the council room. Bo Yusuf joined Princess Yaminah. He was concerned about her. She was often inured during political counsel, but she was more reserved during this particular meeting. Yaminah even walked quicker as she stepped away from the room and headed back to her royal quarters. Bo Yusuf was exerting himself to keep up. When he was side-by-side with the Princess he noticed her focused and enraged expression.

"That's quite a step you have in your walk today, Princess," said Bo Yusuf. Yaminah continued her quick pace. She did not address the Moorish General. Bo Yusuf's demeanor turned to visible concern. "What is the matter, Yaminah?" The Princess scurried through the palace halls, finding her way to her room. She did not address Bo Yusuf. The General's demeanor changed from concerned to frustrated. She entered her room, leaving the door open for Bo Yusuf. He entered and shut the door. He looked at his wife-to-be and demanded, "Speak to me, Yaminah. What is the matter? I demand to know." Yaminah turned around, tears in her eyes. She walked closer to Bo Yusuf and he took her in his arms. "Talk to me, Princess."

"I love you, Bo Yusuf," she said quivering through tears. She wiped and sniffed her tears away. "My mother could sense we have been together." Bo Yusuf backed away to give Yaminah a concerned look. She assured the General, "She's not angry. She's quite happy, actually. She's trying to turn our relationship into politics." She walked away from Bo Yusuf's embrace and took a seat on her bed. Bo Yusuf sat next to her. "And I understand what our marriage would symbolize, but it just hurt. She wasn't happy for me. She was happy about what status our marriage would bring. The powerful union between an al-Mari Ifriq official and a Djenhai Princess. She's worried about our titles and authority once Kemnebi finds brides, especially a Queen of the Second World." She looked up and rolled her eyes. "I wish the three worlds we govern could dissolve and be washed away."

Bo Yusuf did not mean to be rude. He understood that Princess Yaminah was tied to the doctrines of her kingdom, but he could not help but correct her choice of words. "*Two* worlds, Princess." Yaminah reacted. Her tears stopped, and she smiled brightly at Bo Yusuf. He waved a hand toward her and apologized. "I don't mean to correct you about your culture, Princess, it's just—"

Yaminah stroked Bo Yusuf's face gently. "We will be married, Bo Yusuf. I don't believe in keeping secrets from you. There are truly three worlds within the Djenhai tradition. The third world is part of the first world, actually. The second world, of course, is the Mohammedan world. The first is the African world, the ancient kingdoms of the east, Nubia, where the first Djenhai king was born. He brought our people here, trying to follow the black rush into al-Andalusia. But he, and the people he led here, were a part of another culture. They lived in Nubia, descendants of refugees. They were not, as a people, originally from the land. They are a part of our hidden, third world—the world Djenhai honors in secret. The third world extends to a history in Mesopotamia." Yaminah beamed, looking like a child remembering a fantastical storybook tale. Bo Yusuf was intrigued. "It's a legend we Djenhai nobles learn, only the immediate royal family. Not even Feroz Aunun's wife knew of the tale, she being a distant cousin. It's a tale that goes back a long way in history, Bo Yusuf." Yaminah sounded extremely mature when she spoke. "It goes back to when Mesopotamia was still Africa. It speaks of the fractured kingdoms calling out for Africa to send warriors to defend the land. Many kingdoms fell to wandering white tribes coming from the mountains in Europe."

Bo Yusuf started shaking. His movement was subtle. He wanted to interrupt, but he could not find the words. His thoughts trembled just as much as his hands and lips. He just watched as Yaminah continued her narrative while looking away from Bo Yusuf, not noticing his eyes starting to water.

"As the legend continues," the Princess proceeded, "hundreds of years later, there were nomadic black nations within Mesopotamia, descendants of the African warriors sent to Mesopotamia to assist the once black lands."

Bo Yusuf felt as if he was drowning. He wanted to speak, but there was nothing. The air he inhaled was like water, clogging his throat and bubbling in his lungs. He couldn't turn his breath into words, and he felt overwhelmed by emotion.

"The legend talks about a group of five warriors," Yaminah continued. Bo Yusuf's heart skipped. He finally flinched, but the Princess still did not noticed. She turned to look at him, a smile wide on her face. "I loved to hear my father tell the story. Munashe's wife is the best, however. She knows how to spin a tale. Ojodo would love her. I have to get the two to meet." The Princess was so lost in recollection she did not see Bo Yusuf choking with emotion, though she looked directly at him. "Sometimes the story focuses on five warriors. Sometimes its eight, seven, nine. Munashe, ever the concrete realist, says the Mesopotamian kingdom enslaved the entire nomadic nation. There was a revolution. They were not a group descended from the African warriors sent into the land; they were an indigenous black nation displaced, then made slaves in their own kingdom." She shook her head, demeanor now locked onto the happiness of the tale she heard growing up as a child. "I love when the story is told with five warriors. They recognize the kingdom was once theirs, the descendant of the original royal family among them. They stand alone, against a corrupt, barbaric, foreigner reigning as king." She returned her gaze to Bo Yusuf. She finally noticed his appearance. Yaminah reached for Bo Yusuf, she stroked his arm.

The Moorish General stood up and walked away. He took a deep breath. He shook off the quivering sensation running through his body as he exhaled. Yaminah stood up, gently calling her husband-to-be by name. Bo Yusuf responded, turning around slowly to face the Princess. The quivering returned. He breathed harder, trying to get his words out. He straightened himself and said, "I've heard the story of the warriors. *Nine* warriors. They took a kingdom that was once a black nation—their nation." He cleared his throat and looked around the room trying to remember. "Unfortunately, the kingdom did not stand long. A tawny Mesopotamian kingdom, six generations later, marched through and conquered the black kingdom. The nobles fled with the royal army, running back into Africa."

Yaminah was perplexed, but still held a smile on her face. "Did…did Kemnebi educate you, or my father…?"

Bo Yusuf shook his head, no. His lip trembled, his voice quavered. "I learned the story from Chief Mazigh. The Ogunsanwo-Mashek hold the same legend as their origins."

Yaminah was in disbelief. "They must have taken the story from a Djenhai prisoner," Yaminah hollered. "Long ago."

Bo Yusuf shook his head again. "When the nobles of the kingdom fled, running back into Africa, they first settled in Nubia. Correct? There were warriors that stayed behind to fight. These warriors became the Ogunsanwo-Mashek. The nobles promised to return, but there was never word. A group of over a hundred men and women made a long journey into Africa to find the nobles. They settled here and became the Ogunsanwo-Mashek. The nobles became the Djenhai people. I'm sure the Ogunsanwo-Mashek's decision to settle was determined by revenge. Someone among them recognized, somehow, that the Djenhai were descendants of the nobles they served long ago. The first strike, killing a Djenhai king and a prince, was motivated by revenge. A people that felt abandoned by their nobles motivated the first attack against Djenhai. It was generations later, but the emotions were still there. Then there was war, and the reason got lost with time." Yaminah put together the proposed chain of events. She returned to the bed and sat down. Bo Yusuf walked toward her. "Djenhai cannot carry out the enslavement of the Ogunsanwo-Mashek. If you help enslave them, you would be sending your own people into slavery."

Yaminah looked up, horrified. "They killed our King. They killed a Djenhai nobleman. They killed your former Beylerbey."

Bo Yusuf knelt down. He cupped Yaminah's hands tenderly. "Listen to me," he said in an assertive tone. "Al-Jeheuty and I have evidence that the Ogunsanwo-Mashek were not a part of the strikes made on al-Mari Ifriq." His grip on Yaminah's hands tightened. He whispered, "Statesman Ozan, and a host of conspirators—including European slavers—are behind the murders and attacks." Bo Yusuf could feel the Princess' hands trembling. She looked at him as if he, slowly and by way of a horrific and graphic transformation, changed into a different creature. "We have found some of his conspirators. They have been interrogated. They have confessed. We have been acting just as clandestinely. Al-Jeheuty's strikes have been in secret. We're trying to keep Ottoman and European ships from our shores."

Yaminah caught her breath. "Wh—what would've happen had you come across the Ogunsanwo-Mashek while on your campaign?"

Bo Yusuf bit his lip. A guilty expression came over him. He confessed, "I…I was leading the armies to dead sights. The Ogunsanwo-Mashek are in Tunisia, resting on its borders. Chief Mazigh moved his people there on al-Jeheuty's orders. We've been giving them supplies."

Yaminah was calmer than Bo Yusuf imagined. "There can be peace…?"

Bo Yusuf nodded. He smiled and said, "Yes, Yaminah. We need to find your brother and talk to him."

"We talk to al-Jeheuty first," the Princess demanded. "I want to be briefed on everything."

Bo Yusuf stood up and bowed cordially. "Yes, your Highness." He reached out his hand and lifted the Princess from off the bed. "Let's track down al-Mari Ifriq's Beylerbey." The General and the Princess walked from the room and traveled through the palace corridors to al-Jeheuty's quarters. Two guards and a personal servant were stationed outside. The three men bowed on sight of the Princess and the General. Bo Yusuf asked, "Is Beylerbey Anhur Has in his chambers?"

"Yes," answered the servant.

"Let us in, please," Yaminah commanded. "We need to speak with him."

The servant turned to knock on the door. Bo Yusuf moved him aside and knocked against the door hard. "Al-Jeheuty! This is Bo Yusuf, brother. We need to—"

The door opened. Al-Jeheuty was lightly dressed, his loose shirt and billowing pants wrinkled, indicating he had been resting. "Bo Yusuf," he said trying to clear his nap's blur from his eyes. He spotted Princess Yaminah. "Is there a problem?"

"Not a problem," Bo Yusuf replied. "A development in the war."

Al-Jeheuty opened the door wider, inviting the Princess and his brother-in-arms into his guest chamber. He closed the door and took a seat at the table. "Please, sit. I don't mean to be rude by commanding you in your kingdom, Princess."

"That is not a problem, Beylerbey" Yaminah assured as she rested on the bed.

Bo Yusuf continued to stand. Al-Jeheuty looked at him with a bewildered expression. The General took a seat next to his Beylerbey and friend. "Where do I begin?" He took a breath. "Princess Yaminah expressed to me a legend held by the Djenhai royal family. They are descendants of a kingdom in Mesopotamia, a kingdom that was once a black kingdom, taken by whites, and then taken back by the descendants of the original kingdom."

Al-Jeheuty stood up. He looked at Yaminah and said, "The Ogunsanwo-Mashek have the same story, Princess. They are innocent of the attacks—"

"She knows everything, my brother," Bo Yusuf informed. "I told her everything. As of now, between the three of us in this room, we are aware the Djenhai and the Ogunsanwo-Mashek are descended from the same blood."

Al-Jeheuty returned his gaze to Bo Yusuf. He said nothing to him. He walked over to the Princess and said in a trembling voice, "Al-Rinak has marked my wife and your husband for death. I am on that list too. I beg the Djenhai Kingdom to help the Griffins of al-Mari Ifriq put an end to this clandestine conflict, this secret war."

"The Princess of the Second World will assist you, Beylerbey Anhur Has," Yaminah assured the Beylerbey.

Al-Jeheuty returned to his seat. "I know emotions are running high in your kingdom, Princess Yaminah. Your brother's duties as king. Your entire royal family. Could we gain your brother's ear with this information? We would have to establish a secret rendezvous between Chief Mazigh and King Kemnebi. And when I say secret, I mean that not even God knows." He contemplated. "Bo Yusuf, you will be on your way to Tunisia with Ojodo and King Kemnebi. We'll stay in the kingdom longer than planned, long enough for you to complete this mission. Princess Yaminah, find your brother, tell him I'm ill. We need to separate him from your uncle and al-Rinak."

Yaminah's face contorted with concern. "Do you believe my uncle is a conspirator?"

"No," al-Jeheuty said firmly. "Absolutely not. We'll need your uncle to keep al-Rinak busy, or to continue royal duties while your brother checks on me. If we give a more dire excuse, the both of them will come. That could make al-Rinak suspicious. I don't believe he thinks we're on to him. No more than usual."

"Usual," Yaminah questioned.

"Taran is one of his conspirators," al-Jeheuty said in a quick breath. "Mehit's father has been assisting the Turks for a while, his loyalty to Nasir's father lost with time. He conspired with The Four Winds to assassinate Nasir's father. Behar, Bo Yusuf, Rahmis Husani, Ojodo Yerodin, and myself were brought in to take down The Four Winds."

Yaminah moved her eyes from Bo Yusuf to al-Jeheuty. "Then the rumors are true? You plotted a revolution? You killed the heads of The Four Winds?"

"Yes, Yaminah," Bo Yusuf confirmed.

"Feroz Aunun said otherwise," Yaminah said in a low voice. "We opted to believe him. The Second World of Djenhai did not want to be privy to information about a strike against Mohammedans."

Al-Jeheuty said, "Oh, they might have read the scriptures, but they did not follow them. The Four Winds did not come in peace. Believe me when I say, we made war with heretics, one of which was al-Rinak's brother. The Ozan faction had devious plans for al-Mari Ifriq and all of Odongo-Mauharim. You already know the corruption exposed when The Four Winds were eliminated." Al-Jeheuty took a moment to contemplate the actions of their revolution. He said to Yaminah, "I understand if you believe that our actions led to this moment in time. I understand if you believe our actions led to your father's assassination."

"You believed there were militants within the Ogunsanwo-Mashek," said Yaminah.

"Yes," answered al-Jeheuty. "We also believed that al-Rinak was using them too. But he's had no contact with the nation. Two Ogunsanwo-Mashek warriors had plans to kidnap your father and hold him for ransom. This action was to stop your kingdom from selling them into slavery. It was a desperate act. They were also planning a devastating attack on Djenhai, retaliation for a brutal attack made on them by Turkish troops. The attack served al-Rinak's interest. His troops pilfered Ogunsanwo-Mashek warriors of their clothes and weaponry. Conspirators used those outfits as a disguise. It was they who attacked us. We were given confirmation by several of al-Rinak's conspirators."

"What do you wait for," Yaminah hissed. "Al-Rinak continues to plot, and you have men that will give evidence against him."

"Those men are dead," explained al-Jeheuty apologetically. "Punished. Their voices would not have carried much weight. One was a Frenchman. His voice would have caused blatant war had he not been taken care of. We were given permission to eliminate him and another Frenchman. They're gone." He thought about the progress on Traont Coutelier's mark. "Two other conspirators were lowly crewmembers. Al-Rinak could have fought against such accusations. The right conspirators will be arrested. We're doing our best to keep foreign powers from off our shores."

"We're also trying to beat the marks hanging over our heads," Bo Yusuf voiced. "Marks that could be executed at any given moment."

Yaminah stared at Bo Yusuf. Her eyes were filled with sorrow as she replayed her father's death in her mind. Bo Yusuf's likeness was substituted for the former King's. Yaminah stood up. "I will find my brother. The two of you stay here. I know his first activity for the day, scheduled after our meeting. He was going to deal with kingdom finances." The Princess assured her return and then left the room.

Al-Jeheuty and Bo Yusuf looked at one another. Their miracle had surfaced. "It's far from over, my brother," said al-Jeheuty to Bo Yusuf. "But we got him. We got *him*. Al-Rinak."

Bo Yusuf nodded. "I've spent my life looking for that perfect fight. That perfect, violent storm that I could rush into and expend every ounce of anger within me. For the last month, I've done nothing but try and quell every conflict, avoid any war."

"It's a hell of a thing, maturing." Al-Jeheuty lifted an eyebrow. "But don't get too comfortable, my brother. You will have your fight. All two hundred Turkish soldiers will not surrender their arms without a tussle." He took a breath and then expressed, "I wish Nasir could be here."

Bo Yusuf leaned forward, readying himself to leave the chair. "Should I find him?" he asked.

"Yes. Perhaps you should," al-Jeheuty confirmed. "I'll stall if Yaminah returns with Kemnebi." Bo Yusuf stood up and made his way to the door. "Bo Yusuf," al-Jeheuty called. The Moorish General turned around. "Find a bottle of something fermented too. We should celebrate."

Bo Yusuf grinned at al-Jeheuty's command. "I am on my mission, Beylerbey," he said before walking from the room. Al-Jeheuty closed his eyes. He thought of his wife and his family. He thought of Behar, which produced thoughts of all the fallen soldiers in the conflict. He thought of Tegu, Awa, and Nasir's father, even though he never met him. He thought of the unnamed men and women, and he thought of the enemies he put down. He hoped his allies were at peace; and he wished his enemies the fires of hell.

Yaminah returned with King Kemnebi before Bo Yusuf returned with Nasir. The King looked perplexed when he did not find al-Jeheuty resting in bed. The Beylerbey also looked to be in good health and spirits. The King expressed, "Beylerbey Anhur Has. My sister tells me that you're ill."

Al-Jeheuty stood from his chair and paced closer to the King. "I apologize, King Kemnebi. You've received false information. I'm doing well, but I needed to speak with you privately. I did not want to arouse suspicions. Not even among your closest advisors. We wait for General al-Dume to return with Ambassador Sa'ood." It was only seconds after al-Jeheuty finished his statement when there was a knock on the door. "That must be our returning party." Yaminah answered the door. She permitted Bo Yusuf and Nasir entrance. Bo Yusuf held two bottles of Djenhai's traditional, fermented drink made from millet and exotic fruits. The drink was called *kua*, a type of beer. Nasir carried cups for everyone in the room. The bottles and cups were placed on the writing table.

King Kemnebi looked at each person in the room. His perplexed expression showed that he demanded answers. His eyes rested on al-Jeheuty. The Beylerbey cleared his throat and continued, "King Kemnebi, you are a great man and King. You have held your kingdom together through a very difficult time. And you're so young. But you have matured. War has a strange way of making us grow up very quickly."

Kemnebi nodded. "Yes. Truthfully, I was not yet ready to lead, but I've had no other choice but to be a King to my people. We are at war. Djenhai finds itself at a point where it can end a long struggle with a fiery group."

"Would you consider peace, King Kemnebi?" asked al-Jeheuty.

Kemnebi answered, "Absolutely."

"Even at the expense of your ego?" continued al-Jeheuty. "Could you face your people and tell them you were wrong about the factors involved in this war?"

Kemnebi hesitated, but finally said, "Yes. However, I believe we're beyond the point of peace talks. The Ogunsanwo-Mashek have done too much damage to Djenhai *and* al-Mari Ifriq."

Al-Jeheuty locked his hands behind his back. He circled Kemnebi once, and then returned to face the King. "What if I told you there was evidence proving the Ogunsanwo-Mashek innocent, and further evidence that this war has been manipulated by someone looking to execute marks on the reigning officials of al-Mari Ifriq? Myself, the governor, your sister's husband-to-be, and my ambassador here are all marked."

"I would demand to see this evidence," the King replied.

Al-Jeheuty turned away from the King. He returned to his seat and sat down. The King joined the Beylerbey at the table, taking the seat opposite al-Jeheuty. "Unfortunately, the co-conspirators to this plot had to be dealt with severely," al-Jeheuty confessed. "But there are others that we stand ready to arrest. Once detained, they will testify against Statesman al-Rinak Ozan in an Ottoman court. I guarantee that."

Kemnebi sat back in his chair. He rubbed his chin. "So, it is Statesman Ozan that has engineered this war. I don't find that at all improbable. Not one bit. Not with how much he is bent on pushing for war and slavery. I will be cautious in his presence."

"Entertain him," al-Jeheuty instructed. "Don't become standoffish. He'll suspect something. Keep Munashe ignorant too." Al-Jeheuty leaned forward and said in a low voice, "We have been boxing al-Rinak in. We've taken out some of his collaborators. He is, at the moment, unaware they are dead. After the first attack on al-Mari Ifriq, myself, Bo Yusuf, and Roberto Hamaat sought answers from the Ogunsanwo-Mashek's Chief."

"Yes, I'm aware," said the King.

"Chief Mazigh informed us that Turkish soldiers engaged them. Ogunsanwo-Mashek warriors were stripped of their clothes after being executed. The confiscated clothing could have been seen as war trophies. Even with this information, we were under the belief the more militant Ogunsanwo-Mashek had gone rogue. The clothing was used as authentic disguises, a sentiment Chief Mazigh suggested to us. Unfortunately, we discovered too late that he was correct. The second strike occurred. However, al-Rinak's collaborators were sloppy. They left behind clues. We unraveled these clues. It's been the statesman all along." Al-Jeheuty put his hands together. "Please, forgive us for not reporting our inquiries. We had to act silently. Our goal has been to unify Djenhai and al-Mari Ifriq, but greater than that, our goal has been to keep foreign powers from razing our shores. We have been cautious of al-Rinak for a long time. He is the brother of one of the former rulers from The Four Winds Company. One of the four heads whom my brothers-in-arms, Ambassador Sa'ood, and myself assassinated. The stories of revolution are true, which I'm sure you already believed." Al-Jeheuty rolled his eyes.

King Kemnebi said nothing. He took in all that al-Jeheuty expressed, pondering on the information.

"There are more details," said al-Jeheuty. "That was just a summary, a backstory to the actual reason I've called for you, King Kemnebi." The Beylerbey turned to Bo Yusuf. "My Army Official, and General in your army, has come across an amazing discovery. Bo Yusuf."

The General came to al-Jeheuty's side. He took a breath. "Your sister—my wife-to-be—revealed to me that Djenhai is truly made up of three worlds, not two. The third world is more ancient, and it is secret. She recounted the third world's legend. The tale of five warriors taking a kingdom in Mesopotamia." Kemnebi smiled wide, the legend stirring childhood memories. "This was not the first time I heard the story."

"Oh," said Kemnebi, intrigued by Bo Yusuf's knowledge.

"The story I came across was a variant," the General specified. "Same words. Nine warriors instead of five."

"Yes, the number of warriors often varies," the King acknowledged.

Bo Yusuf nodded. "Yes. Nine warriors," he reiterated. "That's how Chief Mazigh, and the Ogunsanwo-Mashek nation, recounts the tale. It is the story of their origin. They are descendants of the warriors left behind when the kingdom fell again. The Djenhai are the descendants of the nobles that left the warriors behind to flee into Africa." Kemnebi's expression returned to the contorted perplexed look. His mouth hung agape, his lower jaw trembling. "Their first attack on the Djenhai was motivated by anger, hurt. That's what I believe. They knew the Djenhai were the nobles that— so they felt—abandoned them. I'm sure only their leaders knew. They died with that knowledge. As the older generation can sometimes do, they did not pass the knowledge to the next generation. Confusion and war remained."

King Kemnebi could not stay seated. He jumped from his seat, his expression never changing. He walked toward the door first. He stopped. He said over his shoulder, "Pour me a drink."

Al-Jeheuty fulfilled the King's command. He stood up, walked to the King, and presented the cup. Kemnebi turned around and took the cup. He knocked back a hard gulp. Yaminah looked at her brother. Her eyes watered. A warm smile was on her face. Kemnebi approached her. His perplexed expression dissolved. He beamed, putting his arms around his sister. "We will change things in our time."

"We will, my brother," she answered in a soft voice, reflecting his smile with her own.

Kemnebi stepped away from his sister. He faced the Moorish officials. Al-Jeheuty said to him, "Don't be too happy, my King. They are not entirely innocent. They have attacked trade caravans. They have been land pirates for the past three hundred years."

"I recognize them as my brothers and sisters from this moment on," Kemnebi declared. "And what would brothers and sisters be without sibling rivalries?"

Al-Jeheuty looked back to Bo Yusuf and over at Nasir. "Bloody and drawn out as this sibling rivalry has been," he said.

Kemnebi took another drink. "Beylerbey. You tell me a devil has seduced my kingdom, killed my father, and that an old world can be re-united. It's far less complicated than making war for the benefit of white slavers, even if we profit from it too. The truth is easier to embrace, even if there is more responsibility to uphold. Make war, and expect retaliation. Make peace. How do you retaliate against peace? With love, I believe." He put a hand on al-Jeheuty's shoulder. "I will meet with their chief. No. I will meet with their *King*. I will meet King Mazigh."

Al-Jeheuty sighed relief. He explained, "Their accent is strong, but you will understand their language. They do know a lot of African languages. They might know the Djenhai tongue."

"We will speak in the language common to us all, Beylerbey," Kemnebi insisted. "We will all communicate in these proceedings. Please, everyone, take a drink." The Moorish officials and Princess Yaminah followed the King's orders. "Do you have a plan, Beylerbey?"

"I do," al-Jeheuty answered before taking a sip.

Kemnebi sighed again. "I hated these people all my life. I wanted them wiped clean from the earth when I believed they killed my father, a Djenhai noble, and your Beylerbey. But I have prayed for peace. Somehow. Someway. I tried to make myself strong for war, but I have been overwhelmed. I said I would sacrifice my hate for peace. So shall it be. I place my hate on an altar, and I offer it to the gods. I wish this information was learned earlier."

"With no offense, King Kemnebi," spoke Nasir. "The information presented itself at the precise time. All hail the start of a new day."

King Kemnebi raised his cup to Nasir. "You are right, Ambassador."

Everyone took a seat at the table. Their attention turned to al-Jeheuty. The Beylerbey described his plan for bringing the two Kings together. Kemnebi agreed. Ojodo was called upon and introduced to the new turn of events. By the next morning, King Kemnebi, Ojodo, and Bo Yusuf secretly slipped from the city.

Chapter Forty-Eight

Al-Mari Ifriq's heaviest gamblers held their breath in anticipation for the grand tournament of games. Chess players, card players, and dominoes players chatted regularly about prize, purse, strategy, and game. *The Siren's Call* was closed in preparation for the games, and Rahmis Husani teased the awaiting participants daily. The fervor was calmed slightly by the games held within *The al-Hammon Palace*. But Rahmis knew how to stir up interest, and keep it billowing. Other tavern's games did not carry the weight of prize or bragging rights that Rahmis whisked into his tantalizing words that defined the might of the tournament that would be held at *The Siren's Call*.

Rahmis' words did not come as a challenge to other tavern owners. They welcomed the inflated sense of accomplishment Rahmis promised. The pot, for each game, was a king's ransom, plus seven precious gems. The small treasure was stored away in the palace, only to be brought to light when the winner of each game was determined. The other tavern owners saw revenue by holding small games, which every gambler jumped into for the sake of sharpening his or her skills. There was profit for everyone. The local owners were only nervous about the more disorderly patrons that the games attracted. Roberto Hamaat's police were on guard at all games, calming the owners' worries. Any sign of disorderly conduct was handled immediately and escorted to the cells.

Most gamblers practiced their games at *The al-Hammon Palace*, believing it a good sign to win inside an establishment partially run by Rahmis Husani. But only skill and luck determined the winners, and the participants eased their gambling routine days before the tournament began. No one wanted to exhaust their skill by using it up in practice games, and the chess players simmered down their gaming earlier than the dominoes and card players. This left *The al-Hammon Palace* in a quiet state several days before the tournament.

It was earlier than usual, but still late enough, when Maurice started to shuffle the patrons from his dive. None of the *Palace's* guests needed extra encouragement to leave. It was two o'clock in the morning. The gambling patrons lost track of time, and needed little motivation other than fatigue to pull them from their chairs to inns scattered around the city. The dancing girls also retired elsewhere, all but one. The Moorish girl named Tendai, the beautiful, slender entertainer that often spent her nights with Maurice, stayed behind to clean. Melusina assisted her.

Fusan continued to drink at a table, taking quick gulps from his cup. He watched his brother interact with Tendai as she cleaned. Fusan stood up and approached the both of them. "I have urgent business to attend to in Tunis," he barked at Maurice. "My crew is prepared. We are taking leave on a ship bound for Turkey, dropping me off in Tunis."

"Fusan," Melusina hissed. The Moorish corsair's tongue was too loose in front of Maurice's mistress.

Fusan retorted over his shoulder, "My point is, Melusina, my brother was supposed to deliver my cargo to the ship. I would like to know if it's been done? I would like to leave immediately at sunrise."

"Then you won't get any sleep tonight," Maurice said not looking at his brother, "because that was not my duty."

Fusan beamed a drunken smile. "Correct. That would require manual labor." He gripped Maurice's left bicep. "These small things couldn't handle a crate filled with clothes, could they?" Maurice shifted his arm out of Fusan's grip. "I did ask you to set the crate aboard the ship. Is your lack of duty another chapter in your tale of revenge? Are you getting back at me for missing my mark?" Fusan was feeling his alcohol. He pretended to cool down. "I asked you, so I take the blame. I should've consulted a man for the job, maybe someone stronger like your mistress." Fusan chuckled. Maurice finally looked at him, anger on his face. Fusan said to him, "Tell the bitch to leave so that we can conduct our business."

Maurice cooled. He turned to Tendai and ordered, "Escort Melusina to her residence." He removed his pistol and handed it to the young woman. "Take this. Be careful." Tendai accepted the weapon and joined with Melusina before exiting the tavern.

Maurice made his way to the large storage area in the back. Fusan followed him and teased, "I can't wait for the day to see you smile, brother. That should be in four day's time. The story of your revenge complete. Tell me, why does Nasir hold your love so much? Zakiy shares his father, should I dispense of him too? Will you kiss Nasir's lips at his funeral? Tell your lover goodbye? You've hated him so long I think you love him."

Maurice did not answer. He opened a hatch in the floor, revealing a six-foot deep hidden storage space. Maurice jumped inside. Fusan watched his brother toss up the Ogunsanwo-Mashek apparel, which he and his crew continued to use as disguises. Pieces of armor were also stashed with the outfits. Maurice carefully placed the pieces of armor outside of the compartment. He jumped out of the compartment and started separating the outfits.

Fusan expressed another taunt. "Do you wish for me to deliver a message to your love?" The taunt was enough. Maurice jumped to his feet and charged his brother. He stopped, standing still, inches away from his brother's massive frame. He balled his fists. "Tighten your fists and clench your teeth," sneered Fusan. "That's all the fight you have in you. If you were a real man, you would've gone on these runs with me, executed your own mark. You can be angry toward me all you want, but you need me to make you complete. You need me to finish your story, because you're not man enough to finish it yourself. I'm surprised you take women to bed."

"Would you rather me take anything that stands on two legs, boy or girl, like you and Captain Piett?"

"I'm still a man," Fusan snarled. "At sea, there are no rules. It's there that I can force anyone to have fun with me." He chuckled. "Tendai fucks you for free, but that bitch is any man's friend if you toss a fair amount of coin in her direction. Just ask me. Her and I are good friends, on occasion." Fusan stroked his brother's chin. "But you're special. She refuses your coin. It must be love." He bent down to look at his brother directly in the eyes. "Are you going to marry her? Just remember, she's nice with you, but she's a whore for me." Maurice trembled with anger. Fusan stood up straight. He looked at his brother's quivering fists and said, "Be careful. If you swing and hit me, you might damage the person you need to help you." He backed away. "Get the rest of the clothes, rugrat."

Maurice stepped away. He turned around and dragged a crate from the corner. Fatigue was starting to set in after the long day and night. He moved the crate to the clothes, opened the top, and started to throw the disguises inside. Maurice put the outfits in first, and then set the pieces of armor atop them.

Fusan yelled from the front room, "Our mother would tremble too, remember? She would wake up at night screaming for our father, shaking with an insane rage. I applaud our mother." Maurice listened, his anger quelled when he heard Fusan express the endearing sentiment. "She sacrificed her life to give me strength at sea. Our father possesses me too." Maurice continued to stuff the crate again, considering his brother's notions silly. "It begs me to ask why you would want to avenge parents that have chosen to abandon you even in their afterlife. It appears they still favor the stronger son."

Maurice closed the crate. He returned to the front of the tavern. "Your supplies are ready," he told Fusan. The burly Moor poured himself another drink, throwing back the contents of his cup.

Fusan stumbled toward the door. He said as he departed the tavern, "I will return with two of my soldiers. We'll carry that crate to the docks."

Maurice exhaled an angry sigh as Fusan made his exit. He stared at the bottle from which his brother took his drink. He thought about Nasir dying, shot to death, the event several days away. By now Nasir should have already been dead, according to Maurice. Nasir should have died in the first attack staged on al-Mari Ifriq. Maurice asked himself if Nasir's death would quell his anger, and he surprisingly answered himself with a 'no'. He asked if Zakiy would have to die too, and then ultimately Afya, Nasir and Zakiy's mother. He could not answer.

Maurice thought of a third option as he grabbed his brother's bottle. He placed the bottle of liquor and two cups onto a table. He went to the backroom and pulled from the cupboard a thick vial containing a powdered substance. He decided to put a little extra spice in his brother's drink. He returned to the front, poured himself a cup, and then emptied the vial's entire contents into the bottle of liquor.

Tendai returned.

Maurice quickly made his way to her. He placed his hands on her shoulders and ordered, "Return to your apartment for the night. My brother and I still have business."

Tendai contorted her face. "I am not returning to the outside. I'm tired. Conduct your business while I sleep in the backroom." She walked past him, putting his pistol on a table.

Maurice turned around, his chest pounding with anger. He reached out and grabbed Tendai's arm, pulling her back. "Our business does not concern you. Leave. You are employed in my services, you prostitute. That is an order."

Tendai moved her arm from Maurice's grip. She laughed at Maurice's display of anger. "Is this your attempt at being a man, giving me orders commanded by your brother? Did he order me gone? Show yourself a man to Fusan and defy *him*."

Maurice's angry actions were quicker than his thoughts. He reached out for Tendai, palming the side of her head and slamming it with great force against a table. The young woman stammered with the brutally hard impact. The strike rattled her senses. The right side of her brow was bleeding, the skin ruptured, her skull cracked. Tendai's feet stepped back a pace, some function and life still left in her body. She dropped to the tavern floor.

Maurice looked at Tendai angrily. He watched as the Moorish prostitute's body convulsed, small tremors quaking through her. Tendai's eyes looked around the room, aimless, confused. Maurice bent down. He grabbed the scantily clad woman by the collar and raised her up. He struck her with his fist, a heavy blow. He then let her go. Tendai's eyes closed. Blood started to clog her throat. Maurice lifted her body into his arms and took Tendai to the backroom. He laid her body on the bed, and covered her with the sheets and blankets. He extinguished the light in the room and returned to the front just as Fusan entered the tavern. He was stumbling, and he was alone.

"I'll make rest here for the night," he grumbled trying to shake the effects of the drink from his head. "Can't do anything now. I'm as effective drunk as you are sober." His eyes were able to gain focus on the table decorated with the bottle of liquor and cups. Maurice made quick steps toward the table and snatched the already filled cup. Fusan poured himself a cup of the bottle's contents. He took a seat. Maurice joined him. "Where's your slut," Fusan asked. He dug into his pocket and removed eight coins. "Give her these. Tell her I'm going to drill her before my ship leaves port." He kept the cup at his mouth, laughing.

"What should we drink to?" Maurice asked.

"I drink to our parents," Fusan answered. He raised his glass and yelled his words to keep them from slurring. "They blessed me with strength and courage. I am thankful they did not curse me with sorrow and anger. They left that with you. What do you drink to?"

Maurice thought. "To the peace in death that you cannot find in life," he told Fusan.

"You are wrong again, brother." Fusan took a heavy gulp. He swallowed half the contents of his large cup. "Life's been good to me. You've watched, haven't you? That's what the cowardly do, isn't it? Watch. You've observed. I've gone forth and conquered. Taran and al-Rinak have entrusted me with the duties of securing al-Mari Ifriq. I am a General. You've been a messenger, an errand boy. You've been misguided in the larger picture. You've only had one goal. You're selfish." He leaned over the table and said to his brother, "Do you believe our father will be proud of you once you've dispatched the *son* of his killer, his murderer already dead. Do you really believe? You've lost sight of the greater picture. You've lost sight of what Taran said that our father wanted most. A secured city."

Maurice battled with his cool and his anger.

"That's why al-Rinak and he do not trust you," Fusan continued. "They trust me. I am a man of action." He finished drinking the liquor in his cup. He poured another. He drank more. "Do you really think you'll have any political power once this is all over? Al-Rinak is not stupid. He says what he knows will get you to work. You can barely run this tavern. Its sophistication comes from Rahmis' hand."

Maurice ignored his brother's taunts and laughter. He said while looking at his cup, "I have been thinking about Nasir's death. I've been thinking about its importance. You're right. It won't stop me from being angry." He attempted to goad Fusan. "I hope you miss your target again. I hope Nasir survives." Maurice thought about his words. He corrected, "He *will* survive. And I will look him in the eyes and curse him when he returns. *I'll* kill him. I'll kill him after I tell him how imperfect his father was. I'll reveal to him how little he knew of his father, that bastard. He will know what his father truly did to us. He will know his father made us orphans."

Fusan finished his second cup. He turned to his brother, his body starting to ache. He put the cup down, an ordeal that caused an unexpected pain. He considered that he drank too much. He guessed that he was about to pass out. Before he dropped unconscious, he went to speak to his brother, to question Maurice about his words. But when Fusan opened his mouth to speak, his words were silenced, choked. He could feel his throat closing. He coughed to clear a passage for air. He had trouble pushing words from his mouth, and now he found himself having trouble breathing. His throat felt clogged, caved in on itself. The beat of his heart quickened to an erratic pace. He felt lightheaded.

Maurice stood up from his chair and walked over to his brother. He bent down and whispered into his ear, "I hate you. I would rather see you die than have you report to me Nasir's death. I will not be in your debt for such a task. I will kill Nasir. I'll deal with al-Rinak's anger. These officials can die at any time. You are, and always have been, expendable, Fusan."

Fusan tried to stand, but moving his limbs burned. His body toppled over, crashing against the tavern floor. Maurice stared at his brother, Fusan reaching out to him. The burly Moor's tongue curled and penetrated out of his mouth. Maurice watched his brother attempt to fight against his eyes rolling back into his head. Fusan continued to wheeze, his coughing ceased. Foam, mixed with blood, gurgled from his throat. Fusan finally let the fight go. His eyes rolled into the back of his head. His body, curled and contorted like a dying spider, straightened and then eased.

Maurice walked around his brother's body. He scooped Fusan's corpse underneath the armpits, and lifted his torso to drag him to the storage room. He dropped the body into the compartment beneath the floor. He closed the compartment, returned to the front room, and extinguished the lights in the tavern. He took rest in an empty backroom, slipping into a bed and going to sleep.

Chapter Forty-Nine

The Giant, the General, and the King penetrated the Tunisian border. They traveled under a blazing sun that switched positions from its early placement at the start of their journey. The sun was now higher and in a more unforgiving position in the sky. The three men's outfits shaded them, light, billowing robes, wraps, and headgear. Bo Yusuf and Ojodo, strapped with an assortment of weapons, flanked King Kemnebi. The Djenhai King made himself apparent. He was unmistakably the high, royal noble of the Djenhai kingdom. He was capped with a woolen crown that was adorned with gold pendants encrusted with jewels. He was clothed in the royal, pastel colors of the Djenhai kingdom. He was distinctive, and holding the attention of the watching eye peering through a spyglass from the mountain range in the distance. Al-Mari Ifriq officials provided the spyglasses to the Ogunsanwo-Mashek warriors to keep an eye on incoming bodies.

The glass from the scope sparkled as it reflected the sun, which Bo Yusuf decided was now good for something other than providing a misery of heat. The General lifted his hand and contorted his fingers into odd configurations, signaling the spying warriors that lay in the distance.

King Kemnebi noticed Bo Yusuf's actions. He asked, "Are we being watched?"

"Yes, King Kemnebi." He pointed with his head toward the mountains. "Look at the reflecting light glimmering from the mountains." He scoffed, "Roberto and I continue to tell them to stay in shadow when using the spyglasses." An arrow cut through the air, shot from the distance at the arriving party. It landed in front of Bo Yusuf's mount. The camel bucked as Bo Yusuf pulled the reins. Ojodo and the King ceased their mounts' forward movements. The three riders stood still.

Warriors rose from out of the sands, forming a circular perimeter around the three mounted men. The fourteen Ogunsanwo-Mashek men stood armed with bows and arrows. Their weapons were drawn back, at the ready. King Kemnebi stayed still, his face motionless, the opposite of his heartbeat. Ojodo remained calm. Bo Yusuf spied five, approaching mounted warriors. The middle rider was Balde-Sih. The Ogunsanwo-Mashek captain held a smile on his face as he neared Bo Yusuf, penetrating the circle of bowmen. He rode up next to the Moorish General and reached out a friendly hand. "Bo Yusuf. It is good to see you."

The General accepted Balde's hand and shook. "Likewise."

Balde examined the intense emotion coursing through Bo Yusuf's face. "Is something the matter?" His eyes went to King Kemnebi. He recognized the Djenhai royal colors, crown, and insignia. "Identify this man," Balde demanded.

"I need to speak with Chief Mazigh," answered Bow Yusuf. "It's urgent."

Balde pointed with a stern finger and again demanded, "Identify this man!"

"I am King Kemnebi Igdobe Djenhai!" the King announced in a royal, authoritative voice. Most of the soldiers understood the language used by the King. They leaned in closer with their weapons, their hands trembling. "I come as an ally. I come as family. I come to unite a lost tribe with a kingdom just as equally lost and separated from its entire history." Balde looked perplexed, his eyes squinted. The King explained, "The Ogunsanwo-Mashek and the Djenhai nation have been offset. We come from a common origin in Mesopotamia."

Bo Yusuf raised his hand to silence the King. He turned and addressed Kemnebi, "Not to be rude, my King." He then said to Balde, "I must speak with Chief Mazigh. There has been maturation in the relationship between the Djenhai and the Ogunsanwo-Mashek. Would you like to be the generation that keeps a war going, or the generation that closes shut the doors of war forever."

Balde yelled a command to the surrounding warriors in their native Ogunsanwo-Mashek language. He said through clenched teeth to Bo Yusuf, "It is always so damned interesting when you Moors show up."

Bo Yusuf retorted with an equally serious tone, "It's always so damned interesting how you greet us."

Balde rolled his eyes and took lead. "Come. To Chief Mazigh." Bo Yusuf, Ojodo, and King Kemnebi followed behind Balde and his mounted troupe. The fourteen warriors marched behind them, weapons lowered. Balde slowed his mount's trot, taking a position next to King Kemnebi. The warrior asked the King in a cordial voice, "You believe our people have a common origin?"

"We have a story depicting black warriors taking a Mesopotamian kingdom," Kemnebi answered. "It is similar to yours. The Djenhai govern three worlds, one a secret. We come from a black kingdom twice fallen.

That kingdom was located in Mesopotamia. We are descendants of its nobles. You claim descendants of its warriors."

Balde bit his lip. He said in a slightly agitated tone, "Warriors left behind by nobles promising a return. That is how our history recalls the tale. That is our side of the story. We were abandoned. Left for dead."

Kemnebi shook his head. "Yes. Possibly. We don't know for sure. However, what is certain is that you warriors would exact your revenge generations later, following us into Africa, tracking us down, and executing a Djenhai King and his son. The assassination almost disrupted our traditions. The King's second son took the helm and the offensive. We have engaged in killing one another ever since."

"We did not kill your former King—your father," Balde barked.

"I am aware of that," said Kemnebi.

Balde yielded. His angry emotion dissolved with a sigh. "The scars made over hundreds of years cannot be healed overnight, King of Djenhai." He looked at the King and said, "But we have to start somewhere."

Kemnebi replied, "I hope your sentiments are echoed in your King."

Balde flinched. He had never heard any of the chiefs referred to as 'king', especially from an enemy. The Djenhai soldiers the Ogunsanwo-Mashek encountered over the many years, in Balde's lifetime and before, chose more colorful terminology. The Captain pondered this as he steered them into the Ogunsanwo-Mashek camp. It was bustling with activity, and staged no different than the sites Bo Yusuf had been through. This site just happened to be close to a mountain range. Though nature supplied little fertile land, al-Mari Ifriq's officials had been shipping the Ogunsanwo-Mashek supplies to compensate them, and the mountains provided a great deal of shade.

The activity filtering throughout the camp paused briefly to view the arriving warriors. Many among the passersby recognized Bo Yusuf. Most marveled at the mounted towering mass that was Ojodo Yerodin. Everyone recognized the Djenhai colors draping King Kemnebi. The Ogunsanwo-Mashek citizens were curious, but continued about their daily routines. Balde dismounted as two servants came to his aid. He looked up at the others and said, "Wait here." He disappeared into the camp. The servants led his mount away. Balde's mounted warriors stayed. The fourteen bowmen moved further into the camp, making their way to the mountain range beyond.

Kemnebi observed his surroundings. It was much like he had imagined, a community living among nature. He was sure the Ogunsanwo-

Mashek had their politics, for better or worse. But for the most part, King Kemnebi observed much of what he had imagined. The community was not a ghetto, but it was not rich either. It was surviving.

The three foreigners could not tell how much time had lapsed. Balde had been gone for a long period, no doubt explaining the King's arrival and its purpose. Bo Yusuf and King Kemnebi took a deep breath when Chief Mazigh finally emerged. Gu-Gurzil and Chwezi flanked him. He was keeping the two men close as of late, using them as guards in order to keep an eye on their activities. Neither man strayed from their orders, loyal to Mazigh's commanding word. Chieftess Nugaymath was also by Mazigh's side.

The chief and the King observed one another. Mazigh held a sly smile. He was dressed in his usual sash and signature black, billowing pants and sandals. To Kemnebi, Chief Mazigh looked organic, like a piece of nature. His demeanor was far from kingly. Chief Mazigh carried himself like a bandit-king; he was a corsair of the land, troops at his command to plunder. He looked young, but Kemnebi could see that Mazigh was matured by circumstance, no different than he.

Mazigh observed the King's demeanor. Kemnebi was stiff with tension, but the Chief admired the King's audacity to march into his site alone. Mazigh stepped closer to the King's mount and said, "I make history with every step, King of Djenhai. Dismount. Let us put hand in hand."

Ojodo stepped down from his mount, the animal looking relieved from the giant's weight. Ojodo made his way to Kemnebi and aided the King from off his camel. By now the Ogunsanwo-Mashek tribe was gathering around, making a slow approach toward the moment at hand. People believed Kemnebi was a Djenhai Ambassador, not the King. Slowly, word started to pass through the mouths of the people that the King of Djenhai was in their presence.

Mazigh and Kemnebi approached one another. Both men extended their hands and gave a cordial shake. Kemnebi wanted to bow and show honor, but he believed that might have been too much, and might have opened the door for the Chief to give a snide remark. He also did not want it reported back to the Djenhai people that he bowed first. He stayed upright.

"Sharing a common bedtime story will not make us the same people overnight," Mazigh voiced. "The Christians and Mohammedans both believe in Moses and Christ. Look at them. The Judaic too. We've had evangelists from your kingdom come through, and more from converted tribes."

"We observe Mohammedan Law for political purposes," Kemnebi explained.

"So I've been told. Come. Follow me." Mazigh then called, "Bo Yusuf. Follow." The Moorish General dismounted. He kept his eyes on Gu-Gurzil and Chwezi. The two warriors looked more relaxed than expected. Bo Yusuf joined the party, Ojodo followed. Their mounts were taken from them. No more was said between the King and the Chief until they walked into a crafted house made from cloth and supported by cords and poles. Ojodo stayed outside, posting up with the guards. He was too tall for the makeshift quarters. Inside were cushions and seating areas for the rest of the party. Mazigh sat in his chair. Chieftess Nugaymath sat next to him on her long seat. Gu-Gurzil and Chwezi flanked their Chief and Chieftess.

Bo Yusuf and King Kemnebi took a seat on the cushions in front of the thrones. Mazigh nodded toward King Kemnebi and said in a sincere voice, "I offer my sympathies to you for the murder of your father. He was ready to enslave our people. There was much hate in our hearts for him and his decisions. Make no mistake. My soldiers that flank me," he looked to Gu-Gurzil and Chwezi, "they had plans to capture your father and force a treaty. We trembled with fear when we heard he was killed, along with a noble businessman, and al-Mari Ifriq's Beylerbey. We already suspected a devil used our skin to commit atrocious acts against al-Mari Ifriq. The devil struck again." Mazigh paused, and then he said with honest anger, "I hated your father." He then relaxed his voice as he continued, "But now, I am hurt that I did not get to know him. I was told your father was a good-humored man. We've never seen that side of Djenhai. Disappointing. Further, I am sad that my father and he did not know one another, or were not, in life, privy to the knowledge about the common origins between the Ogunsanwo-Mashek and the Djenhai kingdom."

Kemnebi nodded his head. "I too am sorry. I'm sorry for every soldier, civilian, and noble that had to learn the lesson through death." The King put his hands together and said, "Knowledge be obtained." He paused for effect. "The devil that has escalated our petty prejudices resides in my kingdom at this very moment."

"Kill him," said Mazigh in a nonchalant voice.

"That can't be done, Chief Mazigh," spoke Bo Yusuf. "You know that. His voice carries weight. We would be endangering al-Mari Ifriq and the Djenhai kingdom. Your people would still face enslavement. But I have devised a plan to take out the Turk's army. Beylerbey Anhur Has, as you know, executed successful strikes on co-conspirators. The remaining conspirators will be arrested, pending evidence."

"Evidence," Mazigh scoffed.

Bo Yusuf understood the Chief's annoyance. He explained, "These are politics that we must engage in order to keep all three nations safe. If there were not the threat of the Empire looming over us, we would've beheaded al-Rinak and all his conspirators upon discovery of the plot."

Mazigh relaxed. "I concede, General. But, you did mention a plan calling for *some* action."

"Yes," Bo Yusuf replied. "Call your warriors together. We are going to cripple al-Rinak's army. I have discussed the plot with Beylerbey Anhur Has. He will seek the approval of our governor when we return to al-Mari Ifriq. We will send a representative from Roberto Hamaat's clan to inform you of our progress. Watch for our messenger." He turned to Kemnebi. "I will lead the Djenhai troops. We will ensnare al-Rinak's army."

Chief Mazigh lifted a hand, ceasing Bo Yusuf from speaking further. He looked at Gu-Gurzil and Chwezi. "Assemble all our captains." They bowed and set about their task, exiting their Chief's house. Mazigh said to Bo Yusuf, "Continue."

The General spoke his final thoughts. "All I have left to say, before your captains enter the room, is this will be the battle that unites Odongo-Mauharim."

Gu-Gurzil and Chwezi returned, five captains with them, including Balde-Sih. They gathered around Bo Yusuf and King Kemnebi. Mazigh addressed his captains. "Has word spread? Our guest is King Kemnebi of Djenhai. We are allies and more. Three hundred years of strife comes to an end, and an understanding." Mazigh then asked smiling, "So, of course, what does this mean General al-Dume?"

The General's tension relaxed. He returned a smile and answered the Chief, "It means you have a reason to hold a festivity tonight."

Mazigh shook his head. "Most definitely. After which, we will prepare for war. For now, we plan the war. General al-Dume, present your strategy."

Bo Yusuf asked for the captains to come closer. He outlined a plan of attack, Mazigh and Gu-Gurzil offering suggestions to tighten the General's strategy. Bo Yusuf incorporated their changes, and the Chief and his captains helped solidify an effective strike on al-Rinak's troops. The plan was shaped over the period of an hour. The General, the King, and the Chief approved the plan, and the meeting was adjourned. King Kemnebi and Chief Mazigh enjoyed one another's company, the Chief guiding

Kemnebi through the Ogunsanwo-Mashek site and introducing him to various people, including citizens, priests, and law keepers.

The day faded into the night's activities. Chief Mazigh summoned his people and briefed them about King Kemnebi's visit. The Ogunsanwo-Mashek people absorbed the wonderful tale, and their Chief spoke at length on the new war and enemy encroaching on all of Odongo-Mauharim. "It is not the tawny Turk. It is not the politics between African nations, fixed or nomadic. It is not a religious war. All the blacks throughout Odongo-Mauharim and Africa stare down the winds of a paradigm shift that will leave our continent buried in rubble. A devious plan for slavery has been crafted. A form of slavery so profitable, no one looking for coin will refuse to participate. We have come across brothers and sisters as willing participants, the gain of coin on their minds shaping their breath to speak devious words. We did not follow them. We did not fall for their words. Some of the Ogunsanwo-Mashek did," he admitted. "These people did not heed warning from my grandfather's words, my father's words, or my words.

"The Djenhai, we can forgive. They are not willing participants. Our war with them, its motive lost with time, is a siblings' quarrel. A devious man, posed as a peacekeeper, wishes to walk into our quarrel, escalate it, and profit from its mediation. He is a devil-minded black. He has tricked the Djenhai. He has tricked us all. He ushers in this white form of slavery like Suma ushered in white barbarians from the mountains, making war with the civilized nations of the world. Let us not hate him either. He is a black. This man, as I have been informed, was reared by the devious education of white politics. It corrupts the words of the gods, goddesses, and all forms of spiritual alchemy, as it is envious of black, magical operations. It twists law and order. It has twisted this brother just the same. We fight a miseducated black. Misguided. Will the gods have mercy on him? If so, let it be. If not, let it be. Who knows? This just might be for the sake of our transformation. A terrible lesson taught to us by Nature, cruel as She can often be. This is our alchemy, our transformation."

The ceremony concluded with dance and with the Chief and King poking fun at one another. Chief Mazigh began the story of the black Mesopotamian kingdom, while King Kemnebi interrupted and corrected the story with the Djenhai's interpretation. It drew laughter as one would say, *"No, you tell it wrong! It was five warriors, not nine!"* This happened throughout the remainder of the tale. The joke continued as King Kemnebi announced, "This is a brand new day for the Djenhai-Ogunsanwo-Mashek nation."

Mazigh jokingly corrected, "You're in my kingdom now. We shall call it the Ogunsanwo-Mashek-*Djenhai* nation."

The crowd roared playfully.

"I believe this is the Griffin Regency," Bo Yusuf joined in as the crowd simmered down in their excitement. His comments ignited laughter and playful jeers and taunts.

Ojodo shook his head. His voice boomed. "We're in Tunisia, may I remind you all."

"Then let us retreat back to Odongo-Mauharim," Chwezi suggested. "Before we have another war on our hands. I'm getting confused about at whom to be angry. Who should I hate again, my Chief?"

"Everyone, just in case," quipped Chief Mazigh. "However, to make this ordeal easier, I believe research is in order, King Kemnebi, to find our original name." Kemnebi agreed. Chief Mazigh relayed his words in the Ogunsanwo-Mashek tongue, and the crowd rejoiced.

Through the air of festivities, Chief Mazigh looked around at his people. There were still great politics to consider. He asked himself various questions on his nation's future, and that was only if they survived the war. King Kemnebi had already promised to bring the Ogunsanwo-Mashek people into Djenhai while the nation's warriors stayed behind to fight.

Bo Yusuf, King Kemnebi, and Ojodo returned to the Djenhai kingdom an hour before sunrise. Al-Jeheuty and Princess Yaminah were briefed on their journey into Tunisia once the trio entered the palace. Kemnebi described to his sister that Chief Mazigh was very inviting. Though the news of peace was comforting, there were many uncertainties that faced the nation. Conversation was not long. The returning party retired to their rooms and went to sleep.

No one questioned the King's whereabouts the next morning. It was announced that al-Jeheuty was 'recovered.' The Beylerbey decided it was time to return home. Their caravan was prepared an hour after sunrise. Ojodo and Adaeze elected to stay in Djenhai. The Moorish titan promised to visit al-Mari Ifriq before he and Adaeze made their way east.

King Kemnebi made a surprising move. The King informed Bo Yusuf that he was keeping the Djenhai unit that was under the General's command. "They will stay here, General, until further notice." Bo Yusuf agreed. Al-Mari Ifriq's officials were escorted to the gates of the city. Their entourage put together, waiting for them outside the city walls. The Beylerbey and Ambassador Sa'ood took their place within mounted carriages. Bo Yusuf joined his friends after bidding Yaminah farewell. Commander Koray, his troops assembled, surrounded the caravan.

Kemnebi parted with al-Rinak last. The King shook the statesman's hand, leaned close to him, and whispered, "You will have your slaves by the week's end. I am making a bold move against the Ogunsanwo-Mashek. I will separate the people from their warriors. Wait for my message."

Al-Rinak beamed a smile. He departed from the King's presence, taking his place within the caravan. The statesman was already on alert, anticipating a strike on the caravan. He relaxed and waited, but there was no immediate strike outside the Djenhai kingdom, as was planned. Al-Rinak started to boil with anger by the third hour of travel. Nothing happened, not even when the party was only an hour from al-Mari Ifriq. The trail was clear. He looked through the drapes of his carriage. Nothing. Al-Rinak sat back. He wiped away his emotions and became patient again. He was silent, saying nothing to the servants that occupied the mounted carriage with him. He did not make an order, not for food or drink.

Al-Rinak was furious when the caravan reached al-Mari Ifriq safely. He was aided from his carriage and ready to question Taran, Maurice, and Fusan for answers. Taran and Wakil greeted the arriving officials. Al-Rinak's anger increased when he saw Taran. The former ambassador's smile was irritating to watch. His daughter was by his side, beaming just as ridiculously at her husband. A handmaiden was with her. Al-Rinak remembered her name as Aludra. She embraced Nasir, which made al-Rinak lift a single, curious eyebrow. His anger faded upon closer inspection of Taran. His eyes glimmered subtly with complete surprise to see the caravan intact. He turned to al-Rinak and cast his expression on him while Mehit and al-Jeheuty embraced. No one was harmed. Al-Rinak was not feigning regret that Beylerbey Anhur Has was dead, or al-Jeheuty's ambassador and Army Official. All was well, for the most part.

"I bring brilliant news," al-Jeheuty said to Wakil, his voice breaking into al-Rinak's thoughts. "Great news." He tried to hide his enthusiasm. "King Kemnebi agrees with our plans. We will put together a false caravan within several days. It will be outfitted with all of the Turkish troops. General al-Dume will assist. The Djenhai soldiers will box the attacking Ogunsanwo-Mashek. We'll take some of their warriors. It won't be a full-scale battle, but it will be enough. We only need to capture one warrior. He will give the location of the party." Wakil squinted at al-Jeheuty. The Beylerbey was speaking quickly. "I'm tired, Governor, as I'm sure all the officials are, soldiers, and our servants too." He said this to Wakil while resting his hand on the Governor's shoulder. "I request a day's rest before we hold a meeting on our accomplishments."

"Absolutely, Beylerbey," Wakil permitted. He looked at the other officials and asked, "Are there any objections?" The other officials agreed, showing no objections among them. Al-Jeheuty ordered Bo Yusuf and Commander Koray to get the troops situated within the barracks. Taran was ordered to see to the servants and guards, escorting them to their rooms within the palace. Al-Rinak and Nasir were dismissed.

Al-Jeheuty took his wife's arm and walked through the rear courtyard and into the palace. Governor Wakil was close behind. "Ojodo and Adaeze opted to stay in Djenhai," al-Jeheuty notified. "They will return before setting out east."

Once inside the palace, Nasir and Aludra, and al-Rinak and Taran separated from al-Jeheuty, Mehit, and Wakil. The governor maintained silence as he followed al-Jeheuty and Mehit back to their private quarters. Al-Jeheuty allowed the governor entrance. He shut the door and turned to Wakil, urgency scrawled on his face.

Al-Jeheuty asked, "Where is Roberto?"

"He's assisting Rahmis with security at *The Siren's Call*," the governor answered.

Al-Jeheuty waved his hand. "We'll notify him of plans soon enough." Mehit excused herself. Al-Jeheuty hesitated momentarily, almost asking his wife to stay. But she too would learn soon enough. Al-Jeheuty shut the door behind his wife. He looked at Wakil and whispered, "Djenhai and the Ogunsanwo-Mashek are at peace. The war is over."

Wakil's expression contorted with confusion. "What?" he expressed.

Al-Jeheuty could not help but smile. "It's over. You wanted peace, Governor-Imam. There's peace. All praises to the Miracle Workers. We are going to cripple al-Rinak's army. He will not see it coming."

"Peace? How?" Wakil was confused, though noticeably excited.

"Remember when Bo Yusuf and I recounted to you and Behar the Ogunsanwo-Mashek's legend?" asked al-Jeheuty.

"Yes," the Governor answered. "Behar and I were intrigued."

"The Djenhai share the same legend," al-Jeheuty said with a smile. "They are descendants of that fractured, black kingdom. The Djenhai are descended from the ancient kingdom's nobles. The Ogunsanwo-Mashek are descended from the warrior-class, which felt abandoned by the nobles when they made their escape." Al-Jeheuty clarified, "The Ogunsanwo-Mashek's first attack was based on anger, hurt, and revenge. They knew who the Djenhai were. The Ogunsanwo-Mashek elders did not share their motives with the rest of their nation."

"And there has been war ever since," Wakil concluded.

"Unfortunately." Al-Jeheuty cleared his throat. "Kemnebi and Mazigh met, secretly. Ojodo and Bo Yusuf took him to the Ogunsanwo-Mashek nation. We will attack al-Rinak's troops on a planned excursion. Djenhai soldiers and Ogunsanwo-Mashek warriors teamed together. With his army eradicated, we'll corner him for his crimes. He will confess. Taran too. Fusan as well."

Wakil warned, "Be careful. Fusan is gone. Men from his crew have gone too. They most likely left on board al-Rinak's ship, supposedly bound for Turkey. Be on alert, especially during these tournaments."

"I will," said al-Jeheuty. "As of the moment, Governor, I'm pondering the weight of our voices in a Turkish court. We have a King connected to them by faith and tradition; we have our voices."

"Al-Rinak might drum up the past," Wakil suggested. "He might site our revolution against his brother, and the other heads of The Four Winds, as probable cause. He would say he acted in the Empire's interests."

"He'll have no evidence," al-Jeheuty disagreed.

"Taran," the Governor reminded.

Al-Jeheuty lifted an eyebrow. He looked at the door as if Mehit was there. He turned back to Wakil and said in a low voice, "Taran won't see the Turkish court. He'll be dead by that time. Trust."

"And what will Mehit know?" the Governor asked. He understood the burden al-Jeheuty carried, he having the same burden for presenting a truth to Nasir.

"The truth," al-Jeheuty answered.

"I'll pray you have an easy time telling her," Wakil said making his way to the door. "There are two updates on your clandestine front." He turned away from the door and faced al-Jeheuty. "Traont Coutelier is dead. Signore Verola sent word. He also relayed that Giovanni Ghislanzoni-Verdi, the former Baron's nephew, is dead from an unfortunate accident. The official report is that he drank too much, and he fell overboard the ship taking him back to Sicily. He drowned. His letter sounded angry, accusing."

"That's fine, as long as we have a good official word," al-Jeheuty stated. "Thank you, Governor."

Wakil left the room. Mehit entered several minutes after. She found al-Jeheuty resting in bed. He was dressed in his pants, nothing else. The woman glided over to her husband and sat down beside him. She rubbed his chest and smiled. Al-Jeheuty wanted to tell her the progress of the war, every last detail, but he resisted. Mehit tapped his chest, kissed her husband's forehead, and stood up again. "I'm off to watch my business. R'uza will be right by my side."

"Good, *mora*," said al-Jeheuty.

"Get sleep," Mehit told her husband. "You've earned it. I'll return when my day is finished." She then stepped away from al-Jeheuty and left the room. The Beylerbey dropped into sleep quickly. He was exhausted.

Chapter Fifty

Maurice's excuse was simple. He helped his brother's crewmembers early the next morning take the disguises to the Turkish ship before the crewmembers and Fusan departed al-Mari Ifriq. That's what he told Taran and al-Rinak. In reality, after murdering Fusan and Tendai, the next morning he called for members of Fusan's crew to take away the crate filled with the Ogunsanwo-Mashek outfits. He advised them that there were new plans. Fusan would catch up with them in Tunis in several days. They were not to make a move until their captain appeared. Fusan's crew departed al-Mari Ifriq without question.

There was a change in plans, considered Maurice. He was going to bring his brother's corpse to their house. It would be believed that Fusan drank himself to death. He would backpedal in his story to Taran and al-Rinak. Maurice would tell the two of them he was covering for his brother, watching over him while he recovered from an extremely disagreeable, drunken binge.

Maurice did just that.

Under the cover of darkness, Maurice moved his brother's body to their housing complex. He disguised himself with heavy robes, and dressed his brother the same. He dragged Fusan as if he was a wounded soldier. He ducked through alleyways, finding a quick route to their home. He brought Fusan to his bedroom and rested him down on the bed. He removed the heavy robes from his brother's body. He took off Fusan's leather vest, opened his shirt, removed his boots, and fixed him properly in the bed. He went back to the tavern and tossed Tendai's body into the underground compartment, and took residence in a backroom.

The next afternoon, while the citizens of al-Mari Ifriq reveled in the tournaments held at *The Siren's Call*, Maurice whispered into al-Rinak's ear about Fusan's whereabouts. Taran was also summoned, and while they walked to Maurice and Fusan's house, Melusina accompanying them, Maurice confessed his false story. Melusina validated Maurice's narrative, recounting Fusan's stumbling, alcoholic behavior the last night she saw him alive. "He was deranged," Melusina said to al-Rinak. "He was ranting about our plans in front of that prostitute girl. I had to silence him."

Maurice concluded the story of Fusan's last moments by informing al-Rinak and Taran about his continued drinking throughout the night. "He was in no state to travel. We fought as I brought him here. I did not want him at the *Palace*. Not in that state. Not while I spent the night with Tendai. The next morning I checked on him. He was in a rage, still drinking. He said he would join his men in Tunis later. But he got worse."

They entered the house, climbed the stairs, and walked into Fusan's room.

The Moorish corsair was still. He looked at peace.

"I blame al-Jeheuty," sneered Taran after a moment of silence. "Grounding Fusan was taking its toll. He lived for the sea." Taran sighed. "Let me alert the Beylerbey." Taran exited the apartment, journeying back to *The Siren's Call* where al-Jeheuty attended the festive tournament.

While he was away, Maurice pleaded with al-Rinak to help him put together an assault that would take out the marked officials. "I have no other choice," al-Rinak answered Maurice's pleas. "However, Sükh Koray will carry out the mark on Bo Yusuf. The General will meet his end in combat. King Kemnebi has devised a plan to separate the Ogunsanwo-Mashek warriors from the people. I'm waiting for a message from him." He said before he exited, "Until then, continue to plot. Melusina, let us return to the games." Al-Rinak and his mistress left the house before the officials arrived. Al-Rinak was not upset. He was disappointed in Maurice and Fusan, but although his plans were displaced, they were not extinguished.

Al-Jeheuty, Roberto, and Nasir were brought in to identify the scene. Roberto's clan members, in use as city guards, removed the body from the house and delivered it to one of the infirmaries. Al-Jeheuty and Roberto followed the guards outside. Roberto continued to the infirmary, al-Jeheuty looked for Governor Wakil to deliver the news.

Nasir gave his greatest sympathies to his friend. "Thank you," expressed Maurice. He looked at the empty bed. "I never saw Fusan more at peace. He was an angry man. We were not the same after our father died." Maurice put his eyes on Nasir. He wanted to tell him, but it was not the time. Nasir embraced Maurice in a brotherly manner. "It's alright, Nasir," Maurice said. "We all rest in peace soon enough. I just hope the truth resides with us when it happens."

Nasir was conflicted. There were scars on his body he believed were caused by Fusan. But Nasir was still sad because of the loss, especially for Maurice. His friend had lost everyone in his family. He was completely alone. "I have my duties as an ambassador," stated Nasir, "but should you need my assistance with anything, I'll be there."

"Rahmis helps with the tavern," spoke Maurice. "I'm covered there. I handle the import of our drinks. I should be fine. I'm sure the Beylerbey stands ready to assign my brother's protection route to another captain. But I will call for your assistance should I need any." Nasir returned to the games. Maurice went to the infirmary to see his brother for the last time.

The scourge of the Mediterranean was dead. The news slowly permeated through the city. It was whispered inside the tournament, but did not interrupt the games. Some of the gambling corsairs, pirates, and privateers toasted to Fusan, to them, a great man. The report was already shuffling through the city by passersby that witnessed the corsair's body being removed from his home. Al-Jeheuty informed Wakil of the matter. The governor ordered the Beylerbey to continue the state of alert. Al-Rinak, desperate, could attempt anything.

Word reached Mehit of her foster brother's death. She was not surprised. She long believed Fusan was marked by destiny and fate for a violent death. Mehit showed considerable and sincere sympathy for Maurice, however. She, along with Laith and Jabari al-Hakam, and Nasir and Zakiy Sa'ood, hosted a small remembrance ceremony for Maurice in honor of his brother Fusan. The gathering occurred at Jabari's house.

The affair did not go well.

Maurice ended up drunk and telling his childhood friends, "You all feign sympathy, but you know the truth. Fusan was a son of a bitch. He was hateful, to all of us. I'm glad he's dead. I'm glad I..." he stopped his words, then corrected himself quickly, only appearing to slur his words. "...I'm rid of him." He wasn't drunk enough to let slip the deed of murdering Fusan, though anger and liquor possessed him. Nasir tried to comfort Maurice, only antagonizing him further. "You're so self-righteous, Nasir. You're clueless. You have no idea. None." He turned to Mehit and said to her, "And you, you little bitch. You never cared for him. Please. Fusan fondled himself to fantasies of defiling you in the most violent of ways." He stood up straight, as best he could. "I ask that you remember him as he was: a shit, a bastard, and a sick fiend. I would be honored by your honesty. The dead pass on, but they do not get a pass."

Maurice passed out. Laith and Nasir carried him home.

For the next two days a festive atmosphere surrounded al-Mari Ifriq, even amidst a small funeral held for Fusan al-Hammon. All the officials attended, including Rahmis. The games continued under trusted supervision. Fusan was buried next to his father and mother, in a private burial court near the house that Maurice and Fusan inherited. Maurice did not apologize for his behavior at the remembrance ceremony, and no one expected him too. Everyone kept a distance from him. Maurice was left alone while the other attendees retired from the premises.

The men, including the Beylerbey and governor, Rahmis Husani, Nasir and Zakiy Sa'ood, Bo Yusuf, and Roberto Hamaat returned to the games. Taran and al-Rinak joined them. Laith and Jabari al-Hakam went about their personal duties. Mehit returned to her bathhouse, accompanied by her mother and Afya Sa'ood.

A messenger interrupted the governor and Beylerbey as they headed to *The Siren's Call.* The rest of the men were ahead of them, but al-Jeheuty called for Bo Yusuf and al-Rinak when the messenger revealed that there was a unit of Djenhai soldiers gathered at the southern wall. "The Commander's name is Abanobi," stated the messenger. "He is with a large group of soldiers, all mounted. It's intimidating."

"He means no harm," assured Bo Yusuf. "He's part of my command in the Djenhai army."

"He declares that his message is urgent," concluded the servant.

"Everyone. Come," ordered Wakil. The officials followed close behind the governor. Taran was included.

Commander Abanobi, surrounded by a mounted unit of forty soldiers, greeted the officials as they arrived at the city's rear entrance. He galloped up to Governor Wakil and said, "We are in need of the Turks' army. King Kemnebi has taken slaves. We found the whereabouts of the Ogunsanwo-Mashek camp. They were in Tunisia. We made a swift attack. The warriors retreated with some of their people. We made a grand capture of slaves."

Bo Yusuf and al-Jeheuty looked at one another with a perplexed expression. Al-Jeheuty addressed Commander Abanobi, "There was not to be an executed move without al-Mari Ifriq's consent."

"We've taken matters into our own hands," Abanobi retorted firmly. "General al-Dume, your services are requested. Statesman Ozan, your army. Ogunsanwo-Mashek warriors have made unsuccessful attacks on Djenhai. There is war. We mean to end it."

Wakil suggested to al-Jeheuty, "Perhaps the King has other plans. Let's see what comes of this." He reminded the young Beylerbey, "We do…have our means secured to end the war in other ways."

Al-Jeheuty exhaled. "Bo Yusuf, gather your supplies." He leaned close and said, "Keep an eye on this situation."

"Yes, Beylerbey." The General turned to Commander Abanobi and assured his return.

Al-Jeheuty addressed al-Rinak, "Find Commander Koray. Put together your soldiers. That will take a great deal of time." He looked up at Commander Abanobi. "Two hundred soldiers need to be assembled and equipped."

"We can wait," said the Djenhai Commander.

Al-Jeheuty ordered, "Statesman Ozan, to your duty. Return to the palace when Commander Koray is found and is in the process of assembling his men."

Al-Rinak bowed and said cordially, "As you wish, Beylerbey." The statesman disappeared through the southern courtyard, Taran in tow. The two men went through the palace and walked to al-Rinak's apartment first. They needed to converse privately. Both men stayed silent throughout their journey, but surprise apprehended them when they entered al-Rinak's residence. Captain Kyler Piett was waiting for them while sitting on the front room sofa. He was dressed in heavy, beige robes and a small turban covered by a hood. It was a disguise. He stood up when the two men entered the room. He bowed to both of them.

"Melusina let me in. She returned to the games to find you," the Captain explained. "I heard about Fusan."

"All the way in Europe?" al-Rinak questioned, his eyes examining the Captain from behind squints.

Piett shook his head. "No. I found Maurice at their house. I saw the grave. I paid my respect. I've fled France." He looked at al-Rinak and said, "But don't worry, Master Ozan. My Dutch contacts sent me here to check on progress. They await slaves, but, I…I stopped in France for a while, to visit an old flame. Much happened. I came across terrible news." Piett's eyes went from al-Rinak to Taran. Neither man spoke, but the Captain knew they had questions ready for answers. "Rene Chaffee is dead." Piett braced himself for an angry attack from al-Rinak. The statesman just clenched his teeth angrily and exhaled. Piett also reported, "Traont Coutelier is dead too."

"What," al-Rinak blared. The statesman growled like an animal.

"Interestingly enough," continued Captain Piett, "Traont Coutelier was killed in Sicily, according to my contacts. Black slaves killed Baron Agusto Ghislanzoni and his administrators. There was a revolt. Traont Coutelier was investing in black slaves in Sicily. Supposedly, he received word from Rene Chaffee to inspect the slaves before purchasing them. Rene was already in Sicily. Greed got the better of our Frenchmen. They were caught in the revolt."

Al-Rinak shook his head. He put his hands on his hips. He dropped his head and took deep breaths. Finally, he looked up and toward Taran. "They know," he said. He walked away from both men. He kicked a wooden tablestand, knocking it over and toppling the decorative floral arrangement resting atop it. He turned around and said to Taran, "Should we find it a coincidence that al-Jeheuty sends Nasir to the baron to barter more revenue with slaves and a revolt takes place? Chaffee *and* Coutelier?"

"Their greed got the best of them," Taran said in a reassuring voice.

Al-Rinak pounded a fist against his stomach. "I know what my gut says, you swine. That dog al-Jeheuty, and all his bitches, knows our plans." The statesman relaxed. "Hell, they've always known." Al-Rinak retreated into thought. He imagined the revolt in Sicily, the death of Baron Agusto and his advisors. He thought of the design of al-Jeheuty's clever plan almost exactly as it was, but he was missing one variable. "The baron's estate goes to his nephew. Perhaps this was not engineered by al-Jeheuty and his Griffin Company."

Captain Piett hiccupped. He hesitated to tell al-Rinak about the news he learned pertaining to Giovanni Ghislanzoni-Verdi. However, he conceded. "The baron's nephew is dead. It was an accident. He drowned after getting drunk. He was aboard a vessel heading for Sicily. He was called home by Lord Donatello Verola."

"Lord?" al-Rinak growled. "Verola? That Sicilian messenger and lapdog?"

"Yes," stuttered Piett. "He subdued the slave riot. His family took control of the region."

"Did they," al-Rinak said in a sarcastic voice that resonated his irritation. He walked to Taran and said, "Commander Koray will stay here with a garrison of fifty men. Koray will assign a competent, lower ranked leader among the troops to lead the charge against the Ogunsanwo-Mashek. They all know their orders. One army will take out Bo Yusuf. The army here will march to take the city. All we need is to kill four men: the Beylerbey, his ambassador, the governor, and Roberto Hamaat. I trust Koray to accomplish such a deed. This city has no army. The only army in this city is at my command." He said to Captain Piett, "Stay here. I will find Commander Koray."

Al-Rinak and Taran exited the apartment, setting out to find the Turkish commander. They found the Mongolian-Turk near the Open Market, and al-Rinak briefed the Commander on the rising situation.

Commander Koray asked, "Do you believe the officials will not become suspicious after you request such a notion?"

"No," al-Rinak answered with confidence. "Round up the soldiers. Make word spread about the Ogunsanwo-Mashek threat. Our leaders will have no choice but to feel compelled to protect the city. I will ask for fifty men to keep watch over the city. I'll even separate you as that unit's leader. Now, go to your task. When you finish, group with the Djenhai unit at the southern wall."

"That will take some time," Commander Koray said apologetically. "Most men are on alert, waiting for orders, but there are a good amount of soldiers just running about."

"Take time," said al-Rinak. "We have it. Make sure word is spread. What's most important is that the citizens are riled up by the news. Do not make it too obvious, just enough to reach our officials' ears. We'll meet you at the southern wall. In the meantime, I will sell water to drowning men." The statesman and Taran left the Commander to his duties. The two men returned to the palace as ordered. Al-Rinak informed the Beylerbey that Sükh Koray was about his duties to round up all two hundred soldiers in the Turkish army.

Hours passed before Commander Koray assembled the Turkish soldiers scattered throughout the city. It took another hour to fit his soldiers with the proper provisions and weapons. Within this time, word circulated throughout al-Mari Ifriq that war resided over its horizon, and not figuratively. The citizens became restless, demanding answers from their officials. Many gamblers, privateers as most of them were, put together their earnings and made their way to the ports to leave the city. Some local citizens involved in the games went home, others convened at the city square, stopped by a large group of Roberto's guards from nearing the palace. Al-Rinak stepped in with his proposal, which was reluctantly granted. Al-Jeheuty silently plotted to have al-Rinak's soldiers covered by Roberto's assassins and Nuru's al-Jasi.

The officials exited the palace to attend to the audience of citizens. The governor and Beylerbey addressed the city's people and their heightened concern and furor. There was silence as Governor Wakil al-Hakam spoke in an assuring tone, "War will not touch our walls again. The Djenhai kingdom has made a bold move in an effort to stamp out the Ogunsanwo-Mashek. The fight takes place at the border of Tunisia. There is a fear that it will reach Djenhai. Al-Mari Ifriq is assisting its ally. We do suggest that you remain in your homes at night. Carry out your daily duties. There will be city guards on alert, and Statesman Ozan has granted fifty soldiers to watch the city while the rest of his army assists the Djenhai people. The horizon will be covered."

The citizens' worries were quelled. The crowd dispersed. Commander Koray, at that very moment, marched his troops to the southern wall, taking a path through the city's western gate, and journeying around the outside of the city to meet with the Djenhai unit.

The officials saw them off.

Bo Yusuf and Commander Koray marched to the horizon with the might of their armies following. Commander Koray separated fifty soldiers from the greater army. He assigned a competent officer to command the larger unit. "Inspect the slaves when you reach Djenhai," he told the Turkish officer named Vedat. "Inform King Kemnebi that Statesman Ozan will arrive after the Ogunsanwo-Mashek warriors have been dealt with." With his orders in place, Commander Koray split from the larger unit, taking command of the fifty soldiers staying behind to guard al-Mari Ifriq.

Chapter Fifty-One

The armies moved over the North African landmass heading south to the Djenhai kingdom. Two hours into travel, Commanding Officer Vedat separated eight soldiers from the Turkish army. The soldiers were assigned another commanding officer. It was there eight soldiers that continued on toward the Djenhai kingdom to inspect the captured Ogunsanwo-Mashek natives. Four Djenhai soldiers were chosen to escort the Turkish troupe. Bo Yusuf and Vedat pushed the army eastward, toward Odongo-Mauharim's Tunisian border.

The army marched in segregated clusters. African Djenhai troops traveled alongside one another, separating themselves from the Turkish soldiers. Bo Yusuf and Commanding Officer Vedat rode side-by-side. There was only military strategy exchanged between the two men, not much more in words. Bo Yusuf kept his eyes on the mountains in the distance as they emerged from the sands, peeking over the horizon. He stopped his mount and lifted a hand. Commander Vedat and all the troops ceased their travel. Bo Yusuf turned to Vedat and gave the order, "I want the Turkish troops to take drag." His voice was firm. His tone was assertive, making sure there would be no argument to his command. Bo Yusuf turned to Commander Abanobi and ordered, "Stay behind my lead." He then addressed both Commander Abanobi and Commanding Officer Vedat. "This needs to be done quickly." He looked toward the mountain range and then surveyed the surrounding area. "Now."

Vedat put up no fuss. He circled around the soldiers in the Turkish unit and shouted commands organizing them into military formation behind the Djenhai soldiers. The Commanding Officer was at the head of his unit. He kept a close eye on Bo Yusuf. With the Moorish General's attention occupied, and his back to the Turkish army, Vedat addressed three of his unit's soldiers with the use of hand signals. His message called for the soldiers to keep their hands close on their weapons until further notice.

From his vantage point, Vedat noticed Bo Yusuf raise his hand again, ceasing the troops from continuing forward. They had only trotted halfway to the mountain range. Vedat believed the Moorish General was being too cautious. He watched as Bo Yusuf turned to Commander

Abanobi. The two men had an exchange. Bo Yusuf turned around to see Vedat. The General nodded his head.

"Is there a problem, General al-Dume?" Vedat hollered up to Bo Yusuf.

"I feel it's necessary that we should negotiate a surrender, Commander." Bo Yusuf replied.

Ogunsanwo-Mashek warriors rose from the sands on the right side of the Turkish and Djenhai army, Gu-Gurzil their captain. Commanding Officer Vedat's trained eye estimated fifty warriors among the militia. The warriors had at the ready arrows locked into bows. Vedat removed his sword. Every Turkish soldier aimed muskets at the emerged army, and it was then that a second Ogunsanwo-Mashek unit emerged from the left side of the Turkish and Djenhai army, thirty-six counting their numbers, with Chwezi as their captain.

Vedat put his eyes on Bo Yusuf looking for a command. The Djenhai troops remained still. Bo Yusuf looked apologetic. He said to Vedat, "What are your terms for surrender, Commanding Officer?" He could see the perplexed expression on Vedat's face. The Commanding Officer was slowly realizing that the Djenhai unit stood together with the Ogunsanwo-Mashek as allies. "These politics are complicated, Officer Vedat," Bo Yusuf continued. "It's been a long time since you've seen your home country," he said. "Surrender now and all of you are granted amnesty by this state."

Vedat surveyed his surroundings. He watched the Ogunsanwo-Mashek warriors creep closer, bows ready to strike. He looked at his unit and signaled his soldiers. He addressed Bo Yusuf, "Odongo-Mauharim *is* our home. We fight to secure it. We fight under the command of our Beylerbey al-Rinak Ozan. There is no bargain, General al-Dume."

Two Turkish troops tossed bombs at the Ogunsanwo-Mashek units. The bombs erupted, coughing up sand and debris and tossing warriors from each unit into the air. Arrows were fired in retaliation. Turkish troops and mounts were cut down. Soldiers, unscathed from the mass of arrows, fired their muskets. Some aimed at the Ogunsanwo-Mashek, killing and wounding warriors. Other Turkish troops fired at the Djenhai unit. Bo Yusuf galloped away from the attacks. He fired a pistol at the Turkish army and managed to strike Vedat in the neck, killing the Commanding Officer amidst the confusion.

Both Ogunsanwo-Mashek units removed swords and rushed the Turkish army. Soldiers dropped from their mounts and engaged the warriors, swords clanging. Some Turkish troops opted to remain mounted, slicing Ogunsanwo-Mashek warriors from atop their camels and horses. Djenhai soldiers joined the conflict, taking aim and firing into the violent mesh of clashing warriors. Their bullets struck the mounted Turks. Ogunsanwo-Mashek warriors sliced their swords across camel and horse, bringing down the mounted soldiers. Men from each army kept their heads low from persisting gunfire, unable to see if the shots came from Turkish or Djenhai soldiers.

Bo Yusuf jumped from his mount and participated in the battle. The Moorish General did not draw out his sword play with the Turkish troops. He cut them down with single swipes from hi sword. He recited the names of Moorish knights he was descended from, male and female. He hollered their names like a war cry, a ferocious mantra to invoke all the fighting blood and spirit in his lineage. He swung his sword with such quickness that he appeared to be made of many arms, hands, and swords. Every swing was effective, taking down one Turkish soldier after another.

From the mountains came another Ogunsanwo-Mashek unit led by Balde-Sih, twenty-one soldiers at his command. The militia was mounted. Balde screamed a warrior's call, aiming his sword forward and charging the bloody foray. The conflict was wild. Gunfire was muted as loaded ammunition from one-shot pistols and muskets became extinguished. The clash of warriors dissolved into a vicious sword battle. The Turkish soldiers, strong in number, diminished in esteem. This was not the battle they were prepared to fight.

Djenhai soldiers and Ogunsanwo-Mashek warriors battled back-to-back, allies against a common foe, and enlivened by their common history and origins. They were a broken family made whole again. The confusion of war did not affect the re-united culture. Their thoughts were clear, and they overpowered the massive Turkish army. The sight of those warriors that fell only made the remaining warriors stronger, continuing the fight invigorated by the spirit of the dead.

Chief Mazigh appeared over the northern horizon, his wife next to him. Both of them led mounted troops, swords drawn. But as they moved closer to the battle, the Turkish soldiers were already laying down their weapons, being subdued and shackled. The Turkish army, once comprised of one hundred and fifty soldiers, was reduced to forty wounded men, most of their numbers slain, and few unscathed. They dropped their weapons and issued surrender, yielding to capture. Unlike their dead Commanding Officer, Vedat Yilmaz, they did not consider Odongo-Mauharim their home.

Bo Yusuf, Gu-Gurzil, Chwezi, and Balde-Sih sheathed their weapons and approached the Chief and Chieftess. The remaining captains among the Djenhai and Ogunsanwo-Mashek soldiers placed the remaining Turkish soldiers under arrest.

Mazigh dismounted from his camel, holding the reins as he approached his captains and the Moorish General. The Chief's smile looked like a sigh of relief as he watched the scene in front of him. Balde-Sih took the reins from his Chief as Mazigh walked past the approaching Ogunsanwo-Mashek captains and Moorish General. He stepped closer to the aftermath of battle. He put his head down, closed his eyes, and said a prayer for the slain warriors.

The Chief's captains kept their distance. Bo Yusuf approached Mazigh just as the Chief lifted his head and heaved a sigh. He turned to Bo Yusuf and said, "I didn't see combat. King Kemnebi advised me to stay within Djenhai walls, to keep safe with the rest of our people. I told him that I was a General-Chief. I should oversee the fight. I didn't offend his manhood. He didn't believe I called him a coward. He understood." He smiled again. It resonated just the same as before, like a sigh. "I told the King not to abandon us again." He laughed. "I told him that we'd hunt his noble court down just the same, start this whole damn fight all over again."

Nugaymath approached Mazigh. The Chief turned to his Chieftess and embraced her. The remaining Ogunsanwo-Mashek warriors and captains surrounded their nation's leaders and started to sing a song of trials and tribulations endured by their people. The song was in their native language. Bo Yusuf and the Djenhai soldiers did not understand the words to the song, but felt its meaning. Bo Yusuf and Abanobi backed away out of respect for the culture.

Bo Yusuf said to the Djenhai Commander, "Mazigh and Nugaymath will escort the captives back to Djenhai with their unit of warriors. Take five soldiers and return to al-Mari Ifriq. Relay a message to Commander Sükh Koray. Tell him reinforcements are needed. Tell him the Ogunsanwo-Mashek are running wild and that I'm dead. That should sweeten the situation. Lead the Turkish army to the mountains. I, and a unit of Ogunsanwo-Mashek archers, and the remaining Djenhai soldiers, will be waiting."

Abanobi agreed. He suggested, "Confiscate the dead of their muskets. Reload them. The army that approaches will be well armed."

Bo Yusuf nodded. "I will, Commander."

The two officers returned to Chief Mazigh when the hymn was finished. Bo Yusuf stated his plans, and the Chief and Chieftess agreed. The wandering camels and horses were gathered. The units organized their numbers. Bo Yusuf led a squadron of Djenhai soldiers, and Ogunsanwo-Mashek warriors under Gu-Gurzil's command, toward the mountains. Abanobi and five Djenhai soldiers headed northwest to al-Mari Ifriq. Chief Mazigh and Chieftess Nugaymath escorted the apprehended Turkish soldiers back to the Djenhai kingdom.

The sun was starting to set.

Chapter Fifty-Two

There was little traffic running through al-Mari Ifriq's streets. Activity simmered down shortly after the Djenhai and Turkish soldiers marched toward war. The city was on alert. Roberto's men took post at different sections of al-Mari Ifriq. The day had come to an unexpected end, and citizens waited anxiously. Rahmis Husani was upset about the sudden turn of events, and he demanded to be alone from escort, servant, or guard. His tournament had been interrupted. He brought Fumnyana to the apartment suite he purchased for her. She lived in the suite on permission granted by her father. Rahmis was continuing to make steps toward procuring Fumnyana as his bride, but he still hesitated in making a formal proposal. Fumnyana did not seem to mind, as long as she stayed in Rahmis' company. Rahmis believed she was just too plain a personality. She had very little ambition, content with her life. It did not serve Rahmis' noble agenda. *It was a shame*, considered the princely Moor. He thought Fumnyana was pretty, and to him, and to all she came in contact, she did have a pleasant attitude.

The noblemoor walked the emptying streets focused on his thoughts. He was upset that activities in his 'kingdom' were put on hold. He returned to *The Siren's Call* just as the sun presented its last hour of light. He returned to finish locking the tavern, and putting away the sums of coin stored in the back. These large sums of monies were not the main prizes for the games. The main prizes still rested safe in the palace.

Rahmis entered his establishment and discovered Maurice al-Hammon occupying a table. He was drinking. He looked up as Rahmis entered. Rahmis smiled at him. He swiped a clean cup from another table, a second bottle, and dropped down into an unoccupied seat across from Maurice. He poured a cup, took a gulp, and looked around the room.

"You're not trying to rob my establishment, are you?" Rahmis joked. "Should I count the coin locked in the back? And you'll pay for that bottle too." Maurice did not laugh. Rahmis continued to try and lighten the air. "Politics invaded my kingdom," Rahmis said. "All my subjects have gone."

"Appreciate the silence," Maurice advised with a scowl on his face.

Rahmis finished the contents of his cup. He poured another. "I cannot in good faith allow you to continue drinking. I heard you caused much of a ruckus several nights ago at your brother's remembrance."

Maurice knocked back the rest of his drink, looking intensely at Rahmis. He poured more into his cup. "Did that brat Nasir tell you about my behavior? Perhaps that cunt Mehit." He took a hard gulp then placed his cup down. "Mehit…she is such an ungrateful child." It appeared that Maurice was already drunk. "Nasir…he's as spoiled as you say al-Jeheuty is."

Rahmis finished another sip before saying, "I say that in jest, Maurice. I also have no problems telling al-Jeheuty in front of his face."

Maurice started to clap sarcastically. "Congratulations for not being a two-face bastard." He took his cup, and with a hard knock back of its contents, placed it back on the table, then leaned forward. "You are as noble as you speak about, though hypocritical."

Rahmis stiffened.

Maurice just laughed drunkenly. "Don't take it personal. I mean, look at you. You walk around here all high and mighty about your noble blood, but for most of your life, until now, your so-called noble blood was cold-blooded. A killer. Or were all your criminal activities against the Spanish Crown noble?"

"Maybe you should go home," Rahmis said in a stern voice.

Maurice sat back, a devious and satisfied look on his visage. "I know you too well, Rahmis. You are so hurtful against that lovely woman you court. You string her along as if she's made of pearls. And why? Because she's content with who she is." He took another hard sip. "You just don't like the fact that Fumnyana is happy with who she is, because you're not happy with who you are, *noble killer.*"

"You have to leave," Rahmis snarled.

Maurice spread his arms wide. "Drag me out, you glorified manservant. You're the Beylerbey of stewards. All hail Rahmis Husani. The Chief Boss of all Custodians." Rahmis didn't move. Maurice continued to drink. "I hate every last one of you. You're as treacherous as Nasir's father. Sa'ad always pranced around as if he was nobler than everyone else. He was so goddamn self-righteous. No different than you." Maurice nodded his head. "He was a noble killer too." He looked away from Rahmis. His expression became sad, watery with tears. "Sa'ad killed my father, do you know? That was his best friend. My father and he grew up together. They were like brothers. And Sa'ad betrayed that brotherhood by murdering my father." Maurice's face trembled as the tears streaked down the sides of his face.

Rahmis remained still. His anger evaporated as he listened to Maurice's sad confession.

Maurice wiped his face and screamed, "Do you curse me, Fusan?" He looked at the floor. "Do you curse me from the pits of Hell because I weep for our father? Does that make me weak?" Maurice lifted his gaze from the floor. "I'm so glad I poisoned your drink," he said in a low voice, whispering to the ethers. "You had love for our father too," Maurice continued. "You were there that night we put bullets in Sa'ad's head, and helped Guyotta snuff him out. You were hurt just as much as I when Taran confessed to us years ago the sin of murder and betrayal Sa'ad committed against our father."

Rahmis wanted to move, but he was still.

Maurice looked at Rahmis. "Don't believe Nasir when he speaks about his father. Sa'ad was a bastard. Foul. He was a bastard just like you, Rahmis. He was a hypocrite, carrying jealousy for his closest friend." He grit his teeth and spoke sharply, "You whine so goddamned much over Bo Yusuf's union with that Djenhai Princess. And now, for some reason, you're crying over Ojodo and his new girl. Is she noble too? Are your friends buying up real estate on a title you believed was exclusive to you?"

Rahmis had enough. He stood up and declared, "That's all with you. You're leaving, and further, I'm placing you under arrest." He took a step forward.

Maurice moved like lightning. In an instant, the bottle on the table was in his grip and then cracked across Rahmis' face. The bottle shattered! Maurice screamed. Rahmis stumbled, and before he could regain composure, Maurice attacked him with a flurry of jabs to his face. Rahmis' body crumpled. He smacked the floor. His robes sprawled out wide, his arms and legs the same.

Maurice tossed away the broken bottle. He kicked Rahmis' body. Two of his attacks pounded Rahmis' stomach. A third and fourth kick smacked the princely Moor's face. Maurice stepped back drunkenly. His hand brushed against the pistol strapped to him. He removed the weapon and thumbed back the hammer as he stood over Rahmis' unconscious body. Maurice's vision blurred as he stared down at Rahmis' swollen face.

"No!" Maurice heard someone scream.

Maurice looked up. His blurring vision watched as a hazy and dark ghost made its way toward him, arms outstretched. He aimed the gun at the hazy figure and fired! The bullet's impact spun the attacking specter around and it dropped to the floor. The sound of the collision jarred Maurice's vision back to normal. He looked closer and saw the lovely Fumnyana lying on the ground, blood pooling underneath her body.

Maurice sheathed his gun. He shook his head to gain a sense of sobriety. He made his way into one of the backrooms and ransacked the area. There was nothing he could pilfer. He checked the tavern's other rooms, finally finding four small chests filled with the tournament's pooled monies. He confiscated two chests, placing them under his arms, and then he left the establishment.

Fumnyana's body stirred minutes later.

She trembled, pain searing through her. Fumnyana gasped. She looked up and saw Rahmis unconscious. She checked her person and hiccupped from the pain coming from her right thigh. Her wound bled steadily from the bullet that struck her. She took a deep breath and then crawled to Rahmis' body. She put her cheek to his lips and nose. She felt his breath and realized he was fine, just unconscious. She inspected his battered face, running a gentle finger along the bruises and swelling. She became angry, determined.

Fumnyana took another deep breath. She reached up onto a chair and dragged her body into the seat. The pain increased when she sat in the chair, her thigh bunching up in the seat. Blood bubbled from her wound. She looked at the spot where she lay and saw her veil on the floor. Fumnyana cursed her luck. She balanced herself on the table and hoisted up on one leg in a single hop. There was another breath. She was sweating. Her thigh tingled, stung, and burned all at once.

Fumnyana limped over to her veil, dragging the chair with her, leaning on it for balance. She took a seat when she came to her article of clothing. The pain pinched her again. It increased when she bent down from her seat to snatch her veil. She lifted her dress and stretched out her bare leg revealing the wound in her thigh. She tied the veil tightly around her thigh, over the bullet wound. She put her dress back down, stood up, and limped to the door.

The outside atmosphere impressed a sense of vertigo on Fumnyana. She stumbled immediately, catching herself on the tavern's entrance. She looked around, the world beginning to expand and rotate. Her vision spotted two guards coming up the street. She screamed, "Help! Help! I've been shot!" The two guards, Suns in Roberto's order, charged toward Fumnyana and caught the woman when she stumbled again.

Fears that had already been quelled resurfaced as emotions entangled Fumnyana. The young woman uttered before slipping into an unconscious state, "My dear Rahmis is dead."

One of the guards held Fumnyana gently in his arms while the other rushed inside and found Rahmis on the floor. The guard inspected Rahmis' body and realized he was just unconscious. He yelled to his fellow guard, "Lord Husani is alive. He's unconscious. Beaten."

"Leave him be," shouted the second guard. "I'll watch the woman. Find Master Hamaat."

The first guard agreed. He exited the tavern and ran off to find their clan's leader. The second guard inspected Fumnyana's wound. He could see her makeshift bandage through the bullet hole in her dress. She would be fine. The young woman was lucky to be found in time. The Sun examined his surroundings as it started to get dark. He kept a careful watch, should the perpetrator of the crime return.

But the guard did not need to worry. The man responsible for the crime rested several blocks from the scene, resting at a table in his own establishment, pondering his escape from al-Mari Ifriq while gazing back and forth between the opened chests of coin and precious gems. Only one lantern burned in the entire tavern, emitting a soft, eerie glow.

Maurice considered his options as the day's light retreated.

Tunis. Algiers. Sale.

Maurice believed he could be found if he stayed in Africa-north. He settled on the Caribbean. He would have to leave on a ship heading to Sale, and then join a crew once there. He had enough coin to spare.

Al-Rinak can have this city, Maurice thought to himself as he reloaded his pistol. He then pondered if he would kill Nasir personally or leave him to al-Rinak. There came heavy pounding on his tavern's door before he could weigh his options. Maurice aimed his gun at the door. The pounding increased, and then softened. From beyond the door came a low hiss calling his name.

"Maurice," the voice spoke. "Maurice."

Maurice lifted from his seat. He cautiously crept toward the door. The voice called again, its tone louder than a whisper. Maurice then recognized the voice as Captain Kyler Piett. He opened the door. The renegado, still clothed in his disguise of heavy Mohammedan robes, had a hood drawn over his head and a sack in his hand. Maurice permitted him entrance.

Kyler inhaled and expressed, "Why do you continue to burn such heavy incense?" He wiped his hand in front of his nose. "Is everything okay? Why such a heavy, sweet odor from the backroom?" He did not allow Maurice to answer. He moved on, putting aside the thick smell of cinnamon and rose petals filtering from the storage room and flooding the front. "Al-Rinak has sent me to find you," Kyler explained. "He's ordered you to stay put. He's making a desperate move. His army will come back into the city. I'm to make a signal for them." He pointed at the sack. "Bombs. I will trigger them. Koray will enter the city with his army. He will investigate. The presence will draw out the Beylerbey, his ambassador, the Governor, and that heretic Hamaat. Bo Yusuf is scheduled to die on his mission."

Maurice lifted an eyebrow, intrigued by Kyler Piett's words.

"Ignite *The Siren's Call*," Maurice suggested to the renegado. "Rahmis' burning establishment will bring the officials running to inspect the scene, especially if there were bodies found inside."

"Bodies," Kyler inquired.

Maurice explained, "Rahmis and his mistress reside there now. Take them by surprise. Killing them would excite the officials to careless action. They would come to investigate. They would have to see the damage with their own eyes. It would expose them."

Kyler nodded his head. "I agree," he said. "Al-Rinak thought it best that I hit Mehit's bathhouse, but I believe that would be too much of a theatrical display. This will serve better. With all the money stored at the tavern, and among the day's hysteria, this will be perceived as a robbery. Excellent. Stay here." He scooped up the sack of bombs. "I will light the sack and toss them into the tavern. Rahmis and his mistress will burn. Commander Koray will drive his army back into the city, take position, and assassinate the officials."

There was no more exchanged between the two of them. Maurice guided the renegado to the door and saw him out. He returned to the table and took a seat. His troubles would be solved. The explosion would burn the bodies left behind. There would be no investigation. He could stay in al-Mari Ifriq, become one of its officials, and assist al-Rinak and Taran in its rule. He waited patiently to hear the sound of *The Siren's Call* exploding several blocks away.

Kyler Piett, at the moment, ducked through alleyways and side streets to keep his presence from being detected. Few citizens roamed the streets during the last half of the day. The sun was now gone, and the night took watch over the city along with the surplus of assigned guards. Captain Piett stayed close to the shadows. He also hid deep inside his robe's hood. Piett decided to discard the outfit once the deed was done. He donned the heavy robes during his flight from France. He had to flee after a scandal broke out, his name attached to the misconduct. Kyler Piett's actions shamed a French noble, being caught having an affair with the aristocrat's twenty-year-old son. The French noble called for the renegado's head before news circulated through the streets. Kyler escaped, returning to al-Mari Ifriq in disguise.

Kyler entered the alley positioned two buildings away from *The Siren's Call.* He peeked from the alley while painted in shadow. He watched closely. Guards already swarmed the building. He waited, keeping an eye on the scene. He counted ten guards flocked around the tavern. Kyler tried to listen to their conversation, but the guards only whispered close to one another. Kyler could not decipher anything from the situation other than the puzzling realization that the guards appeared to be treating the tavern as a crime scene. He reversed his steps, choosing to maneuver the alleys to attack *The Siren's Call* from its rear entrance.

Kyler turned around. He was in mid-step when he saw the sharp point of a blade aimed at his neck. His eyes went wide, fixed on the weapon. Kyler looked up to see the weapon's handler. Roberto Hamaat stared at him with a tough gaze. Four Suns, with one-shot pistols aimed at the renegado, surrounded the aged assassin.

Roberto tapped the dagger's tip against Kyler's neck and ordered, "Hands up." Kyler lifted his arms. Roberto removed the hood from around Kyler's head. He relieved the pirate-Captain of the sack he carried. Roberto sheathed his dagger and stepped back into the comfort of his soldiers. The assassin opened the bag and inspected the contents. "These are illegal to carry in the city, unless authorized, Captain," Roberto declared looking up at Kyler. "Where did you get these?"

Kyler remained silent.

Roberto rolled his eyes. "Did you perpetrate the attack on Rahmis Husani and Fumnyana Maysa? Have you returned to get rid of the bodies by destroying the evidence of your crime?"

Kyler said nothing, but his eyes went wide with surprise at the accusation. He saw Roberto take note of his action. He spoke, "I…I did not." The Captain started to understand Maurice's intentions. He deduced that a dispute must have taken place between Maurice and Rahmis Husani, ending violently. Kyler did not think about whether Rahmis Husani and his mistress were dead. It did not matter to him. He was now angry at Maurice for setting him up. The Captain was frustrated with himself too, but his deed would have been remarkable had he accomplished the task.

Al-Jasi city guards walked up behind Kyler Piett. Roberto ordered them to place him under arrest. The charges surprised Kyler Piett. Roberto proclaimed, "You are under arrest for aiding a conspiracy against the officials of al-Mari Ifriq. Take him to the palace. Beylerbey Anhur Has will want to speak with him." Roberto put the Captain's hood back into position around his head to cover his face.

Kyler Piett was marched through the streets. More guards swarmed him, concealing Kyler Piett's presence, and presenting the appearance that the guards were escorting a Moorish official to the palace. They entered the officials' manor and guided Captain Piett to a small, dark room. He was searched, confiscated of a pistol and dagger, chained to a chair, and left alone. Minutes passed before Roberto Hamaat and Ambassador Sa'ood arrived with the Beylerbey, lanterns in their hands.

Kyler examined their faces. Roberto looked as if he had captured a great prize. There was a wide smile on the assassin's visage as he announced the Captain's capture. Al-Jeheuty did not look as enthused. The Beylerbey sighed and shook his head.

"This man is of no great concern to me," the Beylerbey said to Roberto.

The Chief of the Guard pleaded, "Beylerbey, with no disrespect, this man is part of the plot to—"

"This man's voice carries no weight, Hamaat," al-Jeheuty interrupted sharply. "We need others that are a part of the plot. You've already expressed to me that he's not even the man that attacked my dear friend and his mistress."

"Illegal weaponry was found on his person," Roberto argued.

"And for that, have him beheaded immediately," al-Jeheuty commanded. Shock and horror exploded on Kyler's face. The Beylerbey insisted, "No more time can be wasted on low-level enforcers—"

"Maurice!" Captain Piett shouted, his voice breaking into al-Jeheuty's words. "Maurice al-Hammon attacked Rahmis and his mistress. I have no idea of his motives."

Al-Jeheuty, Roberto, and Nasir turned their heads. The Beylerbey nodded. "Thank you," he said casually. "There. Our crime is solved. It was a small quarrel with big results. We understand Maurice's behavior. He's recently lost his brother. He's in a bit of a mood." Al-Jeheuty turned to Roberto and commanded, "Search Maurice's home and tavern. Arrest him on sight." He then commanded Nasir, "Continue with this one's beheading. Make it quick. I have to meet my wife for dinner. She'll be upset if I'm late. She's pregnant, cranky—"

"No!" Piett screamed. "No. Please, Beylerbey! Grant me mercy. I beg of you."

Al-Jeheuty had no intentions of beheading Kyler Piett. He and Roberto were engaged in a charade only to make the Captain confess. He walked closer to Kyler Piett, standing tall over him like a tower reaching toward the heavens. The Beylerbey bent down, locking eyes with the Captain. He placed his lantern next to Kyler Piett's seat and said, "You were part of the phalanx called The Scourge of the Mediterranean. You terrorized many people while at sea. You were without mercy then, Captain. Now, you make an appeal for it? Should I treat you any different than you treated the men—and I'm sure the women—that begged for your mercy?"

Kyler did not address the Beylerbey's sentiments. He confessed to save his life. "Maurice is part of that conspiracy. He, and his brother, and I…we have helped al-Rinak Ozan in his efforts to kill the city's officials. Taran Zaher too." Kyler made a heavy sigh. He leaned back and said, "But you already know that, Beylerbey. Unfortunately for you, so does al-Rinak." He looked at al-Jeheuty and said, "I heard of Rene and Coutelier's deaths while I was in France. That is why I'm here. I told al-Rinak. He suspects that you are involved in their deaths. He's aware you're onto him. He's become desperate. Bo Yusuf is marked to die in combat. He might already be dead. I was supposed to cause a distraction that would call the remaining Turkish troops into the city. You would investigate the explosion, and the Turks would assassinate you, hidden at strategic points."

Al-Jeheuty whispered into Nasir's ear. The ambassador nodded his head and then left the room. He returned moments later with a man Kyler Piett did not know. The Beylerbey introduced him as a commander in the Djenhai army. Commander Abanobi. "He arrived a little before sundown," al-Jeheuty continued. "He informed Commander Sükh Koray that Bo Yusuf is indeed dead. The Ogunsanwo-Mashek are running wild. The five troops that escorted this Djenhai commander are now heading toward Tunisia with forty of the fifty Turkish soldiers stationed outside the city. They will be led to the mountains and find General al-Dume very much alive. He will be leading an army of Djenhai and Ogunsanwo-Mashek warriors against the Turkish troops. The remainder of al-Rinak's army will either be arrested or slaughtered, much like the Turkish soldiers before them." Al-Jeheuty sighed. He turned to Nasir and reiterated. "Give Captain Piett his punishment."

"Beylerbey!" the Captain yelled. "Please. I have given you all I know."

"You've confirmed what we three already know," al-Jeheuty snapped. "You've told us information that Tobal Lessman and Yan Nuh have already confessed before you. Rene Chaffee too, before he died. Unless you would testify against al-Rinak, then I cannot—"

"I give you my word, Beylerbey," Piett pleaded. "My word is yours. In any court."

"The Ottoman court," al-Jeheuty demanded.

The Captain went silent. He examined the African Moors standing in front of him. His expression was wide and perplexed. "Why not your own? Statesman Ozan has no ties to the Ottoman Empire. He retains his title, but al-Rinak—"

Al-Jeheuty lifted a single hand. "Hold your speech. What do you mean al-Rinak has no ties to the Empire?"

"He and Statesman Sinan Demir were in charge of removing the troops from al-Mari Ifriq," Captain Piett explained. "Instead, they purchased the troops from the Empire and the claim in the Ghanem Company. The Empire has little time to deal with such politics of a corsair-state."

"What about Statesman Demir's attempts to secure the use of the troops for military operations?" al-Jeheuty asked.

"A ruse," answered Piett. "Statesman Demir was looking to capitalize from al-Mari Ifriq's desperation by having monies paid to him by your former Beylerbey. He suggested payment for troops to recoup his losses in the army's purchase. It enraged al-Rinak. The two of them concocted the idea of keeping the Empire's threat real. Statesman Demir left with half of the Turkish army, pretending to head to Turkey and see of the troop's use. Melusina accompanied him. He was poisoned. The troops waited at sea, met by al-Rinak weeks later. Statesman Ozan told you he was going to see about your wife's sister. He was. Savas, her husband, is al-Rinak's contact. It's Savas' voice that has the power. He was backing al-Rinak, his brother, and Taran Zaher. It was he and his money that could influence the Empire."

"Savas died a month ago," al-Jeheuty said. "Fadheela is now married to his brother."

"And his brother wants nothing to do with al-Rinak's ambitions," said Captain Piett. "Their relationship is held together by string. Firat believes al-Rinak's ambition is a waste of money."

Al-Jeheuty looked at Nasir. "Draft a declaration to the Ottoman Empire that al-Rinak Ozan is being brought up on charges of conspiracy. We will still deal with this issue in a civilized manner. Keep Captain Piett alive should we need him." He bid the Captain farewell, took his lantern, and then left the room with the other officials, locking the door behind them. He again commanded Roberto, "Put together a crew. Arrest Maurice al-Hammon. Search his home and tavern." He turned to Nasir. "Find Wakil, inform him of what we've learned. Begin working on the declaration with him." He addressed Abanobi. "Commander, would you assist me in arresting al-Rinak Ozan?"

Abanobi bowed his head. "I am at your command, Beylerbey."

They split from one another after entering an adjacent hall. Roberto grouped with fifteen soldiers from his outfit. Nasir, Aludra at his side, journeyed to find Wakil at the governor's manor. Al-Jeheuty fashioned himself with pistol, sword, and eighteen al-Jasi city guards. They marched through the street, heading toward al-Rinak's residence.

The statesman lay ready. The ten soldiers at his command, along with Commander Sükh Koray, waited by all windows and doors. They were heavily armed. Taran Zaher sat on the sofa. He was nervous being surrounded by the armed Turkish troops that waited for the officials' presence, ready to fire on them. Al-Rinak and Melusina resided in the bedroom suite. He sat down on his bed thinking about the movements he made throughout his secret war.

The statesman was initially confused by Commander Koray's presence. The Commander's appearance was not the result of a building exploded by Captain Piett's bombs. Koray informed Statesman Ozan that Bo Yusuf was dead, a message delivered by a Djenhai Commander. But, the Ogunsanwo-Mashek, running wild, were slaughtering the remains of the Turkish army. Sükh Koray sent forty of the remaining troops to assist them. The rest he brought with him to brief the statesman on the current situation.

Al-Rinak was angry by the Commander's move. He directed Sükh Koray and the troops to post up around the room, taking positions at the windows and doors. Five men stayed upstairs. Five soldiers were positioned on the lower level. Three at the front windows and two stationed near the rear door.

Al-Rinak did not allow Taran to leave, even as it got late. This was the statesman's last effort. There was no explosion that alerted the officials, sending them into distress. Al-Rinak believed something happened to Kyler Piett, possibly while on his way to find Maurice al-Hammon. He guessed the officials would soon arrest him, and his troops would fire on them.

Al-Rinak could still take the city.

Melusina danced in front of him. Her movements would have hypnotized any other man, but al-Rinak was miles away in thought, lost inside his head. The woman spun around, her back facing al-Rinak. She smiled seductively and extended her arms, stating her exotic proposition. "I am French. I am Turkish. Which part of me do you wish to lay with tonight?"

Al-Rinak looked at Melusina's alluring figure with complete disinterest. The only thought on his mind was a frustrating notion that al-Jeheuty had cornered him. The young Beylerbey had won. Al-Rinak erupted in an angry cry, yelling hard and loud. His scream did not lose air, and when it seemed to soften it picked up again.

Al-Rinak's troops jumped to attention.

Taran sprang from his seat.

Everyone stared at the door as the hollering continued. All were too petrified to make a move to investigate. Four troops aimed muskets or pistols at the door. There was a frightening belief that al-Mari Ifriq guards had penetrated the suite through the windows.

Sükh Koray and Taran harnessed enough courage to barge through the closed door of al-Rinak's suite. They found the statesman inside, standing over Melusina's body, his hands still tightly gripped around her neck.

Al-Rinak took a deep breath. He let go of Melusina and backed away from his dead mistress' body. He sat back down on the bed. "Commander Koray, take Taran outside. Use the rear entrance." He looked at Taran and said. "Taran, go home. Separate yourself from this."

"Al-Rinak," Taran pleaded.

"Go," the statesman demanded. "Or I'll have Commander Koray put a fatal bullet in you, unlike the others I've had you hit with."

Sükh Koray tugged Taran's arm and led him from the suite, through the front room door, and down the stairs. He guided Taran to the rear entrance, passed the soldiers stationed there, out the back door, and into an alley. The two soldiers stepped outside with their Commander.

Pistol fire rang out!

The two soldiers were killed, shot in the head and through the heart. Taran dodged and ran down the alley, ducking away from the skirmish and into a shadowy backstreet. The land baron moved his feet as if he was a young man again, winding his way through the city's alleys to find his way home.

Taran left behind Commander Koray to face al-Jeheuty and two al-Jasi city guards. The Commander discarded his pistol and unsheathed his sword, lunging at the Beylerbey. Al-Jeheuty, quick with defense, parried the attack. The two al-Jasi soldiers rushed through the back entrance, tossing a bomb into the downstairs area, and taking cover in the kitchen. The pressure of the explosion tossed the three Turkish soldiers around the room, crushing their bones and crippling them.

Outside, al-Jeheuty and Commander Koray faced off with swords. Koray bombarded the Beylerbey with lightning quick strikes. Al-Jeheuty parried all of them. The Beylerbey dodged a few strikes made at him, turning around and countering with heavy sword swings at the Commander. But, al-Jeheuty resigned the offensive to the Turkish Commander, studying Koray's thrusts and strikes.

Al-Jeheuty considered the Commander's swordplay too predictable. Koray's moves, though impressive, well studied and executed, were conservative and stiff. His strikes, parries, and sword position did not extend beyond the lessons he studied. Al-Jeheuty saw enough. He ended the battle in three moves. His first move was defensive, blocking a downward swing made at him. In the same motion he pushed Commander Koray's blade up and away from him, exposing the Turk's midsection. Al-Jeheuty commenced his second move. The Beylerbey spun around and quickly ran his blade from the lower right of Koray's torso, across his stomach, and up to his left shoulder. Koray buckled, dropped his sword, and bent down. Al-Jeheuty spun around again, ending up behind Commander Koray, and slicing his blade across his back.

Koray dropped to his knees, bleeding from his wounds. He was hurt, with shock running through his body. His wounds were deep, but not fatal. His forearms were against the ground, his eyes concentrated on the blood pooling under him.

Another explosion rocked the building. A bomb was tossed through a front window, killing the five soldiers posted in the second-floor front room. Eight al-Jasi city guards and Commander Abanobi stormed the premises and subdued Statesman Ozan.

Sükh Koray continued to wheeze and gasp, eyes wide. Al-Jeheuty bent down and said to Commander Koray, "We will get you a physician. Your wounds are heavy, but not fatal. I will get you to the infirmaries." Al-Jeheuty rushed inside the building, entering through the rear entrance. He stepped over the debris and crippled soldiers and walked up the stairs. The scene was mimicked on the second floor. Five Turkish soldiers lay sprawled on the ground. Two of them winced in pain. The al-Jasi city guard huddled near the door of al-Rinak's bedroom suite. Al-Jeheuty commanded some of the guards to tend to Commander Koray in the back alley. He walked past the others, into the statesman's room. Abanobi was already placing shackles on al-Rinak.

Al-Rinak smiled at al-Jeheuty as the Beylerbey entered the room. The scene looked grotesque and sadistic to the Beylerbey. Melusina lay dead on the floor. Her life smothered by al-Rinak's hands, like so many before her. The Turkish statesman was grinning as if his entire ordeal of murder and conspiracy was just a game to him. Though al-Rinak lost, his fun was had.

Al-Jeheuty pointed his sword at al-Rinak and announced, "In the name of al-Mari Ifriq, capital city of the State of Odongo-Mauharim, you're under arrest Statesman Ozan."

Al-Rinak continued to smile. He chuckled and then sighed. He looked at al-Jeheuty and presented the Beylerbey with a respectful bow before being carted out of the demolished complex.

Chapter Fifty-Three

Ashir Husani always referred to Spain as al-Andalusia, even though it had been two centuries since the country had been called by such a name. Ashir believed the Moorish taifa he lived in was the last civilized region of the world, coupled with a playful, romanticized mythos that he still resided in Moorish controlled Spain. He was too proud a man to leave the country, even with its dangerous climate and temperament toward the African Moor. He considered the taifa his home. It was where he was born, raised, and educated. Many left for Africa, family and friends alike.

Ashir only went to Africa to find a wife. Her name was Kamaria, a woman from Mali that taught contemporary and ancient African dance. She fell in love with Ashir, his tales of Moorish Spain, and his consistent crowing about how he was connected to many noble bloodlines. His talk was charming. Kamaria married the Moorish shopkeeper while he stayed in Mali, and returned to Spain as his wife. She gave birth to a baby boy in a year's time. They named him Rahmis, and Ashir referred to him as his 'little Prince'.

But there were complications when Kamaria delivered her son. The European atmosphere had its effect on the African woman, making her sick. The energy her body exhausted producing and giving birth to a child made Kamaria susceptible to the non-African environment. The Moorish physicians said it would be best for Kamaria to return to Africa, but in an unfortunate turn of events, Spanish soldiers marched through the taifa to arrest a list of conspirators aiding Moorish revolutionaries against the crown. Ashir Husani's name was on the list, his shop a funnel for weapons and stolen goods for Moorish rebels. He was shot for resisting arrest, Kamaria a witness.

Kamaria did not want to flee Spain, but she needed to breathe the African atmosphere to help restore her body. She left her child with family friends, though she started to question everyone tied to her husband. This particular family of Moors was innocent, but they were good friends to a man named Ameer Las el-Behar, a Moorish revolutionary. Kamaria vowed to return to health, and then return for her child.

Kamaria was captured before she could leave Spain.

She died on a slave ship bound for America.

These moments, lived by Ashir Husani and his wife Kamaria, unexplainably filtered through Rahmis Husani's unconscious mind as he lay resting in the palace infirmary. The memories were accompanied by a maiden's soft, beautiful singing voice. The images melted into a blurred portrait of reality as he emerged from his long sleep. Though Rahmis had his moments of consciousness throughout his two days of rest, he was never completely lucid. Rahmis Husani left behind the images of his parents, never to remember them again. He was left with only his deep, secret conviction that he would give up his noble bloodline just to know his mother and father. And perhaps, be embraced by them.

Rahmis believed his wish was granted when he broke through the last remnants of the past to surface into an unfocused, watery vision of the reality in front of him. Someone was holding his hand. A man and a woman were next to him. The man was standing. The woman was sitting. Rahmis' vision shifted, focusing clear and solid. His eyes noticed the dark skinned Moor wrapped in a physician's attire, but his vision was centered on the innocent beauty of Fumnyana. She was sitting next to him, holding his hand. The physician welcomed Rahmis' recovery, but did not stay long.

Rahmis continued to stare at Fumnyana. His eyes watered as she said, "You're still handsome, Rahmis Husani." She chuckled. "You heal very well. Must be that noble blood." Fumnyana said with a smile, "My leg will be fine. The bullet did not go too deep, but there was a lot of blood. Scared me."

Rahmis sat up in the bed. His vision whirled from the sudden movement. He managed to stay alert. He continued to look at Fumnyana's leg. The young woman lifted her dress to reveal her bandages. She lowered her garments.

"I followed you because I was nervous that you were going to be alone with all that money," she said. "I didn't argue when you escorted me home. I was bringing your gun to you." She spoke casually, as if recounting a card game. "Maurice al-Hammon shot me. He was going to kill you. I think I startled him. He fired his gun at me instead." Rahmis suddenly started to hit his head angrily against the headboard. Fumnyana pleaded, "Rahmis. Stop that childish behavior. You'll do more damage. You just recovered."

Rahmis stopped. He looked at Fumnyana with sad, teary eyes. "I have been terrible to you, *mora*." He slipped back down into the bed, lying on his back and looking up at the ceiling. "I have blocked my heart from…caring for you…because…" He couldn't finish the statement. Rahmis grit his teeth. He wanted to fall back into an unconscious state and hide among the darkness. But he confessed, "I considered myself too noble for you."

Fumnyana let go of Rahmis' hand. She placed her hand tenderly on his chest. "Do you know why I pursued you, Rahmis? Do you know why I fancy you? It had nothing to do with your noble blood, which is of no consequence, and means so very little. It had nothing to do with your looks, handsome as you are. That would be as shallow as you confess to be. Though, your looks do not hurt my ambition." She leaned over him and said, "I saw beyond all that, and I discovered a hurt little boy, desperate for love and acceptance. I felt very sorry for you. If there was anything I saw that was truly noble in you, Rahmis Husani, it was how you went out of your way to make people feel accepted and special. All so they didn't have to share your pain, or just help them forget theirs."

"Do you forgive me," Rahmis asked in a low voice, nervous of the answer.

"I will," Fumnyana said to him. "Many women will question my judgment. I've been your princess by your side, and in your bed—as you like me to be. You have been hurtful, but I extend my forgiveness under one condition: you will let me sing at *The Siren's Call*. I will present to you a schedule, and you will pay me for this service of entertainment."

Rahmis smiled. He remembered Fumnyana's ambitions to sing the poetry she scribed. She was a brilliant singer. "I will," he told her.

"I do have some ambitions," she said shyly. "I just…keep them private. They're hard for me to express. You know me as quiet, unless I sing." They smiled at one another. Fumnyana called for assistance. Two brawny, male servants surrounded Fumnyana and lifted her chair from off the ground. "Having a wounded leg has its perks, noblemoor," Fumnyana teased flirtatiously. She was carried from the room, waving her hand at Rahmis as she departed in her royal fashion.

Rahmis was left to his thoughts. He didn't much like how he felt about himself. He closed his eyes and asked his mother and father for forgiveness, and he drifted back to sleep. The entire Griffin outfit entered Rahmis' room several hours later. He was awake to receive their company. Al-Jeheuty, Bo Yusuf, Ojodo Yerodin, and Nasir Sa'ood stepped inside. "There's the court jester now," al-Jeheuty joked. The men surrounded Rahmis' bed. "The physician told us you were receiving guests. How're you feeling? It's been two days. A lot has happened."

Rahmis sat up in the bed, the dizzy feeling returned. He waited until his vision orientated before talking. He took a deep breath. Al-Jeheuty put his hand on Rahmis' shoulder, comforting him. The princely Moor expressed that he was fine. "I do feel ashamed, however," he admitted to everyone's surprise. "How is it that we can bury secrets so deep that even we might forget them, but a woman can figure it out when they first see you?"

Al-Jeheuty aimed his open hand toward Nasir. "I defer that question to my ambassador. He knows plenty of information on the 'black goddess'." Everyone chuckled lightly. "You and Fumnyana have things to work out?"

"No," Rahmis said in a sad and guilty tone. "I have things to work out for myself, my brother. I can only hope she is there as it happens—as much as I've acted like an ass."

"Well, *we've* stuck around. Haven't we?" Ojodo joked.

Rahmis smiled. "I guess so."

Al-Jeheuty fixed his clothes and announced, "There is news. Good news, to some degree. Maurice al-Hammon has been arrested."

Rahmis' eyes widened. He looked at Nasir and said as he remembered Maurice's confession to him, "He confessed something to me, Nasir. He said your father murdered his father. Maurice is angry. Always has been."

Nasir nodded his head. "I know. I spoke with Maurice at the prison. He was shouting that he had something to tell me. Wakil told me the truth of the matter before I went to see Maurice, however." Nasir looked shaken. "Wakil spoke about how hard it was to tell me. I…understand." He exhaled a heavy breath. "Maurice's father was a traitor to our city. His actions set in motion everything that has come to this point. My father took action against him—personally. Wakil said it tore my father apart. Rashaad—Maurice and Fusan's father—was like a brother to my father."

"Did you tell Maurice the truth," Rahmis asked.

"No," Nasir said sadly. "He already has great burdens on him. I just apologized for my father's behavior." Nasir waved his hand. "It will be over for him in time, the anger. He's set for execution. He'll know the truth on the other side. May he find peace."

Nasir reflected on the ordeal, especially the moment that his mother confessed that she knew about her husband's deed, or at least suspected, never having sought Sa'ad for a conclusive answer. But she knew her husband's routines after a mark was executed. Afya found no coincidence that Sa'ad indulged in his 'after mark' ritual on the morning his best friend was found murdered in an alley. She was also awake when he returned the previous night, having waited for him. Afya confessed to Nasir that she feigned sleep, and the next day, when Taran and Wakil delivered the news, she feigned ignorance, knowing her husband was probably breaking inside. She prayed he would not break too much.

Nasir confided in her the reason Maurice and Fusan's father was executed. Afya understood. She knew that if her husband assigned a mark, there was a good reason. And she too had her reasons for wanting Rashaad dead, knowing what he had done to her many years prior, the memory of her rape at his hands, just broken images and feelings, but enough to find solace in his death. This, however, she did not confess to her son. She did tell Sa'ad many years after Rashaad's death, consoling him with the information after Sa'ad awoke from a nightmare.

Sa'ad never felt guilty again, coping with the sadness and deed.

What Nasir confessed, from what he knew, jarred each of his friends. Rahmis was especially taken aback. He pleaded to al-Jeheuty. "Beylerbey—my brother, I beg you, Maurice al-Hammon was drunk. His actions were wrong, but nothing a month's time in prison, a heavy fine, and community's service could not fix."

"He confessed to killing his brother," al-Jeheuty informed. "Poison."

Rahmis' memory recalled Maurice's low, drunken mumblings, specific words—actions against his brother and Nasir's father. Nasir folded his arms, frustrated as he thought about Maurice's behavior. "He killed a barmaid too," Nasir added. "She was a dancer and prostitute at the *Palace*. We found her body in the backroom. Incense covering her smell." Nasir's eyes began to water. "He also helped kill my father." He wiped his eyes and put aside his anger.

"Let's not forget he shot Fumnyana," continued al-Jeheuty. "Also the fact that he meant to kill you. And more, he's one of al-Rinak's conspirators." Rahmis looked at the Beylerbey surprised. Al-Jeheuty informed, "He's willing to testify in our courts to al-Rinak's crimes, along with Captain Kyler Piett." The Beylerbey took a seat on Rahmis' bed. "We've learned al-Rinak has no power or ties within the Empire. We are covering our tracks by drafting a letter to the Empire speaking of our ordeal with al-Rinak and his army, just to be sure. He is in custody. His conspiracy against al-Mari Ifriq has been quelled, and it has been exposed. Fusan's crew has been arrested, they're being held by our Tunisian associates. Commander Koray is recovering from wounds, but he is under arrest. Al-Rinak's conspirators are subdued. All but one player, and we will handle that particular player in a private court. Tomorrow morning. He thinks he's safe. He believes he's being made Commissioner of Domestic Affairs." He patted Rahmis on the knee. "You continue to rest." The Beylerbey stood up. He dismissed the other officials. They each stated kind words hoping for Rahmis' recovery, and then left the room. "Fumnyana has a lovely voice," al-Jeheuty told Rahmis. "Mehit and I listened to her everyday from down the hall. She sang to you while you recovered. She's a good woman, Rahmis."

The princely Moor shook his head and said, "I hope I can be an equally good man. I have a lot of work to make up."

Al-Jeheuty grinned. "You'll learn." He then told his friend in a sincere voice, "You're a true king, Rahmis. I'm glad you're safe. This city would not be as elegant, or as noble, without you. Behar always said al-Mari Ifriq would be a ghetto without your royal touch."

"Thank you, my friend," Rahmis said. "Please, send Bo Yusuf back. I have an apology to make to my brother."

"As you wish," said al-Jeheuty. He turned and left the room.

Rahmis exhaled, relieved.

Another day had come to a close.

Al-Jeheuty retired to his room for the night. The Beylerbey made occasional trips to Rahmis' room to check on his friend. Bo Yusuf was always there, the brothers-in-arms rekindling their friendship. The physicians attending to Rahmis assured the Beylerbey the princely Moor would make a full recovery. With that, al-Jeheuty went to bed, his mind more at ease. He lay next to his wife and told her, "I have to see your mother in the morning."

"Is everything alright?" asked Mehit.

"She's still shaken by Behar's death," spoke al-Jeheuty. "Before I counsel with your father, I will speak with her. There is no need for her to blame herself for the actions of a greedy man such as al-Rinak Ozan."

"My mother has good days and bad days," said Mehit, hand on al-Jeheuty's chest.

"I hope my words can comfort her," said al-Jeheuty.

"They will. You're a wonderful negotiator," complimented Mehit.

The Beylerbey fell asleep, his wife by his side. In the morning, al-Jeheuty, after being primped and dressed, was fitted with guards who escorted him to Taran's house. The land baron exited his home, surprised by the Beylerbey's presence.

"Is everything fine, al-Jeheuty?" asked Taran.

Al-Jeheuty stepped forward. "Not entirely," he replied. "I have to speak with your wife. I understand she continues to be rattled by Behar's death. I wish for her to ease those troubles. We've caught the perpetrators of the crime."

"Catching al-Rinak and the remnants of his conspirators have brought all these feelings back," Taran sighed. He stepped away from his house's entrance. "Please, Beylerbey. Have your word with her. I will wait here. Tell my wife I permitted your entrance. She is in the gathering room, located at the back."

Al-Jeheuty stepped inside Taran's house and journeyed through the corridors to find Alimah Zaher. After some time, Taran, from the corner of his eye, witnessed Mehit rushing toward the house. Taran turned and walked up to her. "Your husband is speaking with your mother at the moment."

"I know," Mehit said softly. "I wanted to comfort her. I…I think I should be there."

"Let this be a private affair," Taran suggested to Mehit.

Mehit's face contorted into an annoyed expression. "I was there too when the Beylerbey was slain. He protected us from al-Rinak's disguised troops." Mehit relaxed her emotions. "I'm sorry, father. I feel I should be by my mother's side."

Taran smiled softly. "As you wish, dear. Your husband and mother are in the gathering room."

Mehit entered the house and walked to where her husband and mother were located. Al-Jeheuty and Alimah sat on a sofa, al-Jeheuty speaking. He looked up at his wife as she appeared in the wide entrance. Alimah looked back at her daughter, eyes wet with tears. Mehit was frozen, her mouth agape seeing her mother wracked with grief. Al-Jeheuty stood up and walked over to Mehit. He said to her, "Your mother has something to tell you, *mora*. I'll leave you two in peace." The Beylerbey looked over his shoulder at Alimah and said, "Thank you, ma-ma."

Alimah stood up, trembling. Her eyes stayed on Mehit as she called her daughter over. Mehit was afraid to move. Al-Jeheuty whispered into her ear, "Your mother wishes to confess something to you. I will be outside with…Taran." Mehit found the courage to move as al-Jeheuty walked past her.

Alimah embraced her daughter and led Mehit to the sofa, sitting her down.

Al-Jeheuty watched from down the hall. Mehit and her mother were covered in shadow from al-Jeheuty's vantage point. They were conversing silhouettes. The Beylerbey turned away from them and made his way out of the house. Taran greeted him. He spoke in a concerned tone. "How is my wife, Beylerbey?"

Al-Jeheuty looked at the house from over his shoulder. He then addressed Taran, "She'll be fine. I believe she's going through her last weep. Her mourning is over. Let's begin our day." He aimed his hand down the road, ushering Taran to take lead. The Beylerbey caught a glimpse of Mehit. He looked up. His wife was out of breath, leaning against the entrance to the house. Her mouth was agape, trembling.

Al-Jeheuty stopped.

Taran noticed the Beylerbey's pause and turned around. He saw his daughter approach al-Jeheuty, her eyes billowing with tears. Taran stepped toward Mehit and al-Jeheuty as the two embraced, but he stopped short before joining them.

"Behar," said Mehit. "He…he…was…" She sniffed tears trying to regain her composure. "You knew…"

"I'm sorry, Mehit," al-Jeheuty apologized to his wife. "I couldn't tell you. I didn't know how. I was told a day before our wedding. I'm sorry, *mora*."

Mehit nodded her head, understanding. She whispered in a quavering voice, "He's guilty. Isn't he?" Her eyes made a quick motion toward Taran. The baron did not notice.

Al-Jeheuty told her, "The officials and I have a meeting with Taran—" He was cut off by Mehit's sudden choke on tears. She took in a long breath. Everything she just learned overwhelmed her. Ameer Las el-Behar was her father. Mehit learned of her mother's prior relationship with him, she being conceived as a result. She was informed about her mother's split from Ameer Las El-Behar because of an arranged marriage to Taran Zaher, a man with a more respectable title, according to her mother's father. It was a marriage rushed out of necessity for her mother to keep anyone from knowing Behar was the father to her unborn child. Mehit also learned of the affair her mother continued to have when Behar returned to the city and was made Beylerbey.

Reality looked different.

Taran approached Mehit cautiously. He reached out toward her as the tears rolled uncontrollably down her face. Mehit turned to him. Taran almost retracted his hand. Mehit walked over to him. She put her arms around Taran and held him close. Taran controlled the urge to speak. He relaxed into Mehit's embrace, and put his arms around her. Mehit's tears dripped onto his chest. Their embrace was tight. Taran never felt more close to Mehit. She backed away after a long moment, letting Taran go. She gently wiped her fingers along Taran's cheek. Her eyes were lost in sadness, and Taran gazed at Mehit with a perplexed expression as she planted a sweet kiss against his cheek.

Mehit again sniffed back her tears. She wiped her face and patted Taran on the chest as she backed away from him. She kissed al-Jeheuty, and then she walked back into the house. Al-Jeheuty grouped with Taran, and the two officials continued their journey to the council house. Roberto Hamaat, Wakil al-Hakam, Nasir Sa'ood, and Bo Yusuf were already seated when they walked inside. The Governor and Ambassador relaxed at seats on either side of the bed. Roberto and Bo Yusuf sat to the left and right of an unoccupied, low upholstered seat.

"Have a seat, Commissioner," al-Jeheuty directed.

Taran sat down between Roberto and Bo Yusuf.

Al-Jeheuty walked to the kitchen area. A dark skinned, bald-headed male chef met the Beylerbey at the entrance and handed al-Jeheuty a sharp cleaver. "Beylerbey," said the man named Arbazz Aariz, eyes wide and intense, gold, looped earrings dangling from his ears. He said nothing more. He made a quick glance toward Roberto, but the master assassin kept his back to the exchange, missing the intense stare from the initiated Sun.

Al-Jeheuty thanked Arbazz and turned around. He walked toward Taran, hands behind his back. "Governor al-Hakam," al-Jeheuty shouted. "Would you kindly state the business of this meeting?"

Nasir locked eyes on Taran.

The land baron looked attentive, his gaze on Wakil as the Governor spoke.

"We have gathered today," started the Governor, "to discuss the proceedings dealing with al-Rinak Ozan." He put a stern gaze on Taran as he concluded, "And all his conspirators."

Al-Jeheuty lifted the cleaver and slammed it hard into Taran's back!

Pain choked Taran instantly. His body jumped forward with the impact, his mouth opened, ready to scream. But another action made against him kept his voice from escaping, and kept his body from falling forward. Bo Yusuf, seated to Taran's right, removed a curved blade, and jammed the weapon into Taran's chest.

A small noise leapt from the land baron's mouth, a faint breath in his throat as blood gurgled and crawled its way up his windpipe. Taran's head looked upward, eyes wide, mouth still open. His head then slumped, chin to his chest. Taran's body felt like it was on fire, pain caressing every nerve. Taran realized his luck was drained. The venomous actions of his life no longer held a strong poison. He understood the men surrounding him knew everything about him, and possibly more.

But that was not the last thing that went through his mind.

Roberto removed a small, one-shot pistol in a calm and cool manner. He fired the weapon into Taran's skull. The bullet broke through Taran's temple and traveled halfway through his brain, staying lodged inside his head.

Taran's body crumpled onto the floor, lifeless.

Arbazz, along with three Moons, rushed over and attended to Taran's corpse. He was wrapped inside an old, used rug, and taken from the council house. Al-Jeheuty looked at Wakil. "Governor," he called.

Wakil nodded his head. "This meeting is adjourned."

The officials stood up. Al-Jeheuty walked over to Nasir, presented the ambassador with a kiss to each cheek, his hand, and a gentleman's embrace. Their eyes were watery. Wakil and Roberto presented Nasir with the same gestures as al-Jeheuty backed away. Bo Yusuf bowed to Nasir, and the officials walked out of the council house. They made their way into the city, guards surrounding them. They separated once through the gates. Roberto and Bo Yusuf went to check on *The al-Hammon Palace*. Nasir and Wakil headed to the palace to continue drafting the Odongo-Mauharim state letter addressing the Ottoman Empire.

Al-Jeheuty journeyed to the prisons to visit al-Rinak's cell. The Beylerbey found his cunning adversary seated comfortably in the corner of the small room. He looked up through the bars as the Beylerbey entered. Al-Jeheuty informed, "Taran is dead. I've just come to tell you that."

Al-Rinak nodded his head. He looked at al-Jeheuty and grinned, confessing to the Beylerbey. "You are an excellent chess player, al-Jeheuty."

"I hate chess," al-Jeheuty replied. "I never understood it, no matter how much Behar or my father made me practice. I was never any good at it. Always getting beat. There are too many rules for a creative mind to work properly. I believe my pieces should move wherever I'd like them to move, and in any formation."

"You followed the rules trying to catch me," al-Rinak insisted with his wide grin still on his face.

"Then perhaps I'm better at real life than a game." Al-Jeheuty took a breath. "You've done a lot of damage, al-Rinak. You will be sentenced to death, as you know. That is simply the punishment for the crime. It's not malicious."

"Expected," al-Rinak said.

Al-Jeheuty left the prison house and returned to Mehit at her childhood home. Alimah met him at the door. She gave the Beylerbey a warm hug, and then informed al-Jeheuty that Mehit was still in the gathering room. He made his way to his wife and sat down next to her on the sofa.

"He's dead?" Mehit asked after a long stretch of silence.

Al-Jeheuty confirmed with a nod of his head. He felt the need to speak. "Yes...*mora*."

"Is this what it feels like," Mehit started to ask. "The feeling of living with the consequences of a tough decision?" She moved closer to al-Jeheuty, but did not look at him. Al-Jeheuty embraced his wife. He did not answer her question. He considered Mehit always made tough decisions. She went against Taran, schooling, religion, and became a prominent businesswoman, and she decided to marry him.

Al-Jeheuty started to rub Mehit's forehead with a single finger, massaging the center of her brow. Mehit loved the feeling of al-Jeheuty's simple massage. She felt it everywhere, from her forehead to her entire frame. Just as she started to lose herself in the feeling, and just as it began to resonate sensuously, al-Jeheuty stopped and said, "Let me tell you a story, *mora*. It is a tale of a small city in Africa-north that had big dreams."

Al-Jeheuty recounted the last four years, keeping no information from his wife. He told her the story every day, adding more information each time something new occurred in al-Mari Ifriq. Mehit would ask, *"And what goes on in the continuing saga of al-Mari Ifriq?"* and al-Jeheuty would answer his wife by first summarizing the story's previous events, and then concluding with a new occurrence.

One such event was Nasir leaving for Turkey with three other ambassadors. There was Captain-turned-Ambassador Hieremias Sunwil, Ambassador Ras Ali, and Ambassador Rahmis Husani. On return, al-Jeheuty added to the story their successful negotiation, and the Empire's blessing to proceed with al-Rinak's trial and all living conspirators of his army. Mehit's sister, Fadheela, and her children, returned to al-Mari Ifriq with the ambassadors—no longer attached to the brother of her deceased husband. In time, the story would include her marriage to a Djenhai nobleman. She would have two more children with him, and help her sister run her bathhouse, expanding the business into Djenhai, Chieftess Nugaymath and other Ogunsanwo-Mashek medicine-women assisting with the business.

Al-Rinak and his conspirators' trial proceeded. Al-Jeheuty bored Mehit with the details, making her understand how tedious the court system was, even with a guilty man. Al-Jeheuty recounted to Mehit that Governor al-Hakam, Hesam Gandarewa, and Yaminah Igdobe-Djenhai bestowed upon Mehit the title of company boss, her *Prechet Alliance* consolidating the women's services businesses into one system. This was one of Mehit's favorite parts of the story. There was even more information added. He spoke about his brother feeling better and his sister-by-law expecting another child.

Though no official other than Roberto Hamaat attended al-Rinak and his conspirators' executions, the Beylerbey added the events to the story once they were reported to him.

Then the day came when the story expanded into a wonderful celebration consisting of two parts. The first was the announcement of Odongo-Mauharim as a true state. The date was the sixteenth of March. The next day marked the grand wedding of Princess Yaminah-Igdobe Djenhai and General Bo Yusuf ibn Tachfin al-Dume. The ceremony was held in Djenhai, a joyous event that was felt throughout the African Kingdom and all the way to al-Mari Ifriq. Yaminah's mother, A'sharia, Company Queen of The Marjani Company (formerly Ghanem), was genuinely delighted.

City and kingdom were now one.

Nomadic warriors and fixed nobles were re-united as a culture.

And so continued the tale, growing to include the private and quant weddings of Ambassador Nasir Sa'ood and the Moon Aludra el-Amin, Ojodo Yerodin and Princess Adaeze, and Rahmis Husani and Fumnyana Maysa.

The giant and the Princess left the city shortly after, heading east.

Weeks passed when there was nothing more to add to the story, but al-Jeheuty continued to tell Mehit the great tale of al-Mari Ifriq. It was harder for the woman to stay awake as al-Jeheuty spun the tale every night, and soon, the Beylerbey's audience grew.

Mehit al-Tarqiyya el-Behar Anhur Has gave birth to twins, a boy and a girl.

Their daughter, the first delivered of the twins, was named Zalira Anhur Has. Al-Jeheuty's brother, visiting from Nusurika, congratulated al-Jeheuty on the birth of his daughter. Aatif advised, *"It is a girl born unto a man that makes him grow wiser."* Unbeknownst to Aatif, his wife carried twin boys in her womb.

Al-Jeheuty and Mehit's second child, a boy, was named Bruk al-Din Anhur Has. As men often do with the announcement of a son's birth, Rahmis Husani, Bo Yusuf, Nasir Sa'ood, Wakil al-Hakam, Roberto Hamaat, and Hesam Gandarewa cheered loud for al-Jeheuty. The Beylerbey's friends also jumped on him for wanting to name his son *Quantavious*. They praised Mehit for beating al-Jeheuty on the decision. Their celebration took place in *The Siren's Call*. They drank and shared stories with al-Jeheuty's brother and father also in attendance. Ilindia Kali entered the tavern. The men stood at attention. She addressed al-Jeheuty, "It is time, Beylerbey. Come. You may see your wife and children."

Mehit had been advised to rest for three days, letting her body heal. She was to receive no male visitors in that time, not even her husband. Her two children were to stay next to her, and they too were to receive no male visitors, not even their father. Al-Jeheuty's children had been announced to him, but he had not yet seen them. Alimah, Fadheela, Ilindia, Jawhara, Khaira, Fumnyana, Aludra, Yaminah, and Saleema attended to Mehit's delivery.

Al-Jeheuty walked to Ilindia. He was nervous. The elder took him by the arm, and she escorted him to his wife's bathhouse. Alimah, Fadheela, Jawhara, and the other women, greeted al-Jeheuty the moment he stepped inside the establishment. They guided him to Mehit's private room and stepped away as he entered. Ilindia closed the door.

Lanterns at each corner, placed atop a stool, provided light for the small room. Mehit lay in bed. She sat up slowly and carefully as al-Jeheuty stepped closer. She smiled at her husband, and he smiled at her. "How are you doing?" al-Jeheuty whispered.

Mehit produced a soft chuckle. "Giving birth is just the beginning of the responsibility." She silenced her laughter and asked her husband in a soft voice, "Would you like to see your children, al-Jeheuty?"

The Beylerbey kept a shy, boyish, and excited smile on his face. His son and daughter rested in separate cribs positioned next to one another. Al-Jeheuty approached the cribs with soft steps. He took a stool that rested next to the bed, placed it between the two cribs, and took a seat. He looked inside at his daughter, and then at his son. Both children were awake, stirring and groping the air with their hands. He introduced himself to them. He lifted his son from out of the crib and stood up.

Bruk al-Din conformed to the cradle of his father's arms. Al-Jeheuty bounced his son around, smiling. Bruk al-Din smiled back at his father. The Beylerbey walked over to Mehit and handed his son to his mother. He returned to the cribs and retrieved his daughter.

Zalira Anhur Has reached up for her father, putting her fingers into his mouth. Al-Jeheuty moved his head back, removing his daughter's fingers with the motion. "Hey, little girl. You're already training to be an assassin." He looked at Mehit, walking over to her. "That sounds like a story for Ojodo, a title. *The Princess Assassin.*" The two parents chuckled. Zalira relaxed inside her father's embrace, contorting her face to what looked like a sly grin to al-Jeheuty. "Yeah. You can't get over on me," al-Jeheuty drawled. "I know you're just waiting to strike again." Al-Jeheuty bounced Zalira and the baby girl made a noise that sounded like a chuckle. "Already using her feminine charms, like her mother." Al-Jeheuty held his daughter carefully. He moved the stool from between the cribs and placed it next to Mehit's bed. He sat down. He looked at Mehit as she held their son. She looked at al-Jeheuty as he held their daughter.

"Now that I have my audience," said al-Jeheuty. "I have a story to tell you." The Beylerbey smiled, tears in his eyes. "It's a long story, with characters gained and lost." He looked at his son and daughter. "The two of you would be the characters gained. And your grandfather, your mother's father, well…he was a great man lost." Al-Jeheuty then thought about his words. "Well…there was another man that was your mother's father…at least we thought he was your mother's father. I think it's safe to call him a tyrant. I would use other words to describe him, but you're not old enough for that kind of language yet. But he was not the worst. No. The worst was a man named al-Rinak. He caused many storms for al-Mari Ifriq—that's the city you live in. Did I tell you that your father is one of the heroes to this story?" He rolled his eyes and said while looking at his daughter, "I know. I'm jumping around a lot. I'm not as good a storyteller as your Uncle Ojodo. You'll meet him soon. Can't miss him. He might be in Africa-east, but if you look to the horizon, you'll see a giant moving in the distance." Then al-Jeheuty asked to hold his son, and he and Mehit swapped children. Zalira caressed her mother's chin.

Al-Jeheuty said to his daughter, "Oh, is that how it is? You treat your mother nice. I get fingers shoved in my mouth." Zalira did not respond to her father. Mehit laughed. Al-Jeheuty looked down at his son and whispered, "You see that, my boy. We're going to have to stick together against these two." The Beylerbey believed his son beamed a sly grin. Al-Jeheuty looked up at Mehit, an excited expression on his face. "We have ourselves a negotiator. I'd recognize that look anywhere. I've worn it myself quite a few times." He said to his son. "I'm going to have to teach you to hide that grin until you leave the room, or the presence of your mark. Also, you'll never be able to out talk your father. Sorry, my boy, I'm the best at this game." His tears returned. "But enough of your future. Let me tell you about the past." And al-Jeheuty told al-Mari Ifriq's marvelous tale to his new audience of wife and children.

Chapter The Last

North Africa, 1655

Still standing is al-Mari Ifriq, now a grand city bustling with activity, prosperous, and brimming with wealth. The city was larger, with surrounding establishments, smaller cities and villages. Its southern walls extended farther south, the city having doubled in size. The officials' palace was now in the center of the city, and renovated into the Governing Hall where all manner of politics were discussed, and law was studied, created, and enacted into practice. The new officials' palace, located at the far end of the expanded city, was just as illustrious as its predecessor.

Al-Mari Ifriq was the capital of the state of Odongo-Mauharim and was presided over by Governor Nasir Sa'ood, Beylerbey Al-Jeheuty Anhur Has, and their administrative cabinet. Nasir Sa'ood succeeded Wakil al-Hakam when the preceding governor became too ill to continue his duties, ultimately succumbing to his ailment early in the year 1652. He was buried with Nasir's father, Company Boss Sa'ad al-Din Sa'ood and Beylerbey Ameer Las el-Behar. All members of The Griffin Company, Roberto Hamaat and his mistress, Wakil's sons, daughters, wife, and all his grandchildren honored his passing with a wondrous Mohammedan funeral.

At the moment, the city glimmered under the night sky. A joyous festivity commenced. The festival honored Odongo-Mauharim's statehood and combined governments. King Kemnebi, his two wives, and children journeyed from Djenhai to attend the ceremony. Music, song, and dance filled the city's streets. The festival always lasted seven days, with the final day held in the Djenhai Kingdom.

Today was day four.

Citizens returned to their residences as the night concluded. They were anxious for rest, ready to attend the morning and afternoon productions put on by Ojodo Yerodin, his wife Adaeze Yerodin, and their traveling troupe. His productions were held within the renovated structure of *The al-Hammon Palace*. It was now named *The Moorish Scrolls*, a tavern with theatrical entertainment. Rahmis Husani, along with his wife Fumnyana, helped run the establishment when Ojodo and his troupe traveled abroad. The upscale renovation did not lure the more seedy patrons of al-Mari Ifriq. Rahmis, ever the princely entrepreneur, created a dive for them. It was named *The Back Alley*.

Personal rituals began as the blaring music softened. King Kemnebi, with his wives and children, returned to his palace suite. He bid the heads of The Griffin Company, and officials of the city, a good night. Al-Jeheuty and the other Griffin officials watched their wives guide their children home. The women would rendezvous again at Mehit's bathhouse for their own ritual.

The Griffin officials moved into *The Siren's Call*, passersby bowing respectively and offering appreciative smiles toward their city's leaders. Some of the bolder citizens shouted to be blessed by the officials. The mass of guards surrounding the Griffins did not allow the more fanatical citizens to get close. Of course, these overzealous residents were not bold enough to invade the officials' space. They shouted their approvals from afar, extracting a wave from the city's leaders. Both al-Jeheuty and Nasir wondered why these particular citizens could not be as festive throughout the entire year. The same people wishing for a blessing also brought the greatest complaints to the courts and open forums.

The gentlemen entered Rahmis' venerable establishment, guards remaining outside. A table was already set with wine, water, juice, and treats. Rahmis lit the lanterns for the establishment and then took a seat with his fellow Moors. Each man exhaled a sigh, stretched back, and reached for a bottle of water or jug of wine for their cups. Life had become routine for the men. Officials. Husbands. Fathers. They appreciated the mundane schedule their lives became. They were each a little more grey, and lazy with a shave, beards billowing despite their wives' disdain. They were matured now by age, rather than just experiences. A steady, peaceful life was appreciated. They were not entirely lost of their youth, but they were slowly becoming as venerable as the men that reared them to manhood.

Politics offered little more than petty, local disputes, though war reigned on the Mediterranean. Slavery was always a looming threat, and the officials knew that with time, even they would be engaged against slavers' attempts at penetrating Odongo-Mauharim's borders. Until then, al-Mari Ifriq was a safe haven, and considered by all nations as off limits for attack. Their primary source of legal income was trade and protection. But the Governor and Beylerbey still used the more illicit activities of piracy and narcotics trade as additional sources.

French ties dissolved a year ago with the death of Simon Beaumont. Gautier Leolin joined the Sa'ood Company, helping Company Boss Zakiy make strategic strikes against wanted pirates, or assisting them for take of the profit. Company Boss Hesam Gandarewa also helped, his voice strong on the Council of Captains. There were still tough company bosses, but nothing the Griffin outfit could not handle. Al-Mari Ifriq was at peace. Odongo-Mauharim was a calm state.

Al-Jeheuty looked at Ojodo and said, "Gu-Gurzil took another Moon as his second wife. He's trying to show his dedication to the clan. He's made another plea to Roberto to create an extension of the Seventy-Two Points of the Universe. Roberto finally gave him the okay. Gu-Gurzil is excited. He wants to speak with you."

Ojodo placed his cup down after a hard gulp and asked, "Why me?"

"You've been around," al-Jeheuty answered. "Studying."

"As best I can," Ojodo sighed. "Not much remains in Africa. Many of our ancient doctrines have been pilfered. Word of mouth is corrupt. The greater philosophers silenced or remaining silent, suspicious of foreign men, even their African brothers and sisters. It's a wonder Adaeze found out so much of her royal past. The Sicilian did not lie, God rest his soul."

Nasir chuckled. "He's not dead. He was arrested."

"What's the difference?" Ojodo asked with a raised eyebrow.

"A lot," Nasir replied. "He's active. His imprisonment is all politics. Verola was doing nothing wrong. The powers that be just don't have the guts to kill him. The people love him. Besides, Donatello controls his operations from a cell, and as I understand it, he will be a free man soon. His imprisonment garnered him more support among his people. I heard Admiral Carlos LaFregona assists him with running pilfered beers and liquors."

Rahmis smiled and lifted his cup. "He's an Admiral now. LaFregona knows how to sniff out the best drinks for capture. Brilliant. Someone make that Spaniard a Sultan or a King…of drinks, of course."

Ojodo looked at al-Jeheuty and asked, "And what does Gu-Gurzil want with a traveling dramatist?"

"Your research," the Beylerbey answered. "Roberto goes on about ancient doctrines, scrolls, and artifacts, all of them stolen by foreign powers. Roberto says these items of interest now reside in foreign countries. Gu-Gurzil wants to create a mirror version of Roberto's assassins. Though, he would like his outfit to concentrate on theft. He knows you've traveled and studied a great deal. He wants your knowledge as to the whereabouts of these stolen items so his outfit can get them back."

Ojodo beamed. "I will oblige," he said. "There are a lot of doctrines I wish I could've read or held. By the time Adaeze and I showed up, foreign powers pilfered them. Let Roberto's School of Dom-Daniel add another science to it," he laughed as he joked. "Is that old assassin considered the Maugraby of our time because of his devotion to the dark sciences? So misunderstood. Much like Africa has become. Confusion and loss of knowledge scares us into believing lies. Others hold our knowledge sacred while we have become scared of it."

Bo Yusuf shook his head and remarked, "Oh, here comes the philosophy."

The men at the table laughed.

Ojodo pointed to the Moorish statesman and said, "You know what I'm talking about, my brother the nationalist."

"I'm more political," said Bo Yusuf. "And my sons and daughter have tired me out."

Nasir nudged the Moorish titan and stated, "I know what you mean, Ojodo." He turned to al-Jeheuty and said, "I know Aludra will volunteer her services to Gu-Gurzil. Anything to spread the ancient gospel."

"Speaking of which," said Rahmis to al-Jeheuty, "will your children take the *Nature Walk* given by the Ogunsanwo-Mashek?"

"Most definitely," the Beylerbey nodded his head. "Mehit had all the say in the matter. She wants our children to be drenched with the ancient traditions. Our two oldest are getting ready now. They're only twelve, but sixteen is around the corner."

"Fumnyana wants our daughters to do so," said Rahmis. "I don't know. Spending all that time in the wild."

Al-Jeheuty chided jokingly. "Did you forget the magic words every man must know in order to have good relations with his wife?"

Rahmis smiled. "No. I still yield. But…ah, it doesn't matter. I will look at her when it's brought up again and say—"

"Yes, dear," said each man in unison.

"I've already prepared my children," said Nasir taking another sip of his drink. "My son and daughter join me every day to watch the sunrise. I teach them about timing. They are eight and ten, and they appreciate it for different reasons. My daughter commented that it's like the human body, all parts working as one. My son appreciates that no one is arguing," Nasir started to laugh. "He likes how the sun does its job and life responds accordingly. I think I resurrected my father with him." Nasir held a proud smile on his face. He then stated, "But I tell him life is not as ideal even when you're the leader."

Politics did not possess the dialogue spoken by the men. Rahmis talked on end about the success of the horse racing sport introduced to al-Mari Ifriq eight years ago. But, it was family life that took the forefront of their conversations, all the new adventures concerning their sons, daughters, and wives. When the subject of their women came up, each flaunted the copy of the small book given to them by Roberto Hamaat on their wedding day. Holding the book inspired them to adjourn their meeting. It had been two hours. The men rendezvoused with their wives, and each couple retired to bed, engaging in sensual routines before going to sleep.

The Moorish Scrolls was prepared for production early in the morning. Ojodo arrived two hours before noon to oversee the final stages of construction. He met with his wife and both of them prepped the actors in their troupe for the performance. Adaeze then left to sit in the front. Ojodo's children went with their mother.

Guests entered the theater promptly at noon. After all the officials from al-Mari Ifriq and Djenhai arrived, sitting in the front, Ojodo took the stage to a round of applause.

"Thank you," he said to the audience. "I have been asked if there would be anymore adventures concerning Mwindo and the Djedhi Khepri warriors. Unfortunately, there will not. *The Mwindo Epic* is only a six-part story. There are no more chapters to tell. Mwindo's father's rise, fall, and redemption have been told. Of course, in your imaginations, the story will always continue." Ojodo took a breath. "But, today I present a great epic that centers on al-Mari Ifriq and its history. It will begin thirty-five years before this date, and it will recount the politics of al-Mari Ifriq coming under Turkish rule. The story will conclude with Odongo-Mauharim's statehood. The story has fifty-four parts. Not all will be presented today. After this story is told—years in the writing and making, I will begin a new epic. It will be a magical adventure titled *Abyssinia: The World of Three Moons*. Until then, the Yerodin Troupe presents to you, *Al-Mari Ifriq, Moorish Africa*."

Dancers and acrobats took the stage as part of an opening number before the start of the main drama. The audience clapped when the performers exited the stage. A magician was next, wowing the audience with tricks and staged sorcery. Then the drama opened. Four actors sat on round, upholstered seats. They portrayed the members of the *Sa'ood Alliance*. A fifth actor entered playing Roberto Hamaat. The real Roberto, sitting in the audience with his mistress, was curious as to how his character would be portrayed. But the assassin and elder had nothing to worry about. Ojodo scripted the drama with reserve. Roberto's character was simply a police guard. His secret organization would not be mentioned.

Mehit joked to al-Jeheuty that he no longer had the burden of telling the story of al-Mari Ifriq. Al-Jeheuty replied to his wife, "As Beylerbey, I get twenty percent of this production's take." Mehit chuckled silently at her husband's retort. The Griffin officials, with their wives and children, sat back, and with a grand audience in attendance, enjoyed their lives passing before their eyes.

Here was told the story of al-Mari Ifriq, Moorish Africa.

The city's dreams had been fulfilled. Its borders stretched beyond the four directions, its influence infinite. The city's life no longer had bounds. With a healthy surplus of history, al-Mari Ifriq stretched through time. The story of the hierarchy of company bosses, corsairs, and all manner of politics would never be forgotten. The greater history of the Moorish revolutionaries that united maritime companies in an attempt to control the legal and illegal trade routes of the Mediterranean, would forever tuck African children into bed, and guide them to sleep. Each child dreamed of being the embodiment of the heroic African Moorish officials, kings, queens, corsairs, assassins, proprietors, merchants, warriors, and soldiers who fought against tyrants vying for control of the city.

Every child had his or her favorite character.

Al-Mari Ifriq was no longer just a city.

It was a legend.

<u>References</u>

The name *Sa'ad al-Din Sa'ood* is the name of the promiscuous blackamoor at the beginning of **The Arabian Nights: 1000 Nights and 1 Night**.

The funeral rights, wedding, and customs of the Moors (though taken with creative license) were studied from the books **The Land of the Moors, The Moorish Empire, and The Moors** by **Budgett Meakin**.

The name *Lass el-Behar* comes from the Moorish legend **The Legend of El-Minar**. The legend can be found at the beginning of **Pirate Utopias Moorish Corsairs and European Renegadoes** by Peter Lamborn Wilson.

Al-Jeheuty's dialgue "Because when the Djenhai police throw your ass in a cell, and I'm called upon to negotiate your release, this is what I'll say: *What, Officer? My brother? Oh, no. We definitely had different fathers.*'" The table roared with laughter. "Check this out." Al-Jeheuty pointed to himself and declared, "Sun rise," he pointed to Rahmis and said, "Midnight. No way." found in Chapter 23 is an homage to dialogue from the film **Under The Cherry Moon**.

There are many **Star Wars** *'homages'*.

Pirate Utopias Moorish Corsairs and European Renegadoes, p. 32-35 used for the description of musical instruments described in Chapter 14.

Maefil – An Afro-Arabic word for 'union' or 'unify'

"Let us sit upon the ground and tell sad stories of the death of kings." Shakespeare's Richard II Act 3 Scene 2

"The land, through which we have gone to spy it out, is a land that devours its inhabitants, and all the people that we saw in it are of great height. And there we saw the Nephilim, the sons of Anak, who come from the Nephilim, and we seemed to ourselves like grasshoppers, and so we seemed to them." Numbers 13:32-33

<u>RECOMMENDED READING</u>

Othello's Children in the New World
    By Jose V. Pimienta-Bey

Pirate Utopias Moorish Corsairs & European Renegadoes
    By Peter Lamborn Wilson

Golden Age of The Moor
    Edited by Ivan Van Sertima

African Presence in Early Europe
    Edited by Ivan Van Sertima

The Golden Trade of the Moors: West African Kingdoms in the Fourteenth Century
    by E.W. Bovill, Robin Hallett

The Story of the Moors In Spain
The Story of the Moors After Spain
        By Stanley Lane-Poole

<u>MORE TITLES @</u>

www.TwinGriffinBooks.com

www.ingramcontent.com/pod-product-compliance
Lightning Source LLC
Chambersburg PA
CBHW051549100726
47898CB00001B/22